SING THEM HOME

Also by Stephanie Kallos

Broken for You

SING THEM HOME

Stephanie Kallos

Atlantic Monthly Press
New York

Printed in the United States of America

FIRST EDITION

ISBN-10: 0-87113-963-4
ISBN-13: 978-0-87113-963-4

Atlantic Monthly Press
an imprint of Grove/Atlantic, Inc.
841 Broadway
New York, NY 10003

Distributed by Publishers Group West

www.groveatlantic.com

09 10 11 12 13   10 9 8 7 6 5 4 3 2 1

For my parents,

Gregory William Kallos
August 1, 1927–January 8, 2005
and
Doris "Dorie" Arlene Dorn Kallos
October 16, 1931–January 6, 2006

and my friend,

Michael Thomas Maschinot
November 8, 1957–June 22, 2007

SING THEM HOME

Prologue

It's so hard to explain what the dead really want. Not to be *alive* again, heavens no, never that: a passenger buckled into that depreciating vehicle of the body, that cramped one-seater with its structural flaws and piss-poor mileage, its failures and betrayals, its worn, nonfunctioning, irreplaceable parts. Even the body's sensual ecstasies don't have any allure for the dead, not anymore. Symphonic sex; meadowlark song; the silence that follows a prairie snowfall; the sky unzipped by lightning; that handful of nineteenth-century Russian wonders but especially Rachmaninoff and most especially *Variations on a Theme of Paganini;* Doris Day singing "Whatever Will Be Will Be"; eggplants, avocados, asparagus, sweet corn; the smell of warm Crayolas and breast-fed babies' breath; the exposed, downy nape of a child's neck; lightning bugs; infants' feet.

All of this would be pleasant to remember if the dead were capable of looking backward. But they aren't. When it comes to time, the dead are tetherless. Like very young children in this way, they exist entirely in the now. They are blessed with an ability to be fully entranced by what's in front of them.

No wonder the living are a constant source of exasperation. The living—pathetically obsessed as most of them are with calendars, deadlines, delivery and expiration dates, estimated hours of departure and arrival; with measurements, quotas, statistics; always casting their eyes toward the room beyond the room in which they're standing—exude this *energy,* for lack of a better word, that frustrates the dead to distraction, makes them so nervous that they'd jump out of their skins if they had any.

The living are like spinning tops, powered by a need for atonement, or revenge, or by avoidance, guilt, shame, fear, anger, regret, insecurity, jealousy, whatever, it doesn't matter because it all derives from the same pop-psyche alphabet soup and oh Lord here comes another best-selling book on the self-help shelf when really if they would just smash all the time-keeping devices excepting sundials, do a crossword puzzle, study the backs of their hands, notice their breath going in and out, drink their food and chew their water, *relax,* it would be a great step forward in the evolution of the species and the dead would be so grateful.

Here, then, is one thing: They want to be undistracted.

Another point of contention: They don't want buildings named after them. They don't want to be part of the school curriculum. They abhor being the subject of biographies, documentaries, sappy made-for-TV movies. They especially hate public-funded art: commemorative portraiture, statuary. For the most part, the dead are shy. Imagine how they feel, seeing themselves cast in bronze and on display for all eternity! And then there's the theater. The humiliation of learning that one's tribulations have become the stuff of legend and are erroneously reenacted every summer on the stages of community amphitheaters all over the world by bad actors speaking stilted dialogue! It's a nightmare.

The dead aren't always irritated by the living. It is understood that the living mean well, believing that they are honoring the dead when they speak for them, about them. When they memorialize them in these ways. The trouble is, the living are always trying to interpret the dead, but this is entirely unnecessary. The dead aren't like God. They don't need go-betweens. The dead can speak for themselves thank you very much, and they do. All the time.

The sad fact is that the dead have never yet come up with a uniformly successful way of getting their message across. Believe it: They've tried.

Take the Jones children, for example.

For most of their lives, they have been waiting for their mother to come down. To do otherwise, they believe, would be a betrayal.

Other things came down: the ruined Steinway immortalized in a *National Geographic* photograph; the nibbled #2 pencil thrust improbably into the trunk of an Eastern Red Cedar; the red American Flyer, driven down so hard that half of it went into the earth while the handle and one set of wheels waved helplessly in the afterwinds. All these things returned to earth after being whirled about in an unimaginable dance that surely was so wonderful it might have given objects a consciousness, a power to tell tales, at least to one another. But not to them, these children, who didn't share the miracle of these objects' ascension and return.

All these things went up and came down, but their mother never did.

The phrase *waiting for the other shoe to drop* has a special significance for them; it seems more than anything to constitute their curriculum vitae, their professional résumé, their fate. Other forms of evidence and instruction have appeared in their field of view, but these clues have either gone unnoticed or been misinterpreted.

The gift of bones is a profound comfort to the living—little else satisfies—and these children have done without it.

They have begun to suspect that they are insane, that they were born out of nothing. Mythological beasts. Freaks of nature without maternity. Perhaps they entered the world through other means: deposited as bee pollen on a porch step, by accident, forming bit by bit into something vaguely human, but suspect to any who look closely. Maybe they arose from the ashes and mud ensuing a storm, or from the depths of a drop of rain, a spoonful of cookie dough. Maybe they climbed out of one of the bottles of iodine, mercurochrome, or cough syrup nestled at the bottom of their father's medical bag. They could have come from any of these places; all of these possibilities seem every bit as plausible as the idea that they were born out of the body of a woman. Their mother.

Like most siblings, they are different in many ways, but idiosyncratically alike in others. All three of them abstain from the use of blowdryers. They spend inordinate amounts of money on shoes. None of them have ever seen *The Wizard of Oz*. A sense of humor eludes them.

Their mother went up. She never came down.

If only she had a different name, they often think.

The dead just wish they would all stop waiting.

PART ONE

The Tornado Debris Project

People who say cemeteries are peaceful probably have no means of reception for the powerful static of rushing voices that throb there. I don't believe all cemetery visits can be fruitful because there is no reason why, once having discarded the body, the soul should haunt its remains. My belief is that simply as a matter of tact and convenience some souls make an effort from time to time to be present at a common meeting place.
—from *Terra Infirma: A Memoir of My Mother's Life in Mine*
by Rodger Kamenetz

Chapter 1

The Mayor Ignores the Rules

For someone born and bred right here in the rainwater basin of the central great plains, Llewellyn Jones—the mayor and presumptive leader of Emlyn Springs, Nebraska—is showing a sad lack of common sense. His ladyfriend and bedfellow for the past twenty-five years, Alvina Closs, is flummoxed.

"Can't you *wait* an hour?" she is saying. "You can still get in nine holes—maybe even eighteen—after it blows over."

"I've got a tee time reserved," he answers. "I'm expected."

"We don't live in Miami!" Alvina counters, shrilly. "It's not as if there's a crowd of people waiting to play. Why can't you wait?"

"I'm going now, Viney," he says. Just like that. No explanation. No compromise.

"You and your goddamned golf."

He gives her a level, noncommittal look. "I'll be home by happy hour," he says. Then he turns around and walks up the stairs and toward the bedroom, his posture erect, his gait processional. *If he thinks I'm going to follow him up there,* Viney says to herself, molars clenched, *he's got another thing coming.*

Plenty of others share Viney's agitation. The smallest and least civilized townsfolk are the most distraught: the babies, all of them, even the easy ones, are confounding their mothers with uncharacteristic, colicky behavior. The babies have been fed and changed and burped and read to and sung to and walked and held but still they are out of sorts. They are determined to cry, naptime be damned. There are grumpy toddlers, too, throwing tantrums, caterwauling in unison. Family pets all over town are nervous and misbehaving—fluttering, howling, hissing, gnawing, mauling lace curtains, and mangling good leather shoes even though they know better. Premenstrual girls are arguing with their mothers, moping in front of the television, or daydreaming on polyester bedspreads behind violently slammed doors. Teenage boys contemplate their troubled complexions with dismay. Afternoon trysts are not going well. Noses tickle without relief. The carpenters in town curse and measure again, cut again, curse again, measure again. At the Williamses' mansion, Miss Hazel's most promising student strikes a C-sharp. Hazel cringes in the parlor; in the kitchen, her younger sister, Wauneeta, cringes, too. Downtown at the piano hospital, Blind Tom experiences a sudden unaccounted-for burst of tinnitus as he applies a cotton swab saturated with milk to a stained bit of ivory he found last week by the side of the road near Hallam. Next to the old train depot, the aged citizens encamped at the St. David's Home for the Elderly are experiencing intestinal problems; not a one of them, not even Mr. Eustace Craven, whose bowels have emptied like clockwork for every one of his ninety-eight years, has had a decent BM all day.

And in the living room of the house that has been Llewellyn Jones's primary place of residence for a quarter of a century, Viney turns her back on the mayor and plants herself at the picture window—arms folded, mouth adamantly stitched shut, brows lowering, wearing an expression that no one but her dearest friend has ever seen.

Viney rarely frowns. She does five minutes of facial exercises and acupressure every morning and makes an effort to keep her countenance (a word she routinely mispronounces as *continence*) relaxed and neutral. Time needn't be the enemy. A person doesn't have to spend a fortune on face-lifts and creams. Alvina Closs is seventy-four years old, almost seventy-five, but she looks at least ten years younger. Maybe even fifteen.

She scrutinizes the ballooning clouds advancing from the south. The baby-blanket blue of the sky is darkening, graying. She can hear Llewellyn banging around in the bedroom, opening and closing bureau drawers. He must be changing into his shorts.

Viney can't for the life of her imagine what's gotten into him. The mayor is usually so easygoing, a model of the compromising spirit. It's one of the many reasons they've stayed together for so long.

Many positive things could be said of Viney's late husband, Waldo, but a flexible nature was not one of them. They had sex in the same position their entire married life, and Waldo required some form of red meat at every meal. He'd choke down a slice of turkey at Thanksgiving, but that was the extent of it. Chicken? "Dirty birds," he'd say, although that didn't keep him from eating eggs fried in butter eight days a week. Fish? Forget it, even when his friends brought home fresh perch from the Big Blue. It was meat, meat, meat with Waldo, which is why—Viney knows this for a fact—he dropped dead of a massive heart attack when he was only thirty-two years old, leaving her a young widow with four kids. He had a beautiful body. She's still mad at him.

The window needs cleaning. They haven't had a good rain for days—although Viney's oldest daughter said it sprinkled up in Omaha yesterday. The topsoil is parched, the wind has been relentless. There's dust on everything. Viney takes up yesterday's newspaper and her spray bottle of water and Coke and gets to it.

The picture window is a relatively new addition. Waldo installed it back in 1962, not long before he collapsed in the parking lot of the Surf'n'Turf, where they'd gone to celebrate their fifteenth wedding anniversary. Waldo was handy, that was one of his attributes. He made a lot of improvements to the house when he was alive. Up and down ladders, hammering, hoisting, sawing, drilling. All those comforting male noises.

Alvina Closs has been a widow longer than she was married. She's been an adulteress longer than she's been a wife. She would have dried up for sure, grown shut down there—and in her mind and heart, too—if it hadn't been for Llewellyn Dewey Jones, and Hope.

Welly comes back downstairs and goes out through the kitchen door, not exactly slamming it but giving the action just enough *oomph* to set the door harp clanging overenergetically. What's wrong with him?

Viney hears him out in the backyard, thumping his shoes together, clearing off the dirt between the spikes. She pictures great bricks of dense sod being flung about the yard, and then falling into a serene, elliptical orbit with Welly at the center: a small angry god in argyle socks, giving birth to a new solar system in which the terrain of every planet is an immense, impeccably groomed PGA golf course.

Viney resumes window-cleaning. She does a few nasolabial stretches and waits for Welly to reappear. Surely he won't leave without patching things up.

Viney's house is one of the oldest in town, if not the finest or fanciest: a whitewashed two-story saltbox built back in 1910 by her great-grandfather as a wedding present for her grandparents. Her mother, aunts, and uncles were born here, as was Viney, as were Viney's four children. She keeps her house, and Welly keeps his, even though they've been sleeping together since the nation's bicentennial.

In part, it's for appearances' sake—but it's also because the house provides Alvina Closs with a sense of personal and historical continuity. Frankly, she's never cared a good goddamn what people think of her and Llewellyn and their unusual arrangement, and she's always deeply regretted the fact that Welly and the children didn't move in here after Hope went up.

But that's a sore subject and another story entirely.

Welly is in the attached garage now—another of Waldo's contributions—opening the garage door with the remote. Maybe he won't come back inside to say good-bye after all.

The phrase *friable earth* voices itself in Viney's mind suddenly. Where has she heard that expression? What does it mean? She goes to look it up.

In 1966, Viney replaced the family Bible on the lectern with a massive *Webster's International Collegiate Dictionary*. She makes a point of learning a new word every day and then using it in conversation. Staying mentally agile is crucial as one ages. There is no reason why a person should stop learning. Yesterday's word was *sangfroid*.

And then she remembers: One of her granddaughters—the one who's having so much trouble getting pregnant—told her recently that she was diagnosed as having a *friable uterus*. Viney was a registered nurse for over thirty years and maintains a keen interest in the medical field; nevertheless this expression was unfamiliar. She didn't have the heart to ask what it meant at the time, and a good thing, too:

Friable, she reads. *Brittle. Readily crumbled. Pulverable.*

How in the world does a uterus crumble?

Viney looks up. Llewellyn has backed out of the garage and is loading his clubs into the trunk of his Marquis. He's going then, without a word. His expression—normally so benign and handsome—bears a sour residue, the result, she supposes, of their recent spat.

The sex in the beginning was very good, probably because it felt illicit, even though their adultery was completely sanctioned—more than that, *encouraged*—by Llewellyn's wife, Hope.

Viney and Welly still have sex, at least once a month, after lunch. Welly is an improviser, a person who bends, goes with the flow. They have their routines, of course, but overall their life together has been one of freedom, quiet adventure, and discovery—both in and out of the bedroom. Viney has kept them on a semivegetarian lacto-ovo diet since 1980—relying heavily on *Fresh Vegetable and Fruit Juices: What's Missing from Your Body?* and *The Vegetarian Guide to Diet and Salad* by N. W. Walker. She credits this with their physical health, mental acuity, and active love life. Viney pictures the two of them engaged in stimulating conversation over glasses of beet juice until they are well into their hundreds. Dr. Walker himself lived to be 110. No one has yet found any reason whatsoever why the human body should die.

All those years ago, when she charged through the front door of McKeever's Funeral Home, and, ignoring staff urgings to be reasonable ("State law my ass!" she proclaimed), stormed down to the basement prep room to see Waldo's pre-embalmed remains—such a strange word in that context, *remains,* because at that point Wally was still all there— she noticed a protrusion, something like a tent pole, midway down the sheet.

"What's that?" she'd asked, even though she had a pretty good idea. She was thinking about the fact that it was her fifteenth wedding anniversary, her husband was dead, and never once had they had sex with her on top.

Malwyn McKeever repositioned himself so that she no longer had a view of Waldo's nether regions. "It's a reflex," Mal said, clearly embarrassed by the question. "A common postmortem reflex."

"That figures," Viney muttered. She had stopped crying and was starting to feel the undertow of a fierce, angry grief. She was young and foolish enough back then to believe that the worst thing in the world had just happened to her. She didn't know anything.

She was curious to hear about how embalmers deal with postmortem stiffies—imagining this almost made her laugh—but Mal's face was as pink as a medium-rare steak. So she picked out a coffin, signed the papers, and (vowing to never put herself through the experience of laying eyes on him again) bid farewell to her beautiful dead husband's erect remains.

She could never in a million years have gotten Waldo to drink carrot-ginger juice on a daily basis or sit through a program on educational television.

Why, just last night she and Welly were watching one of those science shows on PBS about stem cell research and a whole new branch of study called regenerative medicine. There's a group of doctors now who believe that people with spinal cord injuries can walk again. They've done things like remove stem cells from people's noses and pack them into the spinal cords of people who've broken their backs or necks or are suffering from some other kind of damage to their nervous systems. Lo and behold, those cells start regenerating. People who've never been able to do so much as wiggle a toe have started flexing their feet! They've even done this with a person's heart, a young boy whose idiot friend was playing around with a nail gun and shot him right through the left ventricle. Nobody believed it was possible to regenerate heart tissue, but sure enough, they've done it!

Viney tried to engage Welly in a conversation about the TV show when they were getting ready for bed, but for some reason he was unusually quiet (possibly the subject matter was upsetting given their shared history, the wheelchair-bound, and so forth) so she didn't push him.

Even though they have never officially tied the knot, they are bound together in all the ways that matter—through the rituals of everyday living, dependability, courtesy, and an innate sense of when to talk and when to keep still.

All the emphasis on *honesty* these days is, in Viney's opinion, a bad idea. Living with another human being is a stormy enough proposition without stirring up trouble over this and that and every last little thing. As far as she can tell, this obsession with talking and listening, sharing feelings and so on, hasn't done one blessed thing for the institution of marriage. Just look at the statistics. Viney's own children are example enough of the state of things: one divorced, one separated, one in counseling. None of Welly's kids have ever even gotten married. Viney has always felt sad for them—and for Welly, too, with no grandbabies—but maybe it's for the best. Cohabitation is not for the faint of heart.

Viney regrets getting snippy. She shouldn't have made a fuss, pushed him like that. It's one of those men things, a matter of pride, and there's nothing she can do now to stop him. She watches him slam the trunk closed and walk around to the driver's side door. He could use some new golf shoes. She got him that pair a couple of Christmases ago. It's not like he hasn't gotten good use out of them.

A wind kicks up. The bamboo chimes shudder; the whirligig in the rose bed spins madly. Welly starts the car. A cloud of exhaust is instantly dissipated.

It's August! Viney thinks with sudden clarity. That's what it is, that explains everything. *The Joneses always get owly in late August. Criminy, the whole* town *does for that matter, it's not as if what happened to them didn't happen to the rest of us.*

Welly's children must be feeling it, too—Bonnie a few blocks away, Larken and Gaelan up in Lincoln. Poor kids. None of them are happy, none of them have ever really settled down. Viney glances at the photographs of Llewellyn and Hope's children, prominently displayed on the fireplace mantle along with the pictures of her own blood kin.

Feeling a burst of sympathy and contrition, Viney hurriedly pushes open the screen door and scurries out to the curb to wave good-bye, but it's too late. Welly is already turning the car onto Bridge Street. He doesn't see her.

Viney sighs. That man does love to whack things with a stick. Funny. He's not even very good at it.

She gives an assessing look to the accumulating clouds off to the southwest, checks the thermometer on the garage, and sniffs the air. The wind is high now, and cooling. The thick humid air that's hovered over town for the past few days is being pushed aside.

Viney goes in. She changes into footless tights and a leotard. She'll do her exercise video and then figure out something for dinner.

Maybe he'll get to the club and run into Alan or Glen. They'll have a drink. That's probably what he'll do. He won't tee off when it's sure to storm soon.

Viney shoves *Young at Heart Yoga* into the VCR and pushes the Play button.

While the FBI reminds her of the penalties associated with video piracy, she unrolls her mat, sits down in lotus, and closes her eyes.

It's Friday. They'll have frozen lemon pepper filets and that new Stouffer's Spinach Souffle. She'll whip up a salad from Dr. Walker's cookbook. She'll make a fresh lime and celery juice tonic and mix it with spring water.

The music begins. The steady, sangfroid voice of the yoga instructor encourages her to *relax, relax. Breathe*.

And for dessert, they'll have big dishes of that fat-free rocky road that Welly likes so much.

The living aren't the only ones unsettled. The dead—especially the fathers—are also perturbed by the mayor's behavior.

There he goes, they're thinking: kicking up dust with that gas guzzler he drives, hell-bent to engage in his favorite form of outdoor recreation, putting himself in the path of what any fool could see is a developing thunder cell, and at the worst possible hour of the day.

Idiot.

The dead fathers of Emlyn Springs are obstinate homebodies. They value routine. They keep close to their caskets.

This rootedness isn't entirely owed to the fact that they've been planted in the landscape. For the farmers, it's a matter of habit. They spent their lives knee-deep in loess, spring water, and manure; laying drain tile; planting, tending, and harvesting crops. A shackled vigilance to the soil and to the moods of the provincial sky was essential. It was possible to leave, but for a few hours at most, and only for the most pressing of reasons: a drive into town twice a year without fail to go to church; up to Beatrice to pick up a new transmission for the tractor; over to Branson, Missouri, to see traveling magicians, lion tamers, Up with People, or some other cultural event that the mother of their children arranged, and at which their presence, however grudging, was mandated. Ever black about the face and hands, pungent, abidingly crumby with dirt no matter how much they scrubbed, their bodies over time became so embedded with earth—and most of them lived long—that their skin evolved, adapted, developing a subdermal stratum composed of equal parts skin and soil. For the farmers, the transition to being dead and buried was hardly noticeable.

But even the nonfarmers are perfectly happy staying put. There may not be anything spectacular about the landscape in this part of Nebraska, but it's home. *If you leave, you're gonna cry* is what they've always said, but not everyone listens.

The most compelling reason behind their constant presence, however, is this: The dead are often called into service as what for lack of a better term could be called *outfielders,* catching those disquieted souls who die unwillingly, with rude, terrifying suddenness (victims of car accidents, gun blasts, natural disasters, and the like) and conveying them home. These kinds of deaths aren't common in Emlyn Springs, but the dead fathers maintain a proud readiness.

In the meantime, they are not idle. Far from it.

Several of them are plein air painters. Being submerged in the landscape has given them a new appreciation for it. Their awareness of color is deeper and more refined; after all, they themselves provide at least some of those colors: the robust burgundy of milo seed heads, the eerily dense green of emerging soybeans. Many are engaged in ongoing scientific experiments. Others are linguists.

To label their pursuits as hobbies would be misleading. The dead fathers of Emlyn Springs are not dilettantes. They work long and hard. They postulate formulas and equations with assiduity and then set about the long, slow, solitary business of proof. This makes them very happy. Eternally happy.

Meet some of them. Observe their labors. Tread lightly.

Mr. Merle Funk, farmer (1874–1930), is preoccupied with subtle differences in grasshopper physiology. Waldo Closs, insurance salesman (1930–1962), studies the fragile nervous system of the four-leaf clover. Obediah Purdy, pharmacist and bicycle enthusiast (1826–1899), transcribes dialectical variations in bee-speak. And leading the landscape artists is Dr. Gerallt Williams (1902–2000), family physician and specialty carpenter.

When it comes to the animal kingdom, their studies are focused exclusively on native birds. They're done with cattle and hogs. They're fed up with chickens. Ezra "the Egg King" Krivosha (1888–1982)—who put

Emlyn Springs on the map by promoting it as the Fancy Egg capital of the world—no longer cares one whit about the inner lives of exotic laying hens, but he's fascinated by the social interactions of snow geese. And since his death a hundred years ago, Fritz Bybee, Esq., has been recording the genealogical history of a single family of pied-billed grebes.

Other dead fathers are engaged in researching the impact of weather upon the underbelly of the Nebraska landscape—and, by extension, upon all remains that are there interred: Mr. Roy Klump, owner of Roy's Roofing (1930–1998), records the varying sound waves produced by different sizes of hail and notes their effect upon postmortem hair growth. Myron Mutter (1898–1982), pastor, observes the way that electrical currents passing through the earth in advance of a thunderstorm affect hearing loss. And Mr. Ellis Cockeram, podiatrist and choirmaster (1903–1979), is devising a means of measuring tornado-force winds by observing the escalating sensations that occur in his left fourth metatarsal.

The dead are just as certain as the living that a storm is on its way today, and soon—not by observing the sky, but through a particular chemical agitation in the soil, along with various corresponding skeletal anxieties. (Thankfully, Mr. Cockeram's toes are unaffected.) Their softer remains are growing incrementally more acidic, and the earthworms, preferring a sweeter cuisine, are burrowing away.

Dead fathers don't ask for much: solitude and quiet and detachment from the emotional vicissitudes of the living. They don't thrill to demonstrative mourners. They can't abide recklessness. And nothing upsets them more than willful stupidity.

Ergo, as far as they're concerned, Llewellyn Jones deserves whatever he gets for behaving with such reckless disregard for the rules of storm safety, rules that each and every one of them can tick off in their sleep.

And now the mayor is at the country club, parking his '89 Marquis next to Bud Humphries' '84 F-150, shouldering his bag and heading directly for the first hole tee-off.

What the hell is he thinking?

Decoding the motivating forces behind human behavior is the academic province of dead mothers. In contrast to their male counterparts (those curmudgeons, digging in their fleshless heels, barking out rules with a catechismal self-importance), dead mothers—*ah!*—they travel.

They would insist, somewhat defensively, that travel is a requisite of their studies in cross-cultural behavioral psychology. But truth be told, it's mainly because they are weight-sensitive. When grounded, the dead mothers feel every footstep of every human being all over the world.

It was something like this when they were pregnant. Their children's feet trounced around inside them like so many mischievous elfin sprites. Bubbly, they were. Effervescent when they quickened, like soda pop in the gut. That was how they made their presence known. So lightly.

But now! The heaviness of all of them. The pitter-patter of little feet has become a nonstop cacophony of stones.

The dead mothers' travels are interrupted when something of significance is about to happen, something involving a living child, for example, or a spouse. At such times, they are called back from wherever they are, whether it's across the state or on the other side of the ocean. They come willingly, without resentment.

One among them is being called back now: Aneira Hope Jones (1940–1978). She is halfway around the world, visiting the town of Pwllheli on the Llŷn Peninsula of North Wales. Among the dead mothers of Emlyn Springs, Hope tends to travel farther and stay away longer; but then, she's always been different.

Hope knows this much: Her presence is required, and so she sets out, returning to the land and the people with whom she was once one flesh.

Llewellyn Jones is teeing off. The dead are paying attention.

Rule Number One! Merle Funk barks out. *Don't go under a large tree that stands alone!*

Lightning illuminates the sky. The dead fathers start counting:

One cornhusker, two cornhuskers, three cornhuskers . . .

Llewellyn is in the rough. Hope arrives—her unexpected appearance is barely noticed by her comrades—and she watches with the rest of them.

Rule Number Two! Fritz Bybee chimes in. *Don't stay in a place where you are taller than your surroundings!*

He's certainly played better, muses Roy Klump. *He used to beat me on that hole every time.*

Llewellyn's wedge shot—into the pond—corresponds with the next thunderbolt, as if he himself were summoning the elements.

The air inside the clouds a mile to the southwest is becoming agitated. Groggy humidity is being dragged up from the earth.

Llewellyn is standing knee-deep in water.

Rule Number Three! the fathers cry together, *Don't fish from a boat or stand on a hilltop or in an open field!*

To which Ellis Cockeram adds, *Lightning kills more people than all other kinds of storms put together!*

A tunnel of supercooled air is gearing up to jettison downward.

Llewellyn crests the hill to the green. He sinks the putt. More thunder.

The dead mothers join the fathers, chanting *One cornhusker, two cornhuskers* . . .

Picking up his ball, Llewellyn hurries to the number five tee-off, the highest point of the Emlyn Springs golf course. From here he can see miles in all directions—over to his family's land, long ago vacated by them, not sold, but turned over to more capable and less sorrowful hands. He can see the cemetery where a cenotaph marks the place his wife, Hope, would be buried, if only they could find her. To the north are his two oldest children, out of harm's way, he hopes, out of the danger zone. He imagines seeing his youngest, Bonnie, on one of the back roads, pedaling her bicycle in the furious way she's had since she was small. But no. Whatever else her siblings think of her, Bonnie has a good head on her shoulders. She wouldn't be out on her bike in weather like this.

Here he goes. Burying the tee. Settling into his stance.

What is the fool thinking? wonders Alvina's dead husband, Waldo.

Rule Number Four! warns Pastor Myron Mutter, desperately. *Never hold on to or be near anything made of metal!*

Mayor Jones—whose first name is pronounced with a sound not found in the English language, a palatal push of air—breathes in the sight of his homeland, and then . . .

Llewellyn . . . Hope whispers, sending her breath into the double *l*'s the Welsh way, giving his name the sound of a reticent breeze.

He looks down, prepares, still as granite. Suddenly he swings: his club arcs up—forcefully, theatrically, with intent—and then down, slamming into the ball as the thunder roars again, swinging through, cutting a semicircular swath through space and then freezing momentarily, long enough to form with his club a straight vertical line, a perfect conduit between earth and sky, and then there is a crack and a sizzle and a sword of light.

The motion of the ball outlasts the living force behind it; it hurtles skyward with a marvelous ease, and even after the mayor's heart is stunned into stillness by ten million volts of electrical current, the ball sails onward, upward, disappearing into the roiling clouds, moving in opposition to the hail that is now beginning to fall.

In the clubhouse cocktail lounge—where there's a good view of the fifth-hole tee—the mayor's friends are temporarily confused. They cannot see that the single hailstone that seems to be rising miraculously in resistance to the laws of gravity is really an ordinary pockmarked Titleist 100.

Then their eyes, losing sight of the ball, trace a line earthward and land upon the stilled form of Llewellyn Dewey Jones (1934–2003), physician, baritone, four-term mayor of Emlyn Springs, Nebraska, and now-dead father.

Hail is bludgeoning the clubhouse roof. Bud Humphries, the country club bartender, town council chairman, and volunteer paramedic, snatches up the defibrillator and rushes outside. Hail, obedient, downward-falling hail, pummels his shoulders; he will be sore tomorrow and for weeks to come. This soreness will be fought with numerous applications of Bengay, which he will purchase from the town's only drugstore, Lloyd's Drugs, and here is Owen Lloyd now, pharmacist, war veteran, knocking over his martini glass in his haste to get down from the bar stool and call the fire station. The two other men in the clubhouse, Alan Everett Jones (no relation) and Glen Rhys Thomas, leave their peanuts and pitcher of beer and follow Bud outside, even though the storm is still directly, dangerously overhead. They go because they are men of Llewellyn's generation, few in number, men who have stayed put as their sons and daughters moved away in all four directions, to bigger towns and even bigger cities.

They reach him, their fallen friend. Bud performs CPR, knowing that the mayor is gone, and yet still here, and so deserving of their best efforts. Llewellyn would have done the same for any of them. They could all tell a different story about a time they watched Dr. Jones labor over the body of some poor soul who had clearly passed on—and saw the look on his face when he couldn't postpone that passage.

Owen Lloyd has finished his phone call and hurries outside—as best he can, with one good leg and one prosthetic one. He has remembered to bring a blanket.

These living men, fathers all, cover their friend, standing guard over him in the pelting hail, the pouring rain. They stand: waiting, witnessing. From town comes the sound of the firehouse siren. The volunteer firefighters, who they've known for years, known by their first and middle and last names, are on the way.

The storm subsides, passes. The air is cooling. Bud stops giving CPR. They might as well carry Llewellyn inside.

The babies fall into a tear-stained slumber, so exhausted that they may even bless their frazzled mothers by sleeping through the night. In the bodies of the teenage girls who are not yet mothers the blood arrives. One native son sneezes, another has an orgasm. A teenage boy pops a pimple. A toenail falls off. The carpenter slides the board into place. In Miss Hazel Williams's parlor, the piano student strikes a B-natural. At St. David's, Eustace Craven finally succeeds in moving his bowels.

The dead sigh and look to the place where Llewellyn will be buried, right over there, next to the unoccupied bit of earth that has been reserved for his wife. Cenotaphs are such a waste of real estate.

The rain comes and soaks the ground. Cool and clean, it is a great relief to all concerned. The dead get back to work. They barely registered Hope's presence, so few of them notice that she has already, once again, gone missing.

And above the field that has been in Llewellyn Dewey Jones's family for over a century, three birds, all native to Nebraska but of disparate species, are traveling earthward on a cold downdraft. After uttering a few words to one another—too quickly for the dead ornithologist fathers to translate—they fly off in different directions.

No one notices Llewellyn's Titleist 100, bearing a crescent-shaped cut on one side, looking like a partially peeled exotic fruit. It continues to arc up into the sky until it disappears.

It does not come down.

Chapter 2

The Professor and the Weatherman TGIF

It is the last day of the summer term. Exams are done, papers are graded. All that stands between Larken Jones, BA, MA, PhD, and a two-week hiatus is a bit of paperwork and a conference with one of her grad students, Misty Ariel Kroeger. It has become university policy that academic failure not come as a rude surprise; the bad news must be delivered in person. Every effort must be made to coddle the slacker.

"Hello, Misty. Come in."

Larken sits behind her desk in the basement of one of the oldest buildings on campus. Her office is not a reflective or spacious one. A euphonic description would include the words *penumbral* and *cloistered,* words she habitually uses when describing Joseph's woodshop as depicted in the Mérode Altarpiece, ten-dollar words used with intent, to help her sort the wheat from the chaff, so to speak, among her Art History 101 undergrads. There is one north-facing-daylight basement-type window, the room is slightly bigger than a walk-in closet, but she shares it with no one. It is all hers.

Larken doesn't look up; ostensibly, she is scrutinizing the set of student papers and attendance records arrayed in front of her. She works her mouth in a way suggesting solemnity, a judicial concentration that is the preface to some wise, weighty, and well-articulated utterance. In fact, she is trying to dissolve the last remnants of two Reese's peanut butter cups, one cadged expertly in each cheek.

"Please sit down." Larken has developed an ability to articulate clearly, like Diosthenes with his pebbles, while surreptitiously holding all manner of sustenance in her mouth. Her ability to maintain an unmoving jaw as she speaks only adds to the overall impression that she is indomitable. Larken has overheard students refer to her as General Jones—some with obvious fondness, some with trepidation, others with disdain. Aside from its asexuality and implied hawkishness, the moniker pleases her.

The student facing her now is lithe and naturally beautiful, but has chosen to sully her looks with excessive eye makeup, filthy dyed dreadlocks, and numerous piercings. She is the sort of girl who invests in a radical outward appearance rather than develop her intellect, creative vision, or technique. Misty's work as an artist, which Larken saw in the spring student show, bears the particular blend of personal polemics and bad technique that seems to be more and more common among the grad students these days: Frida Kahlo wannabes; collages of trite images, done-to-death symbols, and personal writings; studied attempts at a primitive style that is really only primitive. Larken hates this stuff, but many of her departmental colleagues seem to encourage it.

"Do you have anything you'd like to say?" Larken asks, looking up from Misty's essay exams, quizzes, and the record of her class (non)attendance.

Misty shifts in her chair, causing it to creak daintily.

"I suppose you're gonna tell me that I didn't do that well."

Larken works her tongue behind one of her wisdom teeth and dislodges a small fragment of chocolate. "You failed the course, Misty. You have to know that."

Misty's eyes widen in a pathetic effort to indicate shock. "You're kidding!"

Larken adjusts her glasses and works up enough saliva to flood her mouth with a last dilute taste of the peanut butter cups. "You missed several classes. You got a D on the exam. And your essay . . ." Larken indicates Misty's paper on the table in front of her. It's fiercely handwritten, barely legible, full of spelling errors.

"What about it?" Misty asks, defensively.

Larken wonders if it would be possible to sneak the last pair of peanut butter cups into her mouth; they're just down there, in the open desk drawer to the right, invitingly unwrapped, nestled in their tiny pleated papers. It would be easy. She slides the course requirement sheet across the desk, pointing with her pen as she enumerates Misty's infractions.

"You've had several unexcused absences, missed quizzes . . . You didn't take advantage of the extra-credit opportunities, nor did you make up late or missed assignments even when I allowed you to do so . . . You basically violated every condition of the class contract. How can I possibly give you a passing grade?" Larken keeps her voice even. It's important in cases like this to maintain one's civility. "You're a first-year graduate student, Misty. I wouldn't even allow this kind of performance at the undergrad level."

"But I really need this credit!"

But I really need this credit—uttered in the desperately plaintive way Misty has just demonstrated—is the statement Professor Jones hears almost as much as *Do we have to know this for the test?*

"You should have thought of that before you missed seven classes and turned in unacceptable work."

Misty, predictably, starts chewing her pierced lip and working up a dewiness around her heavily made-up eyes. "I didn't skip. I had a personal emergency."

I broke up with my boyfriend/girlfriend. I broke my wrist. My cat died. I couldn't pay the rent. My parents disowned me. My computer crashed.

Misty is looking skyward, as if seeking divine intervention. She launches into a well-embroidered fabrication involving distant family members and vague, life-threatening medical conditions. Larken steals looks at the clock above the door. It's almost noon.

". . . so I had to get back to Ogallala to see my cousin every weekend all summer, and it's like a two-hour drive each way."

Professor Jones, who does not travel by plane, has made several car trips across America over the years; she happens to know that getting to Ogallala from Lincoln—even on Interstate 80, even exceeding the speed limit—takes at least four and a half hours. "If you had told me about it I would have been happy to make special allowances."

"But I turned in my paper!" Misty has now passed into the next phase of slacker student protestation. Like patients receiving a terminal diagnosis, students who have failed a class go through a predictable range of phases: rage, denial, bargaining, acceptance, etc. "I worked really hard on it!"

"Misty, it's not even typed."

"The library computers were all down and my roommate left already with her computer."

Larken reads from Misty's paper, circling misspelled words as she goes. "'The Mérode *Alterpiece* is a prime example of the historical artistic *subjegation* of women. It has no *legitmate* place in a post-*femnist* approach to art history.' You can't make an incendiary statement like that without offering proof, without providing more scholarly evidence to uphold that statement."

Misty is giving Larken a slack-jawed, baffled look. "Incendiary?"

"Inflammatory. Fiery. Seditionist. Controversial."

"Well," Misty counters meekly, "it's true."

Larken sighs. The class Misty is about to fail—a special topics class, Feminist Perspectives on Pre-Renaissance Art—always attracts the immature, the strident. Young women who seem to feel that, by virtue of their in-your-face fashion and political attitudes, they're guaranteed an instant rapport with Professor Jones and an unqualified A, when in fact Larken is hard-pressed not to apply an unfairly rigorous standard where they're concerned. She compensates for this by swinging to the other extreme, giving them every opportunity to succeed, even when, as in this situation, it's hopeless.

"All right, Misty, why don't you elaborate on your theory."

Larken makes a show of readjusting herself, rotating and leaning her body slightly so that she can dangle her arm into the bottom-right desk drawer, within range of the peanut butter cups; she brings her left hand to the front of her face, forming a kind of low-hanging awning over her mouth. While Misty regurgitates a predictable barrage of generalist postfeminist slop she's undoubtedly plagiarized, Larken delicately fingers the peanut butter cups out of their wrappers.

". . . blatantly subservient position of the Virgin!" Misty is ranting, not even looking in Larken's direction. "Predatory Peeping Tom presence of the male patron! . . ."

Larken palms the first peanut butter cup and, with one flowing movement, brings it to her mouth. She leans on both her hands now and lets the candy warm and soften, enjoying the way the delicately corrugated ridges on the side of the peanut butter cup contrast with its smooth top and bottom.

". . . the murder of female sexuality!" Misty continues, fervently. "A forced union with a man old enough to be her grandfather!"

It's almost as though these young women have undergone some form of mind control, causing them to spew the same speech. Faking a sniffle, Larken plucks a tissue and swipes at her nose, then leans down to toss the tissue in the wastebasket. On the way up she grabs the second peanut butter cup and slides it into her mouth.

Misty riffs on and on (all she needs is a bass player and bongo drums) about the absurdity of studying the religious painting of the pre-Renaissance Flemish masters—which happens to be Professor Jones's area of expertise and the center of her life's work. Postmodernism is all that matters, Misty insists, these are not the influences on her generation; being required to take this class is a waste of time and money. And after all, who's paying for her education anyway?

That's what I'd like to know, Larken wonders. She's sucked off all the chocolate and is savoring the slightly granular texture of the peanut butter heart.

Misty winds down. "So," she says, looking up at Larken with appealing coyness. Many of Professor Jones's students believe she is gay. Misty herself might be gay. "Is there anything I can do to get a better grade?"

Larken swallows the last of the candy and clears her throat. A positive by-product of chocolate consumption is the way it affects Larken's already-distinctive voice: Something about the combination of emulsified and hydrogenated oils and cocoa lends it a sage, gravelly resonance that is very impressive.

"Rewrite the paper. Type it. Elaborate in writing on the points you just presented, turn it in via an e-mail attachment by the end of the day—no later than four o'clock—and I'll consider giving you a D."

"What?" Misty looks incensed.

"That's the best I can do."

"Fuckin' bitch."

"Excuse me?"

Misty stands up suddenly, dreadlocks flying, all pretense of weepiness cast off. Here comes the acceptance phase.

"You're a fuckin' FAT DYKE BITCH and I hope you die!"

Misty storms out, slamming the office door behind her, no doubt feeling that she's left Professor Jones decimated in the wake of this dramatic exit line. The truth is it's highly unoriginal, just like Misty's ersatz Frida Kahlo art.

Larken has an impulse to crumple Misty's essay into a ball and eat it. Instead, she uses a red Sharpie to draw a thick line down the entire left margin of the page, another across the top, and a third halfway across the middle: a big, bleeding F.

She then scoops up a handful of change from her middle desk drawer and pockets it. She pushes herself out of her chair and heads for the vending machines—conveniently located just around the corner.

Larken has been in the basement for eighteen years, since she herself was a grad student and teaching assistant. She could move into a different office anytime she wants, a more spacious and well-lit one, an aboveground office befitting her rank as a tenured professor and doctor of letters. She's been offered a change of venue often enough. But she prefers it here, in the basement. The proximity of the vending machines is only one reason; it's always cool (woe to the Midwesterner without summer access to a poured concrete basement), usually quiet (hardly anyone comes down here except the photography students, and they are generally nocturnal), and if all that weren't enough, there are the decades-old yellow-and-black signs guaranteeing shelter from atomic fallout in the event of nuclear war.

When Larken assumes the mantle of department chairman—and it's not unreasonable to imagine that she'll be rewarded with that academic pinnacle soon—she'll be delighted to relocate aboveground. Until then, she's staying down here.

Larken starts loading coins into the machine, pausing after each deposit of change to make sure no one is coming. Over the years, Larken has developed her own rulebook governing professorial conduct; one rule states: *It is unseemly for a tenured professor to be caught in the act of buying food from a vending-machine.*

As she struggles to define what she's craving, she hears someone approaching. Sidestepping smoothly to the beverage machine, she takes another handful of coins and deposits them, so that by the time the department's star undergrad photography student rounds the corner

("Hi Professor," he says amiably—Larken loves this about him, that he addresses her as *professor*), she is retrieving a bottle of spring water, innocent and noncaloric as a celery stick.

"Hello, Mr. McNeely." Drew McNeely is one of Larken's rare A students. "Shouldn't you be making your escape from this gulag?"

He laughs. "Pretty soon, I hope. Just finishing up some prints."

"Will I be seeing you next term?"

"I'll be in your Northern Renaissance class."

"I look forward to it."

"Take care, Professor."

After the last echoes of Drew's footsteps have faded and the basement is silent, Larken makes her selection, returns to her office, closes the door, and locks it. She is expecting no more visitors, and if someone comes by she'll pretend she isn't here. There's still work to do, and she wants to get out of here no later than 1:30.

Larken lays a square of paper towel on her desk. She opens and shakes out two bags of Corn Nuts, being careful to contain everything in a loose pyramidal construction within the paper towel's perimeters.

She then starts to reexamine the evidentiary record of Misty's performance one last time. Flunking a student in these whiny, litigious times—even a nonscholarship student attending a state-funded university—is a bold step, and Professor Jones is one of the few faculty members who still invokes her right to do so. Since Misty is exactly the kind of student who'd be likely to lodge an official protest with admin, Larken has to make sure she's scrupulous in her documentation.

Yep, she concludes. *The girl really went out of her way to fuck up.*

Pinching a handful of Corn Nuts out of the pile, Larken starts double-checking all her students' final grades. It's exacting, tiring work—Professor Jones's combined teaching roster contains well over two hundred names—but the repetitive hand-to-mouth motion, oral exertions and percussive sound track keep her focused. Now and then she rests her eyes and replenishes her spirit by gazing at a framed full-sized reproduction of a Flemish triptych that hangs on the wall opposite her desk.

It is a small work—surprisingly small given its significance. Taken as a whole, the three panels of the Mérode Altarpiece measure only about three feet by two feet. It is attributed to a man named Robert Campin, but most historians believe that one of his unnamed assistants did much of the work.

Larken first saw the Mérode in the fall of her freshman year; it was projected in slide form on a screen at the front of a huge lecture hall, where—slouching in a chair in the back row, chewing her fingernails, watching the clock, and desperate for her next cigarette—she was one of a hundred students who'd randomly chosen Art History 101 as an elective.

"And here we have *The Annunciation Tryptych* by Robert Campin," Professor Arthur Collins intoned, "one of the most radical works of art ever produced."

Larken felt as though she'd been hit in the chest with a thunderbolt.

"Would any of you care to venture a guess as to why I've used the word *radical* in reference to this painting?" the professor continued.

Larken's hand shot up. Other hands went up as well, but she was the one who got Arthur's notice. He made a show of squinting from beneath his famously wiry brows and then shielding his eyes, calling up to her as if from the playing field of a sunlit stadium. "Ah!" he cried. "A voice from the cheap seats! Miss . . . ?"

"Jones," Larken replied. "Larken Jones."

"Yes, Miss Jones?"

"She's not in a church," Larken ventured. "She doesn't have a halo or anything."

"'She?'" Arthur prompted with the icy disdain that was his trademark, a tactic meant to condition the faint of heart. "'She' who?"

"The Virgin," Larken replied, ignoring the subsequent wave of giggles. "The one in the middle. She doesn't look special or holy. She's just sitting in a regular room, like a living room or something, reading a book."

"Why is that significant?"

Larken paused, realizing that he did not expect her to simply fill in the blanks of some thought that was already in his head.

"Maybe because—"

Arthur winced theatrically, as if physically wounded. Holding up his hand like a crossing guard keeping traffic at bay, he said, "Never preface your responses with 'maybe,' Miss Jones," he said. "Or use words such as *kinda* or *like* or *something* or *sorta*." His imitation of a waffling student evoked more laughter. "Render your opinion with linguistic authority at the very least, and your listener will be far more likely to give you a hearing."

Larken took a breath. "If an angel can come to the Virgin Mary while she's sitting in a living room, then miraculous things can happen anywhere."

"And why is that important? Why is that radical?"

"Well . . ."

Again, Arthur recoiled, mock-pained. "A *well,* Miss Jones, is a hole in the ground."

Larken persevered. "If God can be anywhere, then how can churches and priests and"—Larken faltered; she was about to say *people like that*—"How will *clergymen* be able to convince people to give them money? If there's no need for churches, then there's no need for collection plates."

Arthur nodded and stared at her for a moment—whatever test he'd put her to, she had passed—and then said, "Good, Miss Jones. Quite good." He resumed his address to the class at large, pretending that she'd faded once again into back-row obscurity. But Larken wasn't fooled; something special had passed between them. She'd been *noticed.*

"Simply by presenting the Annunciation of the Virgin Mary in a commonplace setting," Arthur continued, "an ordinary, middle-class home, and by portraying her as a real, robust young woman without a halo, the artist has done something that has far-reaching, political, and in that sense, *radical* implications."

And that was how it began: with Arthur requiring her to translate amorphous, sloppy feeling into formed language, training her from that moment on to use clear and specific words in the service of clear and specific ideas.

Six characters inhabit the Mérode Annunciation: mother, angel, monk, nun, gatekeeper, carpenter. Larken has been studying them, weaving stories and asking questions about them for over half her life. On any given day, one of them will advance to the foreground of her mind and imagination, demanding scrutiny, while others recede from view.

Today her attention is drawn to the center panel of the triptych, where the Virgin Mary—eternally luminous and young, her face smooth, almost plump—sits on the floor of a small, ordinary chamber in a middle-class

Flemish house. She is reading. She wears a voluminous rose-colored robe—one senses that the body beneath is solid, well-fed, even roly-poly with residual baby fat—and a trick of divine light causes a star to appear within the complex folds of cloth. The angel has just arrived; in its wake, so tiny as to be inscrutable except in extreme close-up, is the spirit of the Christ child. Symbolized by a cherubic naked form no bigger than the Virgin's forefinger, the Son of God shoulders a plain wooden cross and rides toward this unaware girl on golden threads of light that penetrate the room via an unshuttered, circular window.

The candle has just been extinguished. The words of the annunciation are about to be uttered. The Virgin is about to become a mother.

By the time Larken closes her grade book, she's electrically charged with carbohydrates. She needs to ride this high while she can, using it to sustain her through her next (and final) set of obligations: getting her grades turned in to Chris, the art department secretary, whose office is in another building. Then, for the next two weeks, she's free.

She should really take next summer off and do something besides teach. Travel, maybe. Drive to New York, spend some long days at the Cloisters, where she can see the Mérode firsthand. Get overseas, somehow. Rent a room in a Tuscan monastery—lots of academics do that kind of thing. Take a slow boat to the Netherlands.

Larken methodically pushes the vending-machine wrappers deep into the plastic bag lining her wastepaper basket. She ties a knot at the top of the bag, gathers her things, turns out lights, and opens her door a crack. No one. She quickly closes and locks her door, then stuffs the evidence into the large anonymous metal trash can stationed out in the hall.

She takes the elevator and begins her ascent.

Larken always dresses in dark colors; today she wears loose black silk slacks and a maroon rayon shirt with its bottom three buttons undone. Her clothes are nice enough—she orders them online from Lane Bryant—but she spends most of her personal wardrobe and grooming budget on her head and feet: salon haircuts, designer makeup, jewelry and scarves, expensive shoes. She walks briskly, with resolve (even in this heat, no matter what it costs her) and she makes as little noise as possible—habits that have been developed consciously over time.

Emerging from the elevator, Larken immediately starts to perspire; it's at least thirty degrees hotter up here than it was downstairs. This is an old building, warmed in winter by steam heat, cooled in summer by wishful thinking and placebos: half-open windows, rotary fans. Larken starts down the shadowed hall that she must traverse to get to the door nearest her destination. Thankfully, it is a long hall, allowing her to stay indoors as long as possible.

The air outside hits her like a boiler room blast. Instantly, she begins to sweat. Her thighs chafe together as she crosses the commons.

Walking through the university's sculpture garden, Larken passes two of its notable acquisitions: the zaftig *Floating Woman* and the trimmer but still paunchy *Woman in a Box*. She thinks of her parents, of a conversational exchange she heard numerous times when she was growing up:

What a shame! Hope would say, sotto voce, as she often did when they passed a fat stranger. *She has such a pretty face.*

Pretty face, my ass, Larken hears her father counter scornfully. *Pretty is pretty, Hope. Fat is fat.*

It must be hard for Dad, Larken often thinks, knowing that, although the body habitus of his eldest daughter falls short of morbid obesity, it most definitely fits under the less precise heading of "blubber butt" and well within U.S. government parameters for "overweight": Professor Jones is five feet two and weighs one hundred and seventy-eight pounds. She doesn't need Misty Ariel Kroger to tell her that she's fat.

Larken mounts the stairs, determined not to slow her pace. By the time she reaches the level of the entrance, she is drenched and panting. She has walked two hundred paces. Her sugar high is already starting to wane. But sustenance is not far away, just around the corner.

She arrives—*yes!*—and there it is.

Kris, the art department secretary, always has sugary treats on her desk; this week, it's a glass canister of Hershey's Kisses. When Larken sees that Kris has her back to her and is occupied in the copy room, she grabs a handful and drops them into a side pocket of her book bag.

"Hi, Kris!" Larken calls out, adopting the shoplifter's strategy of calling attention to herself. "TGIF!"

"Hi, Larken," Kris calls over her shoulder. "You got that right."

Kris has been the department secretary for eight years. She wears a gold crucifix, small enough to be tasteful, large enough to be noticeable.

Larken likes Kris well enough—she's tremendously efficient and courteous—but she prefers to keep their conversations brief. Larken has an abiding fear that Kris will one day look her in the eyes and ask earnestly: *Are you saved?*

Larken grabs a few more kisses. "Where do you want these grades?" she asks.

Kris comes out of the copy room; she has a high-stepping, energetic way of walking and a tirelessly chipper voice, as if she spends her off-hours as a drum majorette. "I'll take them," she says firmly, holding out her hand—and Larken's heart jumps fearfully.

But she is referring to the grades, of course.

"I had to fail Misty Kroeger," Larken remarks casually.

"No big surprise there, was there?"

"Not really, but still, I hate to do it."

"You are so softhearted. Thanks for getting these in on time. I'm still waiting for half the faculty."

"Well, I'm out of here," Larken says. "See you in a couple of weeks."

She is almost out the door, already unwrapping a kiss in her imagination, when Kris calls her back.

"Hey! Aren't you going to that thing this afternoon?"

"What thing?"

"The cocktail-thingy. You know, at the gallery? Say hello to the new dean, lah-dee-dah?

"Shit," Larken mutters. "I forgot." She glances toward the current chairman's office. "Is Richard going to be there?"

"I imagine so."

Damn. She'll have to go.

"How about Professor and Mrs. Collins?" In spite of being nearly forty years older than Larken, Arthur and Eloise Collins are the only people in the academic community that Larken has a personal relationship with; their presence at any university function at least assures a safe conversational haven.

"Well, Arthur hasn't been in—he turned in his grades a couple of days ago—but I'm pretty sure, yeah. Didn't you get your invitation?"

"Yes, yes, I got it, I just . . ."

Shit! She had plans for this afternoon. She wanted to get home, get ready for tonight, be done with this place.

Larken glances at her watch. "What time does it start?"

"Three-thirty. It goes until five-thirty, but I'm sure you don't have to stay that long if you don't want to. Do you have plans?" Kris speaks in a concertedly offhanded manner. Larken recognizes this tone; it's meant to mask a rabid subtextual curiosity. No one in the department besides the Collinses know anything about Professor Jones's personal life, and even with them Larken is not terribly forthcoming.

Ignoring the question, Larken says, "Okay, then, I'll see you there," and starts making her way toward the exit.

Just before she heads back out into the stifling heat, she gobbles a kiss; it is both a reward for her punctual compliance in submitting her grades and a consolation for having to go to this fucking bloody university thing. Food is wonderful that way; it accommodates all occasions.

Larken has a coveted parking space close to the building where her office and classrooms are located. This is no small boon. Arthur, who held the art department chairmanship at the time, saw to the parking space several years ago, when Larken went from being a stellar, matriculated member of the student body to an eager member of the faculty— albeit an untenured one.

Larken feels eternally indebted to Arthur for this, among many other things. Ever since that day in Art Appreciation 101, Arthur has been her mentor, her champion. His influence on her identity has been as formative as family. It's difficult for Larken to think about what life might have been had he not taken an interest. In spite of Larken's determined efforts, her own father didn't notice her for years.

That's okay. She was fucked up. So was he, probably.

But he's proud of her now. At least professionally. He'll be so happy once she's awarded the chairmanship. Ecstatic. Over the moon.

Larken hefts herself into her car, a 1986 maroon Chevy Nova. It is small. It is reliable. Once she closes the door, she is seized with panic: the interior atmosphere of the car feels dangerous, toxic with trapped heat—like the cabin of a jet with a malfunctioning air pressure system. Frantically, Larken cranks open a window and tries to quiet her breath.

This damn party. Maybe she could beg off, call the dean's office after she gets home and say she's sick.

But no, Kris saw her—sugary, crucifix-wearing Kris—and she's the kind of person who'll go around to everyone saying, *Have you seen*

Dr. Jones? She was in the office at noon, turning in her grades, and she seemed just fine. She said she was coming. You don't suppose she got the flu, do you? Or food poisoning? The road to department chairmanship is paved with publication and cocktail parties. Larken knows that she must attend; moreover, she must suck it up, doll up, make a good impression.

Going home would be the logical solution for most people. Larken has fancier shirts in her closet. Her bureau drawers are filled with eye-catching accessories that are designed to draw focus up, up, and away.

But going home sweet home is not an option. Home, there's no place like home, beckons to Larken with insistence when she is away, holds her with tenaciousness when she is there. She is incapable of dropping by her apartment. "Dropping by" is something birds and insects do. It implies lightness, flow, ease—all qualities of which she is not possessed.

The good news is, after she gets home tonight, she won't have to move for two weeks. She probably will move, but she won't have to. Nothing will be required of her until the first day of the fall semester.

The thick humidity intensifies the smells in the car, vivid smells stimulating memories of fast-food past. Larken imagines festive red-and-white-striped buckets filled with fried chicken, an addicting textural masterpiece that is crunchy and peppery on the outside, smooth and viscous on the inside, pull-away moist next to the bone, and tinged with pink. She visualizes small Styrofoam containers; inside, smooth mounds of mashed potatoes are adorned with swirling islands of gravy. There is such bounty in these Styrofoam containers. They are stuffed so full that their contents are flattened against bulging translucent lids. Larken will peel off the lids and lick them clean, working her tongue into their minute, innermost surfaces, the areas that intersect with the Styrofoam, even though the edges of the lids are sharp enough to draw blood. She will be provided with sporks, and even their peculiar, petroleum-like sheen is tantalizing to contemplate. The back of Larken's tongue curls reflexively, anticipating the arrival of vinegary ribbons of shredded coleslaw, held together by gobs of mayonnaise.

There's a KFC on the way to the mall.

That's it; problem solved. She'll stop at the drive-through, get a late lunch, then hunt down a scarf, an expensive scarf, something colorful and flamboyant, or texturally rich—velour on rayon maybe, or a nubby silk—to offset her plain shirt and draw attention to her face, which she will freshen with a new shade of lipstick. She could look for some new earrings, too: they will be classy but glittering. They will catch the light. Burgundy-colored glass would be nice—ersatz rubies set in black filigree. A 1920s look. A Gertrude-Stein-hosting-one-of-her-Paris-salons look.

Larken would bet good money that nobody ever called Gertrude Stein Thunder Thighs or Lard Ass. If they did, Pablo or Ernest or even big, gay Gertie herself would have hauled off and punched them in the mouth.

Larken starts the car, cranks the window closed, and turns the air-conditioning on full blast. Between the Colonel's chicken, the accessories department, and the cosmetics counter, she can see to all her immediate requirements. She'll put in a brief appearance at this stupid party, conduct herself like Miss Congeniality, and then she'll get out of here.

After that it will be home, home, home where the heart is, because Professor Larken Jones has a long-standing commitment on Friday evenings and nothing in this world could ever make her miss it.

Across town at the KLAN-KHAM studios, Gaelan Jones is about to give the noon-hour forecast. He's on in seven minutes, still wearing the makeup he applied himself at 3:30 this morning in preparation for the six A.M. forecast.

Gaelan leads a calibrated life, on and off camera, one that revolves around numbers: units of time, weights, reps, pressures, precip, wind speed. He studies a fax of the most recent data supplied by the National Weather Service, taking notes. His composure is impressive considering the task at hand: In a very short time, he must stand in front of a live camera and translate multiple columns of numbers into a concise, comprehensive, friendly, and wholly extemporized summary, one that will help the good people of Lancaster and Hamilton counties, among others—farmers and nonfarmers alike—plan their upcoming weekend.

Many people rely on Gaelan Jones. He does his best to never let them down, to earn their continuing faith in his forecasting abilities—even though he is only a weatherman.

This word, *weatherman,* is a euphemism, and fast on its way to becoming obsolete. There was a time when the title carried no secret

connotation, but now it is known by everyone in the television broad-
casting industry to mean someone who is not equipped with a university-
accredited background in hard science:

"Gaelan Jones, with sixteen years of experience, is the hometown
team's favorite weatherman!" Translation: *Gaelan Jones, Nebraska native, small-town boy, got this job because he's naturally charming and the
camera loves him.*

There is another reason Gaelan got this job, or so he suspects, a reason he is even more loathe to acknowledge. He came to the station right
out of the UN's journalism department, as qualified as any twenty-two-
year-old with a 3.3 average could be to land a low-paying internship in
TV reporting. He was hired, but not as an intern, not even as a rookie
journalist. To Gaelan's astonishment, the producers began grooming
him to replace Nebraska's much beloved, favorite weatherman since the
1950s, Joe Dinsdale.

Unheard of. Unprecedented. Unfair.

Gaelan agrees. He knows he skipped to the front of the line. He
understands that his sudden ascent into local TV stardom was, and still
is, deeply resented by many. There's really no way to account for it other
than this: Someone blabbed to one of the producers the story of the Jones
family history, and he was hired for that as much as anything else, as if
having a personal tragedy related to the weather somehow made him
singularly qualified to predict it.

It's a sensational story, as evidenced by the fact that in spite of Gaelan's
best efforts it refuses to die. He still receives sympathetic fan mail. He
regularly declines to be interviewed for such TV shows as *America's Wildest
Weather Tragedies!* and *Truth or Fiction: You Be the Judge!*

Gaelan's professional good luck is one of the many reasons he suffers
from a chronic, diffuse, psychological discomfort that he is unable to
name, much less alleviate; he's like a man walking around in stolen,
unlaundered socks.

His predecessor was a compactly built man with a homely face and a
charmingly diffident air, a man who—like another fixture of American television, Captain Kangaroo—exuded grandfatherly tenderness
even when he was in his thirties. This persona allowed Joe Dinsdale,
weatherman, to be wildly inaccurate in his prognostications on a regular basis and yet never incur the wrath or ridicule of his viewing public.

Gaelan watched Joe's weather reports himself as a child, from babyhood until he was thirteen. Joe was more than a polite guest at the dinner table for all that time; he was family, long before Gaelan encountered him years later in nonpixilated form.

In those days, Joe's forecast came on at six P.M., before anything else. The information he imparted was that important. The tenor of the weather segment was generally professorial, rarely lighthearted, and certainly never flippant. Folks didn't expect weather forecasts to be entertaining. In the glory days of independent farming, when crops and livestock constituted Nebraska's main resources, forecasting the weather was serious business. The family TV was the tribal fire, and Joe Dinsdale—with his honored, top-of-the-hour slot—was the tribal soothsayer. It's possible that coverage of the Kennedy assassination took precedence over Joe's weather report, but that's about the only thing Gaelan can imagine that would have preempted it.

Joe stood in front of a real map, wearing a plain serge suit and wielding a pointer. He talked about today. He talked about tomorrow. He wasn't expected to see much farther into the future than that.

Whenever Gaelan thinks of him, Joe Dinsdale is rendered in shades of black and white. He was the human face of Nebraska weather for over thirty years, from 1955 until 1987, and Gaelan knows that Joe's exit from television represented the end of an era for many Nebraskans, on a par with losing Walter Cronkite. It's one of those historical landmarks Gaelan imagines that people still reminisce about and probably rue: *Now, when Joe* Dinsdale *did the weather* . . .

Joe might not have had the same appeal if he were in the business today. His delivery was famously laconic. The camera was not his friend. But he was a sweetheart. His advice to Gaelan went like this: "They'll say you're stupid if you're wrong, they'll say you're lucky if you're right. You'll never get any respect being a weatherman, but if you can laugh about it—because after all, think about it, son, how many people in the world get paid to predict the unpredictable?— you'll have a lot of fun."

Did Joe predict the tornado that took Hope? Gaelan doesn't remember, he's never been told, he certainly never asked, and it wouldn't have made a difference anyway because, after all, as far as tornadoes are concerned, the phrase *que sera, sera* is never more apt.

Gaelan has often wondered how Joe reported the Gage County tornado of August 1978; these were broadcasts he didn't see, of course, since the Jones television was one of the material casualties of that event. Gaelan always meant to ask him, over a cup of coffee maybe, sometime after his apprenticeship was over and the two of them could relax, converse about matters besides work, but Joe died of a stroke one week after he went off the air, as if his living existence became superfluous with the cessation of his electronically transmitted one.

The other commercial station in town (the one with higher ratings and a broader demographic) has Brock Garrison, *meteorologist:* "First-alert weather brought to you by Brock Garrison, meteorologist! Utilizing the latest tools in forecasting technology, Brock brings twelve years of experience to the people of eastern Nebraska! For state-of-the art weather updates, rely on Brock Garrison, meteorologist, and all the KOLN-KGIN broadcast professionals!"

Gaelan and Brock Garrison share membership in the American Federation of Television and Radio Artists. They go to the same professional dinners. They are frequently invited to be guest speakers at elementary schools all over the state. They are about the same age.

But Gaelan will never feel as qualified as Brock Garrison, meteorologist, because Brock Garrison earned his job by possessing real qualifications rather than leading-man looks and a sympathy vote; he has an advanced degree in earth sciences, one he received (with honors, surely, and a 4.0 average) from the granddaddy of all university programs, the one that inhabits the symbolic epicenter of severe storm reporting: the University of Oklahoma. Brock Garrison has been trained to interpret computer models. He works with a whole other world of numerical data and statistics. Gaelan imagines him pulling numbers out of the air—like a magician conjuring playing cards, coins, bouquets, bunnies—giving them his full attention and then swiping them aside with kingly disdain, making them vanish, retaining their secrets.

Gaelan's forecasts are never entirely wrong. They are never entirely right. They are nonspecific. The data Gaelan relies on, National Weather Service data—which was the only tool available in Joe Dinsdale's day, the one Gaelan was trained to work with, the one that used to be good enough—addresses average conditions. NWS data measures landscape conditions at twelve-mile intervals—much too far apart to calculate the effects of subtle topographic forces.

KLAN-KHAM recently changed hands. Word has come down from above that the new owners are considering making changes in the news department. They desire an edgier, less folksy look, an altered program format. They want to pursue a broader demographic. Gaelan anticipates that these vague, politic phrases will soon translate into one-on-one meetings with the producers. Maybe he'll be asked to adjust his wardrobe, go more casual. He has some ideas along these lines. For one thing, he'd like to forgo suit coats in lieu of short-sleeved shirts; Gaelan Jones is justifiably proud of his biceps.

He's on in two minutes. He's uneasy. Something doesn't jive with this data, but it's a feeling that is completely unsupported by NWS statistics. There's nothing here to indicate anything unusual, certainly not a severe storm. And that's mostly what the viewing public wants to know about, especially at this time of the year: *So tell us, Gaelan, is there a chance of a tornado?*

Gaelan stands up at his desk. The warning light on the camera is on. Just below the lens, the teleprompter scrolls down the text currently being read in another part of the building by one of the news anchors, a story about the health benefits associated with ingesting flaxseed oil.

Gaelan works up a smile. After this, he's off for the weekend. He'll go to the gym and work out, then call Claudia and see if she can get away from work early, fool around, eat dinner, go to a flick. She hasn't seen Arnold's new movie yet. Maybe she'll spend the night. That would be nice.

The words *Toss to Gaelan* appear on the teleprompter, and Gaelan hears the lead-in ad-lib: "How 'bout it, Gaelan? Are we gonna be able to grill a few more steaks before the end of the summer?"

"You bet, Greg! Saturday and Sunday looking pretty good. There might be a few light spots of rain here and there, especially this afternoon in the southeastern part of the state, but I think you can safely put on that 'Kiss the Cook' apron for at least one more weekend."

There is laughter from the news anchors.

Gaelan has a skill set, too, whether or not it's concretely defined by a science degree from an accredited college: He can make people laugh; he looks good on camera, and in a profession that values the way things look, this counts for a great deal. He can bench-press 250 pounds, he can squat 275; beneath his shirt, he is ripped; he adores the company of women and knows himself to be a gifted lover, possessed of an innate, unfailing ability to consistently deliver orgasmic good cheer. And he can say with confidence that it's unlikely a severe thunderstorm will ruin any lives today in southeastern Nebraska.

"Here's what I'm seeing, Greg . . ."

Gaelan Jones, the beneficiary of good looks and capricious luck, proceeds to do his best, pretending to have fun predicting the unpredictable.

This is his last broadcast of the week. In less than an hour, KLAN-KHAM's weekend forecaster takes over, and then, for the next two and a half days, the only thing that Gaelan Jones, weatherman, will have to prognosticate is how many times he'll get laid.

Chapter 3

The Virgin Interprets
the Signs

Bonnie Jones does not identify her-
self by her livelihood, as Gaelan and Larken do—as do all the folks she
has known throughout her life: farmer, physician, nurse, postman, pastor, teacher, mother, mayor. Nor does she equate financial abundance
with success.

Bonnie freely admits to having made a few bad decisions, foolish
decisions, when it comes to her work life. She's been suckered now and
then by back-page print ads and late-night infomercials meant to en-
tice self-doubters and insomniacs. So yes, there were those long-distance
degree programs in medical transcription, handwriting analysis, and
massage therapy—educational investments that were personally enriching but not financially lucrative. In each case, her wages were just
enough to pay off the credit card debt she incurred when she signed up
for the courses in the first place.

But apart from this, Bonnie has always been able to meet her financial needs; moreover, she's a saver. Bonnie's siblings would be astonished
to learn how much money their baby sister has amassed over the years,
working at her various low-paying, dead-end jobs:

Country club caddy, secretary at the farmer's co-op, clerk at Olson's
drugstore, short-order cook at the Little Cheerful Café, door-to-door representative of Electrolux, *Encyclopaedia Britannica,* Avon, and Greenpeace.

She has strung beads and stuffed envelopes: *Stay-at-home Moms! House-wives! Earn $$$ in your spare time! Work from home!* Before her truck broke down, she hauled junk to the county dump, mowed lawns, raked leaves. She's even worked a paper route, arising before dawn (and Gaelan and Larken consider her lazy!), meticulously rolling and rubber-banding the few pages that constitute *The Goldenrod Gazette,* loading them into the panniers of her bike, and delivering them the old-fashioned way. She tried hard to be an exemplary paper girl, but even after a year of determined practice, her ability to toss and aim with precision did not improve, and more often than not she ended up unintentionally obliterating what news her town saw fit to print by catapulting it into mud puddles, birdbaths, snow drifts, wasp colonies, mosquito-infested roof gutters, treacherous stands of blackberry canes, newly shat dog poop.

Bonnie's latest job is as the self-employed owner and operator of a juice and smoothie stand, BJ's Brews. An entrepreneurial effort suggested and funded by Alvina Closs, the business has been up and running since Memorial Day. The hours of operation vary. Bonnie has four regular customers and averages a daily profit of eighteen dollars and seventy-five cents.

But none of these occupations constitute her real work. None of them define her.

If asked to describe her true vocation, the one that gives her purpose and passion, Bonnie would hesitate; there's not an easy title for her line of work. It's something like archaeology, a profession for which she is technically untrained but temperamentally suited.

Generally, she's involved in seeking, excavating, collecting, and restoring artifacts—seemingly inconsequential items that, to the uninformed, would be regarded as roadside trash. She studies them, assigns them historical significance, preserves and places them in an archival setting. If she were to call herself anything at all besides a failure (on this point, she and her siblings are in perfect agreement, although for different reasons), Bonnie Jones, youngest surviving child of Llewellyn and Hope Jones, born in 1971, would call herself a forensic fictionist.

She goes out as soon as she can after a storm. She goes out every day, twice a day at least, sometimes more, even when the weather is uneventful. But the best days are those on which the wind has done its job of scouring, unearthing, rearranging. On these days she finds the most meaningful artifacts: scraps of fabric, rusty lids, pill bottles—sometimes with the prescription name almost legible, bleached pale. These are precious. Any bit of handwriting thrills her—typed pages, too. Metal scraps, because who knows where they might have come from? Farm machinery is the most logical answer, but Bonnie's fervent belief is that any metal she unearths is part of a Singer sewing machine, an IBM Selectric, or a 1977 model Everest and Jennings wheelchair.

And of course she's always on the lookout for anything that might have come from a Steinway baby grand.

It's not unusual to go through periods when the relics seem to adhere to some mysterious organizing principle. They might center around a theme—lists, for example—or relate exclusively to children: pacifiers; single baby shoes; small, orphaned plastic toys that have been separated from their Happy Meals. Artifacts might be related by their size, weight, material—or shape: for weeks now Bonnie's field of view has led her to a preponderance of circles: coins, lids, ponytail holders, condoms, CDs, teething rings.

There is not much litter on country roads. Rural Nebraskans are tidy people for the most part, so the appearance of anything new in the way of roadside debris is easy to spot. Sometimes, rarely, Bonnie finds evidence of carousing teens, young people with new-minted driver's licenses, just up from the Kansas border where they can buy 3.2 beer: cast-off aluminum cans, deflated bags of corn chips. These are of little interest. Bonnie acquires only those relics that can relate to the narrative she has built over the past twenty-five years, one she continues to construct. It is a living history she is assembling, and if she can form a place for a bit of refuse, then she keeps it.

Beer cans don't figure into it, but a scrawled grocery list does.

Everything of significance will be cataloged and categorized and captioned.

Bones are what she longs for. Ribs, phalanges, teeth. She imagines the front-page headlines: *Decades-Old Mystery Solved: Forensic experts used DNA testing to positively identify the human remains discovered by Bonnie Jones of Emlyn Springs, Nebraska as those of her mother, Aneira Hope Jones, who has been missing since 1978.*

But bones are what she never finds—nor anything else with an unmistakable identity, one she wouldn't have to invent, but the real thing, a true artifact.

If only she could find something—one thing—that could be positively, unequivocally linked to Hope. Only then will she know that the time is right, the stage is set for miracles, and the angels are on her side.

On the morning of her father's electrocution, Bonnie steps out of her place of residence, a large converted car shed behind the Williamses' mansion, and checks on the girls. Looking across the expanse of lawn (the grass needs mowing; she'll get to it tonight before the girls go to bed) she sees that the morning newspaper has been taken in; it would have been deposited with unerring accuracy by the current Emlyn Springs paper carrier, Jim and Joanie Llyr's boy, Matthew. The porch light is off, the living room drapes have been parted. The Welsh national anthem is being played on the piano; two strong harmonizing voices, soprano and alto, are singing along. All the evidence indicates that the Misses Williams, Hazel and Wauneeta (eighty-eight and eighty-five respectively) aren't dead yet.

Bonnie turns her attention to the weather. Her sensitivity to the moving currents of the air is exquisite, often exquisitely painful; there is no moment in which she does not associate an awareness of the wind with her mother.

The day is holding its breath, she thinks. It's as though the whole of her town is trapped inside a giant, fevered lung that has forgotten the mechanics of respiration.

Exhale! Bonnie wants to shout, but—not wishing to alarm the girls—mutters instead. *Breathe,* she whispers, reminding herself as well as the wind: inflation, deflation; inspiration, expiration; in, out; breathe.

The wind—what little there is—seems beaten down, puny, too pummeled by the relentless summer to put up a fight. Bonnie does not wilt in this stagnant, oppressive heat, the way Larken does, but she finds it depressing. Bonnie prefers a good strong wind—even if all it does is agitate air that is already stale and soggy, like a fan in a steam room. Motion of any kind is preferable to stillness.

The sun is desperately bright; the sky is clear but brownish, filmy with dust the wind can't rouse itself to disperse. Bonnie imagines swiping a huge, white-gloved finger across the sky, writing *Clean Me You Fucker* the way that kids do, the listless, unhappy kids of Emlyn Springs; embittered, small-time, small-town vandals who can't get their hands on spray cans—and wouldn't dare to use them even if they could—and so make their mark on the backsides of grimy pickups and vans. Kids whose imaginations have already shriveled, who can't even register their rebellion in a way that lasts: *Clean me. Wash me. Fuck. Cunt. Asshole. Pussy. Penis.*

No sign of rain. Bonnie heads back inside.

When Dr. Williams died four years ago, Bonnie was twenty-nine years old and still living at her father's house. Her father was rarely there—for all intents and purposes he lives with Viney—but Bonnie still sensed his disapproval in a million big and little ways. She felt that he was angry and disappointed in her for not going to college like her siblings, for working jobs he considered menial, for staying here instead of moving away, for valuing what she values. For everything, really. She was no longer comfortable being beholden to her dad and wanted her own space.

Knowing that Hazel and Wauneeta would feel lonely and useless—they'd spent the better part of their lives looking after their father—Bonnie approached them about converting the shed into a residence, and they agreed.

Spacious and soundly constructed, the shed was where Hazel and Wauneeta's father spent his postretirement years. Dr. Williams was the town's only physician when Bonnie's parents arrived in 1960. Dr. Williams graciously supported the new doctor, selling his medical office and its accoutrements at a price that wouldn't saddle the young man with decades of debt. He smoothed the passing of the caduceus (as he liked to say) in other ways as well. It's a sad truth that the patients of retiring small-town physicians sometimes behave like the children of divorced parents—punishing the departed parent by making life hell for the remaining one—and Dr. Williams knew that the fact Llewellyn Jones was a native son would give him only a slight advantage in this regard. So he stayed on as an employee long enough to personally introduce every one of his patients to their new doctor, reassuring the doubtful, scolding the curmudgeonly, calming the fearful.

And long after his official retirement, Dr. Williams even continued to make himself available for consultations.

Primarily, though, he spent the remaining years of his life as a carpenter, designing and building hundreds of colorful wooden whirligigs: two-dimensional figures of Welsh corgies, matrons in tall bonnets, barebottomed babies, native birds, hunters, fishermen. Most of these novelties he gave to friends; a few he sold during Fancy Egg Days.

He also excelled at furniture making, and every year, borrowing from an ancient Welsh tradition—a poetry competition called the *Eisteddfod*—Doc Williams designed and built the special prize given to whoever won the title of Little Miss Emlyn Springs: an ornately carved and painted chair, bearing Doc's unique brand of artistic whimsy and skill.

Bonnie is certain that a fragment of red varnished plywood she found one day comes from the wing of a whirligig cardinal that Dr. Williams gave her when she was five. Bonnie remembers stretching out on her bed, day and night, and watching him. He was mounted outside her window on a wobbly ledge that was designed and constructed by her father—one of the two carpentry projects he ever attempted. Spirited, optimistic in all seasons, her cardinal's wings rotated like twin Ferris wheels. When Bonnie thinks of him—dear, undaunted marwing—she imagines him still flying, paddling away furiously, tirelessly, against all odds, eternally airborne.

The ridge of the shed roof is covered with Dr. Williams's whirligigs. Usually they set up a steady clatter; the noise helps Bonnie sleep. This morning they are silent.

Bonnie slices an avocado into eighths; she removes and peels one section and drops it into the glass carafe of her blender. She adds chunks of frozen mango, twelve almonds, three pitted dates, a half cup of soy milk, a tablespoon of flaxseed oil, a pinch of cinnamon. She hits the power button and waits.

Bonnie is on a quest to find the perfect blender, one powerful enough to make frozen smoothies without manual intervention. This one—a Hamilton Beach—is good, but for some reason, as with every brand of blender Bonnie has tried, within a few seconds the ingredients stop circulating. The motor keeps whirring but the contents become inert; the frozen chunks stop making their way to where the blades are. It's bothersome. Bonnie has to press one of her hands down hard against the lid, using the other to steady the base of the blender as she rocks it, vigorously—*thunka thunka thunka!* This shakes things up for a while and gets everything back down to the bottom. She rocks the blender. Success. She waits. Stasis. She rocks it again, and so on. She only has to rock the Hamilton Beach four or five times—it's still not good enough—but eventually, *finally,* there is a continuously spinning vortex with an imploding hole in the center that looks exactly like an innie belly button.

This is what Bonnie waits for: the moment at which the smoothie is thoroughly smoothed. As she contemplates this marvel of kitchen physics—pureed particles of food moving up the sides of the carafe and down through the hole in the center, up the sides, down the center—she sends a few breaths deep into her abdomen.

The blender is Bonnie's single kitchen appliance. She uses it every day.

It wasn't so difficult, making the shed habitable. It was already wired for electricity—Dr. Williams used power tools—and to get it supplied with running water, Bonnie worked out a trade with Pete Earnhart, the town plumber: She maintained his yard for a summer; he dug in underground lines and installed a toilet, shower, and sink. Everything else—insulation, Sheetrock, painting—Bonnie did herself. She's bartered for other improvements to her house over the years: new windows, roof, woodstove, floor. It's a good house, not only because of its soundness, but because it stands for something; Bonnie's house is an accurate reflection of certain values that she holds dear.

As she drinks her breakfast, Bonnie contemplates her first task of the day, one she's been planning eagerly: potting a trio of sprouted avocado pits. She has tended them for months after piercing them, tenderly, apologetically, with miniature skewers—the kind that have yellow plastic ears of corn on the ends.

For two full seasons these pits have sat on the east-facing windowsill, suspended in glass jars filled with water that Bonnie checks daily. There are dozens of other avocado pits in varying stages of germination lining the windows. Bonnie considers the germination of avocado pits evidence of miracles, and yet they are short-lived. If only one of her avocados would survive the transition to being embedded in soil. But all of them, every single one—no matter how well developed their root systems, how sturdy their stems, or how lush their foliage—languish, wither, and die soon after she plants them. Is the shed too cold and dim in the winter? Doesn't she provide them with enough nutrients and affection? She regularly monitors the pH balance of their soil, she programs the CD player to serenade them with music when she is gone, a special anthology she put together herself that includes selected recordings of Welsh male choirs, sound tracks from movie musicals, Rachmaninoff piano concertos, and the best hits of Doris Day.

She has not given up, no, not yet, but she might be starting to despair.

Bonnie begins. She plucks the first avocado pit from its glass jar, gently extracts the skewers, and nestles it into one of three terra cotta pots she prepared last night; each contains a new mixture of nutrient-rich soil, a recipe she has concocted herself. She sings quietly as she works: *There was a seed, in the middle of the ground, the prettiest seed that you ever did see, oh . . .*

Long ago, Bonnie's father traded goods for services. She vividly remembers a late summer morning when she was no more than two and newly walking: in the kitchen, pushing on the magic wall (the one Mommy and Daddy and Lark and Gaelan pass through and then disappear), she does not fall down this time, no one stops her as the wall flies open with a squeak and a bang and admits her outside, by herself, to the back porch where it is sunny, where the air smells different. She feels the dry wood planks warming beneath her bare feet as she toddles farther, toward the swing set and sandbox, toward the clothesline and shirts and sheets like flags in the wind where they play peekaboo, toward the field beyond where she has never been. She means to go on and on, but there on the steps, blocking her way, is something new: a treat! It has never been there before, a bushel basket full of shining fat red tomatoes, yellow sweet corn, cucumbers, purple beans, green beans, beans with freckles, bunches of dill.

Each morning after that she looked for evidence of visitations. The back porch did not always yield a surprise, but that didn't mean they'd been forgotten.

You never know, Hope said each night when she tucked Bonnie into bed and Bonnie asked, *Will there be something tomorrow?*

Other times of year brought other kinds of offerings: apple pies, spaghetti squash, and pumpkins in the fall; brown paper–wrapped parcels of venison meat, pheasant, and quail in November; Mason jars of fruit preserves and tomato sauce in the winter; bunches of daffodils, baby lettuce, leeks, and honeycombs in spring; and once, something with bumpy, dark green leathery skin, tucked into sheaves of tissue—shaped like an egg, Bonnie thought. And until her mother later gave it a name (*Ah-kuh-VAH-do,* a word like an incantation) and explained that it was a rare fruit from a faraway place called *Callie-FOR-na.* Bonnie thought it *was* an egg, one that would hatch into a magnificent dragon, powerful and kind. He would give them rides, guard them forever.

Clearly, her family was blessed. They had been adopted by fairies—the Farmer Elves, Bonnie called them—who ran a home delivery business, traveling from Callieforna on the backs of benevolent dragons with the sole intent of bringing them food. What had they done to deserve such bounty? Bonnie wondered. She asked her friends about it as she got older. But no one else woke up in the morning to find groceries on their porch.

It's a mystery, Bon-bon, Hope said. *Sometimes things happen that can't be explained. Let's just be grateful.*

Bonnie offered prayers of thanks each night to God and the Farmer Elves. She still believed in them when Hope went up, and for some time after.

Maybe they don't know we've moved, Bonnie said to her sister.

Four and a half seasons had gone by without gifts. Bonnie was almost nine.

Maybe I should write them a letter with our new address and leave it out there where the porch used to be. She'd learned that Santa Claus, the Tooth Fairy, and the Easter Bunny were fabrications, but no one had yet disabused her of her belief in the Farmer Elves.

Larken finally told her that there were never any elves. There were only people—townsfolk, people they knew—who paid their doctor bills with food instead of money.

Why did they do that?

Because they were poor, but they still wanted to give Daddy something to thank him for being their doctor.

Daddy knew?

Of course Daddy knew.

But how did he figure out who the food was from? They never left notes or anything.

He had other ways of knowing, I guess, Larken said. She was holding her yellow pencil like it was an ear of sweet corn, turning it, nibbling at it.

Mom didn't know, though, Bonnie stated, firmly. *She would have told me if she knew.*

Larken studied her math homework. *Yeah,* she said, erasing one equation, penciling in another. *Of course.*

But why did they stop coming?

Bonnie wasn't that upset about learning that the Farmer Elves were just plain farmers, but something else was bothering her, something she couldn't articulate.

Larken frowned. *They probably feel sorry for us. They figure we need money more than we need food.*

Why would they think that? Bonnie persisted. *Everybody needs food.*

I don't know, Bonnie, Larken answered angrily.

Can they pay with money now? Aren't they poor anymore?

I don't know! Larken repeated, and Bonnie wondered why her sister was so mad. *Leave me alone now. I'm trying to do my homework.*

Bonnie aligns the beginning of her town's decline with two things: her mother's ascent and the disappearance of the Farmer Elves.

Conversely, the resurrection of Emlyn Springs depends upon the discovery of her mother's remains and a return to the barter system.

Bonnie accepts cash at the juice bar—her customers prefer to compensate her this way—and she pays with cash when required. But the fact is Bonnie doesn't really like carrying money. Having pockets full of currency and coin makes her feel sunk, like a fish that's swallowed a lead lure and has to spend the rest of its life pretending that it likes being pinned down to the river bottom. No more drifting or splashing. No more being carried by the current, or even fighting it.

The juice bar money sees to her immediate needs. The small stipend she gets for being a reading tutor at the K–12 Emlyn Springs School is immediately recycled into the school's library and arts programs. She trades whenever possible.

Some of the less kind-minded folks in Bonnie's town believe she's traded on more than landscape services; Joe Pappas, for example, that nice young widower who moved down from Omaha and works construction up and down the highway, spent an awful lot of time over there putting in those new double-paned windows, and nobody ever saw Bonnie pushing a lawn mower at *his* place.

But they're wrong. The youngest surviving child of Hope and Llewellyn Jones is more of an anomaly than anyone knows.

After finishing her work with the avocados, Bonnie showers, dresses, and prepares to head out on her bike for the first reconnaissance of the day.

It's a slow, steady ascent to the cemetery—southeastern Nebraska is hillier than many people realize—but Bonnie is never winded. She has been riding this road for years, day in, day out, rain or shine. Tall, lean, and lithe as a mullein stalk, Bonnie is the child who most resembles her mother. The dead have come to expect her daily visits, nevertheless; they still can't get over the resemblance, and worry that the young woman has been doomed by physiognomy. More than once the dead have found themselves expecting Bonnie Jones to turn down the blanket of sod overlying her mother's cenotaph and tuck herself in.

She arrives, having seen nothing of note on the way. Propping her bike against the wrought-iron fence that surrounds the grounds, she extracts a Mason jar filled with soapy water and toothbrush from one of the panniers. With the solemn gait of a layperson in a church processional, Bonnie approaches a small headstone at the center of the cemetery; it marks the remains of Gwendolyn Margaret Elfyn (1781–1854). *Beloved Sister and Aunt* it reads, and below that: *The Soul selects her own Society*. Miss Elfyn is a distant relative of Viney's and the first Emlyn Springs citizen interred on these grounds.

And how are you today, Miss Elfyn? Bonnie begins. She must speak loudly to raise Miss Elfyn. Having never been a mother, Miss Elfyn is always in residence, but she frequently naps.

Bonnie! Miss Elfyn begins, in a voice suggesting that this is not an everyday occurrence. *How nice of you to come.*

From the time of her mother's flight, Bonnie reasoned that if anyone knew anything, it would be the oldest dead person in the Emlyn Springs graveyard. In spite of the fact that she has never yet been rewarded with the knowledge of Hope's whereabouts, she persists in that opinion.

I am well, Miss Elfyn. How are you today? Bonnie settles in; today she is cleaning the section of the cemetery occupied by the Mutter family.

Well, thank you, dear. How are the avocados?

I potted three new ones only today, Bonnie answers.

Your hopes are high, then? It is hard to read Miss Elfyn sometimes. Bonnie reminds herself that the word *hope* is not always loaded with the meaning it has for her family. Probably Miss Elfyn means exactly what she says.

Yes, ma'am, Bonnie replies. She is a polite girl, so solicitous of her elders. Quiet, too, forgoing theatrics for simple duty. No wonder the dead are more fond of her than of their other living visitors.

The extremes of Nebraska weather are hard on tombstones. The oldest ones, like those of Miss Elfyn and the Mutter family, are white granite, veined with gray, and in a sorry state. The earth has spun and shifted under them so many times, the prairie wind has assaulted them, and they have become so saturated with rain and snow that many seem to be dissolving, like giant blocks of sugar. Some of them have even fallen over. For the residents under these headstones, Bonnie grieves.

Have you seen Hope? she asks after an appropriate interval. She does not wish to appear pushy.

Miss Elfyn clucks her tongue inside her toothy mouth. Miss Elfyn had impeccable dental hygiene habits. She was ahead of her time in this way. Her longevity was due to her adherence to a strictly vegetarian diet— an unusual choice in the land of beef production, but the Welsh often emulate their patron saint, David, who was known to have abstained from the consumption of meat. He subsisted mostly upon water, it is said, and whenever and wherever he performed a miracle, springs are said to have formed.

Bonnie waits, occupying herself in the interval by scrubbing char-treuse moss from the tombstone of an unnamed Mutter child who died at the age of three days: *Here Lies Our Darling.* There are numerous tombstones like this in the cemetery, too numerous: *The Infant Children of Morgan and Braunwyn Ellis. William and Robert, Our Darling Babes. Their Lives Brief, Our Love Eternal. Much Beloved, Forever Cherished . . .*

There are so many reasons to reject parenthood, to seek out and even embrace childlessness—even now, in these modern, medically advanced times. Children who survive infancy still die before their parents, felled by accidents, illnesses, murderers, wars. The world is overpopulated. Global warming is a fact. Sadness and pain come to us all. There are so many ways a woman could assuage the grief of suspecting that mother-hood, for her, is not in the cards.

But Bonnie finds no comfort in these realities. More than anything in the world, Bonnie Jones wants a child.

And yet her desire to procreate has not yet manifested as a desire to have sex. Any biological urgings she might feel are quickly checked by her fears—fear and desire being siblings, with fear the more im-posing and fierce, ever guarding and protecting its twin. In Bonnie's case, fear will continue to blockade her from any real, that is, con-cupiscent, strivings until she is gifted with a very special kind of proof, a warranty of success.

Only Bonnie knows what constitutes this proof.

At least, she'll know it when she sees it.

Have you seen my mother, Hope? she repeats, more insistently.

Miss Elfyn has a tendency to daydream once awakened. Or perhaps her slowness of speech is due to something else; without the benefit of a countenance, it is difficult to say. Perhaps she isn't daydreaming at all but rather considering, even teasing. Sometimes, especially lately, Bonnie feels it is this latter.

Hope? Miss Elfyn echoes, in a beautifully inflected voice. Miss Elfyn was a fine singer; she has told Bonnie on more than one occasion. *Hope. Have I seen Hope?*

In the Emlyn Springs graveyard there are other women who have been named for virtues: Patience, Temperance, Grace, Modesty. Their names are not used so frequently in everyday conversation, they don't routinely appear in headline news: *MISSING SOLDIER'S FAMILY CAN ONLY WAIT AND HOPE, ANGER SURFACES AS HOPE FADES, VICTIM'S MOTHER HOPES REMAINS WILL BRING CLOSURE, NEW DRUG THERAPIES OFFER HOPE TO PATIENTS.* Bonnie has noticed over the years that the people responsible for headlines like to pair variations on the word *hope* with variations on the word *tragic: TRAGEDY TURNS THE TIDE FOR OLYMPIC HOPEFUL, HOPES BURIED IN TRAGIC MINE DISASTER.*

Perhaps, is the way Miss Elfyn usually answers Bonnie's question. Sometimes she replies with an unequivocal *no,* just to be contrary, Bonnie suspects. But this answer is less cruel than the one Miss Elfyn makes only rarely: *Yes, of course I've seen Hope.*

Where? Bonnie demands on such occasions.

That is for me to know and you to find out is one of Miss Elfyn's typical responses.

Or, at her most infuriating, *You will find that which you seek only when you stop looking*. Bonnie hates that Zen hogwash.

Or, more accusingly, *What does it matter? Why do you care? How would it change things if you knew?*

How indeed? Pastor Mutter laments quietly from beneath Bonnie's kneeling, laboring form. Several other dead fathers nod their heads and murmur in agreement. Bonnie does not hear them.

Today, Miss Elfyn replies, *"Hope is the thing with feathers that perches in the soul, and sings the tune without the words, and never stops at all."*

Sometimes Bonnie gets angry with Miss Elfyn—especially when she is purposely obtuse, like today—and stomps away before they've had a change to discuss other matters. But what good does it do to be angry with the dead?

And to be sure, the dead know the answer to Bonnie's most pressing question—*She's close!* they long to shout, *so close, just over there!*—but, bound by a stringent code of ethics, they are strictly prohibited from divulging the exact whereabouts of the missing. It's for the best, really. The living have to learn to work these things out for themselves.

I love Emily Dickinson, Miss Elfyn says. *Don't you?*

Bonnie sighs. *Yes, Miss Elfyn,* she replies, understanding that this constitutes the end of today's conversation about Hope. *I love her, too.*

An hour later, after Miss Elfyn has exhausted herself by reciting what would seem to be the entire Emily Dickinson canon and then fallen asleep, Bonnie mounts her bike and departs. She needs to get to the juice stand and start chopping up organic celery, apples, and broccoli, snipping flowerets of parsley and blades of barley grass. Mr. Norris is always her first customer of the day, and she likes to have his Green Ginko Power Smoothie ready for him when he arrives at 9:00. Old people's time is so precious.

Business is slow. To Bonnie, it matters little either way: If business is good, she is able to tithe more of her income for projects that are dear to her heart—the Emlyn Springs Cemetery Restoration Project, for example, or the Welsh Heritage Museum—and if business is bad, she can go out on the bike and look for artifacts. It's a win-win situation.

After Mr. Norris comes and goes, a couple of city cyclists show up asking where they can get a latte; Bonnie sends them back to Beatrice. Maybe she should consider investing in an espresso machine; the promise of fancy coffee is a big draw for city people. She'll think about it.

The Labenz boys take a break at 10:30 and amble over for their drinks: Strawberry Surprise Smoothie for Al, Green Apple Pie Smoothie for Pete, and Orange Crush Smoothie for Dylan. (Bonnie worries about them; they drink Coke and eat junk food all day, so unbeknownst to them she always spoons protein powder into their drinks.)

Blind Tom shows up around noon. He's one of Bonnie's occasional customers. She's never quite sure when he'll stop by since his work schedule is erratic and sometimes takes him out of town.

"Hi, Tom," Bonnie says.

"Hi, Bonnie."

"Your usual?"

"Yes, please."

Bonnie takes great pride in her work. Her standards are high, and it's not usual that she makes what she considers a perfect drink. But she makes one this morning for Blind Tom.

"Thanks." Blind Tom sips his Sunny Clime Smoothie. "I, uh . . ." He hesitates. "I have to tell you something."

"Is there something wrong with it?"

"Oh, no. This is delicious. The best ever. It's just . . . I get nervous when you do that thumping thing."

"Thumping thing?"

"With the blender."

"Oh!" Bonnie cries. "I'm sorry. I didn't think about your hearing being extra . . . sensitive."

"No no, it's not that. What I mean is, it could be dangerous."

"I've been doing it for ages. If I don't thump, the ingredients don't all get to the bottom."

"It doesn't seem like the kind of thing the manufacturer would have had in mind."

"I keep my hand on the lid," Bonnie offers reassuringly. "It's perfectly safe."

"Have you ever tried doing it differently? Maybe putting things in one at a time?"

"You have to put the liquid in with the nuts. Otherwise the engine overheats."

Blind Tom smiles.

"I mean the motor," Bonnie adds.

"Maybe you could try grinding the nuts beforehand. I've got a coffee grinder, and I was thinking something like that would grind almonds."

"But then how would you grind your coffee?"

"I could grind it in advance and then freeze it."

"That's really nice, but—"

"Or I could grind the nuts for you."

"No."

"Why not?"

Bonnie considers. "There would be something wrong about you doing the work for me."

"I wouldn't be doing the work. I'd just be helping."

Bonnie frowns. She's starting to feel irritated.

Blind Tom goes on. "All I'm saying is that I'd like to help you with your nut problem."

"I don't have a nut problem."

"I'm just wondering if there's a way to do it that isn't so hard on you."

"It's not hard on me!" Bonnie says harshly, and then immediately feels terrible. Being snippy with a blind man has to be the kind of thing that sends Catholics to confession. "Really, it's no trouble," she amends.

"Okay," Blind Tom says, sounding not at all wounded. "If you say so. I'll see you later."

Bonnie busies herself slicing fresh strawberries from the Williams girls' garden. If no one else shows up by 1:30, she'll close up and take a longer ride, maybe east this time, toward Holmesville or Wymore. She cannot let a day go by without trying to acquire something for her archives.

Chapter 4

The Myth of Protection

Larken arrives at the campus art gallery and ducks into the ladies' restroom before she can be spotted. She is almost ready to make her entrance, but like even the best-rehearsed actor, she has a few remaining preparations to make before she can emerge from the wings and step onstage fully in character.

There are full-length mirrors in the bathroom, but Larken avoids these; she stands at one of the sinks, where the mirrors afford a neck-up view.

She is stunningly accessorized: A beaded burgundy velveteen shawl is draped over her shoulders and she wears new earrings. Her face is beginning to perspire; luckily though, she found metered parking on the street in front of the gallery. If she'd had to endure a long walk in the heat, her face would have slid off. As it is, there's just a bit of shine to contend with, easy to remedy. Her eye shadow and blush are still intact; she only needs to press a cool dry powder puff to her cheeks, forehead, upper lip, and forehead.

With a paper towel, she dabs cold water under her arms and on her wrists. She inserts two minty pellets of gum into her mouth and masticates furiously until she's convinced that all lingering fast-food aromas have been eradicated. She reapplies her new lipstick ("Raspberry Truffle"), perfects the drape of her shawl, takes a deep breath, and then

heads toward the gallery lobby, confident in her looks, sated in her ap-
petites. It is precisely 3:37, early enough to register reliability, late enough
to negate any hint of desperation.

Larken has spent the past two hours purchasing this confidence and
satiety at a cost of just over $300: the scarf was $175, the makeup $70,
the earrings $60, and the food around $15. Larken doesn't consider this
spendthrift behavior. These purchases are necessities. They've made it
possible for her to survive the imminent hell of a university-mandated
schmooze.

The main floor of the gallery is an airy, open place, notable for the
two-story glass wall on one side, the imported Italian marble that covers many of the interior and exterior surfaces. Light-colored—like
cappuccino meringue—delicately veined, speckled, and pockmarked,
the marble has always been Larken's favorite thing about the gallery.

The gallery prides itself on its contemporary acquisitions, and most
of the art is not to her liking. There isn't even one painting in the collection that represents the focus of her area of scholarship: the Virgin as
portrayed by the Flemish masters. Plenty of Christs, of course, no end
to the saints, but not a single Northern Renaissance Mary. So when
Larken is required to visit the gallery, she takes comfort in the marble,
its highly reflective surface, its glassine smoothness. She wishes that she
could walk the museum in bare feet. At a certain time of day—late
afternoon—if the sky is heavy with rain, but there is still enough light
seeping through the clouds, the floors have the look of a frozen pond.

There are maybe seventy-five people here, half students, half faculty
and admin types. The students ring the edges of the group, within easy
access of the catering tables, their plates piled high. Mostly they talk with
one another, and who can blame them? No sign of Drew—one of the
few people she'd enjoy talking to at an event like this. No sign of Misty
Ariel Kroger either, thank God. A jazz trio is playing in one corner of
the gallery. Kris (who has changed her clothes, Larken notices, and
wears a carnelian-colored backless sundress) is embedded in the center
of the room, deep in conversation with the only other woman on the
art department faculty, Dr. Mirabella Piacenti.

There's Arthur and Eloise, arm in arm as usual. Part of a foursome,
they're smiling and chatting with someone Larken doesn't recognize, a
man who must be the new dean. He is squat and balding, rosy of com-

plexion. Larken is dismayed to see that the current chairman, Richard Edgerton Gaffney, completes the quartet: toothy, scarecrowish, wearing one of his Armani knockoffs, taking up too much space as usual, flailing his big hands around, talking and gesticulating like some parody of a wealthy Florentine intellectual (she can almost hear his ersatz British-accented speech) instead of the Southern cracker he really is. Larken has no desire to join this group; Richard holds her in contempt, she is sure of it, so she avoids him whenever possible. She'll get a drink, wait for him to move on, and then do her duty.

Larken approaches the bar. "Do you have something white? Not too sweet?" she asks the bartender, smiling. His view of her, she knows, is much like that she just saw in the bathroom: a tightly circumscribed view that does not include her body.

"I'd recommend the soave," the bartender replies.

He's gay, Larken can tell at once. He's in good shape, moderately buff—but not so much as to be intimidating, like Gaelan—and has bright hazel eyes, dimples, dense black corkscrew curls—and pinned to his crisp white shirt is a name tag that reads *David*. Larken wonders if he wears a yarmulke when he's not pouring wine at dull university functions. He'd look good in a yarmulke.

"I'll take a glass of that then, please."

It's clouding up outside, the light is changing, cooling; oranges and yellows and reds all over the gallery are receding, softening; blues and grays advance. Larken half turns and sees that Richard has moved on and is now holding court with a group of grad students.

Larken picks up her wineglass and takes a sip. "Mmm, this is lovely."

"Glad you like it."

Larken is grateful for the refuge of the bartender's nonjudgmental, asexual male company, his kindness. She wishes she could spend the party here, leaning on the bar, presenting her face and nothing but her face. She'd slip out of her shoes and socks. David wouldn't care. She'd savor the feeling of cool smooth marble against her feet, marble that came all the way from Italy, and talk with him about anything but university bullshit: art, politics, poetry, movies, music, fiction, religion, grief. Maybe he could introduce her to a nice rabbi.

But Arthur and Eloise have spotted her; they wave in unison, and Arthur gestures her over.

Larken sighs. "I'm summoned."

"Too bad. Enjoy."

Larken begins making her way across the room. She knows what is required of her at this event. She knows how to get through this kind of public obligation, painful as it is. She must convince anyone with whom she interacts that they are far more important that the hors d'oeuvres. She has thirty seconds after the introductions to distract the dean from her appearance (clothes and makeup can only do so much) and force his focus elsewhere. Half a minute to banish what will be his first thought, supercede his immediate impression, erase the word she assumes he will be repeating inwardly—*fat*—and replace it with words like *brilliant, charming, insightful, witty,* phrases like *asset to the department, unique perspective on Marian scholarship, ideal candidate for the chairmanship*.

Larken draws closer to Eloise and Arthur and the new dean, mentally readying her first remarks. She walks smoothly, gracefully, as if she is someone well used to navigating a narrow runway, a woman who has won accolades and worn the crown and weighs no more than one hundred and ten.

Milkweed pods close before a rain. They are closing now as Bonnie passes them, like chorusing mouths reaching the end of a song.

Bonnie is reminded of a tradition, one she shared with Hope every August: They went gathering, just the two of them, seeking out wild and untended plants in the roadside ditches and fields: trampled milo, its clustered seed heads like black currants; feathery roadside grasses; sunflower heads, squishy but dry, like empty egg cartons or the vacated nests of wasps; dry verbascum stalks; great bunches of milkweed pods, which looked like sandpapery conch shells filled with swirling mists of silk. Bonnie and her mother arranged their finds in an old milk can that flanked the front porch door. *She* was the one—not Larken or Gaelan— chosen by Hope for this special task. *Fall bouquets,* Hope called them. Bonnie now reflects on this past ritual with dread: a gathering of plants that were dead or dying, desperate to shed their seeds onto ground still pliant enough to accept them. As a child, she felt anointed, special. Now, she feels cursed.

Having biked back up Cemetery Road Hill and offered mental salutations to the dead, she is taking an alternate route back to town because she has yet to see anything today, not even a bit of thread. The roads are desolate. Her pannier is completely empty.

The pods, once closed, are eerily still, as if they are waiting for applause. They seem frozen in that electrified moment after the last note is sounded, when the echoes of music still hang in the air. They continue to close, all along the road, as Bonnie passes; then they begin closing just ahead of her. Leading her? Where?

She follows in their wake, down a paved road, right at an intersection, onto an unfinished road that bisects some farmer's cornfield. Bonnie knows from years of reading *The Farmer's Almanac* that corn ripens as much by moonlight as by sunlight after Lammas Day; even so, the corn in this field is especially ripe, very tall indeed.

The procession of milkweed pods lining the road comes to an end; there are no more.

She dismounts, sets her bike down in the ditch. A single row of corn is bending in the wind, lowering all the way to the earth—what kind of wind, to move with such selectivity, such gentle force? The stalks hinge slowly away from her, forming another road, and Bonnie follows it. Her heart is quickening.

Up ahead she sees something, a small circle of light on the path the wind is making for her. She draws closer. It is an overturned lid, not half-submerged as an artifact should be, but resting atop the flattened stalks and reflecting the late afternoon sun like a mirror, as if it has been placed there recently, purposefully. A signaling device. A sign. Bonnie lifts it up—the metal is cooler than she expects—and gasps. Underneath the lid is a torn piece of paper—a list!—and a piece of floral-print cotton cut into a perfect circle. The lid is rusted, it's been pierced in several places with a nail, the paint is partially flaked off, the lettering half-obliterated, but Bonnie knows what she is holding: It's an old lid from a jar of mayonnaise. Hellman's mayonnaise.

Bonnie presses these newest, precious artifacts to her heart and quickly retraces her steps, out of the field and back to her bike. The unbroken stalks slowly arise to their full height as she goes.

The rain clouds are moving up from the southwest, faster now. It's time to go back. Bonnie secures the relics inside one of her bike panniers and heads home, careening down the hill in high gear, listening all the way to songs of thunder in the distance, milkweed in the ditch.

"She had multiple sclerosis," Gaelan says to no one, in answer to an unuttered question.

It is 3:41, and the front door is closing. It is closing on Claudia, sad, pale Claudia, who fell into his arms three months ago, weeping, and is leaving now, notably dry-eyed, to try to patch things up with her cheating scumbag of a husband. Gaelan telephoned her from the gym, as soon as he finished his workout, and asked her if she'd like to meet him at his place. She stayed long enough to engage in a spectacularly slippery and vivacious farewell boff before announcing her reconciliation. Now she's gone, no hard feelings either way. It's a typical finale to Gaelan's relationships with women. They come, they go, in near-exact accordance with the seasons.

"Don't get up," Claudia had said, turning to face him and suddenly looking very much like a lawyer. She reached out. At first he thought she was going to pet him; instead, she smoothed her hand over the rumpled quilt. "I'll let myself out." Then she picked up her briefcase and left.

Gaelan lingers, aware of the sudden quiet, the cooling sheets, the vacated wet spot.

The Silent Killer of Young Adults. That was the moniker for MS, the tagline that some savvy Manhattan adman dreamed up to accompany public service announcements intended to call attention to Hope's disease (a disease that up to that point didn't have the name recognition of cancer, say, or polio).

MS, the public service announcer intoned bleakly, as the silhouette of an upright, presumably healthy human was seen to shrink incrementally, collapse in on itself, and eventually transform into the silhouette of a feeble, hunched nonentity imprisoned in a wheelchair, *The Silent Killer of Young Adults.*

These PSAs played on television over and over when Gaelan was a child. The ads scared the shit out of him, even before his mother was diagnosed. The word *silent* gave the phrase its insidious threat and terrifying power. A noisy killer would be preferable. At least a person could hear him coming. But a silent killer. Gaelan imagined MS creeping into his mother's bedroom—like Dracula wearing a gray flannel suit and rubber-soled shoes—and offing her while she slept.

Gaelan remembers feeling protected by his quilt—the one his mother made for him when he was a baby, the one that stayed on his bed until they lost everything. A re-creation of that quilt now covers his bed. Claudia didn't ask many questions about it. She may have never asked about it at all; Gaelan doesn't remember precisely.

Theirs was an especially nonverbal relationship, bountifully orgasmic but conversationally sparse. She tasted like lake water; she had a pleasant, weedy smell, especially behind her ears; and she told him once that having an orgasm was like going over a waterfall.

Gaelan always asks his lovers how they experience orgasm. Women have such a way with words. No two of them describe it the same way. It's essential to Gaelan that he give his mind and body over to whatever image his lovers describe—embroidering it, finding his place within it.

He doesn't consider himself promiscuous, no matter how many women he's seeing concurrently. A promiscuous person doesn't invest thoroughly and tirelessly in the specific imaginings of their lovers. A promiscuous person doesn't consider himself a failure if his partner doesn't come.

Is he incapable of intimacy? Hard to say.

During the workweek, after he leaves the studio, Gaelan trains at the gym for two hours. He goes to sleep at seven o'clock; his alarm rings at two in the morning. Saturdays and Sundays are given over to longer sessions at the gym with his personal trainer, errands, an occasional drive down to Emlyn Springs, a movie with Larken. This schedule requires Gaelan to take a certain kind of lover, one who's available to develop a relationship Mondays through Fridays between 3:30 and 6:30 P.M. In Gaelan's experience, this precludes a large segment of the dating population. It narrows the range of possible interactions. On the plus side, afternoon sex always feels illicit, even if adultery isn't involved. Gaelan enjoys this; he assumes the women do, too.

Is he addicted to sex? Possibly.

Without question, Gaelan loves the potency of women, the way his feelings for them translate into something as physically unequivocal as an erection. He loves the grounded feeling that women give him. They seem so enviably secure in their attachment to the earth—which is strange, given their lightness, the funny impractical shoes they wear, their obsession with losing weight. No matter how much Gaelan builds his own body, stacks it with supplements, buttresses it with muscle, he never feels as though he has the same relationship to gravity that women do. But when he is inside them, he feels moored and safe, and he knows that he will not float away.

He will miss Claudia. He misses all of them, every woman who has ever left.

He is not sad, exactly. He is definitely not heartbroken, nothing as dramatic as that. He feels only a vague grayness, a wilting malaise.

He should get up, call one of the other women he is seeing. It's late, it's Friday, but one of them might be free to meet him later, at the movies maybe, where it's cool.

Of course, it's hot and muggy, that's why he's so lethargic.

Kate and Spencer, Gaelan's cats, jump onto the bed. They begin nuzzling the vacant niche behind his knees, purring. He shouldn't nap; it will be that much harder to go to sleep tonight.

The quilt from his side-lying perspective is sharply foreshortened, terrestrial; its folds and patches look like exotically terraced farmland. He could be a reclining giant—like Paul Bunyan, Hercules of the West, savior of small-town America, a hero with the power to reroute rivers, stanch floods, fell timbers, tame cyclones.

Gaelan closes his eyes, just for a few minutes. He'll get up soon and figure out what to do for the rest of the day.

Dead mothers have the ability to see their children not only as they are, but as they *were,* all at once. Their vision is insectlike, prismatic and complex; but whereas a fruit fly, bumblebee, or mosquito sees only the big-screen-close-up NOW—a bumpy, cast-off avocado peel projected from several angles; a geodesic dome of human flesh in the form of a big, juicy, perspiring toe—each plane in a dead mother's eyes presents a scene from a different point in time.

So as Aneira Hope Jones is being borne home on a sudden, supercharged current of energy generated by her living husband, she sees her children not only in what the living refer to as *the present moment;* she is afforded other views. This simultaneity of vision is a gift that Hope is experiencing for the first time; understandably, she is confused by it, not yet in control, more of a passenger riding its power than the entity driving it.

Patience, please. Eventually she will become more proficient.

Here is Larken, her oldest, caught in some falsehood.

Hope perceives this clearly, yet cannot exactly define the nature of the lie.

She is talking excitedly to a small group of people, two men, one woman—all are so much older than she—at a party. She is talking . . .

Can that be right?

. . . about rodents.

". . . and the marvelous innovation in the Mérode," Larken is saying, "one that secures its place, undeniably I believe, at the leading edge of the Renaissance rather than the tail end of the Gothic . . ."

Now Hope understands. The falsehood arises not from what she is *saying,* but from what she is *thinking.*

". . . is this nascent development of a unique and private symbolism. With Joseph and the mousetrap . . ."

Ah. Mice.

". . . Campin radicalizes religious painting."

She is thinking about food.

"He is developing a visual language that originates—for the first time—not from established church doctrine, not from notions imposed upon him by his patrons . . ."

She wants to snatch that brie-smeared slice of bread from the bald man's plate—an act of rebellion—and stuff it entire into her mouth.

". . . but from his own imagination. What could be more modern?"

Why is she smiling when she feels so ashamed?

In other views, Larken is a baby, crying, crying, driving Hope mad.

I do not miss this. Lord, no.

Hope sees that it is hunger, always, that makes Larken cry, not loneliness or fear or overstimulation or fatigue. She is simply hungry.

With Gaelan, Hope knows better.

Easy baby.

Whenever he cries, Hope feeds him, and he is happy.

At the breast, all attention. He could drain me faster and with more ferocity than either of the girls.

"Look, Mama!" Gaelan shouts, three years old and jubilant in bubbles. "My penis is frozen!"

In cotton Jockeys at the age of eight, smiling, sheepish, he comes in to pee while she is trying to apply lipstick. "Mom," he says, his hands held lightly over his erection, "could I please have some privacy?"

At callow sixteen with his first love.

His only?

The hush, the sanctity, the terror, the heat. Young hands mapping new terrain.

"That feels nice," he tells the girl.

An Emlyn Springs girl. What is her name?

Not asking for more, not expecting more, not knowing yet that there can be more, because it is all delicious now, all miraculous, that intersecting bodies can bring such incomparable joy, a heaven on earth. He asks the girl:

Bethan, that's it. The Ellises' youngest. Lived across the highway from us.

"Does this feel nice? Do you like it?"

With everyone since, he keeps his eyelids open the tiniest crack when he's kissing. So restless in his lovemaking. All his women perceive it and in the end it drives them all away.

Home and alone—a man in this view, handsome, not happy—Gaelan dreams of a kite in a cloudless sky. He wonders who is flying the kite; he cannot quite see them and he wants to see. His hand, in sleep, finds his penis, a comfort.

Silly boy. He's the one who's flying the kite.

With Hope's youngest child comes a tangle of visions: screams and cries, spinning wheels, frantic winds.

"No! It's not trash!" Bonnie screams, her small fists clenched around crumbs, stones, empty matchbooks, all manner of garbage. "No! I won't let you throw it away!"

Through all of time, Bonnie rides a bike.

Oh yes. This one. I called her "the little pedaler" when she quickened.

She subsists on nothing. She speaks mostly to the dead and dying. She is almost mad. Hope turns away from these views; they're too plentiful, too painful.

Here's Bonnie, adult in her makeshift kitchen.

Does she really live there?

Outside, as the thunderstorm builds, Bonnie unloads things from a saddlebag contraption: more refuse. And yet she treats these bits of trash with the kind of gentleness afforded to religious artifacts. A torn piece of paper bearing a handwritten list: *Paint the nursery. Buy diapers. The clothes—where*

That sounds familiar.

A circle cut from cotton cloth.

That looks familiar.

A metal lid from a Hellman's mayonnaise jar. As Hope notes the holes punched into it, her vision takes in Bonnie, small again.

This is so confusing.

She is five years old, and there, close by—

At last. All three.

—are her brother and sister, at eleven and twelve.

Gaelan holds the nail—"Ouch! Ouch!"—while Larken hammers the holes—"Sorry! Sorry!"—while Bonnie chatters:

"And tonight after dinner we'll catch them and put them inside the jar very gently and they'll be able to breathe but not get away and Mommy can read to me by their light, that's what she told me. I like main ace, don't you?"

Main Ace. I forgot she used to say it like that.

"I don't like mustard but I do like ketchup. Miss Williams says it like 'cats up.' Did you ever notice that? Isn't that funny? And I like pickles too. But not sweet relish."

"Ouch!"

"Sorry!"

"OUCH! Geez, Larken . . ."

Llewellyn is on the golf course; Hope is with them all.

"Time of death," Bud Morrison, the paramedic, pronounces.

I know him. I know all those men.

Bud looks at his watch as they stand in the rain. "Time of death, three fifty-nine."

And at the instant Hope's husband is borne skyward, riding a small white sphere into the jet stream; something loosens in her living children. Simultaneously they each let forth with fluids:

In Larken's womb, there's a sudden, floodlike sloughing of blood. "Shit," she mutters, mortified, mid-sentence. *It can't be,* she's thinking, *it's not time for my period,* but blood is pouring down her legs. No time for a polite Midwestern exit. She clamps her thighs, knees, and ankles together, abruptly turning away from the puzzled/concerned/shocked faces of the people she was talking to, and starts to waddle toward the bathroom like a bad parody of a graceless geisha.

Who is holding the kite? Gaelan wonders as he dreams. He's anxious. The kite has been let out all the way; it's six miles high, dangerously close to the jet stream. What if the string breaks? What if the end hasn't been secured to the spool? His eyes follow the kite string down, down, down, but he cannot locate the kite-flier. It's a ghost kite without a captain. The string goes taut. It twangs, it vibrates. The kite stops making swallow dives and loops and becomes frozen like a lollipop at the end of a stick. Gaelan wakes as he comes, ashamed, confused.

Bonnie is placing her new artifacts in their archival setting: an oversized, clothbound book, like a ledger. There are many other books like this; they line the shelves of her woodshed, organized by a system that only Bonnie understands. She has already recorded captions (*Quilt Scrap, Mayonnaise Lid from Jar for Children's Lightning Bugs, To-Do List for Baby*), the date (August 15, 2003), and the time (approximately 15:30 hours) when she made her most recent finds. Location? Bonnie pauses. As she retraces her route mentally, she realizes where her artifacts were found—on her family's land, on the spot where the Farmer Elves made their visitations. She gives over to sobs so wrenching that it seems they will never abate.

In unison, their bodies sing: blood, semen, tears.

And now they are scattering again. They were in a singular orbit but have spun apart and are off on different courses.

Hope makes a few quick notes in her diary, characterizing her children as she has newly glimpsed them:

Larken: Heavy, judgmental, fraudulent, afraid.

Gaelan: Closed, disconnected, libidinous, un-self-aware.

Bonnie: Imprisoned, silent, obsessed.

Liars, all of them. And all so humorless!

This is nothing like what I wanted, but probably what I deserve. No one's a bigger liar than me.

The living see only that bit of thread on the spool that has been unwound.

But the dead see everything, through whatever set of eyes they choose. After all, it is all there.

Chapter 5

Annunciation Through the Wires

Viney dries her hands on a dish towel before answering the phone. She has been standing at the sink, washing vegetables and keeping an eye on the weather, getting ready to make a double serving of Dr. Walker's Salad Number 5.

She feels steady and calm after doing her yoga routine. Her third eye is open. The table is set. The oven is preheating. The rain has let up but it's surely too wet at the club to play; Welly will be home soon and in need of electrolytes. Chilling in the fridge are two martini glasses filled with freshly pressed cucumber and celery tonic.

"Hello, Viney."

"Bud. What's happened?"

Alvina Closs, a woman who has received news of many deaths in her life—and of deaths far more terrible and rending than this—recognizes a quality of tone in Bud's voice: sluggish, ponderous, contrite, as if the messenger is already laboring gracelessly under the weight of the newly departed, as if his voice is struggling to hold the coffin and its contents aloft. As Bud tells the story, Viney receives her share of this weight; she sits down at the kitchen nook table and listens. Her hands are blanched in places and shriveled from scrubbing the vegetables; the dish towel is damp in her lap and streaked with dirt.

"He must have misjudged the storm is all I can think," Bud is saying, "maybe thought it was gonna blow over. Believe me, Viney, we did everything we could. He was gone as soon as we got to him. Honestly, I don't think he knew what hit him. It was that fast."

What was the man thinking? Alvina asks herself, at the same time sensing that, if she chose, she could easily penetrate the translucency of this question. She is reminded of that popular novelty: an eight ball, sized like a small cantaloupe and hard as glass. You asked a question and shook it and peered through a tiny triangular window and waited until words floated up, as if through muddied waters, leaving you in suspense until you saw clearly, irrefutably: *Yes. No. Maybe. Not Likely. Try Again. Wait and See.* The answer to Viney's question is already formed, waiting beneath a murky surface. But she can't bring herself to see it, not yet.

Hope? she thinks, and it only takes this one word to summon a palpable presence and the beginning of sorrow, if not acceptance. *What do I do now?*

Easier questions are being posed: Does Viney want to notify the kids herself, Bud wonders, or should he do it? The same with the pastor at the Bethel Welsh Methodist Church. He'd be happy to make the phone calls. All she has to do is say the word.

"I'll tell the kids," Viney answers. "It should come from me. But you can call Pastor Huw if you don't mind, Bud. That would be a help."

"Sure, Viney."

"Is the mayor already over at Mal's?"

"He is."

So it will be this, Viney thinks, all over again: She'll drive the five blocks to McKeever's Funeral Home, make that trip up the porch steps, through the leaded glass door, across the silent, airless foyer with its heavy velvet curtains, and from there to the basement. (The McKeevers and their employees know what to expect from Alvina Closs by now; they won't even try to invoke funeral home regulations to keep her out of the prep room.) She will breathe in that nauseating, sweet, lung-searing cocktail of smells—formaldehyde, putrefaction, paste wax. She will set her feet wide on the slick, bilious-yellow linoleum that's covered the morgue floor since the 1950s, next to the gurney, within a breath's distance of the sheet that Mal—or one of his sons—will draw aside. She'll stand again over that hollow, empty house of horrors that is the body in death. How can this flesh—such a source of joy in our lives—become such an obscenity, and so soon? Only yesterday she and Welly made love.

What was he thinking? she repeats. *Why on earth did he go like that?*

"Good," she says. "I'll get over there as soon as I get ahold of the kids."

"Okay then, Viney. Me and Vonda will be over later to check on you."

"Thanks, Bud."

Viney remains seated. Her eyes drift from the place mats and cutlery to the kitchen clock and coatrack to the colander of new-washed cherry tomatoes next to the sink. They remind her of the rubber balls the girls used to bounce when they played with their jacks on the floor under this table only yesterday, rubber balls attached to rubber bands stapled to balsa wood paddles that the boys loved so, those cheap playthings from Tinkham's Five and Dime, established 1881, out of business since 1980.

Another question is forming. *Was he ever mine?*

The church bell is ringing; Bud must have already reached Pastor Huw. Soon everybody in town will know.

Viney gets up. She dials the Williams house and asks Hazel to summon Bonnie. (*So quiet in her grief,* Viney reflects after hanging up the phone, *as if she already knew. It was the same when her mother went.*)

She telephones Larken and Gaelan up in Lincoln—work numbers, home numbers, cell phones. But all she gets are their recorded voices, so she leaves a brief message, *Please call me, honey, it's important*, after every beep.

She calls her daughters—Julie up in Omaha, Janey in Salt Lake—and leaves more messages; they are both at work and won't be home until later. Her third daughter, Haley, the only one still here, doesn't have an answering machine. Viney knows for a fact she isn't home. It's Randy's weekend with the kids; he lives in Crete and Haley is driving them up there now. It's fine. It's not as though Welly was her father. Viney will talk to her tonight.

It's only after she finally hangs up the phone, turns off the oven, and starts putting the vegetables away that she sees the answers to her questions: He wanted to die. He was not hers. They never really belonged to each other.

The church bell, she notices, has fallen silent.

They never did ring that bell for Hope.

Gaelan is in the dark. His cell phone is off.

He is at the movies, watching the naked, coiled figure of Arnold Schwarzenegger unfurl on the big screen. The sparks are flying. The sizzling force that bore the Terminator from the future to the present zigzags across the desert, igniting tumbleweeds, exploding grains of sand.

Gaelan has seen this movie three times already: with Mara, one of his paramours, on opening weekend; a second time with Jeff, his personal trainer at Y; and then again with Larken a couple of weeks ago. He is seeing it for the fourth time, alone, because staying home by himself on a Friday night was a prospect too depressing to consider.

Gaelan derives great comfort and inspiration from Arnold's projected presence. Arnold is no great actor—Gaelan owns every single one of Arnold's movies (even *The Jayne Mansfield Story*) and watches them with the sound on mute—but he is a great bodybuilder, a marvel of physical solidity. He can stand in his skin like no one else.

Gaelan tries to imagine what it would be like to move through the world with that sure, weighted grace. He still marvels at Arnold's body, which has changed so much since his Conan the Barbarian days. Gaelan's physique has changed too, since he emulates Arnold in all things related to bodybuilding. As Arnold has embraced a leaner aesthetic, so has Gaelan. When Arnold modified his routine, diet, and supplement regimen in the interest of replacing bulk with length, Gaelan followed suit.

Even though Arnold's fame and sphere of influence have grown—he is the governor of California, he is married to a Kennedy, and it is not difficult to imagine that someday the laws of the land will bend to Arnold's upbeat, indomitable force, enabling the possibility of a foreign-born commander in chief: President Schwarzenegger!—Gaelan maintains the status quo sensation of being connected to his long-term hero through his dedication to bodybuilding—albeit at a much humbler level. Usually this is reassuring.

Tonight, however, Gaelan is bothered by evidence that indicates that, however much his commitment to physical fitness aligns him with the former Mr. Olympia, his life is lagging.

Another lover has left his bed. Sleep is elusive. Fall is coming. He is still being stalked by the silent killer.

On the big screen, Arnold has just acquired his wardrobe: tight leather pants, jacket, boots. Here comes the bit with the rhinestone sunglasses. The audience laughs. Gaelan pops another Mylanta.

If only Larken didn't have that regular thing on Fridays; she would have seen this again. Maybe she'll come out with him tomorrow night.

After the initial burst of rain and tears, Bonnie feels better. She is calmed by thunderstorms, and although she's a bit worried about the Williams girls, she remains intent on her archival duties.

What she does notice eventually is the sudden silence, a cessation of wind, dwindling rain. Bonnie disengages from her work and opens the door.

Outside, it has turned winter. The temperature has dropped to freezing. The outgoing gasses from Bonnie's lungs condense instantly, hanging suspended in the air before her. They begin to form a small cumulus cloudbank just beyond her lips that grows and grows with each accelerating exhalation. The ground is white, knobby, studded with hailstones the size of golf balls, and yet when Bonnie looks up she sees that, miraculously, none of the whirligigs have suffered the slightest bit of damage. They begin to spin slowly as she stares at them. There is no wind.

Bonnie practices her own form of augury: As if retrieving a fallen plum, she plucks up a hailstone and puts it in her mouth. It is energetically charged and has a peculiar taste: equal parts iron, salinity, and shoe polish. A chemical reaction commences; as her saliva comes in contact with the hailstone and it begins to dissolve, there is a flash of contained light within Bonnie's oral cavity; her cheeks are briefly aglow.

She starts walking across the lawn, gingerly at first, for she is barefoot and the hailstones are hard, jagged in places, so cold that they sear her skin. But as soon as the telephone inside the big house begins to ring she takes off running, slipping as she goes. She is almost at the bottom of the porch steps when the front door creaks open and Hazel appears, grayed and indistinct behind the summer screen, shrouded in her housedress.

"He knows now, doesn't he?" Bonnie says. "He knows where Mom is."

"I suppose he does," Hazel replies kindly, her eyes filling with tears. Holding the screen door open and gesturing Bonnie in and out of the cold, she looks down and exclaims, "Oh, dear heavens, child! Look what you've done to your feet."

Larken is mincing celery into eighth-of-an-inch cubes; these will go into the carrot and raisin salad. Minced celery is one of the special ingredients that makes Larken's dinner guest prefer her carrot and raisin salad above all others. Larken's other secret: She presoaks the raisins for half an hour in a mixture containing a cup of hot water, a generous splash of orange juice, a dash of lemon juice, a teaspoon of vanilla extract, and whispers of cinnamon and powdered ginger. After the grated carrots, plumped raisins, and celery are mixed with swirls of clover honey, Larken adds the final touch: a protein-enriching sprinkle of sesame and hulled sunflower seeds, unroasted, unsalted, organic.

The pasta is almost done. Larken pours two cups of frozen baby peas into a colander; she will drain the pasta on top. She tends another pot on the stove; it contains a special concoction that she perfected after searching dozens of special-diet sites on the Internet. Larken's dinner guest is lactose-intolerant, and much trial and error finally resulted in a no-cheese sauce that is not just palatable, but truly tasty. Among other ingredients, Larken uses turmeric for the distinctly cheddarish orange that is a requisite visual element of macaroni and cheese.

She stirs the sauce, which is smoothing and thickening nicely, and consciously takes in a deep breath. Everything is going to be fine. She was an angry, nervous wreck when she got home—not the spiritual state in which to prepare food for a loved one. Larken meditates quietly over the pots of steaming pasta and warming sauce, praying that none of her previous agitation has contaminated the food.

She arrived home much later than she'd hoped. As if that pain-in-the-ass university party wasn't enough, there was the sudden and unexpected arrival of her menses—resulting in the need to make an unplanned visit to the drugstore as well as her scheduled stop at the video store—and the stinging shame of imagining what kind of impression she made on the new dean. Traffic was unaccountably congealed—as if the cars themselves were languishing in the heat—and checkout lines were long and infuriatingly slow. As soon as she got home, she kicked off her shoes, turned on the window air conditioner full blast, unloaded the bags, and got right to cooking.

She didn't see the blinking light on her answering machine. She might not have listened to the messages even if she had noticed; Larken hates the assaulting, intrusive necessity of a ringing phone—has hated it since childhood, when phone calls from Dad's patients came in at all hours of the day and night—so she keeps the ring tone on her home phone constantly muted.

Phone calls to Larken's home number are invariably the obligatory, predictable kind: from colleagues, telemarketers, Gaelan, Viney, and rarely, her baby sister. The only other people of significance in her life these days are her upstairs neighbors, and when they need to communicate, they either bang on the floor with the broom handle or holler down the stairs.

They are not hollering now. In fact, it is unusually quiet. There's music playing, but the volume is uncharacteristically low, and there are no footfalls. Maybe they're out—although that too would be atypical at this time on a Friday.

Larken's abdomen is in spasm. The cramps have arrived in full force and she feels as though she is carrying a belly full of bundled rebar. She has already bled through two superabsorbent sanitary pads. She'd best put on a fresh one now, before her guest arrives.

Larken's apartment—part of a house built in the early 1900s—is situated a few miles from campus in a part of Lincoln that is old, well established, and lushly treed. About half the homes in this neighborhood are owned by single families; the other half have been divided into apartments, in this case, three: on the first floor are Larken's one-bedroom and an oddly configured studio (overpriced, hard to rent, currently vacant); the other apartment is a three-bedroom that takes up the entire upstairs. Larken has use of the front porch, which gives her ample space for growing potted flowers, vegetables, and herbs. The bathroom and kitchen have been carved out of other rooms and are not original to the house—they are very small—but the living room remains intact and entire: spacious, with a tiled fireplace, bay window, hardwood floors, and blue-hued stained glass windows that lend the rooms a cool, calm, sanctified light on even the most suffocating and windswept days of summer. Larken's bedroom is behind massive sliding doors in what was once the dining room.

Larken loves her apartment. She has lived here for ten years. She hopes to live here forever.

Overhead, there are sudden signs of habitation and movement: two sets of heavy footsteps offset by the rapid staccato thumping of a third, much lighter individual. Voices are conferring in low tones. Larken cannot ascertain the content, but she perceives a definite tension in the female voice, evidenced by an antagonistic emphasis on the consonants. It's easy to imagine the words being accompanied by hand gestures: jabs, punches, slices, slaps.

Larken's upstairs neighbors, Jonathan Schwartzmann and Mia Hinkley, moved in five years ago. Mia is forty, and possessed of a complicated personal history and a serrated temperament—manifested outwardly by multiple tattoos, aggressively plucked eyebrows, and a Southern accent that she tries hard to conceal. Mia is a performance artist. Larken receives frequent invitations to events in which Mia is a participant; she attends them when it's unavoidable. There's authentic passion in Mia's theatrical offerings, but Larken finds her presentational style odd (it manages to be both self-congratulatory and masochistic), her work disturbingly raw and unformed—like beef tartare.

Jon is thirty-five, holds a lecturer position in the university's English department, and will almost certainly be awarded tenure soon. He's already published two critically acclaimed novels and a memoir. Larken wants academic glory for Jonathan even more than she wants it for herself.

Jon and Mia met in England when Mia's band, Cunt Julep, played a gig in the neighborhood skittles pub where Jon did his writing. (He was the only customer remaining after they finished their first song.) Although their first encounter makes for a hilarious, romantic anecdote, one that Jon loves to tell and Larken loves to hear, they insist that their marriage was a pragmatic affair, a formality undertaken strictly for the papers so that Jon could work in the States.

On the subject of conception, Jon and Mia have remained mum. It's entirely possible that they didn't intend to make a baby; nevertheless they made one, soon after their arrival. In Larken's memory, the U-Haul truck was still parked on the street and they'd only unloaded half their boxes when they went at it on their bedroom floor. Mia is expressive during sex. There's a zoo-animal, primate-in-estrus quality to her coital vocalizations, so Larken knows she heard the sounds that accompanied the conception of Jon and Mia's child, who was born nine months to the day after they moved in.

Larken checks the clock; it is six and everything is ready. Upstairs, the music is being turned off, keys are being jangled, two low and civilized voices are conferring in indecipherable tones. A third voice—high and chirpy—penetrates layers of insulation, aged wood joists, subflooring, and support beams and shouts, "Come ON Jonafun! Come ON Mia! It's time to GO!"

A door slams. Feet are heard descending the stairs; the sound suggests a small pony who has not yet mastered quadruped grace but is making a determined effort to do so. Larken hurries to the door, arriving breathless and opening it soon after a loud and insistent knocking begins.

"LARKEE! HI! HAPPY FRIDAY!"

Only one thing occupies a larger place in the heart of Professor Jones than the pre-Renaissance paintings of the Flemish masters: Jonathan and Mia's daughter, Esmé Veronica Hinkley-Schwartzmann.

"Hi, peanut!"

An exquisite mess of downy white-blonde hair, unlaced shoes, smudges, and jam stains, the love of Larken's life looks like a sherpa-in-training. Her possessions take up more room in the foyer than she does. In one hand, she clasps a canvas grocery bag that barely contains her menagerie of beanbag creatures and finger puppets—unicorn, wolf, dragonfly, Orca whale, turtle, crow, moose, gecko; the other hand grips the handle of her suitcase.

"IT'S MOVIE NIGHT!"

Esmé catapults her thirty-eight pounds up and into Larken's arms. Larken buries her face in Esmé's tangled hair; it is a dizzying mix of odors: crayon wax and Elmer's glue. A bit of glitter anoints Esmé's left earlobe.

"What's your pick this week?" Esmé whispers.

"You'll see," Larken whispers back, "after Mommy and Daddy leave."

"I just KNOW it's gotta be *Nemo*." Esmé snuggles closer, imprinting Larken's cheek with something sticky. Then she wiggles down to the floor.

"You want help, sweetie?"

"I can do it," Esmé insists, and starts dragging her bags into Larken's apartment, fanny first.

Jon is coming down the stairs; he carries Esmé's rolled sleeping bag and pillow.

Larken is always struck by the contrast between Jon's body and his manner of moving: buoyant, fluid, brisk. Accordingly to Mia, Jon is forty-seven pounds overweight and, even given his age, is a poster boy for heart disease. Jon endures with seeming good nature Mia's frequent public reminders of the derision he endured as a pudgy child and her constant efforts to restrict his caloric intake. Larken thinks Jon's body is just right; to her, he has the solid, upholstered look of a leather armchair in a cozy sitting room next to a crackling fire in the middle of winter.

"Larken," Jon says, striding across the foyer and leaning in to kiss her cheek. "Happy Friday."

"How was your day?"

"Well, let me see . . . By mid-morning, I'd become obsessed with the lint balls on my cardigan; around lunchtime, I felt a divine calling to clean the bathroom mirror, which got me wondering if this is the sort of getup a *real* writer would wear; and by three-thirty I was seriously considering going to Hobby Lobby, buying several hanks of yarn, and teaching myself to knit."

Larken laughs. She loves Jonathan's voice.

"Ah! You're amused. But men invented knitting, did you know that?"

"I did not. You are a fountain of information."

"Yeah, well, I'm a fountain of *something,* that's for sure."

It's not just Jon's working-class accent and distinctly Brit-speak manner of expressing himself. His voice reminds Larken of a dinner roll, the kind with faint indentations across the top, perforations that can be eased apart so that, when newly warmed, they fan open, like miniature books.

"In short," Jon continues, "it was a plodding day. A fits-and-starts day. I did manage to establish an especially brilliant place for a semicolon."

Larken laughs again. "I can relate."

Mia appears on the second-floor landing, listening to her cell phone. She's wearing one of her signature outfits—an oversized, striped, vintage men's pajama ensemble that gives her the look of someone who's either just emerged from a rehabilitative stay at a sanitarium or lengthy incarceration as a prisoner-of-war. She moves as if keeping time with a dirge.

"How about you?" Jon asks, casting Mia a look. His voice remains chatty; his expression clouds. "Did you get your grades in?"

"I did." Larken infuses her own voice with an extra dose of jollity. "I am student-free for two whole weeks."

"Congratulations. Please tell me that you ended up failing that girl."

"Misty? Had to. It ended badly. There was name-calling involved."

Jon clasps Larken's arm. "God, Lark. I'm so sorry. Students can be such shits."

Mia has arrived at the bottom of the stairs. She is still listening intently to whoever is on the other end of the phone. Waving and mouthing *thank you* to Larken, she continues her one-woman funeral procession through the foyer and out the front door.

"Well then," Jon says. "I guess we're off."

"What are you guys up to tonight?"

"Open mic at The Night Before. Mia's reading some new work." Jon drops Esmé's gear inside the door. "Hey little girl," he calls out. Esmé is systematically arranging and rearranging her stuffed animals in a semicircle facing the TV screen. "I'm leaving now. Love you."

Esmé races toward her father, colliding into—and then hugging—his legs. "Bye, Daddy! Bye, Jonafun! See ya!" Jon is about to kiss her on the head when she stag-leaps back into the living room.

"Poor child," he says, and Larken perceives that his mournful tone is only half put on. "Terrible separation anxiety. Whatever shall we do?"

"You guys have a *fabulous* time tonight!" Larken cheers. Yes, she is in love with Jon and Esmé—even with Mia—and for this reason and so many others they must not must not must not break up.

Hours later—after Esmé has devoured her mac and cheese and carrot-raisin salad, taken a bath, cuddled with Larken on the sofa, and watched *Finding Nemo*—Larken finally notices the blinking light on her answering machine. There are six messages.

First message, received four forty-two P.M.: *Please call me, honey,* Viney says. *It's important.*

"What's for breakfast?" Esmé yells from the bathroom.

"What's that, sweetie?"

Second message . . .

"What will our hearty breakfast be?"

"How about pumpkin pancakes?"

"I love pumpking pancakes!"

It's me again, honey. Please call as soon as you get this, okay?

"Finish brushing your teeth now. I'll be there in a minute."

"Do you remember that part about Nemo's mom?"

Third message: Larken . . .

"Larkee!"

. . . sweetie . . .

"Yes!"

I need to talk to you. It's about your father. I don't want to . . .

"That part with Nemo's mommy."

"Yes. I remember."

. . . just call me as soon as you can. OK?

"What happened to her?"

"Well," Larken says, making an effort to slow her breathing and control her voice. "We don't know for sure, do we? They didn't show that part."

Fourth message . . .

Larken hears Esmé spit into the bathroom sink and then pronounce, "I think she got killed by that fish with the teeth. Not the shark. He was funny. The other one."

Larken. Viney is crying. *I don't want to leave this on your machine, but . . . Honey? There's been an accident.*

"You remember that other fish?" Esmé prods. "The bearcooduh?"

"That was scary, wasn't it? I'm glad you held my hand during that part."

Your father, Viney is saying. *Your dad . . .*

"Larkee?" Esmé has finished in the bathroom and is padding across the living room to where Larken stands.

"Yes, button." Larken turns down the volume.

"Do you ever cry?"

"Sure I do. Everybody cries." Larken redirects Esmé's body toward the bedroom. "Get into bed now. I'll be right there."

Esmé takes Larken's hand, insistently. "But I want you to come, too. Carry me. Piggyback."

"Okay," Larken says, pausing the answering machine. "But then you have to go to sleep."

Esmé climbs onto a chair, and from there onto Larken's back. "I've never seen you cry," she says.

"That's because when I'm with you, I'm happy."

In the bedroom, Esmé's sleeping bag has already been laid out, her pillow has been fluffed, her favorite stuffed animal—an orca whale— is standing guard.

"I cry when I'm with you sometimes," Esmé observes.

"That's different."

"How?"

"You need to go to sleep now, little bug. Close your eyes. I'm just going to clean up and then I'll be in." Larken heads back into the living room.

Fifth message: Lark, Bonnie says, her voice emotionless. *Dad's dead.*

"Larkee?"

I'm at Viney's. She's gone to bed.

"Don't forget to brush your teeth!"

Call us in the morning.

"Larkee!"

"I hear you, Esmé. I won't forget."

Sixth message received

"Are you coming soon?"

Larken? Gaelan, tearful. *You must have heard by now. I'm driving down tonight.*

"LARKEE! I'm waiting and waiting and waiting for you."

"I'll be right there."

Call, okay? Even if it's late. God, Lark. I can't believe it.

End of messages, the voice of the answering machine declares: an ersatz female voice devoid of comfort.

Larken reaches down to press the Erase button, and then, alarmingly, down and down and down, for the cluttered landscape of her desk falls away, miles away, and she sees typed papers and pictures of Madonnas and angels laid out below her from a great height, overlapping and intersecting rectangles forming a crazy-quilt field of text and color over which she is suspended: sans net, sans parachute, sans wings. She clutches the thick wooden edges of the desktop. Gaelan helped her move this desk into the apartment. It was heavy, even for him.

"My mom is never going to die," Esmé concludes. "Never never never never."

Hope's Diary, 1961:
I could have eaten her, I suppose

Isn't it all just so much list-making? Doesn't it all boil down to this: providing for, fending off, sheltering, feeding, clothing, childbearing: There really isn't much else other than this: seeing to the base needs that we humans are shackled to. Everything else is frosting, so much fluff, and count yourself lucky if you have it. Wait for the inevitable, hope you arrive at death's door before your children and if you must bury them know that the rest of your life will be about nothing so much as moving away from them and yet strangely toward them, toward a reunion much-desired and yet what of the living and their need of you?

I lost the baby.

There are many lists now to be cast into the trash, things like: Paint the nursery (even though Llewellyn is already trying to reassure me, everyone is trying to reassure me, even women who have been through this and oh how eager they are to come out of the woodwork now when something like this occurs and if I sound angry instead of grateful for their commiserating pity it is because I am, I am because their wounds are remote and not still oozing as is this one, as are my breasts from unexpressed and unsuckled milk. I long to run outside at night and spray the heavens with grief).

Paint the nursery.

Buy diapers.

The clothes—where will I put them?

I could have eaten her, I suppose. That would have been a better memorial perhaps. Primal, after the fashion of wild creatures, even country cats. Had I ingested her, maybe I wouldn't be suffering this madness of loss now. She would still be part of me, not separate. I could try to dig her up. Should I?

L. thinks I'm mad. He's right. And here's the most dreadful thing, more dreadful even, possibly (although I don't think so) than the loss itself: it's the certain knowledge that a great divide has sprung up between us. The landscape of our marriage is forever changed, there is an unbroachable cliff, a sheer drop-off over which no bridge can ever be built because there is nothing on the other side. And it's not the pregnancy—we were united then, we were in it together even though it was my body—but it's the death, the death, the giving birth to death, which would have been the truth in any case, even had the baby come to term, I know this now in a way I might not have if this hadn't happened: it's us, always us, the mothers, giving birth and giving death (they give birth astride the grave, which of the Greeks said that?) and now I understand that L. will never never never know this, never feel the way I do. He can never know what this is like the way women do, perhaps, is it so?

He does not see my actions in the correct context.

When I took the strainer from the kitchen into the bathroom and began fishing for her in the toilet—diaphanous, silky she was, and yes I can even call it a she because I know it to be so and require nothing else but that knowledge—he tried to restrain me. As if I were crazy, as if I were endangering myself. But nothing would have stopped me from saving her, nothing could have kept me from giving her a proper burial. The Greeks come again to mind: I could play Antigone now and know her brain-inflamed desperation to bury her beloved brother, her kind, her kin.

L. kept trying to pull me away from the toilet. I kept getting free. There must have been violence involved—I notice now bruises on my legs, scratches on L.'s face. But he must have let me go because I carried her—sheer, unboundaried, a bit more than a collection of cells but not yet in recognizable human form, more like a sea creature—and placed her between two of the squares

Work on the baby's quilt was also on the list

from her quilt. They will always be her colors, there will never be another quilt like this one, never another pattern for any child henceforth

(as if I could ever do this again)

and carried her to a spot deep in the field but easily found, next to a small outcropping of rocks and began to dig.

L. stayed behind, watching, distant. Why couldn't he come and mourn with me? What prevented him? What was he so afraid of?

I could sense him seeing me newly. Horrified? Maybe. Quiet and tolerant in his way, but there it was, another kind of chasm, a deep ravine and what to bridge it?

I dug as deep as I could with bare hands and anointed the ground with blood and milk—blood was running out of me by then, my clothes were soaked so perhaps L.'s resistance was of the simplest kind: he was revulsed by me, by my leakage. Being a woman is so untidy, and here was me, a mess of leaking fluids. Only my mouth was dry. I wish I could have produced something besides dry sounds, a hollowness of grief. If only Mother's mouth could have opened in a song, something to send her on her way, a river to the sea for my little sea creature.

And so I named her: Marina.

It is not that we have the power to give life, this is not the thing that will make my husband and

me strangers for all time; it is the power to give
death. It is the knowledge that we—that I—have done
this.

It really is all our fault. It really is the most
terrible power on earth, given to us, the mothers.

I don't want this.

I can't have this.

And yet and yet and yet

Chapter 6

Blind Driveway

Gaelan is always reminding her that it's a myth—this idea people have that certain places are protected. But he would also be the first to admit that, in spite of every technological advance—the Doppler towers and the mathematical models and the color imaging and the computer-generated simulations—they still don't know what the hell causes a tornado or how it will behave once it's born, and the truth is there never *has* been one that's touched down within the city limits of Lincoln, not ever, so when Larken has put off her departure as long as possible and is facing the inevitable drive away from her tree-lined street in her mythically protected city and toward the danger zone, her hometown, she still can't make herself release the hand brake and step on the gas.

She's been sitting in her car—firmly buckled into the driver's seat, with the engine running and the air conditioner on high—talking to Jonathan. It's been quite a while: long enough for the sun to creep up to her eye line and start searing her vision, long enough for the gas gauge to slip to below half-empty. Larken flips the sun visor down and swigs the last of the coffee Jon brought out when she was loading up.

"Thanks again, Jon," she says, handing over the coffee mug. "I guess I should—"

"Here, Larkee!" Esmé hollers gaily. She holds out a bouquet of squeezed-to-death, gone-to-seed dandelions that she's picked while Larken has been trying to say good-bye.

"Thank you, sweetie! I love these." Larken resists the urge to lick her thumb and start cleaning Esmé's face. She thought she got all the syrupy places after they ate pancakes and watched *Clifford the Big Red Dog* earlier this morning, but dustings of black dirt are stuck to odd, unlikely places: an earlobe, a temple, the inside corner of one eyelid, the spot between Esmé's brows where a jeweled bindi should be. Gritty and sweet, that's how she would taste. Poppy seeds encased in carmelized honey.

"Aren't you going to put them in water?" Esmé asks. "They're dying."

"Oh! Well, I don't have anything in the car to—"

Jon squats next to Esmé and hands her the coffee mug. "Why don't you ask Mum to rinse this out and fill it with water so you can put Larken's flowers in here?"

"Okay. I'll be right back!" Esmé skips up the porch steps and into the house. Jon's eyes trace a path that makes Larken think of Superman and his X-ray vision; it's as if Jon is actually seeing Esmé trundle up the stairs and through the second-floor rooms to the bedroom he shares with Mia, where the window shade is still down. Larken was awake for most of the night, so she knows that Jon came home alone around one o'clock in the morning. Mia got home at four. They didn't make love, but they didn't fight either.

"How does she manage to get Mrs. Butterworth on her eyelids?" Larken asks. She does not want to go. She is needed here.

"It's one of her special skills," Jonathan answers, still gazing up at his bedroom window, as if he has superhero ears as well as eyes and can hear whatever words are being spoken: "'Achieves excessive stickiness.' It's right up there with 'Creates nightly havoc with bedclothes' and 'Performs sword-fighting bits from *The Princess Bride*.' We should all be so gifted." He turns back to face her. "Call me if you need anything, okay?"

She has to go. Her father is dead and she has yet to shed a tear.

"Don't tell Esmé, okay?"

"What do you want me to say if she asks? It's obvious something's up."

Larken nods, considers, and then sighs. "I don't know. Just play dumb."

"Ah! That would be one of *my* special skills."

"Lie, I mean. Tell her you don't know anything. You can lie to your daughter, can't you?"

"Absolutely. It's a prerequisite of parenthood. They won't let you take the kid home from the hospital until you can prove conclusively that you're an expert liar."

Esmé is walking toward them, slowly, carefully, holding the coffee cup.

"Mia was still sleeping," she whispers, "so I did it myself." She arrives car side and holds out the drowned dandelions. Jon dips a corner of his shirt into the water and applies it to Esmé's dirt and syrup spots.

"Well," Larken says.

"We miss you!" Esmé shouts.

Jon hands over Esmé's bouquet and then leans through the open window and kisses Larken on the cheek. He hasn't shaved yet. He smells of coffee grounds and the peculiarly clouded scent that Mia wears.

"I'm so sorry, Larken," he says softly. She loves the way he says her name, like no one else, ever: the dropped *r,* crisp *k,* the vertical spacious-ness of sound—*LAH-kun*—so that she feels herself to be a different person entirely. "Take care, okay? Safe journey."

Good-bye, good-bye, good-bye, they call to one another as Larken backs down the driveway and pulls away. She watches their diminishing fig-ures in the rearview mirror until she can see them no more, wondering how many generations it took for the word *good-bye* to evolve from the phrase *God be with you.*

I'll only be gone a few days, she reminds herself.

But she has a sudden, terrible presentiment that she will never see Jonathan and Esmé again, and she starts to cry before she has even turned the corner.

Larken spends a lot of time this way: coming and going.

She travels to and fro singly, defiantly, American-style, without feel-ing guilty about the price of oil or the global insensitivity implicit in one-person occupancy. She rests in the knowledge that, for this at least, the earth forgives her. Just as there are rules that dictate her professorial conduct, Larken maintains another mental guidebook that keeps her eco-karma on an even keel, assuring that her sins against Mother Earth are expunged by compensatory good deeds: For the sin of single occupancy, she dutifully flattens and recycles every box, feeds her kitchen scraps to worms, turns off the tap when she's brushing her teeth. Atoning for other kinds of sins is more complex, but when it comes to automobile travel, Larken's conscience is clear. Driving alone—especially on the open road—unlocks a peculiar inner landscape that allows a liquidity of thought, heightened awareness, emotional safety, and access to memory that she finds nowhere else. Thus, she does not carpool.

As she motors through town toward Highway 77, Larken becomes curious about the fact that she can weep freely over her upstairs neighbors but not for her father.

Dad is dead, she thinks, waiting at a red light at Ninth and South. She hopes that this unvoiced declaration will alter the torrent of feelings and tears arising from thoughts of Jonathan and Esmé. *Dad. Is. Dead.* Larken is struck not only by the content of her thoughts, but by the fact that the language is so unequivocal, so unlike the language she has used over the years to describe her mother's absence: never *Mom is dead* or *When my mother died* but *Mom went up* or *When my mother disappeared.*

Dad is dead, she repeats, more insistently. Any moment now her nose and eyes will find new reasons to run, her inner monologue will start to reflect the more obvious and appropriate wellspring: her father. Who is dead. Or so she's been told.

The light turns green. Still nothing. She tries an experiment.

"Daddy is dead," she says aloud, evoking the potential power of child-speak, but her nasal passages are so clogged with mucus that she can't manage the plosive *d*'s with any kind of authority and it comes out sounding like "Addy's head."

She tries again.

"D-addy," she emphasizes, "is D-ead." Maybe the effects of sound waves pinging around the interior of the car will incite emotion, find their way through whatever passageways carry the outer world into the inner one, causing matter to be translated into spirit, utterance to be formed into feeling. "Daddy. Daddy. Daddy. Daddy," she repeats, still hoping for an answering sadness in her heart. But the *d*'s evoke comedy, a punch line. *Daddy* may be the right name for her father, but it's the wrong vocal prompt for grief.

She continues south, past new shopping malls and subdivisions that keep springing up farther and farther away from the heart of downtown. When she was a child, there was nothing here but farmland. The subdivisions have phony names bearing no relationship to the landscape—Wilderness Estates, Bison Ridge—and the malls all have delusions of grandeur. In Larken's opinion, the worst kind of American pretentiousness is epitomized by developers who put an *e* at the end of the word *Point* and an *re* at the end of *Center*. Nobody says *pointe* or *centre* in Nebraska—except maybe she and Jon when they improvise conversations in shamelessly nasal, over-the-top, Peter-Sellers-as-Detective-Clousseau accents, a reliable source of delight for Esmé from the time she was six months old.

At another red light, the pedestrian crossing fills with women pushing the full array of what's available in contemporary infant transport: double-wides, triple-wides, three-wheeled jogging strollers, collapsible umbrella strollers, car-seat-to-stroller convertibles, retro-Euro-chrome-framed carriages. Small feet protrude from the strollers as they wheel along, mostly naked, some shod, others with one sock off and one sock on, *deedle deedle dumpling my son John*. The feet exhibit everything from drunkenlike stillness to frantic thrashing. Like pioneers coming across the prairie in Conestoga wagons, the stroller occupants are in the process of casting off cargo that's become superfluous. One rosy foot forcefully jettisons a teething ring. Pacifiers roll out onto the macadam and bounce across the street like minuscule plastic tumbleweeds. Sun hats and booties are flung to the four winds. A small arm thrusts beyond one stroller's confines, ramrod straight and punctuated by a tightly closed, chubby fist, as if the arm's owner is leading a military charge. At the moment it aligns with Larken's steering wheel, the fist opens explosively, becoming a plump pink spider giving birth to hundreds of Cheerio babies. The mothers push ahead, oblivious.

"My father passed away," Larken informs the pioneering mothers and infants. "My father is deceased." Her tears are replenished, but they are not for her dad.

She glances toward the passenger seat, where Esmé's seed heads languish in the coffee cup: frail and ghostly, their stems anemic and hopelessly bowed, they put Larken in mind of the osteoporotic elderly with their degenerating spines and gluey complexions.

Behind her, a horn sounds briefly. Green light. The pioneers have vanished. On she goes.

It's just not real yet, she concludes. It's like reading the obituary entries in the newspaper, beginning the way obits typically do: *So-and-so—born to So-and-so (mother) and So-and-so (father) in Such-and-such a place on Such-and-such a date—has gone home to God, laid down that heavy burden, joined Jesus in heaven* . . . Larken's heart breaks when she imagines the deceased's joyful mother and father on the birthday of this child—a child who is now dead, just as they are dead. The obit continues: *So-and-so moved here-and-there, did this-and-that, is survived by, etcetera etcetera*—all the richness of one life's experience reduced to a ten-cents-a-word run-on sentence delineated by copy editors' commas. Her father's life will be boiled down to an obituary like this, Larken realizes, and it will be sad, but not sad enough to summon any deep feeling.

What will make it real? she wonders, because she does not feel her father's absence in any but the most usual way: He is not here, but it stills feels as though he might be *there,* he might be *somewhere.* In all events, he surely *is* somewhere.

Larken knows that the most reliable place to find someone who is not *here* but surely *somewhere* is in the realm of memory.

She turns on to the highway that will take her most of the way home, a "blue" highway, little traveled, known to few. Her in-breaths expand in response to a landscape unclotted by traffic lights, SUVs, and housing developments. The road ahead is empty and available and waiting. A benevolent metaphor for this country would liken it to stretched, gessoed canvas. Larken's ancestors certainly thrilled to the emptiness of it, lured by the lack of trees to be felled, rocks to be moved, and by black earth that would grow anything, they were told, *anything.* And so it did. However.

No mountains, Daddy used to say when they were in the car and the road opened up like this. *Nothing fancy, but it's home.* There was a funny flatness to his voice—a voice known by everyone for its musical beauty in singing and in speech—so Larken understood early on that Daddy's feelings for this *home* of theirs were complicated.

Sometimes Daddy was yellow—not Mommy Yellow (the color of egg yolks in the mixing bowl, prescrambled and paled by lacings of milk, the color of Hope when they were reading together at bedtime) but his

own special Daddy Yellow: intense, glossy: the pudding-y filling inside
lemon bars served at church *te bachs;* dandelion flowers after a downpour. Daddy could be yellow going the *other* way, to the Indian Hills
Theater in Omaha, say, or the Stuart Theater in Lincoln, and after that
to a fancy restaurant—although his going-away color was usually something Larken described to herself as Clover-Leaf-in-Sunshine. But
Daddy was *never* yellow going this direction: south and then west. He
was never yellow going home.

No, Going-Home-Daddy was a dreary color that Larken has never
been able to completely pinpoint, not even now, all grown up and furthermore a person whose advanced degree and profession requires her
to analyze and describe color in a minute and specific way, to understand the science of color relationships, the way colors play off one
another, react to changes in light. "Gray" was the best she could ever
come up with.

By contrast, Hope's going-home color was a ribald fuschia, the color
of frozen cherries and vanilla ice cream, thawing, melting, mingling.
There was something else to Mommy's color, too, it had fizzy bubbles
and bounce, so that Larken always pictured her mother going home
downstream, happily nestled in an inner-tube tire, sipping a cherry and
vanilla ice cream float made with 7-Up and sprinkled with Sweet Tarts.

This is how it has been as long as Larken can remember, ever since
she was very small, before she had language any more precise than this—
Daddy gray Mommy cherry—to describe the dynamic between her parents and the opposing energies that informed their homeward-bound
car trips. You could align yourself with either one of them, too: If you
wanted to go to Emlyn Springs, you floated *merrily merrily merrily merrily* on Mommy's inner tube, and oars were superfluous. But if you *didn't*
want to go home, you were with Daddy in his cramped rowboat, your
chest tight, your breath ragged, your hands raw and oozing with blis-
ters that broke and healed and broke again.

It is on her father's energy that Larken travels today: an upstream
current that keeps her at the speed limit or below, even though she
knows she should be hurrying to her destination. For this sin of reluctance, there is no atonement.

Larken finds memory on the road of comings and goings like this:
She spirals. Her attention, diffuse at first, circles the landscape, big and

broad and freewheeling, then moving down, the path of thought no longer restricted to a single plane but plunging and narrowing and tightening with the descent. Raptors do this. So do cardiac surgeons and funnel clouds. And then, something is pulled up, whirled about, turned over, dissected, ressected, torn apart, becoming in this process of hyperscrutiny more than what it ever was before: a symbol.

This is what Larken tries to teach her students, how our selective and mindful attention gives an enhanced meaning to what we see, and everything, *anything,* viewed in this way earns significance: A field mouse becomes food, and all that food represents. A diseased heart emblemizes more than the physical body.

And a billboard in a cornfield becomes a symbol of the road not taken.

There it is, just up ahead. *Fetus means "little one."* The billboard illustrator lacks many basic rendering skills, but clearly he means to convince the uninformed and frightened that a human fetus in utero has the anatomical and facial features of a several-months-old baby, complete with a smiling expression and a full set of teeth.

And there Larken goes down the vortex of memory, to events surrounding her first lengthy solo road trip, in the fall of 1979.

The former Little Miss Emlyn Springs is fifteen, already one year and thirty-two pounds past her title-winning days, a motherless child, and for all intents and purposes a fatherless one, too.

"You're absolutely sure that you want to *abort* the baby?" the counselor asks for the fourth time. She is in her mid-twenties, wholesome-faced and aggressively sympathetic, a kind of sorority big-sister type that Larken is not, will never be. "You're sure you won't feel any regrets later about having an *abortion?* There are other options, you know." The counselor's name is Trixie. It suits her perfectly and Larken has never forgotten it.

"Yes, I know," Larken replies without hesitation, and "Yes, I'm sure." She hasn't once responded with uncertainly, and still Trixie has asked and asked and asked, each time regarding Larken as if she were a radial tire with a small leak that she can't quite locate.

"Well, let's just go over everything one more time," Trixie says. "There are lots of social service agencies I can refer you to if you have even the slightest doubt." She is so guileless and unpatronizing that Larken doesn't have the heart to object. "After all, this is a decision that will stay with you for the rest of your life."

Trixie refers to a gray-green sheet of paper with the heading, *Before You Decide: ABORTION Is Only One Option*. She uses her pen to indicate Options 2 and 3 as she speaks, elaborating on each of them at great length, even though they essentially boil down to:

Have Baby/Keep Baby, and
Have Baby/Give Baby Up.

Larken is not an idiot. She understands that Trixie's lecture has nothing to do with disseminating information. Larken holds more data than this in her head when she takes a geometry quiz. This can only be about testing her resolve. Trixie's repeated use of the word *baby* is so blatantly tactical that Larken has to chew her lips to keep from smiling. Maybe other girls succumb, break down, change their minds, but not Larken Jones. Trixie could use the word *baby* a thousand times and this girl still wouldn't change her mind.

Did Lindie Critchfield have to listen to all this crap? Larken wonders. *No way, or Lindie wouldn't have gone through with it.* Larken concludes that Trixie must have been off work that day, at home opening cans of tuna for her twelve foster cats. Or serving lunch at the homeless shelter. Or at the hospital, reading stories to kids with terminal cancer.

Lindie Critchfield is the reason Larken is here. She's a senior, a softball star, and president of the Pep Club. She comes from money, so in that sense she and Larken have something in common. Lindie is nice enough for school royalty—she says hi to everyone and doesn't pretend, like some of the popular kids do, that they haven't all known each other since they were in diapers—but she's not part of Larken's minuscule social circle. (By 1979, Larken doesn't have many acquaintances, let alone close friends. Her best friend is her brother.) The last time Larken and Lindie spoke more than a few words to each other was in seventh grade, when they were lab partners in Accelerated Biology. They shared a frog.

Because royalty is always spotlit, and because Larken's vision is so unique and keen, it is she who notices a subtle dimming of the Glossy Tangerine that has always been Lindie's defining, baseline color. The loss of light is so obvious and alarming that Larken marvels at every-

one else's apparent obliviousness; she fears that Lindie may have con-
tracted some kind of deadly blood disease—leukemia, maybe, or ana-
plastic anemia.

It's true: Larken is paranoid when it comes to illness. She's not hypo-
chondriac, like Gaelan, but having ready access to her father's medical
books has stimulated her imagination to the point where she constantly
looks for symptoms, makes erroneous diagnoses, and visits all sorts of
imaginary plagues upon anyone who looks the slightest bit under the
weather.

When she starts studying Lindie's boyfriend, Matt Moser, Larken sees
that his color has changed, too: the sunny confidence that has always made
Matt universally liked has been replaced with a dark bravado that's turning him into an asshole. It is a glaring transformation as Larken perceives
it, a change that is not just hue but color itself, and texture, and from
wholesome goodness to toxicity: sweet corn to antifreeze.

Larken intuits what has happened. She says nothing to anyone, not
even Gaelan, suspecting that her discretion might earn Lindie's confidence and counsel should she ever need it.

And she does, a few weeks later.

Larken seeks Lindie out at the end of a softball practice when she's
absolutely sure that Lindie's alone. She finds her sitting on one of the low
wooden benches in the back of the locker room, a one-person rain cloud
wrapped in a dingy gym towel, her long bare feet squarely set in the middle
of a puddle that expands with each droplet that falls from her soaked hair.
Lindie's posture—slump-shouldered, bow-backed, chin to chest—makes
her look as though she is staring into the cleft between her breasts, although Larken can't tell from this distance if her eyes are open. She might
be sleeping. She might be praying. Even though Lindie has recovered some
of her color, it still isn't the same, and it's not hard for Larken to imagine
that she's been crying. Maybe even *is* crying.

"Lindie?" Larken says, delicately. The tile walls amplify her voice
though, and Lindie gasps, reflexively clutching the edges of her towel
and drawing it up to her neck, wrists crossed, fists clenched, a perfect
embodiment of the melodramatic heroine under siege by the villain.
Larken feels a sudden unexpected tenderness toward her.

"Larken!" she says, when she recovers her breath. "Shit. You scared
the hell out of me."

"Sorry. I wanted to ask you about something," Larken begins, noticing that Lindie is nervously looking past her, toward the locker room entrance. "It's okay," Larken reassures her. "They're all waiting for you in the parking lot."

Lindie slouches again and starts wringing the water out of her hair. "What's up?" She sounds really tired.

Larken sits down on the bench. "I'm—" Her voice is still too loud, so she slides as close to Lindie as she can without getting wet. She feels like a spy in a James Bond movie. "I'm in trouble," she blurts, sotto voce, inclining her head toward Lindie but not looking at her. "You know the kind of trouble I mean—and I need to get out of it." She keeps her language nonspecific. If anyone comes in, they can deny everything. "You had one, didn't you?" Larken whispers.

Lindie doesn't speak, but Larken hears her intake of breath.

"I just need to know where you went and how much it cost and everything."

Suddenly, Lindie is on her feet, flinging off her towel, all modesty gone. She starts pulling her clothes on over her wet skin, swinging her long thick hair around and dispersing water like a wet spaniel. "I don't know what you're talking about," she says too loudly, as if she suspects the room is bugged. Slamming her gym locker, she hustles past Larken and out the door, still dripping. "See you tomorrow!" she cheers.

"Shit," Larken mutters. Lindie was her best hope of doing this the easy way, and now she's blown it.

Larken retrieves Lindie's towel from the puddle. It's full of hair. Larken mentally accesses some information from one of her father's medical books, a list enumerating what women can expect after suffering a miscarriage (a.k.a. spontaneous abortion, clinical abbreviation SPAB): *It is common to experience fatigue, depression*—some other stuff she can't remember—*and/or postpartum alopecia.*

Larken's hair isn't nearly as lush as Lindie's. Maybe she'll go bald afterward and have to start wearing hats. If anyone at school notices, she can always say that she has cancer.

The next day, Lindie and her crowd pass Larken in the hall after first period. Lindie bumps into her, hard, at the same time dropping a balled-up piece of notebook paper on the floor near Larken's feet. "Hey!" she calls after walking a couple of steps. She picks up the paper and mashes it into Larken's hand. "You dropped this." Lindie's voice has the same jolly sound as always, but her eyes are deadly serious. Larken had no idea that Pep Club presidents were capable of this kind of subterfuge. She vows that she will never again make stereotypical assumptions about high school royalty.

"Don't be a litterbug!" Lindie calls out. She and her girlfriends move on, laughing.

Larken takes the paper into a stall in the girls' bathroom and uncrinkles it against the stall wall. There is no salutation; the note begins with a frantic barrage of words:

You should really think about this before you do anything. I'm really *REALLY sorry that I did it, it was all M's idea and that's the reason we broke up, I didn't dump him because he's been playing so shitty that he probably won't get a scholarship to UN, I know that's what everybody thinks but that's not why, we broke up over you-know-what and now I'm afraid I'll go to Hell. I haven't told anybody so I don't have to tell you that this CANNOT get out. I'm trusting you like I've never trusted anyone in my entire life.* At the bottom of the page is a phone number with an Omaha prefix.

Lindie uses puffy, lopsided hearts to dot her *i*'s. They look like balloons in a state of partial collapse, sighing, sighing. Since Lindie is in charge of Pep Club posters and her lettering style is well known to the entire school, anyone who found this note would know instantly who penned it. (*Dumb,* Larken thinks, reevaluating her opinion of Lindie's intellect and her aptitude for a possible career in covert operations.)

Larken takes out a Sharpee and—using her left hand—copies the phone number onto the stall wall. She locates it between an especially offensive obscenity (*LJ SUCKS BIG DICKS*) and an arrow-pierced heart (*Lindie + Matt*). She'll retrieve it later, when she has more time.

She considers ingesting Lindie's note—that's what a proper spy would do—but decides instead to tear it into tiny pieces and flush it down the toilet. She flushes three times, just to make sure.

She waylays Gaelan on his way to third period.

"We're coming down with the flu," she says.

"What?"

"Rub your head and complain about feeling like you're going to throw up," she says. "I need to skip school tomorrow."

"Why?"

"I'll tell you later. Just act like you're getting sick the rest of the day."

"Okay, but with Dad, too? Tonight?"

"Dad's not gonna be home. The Prohaskas over in Odell are having their twins any second now and he's staying over there until they do. She's high risk or something. Anyway, just act sick and I'll explain it all later. Now go! You're gonna be late."

"Okay," Gaelan says, his brow furrowed. "Actually, I *have* been feeling a little nauseated."

Larken calls the clinic when she gets home from school. After she puts Bonnie to bed, she tells her brother about her plans.

Gaelan pulls a thermometer out of his mouth and sits up. "Geez, Larken." He's been languishing on the living room sofa in front of the TV since after dinner. "Who's the guy?"

"You don't know him," Larken says. She barely knows him either, but she isn't quite ready to divulge the extent of her sexual misadventures to her brother. He's still a baby in so many ways. "Move over."

"Does he know?"

"The guy? Hell, no. He's just some jerk."

"Where'd you meet him?"

"It doesn't matter. He's nobody." She could add—but won't—that he was a backseat fuck in the parking lot of a strip club just over the Kansas state line.

Larken has discovered that, in the right social circles, being fat is no obstacle to getting male attention. In fact, she's sure that a lot of the men she has sex with think they're doing her this big favor. *She's such a pig,* they have to be thinking, *she must be soooo grateful*. So they come whenever they feel like it, pretend they don't know she's underage, tell their friends about that porker from over the state line who dresses like a guy, in jeans and flannel shirts, has a voice like a bull dyke's, blows you for a pitcher of beer, and goes all the way for a plate of nachos. They've got no idea. Larken is grateful all right, but not for the reasons they think. And who knows, maybe somebody from Emlyn Springs will show up some night. It could happen. The word would get out then and no one would have any more illusions about Little Miss Emlyn Springs.

Gaelan shifts uncomfortably on the sofa. He pretends to watch TV for a while. "So you've been, like, doing it?"

"Hand me the chips. Mind if I change the channel?"

"For how long? Why didn't you tell me? I mean, geez."

"You're still a virgin, aren't you," Larken says.

"Well, yeah. Of course. Bethan and I have gone pretty far a couple of times, but never all the way."

"Good. Don't. Give me that." Larken shakes the thermometer and sticks it back in Gaelan's mouth. "You've gotta leave it in for more than two seconds."

They watch a few minutes of a movie-of-the-week. They've both seen it before.

"Dad won't call," Larken says, "but in case he does, you'll cover for me, right?"

Gaelan grunts, nods.

The doomed hero and heroine are falling in love. They look pretty good for two people who are supposed to be dying—at least, dying of cancer. (Hope was dying too—that's what everybody said—but she never looked like it.) If they wanted them to look so good they should have given them another disease. It would have been way more believable.

"I really miss Mom," Gaelan mumbles.

At the commercial break, Larken retrieves the thermometer. "You actually do have a little fever," she lies, "so it's good you're gonna stay home tomorrow. Lie back down."

"How's Bon getting to school?"

"I called the McClures and she's gonna walk with them."

"Are you sure you don't want me to come with you?"

"I'm positive."

"Why not? It's just a little fever. I'm not *that* sick."

"What if Bonnie needs somebody during the day? Besides, I'm not sure how long it's gonna take, and one of us has to be here when she gets home from school. You'll have to make her a snack. She's always really hungry after school."

"Call before you leave Omaha, okay? And be careful driving. Joe Dinsdale says it's supposed to rain all day tomorrow and most of the night."

"I'll be fine, Gaelan. Really. It's no big deal." Larken grabs another handful of potato chips. "I hate this movie," she says, getting up. "I'm going to bed."

"So," Trixie concludes. "Any questions?"

"I'm still sure," Larken answers.

"All right then." Trixie slides the consent forms across the desk. After Larken signs and initials in the appropriate places, Trixie goes on. "Okay. I'm going to explain the procedure and tell you what to expect. It's called a *dilation and curettage*. 'D and C' for short."

Trixie visibly relaxes now that she's stopped using the words *abort* and *abortion*. She barely has to open her mouth to say "D and C."

"A *deenSEE* . . . ," she begins, and she describes the procedure in a blur of barely differentiated language. Clearly, now that Larken has formalized her decision, words have lost their preciousness. Only *evacuate* and *scrape* step forward as noteworthy. Overall, Trixie's speech is like a broad wash of color that has no significance in and of itself, but is background maybe, for whatever the real subject will be.

Larken makes a point of looking at her watch. She doesn't want to hurt Trixie's feelings, but it's already afternoon. She has to get this over with so she can get back to the house in time to fix dinner.

Trixie drones on, sounding like an especially proficient farm auctioneer—not catching on to the ways in which Larken is trying to signal her increasing impatience and anxiety: by shifting in her chair, clearing her throat, jiggling her leg, nodding her head, chewing her lips.

"I *get* it, really," Larken finally interrupts, sounding bitchier than she means to. She backpedals to a more polite tone and adds, "I know quite a lot about medicine, actually," but that comes out sounding snooty.

Suddenly Larken wants to confide all sorts of inappropriate things to Trixie, like, *The reason I know so much about medicine, in case you're wondering, is partly because my father is a physician. He taught me when I was really little that the word* doctor *is inaccurate because dentists are doctors too, and so are professors sometimes, and of course there are medical specialists like neurologists and psychiatrists and anesthesiologists. There are even doctors of divinity, which I don't quite get, it's such a weird concept, don't you think? . . .* Or, *The other reason is that my mom had MS—multiple sclerosis, sometimes they call it demyelinating disease—and I was the person who mostly took care of her for the last two years of her life until she got carried up by that tornado we had last year, just outside Emlyn Springs, which is where I'm from . . .* But she catches herself.

"Okay, then." Trixie is all business now. Larken can almost hear her thoughts: *This girl doesn't need anything in the way of a patch job. She isn't leaking anything but attitude.* "I'll let the doctor know you're ready. Let's get you into a gown."

The *deenSEE* proceeds without complications. It officially concludes when the obstetrician/gynecologist holds out a petri dish for Larken's inspection and says, "Would you like to see what we took out of your body?"

It's late when Larken drives up. She is instantly relieved; Dad's car isn't here. It wasn't at Viney's either so he must not be back from Odell yet.

Her brother is waiting for her in the kitchen, doing bicep curls. It's warm inside and smells like a citrus grove; the kitchen table is covered with orange peels. "Hey!" Gaelan says when he sees her. "It's almost ten o'clock."

"Sorry," she says, shaking rainwater off her coat before hanging it up. "The drive was hell. Is Bonnie asleep?"

Gaelan nods and starts to unpeel another orange. Ever since he began reading muscle magazines and working out, oranges are his favorite food. *All bodybuilders eat oranges when they get hungry,* he tells Larken. *According to Arnold, oranges are the perfect food.*

"So everything went okay today?"

"Yeah. How about with you?"

Larken shrugs. She fills a glass with tap water from the sink and downs two more Pamprin. "Did Dad call?"

"Yep."

"What did you tell him?"

"You and I have the flu. We stayed home from school. We're fine."

"Good."

"Want some of this orange? It's really sweet."

"No, thanks." Larken pulls a can of pop out of the fridge.

"We had tuna casserole for dinner, if you're hungry. I saved you some. It's in there."

"Maybe later." Larken closes the fridge and opens the freezer. "Did the Prohaskas have their twins?"

"Not yet. Dad said by morning, though, for sure."

"Shit," she mutters, "no ice cream."

Gaelan eats his orange. Larken feels his eyes on her as she opens and closes the cupboards.

"We had steamed carrots, too," he goes on. "They were really good. I've been learning a lot about cooking lately. Steaming vegetables is the best way to preserve their nutritional value. It's really easy, too, and fast. I can show you how."

Larken starts moving toward living room, but Gaelan gets up, effectively blocking her way. How did he get to be so big?

"I'll get your plate and heat it up for you."

"Gaelan, stop. If I wanna be fat, I'm gonna be fat. If I wanna eat crap, then I'm gonna eat crap. If I wanna drink, who the hell cares?"

"I do."

"It's *my* goddamned body. I can do whatever I want with it."

"Sis."

Larken turns away from him and bangs open the pantry door.

"I mean I'm really happy for you, really," she says. "I think it's great that you're addicted to this whole health-food thing and becoming Mr. Junior Universe or Little Mr. Arnold or the Teen Hulk or whatever but please just leave me the hell out of it."

Larken stares at the pantry contents, each shelf a phalanx of unappetizing dry goods. She starts rummaging around for whatever it is that she's craving. She'll know it when she finds it.

"Larken."

"Don't you ever do this to a girl, you understand?" she says, bullying her way past the front lines of corned beef hash and condensed milk, toppling boxes of Rice-A-Roni and Hamburger Helper. "Wear a fucking condom and make sure she wears a diaphragm, too." Larken finally locates a large bag of barbeque-flavored Corn Nuts on one of the uppermost shelves—Gaelan probably put it there—and rips it open. Corn Nuts explode out of the bag and scatter like buckshot all over the kitchen floor. "God DAMN it!" She gets down on her hands and knees and starts chasing the Corn Nuts around, using her hands to sweep them into a pile. Gaelan helps her.

Neither of them speaks, but both of them are thinking about the same thing: how familiar this feels—kneeling on a kitchen floor, dealing in silence with a spectacular mess.

They've only retrieved about half of the Corn Nuts when Larken's cramps come back. She curls up on the floor and closes her eyes. Galen keeps on working. The Corn Nuts hit the side of the metal trash can as he pitches them in—an indoor hailstorm—while outside the rain has finally stopped, just like the weatherman said.

The next thing she knows Gaelan is wrapping her in his arms; they feel hard and soft at the same time, and even though Larken can't call up a specific memory to support the feeling—childhood seems so far away—she's reminded of being a kid stretched out on a new-mown lawn in the spring. The way the earth holds you then when the grass is tender, before it goes all bleached and prickly the way it does in late summer.

Gaelan lifts her off the floor and carries her to the couch. She used to be able to outmuscle him in all things, but no more.

She doesn't want him to grow up. She wants to go back to the time before he knew the nutritional value of oranges and steamed carrots, before she learned the meaning of phrases *demyelinating disease* and *compromised reproductive system,* before she was charged with holding secret the knowledge that Bonnie's body would probably never let her make babies.

Gaelan brings hot tea and a heating pad. They sit on the sofa, listening to Bruce Springsteen records, guarding their baby sister as she sleeps, waiting for their father to come back. They listen and keep watch and wait all through the night while Larken bleeds out the last of her little one.

Larken reaches toward her purse, which is open and sitting on the floor in front of the passenger seat. Never taking her eyes off the road, she fumbles around for her bottle of ibuprofen—locating it easily among

an archaeologically complex and layered jumble of handbag contents—
and pops it open.

Hope trained her for this: *Let's play Six Blind Men and the Elephant!*
she'd say, filling a small paper sack with objects—fork, hairbrush, spool
of thread, candle, pocket mirror, corkscrew—and then have Larken
reach inside and identify what her fingers saw. Then they'd glue the
objects together and give their creation a name: *Spooluhpphunt!*

Once the pills are on her tongue, Larken realizes that she's got nothing to down them with. She regards Esmé's dandelions, which have
deteriorated even further and look unbearably pathetic. Time to put
them out of their misery. She picks up the coffee cup and slurps what
little water is left. The taste is noxious: teeth-gratingly bitter and gritty.
Larken smiles, imagining the possible range of her brother's reactions
when she tells him she washed down her Motrin with distilled dandelion juice.

The landscape is changing; mounds of grass-covered earth begin to
arise here and there on either side of the road. After their mother starts
reading them stories of Paul Bunyan and his giant ox, Larken and
Gaelan start calling these mounds Babe's Meadow Muffins.

Immediately adjacent to the road, and on both sides, the earth is
gouged by deep drainage ditches.

There are lots of underground springs around here, Daddy used to say.

Larken wants to ask how he knows this, because in retrospect it's an
odd thing for a physician to remark upon with such authority. *Who told
you about underground springs?* she longs to find out. *And why do you
believe them? Why should I believe them?*

She realizes that, implicit now in every unexplained thing her father ever said are questions that can never be answered. Embedded
too in each question is regret: Why wasn't she a more inquisitive child?
Why didn't she say, *Go on, Daddy, tell me more. Tell me about underground springs and what they are and why they're here and how they are
formed.*

But children never question anything spoken of in a sure, proclamatory
way by their parents. If mothers and fathers don't know everything, then
the world is in terrible danger. So there is nothing for Larken to do but
accept it as fact: There are lots of underground springs around here.

When the weather warms, cattails and verbascum and milkweed flourish in the mysterious spring-fed ditches flanking the road. They provide cover for pheasant and quail then, but they are dying now.

Up ahead on the right, a stand of hundred-year-old red cedars marks the south boundary of the Vance farm. Only someone familiar with local history would know that, since 1978, this stand has been one tree short. The location of that tree's whereabouts is part of a story that will be told again and again (Larken knows this for a fact) over the next few days.

Babe's Meadow Muffins start giving way to small hills, and in the near distance, low, grass-mantled bluffs arise, cutaways in the landscape revealing layers of what Larken assumes to be sand, limestone, shale: monochrome parfaits tinted in places with rust.

The road starts to curve, shaping itself against bluffs that at first are only slightly above the level of the road but soon begin to grow taller. The effect is of sinking, diving. It's as if the road isn't man-made at all, but the remnant of a dried-up, down-flowing river that used to wind through this landscape—and maybe it was. Larken doesn't know anything about geology or the hydrologic cycle. She doesn't come from farming folks, whose business it is to know such things.

The last significant landmark on her journey is about half a mile up ahead, where the road takes a sharp turn and cars have to sling-shot around an especially high bluff.

Small, white wooden crosses, signs, and scatterings of cheap, sun-bleached plastic flowers start cropping up. MICKI AND MIKE, WE MISS YOU! one of the signs reads. The *i*'s are dotted with bloated hearts that look so much like Lindie Critchfield's that it's not hard to believe she lettered the sign herself—although it could just as easily been done by one of her daughters. Three of Lindie and Matt's five kids are girls.

At the top of the bluff, there's a brick-red, wood-sided house, its driveway sloping down to the highway at the curve's apex. The house can't be set back from the road by more than about seventy-five feet, but the combination of hairpin turn and hill makes the driveway completely invisible to drivers coming from both directions.

Blind driveway! Going-Away-Daddy calls out, Clover-Leaf-in-Sunshine. He honks the car horn as they approach and drive past, a long, prolonged honk—a heraldic trumpet!—which delights them all because, even though the gesture is meant to keep them safe and they always know it's coming, it has something of recklessness and spontaneity to it.

Blind driveway, Daddy says when he's Going-Home-Gray, but only sometimes. Sometimes he just honks, and even the car horn sounds sad and defeated.

Larken is considering the best way to memorialize her father— honk or stay silent?—when she spots a white van coming up fast in her rearview mirror, zigzagging dangerously, the first vehicle she's seen in an hour.

Crazily, the van is honking and flashing its lights, trying to pass her just as the road boomerangs, where the double yellow lines reinforce what everyone knows: This is no place to pass. It's a shoulderless road, there's nowhere to turn out so all Larken can do pull as far to the side as possible—slowing to a stop dangerously close to the drainage ditch— and pray that there's no one coming from the opposite direction.

The van passes her, racing around the curve and out of sight. Larken sits in her car, shaking and breathless, her body saturated with fight-or-flight chemicals.

She has never heard her mother's voice as clearly as she now hears her father's: *Don't stay here, sweetheart,* he says. *It's too dangerous.*

Larken pulls back onto the road. The city limit is marked by trees arising from the east side of a spring-fed ravine, which wraps around Emlyn Springs on three sides, and by the population sign, which is draped with a black cloth. The highway becomes Bridge Street as it crosses the ravine. It's the only way in and the only way out.

Even though it's Saturday, Emlyn Springs custom dictates that what few downtown businesses still operate hang CLOSED signs on their doors—all but one, and it is to McKeever's Funeral Home that Larken drives now.

"Hello, Mr. McKeever."

"Larken," he says simply, enclosing one of her hands between his two big beefy ones. Like all children who grow up in Emlyn Springs, Larken identifies her fellow citizens as much by their singing voice—soprano, alto, tenor, bass—as by name. Mr. McKeever is a bass. "I'm so sorry. I'll take you to see your dad."

As she falls into step behind him, she realizes that she never really thought she'd be able to see her father, dead. The idea that he is *dead* is believable enough, but the thought that she will be able to *see* him dead is inconceivable.

Here he is though, dead without a doubt.

As she stares at the vessel that once held him, the emotion that finally ignites her tears is one she least expected. *Thank you thank you thank you thank you* she mouths silently, because it is easy to see that all his colors are gone, there are no more underground springs beneath his skin, and for these reasons Larken Jones knows that at least one of her parents is irrefutably gone.

Habeas corpus, as the lawyers say, is the thought that comes to Larken's mind.

(The dead fathers have been conversing as they look on, and Larken has overheard a comment made by Fritz Bybee, Esq. Sudden, unaccounted-for thoughts in the minds of the living often arise in this way.)

Yes, Larken agrees, noting that Malwyn McKeever has lowered his gaze and is moving away in a show of respect, misinterpreting her tears as those of a grieving daughter instead of a grateful one.

You must have the body.

Chapter 7

Avocado Kitchen

There's a conspicuous abundance of vehicles in front of Viney's house: On the street and tail-to-nose are a light blue Cadillac and a Ford pickup. A chorus line of teddy bears—arranged to mimic the color order of a rainbow—face out the rear window of the Cadillac (their glass eyes make them look like they've been passing a joint and are still in the blithe, nonparanoid phase of being stoned) while the truck is liberally decorated with exclamatory decals and bumper stickers, all red and white: PROUD TO BE A CORNHUSKER! GO BIG RED! CROESCO I GYMRU! IECHYD DA! In the driveway, parked at a perilously close angle to Gaelan's Jeep, is the white van. Larken isn't sure how she feels about having a face-to-face confrontation with the lunatic who almost ran her off the road.

Making her way across the lawn, she tries to guess why the van is here, why the driver was in such a goddamn hurry to get to Viney's, of all places, and who the van belongs to; as far as she can remember, none of the good folks of Emlyn Springs have ever showed any inclination toward vehicular homicide.

When Larken rounds the van and sees the painting on its side, all mysteries are solved.

The artist clearly owes a lot to Robert Crumb, the "Keep on Truckin'" creator of the 1970s. The van painting is an excellent example of imitation as homage; Crumb himself could have done it. A wild-haired, stubble-bearded man wearing gigantic dark sunglasses and swollen-toed, over-sized boots is frozen mid-stride; leaning back in a gravity-defying posture, he holds a cane in one hand and a leash in the other; the leash is attached to a harness; the harness is attached to a shaggy dog—also wearing sunglasses and boots—who is a few steps ahead of his human.

Ah, Larken thinks, appreciating the artists' sly humor and unique contribution to the "Keep on Truckin'" oeuvre. *It's the blind leading the blind.*

The words *Keep on Tunin'* meander over the top of the illustration (the letters are set at varying heights on music staves, as if they're musical notes), while the caption beneath reads "Blind Tom's Piano Service," accompanied by an Emlyn Springs phone number and, to Larken's surprise, a Web site address—proof positive that at least one business in Emlyn Springs (and one of the oldest businesses at that) has not only invested in creative advertising but joined the twenty-first century. *Good for them,* Larken thinks.

From inside Viney's house comes the sound of single piano notes, so it's clear that the current Blind Tom is already at work. Having an immaculately tuned piano is crucial to Emlyn Springs' funeral traditions. Larken rightly assumes that the Closs spinet hasn't been worked on by a Blind Tom since the *Gymanfa* for Viney's son, way back in 1966.

The original Blind Tom, né Trebor Oronwen Mahynlleth, set up shop in Emlyn Springs in 1871 and died in 1897. He's buried in the town cemetery and his headstone benefits from Bonnie's regular attention; its shaded location makes it vulnerable to moss. A combination of deference and naïveté has moved the citizens of Emlyn Springs to address all subsequent piano tuners as "Blind Tom" ever since. Generations of Blind Toms have come and gone; not a one of them has ever complained.

"Oh, honey, oh sweetie!" Viney proclaims, leaping up from her chair as Larken comes into the kitchen, embracing her before she even has time to set down her purse.

No one hugs like Viney. She is so small, such a force, all muscle and sinew. *A ball of fire* is how Daddy described his nurse whenever he spoke of her. *That Viney Closs, she's a ball of fire, a real hard worker.* Larken must outweigh Viney by at least sixty pounds but she feels as though Viney could still easily pick her up and swing her around. In contrast to Hope, Viney was a roughhousing sort of mother. It always seemed to Larken that Viney's maternal instincts derived less from *The Donna Reed Show* and more from *Mutual of Omaha's Wild Kingdom.*

"Don't you worry about being late," Viney half-whispers, her face close to Larken's. "I know you had to babysit that little girl you take care of on Fridays. You would've been here sooner if you could've. I know that." Unique to midwesterners, Larken has observed over the years, is an uncanny ability to make a statement of absolution insinuate blame and incite guilt.

Viney hugs Larken once more in that fierce, protective way, at the same time rubbing the space between Larken's shoulder blades in a circular, rhythmic manner that makes Larken feel as if she's being primed for a nap in her bassinet.

Gaelan is coming toward them—his eyes haggard and rheumy, he looks terrible, as if he's been crying for hours (which he probably has; of the three of them, he's the most susceptible to tears), followed by Bonnie, whose face looks oddly two-dimensional and is as gray as shirt-box cardboard; she looks as if she's forgotten how to breathe. Viney steps aside, still petting Larken's back.

The children come together, arms looping around each other like garlands, swaying a little, unspeaking, holding each other up.

Larken becomes aware of the sound of octaves being played in the next room. The same note in different registers. Blind Tom has been at work since she arrived, the *plunk, plunk, plunk* of notes providing the sound track for her homecoming, but only now—in the silence surrounding this reunion—does she notice.

We're like a tree, Larken thinks suddenly. It's an uncharacteristically simple and sentimental thought from this girl who has never been prone to simplicity or sentiment. *They grow like this sometimes, the ones planted too close together, their trunks butting up against one another over time as they grow, chafing, so that eventually there's no space between them and they graft, become one tree instead of many. I've seen it.*

But as Gaelan starts to sob and Bonnie holds her breath, Larken realizes that that's not quite right. Even in grief, she and her siblings are not so in sync as those old, conjoined trees, as much as she would wish it so. Larken feels caught between wanting to run to the bathroom for a box of tissues for her brother and wanting to perform CPR on her sister.

I should have been here sooner, she thinks, sensing the ache and fear in her siblings' bodies. *They don't blame me now, they don't feel angry, but they will. Bonnie will anyway. I'm the oldest and I should have been here first.*

They pull apart. Gaelan wipes at his eyes and his sobs dissipate; Bonnie recovers her breath in one big, greedy gulp; and Larken finally takes note of the other people present.

Bud Humphries, the town council president, emerges from his place next to the coat tree; Estella Axthelm is seated at the kitchen table in front of a cup of coffee and a plate of cookies (*What the hell is* she *doing here?*); and a gentleman Larken doesn't recognize is positioned on a folding chair at the other end of the kitchen, tucked between the entrance to the living room and the side of the fridge. His posture is slumped, chin to chest; the gap between the top of his socks and the cuff of his pants reveals legs that are white and smooth as candle wax; and his bald, age spot–speckled head has the appearance of a large, luminescent egg. He's wearing spectacles and a KEEP ON TUNIN' T-shirt and Larken isn't entirely sure that he's awake.

Viney's kitchen hasn't been remodeled since the 1970s. The avocado green and harvest gold color scheme has an unfortunate effect on everyone's complexion, lending a bilious cast to the interior light and making them look like members of a club of liver transplant hopefuls.

"You know Bud, of course," Viney says.

Mr. Humphries lumbers forward and takes Larken's hands. "I am so sorry," he says, his eyes tearing up. "We did everything we could for him."

"I know you did. Thank you."

Viney gestures toward the table. "You remember Estella?"

"I do." The witch remains firmly affixed to her seat, feigning frailty and trying to simulate a compassionate expression. *She must be ninety if she's a day,* Larken reflects. *Why do the mean ones always live the longest?* "Hello, Miss Axthelm."

Miss A. holds out spidery, veined fingers in a formal manner, as if expecting Larken to kiss the papal ring. "I'm so very, very sorry about your father," she says in velvety, articulated tones. "What a loss to our community." Miss Axthelm used to make her living as an elocution teacher. She coached Hollywood movie starlets in the 1930s and '40s, girls who came from places like Nebraska, sounded like it, and were taught to be *ashamed* of it, Larken is sure, by people perfectly suited by temperament to such work, people like Miss A. Being far too homely herself to appear on screen, Miss A.'s claim to fame is that she did the voice of one of the elephants in *Dumbo*. She works the muscles of her face to reflect an aggressive and heartfelt pity. "What. A. Shock," she enunciates.

Larken hates her. She takes her hand briefly. *If you're waiting for me to fall apart, you can wait till hell freezes over*. "It is, yes."

Viney gestures toward the fridge and speaks loudly. "And this is Mr.—Oh, I'm so very sorry. I've forgotten your name."

"No problem at all," the man says, craning his neck to the side and struggling to lift his head. "Completely understandable, given the circumstances." Larken realizes that his hunched posture is due to terrible, deforming osteoporosis, and it's a physical effort for him to look at anything besides the floor. He holds out a knobby, arthritic hand. "I'm Howie Barstow. How do you do, Missy?"

Mr. Barstow possesses a wide, friendly face, its friendliness magnified by spectacles with lenses thick as domed glass paperweights. His color (peach) has a translucency that Larken notices sometimes in elderly people. She walks closer and takes his hand.

"How do you do?" she says.

"I'm here with the piano tuner."

"Of course you are."

"This one's very skilled," Mr. Barstow whispers, "and believe me, I've seen a lot of Blind Toms come and go. He can tune five pianos in five hours. I've heard him do it." His moist, magnified eyes grow even bigger, so that his pupils seem the size of chocolate-dipped Dilly Bars from the Dairy Queen. "Of course, I'm a little prejudiced," he says confidentially. "He's my great-nephew."

"I see."

"Don't worry about a thing. Your mother's piano is in excellent hands."

Larken sometimes corrects people who assume that Viney is her mother: *Stepmother,* she'll amend. But not today. "That's a comfort," she whispers back.

Given what must be a severe visual impairment, it's hard to imagine Mr. Barstow being capable of operating a motorized vehicle, much less authorized to do so. Larken doesn't have the heart to say anything about his recklessness on the highway, but she's tempted to ask whether his license is up-to-date.

"I'm very sorry for your loss," Mr. Barstow says, formally, loudly. Blind Tom clears his throat—he's sitting at the piano with his back toward them—whereupon Mr. Barstow ducks his head and cringes in a cartoonish way, as if he's a little boy who's been reprimanded for something he doesn't feel the least guilty about. He makes a key-turning gesture in front of his mouth and settles back in his chair.

It seems suddenly important to Larken that Mr. Barstow's well wishes be acknowledged, so she mouths "Thank you" very broadly—a muscular exertion that for some reason causes her to cry. Embarrassed, she averts her eyes toward the piano.

There are two keyboards in Viney's living room. Compared to the 1950s Wurlitzer, the spinet is new, but it hasn't been played nearly as much; usually it's draped with an afghan and serves less as a musical instrument than as a display unit for a select assortment of Viney's handcrafted angels. She makes them out of old hymnals that have been fanned open, ingeniously scissored to form full paper skirts and paper wings, and affixed at the spine with a doll head.

There are brown-skinned, pigtailed Indian princess angels, black-skinned nappy-headed angels, Farrah Fawcett–style blonde angels—Charlie's Angels angels!—frizzy redheaded angels, and on and on. Some are sweet-faced. Some look saucy and soubrettish. Some are downright homely. All are crowned with garlands of plastic pop beads and wear little outfits custom-tailored in color and design to go with whatever personalities Viney imagines them to possess.

Viney has been selling these angels at craft shows and county fairs and *te bachs* as long as Larken can remember. Larken used to help her make them; her job was hairstylist. "It's so important that all people have an angel they can identify with," Viney used to say. "That's why I make them look so many different ways." For a long time Viney's angels flew—at least figuratively—off the shelves. Their popularity has declined in recent years, however. Today they are definitely not looking their best. To allow Blind Tom access to the spinet's innards, the angels have been evicted from their usual place of prominence and relocated haphazardly throughout the room, stuffed hastily into darkened corner shelves and onto crowded tabletops, sharing the stage

with knickknacks and books and family photos. Coifs askew, they regard Blind Tom with their fringed lids at half-mast, suspicious,
miffed.

Blind Tom is still playing octaves. The sequence sounds familiar.
Larken doesn't have the musical ear of her parents—or even her
brother—but like all children born in Emlyn Springs, she knows
solfege and can identify the names of notes and the way they relate to
one another when they're strung together like this: *Sol-mi-fa-sol-do,
la-ti-do-sol . . .*

Even sitting, Blind Tom is very tall. He must be quite thin as well:
Beneath his white T-shirt, the tips of his shoulder blades are so fleshless
and extruding that they form what look like teepees pitched side by side
on the slope of his upper back.

Next to him on the floor is a black retriever—sans harness, boots, or
sunglasses—forepaws crossed elegantly. The dog registers Larken's presence and then resumes his study of Viney's green shag carpet, which must
have been recently raked, since nowhere does it seem to be flattened by
footprints. Larken wonders how Blind Tom and his dog got in. They
either entered through the front door and took huge, tiptoeing steps to
get to the opposite side of the room, flew, or else Viney raked the carpet
again after they arrived. Which isn't out of the realm of possibility.

La-sol-mi-fa-sol-do, la-ti-do-do . . .

What is that? Larken continues to wonder. *I know I've heard it
before . . .*

Blind Tom moves on to tuning fourths: *Here Comes the Bride.*

"It was nice to meet you," Larken says quietly, turning to Mr. Barstow,
but his head has slumped back onto his chest, and now he truly is asleep
and snoring quietly. He has an impressive ability to produce two separate musical tones simultaneously. Larken wonders how this is physically possible.

"Are you okay, honey?" Viney asks.

Larken starts and turns around. Everyone is staring at her: Bud,
Gaelan, Bonnie, the witch. How long has she been standing here,
daydreaming?

"I'm fine." She strides back into the middle of the kitchen, grateful
for the way her heels sound on the linoleum: percussive and authorita-
tive and completely unenchanting.

"Have you already gone to see him?" Bonnie asks.

"I did, yes."

Viney murmurs, "He looks good, doesn't he?"

His color is gone, Larken wants to say. *His underground springs are all dried up.* She takes Viney's hand. "He looks fine."

"Can I get you some coffee, honey? I've got some made. Oh, wait, this pot here is old. I'm gonna make another one before everybody starts coming."

"You're not supposed to do that, Viney," Gaelan interjects. "Let me."

"Well, I'd like to get a few things ready before . . ."

"Let Gaelan do it," Larken says. "Why don't you sit down for a while?"

"Actually," Miss Axthelm says, "now that Larken is finally here, we should get back to solving our dilemma."

"What dilemma?'

Viney speaks up. "I'll tell you what: Gaelan honey, if you really don't mind making the coffee, I'll go ahead and get changed. That way the three of you can talk with Bud and Estella about . . . you know. Whatever you decide will be fine with me. I'll just be upstairs," and she bustles off in a way that makes Larken sad for her, as if she were being evicted.

"What's going on?" Larken asks.

Gaelan busies himself with the coffee; Bonnie chomps down on her lip and darts her eyes in Miss Axthelm's direction.

"Sit down, why don't you, Larken?" Miss Axthelm says.

"That's all right, Miss Axthelm. It feels good to stand after being in the car."

Mr. Humphries begins. "We've been talking about where to have the *Gymanfa ganu.*"

"Yes?" Larken looks to Gaelan for clues. He is not forthcoming.

"I'll get started on the cloths," Bonnie says. She walks over to the coat closet and extracts a large cardboard box from an upper shelf.

"It's usually held in the home of the deceased," Mr. Humphries says.

"Right. That would be here."

Gaelan blows his nose. Bonnie retrieves the ironing board and unfolds it. It makes a terrible screeching noise. The dog starts to bark.

"Sorry!" Bonnie yells.

"Goodness gracious!" Miss A. intones.

"Hush, Sergei!" Blind Tom commands. Sergei falls silent, and Blind Tom continues with sixths: *My Bonnie lies over the ocean . . .*

"Or Dad's place, I suppose," Larken continues, "although he didn't really *live* there and we'd have to get a piano over there. Is that the dilemma?"

Bonnie gives the atomizer a few preliminary spritzes, aiming it at the part of the kitchen ceiling that is just above Miss A.'s head. Blind Tom moves on to major triads.

Miss Axthelm speaks. "Some people feel that it might be . . . well, *objectionable* to some people to have the *Gymanfa* here."

"What?"

"It might be *offensive,*" Miss A. enunciates. She doesn't appear to notice that there's a fine mist falling on her lofty, lacquered hairdo, causing the slow, steady formation of a kind of sinkhole at its center.

"Why?"

Bonnie takes a folded piece of black cloth from the box, shaking it out with a vehemence that gives it the sound of a thunderclap and then positioning it on the ironing board. Bud shifts in his chair, his leather belt stretching in protestation.

"I don't understand," Larken continues, taking a seat. "Why would anybody object to the *Gymanfa* taking place here?"

Gaelan speaks up from the sink, where he is filling the coffee carafe with tap water. "Because Dad and Viney weren't—technically—married."

Good God, Larken wants to say. Instead, she assumes one of her professorial positions, leaning into her hand and furrowing her brow in a judicious manner. She's starting to yearn for chocolate and wishes she'd thought to bring a private stash; Viney keeps no candy of any kind in the house.

In the next room, Blind Tom switches to minor chords. Bonnie is pressing the black cloth with such force that the ironing board is groaning and seems on the verge of collapse.

"Of course, nobody who knows Viney and your dad well would care," Mr. Humphries says, "but some folks, you know, they might take offense and not come, and of course that would be just terrible. We want everyone to come. I mean, he was our mayor."

The witch pipes up. "Besides, it's not as though Alvina hasn't had a *Gymanfa* here before. She's had *two.*" Her callousness is astounding. "Has it ever occurred to anyone that she might actually be *relieved* to not have to have another *Gymanfa* here? Has anyone thought about that?"

Larken restrains herself from speaking by bringing her lower teeth over her upper lip. Mr. Humphries shifts uncomfortably again. Blind Tom suddenly plays a heavy, fortissimo C minor chord (at this, Miss A. jumps slightly, as if the skin of her buttocks has been fitted with live electrodes) and then sails into Beethoven's *Pathétique* sonata.

"What's the alternative?" Larken asks.

"Having it at the Williams girls', of course," Miss A. says.

Mr. Humphries adds, "It's big over there, of course, and they've got that baby grand—"

"The nicest instrument in town!" Miss A. interjects, triumphantly.

Mr. Humphries gives Miss A. a look. He smiles as only a midwesterner can when they're furious with someone but too polite to let them know. "They've got that nice big second parlor if we need the extra space," he continues. "That would be the main advantage in my opinion."

Viney reenters, wearing high heels, sheer stockings, and a low-cut, fitted black dress that Larken remembers her having since the 1960s when little black dresses were an essential part of every woman's wardrobe. Hope had one, too. Larken hasn't seen Viney in anything but jogging outfits for years. In spite of Viney's obvious weariness and grief, she looks startlingly sexy.

"So, have we reached a verdict?" she asks.

"I need to use the bathroom," Miss A. says suddenly. "Bud, help me."

Mr. Humphries takes her elbow and starts leading her toward the living room.

"Oh no, not that one, take me to the one in here," Miss A. indicates, and Mr. Humphries walks her to the nearby half-bath off the alcove near the washer and dryer. She toddles inside and turns on the fan. Soon after, everyone tries to ignore the obvious indications that Miss A. is experiencing some degree of intestinal mayhem.

"I'm so sorry about all this, Viney," Mr. Humphries says. "I hate to say it, but there's some truth to what Estella is saying."

"Oh, I understand, Bud," Viney says. "I really do, and I'm sure you're right. We had an . . . unusual situation, the mayor and I, and I suppose that even after all this time some folks . . . well, it's a small town and we all know how that can be, the good and the bad. I'm really fine with having it somewhere else."

Larken knows Viney well enough to know that she doesn't mean to sound long-suffering, but she's such a terrible liar.

"They do have a lot of space at the Williams girls' place, you know," Mr. Humphries says for the third time.

"Oh, I know."

"We could fit a lot of people in there. The whole town, practically, if need be."

"That's certainly a plus."

"What do you think, Larken?" Mr. Humphries asks.

Larken knows that the decision has already been made, but some unwritten rulebook of small-town manners requires her to cast her vote. "If it's all right with Viney, then I suppose it's all right with me."

"Good," Viney says, patting Larken's hand. "I'm glad."

Blind Tom must be finished; he's playing a medley of Gershwin tunes. Partly to put some space between themselves and Miss A., and partly because the music is so winning, the five of them drift toward the living room door and listen. Mr. Barstow has apparently gone outside; the shag carpet is flattened in two parallel lines, as if he exited on cross-country skis.

"I never should have got that spinet," Viney muses, still holding on to Larken. "Welly never liked it. He always said the touch was stiff and the tone was stingy. I should have got an upright instead. They're bigger, but the sound is so much fuller."

"It's a fine piano, Viney," Galean adds. He's started crying again, but no one but Larken has noticed. She takes his arm.

Blind Tom concludes with an excerpt from *Rhapsody in Blue*. Everyone applauds. Blind Tom gets up—he must be well over six feet tall—and turns to face them, smiling shyly. His dark glasses look especially dark against his pale skin.

"Well!" Miss Axthelm says, emerging from the powder room victoriously, as if the applause were intended for her. "That's settled then!" Not making any effort to clear her dirty dishes from the table, she gathers up her gloves and pocketbook. "I'm going home to give Sugar her insulin shot, but I'll be back later. Nice to see all you children together in one place," she says, and goes.

"Me and Vonda will be over soon," Mr. Humphries says, making his way out through the kitchen as well. "I'll let Hazel and Wauneeta know about the *Gymanfa*." He gives Viney a quick hug and leaves.

"Blind Tom!" Viney calls, fetching her purse. "Thank you so much. It's been years since that thing's been tuned, as I'm sure you could tell. It was in terrible shape."

"There's not a thing wrong with this instrument, Mrs. Closs," Blind Tom says, shutting his case and taking hold of Sergei's leash. "It just needs to be played more, that's all."

Viney goes into the living room with her checkbook. "We're not going to be having the *Gymanfa* here after all, I'm afraid," Larken hears her say, quietly. "I'm so sorry. I hope you don't feel as though your work here was wasted."

"Nothing's ever wasted," Blind Tom replies. "It's always a pleasure to meet a new keyboard."

"Let me pay you for what you've done," Viney says. "What do I owe you?"

"Not a thing, ma'am. The community council took care of it."

"Oh, that Bud," Viney says, her eyes tearing up. "He really is the sweetest man."

"I'll be off to the Williams place, then," Blind Tom says. "Good-bye everyone!" he calls out in a loud, diffuse way, and then, angling his head precisely in Bonnie's direction, says quietly, "Good-bye, Bonnie."

"See you around, Tom," Bonnie answers.

"All right, children," Viney announces. "We haven't got much time. Gaelan, sweetie, would you bring in Larken's suitcase and put it in the downstairs bedroom? Bonnie, dear, why don't you let me take over the ironing, and Larken honey," she says, pulling a stepstool out from the broom closet and handing it over, "you and your sister can get started on the draping."

"It still smells like Lemon Mr. Clean," Larken says. She and Bonnie have been assigned to the second floor and are covering the windows and mirrors with black cloth. They know just what to do and how to do it; they've covered the windows and mirrors at the Closs house before. Gaelan is helping Viney downstairs.

"So you're staying here?" Bonnie says. "You're not going over to Dad's?"

"No. I didn't even think about it. Gaelan's staying here, right?"

"Viney is so happy to have him here. You, too, of course, but you know how she is with him."

"How about you?"

"I'm staying here tonight for sure. Maybe even all week."

"That would be great, Bon." Larken is surprised. She knows how hard it is for her sister to relinquish her privacy. "It will give us a lot of time to catch up."

"Hand me up another one," Bonnie says.

They're almost through. They've saved Wally Junior's bedroom for last; Gaelan will be sleeping here. "I can't believe they're being so jerky about the *Gymanfa*. I mean, in lots of states Dad and Viney would be considered 'common law,' wouldn't they?"

"They're probably common law *here*, but the people who are being jerks don't give a damn about that."

"How's it going up there?" Viney hollers. "You two about done?"

"Yes!" they chorus.

"Okay then! Larken, you should get changed. Gaelan brought your suitcase inside, and the bathroom is all yours."

Bonnie gets down from the stepstool. It's so dark it feels like midnight. "I wish—" she begins, and then stops.

"What, Bon? What do you wish?"

"Come on, girls!" Viney shouts. "Let's get a move on! People will be here in half an hour!"

"Coming!" Bonnie shouts back, and hurries down the stairs.

Larken listens. The sound of her sister's footsteps is so profoundly familiar—like the seasons, or a color, or a singular piece of music that was playing at the most important moment in her life—that once again, without knowing why it should be happening, Larken finds herself staring at nothing and starting to cry.

On the afternoon following her mother's memorial service, fourteen-year-old Larken stands flattened against a shadowy, faux-wood-paneled wall in the basement of the Bethel Welsh Methodist Church. She is thinking about clothes.

Her two best friends, Peggy McCandless and Stephanie Hansen, are standing with her, but already something has changed between them. There's an awkwardness, a rift. Larken and Peg and Steph have spent so much time complaining about their relationships with their mothers. Larken has never exempted herself from this kind of complaining, even though her mother is wheelchair-bound and supposedly dying, but she realizes that she will no longer be able to be a part of all that. Venting and rebelling are lost to her now. It was hard enough rebelling against a cripple. You can't possibly rebel against a mother who's dead. Probably dead. Missing in action.

"Larken, I'm so sorry for you," Peg and Steph keep repeating, in between nibbles of Welsh cakes and sips of pop, not suspecting that each time they offer up this well-meaning condolence, they become less and less her friends.

She does not want this. She will not cry. She will not fall apart, not in these clothes.

She's wearing a jumper—navy blue, because young girls don't wear black in those days. It's an A-line jumper (the worst kind of outfit for a girl built like Larken, who's already been informed by *Seventeen* magazine that she possesses a pear-shaped body type and should embrace high-waisted Granny-style fashions and forgo starch) and it's dowdy, blocky, with the look of a failed 4-H project about it. Underneath the jumper she wears a stiff, skimpy polyester blouse. It might as well be a Catholic school uniform, and who knows, maybe it is; it would be just like those Catholics, especially those snooty Catholic girls, to donate a faded school jumper to that poor girl down in Emlyn Springs whose mother disappeared in that terrible tornado and who now has nothing, *nothing, NOTHING!* Larken imagines that she and her siblings have already become a closer-to-home substitute for all those poor starving children in Africa. *Wear your new dress!* mothers all over the state will insist, chastising any daughter who dares wear a favorite outfit to school twice in one week. *Don't you know there are girls in southeastern Nebraska who don't have clothes to wear to their mother's memorial service?*

This jumper came to her among the bundles sent down by folks from Lincoln and organized by the Red Cross or some other emergency relief organization that sees to such things. Bad as it is, it was the least offensive thing she could find and the only thing that fit even remotely. Even her shoes are borrowed: they're black Mary Janes—baby shoes!—scuffed and too narrow, so that she feels unsteady, ungrounded. All the clothes came from girls with slim hips and narrow feet and a less full sets of tits, because Larken's tits have arrived, sooner than anyone else's, as has her period.

The sides of the dress keep creeping up and she is in terror of the tops of her hose showing—she's even wearing someone else's garter belt—and the darts do not conform to her breasts.

Gaelan is somewhere; like Larken, he is wearing borrowed clothes. Bonnie isn't here; she's still in the hospital. Larken would give anything to be in her place.

She decides then and there that she'll never wear this dress—or any of the others—ever again. After today, she'll clothe herself in the flannel shirts and dungarees that have been given to Gaelan. Soon Peg and Steph will be so embarrassed and disgusted that they won't want to hang out with her anymore.

Larken is a figure in a tragedy, but her mother is the star and she is only a supporting player. Her father has the male lead, and he plays it well. Larken's girlfriends think Daddy is handsome—usually they giggle when he flirts with them—but they do not giggle now, nor will they ever again refer to Larken's father as handsome. He will henceforth be only Dr. Llewellyn Jones, the widower.

"Do you think he'll every get married again?" Peg asks.

Larken hadn't thought of this, and the possibility opens up a world of imagining, a welcome distraction from the things she doesn't want to think about. If her father marries, she'll have a stepmother, and there's lots of potential drama there. Stepmothers are never ordinary. They paint their fingernails in gaudy colors and border on sluttiness. Maybe her stepmother will be a malevolent character from a fairy tale. Larken feels she deserves an evil stepmother and starts scanning the crowd for women who might make her life hell—just *her* life, though, not Gaelan's or Bonnie's, a stepmother who is secretly vile to her and her alone.

It doesn't turn out that way, of course. A couple of years after Hope goes up, it's clear to everyone in Emlyn Springs that the only person who holds a place of spousal-like affection in Dr. Llewellyn Jones's life is his nurse, Alvina Closs.

Larken is so disappointed. Viney is the farthest possible thing from a wicked stepmother, as innocent as one of her hymnbook angels, and Larken loves her. She'll have to seek out punishment elsewhere.

The clocks are ticking. After Larken emerges, wearing a very expensive, very flattering black linen suit, Viney sits her and Gaelan and Bonnie down in the low sectional sofa where they'll have to remain as the visitors come and go. She holds Gaelan and Larken's hands and addresses all of them soberly.

"Now. Before everything starts, I want you children to know something." She looks each of them in the eye, one after the other. "He loved you. He knew you loved him, each in your own way. And I don't want any of you to ever, *ever* for a moment feel bad about you're not being here, or him dying the way he did. It doesn't matter that you didn't talk to him every day. It doesn't matter that we weren't always together for holidays and things like that. Don't you *ever* think that he wouldn't ride a motorcycle to the moon for each and every one of you." Her eyes linger on Bonnie, who has lowered her head and is weeping quietly. "All right? Promise me you won't feel bad now."

"I promise, Viney," Larken says.

"Me, too," says Gaelan.

"Bonnie?" Viney prompts.

Bonnie looks up. For a fleeting moment, the expression on her face allows Larken to remember what their mother looked like. "Yes, Viney. I'll try."

And then the resemblance is gone. Bonnie looks like herself again and Larken can't recall a single thing about Hope's face.

"Well, this is it, then," Viney says, looking toward the door. "Oh! I almost forgot." Hurriedly, she hands each of them a small, flip-top style notebook; a short, nubby pencil is snugly encased within the spiraling wire that holds it together. Then she sighs and settles deeper into the sofa cushions, giving Larken's hand an extra squeeze. Outside, there's a crescendo of footsteps coming up the wooden front steps and across the porch.

"Let's be extra especially good to one another, dear ones," she adds. "We're in for an allergic week."

Before any of them have a chance to question this odd, fierce woman who is not legally their stepmother, but is that, and so much more, and more even than they know (*What was that, Viney? Did you say "allergic"?*), the doorbell rings, the mourners are admitted, and the three days of silence, the *Tridiau,* begins.

Hope's Diary, 1960:
No one is dead until they've been sung to

Exactly nine weeks, sixty-three (count 'em) 63 days until I'm Mrs. Llewellyn Jones! Sixty-three days and as many nights. Writing it that way makes it seem so far away. Possibly I should have opted for a more complex and peopled wedding, hundreds of guests and many bridesmaids and groomsmen, etc., poetry recitations, soprano solos, string quartets, monogrammed cocktail napkins, buffet tables and a big band at the Elks Club, and so on. Those kinds of weddings take <u>planning</u>. A bride having a wedding like that would be <u>grateful</u> to have 63 more days to get things done. But poor Papa is overextended already—who knew that even a small wedding could cost so much?—and besides, a big wedding isn't my style, or L.'s. I only wish we didn't have to wait so long.

I feel like such a schoolgirl, but never mind—getting married is a universal topic and it's what occupies me completely, or nearly.

All right: Sex. (What sense does it make to be coy in one's own diary?) That's the real topic.

We've talked about it. L. is experienced, of course—one expects that of men. Especially 26-year-old men who are handsome, brilliant, kind, and gifted with a voice so sonorous that surely even the meadowlarks are entranced by it. How did I get so lucky?

Tonight at dinner, looser-lipped than usual from having had two gin and tonics, I pressed him for details.

"Tell me how you lost your virginity," I said.

"Girls are supposed to remain ignorant of their future husbands' sexual histories."

"Yes, and look how well <u>that's</u> turned out! More than half of all English literature for the past century has plot lines arising from that kind of ignorance."

"How can you be so blasé about it?"

"I'm not blasé! I'm intrigued. I hope to reap the benefit of your years of experience. When was your first time?"

"Hope."

"Come on, tell me. How old were you?"

"Twelve."

"No!"

"See, I knew you'd be shocked."

"I'm not shocked." (Although I was. A little.)

"How many women have you—?"

"No. Absolutely not."

"Ah. I see. Too many to count."

"It's different when you grow up in the country."

"You liar! That has nothing to do with it."

"Let's really not talk about this."

"A sexually experienced prude. You would have made an exemplary Victorian."

"And you would have thrived in the Roaring Twenties."

"I have no worries about our sex life. I'd just like to get it under way."

"Hope, I want our wedding night to be special."

"For you, you mean!"

"For both of us."

There was something so sweet and sincere in his expression, I stopped teasing. "I want it to be special, too, and that's exactly why we should get in some practice beforehand."

"Hope."

"Think about it! Would you be able to operate on a patient if you hadn't practiced on . . . oh, what's his name?"

"Who?"

"Your cadaver."

"You've had too much to drink."

"Alistair! You practiced on Alistair. And what kind of a senior recital would I give if I hadn't practiced? Practice makes perfect."

"I'm taking you home now."

"Things can go wrong, you know, on wedding nights. I could be . . . impenetrable, or something. And how special will our honeymoon night be then, Casanova?"

"Right. Shh," he said.

"Make me," I answered.

Instead of the big, sloppy smooch I was hoping for, he popped an after-dinner mint into my mouth, gave me a peck on my cheek, and helped me into my coat—which seemed to have grown an alarming number of sleeves. We left L.'s car at the restaurant and walked back to the sorority house. The fresh air had a sobering effect on my balance but did nothing whatsoever to diminish my ardor. I'm such a cheap drunk.

At the door, L. gave me another too-chaste kiss and made to leave. I pulled him back.

"More please," I said.

He complied.

"Another."

Such an excellent mouth.

L. and I took a break from studying/practicing tonight and went to a movie: The Man Who Knew Too Much. James Stewart as a physician and Doris Day as his wife. Naturally, she was a former music hall celebrity and frequently called upon to burst into song.

Afterward, L. and I went out to Tastee's for malts. "Don't you dare shoot ME full of sedatives if one of our children is kidnapped by international assassins," I said.

He laughed. "I won't. I promise."

We took a long meandering walk back, holding hands. Beautiful early spring night.

"Don't you love the fact that she never lost her voice or neglected her lipstick during the crisis?" I asked. "I'd like to be like that. 'Que sera, sera . . . Whatever will be, will be . . .'"

"She hates that song apparently."

"Who? Doris? How do you know?"

L. shrugged. "I heard it somewhere."

"Well, I like it. That's the song I'm going to request from now on whenever we're out dancing, the one the orchestra will play at our 50th wedding anniversary, is that all right with you, Doctor?"

My answer came in the form of several chocolate malt—flavored kisses.

L.'s grandmother (paternal) died suddenly this morning—a massive stroke, the way we'd all like to go, I suppose, without preamble or struggle, but on the flip side, without preparation—and after telling me about it (midway through breakfast, I should add, and only after I pestered him to tell me what was wrong), L. announced that he planned to attend the funeral by himself.

I reminded him that this is exactly the kind of occasion where I should be at his side, not just at happy gatherings like our engagement party, but real life-and-death events. "In sickness and in health" is how the vows go after all. But he did everything he could to dissuade me from coming.

"Why are you being so resistant?" I finally asked.

"I'm not. I'm just being practical. You'll be missing classes right before finals."

"I can arrange things with my professors. They'll understand."

"I'll be down there for over a week," he said. "Emlyn Springs takes a long time burying the dead." He often talks about his hometown like this—as if it was person.

"A week? That's nothing. You'll want to be there at least a few days before and after the funeral."

"You don't understand. The <u>funeral</u> takes a week. Well, not exactly the funeral, but . . . It's just that there's a whole . . . thing that happens that I have to be there for."

I could tell he was about to go down the conversational rabbit hole again, so I prompted: "Your grandmother must have been very prominent in the community."

"No. They do this for everybody."

When I asked him to explain, he was purposely vague, saying something about there being a lot of rites and rituals to observe.

"You have to know that the more evasive you are, the more determined I'm going to be, so you might as well spill the beans."

"All right," he sighed. "I'll try." He took a sip of his orange juice with the resigned melancholy of a man who will never taste orange juice again. "First there's a three-day mourning period with lots of strictly enforced rules—that happens at my folks'— then there's a parade, a church service, another parade . . ."

"It sounds fascinating."

"It's grotesque, Hope. Truly. I just don't want to subject you to it. It's part Irish wake, part Jerusalem wailing wall, and entirely morbid. The whole thing culminates in this big party at the home of the deceased where the dead guy is laid out next to the cold cuts and macaroni salad and Jell-O and six-packs of Schlitz and everybody eats and drinks and sings Welsh hymns for another three days and after that the townsfolk walk up to the cemetery, bury the poor fool, and then finally thank God it's over." (My dear fiancé: atheist and blasphemer.)

"But not 'some dead guy' in this case," I reminded him, gently. "Not some 'poor fool.' Your grandmother."

"Yes," he said, chastened. "My grandmother."

"A whole town coming together like that to mourn one of its own? It's remarkable."

"It's bizarre. Trust me. It's bizarre for me, and I grew up there. It's even more bizarre for an outsider."

"An outsider? Who would that be, I wonder?"

"You know what I mean, Hope. Don't get bristly." (It's true. I bristled.)

"All right, but I've been wanting to visit your hometown. Under happier circumstances, of course, but this will give me a chance to meet the rest of your family and the people you grew up with."

"How about your senior recital? Don't you need to practice?"

"What, there are no pianos in this town that sing to the dead?"

L. would not be teased, and at this point he assumed that closed, furrowed expression he gets when he's frustrated. L.'s patients surely interpret it differently; to anyone who doesn't know him as I do, this expression must look reassuringly contemplative.

"Llewellyn, your family is soon going to be my family. These people you come from are going to be my people." More Doctor Face from L. I wanted to give him a big indecent kiss but instead dug in my heels. "Fine, then. Go by yourself. I have a driver's license, I can borrow a car from one of the girls, I can buy a road map at Woolworth's, and if Emlyn

Springs is as small as you say, then I should be able to find your parents' house by asking directions of the first person I see."

"I just want to protect you."

"Protect me from what?"

"I can't explain it, Hope," he muttered. "I just think it's a bad idea."

What I did next was below the belt, but in my defense I was frustrated. L. can just be so infuriatingly stoic sometimes.

I summoned my most nauseatingly damsel-in-distress voice and said, "Maybe you're ashamed of me. Maybe that's the real reason you don't want me to go."

That did it.

"No!" he practically shouted, grabbing for my hand. "No! Of course not."

I felt heartily ashamed of myself. In fact I despise women who manipulate men in this way and have always made a point of not doing so. I can see the temptation though, especially when it gets such a dramatic result.

I gave L. a punch on the arm—a chummy, unfeminine gesture if ever there was one—and said, "Stop being such a worrywart and finish your breakfast. I'll call later after I talk to my professors and we'll make a plan for tomorrow, okay?"

No reply, so I gave him a peck on the cheek and left him staring glumly at his fried eggs and hash.

The rest of the day was spent arranging and reasoning and cajoling and coaxing with all parties involved—no one required half as much convincing as L.—and in the end we're clear to leave tomorrow morning.

Must go now. Tired, but leaving fairly early in the a.m. and there's still packing to do.

* * *

Dear Diary (for so I must begin, feeling as if I've
landed in another century!),

What a day—I hardly know where to start.

With place, perhaps: I am ever-so-virginally en-
sconced in the guest bedroom of Llewellyn's family
home (the one in town, that is, as opposed to the
farmhouse northeast of town, which L. has promised
to show me sometime before we go back to Lincoln).

L.'s mother Lillian keeps a very clean house. Already I fear that my abilities as a housekeeper
will fall far short of what L. is used to. The
curtains and bedspread have an odd smell—musty, but
at the same time slightly chlorinated, as if they
had a long and unhappy prior life as bed linens in
a Catholic hospital. Expect my dreams to be visited by towering nuns wearing starched pillowcases
instead of habits.

Everyone has been very nice, but I have the
feeling that there's something improper about my
being here, and that this kind of thing—unmarried
young people sleeping under the same roof—is frowned
upon. Maybe this is the real reason L. didn't
want me to come. After Lillian came by to say good
night, I half expected to hear a key turning from
the outside, locking me in, insuring against any
nocturnal improprieties on L.'s part. (If only
she knew that her son is the one in need of
protection.)

We arrived today later than expected, having gotten
a late start. L. surprised me by saying he'd decided to spend the better part of the morning at
the library, studying. I know he's nervous about
his medical boards, but still, it puzzled me. He
seemed reluctant to get going, which is not like
him, usually all hustle and bustle and brisk efficiency. And once we were finally on the road, I've
never seen him drive so cautiously or obediently.

We would have made it faster had we come by horse and buggy.

On the way, I asked L. about what it was like growing up in such a small town. He hasn't been very forthcoming about his childhood. Not that I think he's hiding something. He just seems so un-affected, as if he sprang into the world fully formed and uninfluenced by anything that came before we met. He's very here-and-now, my L., not prone to journeys down memory lane.

L. admitted that it's a bit odd growing up in a place where your family is an anomaly because they don't ranch or grow corn. "Being a preacher's kid is a stigma wherever you are, but in a farming com-munity you can feel a little . . . left out, I guess, unimportant, superfluous."

"How so?"

"Having a dad who feeds souls isn't exactly like having a dad who feeds stomachs."

"I can't imagine anything more important than giving spiritual guidance."

"Is that what he does?" Llewellyn asked, an edge to his voice. "I thought he just bossed people around."

"Ha! And that's not what <u>doctors</u> do?" I challenged him. "Boss people around while keeping them in the dark?"

"Hope."

"I peeked at your medical ethics essay exam: 'In the case of serious illness, patients should be shielded from detailed information concerning their condition, and even under some circumstances from their prognosis.' What's that if not keeping people in the dark?"

L. was not amused. "That's different."

Recognizing a dead end in the conversation, I decided to try to excavate a bit more about L.'s

small-town upbringing. "So you can't teach me about
raising hogs?" I teased.

"Or cattle or sheep or poultry. Nope."

"You never kept chickens? Not even in the Fancy
Egg Capital of the World?"

"Nope."

"Darn."

"If it's any comfort, I know about detasseling
and roguing corn. That's how the kids around here
earn extra money in the summer."

"Did you?"

"You bet."

"Well, it's good to know that our children will
have gainful employment when they reach puberty."

"Corn, you'll be interested to know, is planted
in male and female rows."

"Let me guess," I broke in. "With males in the
majority."

L. laughed. "That's right."

"Typical," I concluded, and we fell into amiable
silence after that.

One of the things I love about our relationship
is that it embraces silence as well as speech. Being
wordless around L. is a very comfy thing.

As we got farther away from Lincoln and deeper
into the country, I felt what I can only describe
as a kind of a happy, expectant quickening that I
had a hard time understanding—especially considering we were headed to a funeral. L.'s parents seem
to like me well enough, so it wasn't about that.
Nor was I feeling especially nervous about meeting
other members of his family or the town; shy, I'm
not.

I think the feeling arose from the possibility of
being connected to the landscape in a different way,
through Llewellyn and his family. I'm fascinated

by people who live out their lives where they were born—as opposed to my folks, who started out in small towns but left for the city—just as their Nordic and Scots and Welsh and English ancestors did. I've always wondered what it would be like to have a long history of connection to a single place and to people who have always known you and your parents and your grandparents and so on down the line.

What a digression—back to today.

When we got here, the town was already shut down in mourning. Businesses closed, front porch railings draped in black bunting. One would have thought the queen had died.

"They really do this for everyone?" I asked.

"Yep," L. said. "Nothing brings this town to life like a death." There was an almost disdainful edge to his voice.

"But it's lovely, Llewellyn, don't you think?"

He shrugged and I let it go.

We pulled up at L.'s folks' house around 2:30, well after lunch—or rather, "dinner," since that is what they call the noontime meal here. It's the biggest of the day and much was made of our having missed it. Lillian's feelings seemed hurt, and Papa Jones was obviously angry. Lillian had kept plates warm for us, however. She loaded us up the moment we arrived with pot roast, potatoes, gravy, cooked veg, all very heavy. (L. has already warned me about Welsh cooking. "Save room for the Welsh cakes," he said. "Everything else tastes like a punishment.")

Lillian and L.'s father sat with us as we ate. There was a decidedly odd lack of feeling in the room. L.'s dad kept looking at his watch. "Let me know when you're done," he kept saying, as if he wasn't monitoring L.'s every mouthful. "You and I

have to get over to Mal's and back here no later
than four."

"I know, Dad," L. said. He was wolfing down his
food like a teenager. I didn't understand the rush.

After L. and Papa Jones left, I asked Lillian about
it. She explained that—much as L. had intimated—
Emlyn Springs has specific, hard-and-fast rules
governing the mourning process, and all mourning
customs must commence exactly thirty-two hours after
the death. The mandate for this doesn't seem to
arise from religious law, but has evolved in some
other way.

The point is that the immediate family is expected
to view the dead at the mortuary within the first
thirty-two hours. "You're expected to see the deceased," Lillian said seriously, "as soon after the
death as possible." I had to stifle a smile at this;
it seems so punitive, a way of scolding people who
move too far away or can't extricate themselves from
their lives immediately, can't put the dead in front
of the living.

Lillian asked me if I knew what else to expect.

"Well," I stammered, not wanting to get L. into
any trouble by saying "No, not exactly, since your
son is the most tight-lipped man I've ever known."
Instead, I said, "I'd love to hear about it from
you."

She went on to tell me that the family would be
remaining in the house for three days without emerging for so much as a trip to the grocery store.
People would be bringing food and running any other
sorts of errands that might be required. No gossip, no talk of sports scores, all conversation
strictly limited to stories about Grandma Elinor,
words of praise, and barring that, respectful
silence. No radios, no television, mirrors and win-

dows draped in black, and no other occupation. Just sitting and listening.

Furthermore, during these three days, the family is to remain completely silent (!), listening only to words of praise for L.'s grandmother, whether they be uttered as song or poetry or story.

"How do you communicate?"

"We don't. If we need anything—say, something from the drugstore that isn't already in the house—we are allowed to write it down. But the expectation is that we will ask for as little as possible."

Once again, I was struck by how punitive this seemed, and this time I spoke up and said so.

"I suppose it could be looked at like that," Lillian said thoughtfully, "but really it's not meant to be a punishment. A sacrifice, yes, but more as a way of feeling connected to the dead, who do not speak."

Lillian went on to explain that after the mourning Grandma E. will be carried through the streets to the church where a traditional funeral service will be held. Following that, she'll return to her own house, where—for another three days and nights—the townsfolk will sing to her, nonstop.

"Nonstop?" I asked, incredulous.

"In Emlyn Springs, no one is said to be truly dead until they've been sung to in this manner."

They sing in chorus, I was told, in shifts. For seventy-two full hours, no fewer than four people and as many as a hundred will sing to Grandma Elinor at all times, and in the language of her ancestors.

I am so thankful that I came. L. doesn't seem to have any idea how remarkable this all is, how moving. At least to me.

Must close my eyes now. Tomorrow will be another big day.

*   *   *

Days later. So much to write, and I'm very tired, but need to try to get some of this down while it's still fresh in my mind. This is the first chance I've had to write since the day we arrived—or rather, I've had the time but have been too exhausted.

First there was the mourning—I was able to talk and meet people, not being officially part of the family yet, but L. and his mother and father and brother stayed completely silent. The "Treedaw" it's called, although I'm sure that's not how you spell it. L. and I did have a fun time secretly exchanging naughty notes like schoolchildren when his parents weren't looking. I've taped them into these pages.

The funeral was pretty run-of-the-mill—and everyone seemed rather disengaged by this part of the process, as if they were just stepping through the paces. No emotion really, and a bit of uninspired hymn singing. I say "uninspired" although at the time it sounded nice enough—it seems that everyone in town has a fine singing voice—but once we got to Grandma Elinor's house and the real event began, I came to understand what truly inspired Welsh hymn-singing sounds like—a world of difference.

We're back in Lincoln—very tired but must write, as there is big news to impart.

Before we left, I made L. take me out to the old farmhouse—it's about four miles from town—the one that's been in his family for almost a hundred years.

It's magnificent and sad, as it's been quite let go over the years—although L. told me that it is a house with great historical significance: One of his ancestors, a pastor from Wales, led the first church services here. People came from miles around, often on foot. There are tenant farmers living there now and working the surrounding fields. They only occupy the first floor of the house and were gone when we visited. The upper floors have been closed. The main floor was in shambles. There was a smell of mice droppings and alfalfa throughout, and a kind of wet, fungal scent as if there were wool blankets moldering somewhere in the house. Still, much of the woodwork and stained glass is still intact—it has a look that is somehow both humble and elegant—and the layout of the rooms is charming. It was easy for me to imagine what the house must have been like when it was in its glory.

L. said, "I don't know why Dad hangs on to this place. It's literally falling down. It should be bulldozed."

I thought at first he was joking.

"Surely it could be salvaged with a bit of TLC."

"It would take a lot more than TLC. There's too much damage, termites, rats. Plus, the wiring and plumbing are ancient. It would cost a fortune to fix this place up again."

"I'd like to live here."

"Hope."

"Llewellyn, this is a part of your history, the history of the town. You can't possibly be thinking of letting it go. We should at least talk about it."

"About what?"

"Living here—"

"Hope, that's just crazy."

"—in Emlyn Springs, I mean, after we're married."

What L. has told me about the town so far has been obviously meant to discourage me. There's no culture to speak of, the library is small, the women in Emlyn Springs grew up there, they're not going to be stimulating enough company for me, etc., etc. He reiterated those arguments.

"You make me sound like such a snob," I said. "I think you're the one who's being snobbish. Maybe Emlyn Springs wouldn't be stimulating enough for *you*."

"I'm going to be opening my first medical practice. That's all the stimulation I'm going to need for a while."

"Exactly! And as soon as I get pregnant I'll have all the stimulation I'll need as well. We <u>are</u> planning to have sex after we get married, aren't we?"

<u>That</u> made him laugh—finally. L. is so dear, so stodgy in his way. An old man in a young man's body. This is another reason why we're a perfect match—he grounds me, I can make him laugh. I can see us at our fiftieth wedding anniversary, still a couple of complementary colors on opposite sides of the wheel, and yet relying on each other, the way that each child on a seesaw requires the answering weight of the other to make the whole device work.

We took our picnic out to the back porch and sat and ate and talked more, about how the cost of renting an office space would certainly be less in Emlyn Springs than in the city. The fact that everyone in town already knows him is sure to guarantee him patients, whereas in a big city he'd be starting from scratch.

"You'll change your mind about this place, Hope," he said, looking out across the prairie. "It all seems wonderful to you now, I know, and there's a kind of romance to it, but believe me, there's nothing romantic about living in a small dying town. Someday, you'll want to leave."

"No, darling," I said, not to contradict or foil him—which is a game I sometimes like to play—but because I've never felt surer about anything, "I won't."

They say that the reason the Welsh settled here was because the landscape reminded them of the sea: treeless then and windswept, the undulating of the prairie grasses. There is a great, surprising, sad sensuality about this place. I would have been happy to make love with L. right then and there, but he put me off again. I am marrying a man of great resolve and discipline. I'll never have to worry about him being unfaithful, that's for sure.

We talked more in the car on the way home and in the end, it was settled. L. will start his practice in Emlyn Springs.

I've fallen in love, again. First with Llewellyn, and now with the people and the land that bred him.

How blessed we are. How blessed our children will be.

Chapter 8

Welsh Part Singing

"*Groeswen!*" a deep male voice calls out from Hazel and Wauneeta Williams' living room. The piano—newly and impeccably tuned by Blind Tom—answers brightly with two measures, and then they all begin: "*Arglwydd, clywaf, sŵn cawodydd Gwlawa Dy gariad oddi fry . . .*"

It is time now to speak of the Welsh language.

People unaccustomed to seeing written Welsh fear they're hallucinating, or suffering a transient ischemic attack. A cat making haste across a computer keyboard could produce these non-word-looking forms, or an insensible typist with misaligned hands. An unfortunate draw of Scrabble tiles also comes to mind. But surely this is not the look of a designed and spoken language. Everyone has at least a passing familiarity with Irish—*Erin go bragh!*—or Scots—*On the bonnie, bonnie banks of Loch Loman* and *Should auld acquaintance be forgot and days of auld lang syne*—but Welsh? This language is another animal altogether.

The Welsh people will tell you by way of encouragement—for they are a kind and encouraging people—that their native tongue is not difficult to speak, not at all. Every sound is pronounced, they will tell you. There are none of those troubling silent letters one finds in English. Rs are always trilled, and anyone can learn to do it. The accent is always on the next to last syllable, except . . . And this is where it starts, the exceptions, variants, complications, mutations:

1. A *u* can sound like a short *i* ("tin") or a long *e* ("teen").
2. Double *d*'s are pronounced like the *th* in "the."
3. Double *l*'s have no equivalent sound in English; place the tongue on the roof of the mouth near the teeth as if to pronounce "*l*," then blow voicelessly.
4. The pervasive *y* can be pronounced in one of three ways, as a short *i* as in "sin," as a long *e* as in "seen," and as the sound in the word "son." There are rules as to which sound the *y* takes, but nobody knows them.

And so on.

Some advice, then: nonspeakers would do well to simply enjoy the visual anarchy of Welsh, the startling way familiar letters have nestled up to new companions. Released from the need for traditional narrative, one can enjoy the look of Welsh the way one can enjoy an abstract painting.

"*Yn adfywio'r tir sychedig . . .*"

It could be that, in part, Larken's early exposure to written Welsh may have indirectly led her to her chosen profession. It certainly nurtured a visual open-mindedness; this comes in handy when she's teaching a unit on painters like Vassily Kandinsky and Jackson Pollock.

"*. . . Deued hefyd arnaf fi . . .*"

Neither Larken nor her brother has ever learned more than a few phrases of Welsh, although—like all children in Emlyn Springs—they were required to memorize the Welsh words to "Land of My Fathers" ("*Hen Wlad Fy Nhadau*") and "There is No Place Like Nebraska" ("*Ni does unman yn debyg i Nebraska*") and can fake their way through most Welsh hymns. But among the three of them, only Bonnie is fluent.

Larken stands in the middle of Hazel and Wauneeta Williams's kitchen, sipping on a beer that has long since gone warm. She'd like to take her shoes off. She's been standing on this spot for over half an hour, held in place by her own wearing-down politeness: She's pretending to listen to Mr. Eustace Craven, who has been telling Larken an extended version of The Story of Flying Girl, a legendary story in these parts. It's the fourth—possibly the fifth—time she's heard it since the *Gymanfa* began.

The Williamses' kitchen is large, but quite crowded. Larken and Mr. Craven are hemmed in and buffeted by folks who are here to sing the mayor to his official death, but at the moment are giving their tired voices a break and getting food and drink. Larken is worried that if an especially popular hymn is announced, the crowd will disperse and Mr. Craven, suddenly unbuttressed, will fall over. She is keeping a close eye on him.

People take turns in the parlor—like soldiers on watch—so that there always remain at least twenty or so people singing to the mayor at all times, and in harmony. This has been going on, day and night, for three days.

It turned out to be a wise decision to have the *Gymanfa* here; in addition to having the biggest parlor and the finest extant baby grand piano (Hope's Steinway was finer), octogenarians Hazel and Wauneeta Williams are the resident authorities on the Welsh language, and between them they know every Welsh hymn in the hymnal. They know them whether they are called by name—"*Groeswen!*" "*Panytyfedwen!*" "*Penlan!!*"—or by number—"Number 42!" "Number 98!" "Number 13!" for in the old days this is how it was done.

The atmosphere by now is more than jovial; it's bombastic. The occasion could be a rock concert or a national championship football game. No one would suspect that, in the next room, a dead man is lying in his coffin on a catafalque—like John Kennedy's, except that it is draped not with a red-white-and-blue American flag but with a hand-sewn red-white-and-green Welsh quilt, made over a hundred years ago and donated by an early settler for this express purpose.

Of course, some of this ebullience might be due to the fact that everyone here is nearing the end of a three-day, three-night celebration. These people are bone tired, their circadian rhythms have been interrupted, their body chemistry altered. They are as uniquely hallucinogenic as any Depression-era marathon dancers who've been on their feet forever and can no longer remember what prize it is they're trying to win. And they've all been drinking a lot of beer.

"A flying sofa is nothing in these parts!" Mr. Craven hollers. Every version of the Flying Girl story—and there are as many versions as there are storytellers—features this line. "Sofas in Nebraska are flying all the time! Deep freezers, too, and grand pianos and trucks and televisions and tractor-trailers. . . . But a flying *girl*. Now that's something else again!"

Mr. Craven pauses his lengthy narrative long enough to close his eyes, locate from memory his vocal line in the hymn, and join the tenors as they arrive at the chorus.

"*Ie fi!*" Mr. Craven sings—exuberantly, brightly, as the hymnal ordains. "*Ie fi! Deued hefyd arnaf fi.*" As weary as she is, Larken is still charmed by the way a man of Mr. Craven's age—ninety-something—can sound no more than twenty when his voice engages in song.

Not everyone sings in Welsh—there are just as many people singing in an equally impassioned way on the syllable "la"—and those that are have varying degrees of proficiency. Mr. Craven is one of the town's most adept Welsh speakers.

Larken is relieved for this respite from Mr. Craven's story; she uses the opportunity to take a bite out of a Welsh cake that she balances carefully on a napkin held just under her chin.

As the choir in the next room moves on to another verse, Mr. Craven resumes his story. Larken knows how to comport herself at an Emlyn Springs funeral; smiling and nodding is mostly what's required, but she's been at it for hours, for days, and is starting to feel like a bobble-head doll, her brain sloshy and liquefying and losing its definition.

"All the men started singing!" Mr. Craven continues. "We came to the bridge from wherever we were looking once we heard Mr. Koester—his voice carried that far! We started with . . . Oh, what was it? And the boys came too." He elbows Mr. Byelick behind him. "Arnold, what did we sing to the little Jones girl, you know, in 1978, when we found her up in the tree?"

Mr. Byelick washes down the last of his ham sandwich with a gulp of beer. "Oh golly, Eustace, I don't remember all of 'em, we sang for an awfully long time, but uh . . . 'Land of My Fathers' for sure, and—"

"Of course! The national anthem! Everyone knows that one." Mr. Craven sings: "*Mae henwlad fynhadau yn anwyl imi, Gwlad beirdd a chantorion, enwogion o fri . . .*"

"Eustace!" Gladys Byelick enjoins with mock disapproval. "If you want to sing, go in the other room. Goodness. Your voice drowns out everything!"

"Sorry." Mr. Craven swills his beer and continues. "All the mothers were inside by then, it was getting dark you see, but after a while, after they heard us, even they started coming out, some of them with babes in arms. The whole town singing!"

"It must have been something," Larken replies, not so much because she expects to be heard or because Mr. Craven needs encouragement, but so that she can momentarily release her facial muscles from smiling. "Truly," she says, lingering over the vowel sound, grateful for the way it stretches her cheeks. A counterpose.

"We had to sing, you see. To keep the child awake so that she wouldn't fall, because of course we've never had a ladder truck here in Emlyn Springs." Larken rightly suspects that Mr. Craven has forgotten that the subject of his story is her sister. "Never had that kind of money in the city budget, although the mayor, rest his soul, did his best and I think he tried to get us one, but the ladder truck had to come all the way from Beatrice, and of course there were fallen trees all over the county after that storm, and it was hard to get through."

The story of Flying Girl has made its way into the oral history of Emlyn Springs. There isn't a person in town who can't tell some version of it. However, there are elements of the story that have not entered local lore; these are known only to the Jones family, and chiefly, painfully, to Bonnie, on whose body the most significant part of the story is written.

Mr. Craven continues. Larken is familiar enough with the arc of the story to know that it will be at least another fifteen minutes before he comes to the end. She wonders how many times Gaelan has heard it. They'll have to compare notes tonight when all of this is over.

Where is he anyway?

He's in the basement, hiding.

He's in the basement because he can't bear listening to one more version of the story of Flying Girl. Larken doesn't know it yet, but she'd had it easy compared to her brother; he's heard the story seven times to her four.

He's in the basement because the rules no longer dictate that mourners speak only of the dead, and everyone who engages him in conversation either wants to talk about his celebrity, ask why he isn't singing, or tiptoe around the subject of his personal life, especially his bachelorhood.

Also discomfiting is the liberal use of a particular word—a quite ordinary and natural word to use in these circumstances, but one that, when invoked as a conversational prompt, fills Gaelan with leaden dread: *Do you remember . . . ? I remember . . . Remember when . . . ?*

And finally, chiefly, Gaelan is in the basement because it's the safest place to reexamine some significant criminal evidence. He isn't the only criminal; his sisters are guilty too. He's just *feels* guiltiest because he's the one who instigated the crime.

The Williamses' mansion has a big basement with lots of unlit nooks and crannies and doorways, and a damp, chlorinated smell. After ambling around for a while—Gaelan feels slightly unsettled; it really is the kind of sprawling, shadowy basement that served as the setting for the climax of *The Silence of the Lambs*—he enters a remote corner room with a daylight window. Against one wall, there are metal shelving units where the Misses Williamses keep their stash of preserves, shelf upon shelf of Mason jars, all clearly labeled and dated—spaghetti sauce, pickles, fruit jellies, applesauce—and next to that is an ancient, chest-style deep freezer by Frigidaire. This will do fine.

Gaelan closes the door to the room. He takes off his suit coat and rolls up his shirtsleeves. He hoists himself onto the top of the Frigidaire, doing a quick set of sixteen reverse triceps presses before settling down. He listens for a moment to make sure no one has followed him.

Above his head, the sound of the singers is muffled, but he recognizes the hymn; it's one of the few that has a non-Welsh title ("St. Elizabeth"). Perhaps that's why—whenever Number 101 is called out at an Emlyn Springs *Gymanfa*—it's always sung in English.

Gaelan knows far more Welsh hymns than he lets on. He sings along, quietly:

"Flocks that whiten all the plain, yellow sheaves of whitened grain, clouds that drop their fattening dews, Suns that temperate warmth diffuse . . ."

Even though Gaelan Jones, weatherman, is well used to being in the spotlight, he's too shy to sing in public, even in chorus. His reticence is even more puzzling in light of the fact that he inherited his father's voice.

"God to Thee praises be for the gifts thou gavest free. God to Thee praises be for the gifts thou gavest free."

Like his father, Gaelan is a baritone. Unlike his father, he does not read music, so he floats, singing sometimes with the tenors, sometimes with the basses, and sometimes finding the empty spaces between those two male vocal lines. In this way, Gaelan sings a part that is completely unique.

He is not quite the sad oddity that his fellow townsfolk believe him to be—a Welshman who does not sing—what makes Gaelan a truly strange and sad man is that he is a Welshman who sings alone.

The hymn concludes. The basement is temporarily silent.

Reaching into his suit coat pocket, Gaelan extracts the criminal evidence: twenty-three rumpled pieces of paper, torn from the small spiral notepads Viney gave them at the start of the *Tridiau* and bearing short, furtively scribbled phrases. Some of the phrases are in Gaelan's handwriting, some Bonnie's, and some Larken's. They constitute the transcript of an illicit, silent conversation that Gaelan began, so the top page is in his handwriting:

B.E.—*why here?*

(B.E. stands for Bethan Ellis, Gaelan's first—and only—Emlyn Springs girlfriend.)

Larken: *Don't know. Show Bon*
Bonnie: *Husband died*
Gaelan: *Husband who?*
Bonnie: *Weissman, Leo I think. Professor of religion? Philosophy? Met when BE in med school. Older by a lot. Stroke. Sad.*
Larken: *B.E. lives where now?*
Bonnie: *Washington state, island somewhere*
Larken: *MD, right?*
Bonnie: *Radiologist*
Gaelan: *How long home?*
Bonnie: *Few months. Working part-time at hosp in Beatrice*
Gaelan: *Staying?*
Bonnie: *With folks*
Gaelan: *No—how long staying?*
Bonnie: *Don't know. E here too.*
Gaelan: *E—who?*
Bonnie: *Son*

Gaelan: *Whose son?*
Bonnie: *B.E.'s*
Gaelan: *B.E. has son? How old?*
Bonnie: *11 yo, 12? Small, intense, shy.*
Gaelan: *Here? In room somewhere?*
Larken: *SH! Witch looking*

Gaelan shoves the notes back into his pocket. Even though he's read them over several times (in locked bathrooms, coat closets, Viney's attic), he continues to be deeply troubled by the information they reveal.

Since lifting weights helps Gaelan relax, quiet his mind, and center his thinking, he pulls two jars of pickled beets off the shelves and starts doing bicep curls.

Gaelan hasn't had a meaningful conversation with Bethan Ellis for fifteen years. And of course today's contact doesn't really count as conversation; the rules of the *Tridiau* dictate that he couldn't say so much as a thank you when Bethan came over, took Viney's hand, looked at each of them in turn, and said, *I can't tell you how much Dr. Jones's support and encouragement meant to me.* When she went on to remind Viney that *he gave me a job the summer I was fifteen, doing lab work, developing X-rays, and that was when I started to think about becoming a physician,* Gaelan couldn't add *a lot of things developed between the two of us in Dad's dark room that July.* And to Bethan's revelation that *Dr. Jones kept in touch even after I went to med school out in California, right up until a few years ago,* Gaelan couldn't express surprise at the fact that his father had maintained a supportive, mentoring presence in Bethan Ellis's life long after he'd deserted it.

She wears contacts now. She still can't keep from blinking too much when she's nervous.

Homely was the word his father always used to describe the little girl whose family lived across the highway from them.

God but that youngest Ellis girl is homely, Dad would say. *Smart as a whip, but so homely, poor thing.*

To which Hope replied, *Oh, Llewellyn, don't you know it's the homely girls who grow up to be the great beauties?* And Bethan did, but back then she was just this odd, genius girl with a somber face and tight braided pigtails and horn-rimmed glasses and skin so pale that her freckles looked like the last crumbs from a box of Kellogg's Corn Flakes floating in a bowl of milk.

After Hope went up, they moved into the King's Castle Motel in town and waited: for the insurance money to come in, for the new house to be built, for news of their mother.

Months passed; the outpouring of financial aid and material donations and casseroles started to dwindle. Dad was gone a lot, working harder than ever, or maybe they just noticed his absence more. At the same time, Gaelan had the growing feeling that he and his sisters were no longer the subjects of pity but were becoming instead the unwitting dispensers of fear. He could feel people looking at him funny, studying him from a distance, like they were trying to figure out whether or not he was foaming at the mouth and they needed to run and get a shotgun.

When he asked Larken what was going on and did it seem like the kids at school were avoiding them, she snorted darkly and said, *Are you kidding? Nobody wants to see us or have anything to do with us because they all feel too guilty about not looking for Mom anymore. I just wish somebody had the guts to come out and say that she's dead.*

But why does everybody look so scared?

They're afraid of catching our tragic lives or something. God, I wish we could move. At least to Beatrice. It's not like there's any reason to stay here.

But you're Little Miss Emlyn Springs, Gaelan said.

Shut up.

Do you think she's dead?

Of course she's dead. Use your brain. Even if she lived through the storm, she couldn't exactly run away, could she?

Bonnie still thinks she's alive.

Bonnie believes in Farmer Elves. She's a baby.

Yeah, but don't ever say that to her, okay? That Mom's dead. Even if it's true.

Okay.

Promise.

Okay! I promise! You hungry? I'm gonna order pizza for dinner. Bonnie! Get outta the bathtub!

Only Alvina Closs continued to see them in those early months, to be part of their lives—as if she considered herself part of their tragedy, too, or was willing to expose herself to the contagion of the unlucky.

So when there was a knock on the motel room door one night—Dad and Viney were out somewhere on a house call—they couldn't imagine who it could be. Larken answered the door but left the chain on.

A child's voice said, "Is Gaelan here?" and there was Bethan Ellis, age eleven: two years younger than Gaelan but only one grade behind him, notorious throughout school for being so smart that she'd skipped fifth grade. It was raining hard that night and she was soaked to the skin. She must have walked the two miles into town, and in the dark, too.

"This is for you and your family," she said, holding out an aluminum foil–covered pie plate. The surface was dimpled, full of little metallic ponds, and the combination of reflected light and Bethan's pallor made it look as though she was offering up her own reflection. Gaelan received the plate. They would find out soon that it contained a slumped, dissolving peanut butter meringue pie. They ate it later that night, all of it, in a single sitting.

Bethan surprised them further by starting to sing. It was widely known that, in addition to having an extraordinary IQ, and in spite of being born to a people renowned for their gifts in poetry and song, Bethan Ellis couldn't carry a tune in a tin bucket. Nevertheless, she sang all eight verses of "I Sing as a Bird" (at least her Welsh was perfect) while staring at Gaelan's feet.

Then she turned around and started to walk back home. She was wearing her older sister's majorette boots—they were white patent leather and decorated with pom-poms—and a yellow hooded rain slicker with a triangular fluorescent SLOW-MOVING VEHICLE sign ducttaped to the back.

"Hey! Wait up!" Gaelan called, running out after her. "I'll walk you home."

She turned around. "All right. But you should put on some light-colored clothing."

From that time forward, Bethan Ellis was Gaelan's best friend. They became sweethearts in high school, lovers in college. Everyone—even Gaelan—expected them to marry one day. So what if she was going away to med school? A few months apart wasn't so long, not when balanced against the time they'd already been together, all the years that lay ahead. They'd see each other at Christmas.

Gaelan didn't predict the challenges inherent in being twenty-two years old, a TV celebrity, and celibate. He didn't last two weeks.

Bethan flew in on Christmas Eve. He was waiting on the church steps. She came running.

It's weird, isn't it? she said. *No snow at Christmas?*

Townsfolk filed past them, going into the church, smiling, happy to see them together. He hadn't just betrayed her; he'd betrayed all of them.

Yeah, he muttered. *Weird.*

Dad says the weather is changing, she went on. *You think so?*

Maybe.

She tried teasing him. *You're the weatherman.*

He was mute, or as good as—his interjections meaningless, feeble, pathetic.

God, I've missed you so much.

Me, too. He was such a coward.

Gaelan.

What?

What's wrong?

Nothing.

Don't lie. Something's wrong.

It went on like this: Bethan prodding, digging, becoming more and more desperate while he retreated into monosyllabic replies, deepening shame, silence. They were still standing on the church steps when everyone else had gone in and the Christmas Eve service began.

You've been sleeping with other people, haven't you, she finally said. *Just say it.*

But he never did. He's still not sure whether it was the infidelity itself or his inability to speak of it that broke them. Either way, that was that. There's really no way to account for the demise of Gaelan's relationship with Bethan in a way that portrays him as anything but an asshole.

She turned and walked into the dark across that brown, snowless field.

Today, just before she moved on, making way for other mourners and their gifts of praise for the dead, she said, *I'm sorry. I'm so very sorry for your loss.*

Again Gaelan was silent, and his debt of words to Bethan Ellis remains unpaid.

Gaelan has done well over a hundred reps on each side when he hears someone opening the basement door and coming down the stairs. There's at least two people, and their feet have a lightweight, shuffling arrhythmia that makes them sound insecure, or clumsy, or both—as if they're walking on the moon, tethered to the mother ship by a defective NASA cable that could snap at any moment.

"You got the bag?"

"Yeah. Shh. Wait."

Of course: they're teenaged boys.

They continue down the stairs. Gaelan isn't quite sure what to do. He supposes that these boys, whoever they are, are coming down here for the same reasons he has—to escape the *Gymanfa* and to engage in something illicit. There's the sound of more shuffling; they're getting closer. Gaelan's afraid he might be discovered, but their footsteps stop on the other side of the door. Thank God the basement is big enough to privately accommodate more than one criminal.

There's a rustling sound, like a mouse scurrying around in a brown paper bag. Then silence.

"I hate these things," one of the boys says. "I'd rather be in school than go to these funeral deals."

"At least there's a lot of food."

"Yeah. No problem when the munchies kick in. Hey, grab that flashlight, willya?"

A weak, sputtering glow illuminates the space between floor and the bottom of the door.

"That stuff looks like shit. Where'd you get it?"

"There's a patch out past the Johnstons' place, by the bluffs. It grows wild out there."

"No shit."

"Yeah, it's not great, but I haven't been able to use the car to get up to Beatrice."

"Why not?"

"Grounded."

"When? What for?"

"Got a speeding ticket at the blind driveway."

"When? You didn't tell me."

"Haven't had a chance with all this funeral shit. Happened last weekend."

"Lotta kids get killed there, you know."

They fall silent. Gaelan pictures them: two boys sitting cross-legged on the damp floor of a hundred-year-old basement, hunched and intent, one of them rolling a joint of roadside pot, the other holding a flashlight with dying batteries; two boys hiding in a house in a town where the dead get more attention than the living.

"You're really good at that."

"Should be. Been watching Dad roll his own cigarettes my whole life. Here."

"No. You rolled it, you go first."

A match is struck, and then Gaelan hears that unmistakable sound—a tight, high-pitched, lengthy inhale that pulls up short and sudden, then silence, and then an expulsive out-breath that sounds like the single sputter of dieseling tractor.

Gaelan inhales in sync with the boys, remembering the weedy taste, the singeing feel of smoke in his throat. Unfortunately, either his imaginative powers are too keen or the Williams girls haven't swept the basement recently, and at the end of his exhale he starts to cough.

"What was that?" one boy says, lazily. It comes out like *Wuhwuhzzat*.

"Shit!" the other boy whispers urgently. "Somebody's down here. Put it out!"

"Oh hell, Chris, we're gonna get in so much trouble."

Gaelan is as dismayed as they are; he has no desire to bust these boys. He'd also hoped to stay down here a little longer. But there's no choice now: He'll have to come out of hiding. He takes more time than necessary to put on his suit coat and walk across the room. He knocks on the door before partially opening it and peeking his head through.

"Hi guys," he says. "How's it goin'?"

Both boys are on their feet and completely still, but there's a kind of vibratory atmosphere surrounding them, as if the uprising energy it took to get them off the floor is still going and hasn't yet settled back into their earthbound bodies.

"Uh, hi, sir," says the short, husky one. He's holding his arms behind his back and looks mortified: Houdini caught mid-escape.

"Hey there!" says the taller one. He's trying so hard to adopt a lounging nonchalance that Gaelan's afraid he might fall over.

They look about twelve, but they were talking about driving, so they must be at least sixteen. Small-town boys always look younger than boys who grow up in the city.

"We were just, uh . . ."

"We came down here to, uh . . ."

"It's okay," Gaelan says. "I won't tell."

"Gee. Thanks."

"Yeah, thanks a lot. I'm Ricky."

"Hello."

"And I'm Chris."

"Hey!" Ricky says, trying to focus his red-rimmed eyes. "Aren't you that guy on TV? The weatherman? What are you doing here?"

"Geez, Ricky," Chris says in hushing, big brother tones. "Don't you know anything? It's his *dad* upstairs."

"His dad?"

"Yeah, his dad is Mayor Jones."

"Right. Hey! You're really famous."

"Ricky, shut it," Chris continues. "His dad . . . ? Just died?"

"Oh. Gosh. *That* Jones."

"I'm not that famous," Gaelan says. "I grew up here, just like you."

"Still. You're on TV. That's really something."

Some people look completely different in real life than they do on television; Gaelen often wishes he was one of them.

"Listen, why don't you guys go back on upstairs and get outta here for a while? You must be pretty bored by now. Nobody's gonna care. *I'm* not anyway, and I'm family, so . . . go on, why don't you? I'll clean up down here."

"Gee, thanks."

"Yeah. Thanks a lot."

"You should leave the weed with me, though," Gaelan says, holding out his hand.

"Oh! Right."

Ricky comes forward with the rolled, partially smoked joint and a book of matches; Chris offers up the ziplock plastic bag and flashlight. Gaelan feels a surge of affection for these boys—such good boys that they even relinquish the nonincriminating accessories of their crime. Chris and Ricky. Gaelan bets they've been best friends since kindergarten, and that their names are always said together just like that: Chrisnricky.

"Hey, sorry about your dad."

"Yeah. He was a good mayor and all."

"Thanks."

"My mom says he brought me and my sister into the world."

"Yeah, me, too."

Gaelan feels his throat tighten. He nods his thanks. "I'll see you around."

"Bye, Mr. Jones."

"Nice to meet you."

Gaelan tries to imagine what it was like, being in the room with his father when he brought these boys into the world. He can't. He's witnessed plenty of animal births, but never the birth of a child. Did he ever ask to accompany his father on housecalls? Or did he just assume he wouldn't be allowed? What did his father *do* all that time he was away? He'll never know. The realization goes straight to his legs, making him feel like he's tried to bench-press too much weight. His knees start to give way and he has to lean against one of the basement support beams to keep from ending up on the floor.

Eventually he notices that he's still holding the plastic bag of grass and the partially smoked joint. No need to let it go to waste. He sits down, lights up, settles his back against the support beam, and listens. Upstairs, they've started recycling hymns, repeating themselves. The *Gymanfa* is almost over.

There's a sound nearby, and a small boy suddenly materializes out of the shadows several feet away. Gaelan tries to stand but his limbs are sluggish and he's beset with a sudden dizziness.

"Excuse me," the boy says. It's hard to make out his face, but he has a pencil tucked behind his ear and a spiral notebook clutched to his chest. "I wasn't intending to eavesdrop," he continues. "I came down here to *write*." There's a furtive, nocturnal quality about him; he could be

Woodward or Bernstein, whichever one it was who used to meet Deep Throat in unlit parking garages in the middle of the night.

"None of us are supposed to be down here, you know," Woodward Bernstein says. He stares at Gaelan, as if waiting for him to explain himself, and then he puts his head down and crosses the room quickly. When he gets to the foot of the stairs, he stops once more and turns around. "I've been down here for *hours,* but they'll miss *you* if you're gone too long."

And then he hustles up the stairs—on his way, Gaelan feels sure, to call in his scoop to *The Washington Post.*

"We had to sing, you see," Mr. Craven continues. "We *had* to!"

"Yes," Larken says. Mr. Craven has been stuck on this phrase for some time now. She wonders if he hasn't forgotten where he is in the story and what comes next. "Otherwise, she might have . . ."

"That's right! She might have fallen. The way baby birds do sometimes, you know, right out of the nest."

In the adjacent parlor, there is a brief lull.

"*Y Delyn Aur!*" calls a ragged voice.

"Oh!" Mr. Craven says abruptly. "They need me for this one. The tenor part is tricky."

Larken guides Mr. Craven by the elbow into the parlor, where about forty to fifty people are singing in harmony. Some are crowded onto folding chairs, others are leaning against walls (many with bottles of beer in hand). The ladies have the softest chairs, and there are even a few children sitting on elders' laps or on the floor. They sit erectly, for all children in Emlyn Springs know the importance of posture as it relates to breath support.

Mrs. Regina Butts whispers to Larken, aggressively patting the empty chair next to her as if trying to coax a pet to jump up and sit. "Join us, why don't you, dear?" Mrs. Butts was Larken's high school guidance counselor, and Larken suspects she's less interested in augmenting the alto section than in finding out whether her former advisee is still a lost cause, or has bettered her lot since abdicating the title of Little Miss Emlyn Springs for that of Town Slut.

"I'd love to," Larken lies, politely, "after I visit the ladies' room."

Larken gets Mr. Craven settled with the tenors, purloins half a dozen Welsh cakes from the dining room table by shoving them into her jacket pocket, and makes her way upstairs.

Somebody is using the bathroom, so she slips into one of the guest rooms and hides in the closet. No one will think to look for her here, except possibly her brother and sister.

Bonnie is outside, sitting on the new-mown lawn with her long bare legs stretched out, surrounded by chattering children and males in various stages of maturity but similar stages of infatuation: little boys, fifth- and sixth-grade boys, junior high and high school boys, shy boys, peacocky boys, letter-sweater senior boys whose girlfriends stand around the perimeter of the circle and are looking on, sinking into their hips and pouting, trying to be jealous, but it's impossible to hold a grudge against Miss Jones—who is so unlike every other grown-up in Emlyn Springs that she likes them all to call her Bonnie. She's godmother to at least ten of them, including Chris and Ricky Reimnitz who've just emerged from the house to join the group.

In another century, Bonnie would have been labeled a spinster and she would have looked older and more shriveled because of it. The word itself—*spinster*—has a hexing, shriveling power but no one has ever applied it to Bonnie Jones.

It is not sex that the boys want from her, not exactly. There is some quality in her eyes that dissolves such notions, disarms them for reasons they cannot name. Bonnie Jones may be unmarried, she may be a little eccentric—living in that old garage the way she does, going out on her bike and picking up trash—and she may have the worst luck any of them have ever seen when it comes to making a living, but she is a legend, a conduit for all that might be good about their small dying town, and they know it.

Even the five-year-olds can tell a version of "Flying Girl and the Tornado of 1978."

The town's oldest citizen at the time was Mr. Armin Koester. It was several hours after the tornado had done its damage and moved on. All the men were out looking, mostly in the muddy, ravaged cornfields surrounding the Jones place, but any sort of uneven ground was difficult for

Mr. Koester to manage with his walker, so he confined his search to the paved streets of town.

"Bonnie Jones!" he called, over and over, as they all did. "Aneira Hope!"

He was crossing Bridge Street when the sound of the birds drew his attention, singing as they do sometimes at lucky dusk, but with a special exuberance on this evening. And Mr. Koester thought to himself what a day it had been for them, too, poor things, how relieved they must feel, how eager to sing again after that fearful enforced silence that always precedes a tornado, and then of course, the tornado itself, such a terrifying sound no matter how many times you've heard it—and Mr. Koester, a lifelong resident of Emlyn Springs, had heard it plenty. Birds surely have a quota of song time to fill, Mr. Koester thought, and the birds of Emlyn Springs were making up for what they'd lost.

He gazed into the boughs of the trees for several minutes, listening, resting. (He and Mrs. Koester were dedicated walkers, but he'd slacked off quite a bit after she died last spring.) Only then did he realize that something about the angle of one of the tree trunks was off in relation to the other trees lining the ravine, and then he came to understand that that particular nondeciduous tree—a cedar—shouldn't be there at all. Furthermore, it was upside down. It was leaning across the ravine some ways from the bridge, right where the springs are deepest, and just before the creek starts to furrow away from town and connect with the Big Blue.

He didn't believe his eyes at first. The cedar must have been savaged out of the ground, shot like a javelin over the top of the church steeple, and somersaulting into place with its top on one side of the ravine and its roots high up in the air on the other. They found out later it was plucked from the stand of cedars planted on the northwest corner of the Vance place, two and a half miles away.

And there, at the very top (bottom) of the tree, nestled into its ripped, muddied roots, was seven-year-old Bonnie Jones, sitting on her bicycle seat.

How it came to be that she was there, barely conscious and balanced precariously, fanny on the seat and the seat in the roots and the roots on the tree and the tree on the ground, no one save her mother will ever know, but there she was. She must have flown!

The combined miracle of the cedar's age (its root system was massive) and the precise way in which it came to rest (wedged among the limbs of the deciduous, partly denuded trees that lined the ravine on both sides) saved Bonnie's life. The roots of that cedar intertwined with Bonnie's limbs and held her fast—because she could not hold herself.

"God in heaven, there she is!" Mr. Koester shouted. "There she is! There she is!" But no one heard him, and he quickly realized that it would take the employment of his singing voice to summon the others.

Aiming heavenward, he sang the first song that came to mind, Number 65, "*R wy'n Canu*" ("I Sing as a Bird"), with fervor and passion— as if Mrs. Koester herself, and not Bonnie Jones, were up in that tree. As if they were young again, all of twenty years old, and sweethearts.

Soon the men came running, breathing raggedly at first, but in time recovering their voices and joining in. No one dared disturb the tree, the girl might fall, and so, while little Bethan Ellis rode her prize mare Eira all the way to Beatrice to notify the fire department (all the telephone lines within fifteen miles were down), and a dozen other boys and girls rounded up their spooked ponies, talked them down, saddled them, and cleared the highway so the fire truck could get through, they gathered in the ravine beneath her, ankle deep, making a human net to catch her should she fall. And they sang.

They sang to bless her. They sang to let her know that they were there, for who knew what nightmares the poor thing might be having, what horrors she might have seen before landing there among the birds. Who even knew if she was alive? They might even have been singing her to her death.

By the time the ladder truck arrived, every man in town was singing to seven-year-old Bonnie Jones, and a few women and children, too. The person now known as Blind Tom was there; he was thirteen at the time, and his vision had not yet begun to fail. Dr. Llewellyn Jones was there, along with his nurse, Alvina Closs—who stood beside him, holding his hand; Bud Humphries and his sister, Vonda, were there, and the Cravens and the Schlakes and the Ellises and the Byelicks, all of them, everybody who wasn't too badly shaken up or hurt. Gaelan and Larken were not there, nor were they allowed to participate in the search; Viney thought it best they remain at her house, because who knew what kind of shape their sister would be in if and when she was found. Then, too, there was still the matter of Hope.

They sang to Bonnie Jones, who did not yet know that her mother was nowhere to be found, or that the severe internal injuries she sustained when she came down made it unlikely that she'd ever bear children of her own.

They parked the truck on the east side of the ravine, and a young fireman named George Jachulski carried her down the ladder and deposited her in her father's arms. (He later moved up to Chicago to work for the fire department there and got himself killed saving another child only a couple of years later.) She was hurt bad, but she lived.

The main character had to be told her own story, repeatedly and over time, and has integrated it so thoroughly that she now believes she remembers it all, and more. She says she remembers seeing her mother, encircled in the vortex by a hundred other smaller spirals of wind that swirled around her like ribbons, backlit by lightning flashes, as if her suspension in the sky had been cleverly, masterfully engineered, a Fourth of July spectacle. She says, too, that there was someone else there, an angel with white hair who lifted Hope up with immense and powerful arms and carried her away. She says that she remembers hearing the men's voices, and even the sound of the trains—although the trains stopped coming to Emlyn Springs long ago.

The event shaped Bonnie Jones to believe in the improbable, that's sure, and in magic. Of course, she was already predisposed to do so; her mother told her often enough stories of the magic surrounding her conception: how she came to them when her father played the fairy king in that play about fairies and wayward pairs of lovers sleeping in the forest, and potions applied to lovers' eyes, and Jack shall have Jill, naught shall go ill, the man shall have his mare again and all will be well.

By now, everyone has their eyes on the clocks and watches; there is no secret as to when the *Gymanfa* is officially over. It concludes when the townsfolk, standing as they are able, sing two last songs; there's an unspoken expectation that the closest family members will rally before the trip to the cemetery and sing along.

Bonnie comes inside. She notes her siblings' absence but is unperturbed by it, as is Viney. If any two people in Emlyn Springs empathize with the need for privacy, they are Bonnie Jones and Alvina Closs. Neither of them hold Gaelan and Larken's absence against them, or offer to seek them out.

But not everyone has this attitude when it comes to tradition; Miss Axthelm especially feels that it would be entirely inappropriate to end the *Gymanfa* without all the mayor's children in attendance. At her instigation, several citizens are sent to search the house and rout them out of their hiding places. Five minutes go by, then ten.

"We can't possibly begin without them," Miss Axthelm continues to insist.

"We can, Estella, and we should," Viney says. "These folks are tired and need to get on home."

The witch falls silent, but she will badmouth Alvina Closs to her likeminded, mean-spirited friends for weeks to come.

"Let's get started, Hazel," Viney says, and Miss Williams strikes a single note on the piano. There is a short silence as each person in the room hears within themselves their relationship to this note.

And then they begin.

Emlyn Springs has a unique arrangement of the Nebraska Fight Song: sung slowly, a cappella, in Welsh, and in four-part harmony.

O nid oes unman yn debyg i Nebraska . . .

This arrangement is not transcribed anywhere, nor is it accredited; it has evolved gradually over the course of many years and belongs to no one single person.

. . . annwyl "Nebraska U" . . .

In the end, Larken and Gaelan Jones are nowhere to be found, and the town sings without them.

Chapter 9

The Wheel in the Hole and the Hole in the Ground

Larken knocks on the bathroom door. "Are you almost ready, Bon? It's time."

It is late afternoon. Gaelan and Larken emerged from their hiding places as soon as they heard the final chorus of "There is No Place Like Nebraska." Rejoining Viney and Bonnie, they all stopped back at Viney's house for a few minutes to freshen up before heading to the cemetery. Gaelan and Viney have already gone ahead.

Bonnie emerges. She's put on a pair of leggings under her black dress and changed into tennis shoes. "I've got Mom's mouth," she announces in a self-loathing tone, as if she's confessing to adultery or heroin addiction.

"What?" This kind of non sequitur is normal for Bonnie, born on the other side of the decade, on the other side of innocence, beyond the time frame that contains baby boomers. To Larken and Gaelan, it often seems as though their sister was born on the other side of the moon.

Bonnie points at her own lips and traces a quick circle in the air around them. "Can't you see it?"

"Bon-bon, what are you talking about?" Larken is baffled. She used to understand everything Bonnie said; and even if she didn't understand what she said, she understood what she *meant*.

Bonnie goes on. Her voice is still confessional. "Sometimes I'll catch my mouth doing something, and it feels like I'm possessed, like I don't have any control. It's been happening more than ever lately."

"You mean you don't feel like you can control what you say?"

"No, not my voice. My mouth. It's Mom's mouth."

"Sweetie—"

"Don't you remember that little puffing thing she used to do?"

"What puffing thing?"

"She'd pucker her lips and make this little puffing noise. She wouldn't even be doing anything strenuous, she'd just be sitting in her wheelchair, puffing."

"No."

"I catch myself doing it all the time. It's like this." Bonnie demonstrates. Her eyes glaze over, she furrows her brow and expulses tiny bursts of air through vigorously puckered lips.

"I don't remember her doing that."

"She did! I'm telling you. And there are these shapes my mouth takes, these tensions, I can feel it. It's all muscular, like muscle memory, only maybe it's genetic memory, maybe there are delayed mannerism genes that manifest after x number of years, like the genes that cause your hair to turn gray or make you get cancer."

"Bee, I think you're imagining things."

"What if I have it?"

"You mean the MS."

"Yes."

"It's not genetic, Bonnie. It's not inherited."

"They say that, but do they really know? They don't. They don't know anything."

"I'm pretty sure they know it's not inherited, B. You don't have it."

Suddenly Bonnie's face goes hard and clenched. "I've never understood that," she says, and then quickly averts her eyes to a place next to Larken's feet—as if she reined in her vaporizing superpowers just in time.

"Understood what?"

"Why I remember so much more about her than you do. You're the oldest. You should remember everything."

Larken takes a breath. Bonnie is still looking at the floor. "I remember things, Bon. I just remember different things than you do."

Bonnie gets quiet. She does this, falling suddenly silent in the middle of a lively conversation. She might not speak again for the rest of the day. With Bonnie, language exerts itself in bursts, and then, as if the effort has been all too much, goes into hiding. Or maybe she reverts to another kind of language, a wordless language, one in which Larken is not fluent.

"You didn't have to wait," Bonnie says coldly. "I'm not going in the car." No matter how many times Larken has been on the receiving end of her sister's mercurial nature, it still stings: a piercing hot/cold that is the precursor of both frostbite and third-degree burn. "I'll meet you there," she calls, just before the screen door slams, and then she's gone.

Bonnie has her own way of characterizing the unique cries of birds, often assigning words to their songs.

"Oh? Over heeee-re!" say the cardinals. "Hurry hurry hurry hurry hurry!" Another bird sounds like Groucho Marx, chasing a giggling, buxom woman and reaching lewdly for her broad-beamed bottom: "Walka walka walka walka walka." The gossiping birds say, "Really? *Really?!* Tell me tell me tell me tell me," while others impress upon their children the need for careful mastication—the birdsong equivalent of human mothers who remind their offspring over and over again that their stomachs don't have teeth: "Chew chew chew chew chew!"

There are grumpy, nay-saying, pessimistic birds—"Nononono-nononono."—and birds who've escaped from Saturday morning cartoons—"Beebeep. Beebeep." Some sound as though they're toasting their families at a holiday meal: "Cheers! Cheers!" and others sound the way purring cats would sound if only they could sing. There's a gawky, yodeling quality to the cries of migrating geese; they're like sweet, pubescent boys whose voices crack at life's most embarrassing moments. Some birds sound like pull toys, others like a playing card stuck in the spokes of a spinning bicycle wheel. Meadowlark songs are intricate and hard to textualize; Bonnie has yet to come up with something satisfactory for them, but she will. Robins, for all their plump-bosomed beauty, emit a sudden, startled cry; they always sound cautionary and frazzled to Bonnie, like overextended, philanthropic socialites in dire need of a day at the spa.

She loves them all, even the ones whose voices are less melodious: birds who sound like the unoiled hinges of porch screen doors, birds whose voices are metallic and fricative, like the ratchets the Labenz boys use to tighten car parts at the Texaco. And of course, the woodpeckers— many of whom, each spring, try to attract mates by pounding incessantly on the roof of Bonnie's woodshed home. She loves them especially for their persistence and foolishness.

But there is one birdsong Bonnie especially loves: This bird sounds as though it's calling a wayward child with a two-syllable name home to supper.

(*Lar-ken! Gae-lan! Bon-nie!*)

It's a gentle voice—low, calm, patient—and it has the quality of dusk about it, whatever time of day it is heard. These birds always sound far away, too, even when they are near.

It is the faith implicit in these bird voices that Bonnie responds to: No matter how long the children have been gone, no matter how far they have wandered or how many summoning cries have been uttered, they never raise their voices, never feel the need to project their calls in a desperate or territorial manner the way some birds do. These birds know without doubt that, one day, maybe even *this* day, the lost, the strayed, the self-exiled, the banished . . . all will return. All will follow their voices and find their way home.

If they have to go to the cemetery, Bonnie feels very strongly that they should at least be allowed to go like *children,* on their bikes, instead of cooped up in air-conditioned, leather-seated cars, hip to hip with the adults in their tight-fitting shoes and formal clothing. So she's evolved a new tradition over the years, one that she hopes will survive her: When the *Gymanfa* is over, she leads a bicycle caravan of children to the cemetery.

Courtney! Tyler! Jason! Kelsey! calls one bird.

It pains Bonnie that none of these children are hers in a biological sense, even though she loves them, even the smart-alecky girls who wear

T-shirts with slogans like NOT EVERYTHING IN NEBRASKA IS FLAT and I LOVE MY ATTITUDE PROBLEM. Girls in small towns have to rebel more than girls anywhere else, Bonnie knows, if they are rebellious types. She was not, is not. But if there is anything of rebellion in them, they must do it now, because soon they will come to understand that rebellion is no longer possible, they'll settle in to lives that have been templated, become bitter. Bonnie has seen it happen. She only wants them to rebel in ways that do not involve alcohol or drugs or reckless driving or promiscuity.

And so, at the end of these seven days, when everyone has had enough of paying attention to her dead father, Bonnie accompanies the children as they all pedal up the slow incline to the cemetery. She does not always take the lead; there are girls and boys in the back who have already started smoking and are out of breath—although they try to make their position in the group seem like choice rather than necessity, their hanging back an example of the particular kind of nonchalance teenagers always believe is unique to them, when in fact it is the one thing they all share.

The little ones adore her. At thirty-one, Bonnie is old enough to be their mother.

Oh, why can't she conjure a baby out of her own fingertips? Or out of the ionized air on a summer night, right before a storm? Why is there no fairy magic that can birth a child out of an acorn or a leaf? Bonnie thinks it is the worst kind of injustice that babies must be made through human coupling.

"What's a period?" Bonnie asks Larken.

"What?"

"It's the dot at the end of a sentence, isn't it?"

It was two weeks after Hope went up. Bonnie was still in the hospital.

"Who's been talking about periods?"

"I was pretending to be asleep when these people came in, two men and a woman wearing white coats like Daddy does when he's at work. Daddy was here, too, and they were talking about periods and how I might not ever get one and then Daddy started to cry. Why would person need a period?"

"Oh."

"And then I really fell asleep and when I woke up everybody was gone."

Larken nods.

"Where's Daddy?"

"He had to go to work. Gaelan's in the cafeteria, getting something to eat."

"Oh."

"He'll be up soon and we'll all have dinner together, okay? I have a surprise for you."

"They found Mommy!"

"No. No, honey. I just went to the library is all, and brought you some books."

"But what about my period?"

"Well, something in your insides got hurt when you landed in that tree."

"Where in my insides?"

Larken swirls her hand vaguely, as if she's stirring something on the stove. "Around here."

"In my tummy?"

"No, not exactly. A little lower than your tummy."

"I feel much better now."

"I know. And we're all so happy about that. But the doctors say that . . ."

"Physicians, you mean."

"What?"

"Daddy says there are all kinds of doctors."

"Right. Physicians." Larken's voice sounds funny, like she's a soprano instead of an alto.

"So what's wrong with my insides?"

"Nothing, Bon-bon. Really. Why don't I read to you for a while?"

"Does Daddy say it, too? That there's something wrong inside?"

"What would you like to hear? I brought *Goodnight, Moon*."

"That's a baby book."

"All right, then, how about Babar? I got lots of Babar books."

"It's about babies, isn't it?" Bonnie says. "The thing they say is wrong with me. Mommy told me."

"What?"

"She *did*. When I saw her in the sky. She told me, and she said they're all wrong. I'll be able to have all the babies I want when I'm ready. I just have to wait for the right time."

Being steadfast and stubborn by nature—and not unlike her older sister in that way—Bonnie is still waiting.

Another bird is calling: *Ashlee! Jordan! Chloe! Michael!*

Bonnie looks toward the bird's voice and sees that one child has strayed from the group (how did she miss this?) and has headed off on a side road. This happens sometimes, the appearance of a little wayward sheep, although usually Bonnie sees it well before it actually occurs. Different things cause this: a fight, a dare, a duel, an insult. Hurt feelings drive them away. It's rare for a child in Emlyn Springs to go off on his or her own, and those who do, Bonnie keeps a careful eye on. Perhaps one of the others, yes, one of the bullying types has said something unkind or threatening and Bonnie will deal with her later. But now she must go retrieve the wayward one.

She puts an older, reliable girl in charge of the pack and follows the child.

There he is, just ahead, but going so fast. How is this possible? Bonnie's legs are longer, she is pedaling easily as quickly and furiously as he is. She shifts gears. The grade of the terrain angles slightly up, and Bonnie's legs start to burn with the effort; her breath grows ragged.

The child is almost out of sight, looking more and more like a mirage. Bonnie is panting hard now. How far have they come? How long have they been riding? The last bits of light are disappearing behind a stand of silhouetted trees.

She is pedaling in a field, the terrain bumpy and still wet from the soaking it got a week ago. She has her eyes on the child, so when her bike slams into something, she is unprepared. The rear end of the bike tips up as the front wheel comes to a stop, and Bonnie is thrown off.

And then the child is there, standing over her. Except he's not a child.

"Doc Williams?" Bonnie murmurs. He kneels, his face so close that she can almost make out his features, even though it is now quite dark. He lifts her head gently and tips the contents of a bottle of spring water into her mouth. She takes some; a bit dribbles down her chin. After a few more sips, she asks, "Where is your bike?"

He doesn't speak. He hands her a flashlight. He points. She sits up, shining the light in the direction he indicates, back and forth, tracing arcs across the harvested fields, the flattened stalks. She squints. "I don't see it."

When she turns around, he is gone. But she hears the soft motion of wheels and the rustling of wings. He has left his flashlight behind. She takes it into the field. There is something important waiting for her here.

Bonnie wakes herself up.

She knows where she is. She knows too that a change of view, taking a look at something from a different angle, can make all the difference. All the houses on her street look out onto the same park, but she knows—because she has been a guest in the living room of each one of those houses—that each house affords a different view. She notices a different set of details from the Parrys' front porch than she does from the McClures' or Thomases' or the Williamses', so that her eyes never become dead to what is familiar.

It's like berry picking: If you stand in the same place, you'll find good berries. You will plunder what you see. But if you adjust your body even slightly, adjust your level by kneeling or squatting, move even one degree around the berry cane, then a different berry will be revealed, one that you never would have believed you could have missed, its color is so vivid, it is so perfectly ripe.

Bonnie lying on the ground sees something in this field she has missed, something curved and black, submerged—and yet emerging: Paul Bunyan's pocket change, a giant coin that's been stuffed into the slot of a too-full piggy bank. Bonnie uses her hands to scoop some dirt away.

It's a wheel.

Heart racing, she keeps digging. The earth here is still pliable. She'll dig as long as it takes to pull up this artifact. She knows what it represents: Proof. A sign. A message.

She'll dig forever if she has to.

Chapter 10

Sister City

He has been praised at length in both religious and secular settings. He's been serenaded for seventy-two hours straight in the language of his ancestors. He's been paraded through town, planted in sanctified, heavy, nutrient-rich Nebraska soil, and is now being introduced to the society of dead fathers, learning about possible postmortem pastimes. Everyone who wants to can now speak of Llewellyn Jones in the past tense.

All that's left to bring the week to an official close is for the church bell to toll midnight.

Viney has changed out of her black dress and is wearing her bathrobe and slippers. She's feeling that odd combination of exhaustion and restlessness that typically affects the newly bereaved; she can't keep herself from arranging and rearranging the contents of the refrigerator and freezer. "What in the world am I going to do with all this food?" she reflects, not really expecting an answer.

Neither of the other two people in the kitchen hears her anyway. Like Viney, they're tired and antsy, durably encased in their own grief. They're also preoccupied by the absence of a fourth person.

Gaelan is pacing. "You really think she's okay?" he asks. His voice sounds atypically ineffectual and thin, and his question doesn't seem to be directed at anyone in particular. "We shouldn't file a missing persons report or something?"

"I can't *believe* she would do this," Larken hisses. She's parked at the kitchen table, where she's demolishing a plate of leftover meat loaf, peas, and cold mashed potatoes. "What time is it, anyway?"

"Ten twenty-three. I think we should consider calling the police."

Gaelan's anger often manifests as fear; Larken's fear often manifests as anger. This tendency goes largely unnoticed.

"I'm telling you kids," Viney says, "she's fine. She'll be back any minute now."

Larken gets up, taking a forkful of food with her, and stands looking out the kitchen window. Her brother joins her. They are both thinking about the days—how they're growing shorter—and about the absent one—who was last seen wearing black.

"She knew you were leaving tonight, didn't she?" Larken asks.

"Yeah," Gaelan replies. "I told her."

"I cannot believe she would do this!" Larken repeats, trying to articulate around a mouthful of peas and potatoes. "I'm so mad I could spit. The selfishness . . . It's just incredible."

"What should we do?" Gaelan asks. "Keep waiting? I've gotta get on the road soon so I can catch a couple hours of sleep before going to the station."

Larken throws her fork down on the table, sending bits of smashed vegetables into orbit. "We've been waiting for six goddamn hours," she announces. "If she wanted to be part of this discussion she should have been here." Calling across the kitchen as if it were an enormous board room—"Viney! Come sit down with us!"—she resumes her place at the table with the vehemence of a Wall Street mogul orchestrating a corporate takeover.

Gaelan adds, more temperately, "There're a couple of things we need to talk about."

"I can listen from over here," Viney answers. "Go ahead." She's trying to consolidate several pounds of elbow macaroni salad into one Tupperware container.

"Okay, then. Larken? You wanna . . . ?"

Larken sighs. "Right," she says, tightly. Does she *always* have to be the one to lead every family discussion? Can't her brother, just for *once,* take the initiative? "Viney, we need to talk about Dad's house."

"Uh-huh."

"Ask her about the money," Gaelan whispers.

"What?"

"You know, about her and Bonnie sharing the . . . you know . . ."

"You want me to do this or not?"

"Sorry. No. You go ahead."

Larken continues. "Dad left the house to the three of us, but Gaelan and I have been talking and we think—"

"Can't I send some of this food back to Lincoln with you two?" Viney asks. "I'll never eat all this by myself."

"We'll obviously be selling it," Larken continues, "and we'll find a time to come back and do that later, but we wanted to ask you—"

"That's just fine," Viney says. "There's no hurry." In her quest to find room for the enormous tub of macaroni salad, she is extracting all the food from the fridge. A small city composed of buildings with innumerable code violations is forming along the edge of the counter, a doomed skyline of variously sized, precariously balanced Tupperware containers, plastic covered bowls, lidded casserole dishes, cake pans, odd-sized platters, gravy boats. *All this food,* Viney is thinking. *It's obscene.*

"Is there anything over there you want, Viney?" Gaelan asks.

"Over where?"

"At Dad's house."

"Oh, that's sweet of you, honey. Uh, I don't know. I don't really know."

"You should go over and take a look," Larken says. "I expect we'll try to sell the house as is, with the contents and all, so if there are things of Dad's you want, you should take them."

Viney nods. "Can I at least wrap up some of these brownies and cookies and things to send back with you? Larken, how about for that little girl you babysit for? Wouldn't she like some cookies?"

"She's lactose intolerant," Larken mutters.

"What?"

"Sure Viney, that would be great. We can talk about this later, I guess."

Gaelan gets up and looks out the window again. "You really don't think we shouldn't be worried?"

"No," Viney says. "This was hard on her—she and the mayor weren't on the best of terms, you know—and I'm sure she's just having some alone time, you know, on her bike the way she likes to."

They do know. They know all about their sister's special relationship with bicycles—a relationship that began the minute she learned to ride a two-wheeler, at the startlingly early age of four.

After she got out of the hospital, she started sleepwalking; Larken and Gaelan would find her outside in all kinds of weather, sitting on the brand-new Schwinn that was donated by the Lincoln bicycle club, balanced on her tiptoes in the dark. Larken was so terrified that one night her baby sister wouldn't just sleepwalk to her bike but start riding it that she gave it to the Goodwill. She's not sure Bonnie has ever forgiven her for that.

Everyone in Emlyn Springs has seen her often enough on the back roads, as far away as thirty miles in all directions. They don't exactly know what she does out there, although they've all seen her crouched by the side of the road or in the drainage ditches, picking up trash, stowing things in those saddlebag contraptions. Whatever she's up to, it's her business. Odd perhaps, but certainly not disruptive. She rides in all the town parades, and she's been leading that caravan of children up to the cemetery at the conclusion of every *Gymanfa* for several years now. The dead fathers may not unanimously approve, but most everyone else is used to it.

Larken and Gaelan are not used to it. They're afraid of what Bonnie is turning into, cooped up in this small, dead-end, dying place, captive to her own failures and to the way she's perceived by the small-minded people who live here. They do not want their sister to be the kind of person who is described as "eccentric." She's young, but not that young. In three years, maybe even less, eccentricity will cease to be a charming attribute.

They worry about her. They worry incessantly.

"I'd know if there was something wrong with her," Viney goes on, and although neither Gaelan nor Larken understands why that should be so, they believe her, and are temporarily reassured. They notice that Viney has dismantled the village of food containers and found room for everything back in the fridge. There is something of the miraculous about this achievement.

"Gaelan, honey," Viney says, "you should head back to Lincoln. I'll call you, or Larken will, the minute she gets here."

"I think I'll wait just a few more minutes."

"Well," Viney says, "that's your decision." She succeeds in wedging the tub of macaroni salad into place, closes the fridge, and yawns expansively. "I don't know about you two, but I'm bone weary, so if you'll excuse me, I'm gonna head up to bed." She pads across the kitchen and gives Gaelan a long hug. "Drive safe, sweetheart," she says. "I don't like you leaving so late at night. Call when you get home, okay?"

"I will."

She leans down to give Larken a kiss. "Sleep tight, honey," she says. "See you in the morning light. And don't worry about your sister."

I'm not worried about her, Larken thinks. *I just want to kill her.* "Sleep well."

Viney starts to shuffle toward the living room and up the stairs. "My, oh my," she says, sighing. "It certainly has been an allergic week. Good night, dear ones."

"Good night, Viney," they answer.

Once she's out of sight, Gaelan whispers, "So? What does she mean?"

Among the Jones siblings, Larken is the only one who has ever been able to decipher Viney's mispronunciations. "Elegiac. An elegiac week."

"What's that?"

"As in 'elegy.'"

"Ah. Well . . ."

"This is ridiculous. It's almost ten-fucking-thirty."

Gaelan looks at his watch once more and then gets up and dumps the rest of his coffee into the sink. "I hate to go without seeing her, but . . ."

And then they hear the sound of bike gears being downshifted on gravel, followed by quick light footsteps. The screen door creaks open, and Bonnie enters.

She is filthy. She is ecstatic. "Hi, guys!"

Her obliviousness is astounding. "Where the hell have you been?" Gaelan touches his sister's shoulder. "Larken . . ."

"Oh, God," Bonnie says, earnestly. "I'm sorry. What time is it? Were you worried?"

"Were we worried? Were we *worried*? You disappear for almost six fucking hours and you ask me if we were worried? Jesus Christ."

"Please don't use the f-word."

Gaelan intervenes. "Where have you been, Bon?"

"I was out riding is all. One of the kids strayed from the caravan, and . . ."

Larken gets up, making a lot of noise with her chair, and clears her place at the table. After casting her cutlery and dishes into the sink and dousing everything with soap, she turns on the hot water. "I cannot fucking believe this," she mutters.

"Watch your language!" Bonnie shouts.

Gaelan continues. "We just . . . there were things we needed to talk about, and now I have to get back to Lincoln so . . ."

"I found something," Bonnie announces. "That's why I was gone so long. It was buried and I had to dig it up."

Larken turns to face her. "What?"

"It's really, really important. An artifact. You need to come see. I left it outside 'cuz it's pretty muddy, but—"

"Bonnie!" Larken says. "Listen! There are things we need to discuss."

"Don't talk to me like a child."

"Oh? Why would I talk to you any other way?"

"Excuse me?"

"Girls," Gaelan says.

"Why would I talk to you as if you were actually a responsible, accountable adult? You've done nothing but fuck, *screw* off the entire time we've been here."

"And you've done nothing but try to impress on everyone what a big brain you are, how beneath you we all are."

"Girls! Knock it off. We need to talk about the house before I leave."

"The house?" Bonnie asks. "What house?"

"Dad's house," Larken replies.

"What about it?"

"We need to decide on a price, on whether we want to go the FSBO route or get it listed with a real estate agency."

"I'm thinking we should use somebody from Lincoln." Gaelan interjects.

"We also wanted to find out if you'd be willing to share the proceeds four ways, with Viney. Dad didn't make any kind of provision for her in his will, so Lark and I were thinking—"

"No," Bonnie says, using a clear and emphatic voice that startles her siblings into a momentary silence.

"No, what?"

"We are not selling Daddy's house."

"Of course we are," Larken counters. "What else are we going to do with it?"

"Well, we're not selling it."

"It's a nice house, Bon," Gaelan says.

"And it's entirely paid off," Larken adds. "Dad didn't owe anything on it. We'd get the entire proceeds from the sale."

"Is that all you think about? Money?"

"Oh, let's not," Larken says. "Let's not really start talking about money."

"I know what you both think," Bonnie goes on. "Now that Dad's gone, you think you can just cut all your ties to this place and never come back here again—"

"Bonnie."

"—when you *know* that's the last thing Mom would have wanted. We are *not* selling Dad's house! I might even want to move in there myself."

"Jesus Christ."

Gaelan takes up his shoulder bag. "Okay, girls. I've stayed as long as I can. I'm leaving."

"Oh, perfect," Larken says. "That's just perfect. I cannot believe this!"

"Lark, I'm not gonna stay here while you two fight. You're not listening to me anyway. You never listen to me. Look out. The sink's about to overflow."

"Shit!" Larken cries, turning off the water.

"Gaelan, that is so not true," Bonnie interjects, her voice placating. "I listen to everything you say."

"Well," Gaelan goes on, "in any case, I've gotta be at the station and in makeup by three-thirty, which is exactly four hours and fifty-three minutes from now, so you two just . . . duke it out or whatever it is you have to do to settle things, and let me know what you decide."

"I cannot believe you're leaving," Larken repeats.

"Call me, okay?" Gaelan says. "Bye." He gives each of his sisters a kiss on the cheek and leaves.

They stand listening to the sounds of Gaelan opening and closing his car door, starting the engine, driving away. There's a short silence, and then water starts cascading over the edge of the counter and onto the floor, a miniature Niagara.

Larken whips a couple of dish towels off the rack and throws them to the floor; the effort drains her completely. Suddenly she's exhausted, so exhausted that she's bereft of common sense: it doesn't occur to her to pull the plug from the sink. She just stands, ineffectual and dazed, watching the water fall, watching connected pools form in the indented places on the fake brick linoleum of Viney's kitchen. *Isn't that interesting?* she thinks.

When she finally speaks, her voice is quiet. "How could you skip out on Dad's burial service? How could you just wander off like that and not tell us where you were going?"

Bonnie kneels and starts trying to mop up the water with the soaked dish towels. "I know what you think. You think I'm a loser. You think that all of us, everyone here, we're all just losers."

"Here. Let me help."

"I'll do it!" Bonnie pulls several sheets of paper towel off the roll and layers them across the floor; they do not live up to their reputation for superabsorbency. "We're not selling Dad's house," she repeats, glumly.

"It's not about the money, Bon. Neither Gaelan nor I need the money. In fact, we'd really like it if just you and Viney split the proceeds of the sale."

Bonnie looks up. "So you two have already talked about it?"

"A little, but not . . ."

"So you weren't really going to include me in the decision anyway. All this bullshit about wanting to involve me is just . . . bullshit! Just like always, you guys made up your minds because poor little Bonnie can't make any decisions on her own. She's incompetent. She's a failure."

"Bonnie, please."

"Have a great trip back to the city!" the wronged heroine cries, her voice breaking with emotion, and then storms out. Larken can almost hear the swelling music of the player piano. It's a magnificent exit.

Outside, Bonnie pedals away with a furiousness that surely will have her airborne in no time.

Larken stands, transfixed by Bonnie's performance and her own reaction to it.

It's a wonder, really. Only Bonnie has the ability to render Professor Jones completely speechless. Whenever she's in the same room with her baby sister, Larken loses words, loses them by the thousands, and those few words she is able to retain seem to have no meaning. She grows inarticulate—which, for Larken, is the same as growing stupid. Once again, she wishes for a different language, one that would never give rise to hurt feelings. It would require no subtext and allow for no misinterpretations.

Larken summons what little energy she has left to fetch a sponge mop from the broom closet and clean up the floor.

There is something she wanted to say, something she could not access when their energies were in conflict, something important. What was it? Could her body help her find the unsaid thing. If she gestures, will that bring the language forth? Larken can't think of anything but to listen to the night, imagine that she can still hear Bonnie riding her bike back to her garage.

It is hard to accept the idea that her sister is insane. It is more than hard; it is heartbreaking. How can Larken help her? How can she speak about the pacifiers and unmatched baby shoes Bonnie has strung from the ceiling of her shed?—hundreds of them she's picked up over the years. How can she tell her sister that most people do not share her obsession with what they find on the side of the highway? How can she explain that the grocery lists Bonnie tenderly salvages and pastes into the acid-free pages of her scrapbooks with the care of a museum archivist could not possibly have been penned by their mother's hand?

She's dead, Larken longs to say, but she made a promise long ago to never utter those words in Bonnie's presence; she still feels bound by it. If anyone is to blame for her baby sister's madness, Larken feels, it is herself.

She finishes drying the floor. She opens the fridge. The giant tub of macaroni salad falls out; when it hits the floor, the lid explodes away from the container with the force of a nose cone separating from a rocket launcher. Larken spends another thirty minutes cleaning up this new mess, and then, finally—after pulling a soup spoon from the silverware drawer and a gallon of fat-free rocky road ice cream from the freezer—heads upstairs to bed.

*   *   *

Alvina Closs—a woman who cannot technically claim to be either the widow of Dr. Llewellyn Jones or the stepmother to his children—goes to bed hoping to meet Welly in her dreams. Even more than that, she hopes that he'll impart some guidance, a blueprint for how she is supposed to live her life now that he is gone, and specifically how she is supposed to manage all the information she's safeguarded for the past twenty-five years.

She'd like the mayor to visit her the way angels are said to visit: heralded by bright lights and also if possible the blare of a trumpet (for Viney is normally a heavy sleeper). She would not be afraid. A supernatural occurrence would be quite welcome under the circumstances. She would like the spirit of the mayor to hover long enough to deliver a clear directive in his beautiful commanding voice. "DO THIS!" she longs to hear, followed by a monologue delivered in a plainspoken manner.

Ritualizing her readiness for such an occurrence, she places the spiral notebook she used during the *Tridiau* on her nightstand so that she'll be prepared to take dictation—as she often did in her combined professional roles of nurse and medical secretary. Finally, she lays one of the mayor's unlaundered shirts across her pillow.

Tell me what to do, she implores the spirit of her dear, dead, not-husband as she drifts off to sleep. *Tell me tell me tell me tell me tell me* . . .

But she doesn't dream of Welly; she dreams of Hope.

They are the same age in the dream, in their early twenties. They're both dressed in nurses' uniforms, the old-fashioned kind: buttoned up, belted, and pressed shirtwaist dresses with short cuffed sleeves and modest collars, and on their heads those starched white hats that have always made Viney think of miniature baseball stadiums. There's a large red cross affixed to the left chest pocket of Viney's uniform; Hope's cross is placed on the front of her skirt.

Viney feels proud to be dressed as a nurse in this old-fashioned way; after all, she has a good figure. She wonders when Hope received her nursing degree; she's proud of her, too. They're wearing white stockings and white lace-up shoes. All white in those days, like brides, like novices, none of those brightly colored figure-hiding smocks the nurses wear now.

They aren't working as nurses, though. They stand on either side of a very long conveyor belt contraption—it seems to go on forever—and Viney realizes that they're on an assembly line at a factory. They each hold a baby food jar filled with red paint in one hand and a fine, tiny-bristled paintbrush in the other. They have an important job: They're responsible for painting the red lips on baby dolls. It's painstaking work, the kind of work that women are good at. The dolls arrive in front of them, the conveyor pauses just long enough for them to apply two quick curving strokes to the doll babies, one for the upper lips, one for the lower, and then the conveyor moves them along again.

"Bye-bye, babies!" Hope shouts.

There are boy and girl babies in approximately equal number, Viney notices; also, the babies are naked and anatomically correct, a fact that pleases her. She does find it troubling, however, that all of the babies are white.

"Babies come in all colors, you know," she says.

"Not *our* babies," Hope replies.

With that, real human babies start arriving in front of them on the conveyor belt. *It's delightful!* Viney thinks. *We must be in heaven.*

The babies are not newborns, they're Gerber-age babies, four months or so, at that wonderful learning-to-smile stage. And they *are* smiling, which makes Viney and Hope's job even more challenging; it's tricky, painting those moving, smiling baby lips, keeping their hands steady as the babies squirm and try to roll onto their tummies. But Hope and Viney are meeting the challenge, and they are laughing.

And then—oh!—their own babies roll into view: Viney's three girls and Wally Jr. and Larken and Gaelan and Bonnie, and some other babies Viney doesn't recognize who are sound asleep.

These babies have clothes. They are dressed in infant-sized doctor and nurse costumes: the girls in exact replicas of the uniform Viney is wearing (right down to the starched hats and stockings and shoes and red crosses on their front left pockets) and the boys in white pants and lab jackets and white golfing shoes. Every one of the babies clutches a small white medical bag with a red cross on it.

The engine shuts off. The conveyor belt comes to a full stop.

"Break time!" Hope shouts. Viney is worried that her voice might wake the sleeping babies, but they don't stir.

Hope hoists herself to sit on the conveyor belt, unbuttons the top of her uniform, takes Wally Jr. in her arms, and starts nursing him. "Keep an eye on the rest of them, won't you, Viney?" Hope must be the shift supervisor.

"Am I supposed to feed them, too?" Viney asks, looking down at her chest. The red cross on her uniform looks much bigger than it was before, whereas her bosom has completely disappeared. "I'm flat as a pancake!" she proclaims.

Hope doesn't respond. She is rocking Wally in waltz time and singing: "The future's not ours to see, *que sera, sera . . .*"

Viney regards the babies. It occurs to her that painting their lips is really a very silly and unnecessary thing to do. Their mouths are a perfect shade of red—except for the sleeping babies, Viney suddenly notices; they do look a bit pale, and so she takes up her brush and jar of paint and goes to work on them. Her hand is tired; it keeps slipping. She's lost her rhythm, lost the knack. Even though these babies are perfectly still, Viney can't get their mouths to look right. Eventually she realizes that the sleeping babies aren't sleeping at all; they're dead. She wishes that she could cover them with something. She wishes that the conveyor belt would start up again and carry them away.

A wind swirls up, a wind so strong that it starts tearing the red crosses right off all the medical bags and uniforms and sending them flying. Soon they're everywhere, hovering and spinning like helicopter blades. Viney realizes that there is peril in these red crosses; they have razor-sharp edges, and the live babies—entranced—are reaching up for them. Viney scoops Gaelan and the five girls into her arms and places them at her feet. "Shoo!" she shouts, trying to angle her body protectively over the dead babies while at the same time swatting at the wasplike swarm of red crosses.

The conveyor belt starts up again, but soon it's moving too fast, accelerating like a freight train pulling away from the station and making the same rhythmic, clanging sound.

"Hope!" Viney calls. "Welly! I didn't mean it!"

Hope doesn't get off the train. She gathers the dead babies close—they don't look real anymore, they seem to have turned back into dolls—and clasps Wally to her breast. "I've got him, Viney!" she shouts, and the two of them are carried out of sight.

Suddenly there is so much dust and debris in the vortex of the wind that Viney can no longer see anything. Where are the babies? Panicked, she falls to her knees and starts searching for them with her hands, feeling mud and flattened cornstalks against her legs. Her white stockings will be ruined. Eventually she feels small hands grasping at her, desperately, frantically, as the wind howls.

"Aviator grip!" she cries. On either side, hands latch onto her wrists, but they're adult hands, and Viney is suddenly afraid. Who is holding her? The wind howls, the train clangs, the rain is stinging her eyes . . .

The church bell wakes her.

She listens, trying to quiet her heart by matching her inhales and exhales to the sounding of the bell and the resonating space between soundings. It must be midnight.

Is there anything you want from over there, Viney?

Larken and Gaelan's question still hangs in the air, demanding her attention, like something that she must get to but can't quite reach: a serving dish in the high cupboard over the fridge that is hardly ever used, but when needed is needed right away.

She gets up, puts on her slippers, and heads downstairs. Larken and Bonnie's bedroom door is closed; their light is off. All must be well with the two of them and Viney is relieved. She hates it when the children fight.

The kitchen smells of Mop & Glo; Larken must have cleaned the floor. That was thoughtful of her. Viney opens the fridge and pulls out a bottle of spring water, noting a big empty space on the second shelf. *Ah,* Viney thinks. *She must have eaten all the macaroni salad. That girl.*

Is there anything of Dad's you'd like to keep?

Yes, Viney reflects as she fills a glass and drinks it down. *There are many things of your father's that I want, but I doubt they will be found at his place of residence.*

Nevertheless, she realizes that that is where she needs to go.

From the coat closet, she retrieves Welly's light blue cardigan—the one he was wearing when he died—and checks to make sure that his keys are still in the pocket. They are. It suddenly seems strange to Viney that, after twenty-five years of sharing a bed, Welly never had a duplicate set of house keys made for her. Why was that? She had keys to his office, his car . . .

Putting on socks and tennis shoes, and throwing Welly's cardigan over her shoulders, she sets out on foot.

It is a hot and humid night. It has never seemed fair to Viney that heat and humidity should have such a hold on the nighttime as well as the day. She always means to ask Gaelan about that, why it is that some places get relief at night, but not us, not here.

Llewellyn's house is several blocks away, on a big, isolated corner lot at the very northeastern edge of town, just within the town limits. It's a house that's as close to Lincoln as you can be, Viney reflects, without leaving Emlyn Springs.

Welly loved going up to Lincoln—to the college football games mostly, but also to movies, restaurants, plays, concerts. Beatrice certainly offers those kinds of things, and it's closer, but Welly always wanted to get his entertainment farther away.

Was he always like this? Viney doesn't know. She's older than Welly by six years. That's a big difference when one is young, so even though they grew up in the same place, they didn't know each other, not really. Viney married Waldo at seventeen and started having babies right away. That was her life for many, many years—a husband and four children and all that goes with it: diapers and the croup, vaccinations and fever scares, solid food, toilet training, locking up the household poisons (vigilance, vigilance, so much vigilance!) and skinned knees and runny noses and, oh God, chicken pox! Head lice! They cried, she held them, she took their temperatures, patted their backs, smoothed their foreheads, combed and brushed their hair, helped them with their homework. She sang to them, too, and tickled them and wrestled with them, with Wally especially because boys need that kind of thing. And made hundreds, maybe thousands of school lunches and snacks, sat on hard, paint-chipped bleachers in all kinds of weather watching softball games and football games. And saved every Mother's Day card and Happy Birthday card they ever made. And shopped for groceries and cooked and cleaned and went to the Surf'n'Turf with her husband every year from their first anniversary to their last.

That time, how it flew! Her life didn't intersect with Welly's for years, although she knew of him: Llewellyn Jones, the oldest Jones boy, that smart handsome homegrown young man who everyone said could have been an opera singer if he'd wanted, could have had a music scholarship (who hadn't heard his beautiful singing voice in church and at every *Gymanfa ganu* ever held for the dead?) but who wanted to be a doctor instead, a *doctor,* and became one! Not only that, he came back! Came back to his hometown with his tall pretty wife, a girl named Hope who everyone liked at first but soon snubbed for her tallness and prettiness and eagerness, for her passionate love for all of them and their town—everyone except Alvina Closs, another miscreant, another oddball, because who goes to nursing school leaving four children to fend for themselves? Who does that?

For so long, Viney's life was as far removed from Welly's as if they'd grown up on opposite sides of the world. But after Hope and Viney became friends, another life began—a conjoined life. The fact that Hope's been gone for twenty-five years hasn't changed that in the least.

There it is. There's the mayor's house.

It's attractive enough in a 1970s kind of way—solid brick, split level, spacious—but Viney has never liked it. It has always seemed so sterile and uninviting, maybe because it was built from insurance money and in this case stands as a kind of monument to the Jones family tragedy, or maybe because Welly never did anything to make it homey. Outside, no flower boxes, no wind chimes, no flags; inside, white unadorned walls, monochromatic modern furniture. Of course, Hope was the artistic one when it came to decorating. All that work she did to restore the Jones farmhouse, all the care she took to furnish it with period antiques, create something beautiful and lasting . . . All gone.

During the six months it took to build this house, Welly and the children lived in the King's Castle Motel. It was hard arranging time to be together during those months, and it was then that they started having their quickies: after work—when Viney's children babysat Welly's kids at her house—and at lunchtime—when the kids were at school.

Viney is suddenly angry at the house and all it represents. They could have saved that insurance money, taken a trip. Why didn't they? Why didn't Welly and the children just move in with her, appearances be damned? They might as well have; every significant holiday, every birthday celebration—they all happened at Viney's house.

She unlocks the front door. The house has a stale smell. Moving through the darkened rooms, she turns on lights, opens windows. She notices a stray sock at the bottom of the stairs and frowns. Unlike Welly to leave a sock lying about. She looks up and sees that the stairs are strewn with them, socks of all colors, none of them matching. All the lost socks of the world have accumulated on this stairway, like a trail of bread crumbs, but leading where? To what? To the bedroom she never shared with him? To his study?

She's not ready to go up there, not yet. She heads for the kitchen.

Viney starts going through the fridge, throwing spoiled food into the garbage can. There's not much in there. She moves on to the freezer.

It's full of meat.

Red meat.

All kinds of meat.

Beef steaks, liver, hamburger, pot roast, sausages. There's even some venison in here.

She opens the cupboards.

They're crammed with junk food in bulk: endless bags of candy and cookies and chips, all manner of fatty and sugary products, enough to stock a 7-Eleven several times over.

Now she's mad as hell. Now she's *really* had it.

Grabbing a package of M&M's, a bag of Cheetos, and a can of pop, she stomps up the stairs, leaving the socks where they lay. She strides to the mayor's study and pauses at the closed door. Hell's bells, there could be a whole herd of cattle in here. There could be a set of firearms or the makings of a taxidermy business.

Not knowing what to expect, she flings the door open.

Nothing. Just a desk with a leather blotter, a chair, bookshelves, a couple of file cabinets, and, on the floor, more socks.

She moves across the room and stands in front of the file cabinets; each drawer is clearly marked: "Past taxes," says one, "Bills," says another, "House Insurance," "Health Insurance," "Medical Records," and so on. When she spots a drawer marked "Correspondence," she opens it and starts rifling through the files. There's not much here, business correspondence mostly, between Welly and medical equipment suppliers, that sort of thing. If there were love letters from Hope, they would have gone up with her; and Viney and Welly were never a couple to express their affection for each other on paper.

But here's something: a fat file marked "Sister City beg. 1980."

Viney knows from firsthand experience that the mayor kept excellent records (he insisted on making copies of all his outgoing correspondence) and was persnickety about organizing his papers. The oldest letter will be found in the very back of the file.

Bringing the file to the desk, Viney settles herself in the mayor's chair, kicks off her shoes, and opens the M&M's, Cheetos, and pop. She pulls out a carbon-copied letter and starts to read:

Dear Sirs, the letter begins, *and please forgive me if that is not the correct form of address. I have never corresponded with a monastic community before. I am writing in the interest of beginning a dialogue with you, the founders of our sister city. I realize that this may come as a surprise—Emlyn Springs has made no overtures to our sister city since shortly after the war ended. But I am hoping to rectify this state of affairs—partly because, as a newly elected member of the city council of Emlyn Springs, I feel a keen obligation to do whatever I can to keep our small town thriving, but also to act upon an idea that was dear to my wife's heart (she died in 1978). It was always her fervent wish that Emlyn Springs could one day be described in words other than "small and dying" and to that end, I would like to initiate a dialogue . . .*

Viney moves forward in time, letter by letter.

For the first two years, Welly and his correspondent—a monk named Brother Henry—speak in formal, businesslike tones. Viney reads with detached interest. The language of city government—much like the language of football—has always been a reliable soporific as far as Viney is concerned, and several times she finds herself nodding off. She really should go home.

Over time though, she notices Welly initiate a new language, one including words like *family, children, wife, illness* . . .

Another year passes: *guilt, punishment, penance, shame* . . .

Viney begins barreling ahead, reading only Welly's letters, skipping his correspondents' replies. She feels the slamming of heavy doors in her chest, as if she could still contain in that vault the revelations that Welly keeps pouring out onto the page without her permission.

Too late, too late. Her hands are shaking.

The telling of tales, the naming of names.

My wife, Hope . . . my mistress, Alvina . . .

Viney reads the entire file without looking at the clock.

By the time she arrives at Welly's most recent letter—taking note of
the cramped, down-sloping penmanship, the embittered tone . . .

Nothing ever changes . . . the same old story . . . lack of vision . . .

—it's nearly four A.M. The dairy farmers are awake.

. . . nearly twenty-five-years . . . and still I cannot . . . still I feel . . .

They are stirring, the people of her town, casting off whatever lives
they lived in their sleep—lives of gay, improbable adventure, or of
drowning, voiceless horror—and filling their hands with what is real,
what is here, what needs doing: bedclothes, coffee cups, buttons, combs.

Was there nothing of her in what he became? Was it always *wife* and
mistress to him, all the way to the end?

More aware than ever that she doesn't belong here, Viney puts on
her tennis shoes, pulls the laces up tight, and walks home. The stars
are still out.

No real point in going to bed now, she thinks, *I won't be able to sleep
anyway.*

By the time she walks back into her own kitchen the sun is starting
to come up. Larken will be leaving soon. Viney retrieves some textured
vegetable protein sausages from the freezer and a box of Bisquick from
the pantry.

It's a new day. She needs a new word.

She opens the dictionary at random, sets her finger on the page, and
finds "holochroal: having compound eyes with the visual area covered
by a continuous cornea—used esp. of certain trilobites."

What's a trilobite? she wonders, followed by, *How the hell am I going
to use* that?

Hope's Diary, 1962:
Elusive Pancakes

I've become obsessed with pancakes. Who would have believed such a simple thing could be so elusive?

L. is distraught over this, my latest compulsion, but when one's world is defined by domesticity and certain other matters that preoccupy young wives, things like making perfect pancakes take on great significance. All the activities of daily living—and one's successes or failures in measuring up to the title of "homemaker"—become metaphors. Nothing is what it is; it is all something else, it all has the potential to instruct, to give one insights, to condemn.

Buddhist monks probably know all about this. Prisoners too. The more restricted one's view, the more one is compelled to give meaning to what is available. It's how we rise to the challenge. We elevate the mundane. We sanctify the ordinary.

But back to pancakes. It is far more difficult to make a perfect pancake than one would imagine. All those short-order cooks all over America don't get nearly the respect they deserve. I don't remember my mother making pancakes for me. We were not a breakfasting sort of family. Cold cereal, bananas with milk and liberally sprinkled with sugar; once or twice perhaps an egg. Anything special in the way of breakfast we had out, on Sundays, and after church—as if our attendance in the Lord's House earned us an outing. We ate our pancakes at Essie's House of Pancakes in Germantown, where there was a lazy Susan full of syrups with the most unlikely colors. I always wanted to try the lime green-colored one—could it have been lime?—but was never offered the opportunity. Plain syrup was what was poured for me, caramel brown. And lovely igloos of whipped butter that melted instantly and glided across the pancake surface, creating a kind of self-generating skating rink.

Essie's pancakes were big! Gigantic! How in the world were they flipped? Maybe bigger spatulas are the secret. I've already sent L. out several times in pursuit of the perfect pancake-making skillet. I've started a collection.

So. Apart from the cooking implements, pancake success begins with generating perfect batter. There's a particular texture that is crucial—thin, a bit thinner than cake batter, but not much. Not too thin. Too thin produces crepes. Too thick, and the thing never gets done on the inside. There's an oozy, unappealing middle. Uncooked pancake batter doesn't have the allure or good taste of uncooked cake batter or cookie batter. No one asks to lick the spoons and bowls. Then there's the oil question: Should oil be added? Oil makes the batter heat up much more quickly, so there's the potential danger of burning the pancake and I've had multiple experiences with that as well.

Heating the fry pan to exactly the right temperature is also crucial. Not hot enough: The pancake doesn't cook through. Too hot: burning, smoke, fire alarms, the need for extinguishers, emergency professionals on the scene! All very exciting, but when the distraction has passed, one is still hungry for pancakes.

I've taken to writing off the first one. In my experience, it is absolutely impossible to produce a perfect pancake the first time. Or even the second, third, fourth . . . I suppose I'll keep trying. What else can I do?

There were two this time. Twins.

As if losing them one at a time isn't hell enough.

As if I need variations on the theme of miscarriage.

Chapter 11

As the Crow Flies

Rise and shine, princess! Daddy says.

Where are we going? Larken wonders, because his voice has that special sound that means they are taking a trip.

We're not going anywhere until you're ready, screwball! he answers. *Look at the time! Rise and shine!*

And then it's Viney's voice calling up from the kitchen: "Rise and shine! I fixed breakfast!"

Larken blinks her eyes, turns to squint at the other twin bed, hoping to find her sister there. It's still made up, unslept in.

She feels drugged. Evidence of last night's criminal behavior—the empty rocky road carton—has been rinsed and flattened and placed in a plastic bag and from there into her suitcase.

Closing her eyes again, Larken tries to replay the sound of her father's voice on a going-away morning.

Wake up, sunshine!

If they were driving west for a summer vacation, he would burst into her room when it was still dark, bellowing, "Up and at 'em, honey!" and coming over to give her a kiss and tousle her hair. "If we make good time and get to Grand Island by ten-thirty, we can stop for breakfast at Bosselman's. Come on, now. Let's hurry!"

If they were going up to Omaha for the day, to see a movie like *How the West Was Won* or *My Fair Lady,* he'd come in singing. "Wake up, princess! Time to put on your new pretty outfit!" and Larken would jump out of bed and find the outfit already laid out for her just as if it were the first day of school.

Omaha is not so far away, and yet Daddy can never get on the road early enough. They will stop somewhere special for pancakes and bacon and eggs, and at the theater they'll be treated to glossy souvenir programs and popcorn and candy and pop, and the movie will be so long that there will be an intermission, during which they'll buy more popcorn, more souvenirs, and then after the movie they'll have dinner somewhere special, and Daddy will say, "Don't you want another helping? Everybody order dessert now! Come on, let's splurge! It's a special day! No dieting allowed!" And then Mommy will start looking at her watch and saying, "We should leave pretty soon, Llewellyn, we don't want to be driving back after dark, we don't want to keep them up too late."

Finally they will head home, after dark because Mommy can never get Daddy to leave early enough, and when they arrive Larken will pretend to be asleep because then Daddy will carry her into the house and tuck her into bed and this is the sweetest, best, safest feeling in the world. Things look different at night when her father carries her inside; they have a grainy quality that makes Larken feel as though she herself is in a movie, an old-timey one. It's as though everything has already happened and she is watching it happen all over again.

There were so many going-away trips in the beginning, in what Larken has come to think of as the Age of Innocence: before they knew that Hope was sick, when she was just their clumsy, funny mother, always dropping things, always tripping over her feet, and always so sleepy on those rise-and-shine days. "Mommy is just not a morning person," Hope used to say. "I'm not like Daddy. In the morning, I'm as slow as molasses in January."

Larken isn't ready to get up yet. So she dozes again, hoping to summon a happy-going-away memory. Instead she is visited with a coming-home one.

It is twilight. They are driving back from spending the whole day in Omaha, where they saw *Paint Your Wagon* at the Indian Hills Theater, with its huge, wraparound, CinemaScope screen.

Larken is seven years old, all dressed up in an outfit she is wearing for the first time: a purple plaid taffeta skirt, a snug fitted purple velveteen vest with covered buttons, a white satiny blouse with a big floppy bow (she has rearranged the bow to conceal a dime-sized gravy stain she got at the fancy restaurant), white tights, and black patent leather shoes. Daddy likes her in purple—such a rare color for a child to wear, she feels very grown-up—and he bought this outfit for her at Hovland-Swanson, the fanciest store in Lincoln. Larken has been there with him, she's seen how solicitous the salesladies are, how Daddy sits like a king outside the dressing room on an enormous, circular ottoman while she tries on outfits and then comes out and models for him. But Daddy bought this outfit when he was in Lincoln on a football Saturday without her. The outfit was only a little bit small when they left this morning—and it felt nice and fresh and cool against her skin then—but they've been eating all day. The outfit is too small now, the blouse is sticking to her skin in places, and Larken's tummy is starting to hurt. She decides that, since they are on the way home and it will soon be dark, it might be all right if she unfastens the back of the skirt and undoes the bottom buttons of her vest. Maybe she could even untuck her blouse. She decides that she can; she's in the backseat behind Daddy and surely he won't notice. Besides, it's just them now, no strangers to look fancy for. She has a hard time getting the hooks and eyes undone; she has to suck in her tummy even more to do it, but finally she manages—and what a relief it is! Her stomach still hurts, though.

Clint Eastwood was in the movie, and a beautiful blonde actress named Jean Seberg, who Daddy tells her is from Iowa, which Larken finds very exciting since being from Iowa is almost like being from Nebraska. Daddy explains before the movie starts that Jean Seberg will not really be doing the singing. Someone else did the singing for her.

"You'll be able to tell," he whispers, "because her throat won't be moving."

Larken spends the next three hours looking very closely at Jean Seberg's throat whenever she sings. She doesn't understand how Jean Seberg can look like she's singing but not be singing. And if Jean Seberg *isn't* singing, who *is*? Where is the real singer hiding?

"See?" Daddy leans in to whisper every time there's a song. "You can tell, can't you?" and Larken nods, but she can't tell, not really. It looks to her as if Jean Seberg is singing every note.

Larken and her father are the only two people in the family who see the movie in its entirety; Bonnie fusses during the loud parts, and Gaelan gets scared every time there's a close-up of the faces, so Mommy spends most of the afternoon in the lobby with the two of them.

Hope has told Larken that Bonnie isn't as easy a baby as Gaelan was, but she's still pretty easy.

"Was I an easy baby?" Larken wants to know.

Hope always smiles at this question. "You were my *first* baby," she says, as if that explains everything.

Now they are driving home. Gaelan has fallen asleep with his head on Larken's shoulder; Bonnie sleeps in Hope's arms in the front. Larken has a good view of Mommy's face in profile; even in the waning light, she notices that her mother's cherry color is paler than usual.

Larken has perfected the art of playing possum; her parents talk differently when they think they are not being overheard and Larken likes this, likes the private, murmuring sound of their grown-up voices, so when Daddy says, "Are they asleep?" Larken quickly closes her eyes and lets her face go slack.

"Yes," Hope says, and sighs. "They're asleep." They drive on in silence. Larken squints at the stars and revels in the exotic feeling of being out so late at night.

And then suddenly Bonnie starts crying—not a fussy baby cry, but a hurt baby cry, as if she's put her hand on the stove. It's a horrible sound. "What?" Hope is saying, her voice terrified. "What happened?" and Daddy is pulling the car over to the side, dangerously close to the ditch, saying, "Jesus Hope! Did you drop her?"

"Oh, my God," Mommy says. She sounds sleepy or sad. "My hands. I can't."

And Daddy says, "Give her to me," and Mommy says, "No, it's all right, I've got her now. I'm sorry, I'm sorry, I didn't mean to."

Daddy pulls hard on the hand brake. Bonnie is wailing now. Gaelan sleeps on; he can sleep through anything. Daddy comes around to Mommy's side, opens the car door, takes Bonnie from her, and says, "Larken, are you awake?"

"Yes."

He comes back around to Larken's side of the car and opens the back door. Why isn't he closing the car doors? Larken wonders. Three of them are open and it's dark now and this strikes Larken as dangerous. "Hold your sister until we get home," he commands, placing Bonnie in Larken's arms. "Have you got her?"

"Yes, I've got her."

Daddy circles around the car again, slamming all the doors as he goes, one after another (*WHAM! WHAM! WHAM!*) and then hurries around to the front of the car again and gets back in.

Bonnie quiets almost instantly in Larken's arms. *I am good with babies,* Larken realizes suddenly. She has heard this expression; she feels amazed and a little proud to find that it applies to her. *I look good in purple, I have small feet, and I am good with babies.* Gaelan stirs and then goes back to sleep. *And I can stay awake because I'm the oldest.*

Hope cries on the way home. She is trying not to, but Larken can tell that she is because she's sniffling.

When they get to the blind driveway, Daddy pounds on the horn just like always, but quickly, as if the real danger is elsewhere. And when they get home, he doesn't carry anyone to bed. He doesn't even wait for them. He just gets out of the car, slams the door again, and disappears into the house. Larken and Hope and Gaelan and Bonnie are left in the car. Gaelan and Bonnie are still sleeping.

"I did a terrible thing," Hope says quietly. "A terrible, selfish thing."

Larken doesn't speak and they sit there in silence for a while. She thinks that Mommy has forgotten about them, but Hope turns around finally and looks at them. Then she gets out of the front seat and gets in the back with them.

"I'll take her now, sweetie," she says, easing Bonnie out of Larken's arms and into her own. "Gaelan," she says, and Gaelan starts. "Wake up, lambie. We're home. You need to get to bed. You too, Larken. I'm going to sit here for a while. I'll come inside in a bit and tuck you in."

When Larken closes the door, she looks into the backseat and sees Mommy there, looking down at Bonnie and crying. She's moving her mouth the same way over and over again, but it's dark inside the car and Mommy's not opening her mouth very much. Larken can't tell what she's saying but she's pretty sure it's not a prayer.

Years later, Larken and Gaelan drive up to Omaha by themselves and see another Jean Seberg movie. She does not sing in this one. It's terrible, one of those humorless airport movies that have since been parodied innumerable times; they were that bad.

And a few years after that they hear that Jean Seberg has committed suicide. Something to do with Black Panthers and the death of her baby, and they learn that she lived in Europe somewhere and spoke French—even though she was from Iowa!—and encountered in that foreign place a sadness too terrible to endure and so she took pills and died. So did that other blonde actress, Inger Stevens, who was also from the Midwest: she was in a TV show called *The Farmer's Daughter*.

Beginning with Jean Seberg, Larken becomes aware of pretty blonde actresses from middle America who become famous and then kill themselves.

"Larken!" Viney's voice forces Larken into wakefulness. "Come on down now! Your pancakes are getting cold!"

Good-bye and *I'll call you when I get there* and *Don't be a stranger, honey, come back soon* and she is back on the road.

When Larken imagines looking at Nebraska from above, she sees Tornado Alley as an actual boundaried region that is always hovering, ever-present, invisible to Doppler radar but completely obvious with the aid of some other, yet-to-be-invented kind of detection device. She imagines something like that which metastasizes over the earth in one of her most beloved childhood books, *A Wrinkle in Time*: a black insidious blight marking the southeastern corner of the state in the exact shape of one of those photo corners people use to adhere pictures to scrapbooks. Tornado Alley is an energetic curse, the Bermuda Triangle of the Cornhusker State, and Emlyn Springs is smack dab in the middle of it. Usually, Larken is delighted to shake the dust of her hometown from her feet and head north.

But today, as the last one to arrive, the last one to depart, she feels encased in an energy that is neither her mother's nor her father's. What color is she? Vaguely unhappy to go but not wanting to stay, she drives over to the Texaco to fill up the car, expecting to find Bonnie at work. But there's a CLOSED sign on the juice bar.

Pete Labenz appears from the garage wiping his hands as Larken turns off the engine and prepares to get out of the car. "Hey, Larken," he says. "I'll do that."

"Thanks, Pete."

"You headed back up to Lincoln?" he asks.

"Yep."

"Dyl!" he shouts back toward the garage. Dylan comes out, covered in grease.

"Hi, Larken!" he shouts, and then goes to work on the windows.

"Fill 'er up?" Pete asks.

"Yes, please."

The Labenz boys in person are never the Labenz boys as Larken remembers them. Her body remembers them, though—not in a carnal way, for Larken always chose her sexual partners from outside Emlyn Springs, but with shame and fear because who knew if they recognized what a whore she was back then. How could she be sure they weren't talking about her behind her back? And if so, aren't they still talking about her?

There's just no way around it. In Emlyn Springs, she is no one. People are always changing. When they live in close proximity, the change is gradual and everyone is a part of it. But when you move away and then come back, who do you present? The person you were, the one everybody knows? Or the person you are, who (let's face it) is a stranger? Outside the clearly defined protocols of the *Gymanfa*, Larken feels like nothing but a phony.

Al hangs up the phone and comes out of the office. He's put on weight, but he carries it well. "Hey, Larken."

"Hey, Allan."

"Goin' back to Lincoln, huh?"

"Yeah. It's time."

He leans closer. "We'll keep an eye on Viney and Bonnie, no worries."

"Thanks. I appreciate that." She decides to risk a veiled question: "I guess Bonnie decided to take another day off."

"No, she opened and closed early today. You just missed her. Hey, guys! Bonnie say anything about where she was going?"

"Hardware store, maybe," Pete answers. "Said she needed some lumber."

"She told me she was going to the grocery store," Dylan adds.

"That's okay," Larken says. "I just wanted to see her one more time before I headed back."

"You want me to call over to Schlake's and see if she's there?"

"No thanks, Al," Larken replies, already fearing that she's revealed too much. She pays and gets on her way. All three of the Labenz boys wave good-bye.

Surely Bonnie is on her bicycle. Where else would she be? Larken leaves a message with the Williams girls to please have Bonnie call her this afternoon.

She crosses Bridge Street, glancing to her left, where, about half a mile away, Flying Girl's tree still forms a link between the north and south sides of the ravine. Why hasn't anyone taken that tree down?

She could try driving around for a while. She might find her.

But no, she has to get back. Fall term starts the day after tomorrow. Christ! She's had none of her usual prep time.

There's more activity now, signs of life as the folks of Emlyn Springs—released from their moratorium on working and their obligations to Larken's dead father—are on the road. Some have already done their errands and are heading back; she passes several farmers, folks she knows; they lift the tips of their fingers from the top of the steering wheel in acknowledgment.

"Blind driveway," she says, and honks.

The sound acts like the catalyst to a magic trick, releasing a universal perturbation of birds. They spring up from the ditches and explode out from the whiskery vegetation covering the bluff. They seem to come from everywhere and are unaccountably agitated.

Larken leans her head to the side, trying to follow their path.

Up ahead, a large, sleek crow is on the ground being swarmed by smaller birds, starlings maybe, as if the crow poses a threat—but there are no trees nearby, no nests. Is it in possession of something the flock desires?

She drives on, noticing more birds crowd together on the power lines, emit harsh cries, feign injury. But this is not the time of eggs and hatchings and all those protective parental instincts. It's nearly autumn.

There is a sudden swirl a few yards from her windshield, a wild descent as of an unbound manuscript let loose on the wind. It is a moment before she realizes that it is another bird she is seeing, a hawk or maybe even an owl, and all at once the chaotic disorganized shape distills, solidifies, and dives with a spearlike precision to the right side of the highway, into the ditch, where some small inconsequential thing must have been spotted, targeted from up above, and is already dead, or dying.

Here comes the billboard: *Thanks Mom! I got born!* it proclaims. The words inhabit an attenuated cartoon balloon that looks like a cigar arising from a creepy-looking drawing of a newborn with a full set of teeth. Surely the same artist did both sides of the billboard. *God made me,* the billboard reads, *Mom and Dad adopted me!*

And later, back home, she tries to work while she waits for Bonnie to call. She eats the cookies and brownies that Viney sent home for Esmé, achieving the sensation of a full-term pregnancy—a distended stomach, her diaphragm unable to descend on the in-breath, she can only sip air by the quarter-teaspoon—a new sensation arises, unfamiliar and disturbing. Her chest feels like an aviary, alive with papery, irregular flutterings.

So this is it, she thinks, too sated on starch and sugar to feel fully afraid. *Cardiac arrest. They'll find me in the morning, facedown in the chapter on Rogier Van der Weyden and* The Ascension.

But after a time, the birds in her chest quiet, taken down perhaps by something bigger, fiercer, more predatory, more powerful. Or maybe they're simply wearied, exhausted to death by their failed attempts to escape. And whatever else lives in the cage that holds Larken's heart is once again still.

Hope's Diary, December 1963:
All I Could See Was Her

    I'll never ever doubt the occurrence of miracles ever again, never slander my own body, no matter how often it has let me down. All has been redeemed by this little girl, this warrior. Or should it be warrioress? Given what the two of us have been through, I think we deserve a gender-specific version of that title.

    The OB just left. Pompous ass. For a full week he pooh-poohed my insistence that yes, really, truly, the pain is quite severe, it's hard to walk, I think the baby is coming: "Just wait until the pains move around to the <u>front</u>, dear," he kept saying. "Then you'll know you're in labor." The goddamn pains never did move around to the front, and then there were new pains I knew to be wrong and I started bleeding. God knows how many traffic laws Llewellyn broke en route to Beatrice, and in the ER I heard them say, "She's abrupting, get her to the O.R. <u>now!</u>" and then the C-section, the "twilight sleep" they call it, but I battled through with enough awareness to realize that there was no cry, no sound at all, and when they rushed her to another part of the room—a blur of white and maroon, as if she'd emerged from my womb slathered in whipped cream and raspberry sauce—I knew something had gone wrong. L. clutching my hand, his face blanched, his eyes frightened above the sterile mask, and then finally, <u>finally</u> a hearty, pissed-off howl, just the thing you long to hear from your newborn baby, Whitman's "mighty YAWP!" if ever there was one, and then they brought her to me, swaddled and wailing and with eyes big and brown like her father's and wearing a face so fierce you'd have thought she'd been kidnapped. "This is NOT what I'd planned!" she seemed to say with her expression.

Meanwhile, the doctor reappeared, his intrusion triggering a kind of chemical revulsion. I felt allergic to him. He puttered around doing doctorly things and then started asking annoying questions related to my eyesight. Kept demanding that I look this way and that, follow his finger, focus on the little light at the end of his pen, which I found impossible. "Can't we do this later?" I wanted to say. "We are a brave new world unto ourselves, this baby and I, and will not readily admit ready access to this planet that is us. No trespassers allowed! We banish incompetent, heedless obstetricians brandishing penlights and trivial questions! Ask us something important!"

But I remained speechless. I was aware of a feeble light tracing blurry lines through space, like a sparkler, the way a sparkler produces a kind of magical writing, visible for an instant and then you realize that what you're seeing is an illusion, a shadow light, a visual echo that still hangs there. A remnant of time passed, a record of something that only just happened, a vapor trail, a ghost. Something that was, but is no more.

Someday I will tell my girl about the babies that came before her, her older brothers and sisters. But maybe she already knows.

After so long a time, for her to finally be here.

Of course my vision isn't normal, Doctor.

All I can see is her.

PART TWO

The Mother Plant

I am a history
A memory inventing itself
I am never alone
I speak with you always
You speak with me always
I move in the dark
I plant signs

—Octavio Paz

Hope's Diary, 1964:
Hail Mary at the IGA

Larken sleeping, thank God. I should take a nap too but have to write about the morning.

Went up to Beatrice. I wanted to go to the IGA to get a few special things for the dinner party Saturday that I know the Moores don't carry here in town. What was I thinking? Stupid. Larken doesn't take kindly to any deviation from our normal routine. I know this. I know it well so it's my own fault.

She didn't fall asleep in the stroller after our walk—she might be teething, anyway that's what Alvina Closs told me at the post office the other day and a woman with four children probably knows what she's talking about. (There's another reason to feel inadequate: Alvina Closs, young widow with four children, went back to nursing school and is about to graduate. How on earth does she do it?) Anyway, I thought if I put Lark in the car and drove up to Beatrice, she'd go down and I could do some shopping with her sleeping in the cart.

But she still didn't fall asleep and because they were doing road work again at the blind driveway and had everything narrowed to one lane, the going was slow and we didn't even pull into the parking lot until 11:30, almost lunchtime. Still, she seemed fine. Very interested in the clouds today—a big wind, and much shape-shifting in the sky. Maybe she's turned a corner, I thought. Maybe she's becoming more adaptable. All the way in the car she stared out the window and slobbered happily until her chin was glistening and the front of her sleeper was soaked. Totally awake, bright-eyed and bushy-tailed.

I checked her diaper, did a quick change in the parking lot, and by then she was starting to get a

little fussy, but only a little. So we trundled
into the store.

It was as if every other mother in Gage County
had the same idea, all of us stir-crazy at the near
end of winter, home alone with our babies and toddlers, desperate for any excuse to get out of the
house, and what better place than the grocery store!
Cabin fever, spring just around the corner, all of
us dying for some form of social contact even if it
was born out of necessity. The whole crop of new
babes were there. And I swear, every blessed one of
them was asleep except Larken.

I'd made a list—I know I had—but when we got inside the store I couldn't find it anywhere. I hate
it when that happens. And it happens frequently. I
feel conspired against by the wind, the way it grabs
at things you think you've battened down. So I was
shopping without a list. The whole trip was really
doomed from the git-go.

In the produce section, there was a beautifully
coifed blonde woman with an equally blonde and beautifully coifed little girl, three years old maybe.
Dressed in identical dotted swiss mother-daughter
outfits. They looked like they belonged in a
magazine.

I kept wishing my hair was more perfect, my wardrobe spiffier. Shouldn't I be able to be a mother
without losing my good grooming habits? I felt
decidedly unspiffy and wished Larken wasn't slob-
bering so much and was dressed in something besides a sleeper, something like one of those highly
impractical but darling little baby girl outfits
Lillian keeps giving her: pink and ruffled and held
together by impossibly small buttons shaped like
flowers or baby ducks and which my hands cannot
manage even when we're not in a hurry.

The mother gave the little girl a cantaloupe to hold, then went about explaining and demonstrating various squeezing and thumping techniques. The child mimicked her with perfect, calm obedience. The mother looked up once, saw me staring, and smiled beatifically. Her teeth were perfect. There was a newborn in her shopping cart, too, a little boy guessing from the blue blanket. Of course, he was sleeping, hands balled into little fists just under his chin, like a boxer-in-training.

Larken and I look so different—she's got L.'s coloring and physique and a face that belongs to no one but herself. No one would know we were mother and daughter, I don't even think matching outfits would identify us as kin.

In the canned veg section, another mother was speaking angrily to her toddler. That part of it I could relate to—I don't think one ever really comes to the feeling of being at the end of your tether until you're a mother—but she was manhandling him in a way that made me furious.

In frozen foods, another mother—cool as a cucumber to use the appropriate cliché—was trying to buy some Swanson's TV dinners while holding a screaming baby. This must have inspired Larken—or at least reminded her that she hadn't had a nap—and she joined in.

That did it.

Soon, the eyes of the entire store were upon us. My girl can outcry any baby in Christendom, I'd bet everything I have on it. Her cries when she gets wound up are truly horrific, so full of rage and frustration you'd think she was being tortured. I abandoned the cart and fled before someone called Child Welfare Services.

On the drive home (L. fell asleep, of course), I realized that I'd looked at every woman with a child

as competition. There's suddenly this compulsion—
not just to be a "good" mother, but to be the "best"
mother.

No one expects fathers to be perfect. Fathers are
not bombarded with images of themselves, serenely
cradling a newborn, lounging about, immaculately
and stylishly clad with their equally pristine
toddlers.

Why didn't God come into the world as a woman,
one who gave birth? That expression—"God couldn't
be everywhere, so he invented mothers"—is amusing
until one examines its implications. If God came
into the world as a baby girl and lived the life
of a mother, then he would have <u>really</u> understood
something about humankind and the complexity of
love.

When I lose my patience with Larken, I feel like
the world's most unfit mother, but Christ, doesn't
anyone else have a child that cries and cries nonstop for hours on end and then finally out of sheer
exhaustion falls into a sound sleep, but only at
five P.M. so that the hell of it is she'll be awake
again sometime in the middle of the night, nee-
dling, needing, something, who knows what because
the damn thing didn't come with instructions.

I really should take a nap.

No.

SHIT.

There's Larken. Awake.

Help me help me help me help me help me help me
help me help

Well, <u>that</u> was grim.

It's been a few days since I've written. I vowed
not to return to these pages until I was capable of

something besides babbling incoherently, and/or whining.

I'm snatching some time while waiting for Llewellyn—one of his patients just called. Why is it that medical emergencies always begin occurring at suppertime and persist until dawn?

L. takes the issue of patient/doctor confidentiality very seriously. An ethical man, my L. All the secrecy and nocturnal comings-and-goings are starting to make me feel like the wronged wife in a melodrama. Some women's husbands have mistresses; mine has a medical practice.

I am starting to worry about how hard L. is working. His patients come from as far away as a hundred miles in all directions, and L. is rare in that he's willing to travel: a real country doctor, the last of a dying but still much-needed breed. The success of his practice—and its growth—is pleasing, but I can tell that L. is very tired.

Anyway, not sure when he'll return. He said he'd call, but we haven't heard anything yet. I'm keeping dinner warm in the oven in the hope he'll be back soon and able to spend some time with Larken before her bedtime. She's busy at the moment rearranging the contents of the bottom kitchen drawer; my time at these pages is directly dependent upon how long she'll be able to amuse herself. (Note to self: Buy more Tupperware!)

So. I'm feeling better, at least for the moment. Ran into Alvina Closs again, at Olson's Drugstore this time, both of us on errands related to our firstborn children, as it happened: me in search of teething medicine for my four-month-old, she in search of acne cream for her teenaged son. Alvina (she asked me to call her Viney) is one of the few women in town who doesn't look at me like a stranger—

even though L. and I have been here for two years
now.

We had a great chat about colicky babies and those
hellish hours between four and six o'clock in the
afternoon. She commiserated with me on both subjects, was especially funny about the latter, saying, "Why do you think God invented Happy Hour?" I
laughed so hard I almost fell over.

She invited me to her house for a cup of coffee;
I was worried about interrupting Larken's routine,
but I've been so lonely that I agreed, figuring
there would be hell to pay and we'd have to leave
soon. Instead, Viney held the baby and rocked her
until she dozed off. My Larken, asleep in a strange
house! I couldn't believe it.

"What's your secret?" I asked.

She laughed. "No secret. She just knows that I'm
not you."

Viney put Larken down in the first-floor bedroom, closed the door, and we proceeded to chat
for an hour and a half. Adult to adult! What a
treat it was.

Viney asked me why it was that L. chose to open
his practice here, and I told her how it was mostly
my doing, how I'd fallen in love with Emlyn Springs
the first time I came here.

"I can't say that I've ever heard of anyone falling in love with a town before," she said. "At least
not a town like this one."

"You sound like Llewellyn. I know Emlyn Springs
isn't exactly thriving"—and Viney laughed at this—
"but there's so much to love about this place."

"Well, we could certainly use some fresh blood
around here, that's for sure."

I don't know what came over me—probably I just got
carried away by the fact that I was in the presence
of another adult—but I took Viney's comment as per-

mission to give voice to some of the things I've been thinking about, and started chattering: "There's so much I hope to do here once the baby is older and I have some time. Hazel Williams told me there used to be an opera house here, is that true?"

"My grandmother used to talk about that. And a fine hotel, too."

"So many things have been let go—I know that a lot changed when the railroad stopped coming through, but I just don't think that's any reason for giving up on a place. It's beautiful here, people just need to have faith that this town doesn't have to be a dead end. Do you know what I mean?" Having uttered these words (and now transcribed them), I feel a bit Pollyanna-ish, like a billboard for the Better Business Bureau or the Rotary Club, but there you have it: It's how I truly feel. I would like to be part of making some positive changes here: see the library's collection augmented, become involved in restoring the downtown area, maybe get a community theater started up again, a historical museum. All those empty downtown buildings just going to waste. It breaks my heart, when there's a hundred constructive ways they could be used.

Viney patiently listened to me ramble on—I feel so foolish now for having monopolized the conversation.

I told her that I was in awe of her—being able to go back to school while raising four kids.

"You'd be surprised how many people in this town disapprove," she said.

I found this astounding. "I can't imagine anyone not admiring you for what you're doing for your family."

"That's a nice thing for you to say. But when you've lived here as long as I have, folks expect you to behave a certain way. It's as if they've already imagined your life and get truly, deeply upset if you don't play your part the way they've written it."

"But nobody has any expectations of me, surely."

"Oh, but they do, honey!" Viney said. "You'd be surprised."

"Well then, I'll just have to do my best to meet them."

She laughed. "I can't see that happening."

"What do you mean?"

She smiled and shrugged. "I could be wrong. Oh! Here's my kids . . ."

Larken didn't even wake up when I put her back in the stroller; she slept in the car on the way home, and then another hour, and finally woke up cheery as could be. And here we are.

I keep thinking about what Viney said—how people have expectations of me. It distressed me to hear that folks could be so close-minded about her going back to school. She's so brave, reinventing herself after a tragedy. I'm trying to imagine how I'd react if L. died and left me a young widow. It's too awful to contemplate.

Well, in any event, I feel as though I've made a friend.

Viney's graduating from nursing school soon. She told me that she'll look for work in Beatrice. Will talk to L. about hiring her. Lord knows he could use the help. And—quite selfish of me!—if she can work in Emlyn Springs I'll see her more often.

Must go. Larken bored with Tupperware and eyeing the extension cord with interest.

Chapter 12

Wooing Wales

All this time and attention given over to the newly dead has an economic impact, of course it does, but it's minor really and no one grumbles. The cost of living in Emlyn Springs is small. And among the lessons impressed upon youngsters—*Always wear light-colored clothing at night . . . When walking on a street without a sidewalk or a shoulderless road, always walk* against *the traffic, on the left*—is one related to funeral preparedness: *Always have at least one week's worth of money and supplies set by.* Those who are caught unprepared—for whatever reason, no questions asked—are assisted by a closely monitored community fund specifically allocated for the purpose.

The shortest time between deaths—and the longest period of enforced unemployment—was back in 1943, when the town lost three boys from the Groathouse family in a single hour during the Battle of Midway. Those boys were buried side by side and on the same day, as they would have wanted, but they were mourned individually, consecutively: George Jr. first since he was the oldest, then Harold, and then young Jerry. The town shut down for three whole weeks. At the time, it hardly seemed long enough.

The longest they've ever gone without a death was thirty-seven months, and everyone agrees that was a blessed era in the town's history. However, when death finally returned to Emlyn Springs to claim Mrs. Gladys

Hurd Jones (1883–1985) and it was time to bring her *Gymanfa* to a close, folks were horrified to discover that in the interim some of the young people had forgotten the Welsh lyrics to the national anthem and the Nebraska fight song. The community council quickly enacted a measure mandating the singing of those two songs at all town gatherings.

That familiar tourist-enticing phrase, *a bustling small town*—a phrase implying successful commerce, a booming economy, and an energized population—would not be applicable to Emlyn Springs on any day but this, the first day after the last bell is tolled. And even then, "bustling" would be stretching things. *A sauntering small town* would be nearer the truth.

True: YES, WE'RE OPEN signs are going back up all over town, but at a lackadaisical pace and with guarded enthusiam. After all, somebody else could die at any moment and it would be SORRY, WE'RE CLOSED all over again.

The dead fathers are taking up their notebooks and paintbrushes with caution. The dead mothers—usually so eager to take flight—are circling the premises, as if awaiting a go-ahead from the traffic controller.

If anyone could be said to be bustling today, it is the youngest daughter of Emlyn Springs' most recently deceased citizen, Bonnie Jones.

She should be exhausted—the oppositional energies excited by unearthing the Artifact and then arguing with her sister kept her awake all night—but instead she is vibrating, possessed of the glassy-eyed, lunatic resolve one sees in the faces of the sleep-deprived.

Bonnie made productive use of her nocturnal hours. First she opened her current scrapbook to an empty page and wrote the heading *POSSIBLE CANDIDATES*.

She then made a list of every man she knows ("man" in this case being defined as any unmarried male over the age of eighteen excluding her brother). It was a depressingly short and uninspiring list.

This prompted her to turn to another scrapbook page and write, *HOW TO INCREASE LIST OF POSSIBLE CANDIDATES*. She drew a bubble around this phrase and stared at it. As soon as a response came to mind, she drew a line from the first bubble, attached a second bubble to it, and wrote the phrase *MEET MORE MEN* inside.

She went on like this, tethering bubbles together, forming a genealogy of logical responses and questions: the *MEET MORE MEN* bubble led to the *HOW?* bubble, which produced *ATTEND MORE SOCIAL EVENTS,* which gave birth to *ICE CREAM SOCIALS? ELKS PANCAKE FEED? SING IN CHURCH CHOIR? THURSDAY NIGHT CONTRA DANCING IN BEATRICE? GO TO BARS?* and then, triumphantly: *JUICE BAR!* Bonnie has no idea why this technique works, but she swears by it.

JUICE BAR! begat *MORE CUSTOMERS = MORE MEN!,* which begat *INCREASE ADVERTISING!,* which begat numerous generations of ideas, so that by the time the page was full, Bonnie had resolved to make sandwich boards and place them outside strategic locations with reliably high-density male populations (Grumpy's Sports Grill, W.W. Seed Sales, Grell's Ford dealership, Schlake's Hardware, Burke's Auto Supplies, the Farmer's Co-op), put an ad in the Beatrice newspaper, and rename several items on the menu. For example, "Bugs' Favorite" will be henceforth known as "Yang Stimulator," "Orange Crush Medley" will go by the name "Turbo Charger," and "Spring Bee Cleanser" will change to "Man of Steel Tonic."

Bonnie tends to the avocado plants and makes her breakfast smoothie and then sets out for the juice stand. She'll skip her usual trip to the cemetery; Miss Elfyn can't reveal anything more significant than what Bonnie has learned in the past twenty-four hours.

And there's no need to go looking for artifacts either; Bonnie has found the artifact of all artifacts. She's cleaned and polished it at least; it's hanging on a large nail at the head of her bed: an aluminum and rubber star with sunbeam spokes rising over a twin-sized Posturpedic. In time, a plan and a purpose for the Artifact will be revealed. Till then, she'll keep it close. Maybe its proximity will exert a guiding influence on her dreams.

At the mayor's house, Viney too is back at work. She puts in a load of laundry—kitchen towels, bath towels, the *plethora* of unmatched socks. (Viney's mispronunciation of this word conjures visions of a female Welsh wood sprite: *Pleh-THOR-a.*) She vacuums and scours and dusts.

She calls the food bank in Beatrice, asking if they'd be interested in a donation. They'll take it happily if she's willing to drive it up.

Viney considers. She can't bear the thought of donating junk food to people who are already nutritionally deprived; she'll cart it all back to her house until she decides what to do with it.

As for the meat, besides being a symbolic reminder of the mayor's *men-DICK-can-see*, Viney feels repulsed by the idea of spending an hour in a car with thawing animal flesh. "I'll send it by taxi," she says, taking hold of a pen. "What's your address?"

She heads upstairs to the bedroom and starts going through drawers and closets, bundling up Welly's clothes for the Goodwill. She shakes out each item, assessing it thoroughly before refolding it carefully and putting it into a box. She expects at any moment to be moved to sadness by a belt loop or a button. But she feels fine. This isn't difficult. The mayor certainly prided himself on his appearance, but Viney realizes that she's never associated the man with fashion. For years, whenever she's pictured Welly in abstentia he's been dressed simply, informally, either in his boxer shorts or his birthday suit. On his feet: Romeo slippers or Lee Trevino golf shoes.

She's been thinking off and on about a conversation she had with Welly years ago. Or maybe it's many conversations all mashed together. Memory works that way sometimes, condensing time so that one distinct recollection is distilled from many diffuse ones. It's an invention of course, this memory, a kind of lie, but through the passage of time this designed memory acquires authority. It becomes true. It's put into a container and shelved until its relevance becomes apparent. So often, Viney has noticed, certain memories insist on being preserved without letting the rememberer know for the longest time why.

This conversation—in its distilled and designed form—takes place in November of 1980. It revolves around—of all things—city government.

"'Mayor-strong,'" Welly was saying. "That's the form of government we've got here. It means that the mayor has the right to hire and fire city employees without the approval of the city council."

The year suggests at least some of the memory's significance; she and Welly were finding their way, slowly learning to speak of subjects that did not include Hope.

They were at Viney's house, postcoitus, in the early afternoon—this was the setting for most of their significant conversations, no matter what the subject—and Welly was studying the Emlyn Springs charter.

"We're a second-class city," he continued. "In a first-class city like Lincoln they have a mayor-weak system. Everything up there has to be approved by the council."

Viney didn't know a thing about city government. She wasn't really that interested. She'd never run for office—presiding over her own unruly life took all the governing skills she possessed—and she generally found community meetings to be an exercise in frustration. All in all she'd rather spend her time watching a good science program or one of those British comedies on PBS.

But on this day it was so good to see Welly excited about something, enlivened in a way he hadn't been for years, that Viney did what all good women do when the significant men in their lives are earnestly explaining something (the complex mechanism by which disk brakes operate, for example, or the grossly unfair system of ranking college football teams): She *pretended* to be interested.

"Huh," Viney said in a perky, *that's-sooo-interesting* inflection.

Welly had surprised everyone in town—no one more than Viney—by running for city council. His passions had always been medicine and music. He certainly hadn't demonstrated any inclination toward community activism; that was Hope's domain. Harlan Beck, a retired dentist, also came out of the woodwork that year and got himself elected as mayor. Emlyn Springs hadn't seen that much change in city government for decades. The always-reliable naysayers in town were making it sound like a coup d'etat instead of a democratic election.

"I'd never have guessed that," Viney went on, "about the mayor having that kind of power, I mean. It seems to me that the city council rules the roost around here."

"Exactly. That's the problem."

"Estella mostly," Viney added tersely, "and whoever she can bully into going along with her." *I never could stand that woman,* she thought. *Neither could Hope.*

"Estella is in for a surprise. Harlan is going to change things. Get this town running the way it's supposed to."

"Well, I say, good for him for trying. And good for you for getting in there with him."

"I've got a lot of ideas, you know," Welly continued. "Things I'd like to see happen."

"Of course you do."

Viney felt the conversation finally coming to a close. She snuggled closer to Welly. She was ready to move on to another topic, talk about going over to Branson next weekend to see Burt Reynolds doing the Walter Matthau part in *Hello, Dolly!* at the dinner theater. That would be fun.

"She'd be proud of you, you know," Viney added quietly. "Really proud."

Welly gave her a pinched look. "I'm not doing it for her," he said.

The hell you're not, Viney thought, but chose not to share this insight. Welly still sometimes lapsed into treating her like a mistress instead of his dead wife's best friend, like an intruder instead of a co-conspirator—as if their lives weren't entwined by choice, part of a long-standing agreement between the three of them.

"So. What ideas are you referring to?"

"Nothing specific," he grumbled, "and probably nothing I could make happen anyway."

"Don't be so down. You never know."

"It just that, if anybody proposes anything big, anything that takes . . . not work, it's not that, people here aren't afraid of work . . . It's vision, I guess. Farsightedness. Risk. God forbid anything in this town should change for the better. God forbid we should try to succeed, make ourselves into something else."

I've made myself into something else, Viney wanted to say, *and so have you,* but instead she remarked, "I know you're excited about being on the council, and it's a wonderful thing, but you're going to have to be realistic or you'll make yourself crazy. Not everybody here has your drive, Welly. Most people here are fine with the way things are."

"That's exactly what I mean!" he said, flinging off the covers and getting out of bed. "That's small-town life in a nutshell." And then he clamped his mouth shut in a way that made it look like he had a dozen aspirins lodged behind his wisdom teeth and started to get dressed. "We should get back to the office."

He could be that way sometimes, at least in private. Pessimistic. Bitter. A damned pain in the ass, frankly, when he succumbed to that Sad Sack mentality. He seemed to save this side of his personality exclusively for the women in his life; it was something Hope and Viney talked about frequently. In public, he was charming, suave, a real bridge-builder. Everybody loved Llewellyn Jones. But when he was alone with Viney—and even sometimes the kids, she'd seen it—he could turn sour and hurtful, without any warning. *Mercurial* was a word Alvina Closs learned years ago.

"If you hate it here so goddamn much, why don't you just leave?" she sometimes said when he got like this, and then regretted it. *Why don't you just leave?* was one question they both knew the answer to.

Moving on to the study—where Viney has divided the contents of one old file into two new ones (labeled respectively "Sister City Business" and "Nobody's Goddamn Business but Yours and Mine HOW COULD YOU *DO* THIS??!!") Viney calmly examines the contents of the business file a second time, then a third.

Realizing that this set of letters and that single distilled, twenty-three-year-old memory is as close to a divine directive as she's likely to get, Viney sighs, picks up the phone, calls the country club, and gets Bud Humphries on the line.

"Is there much on the agenda for the meeting tonight?" Viney asks. "Besides formally electing you as the interim mayor, I mean?"

"Gosh, Viney," Bud says. "I don't think so."

Viney hears the light, chiming sound of drinking glasses being put away. Like the rest of Emlyn Springs, Bud has gone back to work. He retired from his contracting business a decade ago, but soon after that his wife died, his unmarried sister moved in, and staying at home wasn't to his liking, so now he tends bar part-time at the country club.

"Sorry to bother you your first day back."

"It's no bother. Things are moving pretty slow. How're you doing?"

"I'm fine, Bud. So, the agenda?"

"Hold on a minute. I was just working on it. I've got it here somewhere."

Mayor-strong, Viney thinks. *Shit. Bud's a sweetheart, but he'd fall over if you so much as blew on him.*

"Oh, heck, Viney. I can't find it. Can you stay on the line? I mighta left it back in the kitchen."

"Sure, Bud. I'll hold."

A family death leaves so many emotions in its wake; sadness isn't the only thing. It's not even the most dominant one. All those TV movies about people dying: Viney hates them. They bear no relationship to the way things really are: the dying speaking poetically about their feelings, photographed so that they're all soft around the edges, their suffering accompanied by a musical score that's so corny it's comical. The words of the dying in movies are always significant, too, clearly enunciated, and profound. Viney doesn't buy this for a minute. Who in their right mind would be inclined to speak when they're at death's door?—much less speak with eloquence. If they do have something to say, Viney is sure it would be something like *oh shit* or *Jesus Christ* or *oops*.

And the living! In the movies they are stoically silent and still. They are . . . *complacent,* that's the word—not pissed off and confused and hurt and overflowing with questions that take up so much real estate in the mind that there's hardly room for anything else, not making grocery lists or paying bills or even brushing your teeth. That's how it really is.

Viney has learned that there's nothing for it after the death of a loved one: *Doing* is what's called for, early on when one is still *capable* of doing, before the real face of grief reveals itself and you're knocked to your knees with a particular and uncurable kind of fatigue. *Grief bacon*. That's what the Germans call it.

"Are you still there, Viney?" Bud says, coming back on the line.

"Yes, Bud," Viney answers. In the background, Tennessee Ernie Ford sings about loading sixteen tons and owing your soul to the company store. Viney hasn't heard that song for years. She didn't remember it as being so upbeat, so *bouncy*. "I'm still here."

"Just had a coupla customers come in. I'm still looking. I just can't think where I put it . . ."

Hurry hurry hurry, Viney thinks, because already she is feeling as though the effort is too much, what she is initiating with this simple phone call is a lost cause. "I'll hold," she says, sinking into the mayor's desk chair with a sudden weariness that makes her feel as though she'll never stand up again.

*   *   *

Bonnie arrives at work earlier than usual. The Texaco isn't even open yet. After letting herself into the juice stand, she heads for the cash register, making sure she has enough change for the day.

On the wall overhead is a calendar; as Bonnie starts to flip the calendar forward to September, she realizes that there's something else she must do in response to recent revelations.

Turning back to August, she examines the squares occupied by her scrawled handwriting: birthdays, holidays, community meetings, reminders to pay bills, buy groceries, mow the lawn for the Williams girls, volunteer at St. David's Home for the Elderly. She is looking for a different kind of notation, one related to this mechanical mess called her body.

Because of the damage done to her reproductive system during the tornado of 1978, Flying Girl's menstrual cycle is hardly cyclical; it's not even a reliable monthly occurrence. When she does menstruate, she bleeds weakly and the blood itself is pale and watery, as if her body is just going through the motions.

Up to now, Bonnie has had a perfunctory attitude when it comes to the tickings of her biological clock, only occasionally remembering to note significant bodily occurrences on her calendar. She does this through the use of stickers.

On the day her period begins, she affixes Cinderella's broom to the calendar. Gold stars ranging in number from one to five indicate her period's heaviness. Sometimes Bonnie feels an unusual sensation at the presumed location of her ovaries, a kind of arrhythmic twinging, like a bowstring being inexpertly and hesitantly drawn; on these days she decorates the calendar with Easter eggs—and occasionally a GOOD JOB! sticker.

But she's not been diligent about this kind of record-keeping. She will be now. Now that she's unearthed the Artifact and deciphered its clear directive, she'll have to pay scrupulous attention to her reproductive system—such as it is—and note its stirrings with precision.

Sadly, the month of August is devoid of brooms, stars, or eggs.

As is July.

Well, no matter. Today is a new day. Maybe bodies respond the way dreams do, becoming more prolific once they know the dreamer is paying attention.

Bonnie turns on her five-inch portable TV/radio and watches Gaelan give the morning forecast. He looks tired. Bonnie is sorry about fighting with her siblings, but she's still furious at them, especially Larken. She'll show them. They'll see.

She starts slicing fruits and veggies at a brisk pace. After arranging all the prepped ingredients just so—*Oh, there's nothing prettier than an array of fresh produce!*—she adds the phrase, "LOOK FOR NEW MENU ITEMS SOON!" to the dry erase board. Vowing to consider all comers in an unbiased manner, Bonnie takes a deep breath and unlatches the shutters.

Yes, We're Open.

"Hi again, Viney." Bud has returned.

Viney feels disoriented. She has no idea how long she's been sitting here, waiting.

"I've got the agenda now," Bud adds. "I was just drawing up the order of things. Besides the vote, it's mostly just a bunch of announcements. There's the chili feed coming up, we need a treasurer's report on the Doc Williams funeral relief fund, that kind of thing . . . Nothing much. What was it you wanted to talk to me about?"

"Well, I'm over at Welly's, going through some of his papers, and . . . Did you know about his correspondence with Wales?"

"Gosh, let me see, I think he did say something about that to me once."

"It was with our sister city on Gwynnedd Island. With some monks there. We sent money to them back in the 1940s when their monastery was damaged during the war."

"Huh. I forgot all about that," Bud says, his voice wistful. "I completely forgot we even had a sister city . . . How about that."

This conversation is not going the way Viney had hoped. A more direct approach is required.

"Did you know that the mayor was hoping to get something going with our sister city? Sponsor a visit?"

"You mean a goodwill kind of thing?"

"Something like that."

"Huh. Maybe. He mighta mentioned it."

Shit. She should have thought this out more carefully before she called Bud, maybe even waited a month or two.

But no, she's counting on the fact that the mayor just died to help her get the town to listen to his idea. She's got to bring this to the community right away if she's going to leverage town feeling to incite *action*. It's going to take a lot of energy. Wooing energy. *Shit!* For the first time in her life, Viney wishes that she were a different kind of person, someone with a sweet and accommodating nature. Someone *nice*.

Bud Humphries is nice. He's a milquetoast, but he's nice.

"I'd like to bring up an idea the mayor had, something he's been thinking about and discussing with these monks for years. If it gets introduced right, I think folks might go for it."

"Huh."

"I just want to know if you'd be open to it. Show some positive interest. You know how some of the council members can be."

"I'll back anything the mayor had his heart set on, Viney, you know that. I'm just wondering what I should call it, how I should title it for the agenda."

Viney sighs. "You know, it would be a lot easier if I could tell you about this in person. Could you come over when you get off work, join me for supper? God knows I've got enough food."

"That's awful nice of you, Viney. Five-thirty okay?"

"See you then."

Viney hangs up and surveys the papers scattered across Welly's desk. Twenty-three years of correspondence. It's all here, everything Welly wanted for this town—and Hope, too—and if she has to be the steward for all that (and who else, really?), then she'll do it.

She starts replacing the "Sister City" letters in the folder, in their proper order. At the bottom of one letter, Welly has scribbled something in his famously illegible script.

Henry's e-mail address, she reads, squinting through a magnifying glass, *brotherhenry@saintgwenfrewi.org.*

Viney snaps the file shut, shoves it into the cabinet. Then she goes downstairs, tosses some ice cubes into a tumbler, and pours herself a rum and Coke. (In the process of clearing out Welly's side of the bedroom closet, Viney discovered a substantial cache of travel-size liquor bottles secreted in dozens of shoeless shoe boxes; she's decided to make her way through them, one bottle at a time.)

She's just about to settle down in the living room when she hears a car horn outside. It's the taxi.

Viney gestures the driver to the front door. His face is unshaven and joyless. It seems to Viney that he's far too old to be doing this kind of work.

"Thank you for coming," she says.

"You goin' to Beatrice?" he asks.

"Not me, no. I'm actually sending something with you." Viney hands over the piece of paper with the address. "It's going here, to the Food Bank."

The driver looks perplexed. "What is?"

"Come in. I'll show you."

Viney leads the driver to the kitchen and opens the freezer door.

"That's a lot of meat," the driver remarks.

"Will it be any trouble?" Viney asks. She feels nauseated.

"No," the driver answers. "It's just not what I was expecting."

"Listen. I'll give you ten dollars extra—fifteen—if you'll load it up yourself. I'm not feeling very well."

"Sure," the driver says, his voice softer. "Have you got something to put all this in?"

Viney hands over a box of extra-large plastic garbage bags. "Will this do?"

"Great," he says. "This is a nice thing you're doing, ma'am." He starts loading the bags. "Must be over a hundred pounds in here."

She goes into the living room with her drink, settles down on the sofa, and turns on the TV. There's a soap opera on.

She listens to the driver come and go from the kitchen, intending to get up and thank him when he's finished. But five minutes into *The Guiding Light* she falls into a deep sleep. She won't wake up for several hours, when the civil defense siren goes off, just as it does every Monday at exactly five o'clock.

Startled into a panicked semiconsciousness, she rushes home, picturing Bud Humphries loitering on her front porch, expecting to be fed.

*　　*　　*

When Mr. Norris, age eighty-eight, shows up for his Green Ginko Power Smoothie, Bonnie is fully prepared to give him every consideration. But after hearing him complain about all those noisy misbehaving brats at the mayor's *Gymanfa* and their permissive parents—*This country will be going to hell in a handbasket if these young kids don't straighten up!*—it's clear that he is not the person she is looking for.

After Allan, Pete, and Dylan Labenz come by—have they always been so wounded, so pessimistic, so immature?—Bonnie begins to realize that this process might be more difficult than she thought. Considering the Labenz boys for their baby-making potential has transformed her way of seeing. She feels as though she's meeting them for the first time instead of the thousandth.

She pulls out her list and reluctantly crosses off four names. Only a few hours into the search and her possibilities have already been reduced by 10 percent.

Bonnie regards the list with such dour focus that she fails to notice the arrival of another prospect.

"Bonnie. Bonnie, are you there?"

"Oh. Hello, Blind Tom. Hey, Sergei. Want a treat?" Bonnie holds out one of the organic dog biscuits she keeps on hand for her canine customers.

"Sit," Blind Tom commands. Sergei obeys, accepting his biscuit with the dignity of a celebrant receiving the Communion wafer.

"He is such a well-mannered dog," Bonnie remarks, hoping this observation might get Blind Tom to open up, in the same way that complimenting a parent on their child's good behavior is a reliable conversation-starter. She and Sergei eye him expectantly.

Blind Tom's expression remains solemn. He clears his throat. "He snores."

"Really." Bonnie waits for Blind Tom to elaborate. He doesn't, so she readies the ingredients for his smoothie.

Consider all comers, she reminds herself. Feeling guilty about taking advantage of Blind Tom's disability, she nonetheless studies his face with unabashed interest as she drops mango and avocado chunks into the carafe.

His dark glasses obliterate any real sense of what he looks like—so much of a person's expression is carried by their eyes—but his complexion is pale, and his skin retains deep, puncturelike holes in places, as if he's a plucked cactus.

As Bonnie starts up the blender, she wonders whether she might get a better sense of Blind Tom's identity by meeting him in the land of sound instead of sight. She closes her eyes.

Immediately, she feels disoriented and dizzy. She scowls, scootches her feet out of her tennis shoes, and sets herself into a wider stance. This helps. She hears the blender stall and starts thunking. Deprived of sight, Bonnie discovers that Blind Tom has a point: The sound is unnerving.

"IF IT TAKES TOO LONG FOR EVERYTHING TO GET SMOOTH," she shouts, "IT GETS WARM. I LIKE THEM TO BE COLD, LIKE SOFT-SERVE ICE CREAM."

Tom shouts back. "IT DOESN'T BOTHER ME IF THEY'RE NOT THAT COLD. HAVE YOU CONSIDERED THE DATES?"

"WHAT?"

"I'VE BEEN THINKING ABOUT IT, AND I WONDER IF IT ISN'T THE DATES THAT SLOW THINGS DOWN."

"I USE MEDJOOL. THEY'RE NOT AS STICKY AS THE OTHER KIND AND THEY DON'T HAVE PRESERVATIVES. THEY'RE THE BEST."

"HOW DO YOU PREPARE THEM?"

"WHAT DO YOU MEAN?"

"I WAS ASKING AROUND IN THE BULK FOOD SECTION AT THE HEALTH FOOD STORE UP IN BEATRICE THE OTHER DAY, AND THEY TOLD ME ABOUT DATE PIECES. THEY FEEL LIKE PELLETS, THE KIND OF THING YOU FEED RABBITS AND HAMSTERS AND GUINEA PIGS."

This hints at valuable information. Bonnie turns off the blender temporarily. "Did you keep pets when you were little?" she asks, eyes still squeezed shut.

"Not rabbits or anything, no. When you're visually impaired, teachers are always taking you on field trips that feature opportunities for sensory stimulation. Zoos. Pet stores. That kind of thing."

"Oh." Bonnie turns the blender back on and recommences thunking. She wonders if Blind Tom would prefer being called "Visually Impaired Tom."

The smoothie is ready. She turns off the blender. She considers trying to pour it into the cup without the aid of her eyes, but—not wanting to risk spillage—decides against it.

When she turns to hand the smoothie over to Blind Tom, his expression is different. He's not smiling, but something about him suggests that he's amused.

"So what do you think?" he asks.

"About what?"

"The pellets."

"Oh. They're floured."

"What?"

"I tried them once because they did seem like they'd be convenient. But the way they get them to not stick together in the bin is to dust them with flour, so they give the smoothies this really awful gluey undertaste."

"Darn."

"Why?"

"I bought some for you."

Tom holds out a large plastic bag that has BULK FOODS written on it and contains a huge amount of date pellets. "Gee, Tom, that was really nice of you. Thanks."

"But you don't like them. You don't use them."

"I bet they'd be really good in bread or something," Bonnie says, not wanting to hurt Blind Tom's feelings. It's a sham of an offer, however; there's no oven in Bonnie's woodshed and she doesn't know the first thing about baking.

"Will you be at the town meeting tonight?" Tom asks.

Bonnie hadn't considered this. Almost every man on her list will be there. She hasn't been to a community meeting in ages, but she'd be foolish not to go to this one.

"Definitely."

"I'll see you there."

"Yep. See ya."

Blind Tom and Sergei start to walk away. "Best smoothie I've ever had," Tom comments, "but I still think it's dangerous."

Bonnie watches them go, feeling flat and ambivalent about Blind Tom's potential suitability. Now that she's started looking, she realizes that it would be foolish to rush into anything. She really needs to keep her options open. She shouldn't rule out the possibility of something extraordinary happening, something completely unexpected, *magical* even. Not yet, anyway.

There might be someone out there—someone she hasn't even met!—who ignites a strong, unequivocal feeling, someone whose mere proximity illuminates everything. Attraction can work like that, or so Bonnie has heard. So many love songs have lyrics with words like *heat, fire, sparks, flame*.

With Blind Tom—nice as he is—Bonnie feels no sparks. He brought her a big bag of something she doesn't need and can't use. He's never kept pets renowned for their fertility. What could be clearer? She crosses him off the list.

The kindergarten teacher, Mrs. Prohaska, comes by just after noontime with the new crop of five-year-olds; this year, her class totals eight. Mrs. Prohaska's visit is a beginning-of-the-school-year ritual that Bonnie looks forward to.

"Hi kids!"

"Hello, Miss Jones!"

Bonnie takes orders for the sugarless frozen smoothie pops she's stocked in the freezer: Dixie cups filled with Superman's Strawberry, Madeleine's Melon, Babar's Berry, Harold's Purple Crayon Grape. The children lap up their smoothies on a stick while Bonnie explains how smoothies are made and why they are so good for you.

Then she lets the children help her assemble Mrs. Prohaska's favorite smoothie: a virgin Piña Colada named for Princess Leah: after delivering a lecture on the importance of having grown-up company in the kitchen, Bonnie oversees their efforts with butter knives and soft fruits and then lets them take turns pushing the button on the blender. She does not instruct them in the art of thunking.

"This is the best Princess Leah Pina Colada smoothie I've ever tasted," Mrs. Prohaska declares.

Bonnie dispenses stickers and hands out a basic smoothie recipe for the children to take home and try. After saying good-bye, she starts to close up, counting the till, crossing another day off the calendar. She notices Blind Tom's bag of date pellets. She picks it up, raises and lowers it a few times, switches it from her left hand to her right. *What to do . . .*

Leave it here, probably. She supposes she could give the floured dates another try. Before settling the bag into the fridge, she cradles it in her hands one last time.

Around seven pounds, she concludes. *Maybe seven pounds four ounces.*

The name on his birth certificate is Morgan Geraint Mathias Jones. He is affected by a degenerative eye disorder known as retinitis pigmentosa.

He can see quite clearly actually—within specific, prescribed limits. His *legally blind* status does not arise from having vision that is universally blurred but peripherally limited: he sees the world as two adjacent circles framed in black.

Because retinitis pigmentosa is a progressive disease, the area described by these circles continues to shrink steadily, inexorably.

Once upon a time, these circles were much bigger: backyard trampolines, Conestoga wagon wheels, the steering wheels of pirate ships. They've been inner tubes; extra-large, large, and medium pizzas. They've been the size of Frisbees, floodlights, headlights, dollar pancakes.

Someday he'll look through paper towel rolls, then drinking straws, then the eyes of tapestry needles, and so on until his view constricts to nothingness. Anticipating what this might be like, Morgan sometimes thinks of bagels that have expanded overmuch, so that only the smallest puckered indentation remains to indicate the place where there was once a hole. At other times he likens his eyes to cameras with F-stops that will eventually shutter down completely, a cinematic effect signaling the end of a scene or a cartoon's finale.

That's all, folks.

That's how it will be someday.

But for now, he still has a view of the world, albeit a limited one. If Bonnie really wanted to get an accurate idea of Blind Tom's current capabilities, she shouldn't squeeze her eyes shut; she should walk around looking through a pair of medium-sized mailing tubes.

Autumn is a busy time for piano technicians. The jumble of summer activities is finally over. Schools and community colleges and universities are in session. Piano teachers are welcoming back their old students and recruiting new ones. Church choirs are practicing again. Community theater directors are rehearsing their season openers—big cast, feel-good musicals like *The Music Man* or *My Fair Lady* or *Fiddler on the Roof*. Nursing home activity directors are lining up a year's worth of musical entertainment for their music-loving residents. Finally, lonely pianos that haven't been touched for months are getting attention; and because most of them have not been lucky enough to reside in climate- and humidity-controlled environments, the person doing business as Blind Tom has all the work he can handle.

He loves his job. He only wishes he didn't have to be on the road quite so much; it's hard on his driver. In the sense that making house calls comprises much of their working lives, small-town piano tuners have a lot in common with country doctors.

Blind Tom became Blind Tom when he was twenty-two years old and about to receive a diploma bearing his given name from the Emil Fries School of Piano Tuning and Technology in Vancouver, Washington.

A month before graduation, the current person *dba* Blind Tom (né Phineas William Guffy) contacted the school to inquire if there were any gifted, hardworking students who'd completed their training and might be interested in purchasing a piano-tuning and repair business. Mr. Guffy had owned Blind Tom's for over thirty years. He was ready to retire, move to Arizona, spend more time with his grandchildren, and be listed as *P. W. Guffy* in the Phoenix phone book. He went on to explain that the business was small but well-established. It was located in southeastern Nebraska.

Morgan Jones was the only student to express interest.

"It's a very small town, you understand," Mr. Guffy cautioned. "This isn't Lincoln, or even Grand Island, where there are enough pianos to keep you busy without leaving the city limits."

"I understand."

"This thing is, young man, I don't wanna sell to you if you're not willing to do what it takes. There's been a Blind Tom in business in Emlyn Springs since the 1800s. It's a part of this town's history, you see, and it would break my heart if this place went down. If you're gonna keep it going, you're gonna have to make a lot of dust on a lot of back roads. Can you do that? Can you promise me you'll do that?"

A young man of honorable mettle, Morgan felt compelled to ask an important question: "Do you think it will matter to the people there if I'm not technically—that is, *completely,* blind?"

There was a pause at the other end of the line. "How much vision have you got?"

"Fifty percent," Morgan answered. It was a 15 percent lie. He never would have bent the truth this way if he wasn't positive that his lie would one day be a 100 percent true. "I won't let you down, Mr. Guffy," he added. "I promise."

The soon-to-be-former Blind Tom considered. "Good enough."

The promise was an easy one to make. Morgan had always wanted to go back to southeastern Nebraska. He had relatives in that part of the country, near Blue Springs, and had visited them once when he was thirteen, in the summer of 1978.

It was a strange, eventful visit. A couple of days after he arrived, a huge tornado touched down outside a town not too far away and a little girl and her mother went missing.

Morgan joined the search effort, and in the process of tramping through a flattened, mud-splattered milo field near his great-uncle's place, he came upon the remains of a baby grand piano. It was legless, and its top was gone so you could see its insides: gold strings—like a harp, kind of—and some bolt-looking things, and other parts Morgan didn't have words for.

He'd never seen the insides of a piano. He'd never thought about a piano even *having* insides, really, or about how it produced music, so it had never occurred to him that the crucial and unseen parts of something so outwardly strong-looking and fine could be so horribly damaged.

Morgan was in the crowd watching when Bonnie Jones was rescued. Like everyone else, he was summoned to the ravine by the sound of music. He stood among the people of Emlyn Springs while they sang to her in a language he had never heard before, the language of his forefathers, in many voices that somehow sounded like one, and out in the open air, without a piano or an organ or even a guitar playing along.

After a photographer from *National Geographic* took a picture of the piano, Morgan got permission to have it hauled over to his great-aunt and great-uncle's place. He cleaned it up and took it apart. It was a good project for a curious pubescent boy who was visiting relatives and didn't have other kids to hang around with.

When his visit was over, the adults told him it would be impossible to take the piano back home to Michigan.

"What will happen to it?" Morgan asked.

When told that it would probably get busted up and taken to the dump, he grew upset, confounding his relatives, who knew him as a rule to be reasonable and compliant.

"You have to promise me you won't get rid of it!" he insisted. "You have to save it for me, for the next time I come!"

The adults shook their heads, but they consented; it seemed to mean so much to the boy, and of course he was thirteen, going through all those baffling physical and emotional upheavals that beset young people at that time of life. So Uncle Howie hauled the piano's remains into a corner of the barn, and there they stayed. They all expected that with the passage of time Morgan would forget about it. He didn't visit that often.

It was after that summer that he started having trouble seeing the blackboard. He got dizzy walking down the school corridors. Bright sunlight started to hurt his eyes during the day; at nighttime it became harder and harder to see anything. That summer in Emlyn Springs was the last time he was just a kid, a normal kid with normal vision.

He always wondered about that little girl, whether she was still there, whether her mother was ever found.

So when Phineas William Guffy called and offered Morgan Geraint Jones the chance to answer to a new name and begin his professional life in the place where all those memories and that ruined piano lived, it seemed less like a random coincidence and more like a sign of divine grace.

If the deal was clinched for Mr. Guffy by Morgan's solemn but personable sincerity, the deciding moment for Morgan came soon after he asked, "Wasn't there a tornado in those parts in the late 1970s? A woman and her little girl went missing?"

"There sure was," Mr. Guffy replied.

"Whatever happened to her? What happened to her daughter?"

Mr. Guffy's voice reflected a delighted surprise. "Why son," he cried, "you're talking about Flying Girl!" He then went on to tell his version of the story. Morgan remembers being grateful at the time that the phone call was on Mr. Guffy's dime.

Morgan has always admired the pluck of his younger self. Hope's piano became the only tangible evidence that the events of that summer really happened, that he really witnessed them. That it wasn't all a dream.

He returned to Emlyn Springs, became Blind Tom, and transported the remains of Hope Jones's piano from his great-uncle's barn to the back room of the piano hospital. He felt as though he was finally claiming an identity and a life he'd chosen—or had chosen for him—long ago.

By the time he came back, Bonnie was sixteen. She didn't recognize him; but then, there's no reason why she would. He was just one of a herd of people on the ground when she was up in that tree, a boy then, and a stranger. Now he's someone else.

And yet somehow the same, because he came here, settled here, and is linked to that self and this place by the visual memory of a seven-year-old girl caught up in a tree, the aural memory of voices conjoined in song, the tactile memory of a mud-splattered piano in a field. These memories won't be compromised. They won't fade, even though his eyesight will.

Blind Tom has never been able to think of Bonnie as Flying Girl; to him, she is a sleeping orb in the night sky, her small face lit from below by the hundreds of flashlights the townsfolk carried with them and shone up at her before she was brought down.

She could never belong to him—no more than the moon belongs to the wild creatures that sing to it.

Hope's Diary, 1964:
There's an ordinance against pedal pushers

Small-town life has begun to reveal itself—I should
say, the less generous, mean-spirited side of small-
town life.

Mid-morning, naptime, after some errands in town,
I was taking Larken for a walk in the stroller when
we were gestured near by Estella Axthelm. She was
watering the planter boxes on her front porch. As
I wheeled closer, I thought, how lovely, at last
someone is going to initiate a conversation, maybe
even invite me in for a cup of coffee or a glass of
iced tea. I'd expected that sort of welcome, I realize now, especially since I married a native son.

I wheeled up the sidewalk, smiling my best smile,
strategizing how best to begin the conversation—
say something nice about her flowers, of course!—
and was mid-compliment when she interrupted me.

"You need to go home and change your clothes,"
she said.

"I beg your pardon?" I was sure I'd misheard. I
was slightly distracted by the foreign quality of
her speech, a kind of phony British sound to it.

Larken had begun to stir—any lack of motion she
perceives instantly, no matter how deeply she's
asleep—and so I started pushing the stroller forward and backward. Miss A. continued to water her
geraniums. She didn't even make eye contact.

"That kind of tire isn't appropriate," I heard
her say.

What was she talking about? Truly I felt as though
the woman were speaking another language. Since her
gaze was directed downward, I looked at the wheels
on Larken's stroller. They looked appropriate to
me. I couldn't imagine why Miss A. would be taking
such umbrage at the wheels on a baby stroller.

Then I realized that she was referring to my clothing.

"My attire?" I asked. I was wearing denim pedal pushers, Keds, and a yellow polka-dot sleeveless blouse.

"Mothers in Emlyn Springs don't dress like that," she replied, finally gracing me with the full vituperative force of direct eye contact, which had an especially reproachful weight as she was still standing on the porch and so towered above me. I felt as though I were five years old. At that point, she turned her back and went into her house, letting the screen slam and pulling the front door closed in a way that let me know that an invitation to tea and cookies would not be forthcoming.

By this time, Larken was fully awake and had started to cry. So much for nap time. I stood there for a few more moments, unbelieving. Then I hauled Larken out of the stroller, carried her up to the porch, and let her entertain herself by pulling up every one of Miss A.'s geraniums—hateful, foul-smelling flowers—by the roots.

When I told L. about this—omitting my display of horticultural vandalism until I could gauge his reaction—he was dismissive.

"She didn't mean it," he said. "Small-town folks can be wary of strangers, that's all, and she's always been a prune, that one. Don't take it so to heart."

Needless to say, I didn't mention the flowers, nor the four angry calls I received from Miss A. throughout the rest of the day. I hung up on her every time.

"Darling," I said to Larken at bedtime—still wearing my inappropriate attire—"be kind to people."

Llewellyn doesn't seem to understand how hurtful this encounter was, how deeply it shook me. It set me wondering about other women in town. Do they all feel this way about me? That I'm trashy? That I'm undeserving?

Must go. Larken fussing.

Read a story about the posthumous publication of some poetry by a young woman named Sylvia Plath. American poet with children. Much lauded. I'm wondering if they might have any of her work at the library. I'm not hopeful, based on what I've seen of their collection, but I still plan on going tomorrow. It will be a nice outing for us.

Anyway, at the time of her death, she was married to—but separated from—an equally lauded poet. That must have been hell.

Some people doubt the authenticity of her intent, since she'd prearranged for someone to come to the flat early in the morning. Wasn't she hoping this person would find her and save her? Surely she was bluffing. Weren't her actions a plea for help rather than a real attempt?

Idiots. Of course not. She was seeing to the children, making sure they'd be taken care of when they woke up. I'd do the same. Any mother would.

Chapter 13

Sinkholes Can
Be Self-induced

There's a new face at the gym. Gaelan notices her right away, at the beginning of his workout. He's doing his cardio on one of the elliptical trainers; she's directly opposite him on a stationary bike.

She's praying. That's his initial impression. Her lips are moving and her eyes are closed. Her intensity and self-absorption are unusual. This isn't Gold's Gym on Venice Beach. This is the YMCA in downtown Lincoln. It's a fine facility and perfect for Gaelan's purposes, but it's not the place one expects to see people working out with such an inward-focused, reverential quality of concentration.

After studying her for several minutes, he realizes that she isn't lost in prayer; she's mouthing the words to every song on the *Born to Run* album, in sequence, keeping the beat during the instrumental solos.

By the time she gets to the next-to-last song, "Meeting Across the River," Gaelan is listening to the album in his own head; he can hear the trumpet solo. And by the time "Jungleland" starts playing, he's aligned his body rhythms with hers and they're pedaling in sync.

They dismount their machines. "Hello," he says.

"Hi!"

She's a lot younger than he thought when he first saw her: early twenties, which puts her as much as fifteen, sixteen, maybe even seventeen years younger than he. Normally these kinds of guesstimations wouldn't factor into Gaelan's thinking; today, for some reason, they do—but only a little. She knows Springsteen, she doesn't give off that crazy, desperate, stalker-in-the-making energy that Gaelan has come to recognize and run from after years of experience with female fans, she's not wearing a wedding ring (not that marriage is an exclusionary factor in his selection process, it just makes things less complicated), and she's very pretty in a tall, blonde, Nordic way—defined facial bones, long limbs. It's easy to imagine her gracing the pages of one of those winter sports clothing catalogs, modeling stretch pants and a wool sweater and swishing down a ski slope.

Short of a few delicately phrased inquiries into her sexual history, Gaelan doesn't need to know much more about this girl to make him interested in hosting her in his bedroom.

"You're new here," he says.

"I am, yes." She's extremely cut, but not bulked up, like a bodybuilder. Very lean.

"My name's Gaelan." And then—feeling like an asshole but unable to resist the possibility of impressing her—he adds, "Gaelan Jones. I do the weather on KLAN-KHAM."

"Right!" she exclaims cheerfully. "I thought you looked familiar. She has that condition that causes her eyes to jiggle sporadically; there's a name for it but he can't remember what it is.

"I'm Rhiannon," she adds. "I just moved here a couple of weeks ago."

"Where from?"

"Oregon. I'm here on a grant."

"At the U?"

"Yeah. Geology. Listen, I was supposed to meet my trainer, but he just called and said he was gonna be a little late and I should get started without him. You wanna spot me?"

"Sure."

They head for the free weights. Around her exposed midriff, a smooth, taut ribbon of skin widens and narrows slightly as she moves. She's wearing black, skin-hugging workout clothes: embroidered cropped pants and a spaghetti strap camisole.

Bodybuilders can talk all they want about the aesthetic marvels of a male six-pack; in Gaelan's opinion, nothing compares to the posterior view of a woman's musculature: that beautiful quadrant of glutes and hamstrings, the elegant, gentle slope of trapezieus skimming the shoulders and overlaying the wings of the scapulae.

She can't weigh more than 110, and yet she loads 185 pounds on the bar and lies down on the bench. Is this a joke? Her face is deadpan, so Gaelan gets into the spotter's position: legs set in a wide stance, arms outstretched and available.

"Ready?" he asks.

She exhales into her first press. Gaelan counts.

"One . . . two . . . three . . ."

She doesn't focus on the bar when she's doing her reps; she looks up at him with her strange eyes in a calm and openly curious way that Gaelan finds unsettling. It's not an unfriendly look, but it's not sexual either. It's definitely not the look of a person bench-pressing one and a half times their body weight.

She doesn't stop until she's done twenty reps. *Astounding*.

"Thanks," she says. "I guess it's time to go up."

"Yeah," Gaelan laughs. "I guess."

She peels herself off the bench and starts wiping it down—even though her body has left only the faintest silhouette of perspiration, a kind of shroud-of-Turin effect.

"So what are you studying?" he asks.

"Karsts."

"Karsts?"

"Sinkholes. They can be self-induced. Not many people know that." She indicates the bench. "Your turn."

What to do? This is not his usual sequence. And yet.

"What do you start with?" she asks. "I'll load it for you."

"Two-fifty," he says.

She puts a hand on his bicep. Her skin is surprisingly cool. He feels an answering tug in his groin. "You can do more," she says. "Lie down. Close your eyes."

He obeys, settling himself on the bench while she loads the bar.

When she's done, he asks, "How much?"

"Never mind," she replies, and when he opens his eyes she's smiling down at him. "You know what they say," she adds, winking. "What you don't know won't hurt you."

He reaches up for the bar and stares into her shimmying eyes. "Listen, after this, you wanna go get something to eat?"

"Sure. That'd be great. But first . . ." She furrows her brow, deepens her voice, and puts on an exaggerated Austrian accent. "We're going to PUMP YOU UP! Come on now, baby. Give me eight. You can do this."

She's right. He can. He feels great.

"There are people who would *kill* for these seats, you know," Larken says, fanning her face with a large stack of partially graded pop quizzes. Between the unseasonable heat, the nonstop screaming of several hundred thousand people—most of whom have been drinking alcohol since mid-morning—and the marching band's insistence on playing "There Is No Place Like Nebraska" every five minutes, her head feels like an overinflated dirigible.

"There are people who would probably even *marry* me for these seats," she continues. She swipes at her forehead before another curtain of sweat descends on her brows. "They'd be the same people, actually."

Jon laughs. It's not a real laugh. He's been distracted all day.

"American football tickets as a dowry," he says. "I'll have to remember that when Esmé's of marriageable age."

"Here's a thought: Next year we could scalp them and contribute the proceeds to her college fund."

Jon smiles again, wanly. "Scalping is disallowed, remember?" He squints at the crowd on the opposite side of the stadium as if he expects to recognize a specific person among the squirming sea of red and white.

"Oh, right," Larken replies with mock dismay. "Darn."

They're sitting in the middle of a six-seat block at the fifty-yard line of Husker Stadium. A large cooler occupies a third seat; the three other seats are conspicuously empty. Besides Jon, this week's invitees were Mia, Esmé, and Rhonda, Mia's acupuncturist friend. They were supposed to meet them at the start of the game but fourth quarter has already started and it's obvious that she and Jon have been stood up. Larken's best efforts to engender cheer this afternoon have all failed.

Jon looks at his watch. "I think I'll go call Mia again"

"I'm sure they're okay." Larken chooses not to support this assertion by reminding Jon of Mia's long-standing history as a no-show. "They must have just decided it was too hot."

"Yeah," Jon says glumly. "That's probably it."

It's the last home game. Larken's obligation to her dead father—at least as far as the 2003 season of Husker football is concerned—ends in approximately sixteen minutes.

She's had mixed success filling these seats, and she's never yet managed to fill all six of them. The obvious, first-string choices are her family members. She's invited them, repeatedly, but Gaelan won't give up his Saturday marathon workouts at the gym, and Bonnie is deeply involved in some new doomed-to-failure entrepreneurial effort. As for Viney, she came to the first two games but was strangely subdued, and spent most of both afternoons sitting with her body inclined slightly forward in the seat, chin resting in her upturned, cupped palm, sleeping. She's politely declined Larken's subsequent invitations.

"I'm very involved in planning Fancy Egg Days this year," she explained. "I'm sorry, honey, but I'm sure there are lots of people who'd love to go with you."

Not true. There just aren't that many people Larken wants to spend a Saturday afternoon with. She invited Arthur and Eloise to the Texas A&M game—they brought their two oldest grandchildren—and at the Iowa State game she was joined by Kris and her husband, Dennis, and their eight-year-old son. And now she and Jon are not watching Nebraska get trampled by Kansas State. It's the first home game they've lost all year.

Everyone seems so *remote*.

"I can't believe it's mid-November, can you?" Larken says, feeling her own spirits downslide and making another effort to use small talk as levitation. "Where's the hot chocolate? Where's the *brrrrr*?"

Jon pulls a section of longish hair away from his scalp and starts twirling it with a slow, restrained compulsiveness. Larken wonders if she's watching the nascent development of a dreadlock. She's always wondered how they're made.

The seats are part of Larken's family legacy. Her father purchased them sometime in the 1970s and for a while, before Hope started using a wheelchair, they came up as a sixsome on football Saturdays:

three adults—Mom and Dad and Viney—and three kids. If Larken
thought about it, she might realize that her precise sense of color was
developed on Saturdays, in the streets of Lincoln and in the stadium,
where a thousand or more shades of red collide against one another.
Even the drinks the adults poured from thermoses on those Saturdays
were red: Bloody Marys for the adults, and for the children, Virgin
Marys.

That lasted only a couple of years though. Hope's MS disabled them
all. Things like jolly road trips to Lincoln on football Saturdays were
only one of the casualties of having a mother in a wheelchair.

"Did you ever think about the end of the world when you were a
child?" Jon asks. He's still staring at the mass of Husker fans on the other
side of the field. This may be the first time all afternoon that he's initi-
ated a conversation.

Larken follows Jon's gaze and notices that groups of people are starting to leave; she feels both envious and censorious of these deserters. "It
was hard not to if you grew up here in the sixties," she says. "Civil aid
defense sirens going off every Monday. The shelter signs. And then when
I saw *Fail Safe* and found out about Offutt Air Force Base in Omaha . . ."

"Oh, right," Jon murmurs, nodding.

". . . If there ever was a nuclear war, Nebraska would be the first place
to be blown off the map. Not even a president who looked like Henry
Fonda could save us."

Jon clasps his hands and sits forward in his seat. "I used to think about
the end of the world constantly."

Larken has to mirror his posture in order to hear what he's saying;
the band has launched into another performance of the Nebraska fight
song and everyone around them has stood and started clapping.

In spite of the setting and the noise, an odd sense of privacy envelops
them; the standing bodies surrounding them form the walls of a long,
rectangular, doorless, skylit sanctum.

Jon goes on. "I used to pray as a child, to ask God every night: 'Please,
please dear God, if there's a nuclear war let me be in a bomb shelter with
Mum and Da and my brothers and sisters." He pauses, smiles, looks at
her. "I envisioned a spacious bomb shelter."

"Of course," Larken says. The walls of their little room are still standing. They could live here and never leave. *Don't stop,* she implores him.

"I remember being at rugby games with my dad and wondering, if the rest of the world ended, right now, and the only people left on earth were the people in this stadium . . . would there be someone here who would love me, someone for me to love?"

Larken studies him. She judges it to be more important to tell a small, harmless lie than to speak the commiserating—and possibly dangerous—truth.

"That's funny," she says. "I'd be wondering if there'd be enough to eat."

Her lie reaps the desired intent: Jon laughs, convivially. He stands and stretches; the walls of their room sit down. "Speaking of which," he asks, "do you want anything from concessions?"

Don't do it, she thinks, because she knows it's a ruse. He's going to call Mia again. Why? *Why?* When he was feeling better. When she'd succeeded in cheering him up.

"There's still a lot of food in the cooler," Larken offers, and then regrets it. Of course there's a lot of food; she packed for five, not two and now she's successfully reminded him once again of absent friends.

He gives her shoulder a brief squeeze. "I'll be right back."

The cooler is full of potato salad and cold fried chicken and veggie sticks and raisins and apples and drinks and sandwiches she made especially for Esmé: soy cream cheese and cucumber and olive; tuna and capers and dill; peanut butter and pickle and jam. The sandwiches have been cut into little shapes: stars and ponies and even bells and Santas and Christmas trees because Larken believes strongly that when children are involved it's never too early to start thinking about Christmas.

The score is 38 to 9. If she hears "There Is No Place Like Nebraska" one more time, she'll go mad.

And yet, here it comes again.

In lieu of madness, she opens the cooler and rifles around until she finds the family-size bag of Lay's Potato Chips.

She pulls it out, rips it open, eats.

Season tickets to University of Nebraska football games are to Nebraskans what rent-controlled apartments are to Manhattanites.

They are rare. They are coveted. Their sudden appearance gives rise
to a unique form of desperation among civilized citizens—nice, up-
standing people who have never given any previous indication that they
are deeply opportunistic.

After Larken got back from her father's funeral celebration, she
started receiving baffling phone calls from folks in Emlyn Springs, most
of whom she barely knew. They delivered polite, rambling monologues
in which the caller recounted numerous stories revealing their intimate
friendship with her father—*You may not remember me, Larken, but your
dad used to invite me to at least one home game every season. Of course I
don't have to remind you what a generous person he was. I tell you, the two
of us, we used to have a* blast! *Why I remember one time*—Larken listened
and made monosyllabic responses whenever responses seemed called for;
often she was able to engage the speakerphone feature and work during these conversations: post her online daily communiqués to students,
grade papers, write exams. These phone encounters were often quite
lengthy.

Eventually the caller would come around to the subject of Larken's
weekend plans: *Your Saturdays must be pretty full, what with grading
papers and so forth. I can only imagine how demanding a university teaching position can be. You probably don't have much time for socializing. Has
the university got you taking any trips this fall?*

Viney had to explain.

"They want the tickets."

"What tickets?"

"Your father's football tickets. They're hoping you'll sell them to them
instead of relinquishing them back to the university."

"I don't understand."

Viney sighed. "Call the UNL ticket office, honey. They can explain
it better than I can. Just let me know what you decide so I can tell people.
They're driving me crazy. Bye, sweetie. Love you."

Tell what people? Larken wanted to ask, but Viney had already
hung up.

And so Larken spent almost an entire hour one afternoon in early
September talking on the phone with a remarkably intractable woman
at the University of Nebraska Athletic Ticket Office. Much of the time
Larken was on hold, listening to an endless looped recording of the

Nebraska fight song, complete with hand clapping. The woman never introduced herself, but knowing that she would eventually shape this surreal encounter into an anecdote for Jon's entertainment, Larken realized that the other main character would need a name, and so she christened her.

"You must show up in person to collect the tickets," repeated Mrs. Petra Tabatchnick. "Under no circumstances do we put season football tickets in the mail."

"Because you're worried someone might steal them."

"That would be a concern, yes. These tickets are very valuable."

"So you're telling me I can't just give you permission over the phone to release the tickets?—to friends, say, or my siblings, or my stepmother? I have to come down there. Physically."

"Yes."

"With a notarized copy of my father's death certificate."

"If you are the POA designate, yes. You'll also need to bring a notarized copy of the POA document as well as two forms of photo identification."

Mrs. Tabatchnick's professionalism was impressive. Larken felt a perverse temptation to test the limits of her implacability.

"I can't *believe* this!" she said, attempting to emulate the melodramatic tone she's endured from slacker students over the years. "My father is *dead*. He's *dead*! Are you really going to make me come down there to take care of this?" Larken hoped that her vocal performance was causing Mrs. Tabatchnick to envision a pale, consumptive young woman crippled by the lassitude of grief, prostrate on a rumpled, unmade chaise and draped in a dressing gown: a kind of final-act Mimi from *La Bohème*.

In fact, Larken *was* still wearing her bathrobe and she hadn't made her bed, so that part of the picture wasn't far off.

"These are *football* tickets we're talking about!" Larken-as-diva continued, trying to work up an *I'm-about-to-CRY-I'm-so-distraught* sound in her voice. "It's just plain ridiculous to put people—especially people who have just lost a father—through this kind of . . ."

Larken faltered. Authentically upset as she was, she couldn't bring herself to assault Mrs. Tabatchnick with the word *bullshit,* and besides, Mimi would never say *bullshit*. If anything, she'd say *Merde* and Larken couldn't be sure that Mrs. Tabatchnick was conversant in French, although given Mrs. T.'s articulate poise, it certainly wouldn't be surprising.

"Well," Larken concluded huffily, "it's just *crazy*."

Mrs. Tabatchnick would not be moved. "I'm sorry, Ms. Jones. Could you hold please? I need to answer another line."

"Yes," Larken said, sighing theatrically. "*Fine*."

Oh, there is no place like Nebraska, dear old Nebraska U . . .

By this time—nearly a month after her father's death—Larken has learned that *POA* means *power of attorney*. Along with BA, MFA, and PhD, *POA* is her newest credential.

. . . where the girls are the fairest, the boys are the squarest, of any old school that I knew . . .

As POA, Larken has become well acquainted with a specialized type of Post-it note: transparent around the edges so that it seems to magically emerge from the document to which it's adhered, it is shaped like an arrow and bears a faint yellowish tinge at its center overlaid by the red-lettered words SIGN HERE.

Somewhere among the endless lines of legal-speak, subsections, clauses, addendums to clauses, etcetera, these self-important, specialized Post-its hide, mischievous. Those SIGN HEREs could really be hard to find.

Still, whoever designed them was very perceptive. He or she must have realized that people who are recently bereaved would rather not be required to read. A human being can only hold so much, and grief occupies a large piece of real estate. When it arrives, grief abides by the laws of manifest destiny. Uninvited but entitled, it takes up residence in every seen and unseen part of a person. Reading comprehension is only one of the many countries that grief defeats, oppresses, and occupies.

. . . There is no place like Nebraska, where they're all true blue . . .

It was fatigue that ultimately caused Larken to hang up—that, and the suspicion that Mrs. Tabatchnick had reached a breaking point in their relations and was keeping that pain-in-the-ass Ms. Jones on hold longer than necessary.

. . . We'll all stick together, in all kinds of weather, for dear old Nebraska U . . .

Is she a football fan? No. Did she want this burden? No. If Larken Jones, POA, so concluded, that six-seat block of season tickets at the fifty-yard line in Husker Stadium could go up for general sale. After almost thirty-some years, the territory that had been claimed and defended and occupied by Dr. Llewellyn Jones of Emlyn Springs, Nebraska, could be relinquished. Anyone could have it, and someone *would* have it, eagerly and soon and no matter what the cost, if Larken chose to sign it over, and those six empty seats would be out of her life and held by happier hands.

But she couldn't do it. She knew she'd regret it forever.

There is a small country that forms on certain Saturdays in the autumn within the city limits of Lincoln, Nebraska. On those Saturdays, hundreds of thousands of people gather to cheer on a football team called the Cornhuskers.

In the end, Larken couldn't SIGN HERE—not today, maybe never, because selling her father's small territorial holdings within that Saturday country would be exactly like selling the family farm.

When Jon and Larken arrive back home, they see Mia's car parked on the street. Jon helps Larken haul the cooler out of her car and into her apartment and then bounds up the stairs. Larken puts on a pot of coffee, turns on her computer, and starts sorting today's stack of mail.

Ten minutes later, Mia's voice erupts in a roar: "You just don't get it, do you? You just don't fucking GET IT! I have to have some space. I have to have some time away from you, from her. I don't know who I am anymore besides Professor Schwartzmann's wife and Esmé's mommy."

Larken hears a muffled reply from Jon, then heavy footsteps down the stairs, and then a knock at the door.

Jon stands there with Esmé, half-asleep, in his arms.

"I'm so sorry, Larken, but . . . could you take her for a while? We're having a . . . well, no secret is it? Anyway, she was napping—"

"Is she sick?" Larken asks, reflexively putting a hand on Esmé's forehead. Esmé hasn't taken afternoon naps since she was two.

"Just tired, I think," Jon says. "The heat, you know. I think she'll go to sleep again if it's quiet. I know this is a lot to ask, you've already given up a whole day and I know you have work to do . . . ."

"Jon. Of course."

"She'll be very quiet, won't you princess?

"I will," Esmé murmurs, her brow furrowed. "I'll be very quiet so that Larkee can do her work."

"Here," Larken says. "I'll take her."

"No," says Jon. "I'll do it."

"Da, put me down," Esmé insists. She walks to the sofa, sits, tucks her feet beneath her, opens her Babar book, and starts to read.

Larken isn't sure which is more heartbreaking: Esmé's listlessness or her docility.

"Jon," Larken says quietly, "please, please, don't ever hesitate to ask for help. She can spend the night too if you need more time. It's fine. I love having her here."

They must not must not must not must not break up.

"Thanks again," he says, turning to go back upstairs without bidding a further good-bye to his daughter.

Larken closes the door and turns to face Esmé, who seems troubled by the goings-on in Babar's jungle. "Would you like something to eat? I have some special treats in here."

"Yes, thank you," Esmé replies, not looking up from her book. Larken opens the cooler and fills one of the paper plates with a sampler of sandwiches: Santa, reindeer, tree, star, bell, heart.

"Here you go, sweetie," Larken says, delivering the plate to the coffee table in front of the sofa. "Maybe we can read together later. How would that be?"

Esmé looks up. "Daddy says you have to work."

"I do." Larken moves to the TV. "So how about if you watch a show for a while?"

Esmé frowns and resumes reading. "That would be fine."

Larken doesn't approve of using television as a babysitter, but she's got to get some work done. She turns the TV to the PBS station and then settles down at her desk to start grading a stack of essay exams. By the time she looks up, Kratt's Creatures is over, Miss Frizzle is piloting the magic school bus through the human circulatory system, and Esmé has fallen asleep.

Larken tiptoes across the room and turns off the TV. As she tucks an afghan around Esmé's sleeping form, she notices tiny nibbles around the edges of the sandwiches, nearly imperceptible. Esmé must have just barely applied her teeth to the bread: a nervous dormouse in fear of discovery. And yet she was compelled, in spite of her perilous situation, to nibble every single sandwich, just a little, searching for the right ingredient, hoping to taste the magic potion, the pill, the painkiller, the anodyne. Giving up finally, not finding it anywhere.

Hope's Diary, 1965:
Gravida

I can't believe how long it's been since I've visited these pages. Where has the time gone?

The biggest news to report is that I'm pregnant again.

Note the lack of an exclamation point at the end of that sentence.

I'm trying to hold my emotions in check and not get my hopes up, given how many of Larken's older siblings never made it to term. So, no baby showers, no shopping sprees in the layette department of JCPenney, no sitting around making lists of possible names . . . I'm not telling anyone, not even Viney. It's hard to be so sedate, but I can't bear the idea of falling in love with another baby only to lose it. I just hope whoever's in there doesn't feel neglected.

Don't worry, sweetheart. I know you're in there.

Ah. Now I understand why I haven't written. I've been afraid. Just penning these few words, giving over these few lines to this baby on these pages has already stirred my hopes.

Who am I kidding? I'm already feeling plenty for this child. Impossible not to.

Anyway, so far so good and that's all there is to say about it. Llewellyn and I certainly didn't expect this so soon (who knew that even physicians could be taken in by the myth that breast-feeding has a contraceptive effect!), and the reality of having two babies under the age of two hasn't really settled in yet, but I'm hardly complaining. Llewellyn seems worried, but the truth is, I feel wonderful. Lots of energy. Fingers crossed our little girl will be getting a sibling for her first birthday! (Oops. That exclamation point got away from me . . .)

Other news: I've taken on the work of volunteer
costume designer and seamstress for a production
of "Romeo and Juliet." The house is a riot of fabric. Larken is having the time of her life, winding
herself up in mock brocades and silks. A sensual
heaven for her. She entertains herself while I
treadle away. It's a happy time.

Emlyn Springs hasn't done a play for something
like ten years, Hazel Williams told me. Apparently
pageants and the like used to be a big part of life
here, and for a long time a retired English professor named Dr. Stubblefield used to put on a Shakespearean production at the high school gym once a
year. After his death, no one stepped forward to
organize anything, and that was the end of it. There's
been no effort to resurrect any kind of stage production—at least not until that uppity outsider with
the inappropriate attire, the doctor's wife, arrived in town . . .

I know I shouldn't be so hard on Emlyn Springs,
but sometimes the resistance to anything, anything
that hasn't been proposed by someone over the age
of sixty is astounding. No wonder so many young people
move away. There just doesn't seem to be any appreciation for new ideas—or even old ideas, resurrected!

After letting Hazel Williams in on my plans (such
a dear, she pledged her support right away), I made
a presentation at a community council meeting, proposing a comedy, something light like "A Midsummer
Night's Dream" or "As You Like It," but the reliable naysayers (Estella Axthelm, Greta Hallock,
etc.) wanted something with more "dignity," more
"weight." (I think what they really wanted was
something with starring vehicles for middle-aged
divas. They probably would have chosen "King Lear"
if they'd had unilateral powers.) In any event, the

majority vote was for "Romeo and Juliet."

I'm just happy that we're doing some kind of cultural event. It's so important for our children to
see that we value the arts. And it's been wonderful
seeing people come together for this, even if it's
meant enduring Estella Axthelm's scenery chewing.
The play isn't called "Juliet and the Nurse," but
that seems to be a negligible detail in Estella's
mind.

I still notice disapproving looks from certain
elements of the population when I stand up at these
meetings and propose what I expect seems like one
hare-brained idea after another, but I don't care.
There's nothing I want more for this town than to
see it reinvigorated, and there's nothing standing
in the way except for small-minded people.

At least I've made a dear friend in Viney. Now
that she's gone to work for L. I see her every day.
Fellow anarchist! She's funny and wise and seems
to have made peace with small-town life.

Chapter 14

Corpse Pose

In the back of the room and as close as possible to the exit, Gaelan is playing dead. Rhiannon—also pretending to be a corpse, possibly with greater success—occupies a mat next to him.

Let your body relax, the instructor is saying. *Allow your mind to empty . . .*

Viney would be so proud. She's been trying to get Gaelan to do yoga for years.

He remembers the first time he saw *Pumping Iron*. He was fourteen, maybe fifteen—it was before he had his license anyway because Viney was the one who drove them up to Lincoln to see it. The very beginning of the movie gave her the vindication she'd been seeking. "See!" she whispered ferociously, as they watched Arnold Schwarzenegger and Franco Columbu standing at a ballet bar, doing port de bras with a professional ballerina. "If *he* thinks flexibility and grace are important, then you should, too!"

Gaelan would have gone to a ballet class if Rhiannon had suggested it; as it is, she prefers yoga when it comes to rounding out the fitness triumvirate: "You can't just do cardio and strength," she insisted soon after they met. "And you can't just do five minutes of half-assed stretching at the end of your workout, Gaelan. You've got to build in more flexibility training, or—trust me on this—you're going to end up with injuries. I've seen it happen with so many bodybuilders."

Gaelan wonders how many of Rhiannon's bodybuilding ex-boyfriends are languishing back in Oregon because they didn't learn to salute the sun. He's not about to ask; nor has he offered any resistance. He's been coming to yoga classes with Rhiannon on a daily basis ever since they first worked out together.

. . . Clear away any chatter in the mind, surrender your efforts to the earth . . .

Experience has taught him that complying with *any* request from a woman—even if it's completely unrelated to sex—is the best way to expedite a sexual relationship and ensure happy times between the sheets. Women need compliance. In fact, Gaelan has concluded, the more compliance women receive outside the bedroom, the more eager and aggressive they are in the sack.

Sexual attraction isn't a separate entity for women, something they wall off from the rest of their lives; it arises from and connects to everything. Women carry different things in their heads, Gaelan suspects, when they come to bed. For men—and he's no different, he'd be the first to admit it—sex is a simple here-and-now experience. But a woman in bed might be remembering how you quibbled about buying artichoke hearts, forgot to hold the door open, or didn't take the shortcut. You have to *prove* yourself to women in these little ways all the time. They remember everything that happens outside the bedroom and bring it in, even though they don't always know that they're doing it. It's really best to just lay low and do as they ask.

. . . If thoughts do arise, simply take note of them as if they're clouds passing across a perfectly blue sky . . .

His willingness with Rhiannon is paying off: Today after class they're going to his place for the first time. Back at his condo, everything is ready.

There is nowhere else you need to be, nothing else you need to be doing . . .

They're playing dead longer than usual.

At his first class, Gaelan wasn't sure about Corpse Pose: *svasana*. He just didn't get it. At one point he actually sat up and looked around the room, making sure that there wasn't more to it, that lying on your back with your hands palms up and your feet slightly apart and your eyes closed was really what everyone was supposed to be doing, that he wasn't the butt of some yoga-class-initiation prank. But scattered throughout the room were thirty-some men and women all pretending to be dead. Gaelan noted that many of the male corpses had hardons. He was reminded of miniature golf courses. All that was missing were the flags.

He understands the point of it now, sort of. The physical part of it at least is starting to come more easily. But clearing the mind? It's impossible.

He wishes this were not so. He'd like to stop thinking about what he learned during his father's funeral celebration—that the girl he broke up with fifteen years ago is a widow with a (*11? 12 yo?*) son, living within a seventy-five-mile radius. He wishes that this knowledge didn't keep asserting itself at inappropriate times, like now.

If his mind is going to chatter, he'd rather have it chattering about Rhiannon. If his sky is full of clouds, he'd like them to take the shape of Rhiannon's body when she's doing revolved crow balance or standing splits.

. . . sink deeply into your center now, finding contentment in simply being . . .

Maybe she's having as hard a time of it as he is.

Rolling his head to one side, Gaelan squints his eyes open, hoping to find that Rhiannon is sneaking a look at him as well, that she's just as eager for class to end and is anticipating, imagining what will happen between them when they get to his place.

But no. She doesn't look like she's anticipating anything.

How can she? She's dead.

There's a memorial in Gaelan's condo. He doesn't think of it that way, but that's what it is. It waits behind a closed door, the last thing to be revealed to the women he brings home: a reward for their patience, a confirmation of their hopes, because their first impressions of Gaelan's habitat are not positive.

With minor variations, this is what the women experience:

For two weeks, they partner through a series of steadily accelerating intimacies: from flirting over coffee to exchanging dessert spoons at lunch to neck-nuzzling over martinis to French kissing in the parking lot to heavy petting at the movies. So far, so good.

Then (*finally*) they're invited to his condo.

The first thing the women notice about Gaelan Jones's place of residence is that it's very clean—not necessarily a bad thing, but it's also disturbingly tidy, as if the occupant is the sort whose nervous system short-circuits if the magazines aren't perfectly aligned and the steak knives aren't set uniformly at a thumb-joint length from the table edge.

The stereo is on, tuned to a radio station that plays insipid pop hits from the '60s, '70s, and '80s: "Peaceful Easy Feeling," "Rainy Days and Mondays," "Up, Up, and Away." Perhaps it's been left on to sedate the cats. (The cats are not in evidence, but the women have been told he has them.) It's the kind of music that accompanies dull working environs, sonic pabulum for people who labor grimly in windowless cubicles. It is, Gaelan's women imagine, music that their mothers listened to while rubbing Lemon Pledge onto the coffee tables or ironing spray starch into their dads' dress shirts.

Gaelan presents them with cocktail-hour refreshments: wine or beer, slivered vegetables, stoned wheat crackers, dip, nuts . . . The women sip their drinks and scan the room: There is sleek, nondescript furniture in shades of beige, a set of free weights, a glass-fronted entertainment center, a high-tech elliptical trainer. No posters, no plants, no family photos. Even the dishes and wineglasses are bland and featureless.

Gaelan settles on the sofa next to them, one cushion away. The women feel the structure beneath the upholstery—timber frame, steel springs—respond to his weight in incremental stages: compression, resistance, stasis, support. They are reminded of his bulk, his sculpted physique. Gaelan Jones: weatherman and bodybuilder. These are the facts they all know—the only facts they know, really, now that they think about it. The women bite into celery sticks. The sound is deafening; massive wood beams being razed by bulldozers.

They chat. To his credit, Gaelan is a very good listener, but in this sterile setting, the women feel as if their previous history with him has evaporated. They find themselves recycling stories they've already told, imparting information they've already shared. The conversation keeps them circling one another, wary, decorous—like wrestlers in a way, except that the actual wrestling match might not materialize; it could be canceled due to the sexual side effects produced by Easy Listening FM and monochromatic home decor.

Gaelan's women begin to doubt the wisdom of undertaking a liaison with this man. Maybe his television persona—and his impressively buff, swoon-inducing physique—is all there is. Maybe he's all looks and no substance. He's a decent, if somewhat restless kisser; but what if the sex doesn't measure up? What if it's as careful and mediocre as the surroundings? Maybe they were better off having a relationship with his televised form; they could invest in a ten-inch portable and lug him around. They wouldn't feel any awkwardness then, any pressure to touch or be touched.

(But didn't they come here in hopes of being touched? Aren't they looking for sexual diversion? Poor Gaelan, he attracts only the rebounders and the chronically confused.)

Their host, on the other hand, shows no sign of being ill at ease. He is affable and polite, the antithesis of naughty. The women wonder if there isn't a chaperone somewhere, stashed in the broom closet maybe, or secreted in the vegetable crisper. The women keep their voices low and abstain from further encounters with the celery and crackers.

"Would you like to see the rest of the place?" Gaelan asks, after an interval of thirty to forty-five minutes.

"Okay, sure," the women reply, polite but nonplussed, knowing there is only one other room to see. They haven't even kissed yet. They've barely touched. How exciting can it be?

The women check their watches and think about buying groceries, doing laundry, reading legal briefs, grading student essays on *The Scarlet Letter*. They ponder whatever tasks they're avoiding by being here, whatever obligations await them when they leave, which will be any minute now because this rendezvous with the weatherman isn't going the way they'd hoped.

(And what did they imagine? They didn't expect him to jump their bones right away, did they? That can't have been what they had in mind.)

Gaelan gets up and walks down a short hallway, stopping in front of a closed door. They follow, drinks in hand. He nudges the door open.

The shrine is revealed. The women are mesmerized.

It's a quilt, but nothing like the quilts their grandmothers have passed down, quilts that are packed away in hope chests, folded between sheets of tissue paper, surrounded by moth balls that are hard as hailstones and stink of camphor, quilts that are cherished but unused, being far too prudish and compliant-looking to grace the beds of modern women—unhappy women in this case, since Gaelan's women are universally unhappy as well as confused and have no appetite for commitment, not now anyway; they are here because they possess a keen desire for boisterous, vengeful, heart-pumping, healing, and/or illicit sex. The quilts belonging to Gaelan's lovers are rendered in dainty modulated patterns (Flower Basket, Flying Geese, Wedding Band), patterns featuring large expanses of white cotton that has been salvaged, surely, from the honest, plain white sheets of their ancestors' marriage beds. These fields of white, virginal as wedding gowns, underline the makers' belief that to rely overmuch on pattern and color is to invite danger; looking too long at a complex design might incite the viewer to commit morally complex acts. The quilts belonging to Gaelan's lovers were made by nice Nebraska housewives who never laid down naked with any man but their husbands; the hands that stitched them were guided by hearts and minds that would not approve of late-afternoon trysts with a thirty-eight-year-old television celebrity, a man of dubious talents, odd obsessions, and a bachelor to boot.

But this quilt! The weatherman's quilt! A blast of artistic unconventionality, a free-for-all of swirling, angled shapes, the colors of culinary spices and tropical florals. Who would have guessed?

Here, too, are the cats they've heard about, dozing in the middle of the bed: orange tabby and calico. Their coloring makes them look as if they've been stitched into the design. Their bodies are curled together like intersecting commas. As the women draw closer, the cats' eyes wink open, and they register the arrival of visitors with opera diva stretches and vocalizations. For some of the women, Spencer and Kate are a boon; the dog lovers could care less; the allergic begin to sneeze. But for all of them, the prospect of generic, beige-colored sex has been eradicated. The quilt, so charged with eroticism it could be the cover art for a new translation of the Kama Sutra, changes everything.

"What a gorgeous quilt," the women exclaim—or murmur, muse, sniffle, coo, depending upon individual temperament and the degree of sexual heat surrounding that revelatory moment.

"Thanks," Gaelan replies. He's glad that the women like it, but he prefers to downplay its significance, not acknowledging that the quilt can't help but be the most remarkable thing about his domicile—and his psyche.

"Where did you get this?" the women continue. They are moving toward the bed now to get a closer look. Spencer and Kate, knowing they will soon be displaced, vacate the room.

"My mother designed it." None of the women notice that this isn't an answer.

It's true, basically, but Gaelan omits the fact that the quilt Hope made was carried skyward twenty-five years ago, and that, years later, after making dozens of thumbnail sketches and paintings, he re-created it from memory, handing over his renderings (and his first two paychecks as KLAN-KHAM's weatherman) to the fabric artist who constructed this fascimile.

So it is Hope's quilt, yes—but it's Gaelan's, too, for it is his memory that intensified the colors: turmeric, paprika, curry, lime, periwinkle blue, hibiscus red, black pepper, stamen pink. It is his memory that created the quilt's patternless geography, with bits of fabric veering off, meandering, spinning apart like planetary bodies that have fallen out of orbit. Hope's quilt was an orderly, dilute version of this one, an early draft.

The women make a natural but erroneous assumption.

"Your mother made this?" they say, aghast.

Gaelan doesn't respond, preferring to regard this question as rhetorical.

The women then ask something along the lines of "Is she a professional artist?" "Does she sell her quilts anywhere?"

To which Gaelan must reply, "Actually, she's dead."

"Oh, no!" the women cry. "When did she die?"

"A long time ago, in 1978."

"I'm so sorry."

The women set aside their wine glasses. Bending over the bed, they begin smoothing their hands over the quilt. Gaelan moves behind them. He presses the concavity of his body against the convexity of theirs. He reaches around them. For a while, their hands and Gaelan's explore the quilt together. The women are able to lean into the circle of the weatherman's beautifully cut arms without hestitation or worry now. Everything feels right.

Soon, clothes are shed. Auras start changing color. Pheromones begin discharging with the force of firearms.

The quilt has beguiled them, that is how the women feel. The quilt—with its suggestive colors, its cascading shapes—has charmed them out of their confusion, malaise, melancholy.

Gaelan never meant for the quilt to be the trump card in his sexual life, really he didn't, but the truth is, nothing closes the deal on sex like a sad story, even if it's not the whole story.

Eventually, the women get over whatever troubles brought them here. Healed, they move on, long before it occurs to them to probe more deeply into the history of the decorative anomaly that graces the weatherman's bed. In the end, he's nothing more than a great lay and the quilt is just a pretty bedspread.

"My folks met at a Fleetwood Mac concert."

"I remember," Gaelan replies, *in 1975.* "Beer or wine?"

"Beer's good if you've got something low-carb."

"I do." Gaelan is in the kitchen area of the condo. As he pours the beer into a glass, he gazes at the back of Rhiannon's head. She's sitting across the room on the sofa, absentmindedly playing with her hair, looking around. She seems distracted, tired. Maybe her blood sugar is low. "Help yourself to the hummus," Gaelan reminds her.

"According to Mom," Rhiannon continues, "I was conceived while they were listening to a bootleg recording."

"That's such a great story," Gaelan says, coming back into the living room. "Here you go."

"I'm just glad they didn't name me 'Stevie.'"

Gaelan laughs as if he hasn't heard this before. He settles beside her, stretching an arm across the back of the sofa, fingering a few wisps of her hair. Her neck is warm, still damp. They both showered at the gym right before coming here. "'Stevie' wouldn't suit you at all," he murmurs. "You are definitely a Rhiannon."

He likes thinking about how the two of them were naked together (at the same time but in different rooms) only half an hour ago. She smells like melted candy canes. He can't wait to taste her—but he will. Waiting, even a little bit, makes it all that much better.

She adjusts her body on the sofa. Gaelan removes his hand, takes a swig of beer. "I think somebody told me once that it's Gaelic or something," she adds. "Irish, maybe. Or Welsh."

"Really." This information is new. "I've got a book about Welsh mythology. Let me see if I can find it. Can I get you anything while I'm up?"

"No, thanks. I'm good."

"Be right back." Gaelan goes down the hall into his bedroom. He thinks the book is in the closet with some other stuff he never looks at: old yearbooks, college textbooks, letters. There isn't much; Gaelan isn't the type to hoard mementos.

Yeah, here it is: *Land of My Fathers: A Collection of Welsh Lore and Poetry*.

He opens to the inscription on the flyleaf: *To my big brother, a Welshman through and through and my hero always. Love, Bonnie. Christmas 1984.*

"Found it," he calls out.

Nineteen eighty-four. *Shit.* In 1984, the woman in the next room was nine.

Gaelan thumbs through the book till he finds what he's looking for. "Here we go: Rhiannon," he calls out.

"What?" Her voice sounds startled, as if she was dozing.

"Here's what the book says about your name."

"Oh. Right."

"'Rhiannon is the great Welsh goddess, able to take many forms.'"

"Huh."

"'She often appears as a white horse and is accompanied by three sweetly singing birds . . .'"

"Are there pictures?" Rhiannon calls out. "Let me see."

As Gaelan starts to leave the bedroom, something falls out of the book. It's a letter. He stoops to pick it up; realizing who it's from, his chest constricts: a fabric of sinew and tissue being pierced with too-small sutures, too close together, pulled tight.

"Oh my God," Rhiannon says, her voice close.

"What?" In a panic, Gaelan looks up. But she's not looking at him; she's standing a few feet away from him at the bedroom door. "What?" he repeats more evenly, stuffing the letter back into the book, hiding the book behind his back.

"Your quilt," Rhiannon says, breathless. "It's gorgeous."

"Thanks."

"Where did you get it?"

"It's a family heirloom, kind of. My mother designed it."

"You're kidding. Hey, is that the book?" She takes a few steps toward him and reaches for it, but Gaelan redirects her hand, pulls her into his arms, lets the book fall to the floor and—as they start to kiss—kicks it under the bed.

"Lucky me," he murmurs between kisses, as the clothes come off, as they segue to horizontal, "I brought a goddess home."

Two orgasms later (hers, not his), Gaelan takes a break.

"That was soooo nice," Rhiannon says, sighing and stretching.

She seems sincere. That's a relief. After the alarming realization that he was having a problem with his dick, Gaelan redirected the proceedings with the liberal application of his fingers and tongue.

He asks, because he always enjoys hearing about it (women are so inventive and vivid in their descriptions), "What was it like?"

"Hmmmm," she muses, closing her eyes. She really does look pretty happy. "There was a kind of whiteout sensation, like being snow-blind." She stretches again. "And it was minty." She kisses him, making slow circles with her tongue around the inside of his mouth, pulling lightly at his lips with her teeth.

In Gaelan's netherlands, nothing. Not a damned thing.

"Are you sure you don't want to try again?" she whispers. She starts to reach for him, but he catches her hand, pulls it to his mouth.

"Not today," he says decisively, as if this was his plan all along. He moistens her fingers and then directs them back under the sheets and inside; her vaginal walls are still warm, engorged, wet. "Let's just focus on you."

Rhiannon gasps, closes her eyes.

It's not so bad. It's nice, actually, knowing he can send a woman somewhere, even if it means going away from him.

Inside of her, their fingers move together with escalating urgency. Rhiannon moans, arches her back, sails away.

"That's it," Gaelan whispers, as she goes farther and farther. "Come on, come on, let's make a blizzard."

They'd originally talked about going to a movie, but only in an iffy kind of way. In the end Rhiannon decides to go to the library. They'll meet up tomorrow, at the Y.

"I feel a little guilty," she says as he walks her to the door. "You know, about . . ."

"Don't," Gaelan breaks in. "Guilt is a completely useless emotion." It's a stock line offered in response to a frequently heard sentiment, but it seems to be reliably reassuring.

They kiss. She leaves. In spite of certain disappointments about the way the afternoon played out, Gaelan has every reason to believe that they'll be seeing a lot of each other.

After reassuring himself in the shower that there's nothing wrong with his *equipment* per se, Gaelan decides to stay in; he'll order a pizza, watch a DVD from his collection. Maybe a comedy like *Twins* or *Kindergarten Cop* or *didn't Arnold make a movie with Dolly Parton?*

He strips the bed, stuffs the sheets into the washer, and cleans up the dishes.

He calls Godfather's Pizza and places his order for delivery.

He sits down at his computer and does a Google search.

This leads him to learn that the psychological causes of *erectile dysfunction* include stress, anxiety, guilt, depression, low self-esteem, indifference, bereavement, nerves, relationship problems, exhaustion, and latent gayness. A UK-based Web site implores him to not do anything like purchase pills or potions off the Internet or from blokes in pubs. Another site reassures him that with the advent of prescription drugs, things like penile injections, internal splints, and pellets inserted down the urinary pipe (*Shouldn't that be* up *the urinary pipe?* Gaelan wonders, fending off a wave of nausea) are rarely necessary options.

It's only that this kind of thing has never happened to him before, not even a little. He's always just *been there* in full force when called upon to perform.

Enough. He gets up, remakes the bed with fresh sheets and pillowcases, replaces the quilt. He makes smooching noises. Kate and Spencer emerge from wherever they were hiding, trot over to rub against his legs, and then jump onto the bed.

When he leans in to pet them, his foot touches something.

The book. He'd forgotten all about it.

Tucked inside is a fifteen-page pamphlet (*A Spoonful of Love: The Story of the Welsh Love Spoon* by Elwyn Hughes) and the letter from Bethan that he didn't remember was in there, and which he didn't want Rhiannon to see. He sits down on the bed and reads:

Dearest G, I would have made one of these for you if I could . . .

Gaelan remembers the gift that accompanied this letter. He hasn't seen it for years. He has no idea where to look for it.

Bethan's letter continues: *I hope you like it. I had Dad and Mom on the lookout for someone who'd carve a custom-ordered Love Spoon for me last summer when they were in Wales. (Knowing it was for you, I provided <u>very</u> specific instructions.)*

Here's what it all means:

The heart is a pretty obvious symbol, likewise the keyhole and key, but I don't care. You are the gatekeeper to my heart. ☺

The vines symbolize the growth of love—and of course remind me of Viney. Twisted together like this they're also meant to show two becoming one.

The four-leaf clover is for that old poem by Ella Higginson. And your mom, of course.

And finally, there's the comma/teardrop shape, known as the "soul" motif. No one knows exactly how this symbol got to Wales and started showing up on gravestones and Love Spoons. Some people think it arrived via Arabian pirates incarcerated on the Isle of Mon—isn't that a tale?—who, as practicing Muslims, would have used this shape as representative of the soul (the soul originating from the breath, the breath/soul entering and leaving the body through the nostrils, thus the nostril/comma/teardrop shape). I know: nostrils aren't exactly romantic, but the main thing is, the shape symbolizes eternal devotion. Which is what I give you, my love, now and forever. Bethan.

Gaelan tucks the letter and the pamphlet back into the book and sets it on the nightstand. He should feel something. Regret, shame, longing, something.

He stuffs the sheets into the dryer. He turns off the radio, feeds Kate and Spencer their dinner. He inserts *True Lies* into the DVD player, muting the sound.

Then he settles back on the sofa, lights a joint, and waits for the pizza man.

Everything looks just the way it did before Rhiannon arrived. It's as if she was never here.

Hope's Diary, 1965:
A Spilling Over Life

Now I know the meaning of the expression "easy baby." I can't believe the effect that Gaelan is having on his sister. It's as if he's the twin she's been expecting. "What took you so long?" she seems to be wondering. "I've been waiting and waiting and waiting for you."

They stare at each other until they fall asleep.

Here's how I manage the embarrassment of household chores, my inability to keep up: Somehow I feel that if I leave the clean laundry in the basket, it's contained and thus tidy. Ditto with the dishes: If I fill the large soup pot with dishwashing liquid and plop the dirty dishes and silverware in there, it's more acceptable than just leaving them about on the counter. I take on the dishes one at a time, resting in between.

I do not always feel kind to them, these babes who bless me, torture me, provide me with my greatest joy and my deepest sorrow. They are the ones, after all, who generate most of this mess. There is evidence of them everywhere—of Llewellyn and I, there is barely a trace. The children make themselves known with clutter; we, the adults, with our compulsive tidiness and grown-up ways, have erased ourselves. No one would suspect that anyone lives here except a tribe of feral homo sapiens. Our own little "Lord of the Flies" island.

Motherhood is changing my reading habits, of all things. Reading more short fiction vs. novels now, also more poetry—which seems to be the only thing I can manage at the end of a day spent with two children in diapers. A good poem gives me more food for thought than two hundred pages of "War and Peace."

I quip. I really have no idea. I've never read "War and Peace," nor am I likely to anytime soon.

Both babes teething and nothing to be done. Pretended I was in Italy and had an early drink. It was that or give over to the too tight stringing sensation in my nerve endings and scream back at them. A glass of red wine at eleven-thirty in the morning wouldn't be out of place in Florence. That was my justification.

Larken has earned a new nickname: the little shark. She bit Gaelan on the arm the other day so hard that she drew blood. She's been using her teeth as weapons more and more lately—although up to this incident, her primary targets were teething rings and Mommy. With me, she's been testing: First there were little rhythmic nibbles, then the gentle chomp, then the full-fledged (and painful) bite. Her impulse doesn't seem to arise out of a desire to hurt so much as curiosity, overwhelming affection, and/or excitement—feelings that are so big that they cannot be contained in her tiny body.

Nevertheless, it's unacceptable.

I'd been consistently ineffectual in my efforts to break her of this habit, using the same tactic over and over again, rebuking her with a harsh voice— "No biting!" (as if she were a puppy)—but when she bit her brother I couldn't stand it anymore; I grabbed her, applied my fully formed adult teeth to her chubby baby forearm, and bit her back—not hard enough to break the skin, mind you, but <u>hard</u>.

For a moment she was so shocked that she forgot to cry. I almost laughed.

This passed, of course, and after that she howled inconsolably for a good forty-five minutes. Since Gaelan was still crying from his injury, it was a noisy morning.

I doubt that this is the sort of disciplinary tactic recommended by Dr. Spock, but in my defense, she hasn't bitten any humans for three days.

On the flip side, she hasn't bitten <u>anything</u>, not even a zwieback. She flatly refuses any form of nourishment that has not been pureed. Which of course means that I must spoon-feed her everything.

My clever, obdurate girl. I believe she is taking her revenge.

Viney took the children for a while today after work—angel that she is—so I could get a decent rest. Which I did, thank God. Feel like a new woman!

Kids are home now and outside—I'm watching them from the kitchen window—so I thought I'd scribble a bit while they're entertaining themselves. Sitting down to do this practically guarantees that they'll be here momentarily, however. They have some sort of sixth sense about my music and/or writing time; they can be ignoring me all day, happily playing, but within seconds of my sitting down at the piano or with my diary, it's "MOMMY MOMMY MOMMY!" and then I must go and

God. This is pathetic. Whining about my children on a day when I've even had a respite from them.

I remember that old calendar in Uncle Jim's store, the WWII one. The images on that calendar are still so clear in my mind. Mothers, stoically gazing over the bowed heads of their children as they prayed for Daddy to come home. I loved those images. I loved that idea of motherhood.

Here they come. More later.

*   *   *

It's always fun to try to divide people into two groups, as in "There are two kinds of people in the world: those who see the glass as half-empty and those who see it as half-full."

Today I am thinking of another way to polarize humans: It seems to me that there are people in the world who are able to contain their lives, neatly, calmly. They create boundaries that allow them to function in whatever way is called for at the present moment. They ignore their children, for example, when that is an appropriate response. They pay their bills precisely at the same time every month, clean the bathroom on Wednesdays, plan a week's worth of menus.

I am in the other category. There is spillage everywhere, even in the garden. When I'm angry at Llewellyn, I take it out on the rosemary bushes, which are spilling into the thyme bed, selfish rosemary bushes that I used to long to grow as a badge of my own virtue, since it is said that the Virgin cast her cloak upon one.

Motherhood is messy in so many more ways than I expected. A chaos of emotions and laundry. A life without boundaries, splitting at the seams and spilling over everywhere.

Chapter 15

Kummerspeck

Something is wrong with the weatherman. His face has a peculiarly dewy expression, as if he's in the process of becoming his own graphic, a kind of human cartoon in service of the ten-day forecast: cloudy with a chance of showers.

People all over Lancaster and Hamilton counties are worried. It's not the first time in recent weeks that the KLAN-KHAM viewing audience has found their attention straying. Ever since Gaelan Jones, weatherman, returned from his brief hiatus in late August, he's failed to exude his usual confidence and charm. Some viewers—including scores of women—have even jumped ship, changed the channel, and started watching Brock Garrison, Meteorologist. Brock Garrison isn't as easy on the eyes as Gaelan Jones, but at least they don't find themselves fretting about his emotional health.

It's true that Gaelan has been experiencing unaccountable and sudden bursts of feeling during his live television segments. Up until today, he's been successful in containing and sublimating these feelings—or so he believes: The truth is that the camera sees everything, reveals everything. The merest suggestion of a sad or errant thought is easily perceived. This is why the viewing audience is leaving, the ratings are down, the sponsors are worried, and the station owners are making contingency plans.

Galean never knows what will prompt these emotional stirrings: a lighthearted comment by one of the anchors, the swelling of the KLAN-KHAM news team theme music, the cameraman's shoes. It used to be that, once he was on the air, nothing else got in; it was like being in a tightly circumscribed spotlight. But the boundary that has always kept him focused and held his awareness of the rest of the world at bay has been invaded somehow, breached.

It's the dead. They're the invaders.

These are their portals: music and dreams, chiefly, but sometimes they get in by other means: through gestures, objects, symbols.

And in the same way that a body weakened by a compromised immune system is susceptible to illness, a spirit newly underpinned with grief is susceptible to communiqués from the dead. Such communiqués may not be solicited, expected, or even welcome. They are frequently inconvenient.

Gaelan has used the raindrop graphic for years without encountering any emotional hazard. Furthermore, raindrops caused no problems earlier in the day, when they made their on-screen appearance during the six A.M. broadcast.

But now, during the noon segment, something is loosed when he sees himself on the monitor pointing to a queue of water droplets.

"Sorry to put a damper on your weekend plans, folks," he is saying. "No pun intended, but . . ." He starts to experience an agitated, spiraling sensation at the base of his throat. His voice grows tight. His lachrymal glands go into hyperdrive. His corneas itch. ". . . What the radar picture seems to indicate is that we'll be experiencing an extended period of . . ."

Gaelan stops speaking. The shapes on the screen have ceased to symbolize a prolonged likelihood of precipitation; they've turned into commas, nostrils, symbolic representations of the soul and undying devotion. He thinks of incarcerated Arabian pirates. Of Welsh Love Spoons. Of spooning. Of yin and yang. Of . . .

". . . gravestones."

There is a pause. Did he say that out loud? He thinks perhaps he did.

"Grave showers," Gaelan says emphatically. "Scattered spoons." He clears his throat and speaks slowly. "An extended. Period. Of. Rain. Turning to. Scattered. Showers."

He becomes aware of other people in the studio: the cameraman, the sound man, the production manager, the news anchor. Some of them look perplexed. None of them look happy.

Gaelan has made mistakes before. He knows that the situation calls for him to elaborate, banter, embroider, bullshit—in short, *recover* so that he can fill up the fifteen or thirty or forty-five or sixty seconds remaining in the time that has been allotted him—but as soon as his eyes return to the monitor, he becomes transfixed once again by the solemn parade of apostrophes.

"Back to you, Greg," he says dully, but before he can finish, his screen goes black. He's off camera.

"Well, thanks, Gaelan!" the news anchor bellows jovially from the other side of the sound stage. He lets slip with a politically incorrect comparison between Eskimos and weathermen, and then, beginning with "Singin' in the Rain," launches into a chronologically ordered medley of weather-related tunes in a hearty but slightly desperate-sounding voice. He gets all the way to Bob Dylan's "It's a Hard Rain Gonna Fall" when finally, mercifully, someone cues the theme music.

The show is almost over. Gaelan starts to unclip his mic.

"And that's it for the midday news," the anchor resumes, regaining his composure as the music crescendoes. "Have a great afternoon, folks. Stay dry out there, and be sure to join us again this evening at five as the KLAN-KHAM team brings you the latest in national and local news, sports, and weather."

Music up, Gaelan thinks, trying to command his awareness back into the here and now. *Picture and sound out. Go to commercial.*

He strides toward the sound stage exit. He doesn't speak to anyone. He doesn't change out of his suit or take off his makeup. He snags his gym bag from the dressing room, puts on his sunglasses, and heads straight for the Y.

"She calls that *art*? You've gotta be kidding."

Professor Jones is running through a slide presentation that she gives near the beginning of each semester in Art Appreciation 101; it's a twenty-minute visual anthology of two hundred or so significant painted works dating from prehistory to the present and shown in nonchronological order.

Larken shows the slides lickety-split, saying little. They're strung together in what to an untrained eye would seem to be a dysunified way: da Vinci's *Last Supper* next to Andy Warhol's Elvises; a Dutch still life next to a dreamscape by Salvador Dalí; a Hockney swimming pool next to one of Constable's landscapes; the symbol-rich Mérode—with its blue and white pitcher, water basin, white lilies, snuffed candle, song birds, rose bush, mousetraps—next to one of Frida Kahlo's self-portraits. And so on. Larken usually has a lot of fun putting this presentation together, changing it every semester. But this year—not having had her usual prep time—she's making do with a rerun.

She feels vacant, disengaged—like a reliable actor who's doing the thousandth performance of a great role in a brilliant play: skilled, but uninspired.

Currently on the screen is one of Jackson Pollock's action paintings: *Lavender Mist*. Every semester there is invariably one naive, callow-faced boy who mutters something at this point and, in so doing, unwittingly becomes the prime designate of Professor Jones's attention for the next three months.

Larken freezes the slide show, letting the Pollock linger.

"Did someone have something to say?" she asks. "Please speak up."

From near the back of the lecture hall, a hand is raised. "Anybody could do that," the boy continues. "It looks like he dribbled a bunch of paint on the floor."

"He did, actually," Larken comments. There's an eruption of constrained snickers. "Why, in your opinion," Professor Jones continues, "does that disqualify it from being 'art'?"

"It doesn't *look* like anything," the boy says, confident that he's making an entirely unprecedented observation and speaking on behalf of everyone in the room. "I mean, what's it supposed to *be*?"

"Tell me, Mr. . . . " (She pauses to examine her roster. This is purely for effect since Larken has a near-photographic memory and learns all her students' names by the third day of class.) "Houser. Why does it have to look like something to be art? Does that really matter?"

He doesn't know what she's talking about. None of them do, not yet. But that's okay. That's what she's here for.

"What if we define 'art' differently?" Larken continues. "In the case of this painting, for example: Can it be interesting? Can you be curious about it, ask questions? Can you have a *relationship* with it?"

It has always been a source of grief to Larken, the metaphors through which American culture—and especially Nebraskan culture—instructs its boys. The prevailing belief seems to be that all of Life's Lessons can be learned through engaging in bone-bruising sports and/or enlisting in the armed services, and summed up by expressions like the ubiquitous *No pain, no gain* and *Pain is only weakness leaving the body*.

Professor Jones is tenured. She doesn't have to teach a class like Art Appreciation 101; she chooses to because she feels called to affect the viewpoint of freshman farmboys and ranchers' sons: boys whose ideas about art come from the home furnishings department at JCPenney's, or the Sears catalog, or from gas station and farm co-op calendars, or from county fairs where vendors sell the dead on velvet; small-town boys of beefy build who are here on football scholarships and are only taking Art Appreciation 101 because they need an easy credit; boys whose lives are hard and blunt, and who without her influence will grow into hard blunt men who'll fuck young girls in the back seats of trucks parked outside nameless bars and strip clubs on the fringes of border towns.

Larken continues. "The artist Pierre Bonnard said, 'A painting is a little lie which adds up to a great truth.' Let's talk about that statement in the context of Mr. Pollock's work."

She's interrupted again—this time by the sound of the lecture hall door opening. Larken turns, expecting to deliver a public chastisement to a tardy student; instead, she sees Chris hovering in a thin slice of light at the room's entrance.

"I'm sorry, Professor Jones. May I speak with you for a moment?"

There is sedate muttering. Larken excuses herself and then vacates the podium and follows Chris into the hallway.

"It's Professor Collins," Chris begins hoarsely, her eyes glistening, hyperreflective. "Arthur. He collapsed in his classroom, the paramedics were just here, they've taken him to LGH . . ." She goes on and on, her eyes leaking with the irritant of grief, her words ferrying more and more raw feeling out of her body: an airborne affliction, a virus that Larken must not catch, not here, not now.

She covers her mouth with her hand and looks at the floor, enfolding herself in a compensatory darkness and protective silence.

Shut up, she wants to say, because the unguarded human voice is such a responsive vessel, clear as glass; as soon as *It's Arthur* was poured freely from the heart to the mouth, Larken knew everything she needed to know so *shut up shut up SHUT UP.*

Chris has stopped talking and is staring at her. "Larken. Are you all right?"

"I'm fine. Is he—?"

"I don't know. They think it's a stroke. Eloise went with him."

"Lincoln General, is that what you said?"

Chris nods, tears up again, and then swipes at her nose with what's left of a tissue. "She'll call the office as soon as there's any news, but . . . Well, I know how close you are to them, and I thought—"

"Yes, yes . . ." Larken will not think of anything beyond what's called for in this moment—the practical actions of a commander under siege.

"Cancel my classes for the rest of the day. I'll check in later."

Without waiting for a reply, she hurries away, down the hall, into the elevator. Office, coat, purse, and then up and out and as quickly as possible to the car, the car, she must get to the car: a staging area where emotions can be contained and expressed in private.

Meanwhile, the students of Professor Jones's Art Appreciation 101 class—abandoned, uncertain, increasingly restless—have lost interest in having a relationship with Jackson Pollock. Without the benefit of Professor Jones's insistent queries and intimidating presence, they can't be bothered with redefining their ideas about art.

"Did you say *catheterize*?" Viney asks.

"No, no: '*kasherize,*'" Bethan enunciates. She's standing at the stove in Viney's kitchen, warming up some soup and explaining why it is she brought her own saucepan. "It means to make a kitchen kosher, which means observing certain rules about preparing and serving meals."

"Kasherize." It's an exotic-sounding word, and uttering its peculiar admixture of sounds has a pleasant, empowering effect, as if it invokes magic. Viney decides to direct it toward the framed photo on the wall, the one she and Welly had taken last spring at that professional studio up in Lincoln. "Kasherize," she repeats, and then waits.

Nothing happens.

Viney sighs. "What kind of rules?"

"You can't eat any kind of dairy in the same meal as you're eating meat, for example; you have to have separate cookware and dishes for meat and dairy; eating pork in any form is prohibited . . ."

"Not even bacon?" Viney asks.

"Nope," Bethan chuckles. "I have to admit, it's the one thing I really miss . . ."

No bacon, Viney muses. *That's just bizarre.*

It was kind of Bethan and her son to deliver a hot meal and help with the yardwork—Eli is outside, raking leaves—but Viney had completely forgotten they were coming. She was napping on the living room sofa when they arrived, blinds closed, still in her bathrobe. The house is a mess.

"Leo, my husband, wasn't religious," Bethan goes on, "even though he was a professor of religious studies, isn't that funny?"

"Mmmm." It's the most Viney can manage.

"But it was important to us that we observe some of the Jewish laws and traditions, for Eli's sake mostly. The same way I've tried to keep up the Welsh . . ."

It's just that she's so tired. She's barely able to speak, much less understand the complexities of the Jewish faith as it relates to cooking.

". . . It's been a comfort to me, too, I guess, a way of staying connected to . . ."

Bethan's voice trails off. She opens the oven and checks on the potatoes.

Viney hopes Bethan isn't planning to leave her with a lot of leftovers. She only just got the fridge emptied out; it smelled awful. Everything people brought after the mayor died had gone bad. It was just too much trouble—heating things up, dirtying the dishes. She ended up throwing it all away.

Outside, there's the rhythmic sound of dead leaves chafing together as they're being raked into a pile. A universal sound, a seasonal sound. If she closes her eyes, Viney can imagine that it's Welly out there, or Wally Jr., or Gaelan, even Waldo or Papa or Grandpa Edryd. She can see each of them in her mind's eye so clearly: the individual shape and carriage of their strong male bodies, and she's always had strong men in her life. She could identify every one of them in silhouette from a great distance.

She can't picture Bethan's boy, though; she doesn't know him well enough.

"Viney?" Bethan's voice startles her. "Why don't you go back in the living room and have a rest? I'm sorry about our timing. We interrupted your program."

"Oh, no, don't be silly. I just turned it on so I could watch the news."

This is a lie. Viney spends most of the days now dozing on the sofa while cosmetically perfect people in fictional small towns with ridiculous names commit adultery, endure scandals, and never miss a manicure. In the world of daytime television, even the elderly are glamorous.

"Really, Viney. Go watch your show. I'll call you when it's ready."

"Well, all right then," Viney says. "If you're sure I can't do anything to help."

"Not a thing."

She drifts into the darkened living room and sits back down on the sectional. On TV, a bunch of people are standing in a hospital waiting room. Their expressions run the gamut from worried to smug to sinister to overwrought to hysterical. A doctor enters the scene, wearing scrubs and a surgical mask. The camera pans the crowd as everyone turns to face him, expectant, desperate for information. Slowly, the doctor pulls down his mask and regards each of them in turn. He does not speak. His expression is impossible to read. The screen fades to black.

Viney throws a sofa cushion at the TV.

Across the room, one of her hymnbook angels skydives off the piano.

It was Viney's next-door neighbor, Mrs. Bauer, who introduced her to the concept of *grief bacon*. Viney was ten.

In the weeks following the death of Viney's grandfather, the significant adults in her life—especially her mother, her aunts, and her grandmother—seemed half-asleep, distracted. They never seemed to be *looking* at anything, and they kept saying things like, "Don't bother Grandma right now. She's taking a rest." Or "Play by yourself, can't you, Viney? I have to lie down for a while." Viney had never seen the

womenfolk in her family like this. It disturbed her terribly, because
their behavior could only mean one thing: They had succumbed to a
terrible sin.

One day, Viney was moping around the front yard. She'd been banished from the house because she was being too noisy (even though she
wasn't being any noisier than usual) and was protesting this injustice
by pulling up hanks of grass and throwing pebbles into the street. A
distinct sound coming from next door let Viney know that Mrs. Bauer
was down on her hands and knees, scrubbing her front porch.

Viney worked up a loud belch.

Mrs. Bauer poked her head around the porch wall. "What is the
matter, Alvina?"

Viney answered with authority. "My grandmother is going to hell."

"Really?"

"So is my mother and Aunt Molly and Aunt Lizzie."

"You don't say."

Mrs. Bauer got to her feet and started across the yard. She was wearing a floral print apron—women always did in those days—and as she
walked she bunched up the apron, first in one hand, then the other, using
it like a towel. It was a gesture Viney had seen her mother and grandmother do hundreds of times, their hands shriveled and scalded red like
Mrs. Bauer's from being too long in hot water. Watching Mrs. Bauer
cross the yard while wiping her hands on her apron gave Viney a funny
feeling in her throat, and so she looked down and yanked up another
big fistful of grass.

"Tell me, Alvina, why do you think this about Grandmother and
Mother?"

"The laundry isn't folded. There are dishes in the sink." Viney whispered the most condemning evidence. "They've been taking *naps*."

"I see."

"They're *lazy*. That's another word for *sloth*." Realizing that Mrs.
Bauer's English vocabulary might not include this word, Viney added,
"Sloth is one of the seven deadly sins."

"Ah," Mrs. Bauer said. She knelt in the grass next to Viney. "Well,
Alvina, first of all, we should not judge what we have not lived. Do you
understand?"

"No."

"You lost your grandpa. That is *your* sadness. But have you lost a papa, like your mama has? Or a husband, like Grandmother?"

Viney was confused. Why was Mrs. Bauer talking about her grandfather?

"No, of course not."

"So you cannot know how this feels, can you? This loss of Mama and Grandmother."

Viney frowned. Grandfather's *Tridiau* and *Gymanfa* happened a long time ago, in February. She was sad when he died. She'd cried and sung along with everyone else, but wasn't that the end of it? Weren't they all done being sad? Viney started tweezering single strands of grass out of the ground with her fingers and flicking them onto her outstretched legs.

"Also," Mrs. Bauer continued, "your grandmother is not going to hell. Believe this. And lazy she is not either. Nor Mama. They have the grief bacon."

"The what?"

"Hmm." Mrs. Bauer paused and looked away, thinking. She brought one of her red, veiny hands to her face, burying her thumb in the fleshy spot beneath her chin, fanning her fingers out over her mouth. She started tapping her fingers across her lips, slowly, one by one, as if she were playing piano, the same four notes over and over again. It was an odd gesture, and for some reason it made it very easy for Viney to imagine how pretty Mrs. Bauer must have been when she was young.

"It is difficult, but I will try to explain," Mrs. Bauer said finally. "When someone we love very much dies, it makes us tired. Very tired. It makes us want to sleep and sleep, the way the animals do. You know the word? For what the bears in winter do?"

"Hibernate?"

"Yes. Hibernate. It is the body's way, this tired. And like the bears, the body sometimes grows heavy, puts on . . ." Mrs. Bauer gestured as if she were dressing to go outside in the snow.

"Layers?"

"Yes. Layers. To protect. To keep . . ." She gestured again, shrugging her shoulders and crossing her arms in front of her body as if she were wrapping herself up in a heavy blanket. "It is hard to say, to translate, to English. My family called it *Kummerspeck*. The grief bacon."

Viney considered. "Well, I don't like it. I don't like the grief bacon."

"Think of it this way, honey. Maybe our bodies do this so that the dead—who are still near to us—can visit our dreams before they get too busy."

Viney didn't feel exactly comforted by the notion that the dead could not only appear in dreams, but get busy (*doing what?* she wondered), but it was reassuring to hear that, in Mrs. Bauer's opinion anyway, being a bad housekeeper and taking naps in the middle of the day weren't sins. This meant a lot, considering the source. Mrs. Bauer had the shiniest windows and the cleanest floors in Emlyn Springs. At least that's what Mother always said.

"Oh, look!" Mrs. Bauer said. "I find a four-leaf clover for you! You know the poem about four-leaf clovers? By Miss Ella Higginson?"

Viney shook her head.

Mrs. Bauer recited: "'One leaf is for hope, and one is for faith, and one is for love, you know, And God put another in for luck. If you search, you will find where they grow.'"

Viney regarded her clover: four oval-shaped leaves attached to a stem. One of the leaves was shriveled and tinged with brown; in Viney's mind, this surely had some dire significance that undid whatever good luck the four-leaf clover might bestow. She accepted it to be polite, but planned to get rid of it later.

"Mother and Grandmother will be okay," Mrs. Bauer went on, giving Viney's shoulders a sqeeze. "You'll see. Now, come over to my house, why don't you? I have icebox cookies and nice cold milk. And while you have your snack I will copy down for you Miss Higginson's beautiful poem."

Viney is awakened suddenly by the sound of someone opening and closing the front door.

"Wally, honey, is that you?" she asks, squinting across the darkened room.

"No, Mrs. Closs, it's me, Eli."

"Eli?" Viney sits up and rubs her eyes. "Oh, yes. Eli. Hello." How long has she been asleep? What time is it? The TV is still on—a commercial—but the sound has been muted. There are three TV trays set up, and somebody put an afghan over her. Bethan must have come in and found her asleep. How embarrassing. This just won't do.

"May I please use your washroom?" Eli asks.

"Of course, honey. There's a bathroom back there." Eli starts to cross the room. He has that terrible, wooden way of walking that boys get when they're trapped between childhood and puberty, their bodies growing and changing so fast that it must feel as though they wake up every morning to find that someone snuck into their bedroom during the night and replaced their perfectly good arms and legs with an ill-fitting set of prosthetics.

"Thank you so much for your help," Viney adds. "It's been hard keeping up with the yardwork since . . . Well, I really appreciate it."

"You're welcome."

Eli goose-steps into the bathroom. Poor thing.

The news comes on. Viney unmutes the television: *Welcome to the KLAN-KHAM midday report, where we bring you the latest in local and national news, sports, and weather, with our team of professionals . . .*

And then there's the sex part: wet dreams and uncontrollable erections and all the shame that goes with it. It's so much worse for them, in Viney's opinion, because boys aren't good at hiding the way girls are—behind clothes and hairdos and makeup and a predisposition for cruelty—and because they wear their sex *outside* their bodies. What was God *thinking,* for heaven's sake, making males so guileless and vulnerable?

Our top news story this hour . . .

Viney has always regretted the way that she—and especially Welly—let Gaelan down when he was that age. And they did, she knows it. When he was going through all that, they were both still reeling from Hope's death, the guilt, the shame, the not knowing . . .

Eli comes back. "This was on the floor," he says, handing Viney the fallen angel.

"Oh, thank you," Viney says. The angels' hairdos date them; this one, with her layered Farah Fawcett curls—must be pushing thirty.

"You make those, don't you?" Eli asks.

"I did, yes. I used to make them all the time. Not so much though, anymore," Viney says, feeling suddenly sad and guilty about neglecting her hobby. The hymnbook angel population hasn't increased in years. She really should get going on these again.

"The Jewish faith doesn't allow physical representations of angels," Eli replies. "It's considered idolatry."

"I see," Viney comments. He really is an odd child—an old man in a young body. Sweet, though. "How do *you* feel about it?"

Eli shrugs. "I'm ambivalent."

"Would you like to sit down?" Viney offers. "I'm sure you're tired. Raking leaves is hard work."

"Thank you." Eli takes a seat on the sofa next to Viney. He seems very interested in the news; the program is half over before Viney registers the strangeness of his presence here in the middle of the day.

"Say," she asks suddenly. "Why aren't you in school?"

"I'm homeschooled."

"What does that mean?"

"My mom and I decide what I'm going to study and when."

"But you don't go to school? With other young people?"

"Nope. I do most of my work on a computer."

"Isn't that lonely?"

He looks away from the TV. "What do you mean?"

"Well, school isn't just about learning. It's about friends and class parties and dances and trying out for sports and things."

"I'm shy at dances. I don't really do any sports. I'm planning on being a writer."

"Still."

. . . and now with a preview of our five-day forecast, here's Gaelan Jones . . .

Eli's attention snaps back to the television.

"Well," Viney murmurs, "*my* boys would find it lonely, anyway . . ."

Gaelan begins his segment: *Sorry to put a damper on your weekend plans, folks, no pun intended, but . . .*

"He looks tired," Viney says to herself.

"Besides, we're not staying in Emlyn Springs," Eli adds.

"You're not? How come?"

"We're just here until, well, until my Mom feels better."

. . . what the radar picture seems to indicate is that we'll be experiencing an extended period of . . .

"What's wrong with your mother?"

"My dad died last spring."

Oh my God, Viney thinks. *How could I be so stupid?* "I'm so sorry, honey. I forgot."

. . . gravestones . . .

"And anyway," Eli says distractedly—like Viney, his attention is focused on Gaelan's petit mal mini-breakdown—"I have to go back for my bar mitzvah."

Viney is confused. "Did he say 'gravestones'?"

"I think so."

. . . grave showers . . .

"Your mother is much too young to be a widow," Viney adds.

"My dad was kind of old. He had another wife before my mom, and they had kids together. They're like almost Mom's age."

. . . scattered spoons . . .

"I see."

"Mom and Mr. Jones were boyfriend and girlfriend once," Eli comments.

Viney looks at him. "That's right."

"Why didn't they get married?"

"That's private, honey, between your mom and Gaelan."

There's a noise at the kitchen door. Bethan is standing there, holding two plates piled with food. She too is staring at the television.

. . . an extended period of rain turning to scattered showers . . . Back to you, Greg.

Bethan crosses the room quickly and sets the food down on the TV trays. "Excuse me," she mutters, and then rushes past them toward the bathroom.

"This looks absolutely delicious," Viney observes.

Eli adds, "It's kosher."

From the bathroom comes the sound of Bethan, sobbing. "Is your mother all right?" Viney asks. "Is there anything I can do?"

"She'll be okay," Eli remarks, digging into his dinner. "She always gets sad when she sees him on TV."

Bonnie is kneeling on the wood planks of what used to be Tinkham's Five and Dime, setting out mousetraps.

She found the mousetraps online after Googling *humane rodent control*. Technically, they're called mouse "houses," and they consist of a rectangular, green-tinted Plexiglas box with a small sloped roof—exactly like a little one-room house. They're ingenious contraptions: you slide out one of the walls, press down on a sprung platform, place a fragment of peanut-butter-smeared cracker inside, replace the wall, and then when a mouse sniffs the cracker and steps in, the spring is triggered and the trap closes, leaving mousie with a food supply and air holes until s/he can be relocated. The traps were on sale. Bonnie bought thirty-two.

Her newest entrepreneurial undertaking—BJ's Bikes and Repair—is housed in the same building as Blind Tom's piano hospital. Wanting to prove herself a responsible tenant in her conservation of utilities, Bonnie is working in the dark.

When Bonnie stood up at the town meeting and talked about how nice it would be to make better use of some of the downtown buildings, Blind Tom jumped right in and supported her. Noting that he had twice as much room as he needed to display his restored pianos, he offered to share his space.

The only major impact to the piano hospital has involved an entrance change: since the front door of the building is on Bonnie's half, her customers enter there; Blind Tom's customers are now directed via new signage and an arrow to park and enter through the back. Bonnie was initially very worried about inconveniencing Blind Tom and his patrons in this way, but Blind Tom reminded her that, having been an Emlyn Springs fixture since 1871, his business has excellent name recognition and would likely survive this new arrangement with minimal negative impact.

Blind Tom is on the other side of the plywood wall that divides their workspaces, tuning a recently restored piano that is ready for sale. It's a comforting sound, the sprinkling of single notes in octaves.

"You can turn the lights on, you know," he calls.

Bonnie is puzzled. She wonders how he knew that the lights were off, but decides it would be rude to ask. It *would* make it a bit easier if she could see what she was doing.

The piano falls silent. Blind Tom wanders in with Sergei.

"How's it going?" he asks.

"Almost done. I'll have to check these at the same time tomorrow. The manufacturer says they don't live longer than twenty-four hours in these. Okay if I give Sergei a treat? It's organic peanut butter."

"You're gonna spoil him."

"He deserves to be spoiled. Here, Sergei."

"Thanks for doing this," Blind Tom adds. "The traps, I mean."

"No problem. I like mice as well as the next person, but I don't want them making nests in the piano strings or the wheel spokes."

Blind Tom laughs. "It has been a problem, yes."

Bonnie has a sudden thought. "Have you ever been on a bike?"

Blind Tom considers. "Gosh, I guess I must have been, but it would have been a long time ago. I don't exactly remember."

"You never forget, you know."

"That's what I've heard."

Bonnie has the strange sensation that he can see her.

"Do you know what Mouse represents in Native American culture?" he asks.

"No. What?"

"Scrutiny."

"Really? That's interesting."

He stares at her—or rather, appears to stare at her; his downward tilting face is aimed in her direction. Bonnie waits, expecting to hear more about Native American wisdom on the subject of mice—she loves animal stories—but after a few moments he calls Sergei and turns to go.

"I'll leave you to your work," he says.

Bonnie wishes he didn't wear those dark glasses all the time. She'd like to be able to see his eyes.

Chapter 16

The Speed of Prayer

On the morning it arrives (par avion, bearing exotic stamps, postmarked the day after Welly's death, covered with handwriting she's never seen before), Viney rips the envelope open—a gesture executed with more energy than she's expended in weeks. She withdraws the letter, snapping its folded pages open with a sense of entitlement and righteous anger, as though it's an enemy combatant she intends to give hell to.

Dear Llewellyn, the letter begins. *You sound down. You must be experiencing one of those spiritual eclipses we have spoken of before. I am sorry to hear you so pessimistic, so discouraged. I wish I knew how to be of comfort.*

These temperate words—written by this stranger, this intruder whom Welly invited into their lives without asking permission—have a softening effect that Viney doesn't like. She skims the rest of the letter, only slowing down again near the end:

Some people are beset with a terrible disunity of spirit—that is how I think of it. It is as though their outward achievements have advanced to the front of that long line of identities that make us what we are, that parade of selves. These confident selves—professional success, financial success, good reputation—march on, oblivious to the tender, untended soul at the end of the line, barely keeping up, holding no one's hand, never reassured, always afraid.

You have achieved so much in this life, Llewellyn. Given so much—to your family, your patients, your community. Try to remember that. Hold that knowledge close.

The dark night comes to us all. But for you, my friend, it seems there are words that can never be heard enough, and so I will remind you of these simple truths:

God does not hold grudges.

You are a good man.

You have paid for your wrongs.

You are forgiven.

Viney refolds the letter and slips it back into its envelope.

She has informed the unknowing. She has acknowledged every condolence that came her way. It's only polite that she reply to this letter as well—even if it means consorting with the enemy.

"I need to learn how to use one of those," Viney blurts, pointing to one of the library computers. "Is there anyone who'd have time to help me?" she asks the librarian at the information desk.

Having failed several attempts at a handwritten reply to Brother Henry (the addition of liquid courage led consistently to a vitriolic tone, not to mention illegibility), Viney has concluded that a new approach is called for. To that end—and riding a burst of energy and resolve—she's driven all the way up to Beatrice.

I can do this, she tells herself. *I can learn something new.*

Of course, she could have gone to Wymore and been there half an hour ago; the Wymore library has computers and the Internet and all that, she knows because Larken and Gaelan go over there sometimes when they're visiting to check their email.

But Viney knows the librarian in Wymore. If she'd gone there Betty would've asked all kinds of personal questions and Viney is just not in the mood to be showered with sympathy or listen to someone kvetch about how terrible it is to be living alone at this time of life and how important it is that you *get OUT* now and then, *TREAT yourself, SO-CIALIZE.* If she's going to make the gargantuan effort to get dressed and leave the house in the first place, the *last* thing she wants to do is waste her time chitchatting with other lonely old women.

"I'd be happy to help you," the librarian says, coming out from behind the information desk. "Follow me." This librarian is no pinched, spinsterish matron wearing a cardigan and spectacles. She's a big girl, twentysomething, and she walks like a man. She has greasy hair held in place by numerous rhinestone-covered bobby pins and she wears fishnet stockings and hideous shoes and a name tag that says ADDISON. Young women have such interesting names nowadays.

"Have a seat," Addison says when they arrive at an unoccupied study carrel.

"I'm here to write an email letter. Can I do that?"

"You bet." The girl lays her hand on a silver, dinner-roll-sized object on the desk and expertly starts sliding it around. Periodically, it emits a single, light, ticking sound. It puts Viney in mind of the voices of fledglings and fox kits and she finds it oddly soothing. A thin gray cord flows away from it and down through a circular hold in the desk where it joins up with a lot of other cords.

"This is called a 'mouse,'" Addison remarks. "Sadly, it's the only named part of a computer that has any poetry."

"Aaaah," Viney says. A mouse. Clever. She likes this.

Addison keeps moving the mouse around, causing images on the computer screen to come and go so quickly that Viney barely has time to register what they are. "Okay. Now. Let's get you set up with a user name so you can write and receive mail online."

"Can't I just write a letter without doing that?"

"The person you're corresponding with needs to be able to write you back. Sooo . . . you need to come up with a name."

Viney refrains from reminding Addison that she already has one.

"It can be really simple, like your first initial followed by your last name, or your name followed by a number: how many children you have, for example, or a significant year. It can relate to your profession or your interests. Or it can be whimsical. Completely made up."

In Viney's experience, the people most likely to invent names for themselves are movie stars, strippers, and crooks.

"But whatever you pick, it should be at least six characters long with no spaces. While you work on that, I'll go help those folks at the counter. As soon as you've got something we'll get you started, okay?"

"Got it. Thank you."

Addison clomps away. It's a good thing the library is carpeted. But then, maybe silence is no longer the commodity it once was.

Pondering her assignment, she takes up a piece of scratch paper and a short, sharp pencil and prints her name across the top:

ALVINA CLOSS

Beneath this, she writes *Acloss.*

She doesn't like this, the way the word *loss* jumps out at her.

Alvinac.

A prescription drug for intestinal distress.

Vineycloss. Vineloss.

Maybe backward?

Yenivssloc.

Slavic—in a threatening, Iron Curtain, shoe-pounding Nikita Khrushchev kind of way.

Acloss1929. Mother1948. Widow1962. Mistress76. Angelofdeath78.

A name. She has to come up with a name. A *new* name. She really should be having more fun with this. After all, how often does this happen? How often does a seventy-five-year-old who's lived in the same town her whole life and never been called by any name but the one she was baptized with get asked to invent an alias?

Addison is back. "How you comin' along?" she asks.

"Maybe if you gave me an example. What name do you use?"

"'Sad bison at gee mail dot com.' It's an anagram of my first name and my middle and last initials. But it doesn't have to be that complicated. Do you have any hobbies?"

Viney considers. "I'm interested in nutrition. I do yoga."

"Fantastic! Just for now—what's your first name?"

"Alvina. I go by Viney."

"Perfect. Let's try"—she types—"nutriyogavine." She hits the Enter button as if she were cracking a bullwhip. "Congratulations! You've got an e-mail name."

"I could change it though, if I wanted to?"

"Absolutely. Now we need the e-mail address of the person you're writing to."

Viney pulls a notepad out of her purse, flips it open, and hands it over.

Addison types *brotherHenry@saintgwenfrewi.org*. Now that Viney understands the range of decisions involved in choosing an e-mail

identity, she's grateful to Brother Henry for making such a traditional choice. She'd find it difficult writing a letter to a stranger with
a name like *Sad Bison*.

"Now," Addison continues. "We'll get the cursor moved down to where
you need to start writing . . . Now you just start typing the way you would
on a regular typewriter." Addison's fingers move with incredible speed.
She demonstrates dragging, cutting, pasting, backspacing, highlighting,
deleting. "Once you're happy with everything," Addison concludes, "you
move the cursor here, click on the Send button, and that's it."

"I see," Viney says. "Wow."

"You'll do great. I'll be right over there if you have any questions."

Viney settles in. Well. Aside from all that naming business, this *has*
been easy. Why has she been so intimidated about computers for so long?
For some reason she thought you had to know all about the insides of
the things before you could use one. But that's silly. It's just another
appliance after all, another tool. She operates plenty of machines without knowing about their insides. Does she know how her car works?
Her Juiceman? Her Electrolux? Hell, no.

And she's an excellent typist. Or used to be. It shouldn't take too long
to get her skills back. This will be a breeze.

Dear Brother Henry

She deliberates over the punctuation. Colon or comma? He's a monk
after all, and they've never met. She opts for the formal choice:

:

It's a letter of introduction. An invitation. Being polite and straightforward is what's called for. Viney typed lots of correspondence for
Welly in her capacity as his medical secretary, so this should be simple.

Dear Brother Henry: My name is Alvina Closs and I am following up
on an invitation made by my long-term friend employer partner common-
law husband the man with whom I shared a bed for the past

Dear Brother Henry: I recently came across your letters to my
I am writing on behalf of
I am writing to inquire if

Are you still willing? I am asking you to please come
It would mean so much to our town, to me and Hope and Welly
It would mean so much to our children if
Dear Brother Henry: You may know of me through your correspondence with Llewellyn Jones, the mayor of Emlyn Springs as I believe
he mentioned me once or twice as his wife's best friend and as his
I have the sad task of informing you that your longtime correspondent and the mayor of Emlyn Springs, Dr. Llewellyn Jones
Dear BH: I was snooping around the office of the dead mayor and
by the way it might interest you to know that he was struck down by
lightning on a golf course and perhaps you as a man of God would have
a unique perspective on that I personally believe he was carrying out
a sentence that he leveled against himself many years ago and you
may also be intrigued as I am by the fact that he pretended for over
twenty years to be a juice-drinking lacto-ovo-semi-vegetarian and was
not as it turns out he kept a lot of secrets which shouldn't surprise me
at all since we've been keeping a very big secret around here for the
past twenty-five years and I know you know what I'm talking about
and
Hello there! I'm Alvina Closs, Dr. Llewellyn Jones's former nurse,
longtime mistress, and one might add co-conspirator since we plot-
ted a murder and got away with it

Alvina removes her hands from the keyboard. With the help of her
mouse she deletes everything she's written. Then, inclining her body
forward so that she can take advantage of the semiprivacy offered by
the study carrel walls, she opens her mouth as wide as possible, sticks
out her tongue, takes a large breath, and exhales forcefully, producing
a kind of unvoiced roar.

When she feels composed and focused enough, she begins again:

Dear Brother Henry:
My name is Alvina Closs. As a member of the Emlyn Springs community and a longtime close acquaintance of Mayor Dr. Llewellyn
Jones, I have the sad task of informing you of the mayor's sudden death
in late August.
I know that the two of you corresponded for many years on the subject of deepening the relationship between our Sister Cities. I am also

aware that you and Dr. Jones discussed the possibility of establishing a second monastery in southeast Nebraska, not only in the interest of expanding the presence of the Benedictine Order here in the Midwest, but also with an eye toward enriching our community's social, cultural, and economic life. Although Dr. Jones encountered some opposition in the past, our community is now eager to explore this possibility with renewed resolve. There could be no greater memorial to the mayor than to see his hopes for an invigorated Emlyn Springs come to pass through an alliance with the brothers of Gwynnedd Island.

To that end, we would like to extend an invitation. You would of course be welcome to visit us at any time, and we are very much looking forward to showing off our little bit of Wales in Nebraska whenever your travels bring you to the States. However, we are especially hopeful that you will consider joining us next summer during our annual summer festival, Fancy Egg Days. The festivities include a number of Welsh-inspired events which you and your fellow brethren might find especially enjoyable.

I look forward to hearing from you.

Sincerely yours,

Alvina (Viney) Closs

After doing a thorough proofread, Viney impulsively clicks on the Send button without consulting with Addison.

This really is just too easy—writing a letter that doesn't exist in any kind of physical form—and Viney fears the global effect of e-mail correspondence upon human morality. Who knew she'd have such an easy time of it, lying by omission to a Benedictine monk? If she'd written this letter the old-fashioned way and then had to stamp it, take it over to the post office, and hand it to the mailman, she never would have followed through. She would have been shamed by the physical evidence.

The words *Your email to brotherhenry@saintgwenfrewi.org has been sent* appear on the computer screen. Not exactly reassured—and certainly not absolved—Viney nonetheless feels a sense of accomplishment.

She drives home, barely able to keep her eyes open. Knowing that she's done all she's capable of today, she changes out of her clothes and into her bathrobe, draws the blinds and curtains, takes a couple of bites out of a stale powdered-sugar doughnut, and then lies down on the living room sofa and goes to sleep.

Larken is making her way through the catacombs of Bryan/LGH Medical Center for her daily visit to the ICU.

Her experience with the inner sanctums of intensive care units has been thankfully limited: other than those terrible visits to Bonnie back in 1978, before she regained consciousness, summons to hospitals have been more like social invitations. Larken has delivered balloons and Get Well cards to acquaintances recuperating from rhinoplasties, knee replacements, rotator cuff repairs. She's visited Mia in the hospital twice; both occasions were celebratory, although one was slightly less so than the other. (Larken has always believed that Mia's joy following Esmé's birth was muted by the sedatives she was given during her complicated labor and emergency C-section. Two and a half years later, however, narcotic aftereffects notwithstanding, Mia was boundlessly jubilant following her tubal ligation, which went without a hitch.)

Larken's oldest memory related to hospitals arises from her early adolescence: it's a distillation of countless hospital visits that occurred between 1973 and 1978.

Most people experience the visual magic trick called "perspective" and the concept of "vanishing point" by staring down a railroad track. Larken and her brother and sister became familiar with this phenomenon by watching their mother and father walk down many very long hospital hallways, their figures growing alarmingly smaller with each step, until they disappeared behind heavy metal doors that clanged shut in a loud, emphatic way: the sound of a castle fortress being secured before battle, a maximum-security penitentiary at lockup. But who was being protected? Larken often wondered. Who was in prison? Her vanished parents, or she and her siblings?

They waited with nothing to do. Larken pretended to read grown-up magazines—*Life* and *Newsweek* and *Time*. If there was a vending machine nearby, she bought candy bars and peanuts and cookies and pop for herself and her siblings. (As the oldest, Larken was entrusted with a small amount of money to spend as she saw fit while their parents were beyond the vanishing point; she eventually began using part of the money to buy cigarettes, swearing her siblings to secrecy.) If there were any *National Geographic* magazines around, Gaelan looked at those. Barring that, he played with a deck of cards that he always carried with him. He knew a million versions of solitaire; he also enjoyed the physics of shuffling and house-of-card construction. Sometimes they played gin rummy or war or spit. Bonnie could entertain herself for hours working on the "Hidden Pictures" pages of *Highlights* magazines. She never got tired of those.

Whenever Larken suggested that they leave for a while, go to the cafeteria maybe, or walk around, just to stretch their legs, alleviate the boredom—because after all, Mom and Dad never said in so many words that they *had* to stay in the waiting room the whole time—she and Gaelan could never get Bonnie to go.

What if they come back while we're gone? she'd always ask. *They'd be really scared if we weren't here. You can go if you want to, but I'm staying.*

Their baby sister's compassion and bravery moved them, shamed them, and so they stayed in the waiting room, waiting. Of the three of them, Bonnie was the one who never doubted that their parents would reappear, two tiny dots on the horizon, and make their way back to them.

Larken is almost to Arthur's room when someone calls out.

"Ex*cuse* me, ma'am. Visiting hours are *over*." Larken has been here every day since Arthur's stroke but hasn't encountered this person before. She backtracks to the nurse's station.

So many of these health care providers look sick themselves. This woman has pale skin glistening with excessive sweat or sebum or both, it's hard to tell, and her blonde hair has been yanked back from her face and squeezed into a punishingly tight topknot. From buttocks to crown her shape is perfectly conical, giving the impression of whipped cream that's been beaten vigorously until it forms stiff peaks. It can't be easy being an ICU nurse. It can't be easy being *any* kind of nurse. Larken can't imagine how Viney did it for so long. Nurses are saints; that's the only explanation. These people don't just check vital signs and draw blood, they hold the line, guard the gate, admit only the worthy.

"I'm here to see Arthur Collins," Larken says. "I'm expected."

"I'm sorry," the nurse begins, "but . . ."

"She's family, Teresa." Larken looks toward Arthur's room and sees Eloise peering around the door frame. "Come on in, dear," she says, gesturing Larken to approach and then drawing her into an embrace.

Eloise exudes an aura that is warm but regal, removed. Even in close physical proximity, there's a sense that her molecules abide by social laws rather than scientific ones and would never think of mingling.

In Larken's mind, Arthur and Eloise are reincarnates of some rare monarchial couple, inhabiting a time (and there was such a time, wasn't there?) when figures of authority could be benevolent, magisterial, humble, circumspect, and wise; a time when world leaders did not appear in supermarket tabloids, wear tacky outfits, behave badly, speak idiotically, become spokespeople for Weight Watchers, mispronounce the word *nuclear;* when their imperfections made them so accessible, so commonplace. Larken prefers her heroes to be unassailable and shrouded in mystery. Eloise and Arthur stand alone in her imagination; their colors are so complex as to defy definition. To say that she loves them would be correct, but it's a love that waves from a distance.

"How is he today?" Larken asks.

"He's starting to demonstrate purposeful movement," Eloise replies. "Last night, he even opened his eyes for a few moments."

"I'm so glad." Larken moves toward the bed. "Hello, Arthur."

"He looks handsome, doesn't he?" Eloise remarks. "His color is much better."

"Very good," Larken concurs, although she is still struggling to define what he looks like, as if the right description would be a comfort somehow.

When she teaches her unit on Southern Renaissance painting, she begins by eliciting descriptions from her students about the quality of the figures:

How do they look?
Totally flat.
Why?
There's no light, no shadow.
Tell me about the colors.
They're pale. They look bleached out.
What do you imagine their skeletons to be like? Are their bones stout or thin, strong or brittle?

They look like they could snap in two, like they're made out of pretzels.
What does that say about their weight?
Like they don't weigh anything.
They look fake. They look prissy. They look like bad actors. They look
like paper dolls.

Once she's managed in this way to get her students beyond any entrenched attitudes they may have toward religion in general and Mother and Son in particular, she queries the significance of these portrayals:

So, now that we've agreed that no one looks like this, what do you think
the artist is trying to say about his view of Christ? What is he saying about
the Virgin Mary? How do you think the artist wants you to feel about these
characters? What does it mean that they are rendered in this very specific and
nonrealistic way?

How could Larken know that she's been wrong all these years? She'd never lie to her students intentionally, she'd never disseminate information that she didn't believe to be true.

Arthur looks like Christ off the cross, but not Van der Weyden's Christ. His torso, flattened against the bleached hospital bedding, is angled up slightly, and flat, as if he's made of creased shirtbox cardboard. His long-fingered hands, palms up, look fleshless—they're emaciated starfish on the bottom of a sunless sea. The tubes arising from his arm are like tendrils. Everything appears so thin and insubstantial. Larken can almost see his ribs; certainly she can imagine them—brittle as breadsticks—under the hospital gown that has been washed so frequently that whatever pattern was once there is a shadow of color, bleached beyond tone or variation. Arthur is one with the bleached cloth and the overlaundered bedding. He has been absorbed into the smells of alcohol and rubbery stale hospital food.

The oxygen tube obscures his mouth; its curving length and centered position make him look like Fu Manchu in meditative repose. Or,

. . . like Boris Karloff before the animating bolt of lightning. Or,

. . . like Dashiell Hammett sleeping off last night's binge. Or,

"He's just resting," Eloise observes.

It is surely meant as a reassurance, because he looks like nothing so much as Death.

Larken and Eloise settle in and make small talk. Eloise is needlepointing a Christmas stocking for her newest grandbaby. She looks toward Arthur occasionally, as if the three of them are having a normal conversation and Arthur has merely fallen silent. Any moment now he'll have something to say.

The nurses and orderlies and aides come and go with their smiles and clipboards, seeing to Arthur's needs, checking tubes and monitors.

At Eloise's request, a cafeteria worker brings a small pot of hot coffee for Larken.

A candy striper delivers more flowers, a gorgeous spray of autumn mums, willow branches, exotic dried seed heads. Larken is reminded of the bouquets her sister and mother used to gather in the fall.

"Oh!" Eloise remarks, reading the card. "How lovely! Aren't these lovely, Arthur?"

Eloise shifts to another subject, inquiring about how Larken's classes are going so far, whether any of this semester's students seem especially promising, has it been a terrible burden, taking over Arthur's classes as well teaching her own?

Larken feels a heavy, fluttering dread begin to gather in her chest. She should excuse herself and get home.

"It's no problem at all," Larken says, glancing at the clock and shifting in her chair. It's nearly nine o'clock. She still has papers to grade, a lesson plan to review. She's going to be up well past midnight and there's a faculty meeting at eight A.M.

When Eloise finally asks the question—and it's a testament to her patience and sense of propriety that she has waited nearly two hours to do so—she does not look up from her needlepoint and there is no change in her voice. "You know," she begins, "I've been thinking about the trip Arthur takes to Europe every winter break, ever since . . . well, since you were an undergrad, isn't that right?"

Here it comes. "I believe so."

"Did you ever take that trip?"

"Just once." *She doesn't remember,* Larken thinks, incredulous, *or else she's just being polite.*

Not knowing whether to feel relieved or ashamed, Larken diverts her eyes toward a bowlful of flabby Jell-O cubes on the hospital tray next to Arthur's bed; they've been sitting here all night, gradually dissolving. Something about their insidious decline, their slimy texture, and their color—bright red—makes Larken wonder if Jell-O isn't used for special effects in horror movies. She'll have to ask her brother. He's seen every scary movie ever made.

"Then you know!" Eloise continues, her voice blithely devoid of subtext; she really seems to have forgotten what happened on the plane all those years ago. "Arthur has done it so many times that it's planned to the millisecond. You know how he is. The curriculum, the day excursions, the accommodations, it's all been arranged, every detail worked out."

Larken attempts a smile. "I don't doubt it."

"There are twelve students signed up. Arthur was planning a unit on Constable—there's an exhibit on at the Tate, you know—and Mirabella is teaching the Raphaelites."

The flock of birds invades Larken's chest. She imagines reaching out and grabbing the Jell-O cubes, stuffing them into her mouth and gulping them down as if this action would sate them, make them still.

Eloise continues. "My point is, even though I'm sure Arthur will be up and around by Christmas, I doubt that he'll be able to travel, so I was wondering . . ." She has risen from her chair and is standing next to Arthur, holding his hand. "There's no one on the faculty like you, no one else who knows Arthur's work as well and is capable of teaching his syllabus in the way he'd want it to be taught."

For a moment Larken has the impression that Arthur is speaking through her, they are ventriloquist and dummy. What a relief! All this time, Arthur has just been pretending!

Don't ask don't ask don't ask don't ask, Larken implores.

But she will, of course.

Gaelan has been summoned to the conference room. It's very crowded. The segment producer is here, the news director, a couple of KLAN-KHAM's long-term sponsors, and the new station owners: two suits whose names Gaelan has never been able to retain, possibly because they have a shape-shifting quality Gaelan has noticed among rich and powerful males; their identities seem to be constantly in flux.

Noticeably absent are Gaelan's on-air colleagues; why would an announcement related to the workings of KLAN-KHAM not involve them as well?

There is a lavish floral arrangement and a cornucopipa-like spread of deli items laid out on the sideboard: fruit, pastries, salads, condiments, cold cuts. It's so unsettlingly reminiscent of his father's *Gymanfa* that for a brief moment Gaelan wonders where the body is.

The station owners facilitate the proceedings. They're cordial: they offer Gaelan a bottle of sparkling spring water—which he accepts— and his choice of a deli sandwich (ham, corned beef, roast beef, or pastrami) and chips—which he declines. They offer him a seat. They express their condolences over his recent loss. And then, without much else in the way of preface, they suggest that he enroll in an accelerated online degree program in broadcast meteorology at Mississippi State University.

In the ensuing silence, Gaelan wonders if he hasn't missed something; the suits are smiling at him in a suspiciously anticipatory manner. Perhaps he's the entrée.

"You want me to go back to school," he states, just to clarify. "Get a degree in meteorology."

Led by the suits, there are happy nods of assent throughout the room, less threatening now: an assembly of bobble-head dolls.

Gaelan tries to keep his voice level. "How exactly do you imagine I'll be able to do this?"

There's a simultaneous, collective reshuffling of the room's energetic field: cleared throats, altered expressions, sliding feet.

Gaelan continues. "I mean, I'm trying to understand how it would be possible to carry a full class load at the same time I'm working full-time. Not to mention *study* . . ."

The suits exchange a grim look—negotiators drafting a peace accord at Camp David—and then go on to say that of *course* they didn't expect that kind of sacrifice, what they're offering is several months of partially paid leave, because he's an asset, really, with his years of experience and dedicated following, and *extremely, tremendously* valuable asset to the news team.

"Look," Gaelan says, "I know I've been a little off the past few weeks, but . . ."

The suits break in to assure him that his *performance*—and Gaelan can't help but feel knifed by the emphatic use of that particular word, given its sexual associations and the fact that his penis seems to have lapsed into a semivegetative, possibly even comatose state—has *nothing whatsoever* to do with their proposal; they'd planned to bring this to him before his father's passing. Furthermore, they're fully prepared to sweeten the deal in any way they can just to ensure Gaelan's continued association with the KLAM-KHAN. He'll be a key player as the station transitions to its new identity. He's a big man in their vision of the future. They *need* him.

And yet, the sensation in Gaelan's body is that of shrinking, shriveling, of fluids being siphoned away in a slow but inexorable process that, by the time this meeting is over (*will it ever be over?*) will leave nothing in his place but a dessicated hull. Even his bones will crumble. It's an end that comes to evil inhuman creatures in certain horror movies: vampires, demons, aliens. He'll try not to shriek. Woe to the janitor with his broom and dustpan; what a job he'll have. Or maybe a good stiff Beaufort 5 will blow through the conference room and carry his powdery form aloft—like cremains.

"Give it some thought," the suits conclude, smiling, glad-handing, "and get back to us." The suits have switched identities once again: Now they're candidates who've already bought the election and are guaranteed to win by a landslide.

It's clear to Gaelan that his future depends upon agreeing with a decision that's being foisted upon him as a suggestion. He understands that he's been dismissed. He exits without shaking anyone's hand, afraid that the lightest physical contact will initiate his horrific demise. It wouldn't do to turn to dust before he leaves the building.

He rushes to his car, so upset that he's lost his habitual physical awareness and control; he's completely unconscious of walking in a way he was shamed out of decades ago, with a pronounced farmer's swing.

In a way, it occurs to him, what's just happened is a relief.

For years, he's felt guilty about his unwarranted early success, agonized over the precariousness of his professional standing. He's held fast to the possibility that the offerings of sincerity and effort have compensated for his unearned luck. He's prayed for absolution.

Now at least his prayers have been answered: He finally knows that it all counted for nothing.

Bonnie, disheartened by a continuing lack of clarity about how to proceed, decides to work on a special subset within the archive. She's pulled out a shoe box in which she stores various sized bits of paper that she's collected over the years: recovered fragments from her mother's diaries. Some of the pages are handwritten, some typewritten, some barely legible. All are torn and their content is fragmented, incomplete.

Out of this refuse—using an acid-free glue stick and the artful application of her intuitive powers—she composes an epistle:

> *Dear Diary,*
> *I am such a cheap   perfect eggplant*
> *Not pregnant   thank you very much*
> *who keeps track of such   hormonal wars*
> *Any mother would.*
> *(oh say what you mean you coward)*
> *I may never be able to   produce*
> *But   I found a pair of   baby   shoes,*
> *Can't we wait?   I heard her say*
> *Wait until what?*
> *My dear babies.*
> *mommy   Bonnie ?*
> *why should I have to wait so long?*
> *poor me*
> *I'm growing bit by bit   crazy*
> *Losing my mind.*
> *my vision   imperfect*
> *nothing to be done*
> *and yet and yet and yet*
> *mother-daughter outfits   coiffed   my obdurate girl*
> *these babes who bless me   hearts and hands   and hands and feet*
> *they are the ones   the twin that she's been expecting*
> *oh, how we labor*
> *help me help me help me help me help*

Bonnie presses the heels of her hands against her eyelids until her tears are reabsorbed. She can't do any more today, and so begins to gather up the unused scraps of paper (there are so many) and replace them in the shoe box.

Here's one:

. . . calling this baby the little pedaler, so busy in the . . .

Bonnie is startled by an eerie sound: a quiet hum, a high-pitched sigh. It's coming from the Artifact: the wheelchair wheel. Bonnie remembers her mother speaking to her of sonic magic in relation to the piano: of *sympathetic vibrations* and overtones and harmonics, the way strings can be set to singing not just via the direct action of the hammer, but through the invisible influence of a migratory sound wave. And then the sound is gone.

What set up the vibration? What awakened the Artifact's voice?

Bonnie's eyes take in another object, one that usually resides elsewhere. It's on a table next to her bed, and so linked to the Artifact not only via its size, shape, and purpose but by proximity: a wheel from her bike. She brought it inside after her morning ride and put it in the wheel jig. It's in need of truing.

The obviousness is comical; the realization hits her like the infusion of a spring breeze. *That's it,* she thinks, and whispers words of gratitude.

Hope's Diary, 1966:
Little Sandwiches and Blind Hands and Feet

Losing my mind. I make sandwiches and cut them into appealing little shapes—hearts and hands and ponies and stars—and then children drop them. I feel myself scowling as I clean up, my voice sounding tight and overcontrolled even to me, so surely they recognize the tension.

I feel chronically unprepared for all my body is called upon to do. My hands have lost their grace. They used to be graceful. There was a time when Larken and Gaelan were babies, even—not so long ago!—that my hands felt blessed and competent, when supporting the backs of the babies' heads, say, when things were simpler. (When they had no personalities, is that what I really mean? When they had no will? HA!)

They have wills now, and the ability to assert themselves and ask for things and express preferences and spill the milk and topple the lovely plate of sandwiches, butter and cucumber and cream cheese and olive, a real tea party, I told them, the way children in England would do at this time of the day, four o'clock, and no wonder, since it is the worst, the absolute worst time for motherhood, the time when all pretense of good humor has dissipated and all one wants to do is have a large stiff drink or slit one's wrists or both.

About my hands: They've acquired a blurriness, that's the only way I can think to describe it, as if they were sighted. They seem to not know where they're going, are frequently running into things, miscalculating the distance between one place and another. I've had the same experience with my feet.

My hands need glasses! My feet are going blind!

All this has given rise to a whole set of invented blindfold games: In our variation on "Six
Men and the Elephant," I fill paper bags with odd
household objects, blindfold the children, and have
them guess what's inside. Our version of hide-and-
seek requires us to not only be sightless, but crawl.
I place Hershey's chocolates on various places on
the keyboard; if they can correctly identify the
note, they get a kiss.

Funny image really. I like the idea of bespec-
tacled hands and feet.

Chapter 17

Wrens in Winter

Larken wakes up with the first rays of December light; upstairs, the three bears are hibernating. She wishes she could join them. The passage of the solstice may mean that Earth is technically tilting toward the sun, but it will be months before Larken's body will believe it. She never feels heavier or more shadowed than in winter.

Wearily, she opens the bedroom closet and starts pulling out shopping bags full of presents, most of which are still unwrapped and wearing price tags. Usually Larken derives great joy from questing for the perfect gifts. This year she's unsure of many of her choices—so unsure that she's saved the receipts.

Three boxes are wrapped and festooned and ready.

For Mia, there's a first edition of *The Collected Poems of Audre Lorde*. Larken braved snowy weather last week to drive up to a used bookstore in Omaha to get it; she doesn't know the poet's work, but Lorde is one of Mia's literary idols and Larken is familiar enough with Jon and Mia's library to know that they don't have it.

Jon is getting a handknit, cabled lamb's-wool sweater in a rich emerald green; Larken ordered it online months ago from a specialty shop in Wales.

Esmé's gift is gigantic, more unwieldy than heavy. It took three rolls of paper to wrap it. It will not escape Mia's notice that there are actually several presents inside the box: from Italy, a gorgeous handpainted puppet theater—complete with curtains and scrims and scenic elements—and a set of hand puppets: King, Queen, Prince, Princess, Wizard, Knight, Sorcerer, Dragon, Peasant, Pony, Barn Swallow, Dog.

Larken understands that this extravagance represents a violation of the established rules. Every year at this time, Mia reminds them that if we're really celebrating Jesus's birthday, we should remember that the Wise Men brought three presents, *period,* and that invoking the spirit of Christmas as an excuse to ransack Toys "R" Us and max out the credit cards is *bullshit*. Mia is a stringent advocate of experiential, versus material, gift-giving. She's happiest when Larken presents them with tickets to the Children's Museum or day passes to the zoo.

Larken doesn't mean to usurp Mia's maternal authority, disregard her wishes, really she doesn't; but this year she just couldn't contain her love for Esmé in an envelope.

She pulls out her overnight case and puts on the coffee. She scribbles a note to Jon (*J—Happy holiday. I'll call tomorrow. Hope M isn't too pissed and lets E keep everything. Give her a big hug and kiss from me. Love, L*), and while the coffee brews, she sets the gifts just inside the front door to her apartment. In his role as Santa, Jon will use his key to get in later tonight, after Esmé is asleep. He'll bring the presents upstairs and place them under the tree.

At least she's only going to be in Emlyn Springs for a couple of days. She has a shitload of things to do before she leaves for Europe. She probably shouldn't be going at all, but this Christmas more than any other she feels obliged to go, for Viney's sake if for no other reason.

This is the first time ever that she and Gaelan are not driving down together on Christmas Eve. She regrets this—knowing how much her brother hates to drive alone—but it's unavoidable, since her flight leaves very early on the twenty-sixth. *Shit.* She's so unorganized. She'll have to wrap the rest of the gifts tonight after everyone else is in bed.

By the time she starts loading up her car, a fleet of ragged-edged, dingy clouds has started creeping in from the southwest. A storm is coming. Stopping at the South Pointe Super Saver on the way out of town, Larken loads a grocery cart with six ten-pound bags of kitty litter in case she gets stuck; the streets are already wet and treacherously slick. In the parking lot, the snow is starting to fall.

She loads the ballast into the trunk, turns on the defroster, puts the Chevy in low gear, and drives onto the highway and into her past.

On December 14, 1977, the future Little Miss Emlyn Springs—accompanied by her mother—is spending the morning of her birthday at the Nebraska State Department of Licensing in Beatrice. She's standing at the counter, weight-shifting from hip to hip in what she hopes is a slouchy, righteously pissed-off way, one that will register her disdain to the other people in the room, because when it's your birthday and your father is a small-town physician and your mother has MS you just *know* that everyone is watching every move you make.

There's a cold front coming in, a real bad one according to Joe Dinsdale; he says they might get up to a foot. It wasn't supposed to start until much later but it's been coming down for about fifteen minutes now. Big surprise. The whole day has been a complete disaster.

They left early—Viney drove—the idea being that they'd get everything taken care of and be back home by early afternoon. The plan was that Viney would drop them off and then run errands while Larken got her learner's permit. It shouldn't take long. Viney wanted to stock up on groceries in case they got socked in; she also wanted to get to a hardware store and buy extra propane for the cookstoves, extra batteries for the flashlights, and a few bundles of firewood.

Getting a learner's permit at fourteen is a state-sanctioned accommodation usually reserved for boys from farming families, but by 1997, Larken's family needs her to be legally authorized to drive the Pontiac every bit as much as the families of her male peers need them behind the wheel of a tractor.

They arrived right on schedule, soon after the doors opened, but it took awhile to get Hope out of the car, up the stairs, and inside. Because the Americans with Disabilities Act won't be signed into law for another thirteen years, the Beatrice Department of Motor Vehicles offers no handicapped-designated parking spaces, no ramps, no elevators, no wheelchair-accessible bathrooms, no widened hallways, no special seating areas.

Viney left the car double-parked and idling at the curb while she and Larken unloaded Hope and settled her into her wheelchair. It was cold when they got here, but not bad—not the piercing, eyeball-chilling cold that comes after a snowstorm, but the cozier, cloud-roofed cold that comes just before.

Larken pushed her mother to the bottom of the stairs and waited. Viney drove around and around the block looking for a place to park. This was an exercise in futility, since the residents of southeastern Nebraska weren't just out and about gathering provisions in preparation for a killer snowstorm, they were panicked by the knowledge that there were only ten shopping days left until Christmas. Viney waved each time she passed, her face and her salutory style reflecting a steady, declining progression from shining optimism to teeth-grinding ire.

Finally, she came charging toward them. The heavy, urgent clack of her boots against the sidewalk made her sound at least fifty pounds heavier. "I'm so sorry," she said. "Can you believe it? I had to park in a *lot*! Six blocks away!"

"No worries, Viney," Hope said, squeezing her hand.

Larken hated how close they were. She hated herself for hating it, but she couldn't help it. They were both so *good* it set Larken's teeth on edge.

"You ready?" Viney asked.

Hope nodded. Using her cane, she pushed herself to standing. She took two shaky steps away from the wheelchair and then balanced precariously.

"Aviator grip!" Viney ordered. She and Larken quickly clasped each other's forearms behind Hope's back at the level of her bum. "Ready!"

This was Hope's cue to sit. She eased herself into their four-armed chairseat and spread her arms, settling them across Larken and Viney's shoulders. The three of them then made their way: Hope in the middle, Larken and Viney on either side, bearing her up and up and up.

Once they reached the top of the stairs (all breathing heavily, all wondering why the entrances to federal buildings invariably demand mountaineering skills), Larken and Viney set Hope back on her feet. While Viney skittered back down and up the stairs to fetch Hope's wheelchair, Larken buttressed her mother's body with hers to keep her upright and steady.

"All right, then," Viney said once Hope was back in the wheelchair. "You two go on in. I'll be back as soon as I can" She looked at the sky and grimaced. "Shit!" she said, and then gave each of them a kiss and hurried away.

"Agile," Hope remarked, "isn't she?"

When they finally got to the waiting area—which was decorated with uncomfortable-looking plastic furniture and government posters—they found that it was packed. Dozens of people had already taken a number and were sitting down.

Larken pushed her mother's wheelchair so that it was positioned next to the front row. Since there were no available seats, she slouched against the nearest wall. After a minute or two, Hope turned to the surly, multiple-chinned man next to her. "My daughter," she said pleasantly, "needs to sit." He didn't budge, so she glared at him until he left. Larken sat down. Her mother reached for her hand.

They waited. Numbers were called. Larken went outside a couple of times to take cigarette breaks, staring down any adult who gave her the hairy eyeball.

By the time #48 was called, over an hour had gone by. Larken walked to the counter and presented her number and her birth certificate to a mousy-looking woman with a bad perm. She explained her family's special needs and then handed over a letter of permission from her physician father; the letter detailed her mother's condition and attested to the need for someone to take on the responsibility of driving Hope to her medical appointments.

Looking at the employee made Larken nervous. She was a blinker; as she perused Larken's paperwork, her heavily mascaraed eyelashes kept colliding with her corkscrewed bangs, causing them to bounce up and down like a row of manic, uncoordinated Slinkys.

"Your situation is unusual," the employee said finally. "I'll have to consult with my supervisor."

So, here she is: Waiting. Again. At least she's missing her Health Ed final.

Today as always, Larken is torn between pretending her mother is a total stranger and proclaiming their connection to the world at large. Having a mother in a wheelchair may be a pain in the ass and embarrassing, but it makes her very, very special. In fact, it's Larken's specialness on this score that accounts for her being here today. It accounts for just about everything, actually.

The last time Larken checked, her mother was still awake, moving her lips slowly as if in prayer, reading one of her poetry books. But when Larken turns around she sees that Hope's eyes are closed, her head is listing to one side. Hope can fall asleep anywhere lately. It's mortifying. She'll be drooling soon and wetting her diapers too, if she hasn't already.

Larken sniffs.

Yep. There's piss in the air.

The mousy employee returns with her supervisor; hard as it is to believe, her perm is even worse than her subordinate's.

"She's not going to use it to drive farm equipment," the mouse whispers to Poodle.

"Why not?"

"Her father isn't a farmer. He's a doctor."

"*Physician,*" Larken interjects without thinking. Mouse and Poodle look at her. "The word *doctor* is imprecise."

They resume their conversation.

"She says she needs it to drive her mother around."

"Her mother doesn't drive?"

"My mother can't drive," Larken explains again, wearily. "She has multiple sclerosis. She's in a wheelchair." She indicates Hope.

"Well, I'll need to speak with your mother then," Poodle snips.

Larken grits her teeth, but tries to speak politely. "She has MS. Speaking is difficult for her. And as you can see, she's asleep."

Suddenly, Mouse and Poodle are looking past Larken, their mouths agape, their eyes wide. Larken turns, expecting to see a madman with a gun, but what she sees instead is her mother, trying to stand with the use of her cane. She takes two shaky steps and then crumples dramatically to the floor.

"Ooohhhhhhhh!" Hope cries. "Aaaaaaaah!"

"Oh my God!" Mouse and Poodle start running toward her, but Larken gets to her mother first.

Hope leans close to her. Her eyes are still closed and her brow is furrowed as if she's in pain, but there's the trace of a smile on her lips. "Just let them *try* to say no now," she whispers.

After Mrs. Jones has been resituated in her wheelchair (she shows no outward injuries but wears a pained expression and continues to moan softly), the supervisor makes a big show of giving Larken's paperwork another look.

"Oh, wait!" she says. "Jones? Larken Jones? Why you're Doc's daughter, aren't you? My family, all my kids, we all had your dad as our doctor since before you were born." She quickly pens a large, loopy signature at the bottom of Larken's application and hands everything back to the mouse. "Congratulations, hon," she says. "You've got your learner's permit."

By the time Viney returns—the backseat of her car loaded with enough provisions to outfit a military regiment in Siberia—the blizzard is in full force.

When they pass the Beatrice City Limits sign, Hope makes a suggestion: "Let her drive, Viney."

Larken is astonished. Her mother has to be joking.

But Viney shows no sign of being amused. Nor does she register disagreement, shock, or any other reaction that Larken would deem appropriate; in fact, and to Larken's horror, Viney actually seems to be considering this insane idea. During the ensuing silence—which is punctuated by grunts, hums, shrugs, suspenseful in-breaths, and purgative sighs—Viney and Hope appear to be having a telepathic conversation.

Finally, Viney speaks. "You're right. If she can drive in this, she can drive in anything."

After pulling over at the first available turnout, Viney puts on the emergency lights, pushes the car door open—briefly admitting a roaring wind and a scattershot of ice crystals—and gets out. A full two minutes later, she reappears on the passenger side and knocks on the window.

"YOU'LL BE FINE, HONEY!" she shouts. Quarter-inch drifts are already covering the eaves of her brows; there are small stalactites extruding from her nostrils. "YOUR MOM AND I WILL HELP YOU!"

Hope pats Larken's hand and nods.

"SHOVE OVER, SWEETHEART!"

With exaggerated difficulty and an angst-ridden huff, Larken climbs over her mother and into the driver's seat.

And so, within an hour of receiving her learner's permit and on the occasion of her magic birthday, Larken gets her first driving lesson during a blizzard so severe that it ends up dumping twelve inches of icy snow on southeastern Nebraska and knocking out power for a week.

It takes them six hours to get home, but Hope and Viney were right: ever since Larken turned fourteen, she's been able to drive herself in anything.

There are worms that live in snow. And mosquitoes from the genus *Aedes* whose larvae develop in the snow broth of early spring. It is strange to think of these kinds of creatures thriving in cold temperatures.

Gaelan has never had magical powers, nor has he desired them. He does not believe himself capable of commanding events, especially those involving the weather.

"Let's make it snow," Rhiannon says. She has materialized, standing in a distant door frame, and advances toward him with an eerily smooth and steady motion; as she comes toward him, he sees that she's riding in a self-propelled American Red Flyer.

She stops. She is much too close.

Gaelan expected at least a little preamble. "I have hickory-smoked tofu," he says, wanting to slow things down. "Chipotle cheddar. Roasted pistachios. Hummus."

"Hummmmmmmm . . ." she says, and starts taking off her clothes. They flutter to her feet, forming a snowdrift of white cotton and lace: T-shirt, gym shorts, lingerie.

There is a weightless quality to falling snow, even in its multiple forms, the various ways it can come down. Many people find it entrancing; to them snowfall is magical. Such people do not associate meteorological events with the disappearance of a parent, and so perhaps understandably given his family history, Gaelan does not prefer snow in this down-falling, vulnerable state; he feels much better once the flakes arrive on the ground and begin accumulating in that clubby way that gives them weight.

"Let's make it snow," Bethan repeats.

Bethan?

She's naked, and now she is pulling the wool sweater over his eyes, obscuring his vision. There is nothing heated about the way she is doing it; he could be five years old. She could be a babysitter helping him get ready for bed.

"It's not in the forecast," Gaelan says inside his sweater.

"Some things are impossible to predict," she answers, and her mouth is on his soon after that.

He sees them having sex in a series of quick snapshots. He's on top, she's on top, they're rolling over, they're on their sides . . . It's very cinematic; there's even a sound track. It reminds him of some movie he's seen a hundred times but can't quite remember the name of.

She has an orgasm.

He asks, "What did it feel like?"

She stares past him—toward the light coming through the window. It casts her face in gray and pale blue shades that give her skin the look of moonstone.

"Gaelan," she whispers, "look out the window."

But he doesn't want to look. He pulls his Intro to Meteorology textbook off the nightstand and reads: "'Snow consists of ice crystals that have coalesced to form flakes. Snowflakes have no set form. They can be needles, columns, stars, or flat plates, depending on the temperature and the concentration of water vapor.'"

"Let's make a blizzard," she insists. Her hands start moving again and Gaelan is suddenly nervous.

He continues to read: "'Snow is caused by precipitation forming when the temperature of water vapor drops below the vanishing point.'"

The wind picks up. Some coincidental angle of snow, light, object, and shadow causes Nefertiti's silhouette to materialize on one of the bedroom walls.

"No!" he cries, frightened now. "I didn't predict this!"

Trying to call out, he wakes up and finds himself on the sofa.

He only intended to rest his eyes—he's been studying all morning. The room is cold and bathed in a distinct, steely light and peculiar quiet. He becomes aware of Kate and Spencer, basking in the radiant heat generated by the small, domed, tropical island formed by the top of his head. Extricating himself gently so as not to disturb them, he gets up and turns up the thermostat. He checks the time—it's much later than he realized, almost noon—and then moves to the window and gazes outside, where, as he surmised, and without any assistance from the National Weather Service, it has started to snow.

* * *

Gaelan has had difficulty focusing on his online studies. He's not a long-distance type as learning styles go. He prefers real people and real classrooms. And it's so easy to get distracted, working from home. There are the cats and the computer, his free weights and treadmill. The quiet is unsettling. It's also hard to resist turning on the TV to check in with his former KLAN-KHAM colleagues.

He turns it on now and finds his substitute mid-segment, gesturing toward the Doppler image of the storm system that he already knows is coming.

The newest member of the KLAN-KHAM news team is a very young, very bright woman with big hair, a small waist, and prominent eyeteeth. Her name, Riley Calder, strikes Gaelan as suspiciously euphonious and perky—designed for its upbeat appeal. Ms. Calder used to be, Gaelan senses, someone else, and is in the process of reinventing herself for the American mass market, in this case, commercial television. She's the kind of person who has simple motives: She wants celebrity however she can get it, and a chance to climb the corporate ladder of her choosing with a name that will assist that ascent. For example, if she aspired to stardom as a writer of Harlequin romances, Gaelan is sure she would have chosen another nom de plume, something like Ashleigh du Printemps or Clarissa de Winter. She probably grew up being called something she considered ordinary, déclassé, unassertive: Sue, Nancy, Doris, Lynn.

Based on the time they spent together—with Riley shadowing him during his final week on camera and Gaelan sitting in on her broadcasts—his impression is that this job is nothing more than a milk stop. She'll be more than competent as KLAN-KHAM's substitute forecaster, she'll do all the right things, but Gaelan imagines that her future plans extend well beyond the limits of Lincoln, Nebraska, and include the appearance of Riley Calder™ in the national, perhaps even international market: a syndicated talk show and women's magazine; book endorsements; a line of gourmet frozen foods and/or designer furniture: the Riley Calder Collection.

Riley already has her meteorology degree; she received it this past spring and this is her first job. Even so, she's quite accomplished and savvy; when Gaelan was training her she seemed to already know everything and was more interested in standing too close to him than in learning the ropes.

He turns off the TV and checks the time again. He should get on the road, start heading down to Emlyn Springs now—he's expected at Viney's for supper at five, and this storm shows no sign of slowing—but he really wants to get in one more gym workout. So—after loading the car and dropping Kate and Spencer at the vet's (where they'll board in kitty condo luxury for the next week), he heads to the Y.

Maybe Rhiannon won't be there. It's Christmas Eve, after all. She may already be on a plane, heading back to Oregon to visit her family and pay condolences to the squadron of lovelorn bodybuilders still languishing in her wake.

He's being dramatic. She didn't break his heart. Not at all. They've continued to see each other at the gym and maintain friendly relations. She's a nice girl, a smart girl, a class act. So it didn't work out between them—she hasn't been back to the condo since that one time or offered even once to spot him again on the bench press. It's fine.

It's not like there were any stated expectations on either side. Technically, they didn't even sleep together. They flirted, they fooled around, she was engaging company for a couple of weeks, and that's it. She can't say she didn't *enjoy* herself that afternoon; it's just that neither of them took up the reins of a sexual relationship beyond that day. There doesn't have to be a *reason* for everything.

And anyway, soon after their two-week-whatever-it-was, it became clear that she was seeing someone else: one of the Y's personal trainers (indeed, *Gaelan's* personal trainer): a guy known simply as Jeff, or "Buff Jeff" in some segments of the Y-going population; personal trainers don't possess surnames.

Jeff competes as an amateur. He's been to the Arnold Classic twice.

It's been mildly distracting, having to face them every day in this setting, catching glimpses of the discreet nuzzlings and brushings and whisperings. Not that Gaelan can't handle it. Still, he sometimes catches Rhiannon looking at him like he's a three-legged puppy. And then there's the obvious, more vexing concern: Has she confided in Jeff about his Problem?

The end result is that Gaelan is afraid of staging a repeat nonperformance in bed. He hasn't invited any woman home for weeks, not even the women he was already sleeping with when he and Rhiannon started going out. For a while, they kept calling, asking him to come out and play. He had a ready excuse (*I'm just so tied up with this online study class . . .*) and took pains to assure them that it wasn't *them,* it was *him,* and that he'd call when he got out from under all this schoolwork.

They've stopped calling now, moved on, like migratory birds in winter. They must be dancing the commiseration tango with other partners.

Actually, a period of enforced celibacy might do him good, help him focus on his studies—although it hasn't so far.

Gaelan parks the car and heads in, scanning the workout room on his way to his locker.

No sign of Rhiannon.

But after he changes into his sweats and reemerges, she's there, standing near the reception desk.

"Hi, Gaelan!" she says. "Merry Christmas." She's wearing a hat, scarf, gloves, boots, and there's a big winter coat slung over her arm.

"Merry Christmas." Gaelan loves it when women dress for cold weather; all those clothes to remove. There's an overnight bag at her feet. "Are you on your way out?"

"Yeah, we . . . I already worked out today. The weather forecast, you know, and the early closing, holiday hours . . ."

"Oh, right. I forgot about that." *Damn.* He'll have to do a truncated, more aggressive version of his workout. "You doing anything special over the break?"

"Well, I'm . . ."

"Hey babe!"

Jeff erupts from the sales office and starts striding toward them; he has his designer jacket slung over one shoulder, tie loosened, shirt sleeves rolled up just enough to give a teasing peek at his mammoth biceps. No hat, no boots, no gloves, no topcoat. Clearly as a man so inherently *hot* that he doesn't need protective gear in subfreezing temperatures.

"Hey Gaelan!" Jeff pulls Rhiannon to his side. He nuzzles her jaw and then flicks his tongue against a pulsing spot on her neck with reptilian precision. "Yum," he murmurs, and then winks at Gaelan.

She's told him. She's told him everything.

"You got any special plans for Christmas?" Jeff asks.

"Not really. Headed down to see my stepmom and sisters."

"Don't forget your free weights, buddy. Keep working your lats and pecs, okay? Come back with those New Year's Resolutions."

"Will do."

Jeff turns to Rhiannon, yanks her by the waist, pivots her so they're groin to groin. "You ready, babe?"

"Yep. Bye, Gaelan."

"Bye."

He moves toward the locker room to the sound of Jeff singing the song that brought Rhiannon's parents together, her answering laughter, and then an inner voice from years past:

That's quite a farmer's swing you've got going there, buddy . . .

Gaelan pushes himself hard on the elliptical trainer, does an extra round of reps on the Nautilus machines. It's late, and it's getting dark outside. If he skips his postworkout stretches, he'll have just enough time to do some heavy lifting with the free weights.

He settles in for the bench press. How much?

You can do this, she said, so he loads up the bar.

He has a great workout and doesn't leave the Y until 3:30. It's another hour before he makes it beyond the Lincoln city limits. The roads are slick, the snow is starting to accumulate, and traffic is crazy. He calls Viney from his cell phone to tell her he's going to be late and they shouldn't wait supper.

His shoulder is starting to bother him. He must have overdone it a little. He pops some ibuprofen, puts in a Springsteen CD, and settles in for what's bound to be a long drive.

Oblivious to the way he's undermining the holiday cheer of his fellow travelers, Gaelan keeps his emergency lights blinking and propels his Jeep toward Emlyn Springs at the speed of a golf cart moving through the rough.

"That's quite a farmer's swing you've got going there, buddy . . ." His father's voice is lightly teasing.

Gaelan keeps walking, but he immediately shortens his stride and brakes the pendulum action of his arms by stuffing his hands into his pockets.

"Sorry I was late," Dad goes on. He's slowed the car and is calling across the highway through the open car window. "Come on, get in. I'll give you a ride the rest of the way home."

"No thanks," Gaelan replies. "I'll walk." He waited for an hour at their appointed meeting place by the bridge before giving up. An hour, while his friends drove by and waved, while townsfolk kept stopping to ask him what he was doing and did he need a ride anywhere?

No, that's okay. My dad's gonna pick me up.

He fixes his eyes on the horizon and quickens his pace.

"Come on, son, don't be that way. I got hung up . . ."

There was a car crash, a thresher accident, an amputation, a heart attack, a birth, a death, a stroke, a fracture . . . Dad's excuses for failing to appear are predictable. And yet, how can you make claims on your father's time or be pissed about him standing you up when he's just sewed some kid's fingers back on?

"We can have a driving lesson tomorrow."

Can't he at least say he's sorry?

"Don't bother," Gaelan mumbles. "Larken said she'd teach me."

There's a pause, and for a while the only sounds are those made by the the two of them, a father and son moving in the same direction on opposite sides of the highway: the skittering of loose gravel and road-side trash in the wake of Gaelan's footsteps, the slowed rpm's of the engine as his father keeps the car creeping along beside him.

"Fine, then," Llewellyn says finally, sharply. "Be that way. Pout like a little girl." Gaelan's heart thuds in fear, but he also experiences a certain satisfaction: *I made Dad angry. He noticed me.*

Gealan hears Dad gun the engine, watches as he speeds on ahead and disappears into the vanishing point of the horizon. He spends the next four miles trying out various ways of walking that won't identify him as a dolt, a misfit, an embarrassment, because nothing could be worse for a thirteen-year-old boy than to be identified in teasing tones as having a farmer's swing by your saintly physician father.

What Gaelan doesn't know, will never know, is that his father's seemingly out directed anger is a function of guilt: He's doesn't have any legitimate medical excuse for failing to meet Gaelan at the appointed time and place; he's late because he was having sex with his nurse and forgot to keep his eye on the time.

And Llewellyn didn't know—the way parents often don't—that it's often the semiconscious comment, the teasing remark, the snippy chastisement uttered in frustration at the end of a trying day that will be one your child remembers and clings to and incorporates into the mold out of which they'll re-form themselves. Not the countless times he's said *Good job, son,* or *I'm so proud of you,* but the single time he barked, *Why can't you take up a regular team sport like swimming or football?* and *Don't be an idiot: bodybuilding isn't an athletic event. It's vanity. It's a freak show.*

If only Llewellyn had made himself available to spot Gaelan when he started lifting weights. If only Hope had still been around when Gaelan discovered Springsteen. She would have chastened her husband for treating their son's first great musical love with disdain. She wouldn't have allowed him to banish *that twangy crap* from the stereo.

Hope believed that certain pieces of music qualify either the composer or the interpreter for a spot in heaven. And not just "classical" music either; Hope was no snob. On her list of Free Admission to Heaven performances (and she continues to build this list) is "State Trooper" by Bruce Springsteen and "Que Sera Sera" as performed by Pink Martini.

If Hope had lived longer, Gaelan wouldn't still be waiting for his father to sit down and listen, really listen to a Bruce Springsteen album with him.

Of couse, if mothers continued to think about all the ways they could advocate for their children, they'd never leave.

The snow stops falling when he pulls onto the bridge; strangely too and at the same time, the Jeep stalls out. Gaelan relaxes, momentarily becalmed by the sudden silence and stasis. He lets his eyes travel down Main Street in advance of his body, taking in the sight of colored Christmas lights twining around lampposts like Maypole ribbons; glowing plastic Santas and reindeer and crèches. Gaelan realizes that this is the first year his father wasn't up on a ladder decorating Viney's place.

His father's gracelessness while trying to do anything "handy" (and he did try) embarrassed Gaelan when he was young; every other kid he knew had dads who could fix things that were broken, build things without them falling apart. But later, when Gaelan thought of his father—who was so full of grace and competence in every other aspect of his life—precariously perched on a ladder, wearing a tool belt that always looked brand-new, bending every nail he tried to hammer—he felt for his father an inexpressibly deep and mournful tenderness.

Did anyone step up to the tasks vacated by his father at Christmastime? Did anyone else stand on a ladder for Viney? Help her put up lights? Decorate the tree?

He poses the questions; he knows the answers: *No No No* and *It should have been me.*

The temperature has dropped again. The bridge is covered with several inches of dry powder, but there's an underlayer of ice. Gaelan restarts the Jeep and makes his way carefully across the ravine and into town, which at this hour and on this night looks—and is—almost completely deserted.

The porch of Viney's house wears only two holiday decorations: a flocked, faux-evergreen wreath, and a choir of three life-size angel children, plastic triplets conjoined at the wings and holding hymnals. These characters haven't made a holiday appearance for years—*Where have they been all this time?* Gaelan wonders—but he remembers them clearly: Their mouths are frozen in perfect *o*'s as if some character from an episode of *The Twilight Zone* gifted with the power to stop time zapped them just after they sang the first syllable of "O, little town of Bethlehem!" or "O Holy Night!" They derive their inner glow from an extension cord that snakes out from beneath the back of the middle angel's robe and travels into the house through a partially opened window. There are lights on inside, but it is well past six and Gaelan knows that everyone has already left for church.

He finds a note on the kitchen table: *Welcome home, honey! Hope the drive wasn't too bad. I'll save a seat for you at church. If you're hungry, feel free to depredate the pie. Love, V.* After he unloads his car, he grabs a flashlight, bundles back up, and sets out for the two-mile trek.

Among the Welsh of Emlyn Springs, it is a tradition to come to Christmas Eve services on foot—or by any other means that doesn't burn fossil fuel or unduly mar the quiet. Not everyone keeps with this tradition, but many do. There are folks who ride their horses or employ them to pull sleighs, wagons, or pony carts; parents with young, nonperambulating children stand in as sled dogs; if the snow is deep and powdery dry, like tonight, some people arrive on snowshoes or cross-country skis. Bonnie rides her bike.

Gaelan can't remember ever walking to church by himself on Christmas Eve. As he swings his flashlight beam in an arc, he's surprised by the number of footprints; he would never have guessed that this many people walk to church.

Townsfolk would give different answers to the question of why this tradition has endured. Certain factions would insist that it's a way of exposing young people—for whom everything is so *easy*—to a hardship that many of them endured on a daily basis. Others, of a less puritanical but still catholic disposition, would remark that there is something of the saints' pilgrimage in this *volkswalk*. Others cleave to this custom because they remember that there's a special sweetness in community that is hard-won. These wise souls would say that whenever light and fellowship and warmth and song are the promised rewards, even the heaviest hearts can soar.

But Gaelan feels none of this: neither light nor lightness nor hope nor anticipation. As he trudges through the snow, he feels nothing so much as dread. He thinks of that poem about a man walking alone through the woods in winter—the poem Larken recited for the talent part of the Little Miss Emlyn Springs competition the year she won—and he wonders what on earth made it his mother's favorite.

Up ahead, he sees the white clapboard church, its steeple like a needle puncturing the dark pillow of the sky, its tall windows emiting a citrus-colored glow.

Suddenly, Gaelan stops, listens. His townsfolk are singing. The song is a famous one, perhaps the most famous of all Welsh airs. Its English title is "All Through the Night" but in Emlyn Springs the song is known as "*Ár Hyd Y Nos*" and sung in Welsh.

Town tradition dictates that a soloist—a gifted young person chosen by the church pianist, Hazel Williams—sings in a call-and-response manner with the congregation.

Gaelan makes his way up the wooden stairs. The intense lemony light bursts out of the church wherever it can, revealing the uncaulked seams, the unweather-proofed cracks. There's a confidence in this light; if only someone would fling the doors to the church open, this withheld light would warm the entire night.

Gaelan opens one of the doors and peeks inside. The church is packed, but hushed. Every seat is taken—except, he imagines, the one near the front that Viney is saving for him, next to her and his sisters. There's a clear view down the center of the aisle, so he can easily see the young man—he's probably sixteen or seventeen—who stands in the front of the congregation, singing. Surely everyone inside knows him, but Gaelan doesn't.

O mor siriol gwena seren, the soloist sings.

Ár hyd y nos, the congregation answers.

I oleuo'i chwaer-ddaeren, he sings again.

Ár hyd y nos.

Gaelan opens the door a bit further, just enough to slide his body into the vestibule.

Holl amrant au'r serddywedant . . .

Ár hyd y nos.

Dym a'r ffordd i fro gogoniant . . .

"*Ár hyd y nos,*" Gaelan sings. Those few notes begin to unlock a reservoir of feeling, so he sings no more, makes his way back outside.

It's snowing again. He's about to start down the stairs when he's startled by the sound of someone clearing their throat.

"Hello." It's Woodward-Bernstein.

11 yo? 12? Small, sad, intense.

Bethan's son.

"Sorry to scare you," he says.

"It's okay," Gaelan answers. "What are you doing out here in the cold?"

Woodward-Bernstein gives him a quizzical look, as if he's trying to decide if Gaelan is truly uninformed or simply pulling his leg. "I'm Jewish," he says, giving Gaelan the benefit of the doubt.

"I see," Gaelan lies.

"My name is Eli Ellis Weissman," he continues, holding out his hand.

"How do you do? My name is—"

"Oh, I *know* who *you* are," Eli says, and then, assuaging Gaelan's sudden terror that Bethan has told her son everything about him, he adds, "You're the television weatherman."

"Yes. That is correct." For some reason, Gaelan feels the need to eliminate contractions when speaking to this boy.

Eli fumbles around in a leather satchel that is slung over his thin shoulders. "I was hoping I might see you here this evening. I've been waiting for you, actually."

Gaelan doesn't know what to make of this. He's been stalked before, but never by a preteenage boy wearing a yarmulke.

Eli extracts a large notebook and clasps it against his chest. "My play won first prize in the Pageant Play Competition and will be performed next summer during the Fancy Egg Days Celebration."

"I see."

"I'm hoping that you will consider auditioning for the role of the Custodian. It's the lead." Gaelan opens his mouth to speak but Eli quickly presses on. "Auditions won't be held until May but I would like you to get a head start. These are your sides." Eli reaches inside the notebook and pulls out a sheaf of loose papers. "Merry Christmas," he says, and then—before Gaelan has a chance to respond—he tromps down the stairs and disappears into the night.

Gaelan looks at the pages. By the light coming from the church windows, he reads, *You might not believe that there's such a thing anymore as magic. Magic is a hard thing to come by these days. But folks, I'm here to tell you that inexplicable and miraculous things are happening all the time. You just have to know where to look. If there's any place in the world that can bear out the truth of that, it's our town, Emlyn Springs. Our little Wales.*

Gaelan sits down on the church steps. Something hard smashes against his hip. Wincing, he reaches into his coat pocket and pulls out his flashlight.

He pictures Woodward-Bernstein walking alone through the dark: his narrow shoulders and dark, serious eyes. He wasn't wearing one scrap of light-colored clothing, and against the cold, no gloves or muffler, just an odd, oversized overcoat.

A man's overcoat, Gaelan realizes, and then, feeling a terrible remorse, he weeps.

Hope's Diary, 1967:
A pilot could fly over it

Family relationships cannot be perceived directly, or even through meaningful words. A family is like a small city at night, seen from across a prairie, its lights glittering. At times, its shape is almost graspable, the contours of its skyline are clear, the pinnacle, the organizing principle, all are fixed and for a moment comprehension is possible. The skyline is a shape that any child could draw. A pilot could fly over it. An artist could paint it. A particularly brilliant mathematician could create a proof to account for all its complexities.

But then one light goes out, another is turned on. Lights dim or brighten, and in an instant what was almost accessible is lost again. Not even this small city can be described.

There are truths, unbelievable truths, truths so terrifying that we hide from them. Perhaps this is wrong. Perhaps we should force ourselves to say these true and terrible things every day.

Someday, my mother will die.

Someday, my father will die.

Someday, my husband will die.

Someday, my children will die.

It is sure. These things are sure.

But who could do this? Who could subject one's own heart to so much truth without turning it to stone? Who can believe in death and still live?

Viney's firstborn, Wally Jr., was killed. His helicopter was shot down in South Vietnam. He was nineteen years old.

There are no words for this.

Chapter 18

Secret Santas

"LOOK AT ME, EVERYBODY! I'M A VOLCANO! BOOM! BOOM! LOOK OUT FOR THE LAVA!"

"LOOK AT ME! LOOKIE! I'M A HER CANE! HERE COMES THE SUE MOMMY!"

Viney's two youngest grandchildren, Dylan, age three, and Zeke, age five, are entertaining themselves with the refuse of Christmas morning. Zeke repeatedly immerses himself in a large cardboard box filled with Styrofoam peanuts and then springs out like a Vegas showgirl emerging from a giant cake; Dylan bounds through fields of crumpled wrapping paper and bows, swirling his arms and scattering debris with the force of a Dust Bowl windstorm. In spite of the unvoiced hopes of the six adults assembled in the room (Viney, Viney's youngest daughter, Haley, and her estranged husband, Randy, Larken, Gaelan, and Bonnie), neither child shows any sign of winding down or developing laryngitis.

According to their mother, Dylan and Zeke were up at six A.M. They finished opening Santa's presents by 6:30 and had emptied and eaten the sugary contents of their stockings by 7:00. They got to Viney's around ten o'clock and for the first hour or so, their antics were encouraged. It's Christmas, after all. Most of the adults even took turns contributing to the chaos. But it's almost noon now. As if they could inspire by example, the adults have started making themselves as small and quiet and polite and inconspicuous as possible. With the exception of Dylan and Zeke's father—who has fallen asleep—they sit up straight with their feet close together and their elbows fastened to their sides. They sip coffee and nibble crumbly squares of cake. Viney usually makes *Teisen Ffrwythau Landudno* from scratch, but this year she's serving store-bought fruit cake. They don't speak unless spoken to.

Larken unwraps the last present. It's from Viney.

"They're MBTs," Viney says brightly after Larken has withdrawn her gift from its box.

"Thanks, Viney," Larken says, feigning delight. "These are great!"

"You don't already have a pair, do you?"

"No. No, I don't."

"Oh, good. I was afraid you might."

"OOOOOO!" Zeke says, snatching up the shoe box bottom and shoving it onto his head. "LOOK, MOM! I'M DARTH VADAR!" He starts stalking his brother and intoning in the deepest voice a five-year-old can muster, "I AM YOUR FATHER LUKE. I AM YOUR FATHER LUKE. I AM YOUR FATHER LUKE . . ."

"STOP THAT!" Dylan says. He extracts a long cardboard tube from the landfill of wrapping paper and starts whacking his brother on the head.

"MBT stands for Masai Barefoot Technology," Viney continues.

"Ah." Larken thought it might stand for *Most Butt-ugly Tennies.*

"I'm surprised you don't know about them."

"I've heard of them," Gaelan says. "They're physiologically designed. They make you walk the way we're all supposed to walk."

"That's right," Viney says. "Like you're barefoot."

"Let me look at those," Bonnie says. "Gosh, Lark," she says, holding the sole of one shoe against the bottom of her foot. "I always forget how little your feet are."

Viney continues. "Anyway, you're so hard to buy for, and I figured you'd be doing a lot of walking while you're in Europe, and . . . Oh, honey," she says, her voice suddenly tearful. "If you don't like them you can certainly take them back and get something else."

"No, Viney!" Larken reaches an arm around her shoulders and hugs her. There's an odd, cushiony feel to Viney's flesh, as if she's put on weight. "I love them. And you're right: These will be perfect for London."

"MOM!" Zeke shouts. "DYLAN WON'T DIE AND I JUST CUT HIS ARM OFF WITH MY LASER!"

"DID NOT! DID NOT!" Dylan says, starting to cry. "I GREW A NEW ONE!"

"Viney doesn't seem right, does she?" Gaelan asks.

"How do you mean?" Larken replies, somewhat breathlessly. Between Bonnie's brisk pace and the irregular, snowy terrain, she's struggling to keep up.

After everyone said their good-byes to Haley, Randy, Dylan, and Zeke, and then helped clean up the house, Viney excused herself upstairs for a nap and Bonnie announced that she had a surprise for her siblings, one that would require them to bundle up and follow her outside. Larken doesn't know where their sister is leading them or what she's so eager to show, but they're headed in the direction of downtown—a prospect so depressing as to impede Larken's progress even further.

Gaelan slows his steps and takes Larken's arm. "She's just . . . off somehow," he says, frowning. His voice has an imploded, held quality; his words are carried on expulsed breaths so miserly that there's barely a trace of them in the freezing air. "She doesn't have her usual . . . glow. And she was so . . . I don't know, *distant* with Haley's kids, didn't you think?"

"Well, holidays and all. December without Dad. It's got to be hard."

Bonnie scampers along with the animal grace she's had since childhood, giving the impression of having four hooved feet instead of two shod ones.

"Jesus," Larken gripes. "Do you have any idea what this is about?"

Gaelan shrugs, noncommittal.

Bonnie turns and shouts: "Come *on,* you guys! Why are you so *slow?*"

Being in her sister's presence when she's vibrating with this kind of energy makes Larken feel ancient. "Why couldn't we have driven?" she mutters.

"I wish you didn't have to go," Gaelan says, his voice so somber and mournful that she has to look at him to make sure he's not crying.

"Me, too," Larken answers. "But I've got to get back tonight. I've still got so much to do and I have to get up tomorrow at an ungodly hour . . ."

"No," Gaelan cuts in. "I meant, to England."

"Why?"

"When's your flight?"

"Early. We leave Lincoln at six-fifteen."

"How're you getting to the airport?"

"Cab, probably."

"Six-fifteen," Gaelan repeats, with strange solemnity. "I'll remember."

"Are you okay?"

"I'm fine."

He's never this closemouthed. Something must be up. "Did you get to talk to anybody at church last night? Bethan was asking about you."

"I was late, remember?" he replies, his voice uncharacteristically edgy. "I missed everything."

"Hurry up!" Bonnie yells with glee. "We're almost there!" They've arrived in the mostly boarded-up area of Emlyn Springs that is still euphemistically referred to as "downtown." Larken can't imagine where *there* might be.

The two of them pause and watch Bonnie pause briefly to look both ways before rushing across the wide empty street. When they were kids, Larken and Gaelan had to constantly remind their sister to *stop, look, and listen* when crossing Main. They trained her well. There was need for that vigilance then, but no more.

To Larken's dismay, Bonnie is making her way toward one of Emlyn Springs' oldest and shabbiest structures: the Tinkham Building. Once housing a single prosperous enterprise, it suffered the fate of many downtown structures and was bifurcated years ago. At present, one half serves as the place of business for Blind Tom's Piano Repair; the other half has been vacant and in disrepair for decades, its door scarred and padlocked, its windows opaqued with grimy swirls of soap.

And yet it is here that Bonnie stops and pulls a set of keys out of her coat pocket.

"We're here!" she cries as she flings the door open; within, there surely awaits an angelic choir singing "Jubilate Deo." "Come on, you guys! Come in and see!"

Gaelan takes Larken's arm again and they approach the intersection of Bridge and Main. For whatever reason—out of long habit, out of respect for their dead town's former glory, or as a way of sheltering their baby sister from the truth (that her hopes are in vain and her faith will never be rewarded)—they still look both ways before they cross.

Blind Tom and Sergei are also making their way downtown. They've spent the day with Uncle Howie, meeting him at noon in the basement of the community center, where the ladies of the Cly-ta Horticultural Society provide a traditional Welsh-themed Christmas dinner for all of Emlyn Springs' disenfranchised citizens—mostly solo-dwelling divorced and widowed men possessing neither the skill nor the inclination to cook a holiday meal. Then they moved on to the social hall of St. David's Home for the Elderly, where—in what's become a yearly tradition—Blind Tom provides piano accompaniment for the Christmas Carol Sing-Along and Secret Santa Gift Exchange while Uncle Howie and Sergei work the room in their respective capacities as octogenarian bachelor and therapy dog.

As they walk, Blind Tom whistles a call-and-response duet with one of his favorite native birds, the one that sings the first four notes of a Beethoven symphony.

It's been a fine day—but the best is yet to come.

Reaching inside his overcoat, he lays his palm against his torso in the area of his lower right ribs; it's silly, he knows, but he seeks reassurance that there's still a rectangular wafer of ivory pressed snuggled into the pocket of his red vest.

It's there.

Feeling its unique contours, even through a gloved hand, fills him with a mischievous, ecstatic happiness, as if he's secretly in possession of a significant relic—which, in a way, he is—and causes him to laugh. Sergei looks up and smiles, happy because his master is happy.

Blind Tom quickens his pace until they are almost jogging. "Come on, Sergei!" he cries, coattails flying. "Let's hurry!"

Who but a blind piano technician would derive such joy from such a small thing? Who but a confirmed odd duck would absent himself from the warmth and comfort of society (and on Christmas Day no less!) in order to ply his trade in a darkened, ramshackle warehouse, anticipating such occupation as a blessing?

Even Blind Tom knows that his eccentricities put him at the fringes of normalcy.

How lucky that he landed here, in this small, benevolent, provincial place insulated by geography and human will, where such eccentricities are more than accepted: They are ignored.

"Tada!" Bonnie flings her arms out theatrically.

They're confronted with a mess of scattered boxes—some opened, some still sealed up—as well as tools, bike parts, printouts of bike-building instructions. There's a single, long, filthy fluorescent light blinking from the ceiling—a kind of tubular crypt, its innards are darkly speckled with generations of dead bugs. It dangles precariously from four chains of unequal length; its spastic glow periodically illuminates a single wheel that is roped to one of the exposed rafters, hung horizontally—like a chandelier—and decorated with tinsel and twinkle lights and garlands of popcorn and cranberries. It's so cold inside that they can see their breath. The place has that distinctly complex smell of singed wiring, mildew, and mouse turds, which indicates that a building is so structurally diseased that its best hope is to be gutted, if not razed. In one corner, a metal trash can is full to overflowing with beer cans and bottles. All of the walls have been spray-painted with graffiti.

Larken remembers the Midwesterner's Golden Rule—*if you can't say anything nice, don't say anything at all*—and shuts up. She keeps her facial muscles consciously slack.

"Gosh, Bon," Gaelan offers. He starts strolling around, opening and closing cupboards and doors, examining electrical outlets. "You've really done a lot of work here." His voice is affable, but Larken knows that his building inspector routine is just a way to avoid looking their sister in the eye.

"It's a mess right now," Bonnie hastens to say. "Sorry I haven't had a chance to clean up. I had a lot of orders for Christmas, you know, from parents who didn't feel comfortable putting bikes together and wanted someone else to do it for them. It was so much fun! I felt like one of Santa's elves."

"I hope you let people *pay* you for doing that," Larken says. "In *money,* I mean." The words are out before she can censor herself.

"Yes," Bonnie says, only a little testy. "They paid me in money."

Gaelan speaks up. "This building used to be the variety store."

"Tinkham's." Bonnie starts following Gaelan around. "It was huge. We came here all the time, remember? There's even some old stock, from when it was a five-and-dime. And funny things keep showing up."

"Dead rats?" Larken mutters under her breath. "Drunk teenagers? Toxic fungi?"

"I'm always tripping over those little red balls, you know? The really bouncy ones that came with jacks."

"Huh," Gaelan says. Larken can tell that he's every bit as dismayed by all this as she is, but he's much better at keeping his opinions to himself.

"When Tinkham's went out of business," Bonnie goes on, "they closed the building up for a while. And then it got divided in two; this part's been empty for a long time, but Blind Tom moved into the other half back in the eighties."

Larken picks up a piece of paper at random. It's a shipping receipt.

"I mean, I'm not gonna get rich or anything doing this," Bonnie says, glancing at Larken, "but the rent's really cheap . . ."

I'll bet, Larken thinks.

". . . and I've gotten a lot of good advice off the Web."

Larken says continues to study the shipping receipt. It cost a small fortune to get these bikes here.

Gaelan opens a door at the back of the shop. "What are all the piano parts?"

"Blind Tom uses the back for storage. Once the bike business takes off, he'll move all that out and I'll take it over for building and repairs, and this front part here will be turned into a showroom. You couldn't ask for a better location. I've got great visibility."

Gaelan disappears into the back room.

"So," Larken says, carefully, "does this mean you're giving up on the juice bar?"

"No. Not at all. This article I read—let me find it for you—said that you shouldn't expect to make your bike shop provide your main source of income for at least—here it is—a year." Bonnie hands over some loose pages.

Larken looks down to find a computer printout of an article from *Mother Earth News,* labeled Issue #26 and dated March–April 1974. "This is what you're using?"

"Like I said, it's really useful."

"Bonnie, are you sure this is still current?"

"The prices are obviously not right, but the basic information is really sound."

Gaelan emerges. "This all looks . . . pretty . . . good, Bon," he says, "but I'd feel a lot better if the wiring was updated and the back door got repaired."

"I know. I've talked to Tom about that and he's gonna contact the owner."

"Who is the owner?" Larken asks.

"Um, not sure. We've had a little trouble getting hold of him. He might be dead."

"I see."

"But," Bonnie resumes brightly, "there's gonna be a real effort to contact all the owners of these downtown buildings and get them spruced up."

"Why is that?" Larken asks.

"Because of the Welsh delegation. The Sister City project." Bonnie speaks with the mildly irritated tone of someone who's thinking, *Weren't you listening?* "It's been all over the newspaper for months . . ." Bonnie has tucked a yearly subscription notice to *The Goldenrod Gazette* into her siblings' Christmas stockings every year since they moved away. Larken doesn't know about Gaelan, but her newspapers usually end up either in the recycling bin or the fireplace.

"Haven't you guys been reading the minutes from the community council meetings?" Bonnie asks.

"Sorry, no," Larken says. "Why don't you just tell us about it?"

"Well," Bonnie sighs. "There'a lot going on, but I'll try to give you the short version. After Dad died, Viney was going through his stuff and found out that he'd been corresponding with the monastery in our Sister City. You know about our Sister City, right?"

"Of course," Larken lies.

"You bet," Gaelan adds.

"Dad's idea was that we invite a delegation of monks here, show them around, and see if they'd be interested in opening a second monastery."

"Why would they want to do that?" Larken asks.

"Because of our connection," Bonnie replies, as if the answer was obvious. "Because we're Sister Cities. And for financial reasons, too. These monks are really successful and they might want to grow their market, establish a presence in the States."

Invoking phrases like *grow their market* and *establish a presence* sounds strikingly un-Bonnie-like. Larken wonders if her sister isn't improvising at all but has been working on this speech with help from members of the Better Business Bureau.

"They've got a thriving cottage industry, so they'd be bringing their business to town. Not just that, but tourists, money, jobs . . . It could be incredible."

Yeah, Larken thinks, *and it would take the length of an Ice Age.*

Gaelan breaks in. "It's a great idea for no other reason than Dad wanting it."

Bonnie goes on. "So Mr. Humphries contacted the monks and they're sending a delegation this summer, during Fancy Egg Days."

Bonnie elaborates on all the ways their town plans to reinvigorate a festival that once included a full week of nonstop, celebratory events, but for decades has consisted of little more than a ragtag parade, a hen-laying contest, and a tractor pull.

Larken and Gaelan smile and listen. Their sister is infinitely loveable. It is so hard not to be disarmed by her. Having never left the landscape of her childhood, Bonnie has never abdicated it; this is why it's next to impossible to reason with her as if she's an adult.

"As for the shop," Bonnie shrugs. "I actually got the idea a while back, before any of this other stuff happened, and then it just all fell into place. Like it was meant to be."

Who can argue with *It was meant to be?* In their sister's worldview, the ridiculous, the impractical, the hopeless—all acquire an *a priori* authority.

"So," Bonnie concludes, arms outstretched, making a three-hundred-and-sixty-degree turn, "what do you think?" She ends up stationed directly beneath the fluorescent light and hanging wheel, which Larken notes with alarm are both swaying slightly. She has to grab Gaelan's arm to keep herself from running at Bonnie and pushing her out of harm's way.

"You've given this all a lot of thought, Bon," Larken remarks. It's a harmless statement, and true, and at the moment it's the best she can do.

"I mean, about that," Bonnie said, pointing up. "That's what really started it all."

"What?"

"The wheel. I found it, remember? The day we buried Dad? That's why I didn't make it to the cemetery."

"Ah." It would be useless to remind Bonnie that *we* didn't bury Dad, that she's explaining her behavior four months after the fact, and this is completely new information.

"You know how businesses frame their first dollar bills sometimes?" she goes on. "Put them on display? I decided I'd display my wheel."

"That's great, Bon."

Bonnie's expression darkens. "You're not even looking at it."

"Okay," Larken says slowly, looking pointedly at the wheel. "I see it, Bonnie. It's . . . wonderful. A wonderful idea, I mean, to keep it hanging there. It's the perfect symbol for what you're hoping to do here." *Whatever that is.*

"You don't see, do you? You just don't get it."

I am not going to fight with her. Not today. Not on Christmas, not on the day before I have to get on an airplane. "See what, honey?" Larken says in the most conciliatory tone she can manage. "Get what? What is it?"

"Nothing. Forget it." Bonnie turns away and gets busy corralling cardboard boxes into a corner of the room. "Thanks for coming, anyway. I know you're in a rush, so if you have to get going, I understand."

Larken checks her watch. "Yeah, I should probably start back. Are you guys staying here or what?"

"I have to collect the mice," Bonnie mutters.

"Collect the what?"

Gaelan pipes up. "I'll stay and help." He gives Larken a look, his subtext clear: He'll see if he can get any more information from Bonnie and then report back to her.

"I love you, Bon," Larken says. "Merry Christmas."

"I love you, too." Bonnie allows herself to be hugged and then goes back to work.

"Drive safe," Gaelan adds, "and call when you get to Lincoln."

Larken starts trudging back through the snow, setting her feet into the indentations she and Gaelan made on the way here; they're already losing their definition; it's starting to snow again, fine and light: confectioners' sugar sifting down from the sky.

Without the buoying support of her brother's arms and her sister's enthusiasm, the trek seems overwhelming. She might as well be crossing the Russian steppes. Maybe it will take the rest of the day and all night to get to Viney's. She'll miss her plane and that will be that.

The snow makes everything so quiet.

As she becomes aware of a familiar gathering tension in her chest, Larken hopes that she hasn't just seen her siblings for the last time.

Twenty-five years is a ridiculously long time to spend on a single instrument; Blind Tom has restored other severely damaged pianos in as little as fifteen months. But those projects were undertaken for monetary reasons; either his efforts were commissioned by the instruments' owners or he was laboring with an intent to sell.

This piano is different. It is not spoken for. No one awaits its return. It will never be put up for sale.

Blind Tom isn't even sure that this project qualifies as a restoration, strictly speaking, since he is not concerned in this case with returning the instrument to its factory-perfect condition, but to its status as the functioning but idiosyncratically flawed instrument it was when it was carried into the sky. After all, this piano produced music—magnificent music, surely—right up until that moment.

Piano technicians—not unlike vintage car enthusiasts—are notorious for acquiring bits and pieces of pianos in the hope that someday they'll get around to using them. Sets of ivories intended for piano keys—brought into the country before such importations became illegal in the 1970s—have been bought and sold for years, passed from one piano technician to another, through estate sales or e-Bay auctions, by technicians who just never quite got around to using them. Blind Tom imagines that the deathbed confessions of piano technicians often involve the location of secret stashes of contraband ivory.

He is extremely fortunate in that he inherited just such a set from his predecessor, and he makes withdrawals from it to replace those ivories that were lost or too ruined to reuse. If he chose, he could use ersatz ivory—Yamaha makes a very good facsimilie that has none of the plastic feel of other brands. But for this piano, he prefers to use the real thing.

Another bit of luck: The white keys of a piano are not—as one might assume—made of separate blocks of wood, but of a single piece, usually sugar pine, which is cut with a band saw–like tool; thus, if any part of that single piece of wood is damaged, one must start from scratch. The keyboard of Blind Tom's special project piano survived intact.

With all his restoration projects, not just his special one, Blind Tom likes to parse out the work in a way that lends significance to the process. Since the piano alphabet only goes from A to G, this limits the possibilities, but not much.

For example:

He might affix an A ivory on Advent, All Saint's Day, the Autumnal Equinox, or the birthday of Clarence Acox.

Luckily, there's a happy abundance of notable musicians with names in the prescribed parameters: in addition to the obvious ones—Bach, Beethoven, Borodin, Brahms, Britten, Chopin, Copland, Debussy, Dvořák, Elgar, Fauré, Grieg, et cetera—there are also many of Blind Tom's personal favorites:

Adderley (Cannonball); Bernstein (Leonard); Brubeck (Dave); Bennett (Tony); Cassidy (Eva); Clooney (Rosemary); Carmichael (Hoagy); Desmond (Paul); Ellington (Duke); Fats (Waller); Forbes (China); Getz (Stan); Gershwin (Ira and George); Grappelli (Stéphane), and so on.

A D might get its ivory crown on St. David's Day, an E on Easter or Epiphany.

He likes affixing Fs on full moons, and Gs on any day there's a *Gymanfa*.

On Christmas Day, then, the choice is easy.

But on this Christmas he's not just affixing the ivory to any old C, but to the Northern Star of the piano keyboard, that key from which all pianists' earliest orienteering efforts begin.

Furthermore, this ivory displays what piano technicians call "dishing"; that is, its surface, through years of wear, has developed a subtle concavity. In comparison to its neighboring keys, this dishing is obvious and distinct—to the hand if not to the eye. Were this bit of ivory to be left outside in the rain (and indeed it was, in 1978), a small shallow pool would form in its center.

Along with all the other ivories belonging to Blind Tom's special project piano, this one was carefully removed, cleaned, and cataloged, and has been waiting patiently, without complaint, with utter faith, as other ivories have been reattached to the keyboard. There is no more perfect symbol in the world for patience than an unattached piano ivory.

Today, the flawed ivory in Blind Tom's vest pocket will finally return it to its original home: at middle C, on the sugar pine keyboard of Hope Aneira Jones's 1918 Steinway baby grand.

"Gae?"

"Yeah, Bon?"

"Do you think I'll ever have children?"

This without any conversational preamble: Following his sister's lead, Gaelan has been working in silence, first flattening cardboard shipping containers and bundling them together with twine, then gathering up small, green-tinted Plexiglas boxes from around the fringes of the room and placing them into an old wooden crate. The boxes contain rodents in varying degrees of distress. Gaelan has been intently studying an especially glum, resigned-looking fellow, which is why he asks Bonnie to repeat herself.

"I said, do you think I'll ever be able to have a baby?"

Gaelan hesitates before responding—this is a tender subject—and then, as if she, too, is scrolling through the list of possible responses going through his mind, Bonnie adds, "And I don't mean *adopt* a baby, although I've got nothing against adoption. I'm talking about getting pregnant. The regular way. Like a normal person. You know, by having"—she stops mid-sentence—"sexual intercourse." These last words are spoken with a grim, wincing emphasis, as if Bonnie has only just accepted the fact that babies aren't delivered by stork. "Do you think it's possible?"

Telling Bonnie the truth is not always the best solution. In fact, when it comes to matters of the heart, it's probably *never* the best solution. Gaelan understands this instinctively; Larken does not, and that's why she and Bonnie fight so often. In this situation, for example, Larken would automatically deliver the truth, albeit gently. But Gaelan knows that Bonnie only seems to be asking for an honest response to a real question; what she's really doing is offering up a bowl of bleeding viscera as currency for the lie she wants to hear.

Gaelan finds it best to treat her like a topographical fact of nature that can sometimes, with the careful application of force and engineering, be redirected—like a river.

"I think you'd be a wonderful mother," he says.

"I do, too," Bonnie replies. She sits down on a vacant lot in the subdivision of trapped mice and starts to cry.

Gaelan gets on the floor with her, pulls her close, waits.

A jingling of bells followed by the sounds of feet and claws indicate that Blind Tom and Sergei have arrived in the other half of the store. Whoever partitioned Tinkham's didn't make much of an attempt at soundproofing; all that separates BJ's Bikes from the piano hospital is an uninsulated wall and a hinged piece of plywood.

Bonnie tries to get her tears under control. "Hi, Tom," she calls out nasally. "Merry Christmas."

"Merry Christmas, Bonnie."

"Gaelan's here, too."

"Merry Christmas, Gaelan."

"Merry Christmas, Tom."

Bonnie pulls a tissue from her coat pocket and snuggles deeper into her brother's arms.

In no time at all, as Blind Tom goes about his quiet work and Sergei settles at his master's feet, Gaelan and Bonnie lapse into a kind of social amnesia, completely forgetting that they're not really alone. Whatever noises there are have the quality of ambient sound—unattached to any living, sentient presence.

"You've had a lot of girlfriends, haven't you?" Bonnie says.

"Well, I don't know about that . . ."

"Oh, come on, Gae. You know what I mean. You're experienced. You've done it a lot."

Not lately. "Yeah, I suppose."

"What do men like?"

"What do you mean?"

"What makes some women better . . . in bed . . . than others? What makes them more attractive?"

"Those are really two different things, honey. There's attraction, and then . . ." He can't believe he's having this conversation with his thirty-two-year-old sister. Wasn't Larken supposed to cover this kind of thing, like, twenty years ago? ". . . there's sex. They're not the same."

"Define attraction."

"Okay, well, uh, it's something you see in the other person, something that catches your attention, like . . . their face, or their body, or—"

"I get that, silly."

"Well, you asked me, and in my experience that's mostly where it starts."

Bonnie is dismayed. "So it's all based on looks?"

"No, not always. There's . . ." What? He used to know this. "There's . . . personality." *That's it.* "A shared sense of humor, common interests . . ."

"But wait a minute. How about with you and Bethan?"

"Me and Bethan?"

"Yeah, it couldn't have been based on looks with you guys, because you knew each other a long time before you had sex, right?"

This is the risk one takes when conversing with Bonnie. One minute she's falling apart and the next she's shining a penlight into your inner ear, looking for scar tissue. "I don't understand what that has to do with—"

"It wasn't like one day you just woke up and, wow, Bethan was suddenly this beautiful girl with this great body. You knew her forever, way before she was beautiful, from when she was a little girl and was even kind of dorky-looking."

"I was pretty dorky-looking back then, too, if you remember."

"You were *never* dorky. And then there's Dad and Viney."

This is another thing: You start out feeling prepared, strong, confident, the wise older brother who's offering good counsel and the benefit of years of experience, and then she goes off on some tangent and you find yourself in a quagmire of complete ignorance.

"Dad and Viney," Gaelan repeats, giving up now on trying to advise, trying only to follow the conversation.

"I mean, how did they get together? Haven't you ever wondered about that? She was Dad's nurse for a long time, and Mom's best friend, and then poof, they fell in love, or something, didn't they?—and stayed together for the rest of their lives. What happened to make that happen? What changed?"

"I have no idea."

"Of course," Bonnie remarks thoughtfully, "they didn't have any babies . . ."

How did this start? Gaelan asks himself. He can't remember.

"So," Bonnie says. "You've never had sex with someone you weren't attracted to."

Gaelan considers. "No."

"But you HAVE had sex with someone you didn't love."

"Yes."

"Why?"

"Because . . . well . . . because I was attracted to them."

"But you didn't want to make babies, or anything. You just wanted to have sex?"

"Uh-huh."

"What was that like?"

"What was what like?"

"Having sex with someone you're attracted to but don't love and don't have any intention of making babies with. Did it work out okay?"

"It depends on what you mean by okay."

"Was it pleasant?"

"Bon, honey, what are you asking me?"

"I don't know what I'm asking. That's the problem." Bonnie sits up and regards the mice. "We're going to have to let them out pretty soon or they'll suffocate."

"Okay."

Picking up one of the mouse houses, Bonnie initiates a staring contest with its resident. "Here's the thing," she says. "I'm going to tell you something I've never told anybody and you have to promise you'll never repeat it to anyone, not even Larken. *Especially* not Larken."

"All right."

"Promise."

"I promise."

"I've never done it."

Gaelan's mind fast-forwards to a time years from now: his baby sister, the town spinster, referred to in fond but pitying tones as *the Jones girl* in the same way that Hazel and Wauneeta are still called *the Williams girls.* At least they have each other. Bonnie will have no one.

The happy version of this future finds Bonnie living in Dad's house (*poor thing, never married*), going to committee meetings, crocheting afghans, wearing support stockings and Hush Puppies, warming up Healthy Choice microwave dinners, dying in her sleep at 114 under the watchful eyes of the staff of St. David's Home for the Elderly.

In the worst-case scenario, she'll keep on living in that woodshed and hoarding roadside trash (*poor thing, never married, not all there*), one of those sad people you hear about, usually living anonymously in a place like New York City, in an apartment that no one has been inside for decades, and then one day there's a ghastly smell and someone gets the superintendent to open up the door and there they are, dead for weeks, decomposing somewhere among the piles of moldering newspapers and books. (Actually, when he thinks about it, this couldn't happen in Emlyn Springs; in small towns, for better or worse, no one is invisible. People are noticed. Dying without anybody noticing is the kind of thing that would be more likely to happen to him, although his prolonged absence from the Y might be noticeable.)

The point is it's easy to imagine Bonnie turning into Donna Reed in the scary version of George Bailey's future. Without love (and sex), she'll shrivel.

"Gaelan, what are you thinking?"

"I'm not thinking anything."

"I just don't see the point of having sex if you're not trying to have a baby. I know that's weird."

"It's not weird at all."

"Have you ever wanted to make a baby? Like, with Bethan, if you hadn't broken up, do you think you would have had kids?"

"That was a long time ago, Bon."

Bonnie considers. "I'm asking you because you more than anybody I know have had everything. You've had a true love and then you've had, well, whatever you call the other women you've had sex with. I'm just wondering how you find the right person. The person you're supposed to be with."

"You know, honey, there are plenty of people who think that there isn't just one person out there, one great love who's the only one you can be happy with . . ."

Bonnie sighs. "I know. I'm just not one of them. Thanks for talking about all this, Gae. It really helped."

"It did?"

"You listened. You helped me figure something out."

She stands and stretches and inspects Mouse Town. "Okay. Let's take care of these guys."

"What do we do with them?"

"First we name them." She consults with a small notebook on her worktable. "I alternate gender names, you know, like hurricanes. Right now we need a boy's name beginning with 'M.'"

"Okay."

"Then we take them over to the ravine and let them go. There's lots of cover there, places to burrow, so they have a better chance of surviving predators."

Gaelan thinks about asking his sister how she's sure that she's not just catching the same mice over and over again, but thinks better of it. He's sure that, to Bonnie, it wouldn't make a bit of difference.

They leave without saying good-bye; in all likelihood they've forgotten he was here.

He's not offended; this kind of thing happens all the time. Blind Tom's experience indicates that, when people are in the presence of someone who can't see, they believe themselves to be invisible. This gives him access to all kinds of useful information.

Middle C has been glued and clamped to the keyboard. His work is nearly done.

Before leaving, he retrieves a wrapped gift and sets it inside Bonnie's half of the store. He hopes she likes it. *Consumer Reports* says that the Vita-Mix 5000 (with its 1380 power wattage, sixty-four-ounce jar, and seven-year warranty) gets raves from owners, who testify that, for those who uses a blender daily—particularly for tough jobs—this is the one to get. It pulverizes whole fruits and vegetables, turns ice to snow in seconds, crushes wheat berries into flour, and its blades spin quickly enough to turn room-temperature ingredients into hot soup in about five minutes—all of which Blind Tom finds tremendously reassuring, since it gives him reason to believe that Bonnie's days of thunking will finally be over.

Viney has been waiting all day for this moment.

Weeks ago, she moved Welly's shoe boxes over from his house and arranged them on the floor on his side of the walk-in closet: boxes containing shoes are grouped in one area; boxes containing liquor occupy another.

Viney is in the walk-in closet now, sitting on the floor. Closing her eyes, she reaches into one of the liquor boxes at random and pulls out two bottles: Bailey's Irish Cream and Kaluha.

From her side of the closet she brings a wrapped box out of the garment bag where it's been hiding for the past month. The tag on the box reads: TO WELLY, WITH ALL MY LOVE, V.

She opens the box. It's a new pair of golf shoes. They were expensive, but he needed them.

"Merry Christmas, honey," she says, raising her bottle. "Here's to us."

Hope's Diary, 1968:
The Censorship Capital of the World

I fell down the stairs today.

Not all the way, thank God, just the last few steps. It was just after I'd finished reading to the children and tucked them in for an afternoon nap.

Not all of it can be blamed on the glass of wine I poured for myself as soon as we got back from the library (another trip to Italy!). I was walking too quickly and wearing toe-numbing high heels. Also, I was still distracted and angered. Bad combination.

Late afternoon now. Waiting for L. to get home for dinner and assess my bruise.

We're on the back porch, Larken and Gaelan playing in the sandbox, Mommy holding a package of frozen peas and carrots to her hip.

I can't believe I actually dressed up for that bitch. Not just high heels either but a skirt and blouse and hose and even hair spray and makeup.

Began the day with such high hopes. When I told L. of my plan he said, "You might want to reconsider."

"What do you mean?"

"Think about it, Hope. There's a reason the library's collection is a little . . ."

"Archaic?"

"Conservative."

I laughed. "It would be nice if the people of Emlyn Springs had the option of reading something that was written in the twentieth century."

"Don't be sarcastic. You're not going to make any friends talking like that."

"I'm not making any friends, period," I reminded him. "Except Viney."

L. shrugged. "Good luck."

So, feeling like Mrs. Claus (in high heels), I loaded the books and the kids into the car first thing this morning and drove into town.

Wanted to get Larken and Gaelan busy in the children's corner before talking with the librarian, so I set them up with viewfinders. Sitting on the floor holding those oversize, ungainly devices to their eyes, they look like chubby exotic bugs. They love the "Wonders of the World" collection: Larken prefers the architectural wonders (Notre Dame, the Parthenon, etc.) while Gaelan loves the natural ones.

Taking up my box of books, I wobbled toward the front desk and greeted Mrs. Burchett by saying, "I'm here to make a donation."

She peered over the top of the box. "That's nice," she answered. As librarians go, Myrtle Burchett is a caricature of repression. Hard to believe she's married and has kids.

I forged on. "I thought you'd like having some of these newer titles."

"Thank you."

For the next hour or so the children and I looked through the viewfinders, did wood puzzles, read. I found a couple of lovely picture books and a collection of American folktales for them, and for me, Hazel Williams's self-published "History of Emlyn Springs" and a how-to on raising exotic hens. Figured it was time to explore what it means to be living in the former Fancy Egg capital of the world.

Near noon, the children starting to get hungry, we took our selections to the front desk. My box was still sitting there. Clearly the contents had been examined; the books were now spines out and alphabetized by author.

Mrs. Burchett started stamping due dates with a grim, measured determination. "I'm afraid we won't be able to use those," she said.

She pushed the box toward me as if it contained decomposing roadkill.

"What's wrong, Mommy?" Gaelan asked.

"Nothing, sweetheart. Here are your books."

"Let's go," Larken said, tugging my hand.

"In a minute, honey." I turned back to Mrs. Burchett. "Could you tell me what your objections are?"

"Well, this volume of poetry, for instance. It's obvious why we can't accept this."

"It's not obvious to me." I swear I was trying to keep my voice civil.

Mrs. Burchett clenched her teeth and opened the book. "This title," she whispered, pointing. "This word. I'm sure you can understand what's inappropriate about that." She then busied herself with stacking books on a small wheeled cart.

"Can I have these?" Larken was foraging through my jacket pockets and found some after-dinner mints.

"Yes. Share with your brother."

Mrs. Burchett looked up. "There's no food allowed in the—" she began, but then stopped herself. She must have decided to make an exception for my poor dears because they're being brought up by a woman who's familiar with the word masturbate.

Putting herself at the helm of the cart, Mrs. Burchett sailed out from behind the desk toward the stacks.

"How about this," I said, chasing after her with Harper Lee in hand.

"The library board has already reviewed that one. There are issues of content."

I reminded her that "To Kill a Mockingbird" won the Pulitzer Prize for Fiction, but she moved on, stranding us among the library's vast Harlequin Romance collection. I spent a few minutes de-alphabetizing. Larken threw a tantrum. Gaelan peed on the floor, I snatched up my box of censored books, and we made our exit. At home, lunch and Paul Bunyan tales and naps for them, a glass of wine and a tumble down the stairs for me.

Back to my bruise: It's spectacular. I've never seen anything like it. I regard its gorgeous mottled purples with awe. I have a perverse desire to mentally replay the incident, watch it in slow motion. The physics of my fall must have been fascinating, the arrangement and movement of my limbs as I fell could have supplied the curriculum for a whole course at the university.

It hurts to breathe—I slid down part of the way on my side, the wooden stair treads hammering against my ribs—but I don't think I've broken anything and there are no bruises anywhere but on my leg. Henceforward I will behave more sensibly when wearing unsensible shoes.

Must go now. Children calling for me to come play.

Chapter 19

The Gatekeeper Deserts
Her Post

The cab does not come. This affirms Larken's chronic anxiety about putting someone else in charge of her transportation; moreover, it's ominous: If a cabbie is this unreliable, how can she feel unfettered, enthusiastic confidence in the pilot of a transcontinental jet?

She creeps upstairs and knocks on the door. Jon answers. She's not sure what she expected of his sleepwear—BVDs and a T-shirt maybe—but it wasn't plaid flannel pajamas. He looks disturbingly adorable.

"Sorry," Larken whispers. "I'm so sorry."

"What?" Jon says. "What's wrong?"

"It's late, I mean, it's early, but my cab hasn't arrived and I'm supposed to be at the airport"—she glances at her watch—"fifteen minutes ago."

"You gave the cabbie the wrong address, didn't you?" Jon teases.

Larken considers this. It's not out of the realm of possibility. "I don't think so. Anyway, so sorry, but could you drive me?"

"Of course."

She waits on the threshold while he shuffles back into the apartment—on argyle slipper socks!—and pulls a bathrobe on over his PJs; it's one of those old-fashioned ones that looks like it's made from a blanket. He dons a vintage cashmere wool coat over the whole ensemble, slips his feet into faux-fleece snowboots, and tugs a knit hat onto his head. He scribbles a note and leaves it on the kitchen table. Only after he finishes putting on his gloves does he turn to face her.

"Shall we?" he says. His face—the only uninsulated part of his anatomy—is flushed in places, full and smooth, and makes her think of ripe nectarines. Suddenly he looks very alert; but then, of the two of them, he is the morning person.

"Right," Larken replies. "Do you mind driving?"

There's a small sniffle; the two of them turn to see Esmé padding out of her room, half-asleep, tangled in her blanket and holding her orca whale by one worn fin. Blearily, she takes in the two of them. "Up," she says, and—letting blanket and orca slide to the floor—holds out her arms.

"Oh, no," Jon sighs. "I'll never get her back in bed now."

"Up," Esmé murmurs again, arms and head and eyelids drooping.

"We can take her," Larken says, scooping Esmé into her arms. "I'll grab her car seat if you can get my luggage."

"Okay, I'll just tell Mia what's going on."

Larken hoists Esmé onto one hip, grabs the blanket and bundles it around her, picks up the car seat, and heads downstairs and outside.

"It's dark," Esmé says as Larken climbs into the backseat with her and starts buckling her in. "Where are we going?"

"You and Daddy are taking me to the airport."

"Why?"

"I'm going on a trip, remember? I told you about it."

"You're always saying good-bye to me, Larkee."

"I know it must seem that way, sweetie, and I'm sorry to be going."

"So why are you?"

"Because I made a promise to a friend."

"But you promised to come to my party, too."

"I know, sweet pea. But my friend got very sick, and he needs my help."

Esmé ponders this statement for a while. She grabs a section of her flyaway hair and starts twirling it.

Larken goes on. "You know I love you very much, and I'm very, very sorry to be missing your party."

"You're going to where Daddy was born."

"That's right. I'm going to England."

"Wait, wait! Where's Grentha?"

"Here she is," Jon says, arriving next to Larken and handing Esmé her orca whale. "And here's a hat and slippers for cold toes."

Esmé submits to being shod and capped. "Larkee's going to England, Da," she says.

"That's right."

"And you know what?" Larken adds, giving Esmé a kiss. "I can write you an e-mail every day while I'm gone."

"Okay."

Jon and Larken settle into the front of the car, Jon cranks up the heat, and they're off.

After a few blocks, Larken glances over her shoulder. "She's asleep."

"Remember how we used to have to drive her around for hours so she'd go down for a nap?"

Larken laughs. "And then she'd wake up the minute we got in the house."

Jon smiles, but he seems subdued, melancholy.

"Did she like her present?"

"Oh my God, Larken, it was brilliant. She played with those puppets all day, acting out little dramas. Thanks to you she'll probably believe in Santa until she's thirty."

I hope so, Larken thinks. She swivels around. Esmé is snoring a little now. One of her hands rests on the pillow near her earlobe; she's been rubbing it in her sleep. She's always done this: It's an unconscious gesture that she discovered in babyhood and has remained reliably self-comforting when she's tired or anxious.

Larken continues to stare at her, remembering another gesture Esmé had when she was a baby. She did it from the time she was six weeks old until she started talking, and although Larken and Jon were thrilled by the development of Esmé's *verbal* vocabulary, they were saddened by the diminishing of her gestural one. Suddenly, her eyes would get a faraway look and she'd bring a cupped hand to one of her ears; and then, with a kind of slow, controlled grace that a newborn baby should not possess, she would start to draw a kind of parenthesis near her ear, over and over, as if she were outlining it in space. The first time Larken and Jon saw her do it, they were in Larken's apartment; Esmé was in her high chair, and

Jon was attempting to feed her a puree of pumpkin and avocado. Her concentration was so complete and deep, it was mesmerizing.

It's as if she's tuning a radio, Jon had whispered. *Trying to find the right frequency.*

Larken nodded and whispered back. *Like she's getting a signal from deep space.*

Eventually they found the perfect description: She was getting e-mail from the angels.

It's true that 9/11 launched a national period of grief and instilled in many Americans a paralyzing fear of flying—grief and fear being often emotional twins—but Professor Jones's pathology is much older.

Growing up, she was rarely called upon to fly. There were occasional family trips to Nebraska bowl games—Florida, California, Texas —infrequent visits to relatives who lived far enough away to make driving impractical. They were uneventful. She doesn't remember them.

But after 1978, she started having nightmares, all obvious variations on a theme: She'd be forcefully jettisoned from strange orbed vessels that were surveilling Tornado Alley—a UFO abductee reject!—or find herself skydiving with a failed parachute, released from a giant raptor's talons, blown from the top of the Eiffel Tower or the Empire State Building. Once she dreamed of being on top of Lincoln's state capitol building with its huge bronze figure of the Sower, cradled safely at first in his giant sloped sack, so like a hammock, it even swayed gently, but then he reached in without warning, blithely scooped her up, and cast her out as if she were nothing more than a handful of grain.

Larken's fear crept up upon her insidiously, like a passenger who comes to sit next to you when you're sleeping: One minute they aren't there, the next minute they are, and far too close and breathing in your ear and even being so bold as to rest their head on your shoulder. Because she and her family never traveled anywhere farther than Omaha after Hope went up (they didn't dare; unspoken among them was the feeling that she still might show up and come looking for them), it was an unexpressed condition.

And so Larken didn't realize how experience and dreams were forging her fear of flying—not until she was a college sophomore and signed on for one of these winter break trips herself. It was a trip Arthur organized and chaperoned when he was chairman. Eloise came, too—then as now, they went everywhere together.

It began just as the engines revved up in preparation for takeoff. Larken's palms grew sweaty; her breathing became rapid.

"This is really your first time flying?" her seatmate asked. A fellow student, he was a boy whose parents had taken him to Europe from the time he was ten. He'd seen all the paintings they were about to see at least three times. Larken had a little crush on him.

She hadn't been able to answer. Something was wrong with her lungs.

"Larken?" he repeated. Then he pushed an overhead button and summoned the stewardess.

"What's the problem? We're about to take off." Larken saw in the face of the stewardess the extent of her illness, the way a mortally wounded soldier in the field might not realize that his guts were strewn about the field until he looked into the eyes of one of his comrades. She became aware, too, that passengers were staring at her: fascinated, repulsed, annoyed, amused.

Was there a doctor on board? (*A physician!* Larken wanted to shout, but the rapidity of her breath wouldn't allow her to speak.)

There wasn't. They had to stop taxiing, turn off the engines. Everything came to a halt.

It was Eloise and Arthur who came to her rescue. They moved to sit with her—Arthur in the window seat, Eloise in the middle. Eloise held Larken's hand, gave her a Valium, and got her to breathe in and out of a barf bag.

Thus sedated, she made it to Europe for the one and only time, barely able to register any feeling at seeing the glorious paintings she'd studied and longed to see, the whole time dreading the inevitable horror of having to fly home. Before they left, a French doctor administered a powerful sedative and she was able to sleep the entire way. She never flew again.

It hasn't been a problem really.

True, Professor Jones's fear of flying may have kept her from cultivating the kind of egocentric visibility that many acamedicians crave:

appearances at various conferences both in the States and overseas, sitting on panels, presenting papers, that sort of thing. Who cares? That's not Larken's style. Furthermore, she does enough mandatory schmoozing at home; she's not about to fly halfway around the world to have cocktails.

Curbside, Jon reminds her to stay in touch. "I'll be expecting daily e-mail updates."

"Is there anything you want me to bring back from your homeland?" she asks, ignoring the time, ignoring everything but the movie that's playing in her head, based on the real-life tragedy involving the crash of a jet carrying a group of University of Nebraska college students and their professors to England to study the landscape paintings of Turner and Constable and the Pre-Raphaelite Brotherhood of portraitists. There are no survivors. "A case of Marmite? A gift assortment of biscuits and cheese? Tony Blair's head on a platter?"

He laughs and kisses her on the cheek. "Just bring yourself, Larken. Safe journey."

Larken steals a last look at Esmé—flushed and jowly, wisps of hair matted to her forehead—and then heads inside.

Even though the Lincoln Municipal Airport is small (planes depart and arrive from Gates 1, 2, 3, and 4), and theirs is the only flight leaving at this time, Larken nonetheless insisted in her titular role as group leader that students arrive ABSOLUTELY NO LATER THAN 4:45 A.M. When she pulls her luggage into the ticketing area at 5:30 to find that all of the students have not only arrived, but are checked in and waiting in a clump at the foot of the escalators, she feels like shit.

Luckily no one notices her at first. The kids—who'd be comatose if asked to come to a class this early—are upbeat, animated, and chatty in that self-involved carefree way of college students on holiday. There are a few sets of older adults, presumably parents, lurking around the fringes of the group; their expressions—sheepish, grim, amused, wistful—reveal everything about their relationships with these adult children, to whom they are now nearly invisible, expendable.

Mirabella Piacenti, the other faculty member on the trip, stands among the students, laughing, talking, poised, tall; she gives the impression of somehow being both *of* them and *apart* from them. It's a quality Larken lacks.

Larken slinks toward the ticket counter, hoping to go unnoticed at least until after she gets her boarding pass. But Misty Ariel Kroger suddenly pivots and glares at her, giving the impression of a penitentiary guard eyeballing an escaping prisoner through the sights of a rifle. She stares Larken down for longer than necessary, her face expressing a perverse satisfaction; then whispers something to Mirabella—who looks up and waves across the expanse, princess-style.

Larken waves back. "Sorry I'm late!" she half-mouths, half-speaks, and then immediately regrets it: *When in the presence of students, never, ever apologize.*

But then, her position has already been weakened. The tone has already been set. Mirabella was here on time—the good, reliable parent—while Larken was tardy. Stupid. She'll have to work like hell to recover her authority.

She mimes her intention to check in at the ticket counter. Mirabella nods and smiles and then turns her attention back to the students. She looks remarkably fresh, as if getting up at four in the morning is de rigueur. Who knows? Maybe it is. Just as Larken makes sure that her colleagues know next to nothing about her personal life, she knows next to nothing about theirs. She hopes Mirabella doesn't expect them to become fast friends during this trip. Besides surviving the flight, Larken has no desire to do anything other than teach Arthur's syllabus, visit the Tate, and hunker down with whatever trashy paperback romance catches her eye at the airport concession store.

"One of your bags is overweight," the ticket agent remarks after Larken shows her ID.

"What do you mean?"

"We have a fifty-pound limit for checked baggage. You can either pay extra or you'll have to step aside and repack."

"Repack?" The thought is horrendous. It took Larken forever to figure out what to bring and she's still not sure she's got everything she'll need. "I'll just pay the fine," she sighs. "How much?"

"Here's your boarding pass, Miss Jones," the agent says after collecting Larken's money. "Upstairs to Gate Three."

"Let's head upstairs, everyone!" Larken hears Mirabella announce, and there's a mass migration toward the escalators. Mirabella lingers behind and they ride up together.

"Good morning," she says. "Tough getting going this early, isn't it?"

Larken is irritated by extremely beautiful and statuesque women who also happen to be kind. "Thanks for getting the kids all checked in."

"It's going to be a great trip. I'm very excited."

As they approach security, Larken remains in the rear and takes her cues from the students. She watches them strip off their coats, remove laptops from their cases, place keys and cell phones and spare change in a plastic bowl, take off accessories with alarm-triggering potential: earrings, nose rings, belly rings, metal-studded wrist bands. Nothing beeps or dings or wails. Perhaps flying post-9/11 skies isn't as terrifying as she'd thought.

But when she goes through, an alarm sounds. Instantly the eyes of the entire group of departing passengers are upon her. As if this weren't a large enough audience, the waiting area is flooded with disembarking passengers. She is asked about the contents of her pockets. "I think they're empty," she mutters, but goes through them just to make sure: lint, crumpled napkins, a ticket stub from *Terminator 3,* candy wrappers. She tries again, and again her guilt is loudly proclaimed. She is ushered to one side and told that she'll have to be wanded.

"Out here?" she asks, terrified. "In front of everyone?"

She's instructed to place her feet just so and extend her arms to the side. This is what being put in the stocks must have been like.

Meanwhile, Mirabella passes through the portal silently and with grace. One of those seasoned transcontinental travelers—Larken knows this much about Professor Piacenti: She has a cottage in Tuscany where she goes every summer with her law professor husband and their two young children—Mirabella wears Italian leather boots and a flowing taupe-colored ensemble accessorized with a silk scarf. Larken suspects this outfit to be part of a coordinated collection of clothing, an array of separates in nonwrinkling, lightweight fabric that can be reconfigured in an instant, allowing the fashion-conscious globe-trotter to go from a day at the museum to a night on the town with ease and elegance and the use of a single compact suitcase. Larken packed an iron.

"Good-bye, Mom!" she hears one girl call, and this intiates a call-and-response litany between the students and their parents.

Good-bye, Dad! Good-bye, Honey! I love you! I love you, too! Call us as soon as you get there, okay? Be safe! Have fun! Drop us a postcard! We'll miss you! Have a good flight! Good-bye! Good-bye! Good-bye!

Larken is once again sent to the back of the line.

Finally, sans MBTs, she passes inspection.

"May I please change places?" Larken asks the flight attendant, who is frazzled-looking, well into her fifties; Larken imagines that she's been at this occupation since flight attendants were called stewardesses; over time, her body seems to have adapted and evolved in relation to her surroundings; her backside has expanded to the exact width of the aisle.

"I can't be in the middle," she says, lowering her voice to a whisper. "I get claustrophobic. I have . . . anxiety issues."

"You'll have to be patient, ma'am," the attendant says. She's slightly out of breath, and her determinedly sweet voice only accentuates her obvious annoyance. "We need to get everyone on the plane first."

"I'll take the middle, Professor Jones," Drew offers.

"That's kind of you, Mr. McNeeley."

Having an aisle seat should help, but after buckling up, Larken experiences a tingling sensation that begins in the soles of her feet and soon starts to metastasize. It's as though an inoculate containing millions of gerbils has been shot into her nervous system. They start racing up and down the meridians of her spine, her arms, her legs, collecting en masse to ride a merry-go-round in the vicinity of her sacrum, a riot of furtive rodent energy, scuttling across the slippery surfaces of her insides with their tiny boned and clawed feet.

"Larken, are you all right?" It's Mirabella, across the aisle, with her velvety maternal voice and her Italian accent.

Pissed as hell even as it's happening, Larken starts to hyperventilate. She feels tears leaking from her eyes as she clasps Mirabella's hand.

"Larken?" Mirabella repeats, her face apprehensive.

Larken tries to speak, but cannot.

It's such a cheat being a European foreigner in the USA. People love you no matter what. Students are fascinated by your exoticism. Colleagues reward you with tenure and then fall to pieces under your compassion-ate eye.

Larken becomes aware of an arm encircling her waist, bracing her back, and of being almost lifted off her feet. She allows herself to be steered down the aisle, dimly aware that everyone else is seated and star-ing at her.

"Don't worry," Mirabella says in a low voice, "they'll think we're just going to freshen our lipsticks."

On the way, they stop for a moment; Larken hears Mirabella speak quietly to one of the flight attendants, requesting that she check the passenger manifest for medical personnel.

"Just hang on, okay?" Mirabella murmurs. "Try to slow your breathing."

After Larken is guided into a seat, someone presses a damp paper towel to her forehead.

They're still racing around in there. Larken pictures her thoracic cavity as one gigantic McDonald's Play Place for gerbils, her heart one of those wire mesh exercisers she's seen in pet stores, her spine and ribs gerbil monkey bars, her diaphragm a gerbil trampoline, her lungs two big inflatable rooms filled with thousands and thousands of balls that the gerbils jump into, over and over again, wade around in, throw at each other, don't these little fuckers ever sleep?

"Larken? Larken," Mirabella's voice is saying, "the doctor is here."

Physician physician physician, Larken thinks. *Christ, can't you people ever get it right?* and then there's murmuring, Larken has trouble fo-cusing on it but when asked pointedly if she is giving her permission to be treated, she nods and says as clearly as possible, "Yes."

"I'm going to administer some intravenous Ativan," a woman's voice says. "You're going to feel a little sting."

Time passes. How much?

"Is that it?" Larken manages to say. She didn't feel a thing.

She hears people engaged in quiet conversation overhead, a discus-sion she comes to realize of procedural and medicinal protocols related to a person with severe flight phobia, and whether or not she should be allowed to remain on an overseas flight. The consensus seems to be that she's too ill.

The sound of a door banging open directs her attention to Misty Ariel Kroger, emerging from one of the bathroom cubicles.

"Is everything all right?" Misty asks. Even pharmaceutically altered, Larken has no trouble perceiving the sudden, potent surge in Misty's color, from wimpy, watered-down putty to a thick impasto of dogshit brown.

"Everything's fine, Misty," Mirabella says. "Would you please let the group know that Professor Jones and I have been detained?"

"Of course," Misty says, smiling. She swaggers away.

More conversation. Being eye-level with a consortium of waists causes Larken to picture talking belly buttons . . . *umbilici?* . . . *umbilicuses!*— and she starts to laugh.

But then they start to converge, hemming her in, can't they give her some room, for chrissakes? They're a cloud of insects now, invasive, insistent, buzzing in her ears, and she starts flailing her hands, trying to bat them away.

One of them leans close and whispers, "We're going to take you off the plane, Larken." One of those exotic burrowing bugs from Southern Italy. "It's for the best."

Pesky chigger. Larken slaps her.

Red-haired St. Michael appears (*It's The Last Judgment*), disguised as an airport employee. He's at the helm of a wheelchair, his expression neutral.

Heaven or hell? Larken wants to ask, but the gerbils have all nestled into her vocal folds and fallen asleep.

As Larken is resituated and transported down the aisle in full view of her students and colleague—a large, heavily sedated mammal en route to the meatpacking plant (*hell it is, then*)—her humiliation is complete.

The gatekeeper is moving out of position, toward the viewer, into the foreground, into the space that is normally occupied by two kneeling penitents—nun and monk—but is now vacant.

Where are they? Larken wonders. They're nowhere else in the painting; they haven't inserted themselves into Joseph's carpentry shop or crashed the Annunciation party in the Virgin's living room. They're not far away, she senses, just out of sight. Maybe they've walked deeper into the painting, through the narrow, open door where the gatekeeper usually keeps watch. Maybe they've finally gotten off their knees—they must be so sore!—and left the walled courtyard, gone into town to do some shoe shopping.

The gatekeeper arrives in the foreground of the painting. *Is he about to step out of it?* He holds his straw hat flattened against his torso. For the first time, Larken notices the anatomically suggestive placement of the hat, the way a tiny protrusion at the very center of its crown resembles the outpushing belly button of a pregnant woman.

He looks at her for a moment, wearing the same mournful, distracted expression that has been on his face since circa 1420–1430. *Is he going to leave?* she wonders again, feeling anxious.

But no. There must still be a barrier between his world and hers that denies him access. He turns away and starts to climb the steps, as if he intends to pass right out of the frame, from the left side of the triptych into the midsection.

He continues to ascend the stairs, stairs that she's never seen before, that she never even knew were in the painting, not even after all the years she's spent studying it. How is that possible? Maybe they're hidden between the panels. Maybe there's a secret door linking the panels that has gone undiscovered! What a find that would be.

And then Larken is the gatekeeper. She's going up and up and up on wrought-iron stairs with no visible means of support. They seem to go on forever, straight up at first, and then spiraling, getting narrower and narrower the farther she climbs.

Finally she's at the top. There's a door here, a heavy wood door with metal hinges and a lock. She has keys in her hand. She starts trying the keys, one after another; there are so many of them. They are skeleton keys and none of them fit, and then she realizes how high up she is and she starts to feel afraid. A plane flies by, dangerously close, close enough for Larken to see the faces of her mother and her father and herself in the windows, and then one of the plane's wings clips her staircase, dislodging it from whatever structural support has been keeping it in place, and then she is falling, falling, trying to scream.

She wakes up, her heart beating erratically, her breath coming in panicky gasps.

Is it morning? Did she really sleep an entire day?

Yes.
What time is it in England?
Who gives a shit?
What time is it here?
What does it matter? She's on winter break.

She starts to cough: a full-fledged, uncontrollable hack, the kind that emanates from deep within the lungs and produces the phlegmy metallic taste that indicates that it's too late for preventative measures.

She's on winter break and she's sick as a dog.

Overhead, someone else is coughing with the same lung-searing vehemence. Perhaps she's not home at all, but in the terminal tubercular ward of Lincoln General. Perhaps she's still dreaming.

Dragging herself to a standing position—the synovial fluid in her joints feels like cement—she shuffles into the bathroom, pees, and then sweeps the contents of her medicine chest into the wastebasket so that she can transport the whole pharmacy back to bed. There must be something here that will help.

After leaving a message on Gaelan's answering machine (*Didn't go, I'm here, sick with flu or something, let Viney and Bonnie know, call you later*), she collapses back into bed and spends another twenty-four hours in a semicomatose condition, the victim of viral invaders and shame, awakened only occasionally by the sound of her own coughing and the echoing response of her unidentified, consumptive sanitarium-mate upstairs.

"They're gone," Jon croaks.

"What do you mean, they're gone?" Larken croaks back. "You shouldn't be alone. Someone should be taking care of you." The feeling in her lungs is still dark, boggy, and dangerously virulent, but at least she's managing bouts of semiconsciousness, vertical orientation, and an ability to speak.

"I mean, they've left." Jon, too, has been laid low with some sort of bronchial catastrophe; they're talking on the phone because neither of them feels strong enough to make the trek up or down the stairs. "Mia's left." He erupts in a fresh round of coughing.

"What?"

"Me," he manages, eventually. "She's left me."

"Jon. What are you saying?"

He emits a horrifically phlegmy, emphatic *hurk* and then announces, "She's taken Esmé and left me for another woman."

"Oh, no. No."

"Things were actually going cock-up before Christmas," Jon continues. "I wanted to tell you, but I also didn't want to spoil your holiday or make you worry."

"Jon . . ."

"Oh, fuck all. I was in denial."

"I'm coming up . . ."

"Are you sure? Can you?"

"Be right there."

"I'll put on the kettle."

"Need anything?"

"Bourbon if you have some. I'm out."

So she drags out of bed, crawls into her bathrobe, locates the Jim Beam, and starts hoisting herself up the stairway.

She's halfway there when she hears the sound of the door opening. Jon stands at the top, waiting, smiling faintly, and wearing his pajamas, robe, and slippers. He looks terrible: skin palid, eyes lodged in the depths of shadowy craters.

"Oh, my God," he murmurs, and Larken realizes that they must look much the same: a couple of extras from a zombie movie. "Can you make it?"

"Yes," she mutters breathlessly. "Just give me another half hour or so." She grips the handrail more tightly and continues to yank herself toward him.

"Hey," he says wonderingly, as if making a sudden realization. "You're supposed to be in England."

"And yet, here I am."

"Are you all right?"

"Aside from the minor psychotic break at the airport," she coughs, "wasn't it in the papers? I'm hunky-dory."

Finally, she arrives.

"Hello," Jon says.

"Hello."

"I'll tell you my sad saga if you tell me yours."

"Deal."

They go inside. "Welcome to the den of contagion," Jon says. "I'll ready the tea."

Illness and depression have made the same imprint upon Jon's living space as they have upon hers: With the shades and curtains drawn, everything is murky and colorless, the decor is aggressively disarrayed, with misshapen pillows and mangled comforters lying about and unwashed dishes on every table, and the air has the peculiarly rank, sour, and stagnant quality of the sickroom. The Christmas tree is dead; the TV is turned to the same channel that Larken was watching downstairs.

She joins him in the kitchen. As he steeps the tea and she makes toast, they start rewinding the experiences of the past few days. When everything is ready, they take it to the living room, settle on the sofa, and start amending the Earl Grey with generous quantities of lemon juice, honey, and booze.

"I mean, the irony is unbeatable," Jon is saying. "We live in one of the most socially conservative states in the U.S. and still she manages to find the one lesbian in all of Nebraska"—Jon takes another gulp of his toddy—"and I don't care how sexist and/or politcally in-fucking-correct that sounds."

"I'm so sorry. I wish I knew what to say." Larken pours more tea. "She'll regret it. What goes around comes around. I speak from personal experience."

Jon's marriage is failing, her professional standing is in disgrace, but this is infinitely better than being alone. She feels unreasonably happy.

"We're having what's euphemistically called a 'trial separation,'" Jon continues. "From what I can tell, this means that she's living in unfettered bliss and lust with this woman she's fallen for and I'm . . . well, as you see."

"It sucks." Larken has a thought. "Do you think it would suck less if she were being unfaithful with a man?"

Jon considers. "Maybe. No. I doubt it."

Larken sighs. "I suppose not. Infidelity is infidelity. An asshole is an asshole."

"I mean Mia's always said that she's bi, so I can't claim that I entered this marriage with closed eyes, but I supposed I hoped that she'd just

. . . how's this for sounding pathetic? Settle down. Choose me. God. I sound like my father. I sound like my father's father. I sound like an old man, which is exactly how I feel."

"You're not old."

"Truthfully, if she doesn't come back, I'll find it difficult to stay, knowing I could run into her in the produce section or at the movies, making out with her girlfriend." He stares into his teacup. "Fuck. I'll have to move back to England."

"Don't say that." Larken sits up, grabs the lapels of his bathrobe, and cries, mock melodramatically, "Don't ever say that, darling!" The tone is meant to obfuscate her real desperation. He must not must not must not leave.

Jon gives her an avuncular, bleary look. "Stay here tonight, can you? We can watch the *Law & Order* marathon and binge on the care package Mum sent from jolly old England."

So she does. She doesn't dream. She doesn't wake up until the next morning. And when she does, they're still sacked out on the sofa, tangled into a swirl of sour-smelling comforters. They fell asleep sitting up, their bodies listing toward each other as if forming the sides of a poorly erected pup tent. In the apartment, there's not a single sound, no movement, no trace of anything to indicate that there's anything in the world but them.

She stares at his face, willing him to wake up. A bit of currant jelly dots a corner of his lower lip; a few biscuit crumbs are adhered to the spot.

His eyes are closed when he mutters, "Good morning." They stay closed as he pulls her close and his hands find her breasts. He finally looks at her as he begins to drag the heavy folds of cloth aside.

They fall into kissing and fondling with Victorian desperation and propriety. No need to fret about the body's flaws with *en dishabille* fucking. Rolls of flesh, his and hers, remain hidden, the flannels stay on. In another century, this would be just how it's done.

Does he say her name? She might only imagine it. But as she swoons into the viral and sexual heat and urges him into the slippery folds of her body, she is already fast-forwarding to their future, an Arthur-and-Eloise retro-romance with inspired variations: a cozy cottage in Cambridge, painted gate, flower garden, walls lined with books, teaching jobs, a circle of close friends with links to literature and the arts—all of whom will have their own children because it is not their passions alone that shape this fantasy: It is a life that must accommodate their daughter Esmé.

And, perhaps, others.

Her body swells and opens, a flood plain of fluids, a vast intake of breath, a quaking release, and then breathlessness. The two of them laughing.

How could she not have seen? It should have been this way from the beginning.

Hope's Diary, 1969:
Mommy Dropped the Mayonnaise

I grew a perfect eggplant. The thing looks exactly like a uterus—at least given what little I know about it. I grew it—from seed, no less!—kept it safe from the claws of our marauding cats, who assume that any well-tilled patch of land is their personal litter box. I don't know what possessed me. Tomatoes, yes, certainly, and a few stalks of sweet corn. You can't call yourself a Nebraska woman unless you grow beefsteak tomatoes and sweet corn. And they've done well, too. It's been hot this summer, not too soggy, not too relentlessly windswept, but hot hot hot, which is excellent for tomatoes and corn if not for me. I've also grown the requisite beans—so easy, and the children love seeing them pop up so quickly—some trellis cukes and God help us zucchini and some herbs. But eggplant? What was I thinking?

It's the color, I think. This is how nature fools us, entices us: with color. It works for the birds and the bees, why not for humans and veggies? "Grow me!" eggplants command us with their exotic skins. It's regal, purple—the color of royalty.

Back to my eggplant: it _was_ perfect (she says mournfully); the exact size and shape of what I imagine to be the unpregnant (as I am, again this month) uterus. I had to throw it away today—the eggplant, I mean, not my uterus. I'd parked it in the basket with the potatoes and by the time I located a recipe for Greek moussaka it had shriveled inwardly and lost its glorious bourgignon sheen.

Boohoo.

The purple of my perfect eggplant reminded me of the purple of my spectacular bruise from my tumble down the stairs months ago (the bruise persists, a

sad watered-down shadow, however, of its former self)
and with that reminder comes the realization that
I've grown chronically clumsy.

Chronically as opposed to occasionally. It, the
clumsiness, doesn't seem to come and go as it used
to. It's a constant, or nearly so.

Which brings me to this afternoon, when I was
making the children a snack.

I dropped the mayonnaise. Except it didn't actually feel as though I dropped it. The crash itself
and the explosive mess that followed seemed to happen
without my participation. There was a cause and
effect that I was not a party to. I mean to say.
Shit. The jar. It was in my hand, then it wasn't.

Curious.

All right, more than that or why the hell am I
giving over so much space in this book to write
about it? Troubling. Surprising, certainly. I
started laughing, that kind of hysterical laughter
that overtakes me sometimes when I'm exhausted.
Luckily, the children didn't register the hysteria; after the initial shock of the crash, they
took my laughter as a good sign and started laughing, too.

Nothing to do but make a game of it—"Look! Mommy
is finger painting with food!" I said, proud of my
improvisational powers, not anticipating the result: Larken and Gaelan immediately jumped up and
started to cross the floor to me—little bare feet
and glass everywhere—and I reflextively screamed
"STOP! STOP!!!"

They stopped all right. They looked terrified.

"Just wait until Mommy gets the glass out of the
way," I added, "and then you can come down on the
floor and fingerpaint, too!"

I couldn't get my legs to resume their evolved
relationship with the planet; they were like faulty

folding table legs. No card games tonight, dearie!
I managed to drag myself over to the cupboard, pull
out a spare roll of paper towels, and get the glass
into the garbage can. And then the three of us stayed
on the floor, for about an hour, finger painting
with Hellman's.

They came back, eventually—my legs, I mean—and
so exhausted that I knew I couldn't get the job
done on my own, I enlisted the aid of my five- and
six-year-old children and made another game out of
finger painting with soap and water.

The kitchen floor has never been so clean.

Llewellyn home. More later.

Chapter 20

The Virgin Doubts Her Calling

During the winter of 2004, the residents of Emlyn Springs—and most of the rest of southeastern Nebraska, for that matter—are interested neither in riding bikes nor drinking smoothies. They've hunkered down. It's all they can do to get from home to work and back again, with occasional trips to the grocery store in between. Many of them are simply making do with canned goods and the contents of their chest freezers.

The dead, too, are far from impervious to the season. Their circulatory systems, although exsanguinated, are not empty; veins and arteries still serve as conduits for whatever waters flow through the underground springs. It is not surprising, then, that when the ground freezes and the springs grow sluggish, the dead slow way down. Their voices drop an octave. They feel a keen desire to do nothing. The dead fathers are especially lethargic.

On the plus side, the insulating layer of snow allows the dead mothers a respite from the incessant, brittle clatter of human feet. Under these conditions, the feeling against the inside of their bellies is much altered: To some, it is like containing a room full of spongy, bouncing Nerf balls; others are reminded of percolating microwave popcorn. In all events, deep snow creates a light, soft, muffled sensation, unpleasant only insofar as it is unceasing. But compared to what they usually endure . . . What a relief!

Experiencing the footfalls of humankind in this gentler way allows many dead mothers to give up traveling during the winter months and catch up on much-needed sleep. A few continue to globe-trot in service of their psychological studies; others limit their observations to the local population. Goodness knows there's enough interpersonal complexity here in Emlyn Springs to keep any one mother busy for an eternity.

Their life experience taught them that after giving birth a woman's sense of self is tremendously altered. They remember this much: Motherhood dismembers boundaries in a way that no other love can—not just corporeal boundaries (although that is certainly part of it) but ethereal ones. They sensed their children as much as felt them. A kind of spiritual echolocation allowed them to be affected by their children whether or not they were in close physical proximity.

Strangely enough, Bonnie Jones—who not only isn't a mother but unlikely to ever become one—has this ability, at least when it comes to the children of her hometown. She intuits their presence, senses their distress, feels the quality of their energy. Not a mother, yet she understands and embraces the mysteries of maternal intimacy.

An interesting case, that girl.

The dead mothers have their eyes on her.

Bonnie tries to keep BJ's Brews going for a while; she even borrows a promotional idea from the Runza Hut up in Beatrice: YOUR SMOOTHIE COSTS TODAY'S TEMPERATURE! But by late January, only the Labenz boys and Blind Tom continue to show up, so she posts a CLOSED UNTIL SPRING sign and moves her blender and dorm fridge into the bike shop, along with a small camping stove and a large electric heater. She starts stocking healthy snacks and board games. She barters one of her new bikes for a used color TV with a built-in VCR and several kids' videos.

Since then, the bike shop has evolved into an ad hoc teen and child care center. Some kids show up at Miss Jones's place because it gives them a respite, a place to warm up before walking the rest of the way home, others because whoever was supposed to pick them up has spun out into a snowbank and can't raise a tow truck.

The young people of Emlyn Springs couldn't be happier about BJ's Bikes—not because of the merchandise but because there's a door, there's space for them, they can get in, they can be close to her. At the juice bar, their view of Miss Jones was limited and their access was blocked. Something about her makes them want to stand close, as if she were a full cookie jar or a medicine chest mirror.

Being surrounded by kids has been an emotional boon for Bonnie as well, their impromptu gatherings like a benediction on her efforts. Their presence might even have the power to jump-start her ovaries; it's certainly shaken her out of a period of inaction, and she's feeling inspired once again to get proactive about procreation.

As a child, Bonnie loved the Arthurian tales that her mother read to them. She loves them still, and prefers the way these ancient stories are rendered in books for children. Her favorite stories play out in Wales, in settings that are secret, underground, enchanted: the hidden cave on Anglesy where Arthur took shelter from battle; the subterranean lake in Dans Emrys where a red dragon and a white dragon engaged in combat; the invisible house on Bardsey Island where Merlin still sleeps.

Whoso pulleth out this sword of this stone and anvil is rightwise king born of all England.

It is an old notion, and one much beloved by Bonnie: that worthiness is determined through deed.

The task is set. The test is in place. Bonnie has summoned the first of her unknowing suitors and waits, expectant, for him to appear.

Beyond locating the candidates—and she's located five—getting them to the test site presented Bonnie with her next biggest challenge: none of them have shown even the slightest interest in cycling. They might feign such an interest—Bonnie is not unaware of the fact that, although none of them are interested in cycling, all of them are interested in *her*—but that wouldn't do.

Ultimately, it was the candidates' universal disinterest in cycling that gave Bonnie an idea about how to lure them. Her invitation came in the form of a promotional flyer/questionnaire that she hand-delivered to each of them in their places of work:

FREE OFFER! PROMOTIONAL GIVEAWAY! FILL OUT THIS QUESTIONNAIRE AND YOU'LL RECEIVE A PRIZE! *Are you interested in cycling? If so, do you own a bike? How often do you ride it? If not, why? What would make bike-riding more attractive to you and your family? What kind of services and information would you like to see offered at a neighborhood bike shop? How could a bike shop best serve you, your family, and your community?*

Present this filled-out questionnaire to Bonnie Jones, owner and proprietress of BJ's Bikes, 1302 Main Street, Emlyn Springs, Nebraska on _____ (and here Bonnie scheduled each of the candidates on successive nights) *and you'll receive a healthy complimentary smoothie!*

It's almost time. Bonnie takes out her clipboard and reviews her list:

Tonight she'll see Harold Schlake Jr., father of three, co-owner with his dad of Schlake's Hardware. Not an attractive man, and divorced at forty, Harold is nevertheless observant when it comes to nuts and bolts and always holds the door open for her.

Tuesday's candidate is Mike Lawlor. Estranged from long-term girl-friend, Mike works in Women's and Children's Shoes at JCPenney's. He sat next to Bonnie at the Beatrice library one day when she was looking at bike building sites on the Internet. He was checking out online dating agencies.

Wednesday she'll be visited by Ed Loerch, activities director at St. David's, and a frequent juice bar customer. Separated, no children. He's always taken note of the cute stickers on Bonnie's calendar and frequently remarks on her choice of clothing.

Dimitri (last name unknown) will come on Thursday. Never married, he's the single father of one, head cashier at the health food co-op in Beatrice. He keeps his piercings very hygienic and is a die-hard vegan.

And on Friday she'll see Brody Canaerfan, high school health ed teacher and wrestling coach. He has been extremely enthusiastic about Fancy Egg Days. Even though he's a bit on the short side, he's not bad-looking, has a great body, and loves kids.

At seven o'clock sharp, there's a knock. Bonnie smears some grease on her face, musses her hair—this is not the scene of a seduction, after all, it's the setting for an exam—and unlocks the door for the first candidate.

"You'll need an upgraded electrical panel in here, that's for sure," Harold is saying. Bonnie follows him around the shop with a clipboard and pen, ostensibly taking notes on his recommendations. "A whole new system."

Solid, she writes. *Dependable. Sees the big picture.*

"The wiring in here is ancient. It's real dangerous."

Serious. Practical. Safety-minded. Will insist on childproofing.

"Who owns this building, anyway?"

"I'm not sure," Bonnie replies. "Tom pays rent to somebody in Arizona, but the last two checks have come back stamped 'RETURN TO SENDER.'"

"Tom?" Harold says.

Suspicious. Bonnie writes. *Jealous type?*

"Blind Tom," she answers. "You know, he runs the piano hospital next door?"

"Oh," Harold says. "Right."

Definitely jealous. "I'm kind of like subletting this half of the building from him. He stores some of his pianos back there."

"Pianos, huh?" Harold says, marching toward the back room.

"Unfinished pianos, piano parts . . ." Bonnie says. She feels suddenly protective on Blind Tom's behalf. "That's all his stuff back there," she says. "I don't go in that room."

Harold ignores her and peeks in anyway. "Yep," he muses darkly. "There's not a single thing in this whole building that's up to code."

Lack of imagination, Bonnie scrawls. *Not a music lover.*

They walk around some more. Harold kneels to scrutinize every outlet in the shop. Half an hour later, his explorations still haven't led him him to look up.

"What do you think about that light?" Bonnie finally asks, indicating the overhead fluorescent.

"Whoa," Harold says with distaste. "Look at all those dead bugs." He stands directly under the wheel and squints toward the ceiling. "Well, I'm guessing that wire is carrying too much current, for one thing. And we should definitely get you fixed up with some different chains."

"Great," Bonnie says. Feeling that she's given Harold every opportunity to succeed, she strides to the front door of the shop and pulls it open.

Harold's expression—a default scowl—grows even darker. "I can climb up there and take a closer look if you'd like," he offers.

"That's okay, Harold," Bonnie says. "I appreciate your coming over."

Harold remains in place, looking dazed and bullish. He regards the door with skepticism, as if walking through it would have dire and embarrassing consequences. "I'm . . . concerned, Bonnie," he says. "I don't like seeing anybody do business in such hazardous conditions."

"Don't worry, Harold," Bonnie says. "I'll get on those changes right away."

"All right, then. Bye," Harold grunts, and stomps out.

Bonnie shuts the door and crosses him off her list. It's not until hours later, when she's back home and tucked into bed, that she realizes she forgot to reward Howard's participation with a free smoothie.

On each successive night, Bonnie trudges through the snow to meet with the candidates. In each case, she ends up having to nudge their visual explorations: *Feel free to take a look around. Would you mind turning on the overhead light? Do you like the unfinished look or should I put in an acoustic ceiling?* None of them want to do anything but talk. They all fail the test; they all leave with complimentary smoothies.

She has high hopes for her fifth and final candidate, Brody Canaerfan. His questionnaire is very promising; in response to *What would make bike-riding more attractive to you and your family?* he wrote, "One-on-one cycling tours with the owner of the shop."

A few seconds after Bonnie remarks, "I guess it's time to take down those Christmas decorations"—casually, of course, and with only the slightest upward tilt of her chin. Brody looks up, his expression riveted.

With warriorlike determination, he drags Bonnie's heavy worktable across the floor so that it is centered directly under the wheel. After climbing onto the table, he pulls himself up into the rafters, balancing impishly on the same two beams that support the wheel and grinning down at her.

This is it! Bonnie thinks. *He sees it! He's the one!*

It's at this point that Brody starts telling Bonnie about his years as a competitive gymnast and his desire to start up a gymnastics team at the school. When he decides to use the rafters to demonstrate some of the saw horse maneuvers that made him three-time state champion, things turn decisively disastrous.

Brody Canaerfan, Bonnie's fifth and final candidate, ends up drinking his complimentary smoothie in the county ambulance while getting a complimentary ride to the emergency room.

"Tom?" Bonnie calls across the partition—a sudden noise having drawn her attention to the fact that he's here.

"Yes?"

"Do you think the bike shop is a good idea?"

"I think it's brilliant."

Bonnie sighs. Once she turns out the lights, the building is cast in complete darkness. "I'm heading home," she says. "Are you leaving soon?"

"No. It's Claude Debussy's birthday."

"Oh. Well . . ." Bonnie has no idea what to make of this information. "Good night, then." Blind Tom, she's concluded, is by far the oddest man she's ever known.

Hope's Diary, 1970:
Fairy Mischief

"Midsummer Night's Dream" opens this weekend, the
sixth annual production of the Emlyn Springs
Shakespeare Troupe! Viney and I nudged and cajoled
and nagged and flattered Llewellyn until he had no
choice but to audition, and of course he's a perfect King Oberon. Hazel inserted some Welsh folk
music into the production—our fairy forest is in
Wales, naturally!—so L. gets to show off his singing voice as well.

True, there are painful moments in the production. Plenty of people thrill to Estella Axthelm's
mannered performance and self-aware command of the
language, but I regard Titania's appearances onstage
as opportunities to nap. Hazel was politic enough
to give her and Llewellyn the final bow at curtain
call. Overall, though, I'm extremely proud of our
efforts.

I found a pair of dice on my socks this morning.
I've never seen them before, nor has Llewellyn or
the children. They're old, wooden. A poltergeist?
Elfin sprites? The cat? Tornadoes do this kind of
thing, deposit mysterious items in unlikely places,
but the only funnel cloud that has visited this
house is the one the children kick up every day.
I'm dumbfounded.
Finding the dice was a nice distraction. It happened when I'd crawled to the foot of the bed and
was fumbling around trying to locate my bathrobe.
Light was finally creeping in from the direction of
the window, warming my face, blurred shapes at the
periphery. At that point, Llewellyn was downstairs
talking on the phone with a neurologist colleague

up in Omaha. Personally, I think he was overreacting, even now.

I've been using my eyes a lot, after all. Hands too—they've been almost constantly numb for the past week from hours of hand-sewing hundreds of sequins onto dozens of pairs of fairy wings. But oh, how magical our fairies appear! It's all been worth it.

"Llewellyn," I said when I woke up this morning, "are my eyes open?" At first I thought I was dreaming.

"What?"

"I can't see. Am I awake?"

"What do you mean you can't see?"

It sounds so funny written down like this, like a burlesque lacking a punch line.

"Hope," Llewellyn said. "Look over here. Can you turn your eyes to where I am?"

"Of course," I said. I heard L. moving about in the vicinity.

"Stay here," he said finally. "I'm going downstairs to make a phone call."

"Llewellyn, I'm sure it's nothing."

"Stay in bed. I'll be back."

"What's wrong, Daddy?" It was Larken in the hallway outside our room.

"Nothing, pumpkin. Mommy's just not feeling well."

"Is she throwing up?" Gaelan asked.

"No no no, nothing like that," L. said, "she's just got a little headache." I heard him descending the stairs, urgent and graceful—so unlike his clumsy spouse. "Leave Mommy alone now," he called out on the way. "Let her rest."

I sensed the children before I heard them—Larken standing in the door, Gaelan taking a few steps in—and pressed my palms to my lids to make sure my eyes were closed.

"Mom?" Gaelan said.

"Good morning, sweetheart."

"What's the matter with you?"

"I just have a little headache."

"Are you going to make breakfast?" Larken asked.

"Daddy will, in a minute. He'll fix you something, or I will when my headache goes away. You can watch cartoons until then."

Gaelan came closer. I knew it was him; his footsteps are more cautious than Larken's, more tentative. I could picture her frowning at me from the bedroom door. I felt Gaelan's body before he actually touched me.

He petted my hand. "Feel better soon, okay?"

"Okay. I will. Give me a kiss."

He complied. Larken kept her distance.

"I love you," I said to anyone within range, and then listened to the two of them go down the stairs together, their footsteps getting softer and softer and all of a sudden I had a terrible intimation of death, theirs or mine, the whole horror that comes over me now and then, the veil of what is bearable being torn off so that one knows one has given birth and given death, all in one.

That was when I started to cry and thought, this is ridiculous, Hope, get ahold of yourself, and crawled to the foot of the bed in search of my bathrobe.

Soon after, my vision returned—I'm sure it was the cleansing effect of tears that did it—and the first thing I saw, staring at me from the pile of dirty laundry I'd cast onto the cedar chest at the foot of the bed last night, were those mysterious wooden dice.

Snake eyes. Double ones. Lucky or unlucky?

Don't know. I've never been much of a gambler.

* * *

Lucky, apparently, because (surprise) I'm pregnant again!!

(Note exclamation points. I don't care.)

L. and I were carried away by all that Shakespearean romance, and I like to think that his performance as Oberon invoked some sort of fairy magic in support of our procreative efforts.

So there!!!!!!!!!!!!!!!!!!!!!!!!!!!!!

Haven't told L. yet. Will do tomorrow.

Chapter 21

Weatherman Encounters
the Coriolis Force

Three-dimensional Gaelan is at the gym on a stationary bike; he's watching two-dimensional Gaelan on a black-and-white flat-screen plasma television at the Y. It's great that he can be in two places at once.

Two-D TV Gaelan is standing in front of a Doppler radar picture that shows a low pressure system making its way into southeastern Nebraska. He's naked, except for a skimpy black Speedo, and he runs through a posing routine while he talks about the weather. "We'll be seeing good symmetry in this front," he says, flexing his pectorals, "with accumulating traps." He turns his back to the camera. "We'll have especially nice definition right here in the lateral obliques."

I look great, 3-D Gaelan thinks as he regards his 2-D self.

Then he switches places: he's inside his body, no longer watching it, and no longer on TV. He's standing on an empty stage, looking out to where an audience should be. It's a vast, starless universe out there. Is he still on the air? Where's the cameraman?

Suddenly, a kind of strobe effect begins: Intense, highly focused explosions of light start going on and off everywhere. Trying to track them causes his eyes to dart around, pinball fashion. It's painful. What's he seeing? Dying stars? Lightning bugs? Flashbulbs?

He's not alone. When the lights stabilize and steady, they illuminate the entire stage: It's a huge, white, circular platform ringed by hundreds of bodybuilders. Each one stands in front of his own blue screen, pointing to radar pictures of various pressure systems, running through individual routines while Springsteen's "She's the One" blasts through the PA system. The mood is upbeat and celebratory, like a rock concert.

Now he understands: It's the Mr. Weatherman Universe competition! Contestants will be judged not only on their physiques but on their camera skills and their forecasting powers.

Arnold is standing next to him, only a couple of feet away, on his left. He's wearing his Conan the Barbarian outfit. Lou Ferrigno is on his right, dressed as the Hulk. Was he supposed to have worn a superhero costume?

He looks down. His Speedo has a red "S" on the front and he's wearing Superman boots that obscure his lower legs. That's okay. He's never been proud of his calves.

Arnold and Lou stand in front of Gaelan and start performing their weather forecasting/posing routines. Gaelan must be a judge; he's holding a small spiral notebook and pencil. It's a struggle to understand what Arnold is saying; his accent is stronger than ever and he's very stiff. He should take a yoga class. And Lou Ferrigno's complexion has a sickly green cast; he looks terrible on camera. Neither of them has any experience predicting the unpredictable. Gaelan writes a zero on his notebook and holds it up.

There's a man standing on the opposite side of the circle. He's very far away and he's wearing a gray flannel suit. He doesn't seem to be part of the competition; Gaelan has the feeling that he's another judge. He's moving his mouth, but Gaelan can't hear what he's saying. He'd like to get closer, but he'd have to go all the way around the circle and disrupt the other contestants' presentations. They really should have built a bridge.

Or maybe not. Something about the man is vaguely disquieting and Gaelan isn't sure he really wants to hear what he has to say.

Gaelan starts doing yoga. He's extremely flexible. He's the first bodybuilding weatherman in the history of bodybuilding weathermen to do yoga as part of his routine.

He comes out of bridge pose to find that he's on the back porch of their old house, looking out at a cornfield. The corn is tall; it must be late summer. There's a big basket of eggplants and asparagus sitting on the porch steps. That's his prize. He won the competition.

He spots Rhiannon way out in the middle of the field. She's a scarecrow. There are a lot of scarecrows out there. He can almost see their faces, but not quite. They're too far away.

She comes down from her scarecrow crucifix. She steps up out of the field and onto the porch. "Wear these," she tells him, handing him a pair of dumbbells. They're very heavy. "Sinkholes can be self-induced," she says, and then she starts leading him farther into the cornfield.

They arrive at a place that seems familiar. He knows it, doesn't he? Hasn't he been here before?

"Not everything in Nebraska is flat," she tells him. "There are a lot of underground springs around here."

A door opens. It's like a root cellar door, but it opens to an underground cave. It's dark down there.

"We've got to get to the basement," she says.

"Are you sure it's empty?" Gaelan asks.

She extends her arm skyward, fingers spread wide, and starts circling her arm in a clockwise direction.

"I thought the Coriolis force moves counterclockwise," Gaelan says. "At least in the Northern Hemisphere."

"Not always," she says. "It depends on your point of view."

And then he is up there, looking down. She's tiny and winged, like Thumbelina, and she's in his bathroom sink. She's sitting on the rim of the drain and sure enough, from this perspective her arm is moving counterclockwise. She's commanding a continuously moving, shallow pool of water. It spirals around the sides of the sink until it disappears down the dark hole of the drain.

And then they're at the Y, in a spinning class. She's the teacher. His sisters are there, too—and Viney and Dad and even his mother, who is taking the class in a stationary wheelchair.

He is so happy to see them, but they're all so intent; they don't seem to notice him at all. Everyone is pedaling backward. Perhaps there's a different set of muscles involved in backward biking.

"Okay, everyone," Rhiannon shouts. "Let's really push it now. Let's make some cumulus clouds!"

His bike is special. There's a weight bench between the handlebars, and there's a woman there, bench-pressing an odd-shaped weight that keeps wiggling. Clearly it's too heavy for her. She's floundering. He needs to spot her.

He tries to get off his bike and into the spotter's position but he can't move fast enough and then she drops the baby—*No!*

—and that's when he wakes up, facedown in his Intro to Meteorology textbook, his body compressed awkwardly against the desk, his left shoulder enveloped in a firestorm of pain.

With his right arm, Gaelan reaches for his OTC meds—his left arm is closer, but when his shoulder flares up like this, even lifting a bottle of Advil causes him to wince. He swallows two pills, assesses his discomfort, and then downs a third.

Restless sleep, vivid, disturbing dreams, and waking up with some degree of shoulder discomfort has become a regular routine. But as long as he keeps a stash of NSAIDs on hand, he's able to work out. He's taking it easier with certain elements of his routine, too: bench press, lat pulls, flys, push-ups. Fewer reps.

His computer has gone into sleep mode; he jiggles his mouse to wake it up. The results of his most recent Google search appear on the screen: a Web site called "Bad Coriolis."

One of the challenges Gaelan has faced as a distance-learning student is the way a simple question can lead to an Internet search that can lead to hundreds of Web sites, that can lead to spending hours reading information that is not part of the class curriculum but is infinitely more interesting than what he's supposed to be studying. He doesn't even remember how he ended up at the "Bad Coriolis" Web site, but he makes frequent visits there; it's one of the most interesting and informative sites he's found in his cyberspace wanderings.

The site is maintained by a Mr. Alistair B. Fraser—a man dedicated to the debunking of certain widely propagated science myths, and to the proposition that "it is better to communicate good information than to offer misinformation in the name of good communication."

For example, Mr. Fraser's "Bad Rain" page reminded Gaelan that the universally accepted raindrop-as-teardrop symbol enforces a fallacy. Raindrops look absolutely nothing like this: small ones are spherical; large ones are shaped something like hamburger buns.

Gaelan plans to support Mr. Fraser's efforts by proposing several changes to the KHAM-KLAN weather graphics when he returns from his leave of absence. He's confident that his viewing audience will not only embrace the use of spheres and hamburger buns as symbols, they'll welcome the accurate scientific knowledge.

The phone rings.

"Gaelan, you've got to get down here now." It's Bonnie. Her voice sounds strained and congested, as if she's been crying. "There's something wrong with Viney."

"What is it?"

"It's hard to describe, but she's acting really strange." Bonnie fills him in on the details; Gaelan tells her he'll be there as soon as possible.

In case he has to spend the night, he throws a couple of things into his gym bag. He fills the cats' food and water dishes. No time for coffee, so he fills the bathroom sink and splashes cold water his face. He's barely aware of the fact that he performs all these actions with the use of his right arm and hand only: from shoulder to elbow, his left arm stays glued to his lower ribs; the left side of his torso remains practically immobile, as if contained in a body cast.

He pulls the plug from the basin and rushes out before observing a scientifically impossible occurrence: The spiraling water empties into the drain in a clockwise manner.

It's after midnight when he arrives. The meds are already starting to wear off; the pain in his shoulder is starting to fire up again.

A wet snow is falling hard. Bethan stands on the front porch, an afghan wrapped around her shoulders. Eli is inside, peering through partially opened curtains, looking over the back of Viney's sofa.

"She's in the backyard," Bethan says, pushing the door open for Gaelan as he comes up the porch steps. "Bonnie's with her. Let's go through the house."

Inside, Eli is now standing at attention. "Hello," he says.

"Hello," Gaelan replies.

"Wait here, will you, honey?" Bethan calls over her shoulder as they pass through the living room. Eli frowns but does as he's told.

They make their way toward the back of the house. "So what happened exactly?" Gaelan asks.

"Bonnie called her this morning—I guess she checks in with her every day—and when she didn't get an answer after several tries, she got worried. Haley couldn't get away because of her kids, so Bonnie came over and found Viney outside, like this."

"In the snow."

"No hat, no coat, no gloves."

"This was when?"

"Right before she called you, I think. Around ten-fifteen."

They arrive in the family room addition at the rear of the house, where sliding doors lead onto a concrete patio. The motion-detector lights are on, sending a harsh light out toward the backyard, casting the falling snow in relief against the black night beyond. The snowflakes are falling in perfectly parallel, vertical lines, as if chasing one another down to the earth, sliding on a construct of invisible threads.

"Bonnie asked me to come over, thinking I could figure out what's going on," Bethan continues, "but I can't do any kind of exam in the state she's in. She's not answering questions, and we can't get her to come inside."

Gaelan draws closer to the sliding door.

"At least she let us put a coat over her," Bethan says. "You see them?"

He pushes the heavy door to one side and steps out onto the patio. Even under the eaves, the wet snow is falling so hard that he can feel it rebounding off the concrete, striking at his feet and ankles, dampening the cuffs of his khakis. He squints into the backyard. It feels colder to him now, but maybe it's the strangeness of the scene that chills him.

At the very edges of the light, where it starts to diffuse, about fifty feet from the patio, there are two figures: The falling flakes make them look like newsreel figures, rendered in grainy tones of black and white. One figure is kneeling with her back to him; the other hovers nearby, holding a large umbrella.

"She's been out there for a couple of hours that we know of, maybe even longer," Bethan says, joining him outside. "She's not herself, Gae, there's something really wrong, but without looking at a CT I don't know a thing. We need to get her up to the hospital."

"She's crying," Gaelan says, half to himself.

"How can you tell?"

He continues to stare at Viney. "Bonnie said she was asking for me?"

"Every time we try to get her inside, she says she's not going anywhere 'until my boy gets here.' We figured that had to be you."

"How is she?" Eli has joined them and stands just inside the house.

"Oh, honey," Bethan says, putting an arm around him. "I'm sorry about this. You're such a trooper. I just didn't feel right about leaving you alone at home."

"I'm fine, Mom," Eli says, shying out of her embrace. He turns to Gaelan. "What are you going to do? How are you going to get her to come in?"

"I don't know," Gaelan says.

"Oh," Eli says. He seems disappointed. "Well, maybe you'll figure it out once you get there."

Putting up the hood of his coat and making his way out to the garden, Gaelan wonders why a few words from this twelve-year-old boy should have such an armoring effect, and why making a success of his task matters so much more because of Eli's presence.

As soon as he's close enough to see her face, he knows he was right: Viney—who rarely cries and, when she does, gives the impression that everything in her body is telling her not to—is kneeling in the snow, in the strawberry bed, shivering, muttering, weeping. There's a coat thrown over her shoulders; her legs are bare and, along with her shoes, covered in snow and mud.

Bonnie stands over her; when she sees Gaelan approach she gives him a sad, scared smile; she's been crying, too. She's holding Dad's big green and white golf umbrella, adjusting it with precision each time Viney shifts her position so that it remains over her. It's a kind but useless gesture; Viney must have been out here long enough before Bonnie arrived to get soaked to the bone.

Gaelan reaches down and lightly touches the top of her head. "Hi, Viney."

"Oh honey!" she cries. She gets to her feet and hugs him, mud and all. He flinches with pain but doesn't pull away. "I'm so glad to see you!

There's so much work to be done here." Before Gaelan can restrain her, she kneels again and pats the soggy earth next to her as if it were a sofa cushion. "Come on. Help me." She starts digging again.

He kneels beside her. "What's the matter, Viney?" Her eyes are glazed; she has an energy that is both manic and diffuse.

"Nothing's the matter, sweetie, nothing! I'm just behind is all. I haven't kept this bed up like I should."

"What do you mean?"

"I've let these runners get too far from the mother plant. These runners. These runners . . ."

Gaelan looks toward Bonnie. Her face is creased with concern.

"Come on, honey," Viney insists, grabbing his wrists, sending another electrical current of pain into his shoulder. "Help me!"

"But how can I help, Viney? What can I do?"

"Dig, sweetie, that's all. Just dig! Like this. Oh, I'm so glad you're here. I've done a terrible thing, you know, letting it all go like this."

She resumes digging, but Gaelan senses that she's wearing down, giving over to the exhaustion, and he realizes that perhaps he doesn't have to do anything but simply be here. His physical presence—and whatever it means to Viney—is enough. Saying the right words is not required.

"A highness sin," she mumbles after a while. "Horrible and highness. And now there is punishment."

Gaelan looks to Bonnie for clarification. Bonnie shrugs and shakes her head. When he turns back to Viney, she has stopped digging and is staring fixedly at her muddied hands, her body rigidly still. He has the feeling that her heart is beating too fast, like a small creature that's only narrowly escaped being roadkill, or is hiding from some looming predator. "Viney?" he says.

She does not answer. She is crying again.

He picks her up—tiny as she is, the action makes his shoulder feels as though it's being ripped apart—and carries her inside.

"Oh, honey," she repeats, "I'm so glad you're here." Her body relaxes into his; her limbs go limp.

As he brings her into the kitchen, one of her mud-splattered shoes falls onto the floor: It's a golf shoe. One of Dad's.

*　*　*

Viney rallies for a while after they get her cleaned up. They settle her in the backseat of Gaelan's car with pillows and layers of blankets, and then start off for Lincoln, Gaelan in his car, Bethan following in hers. Bonnie will stay behind and look after Eli.

For the first few miles, Viney remains awake and chatty.

"I should have known that those runners would get away from me," she says. It's not clear whether she's talking to him or to herself.

"You just can't keep things hemmed in like that, not forever," she continues. "Welly and I should have figured that out, and now that S.O.B. has left me with the whole damned mess and not a word of direction, not a bit of guidance. Isn't that typical? Isn't that just like a man?" She goes on like that for a while, but eventually she wears down and by the time they pull up to the Emergency Room entrance, she's fallen asleep.

Ignoring his body's last desperate entreaties—because no one else can do this, it's his responsibility, his weight—Gaelan hoists Viney out of the backseat and transfers her to a wheelchair. The pain now is nauseating; he has to steady himself against the wheelchair for a moment before taking her inside.

Bethan is already standing at the triage desk and describing Viney's symptoms—disoriented, manic, verbally confused, possibly hallucinogenic, jittery—and ordering a CT. She requests that the on-call neuroradiologist notify her for a consult when the results are back. A hospital orderly transfers Viney to a gurney and wheels her away. Bethan and Gaelan take a seat.

None of the other people in the waiting room appear to be in any acute distress, medical or otherwise, so in most cases Gaelan can't tell if they're to be seen by a doctor themselves or are awaiting news of someone else:

A middle-aged, heavily made-up woman in an overly tight, hot pink jogging outfit is dozing in one of the chairs (something about her makes Gaelan suspect that she's drunk); an exhausted-looking man and woman pass a cranky toddler back and forth, trying to get him interested in watching a Disney video; three men who look like they might be father and sons—but who are completely ignoring one another—sit on a sofa, all are enormously overweight and wearing grimy overalls; and a pale, emaciated girl in the corner appears to be holding a shaggy, languishing, long-haired pet, but when Gaelan looks closer he sees that there's someone

sitting next to her with his head in her lap. They form a disconcerting
tableaux—both of them so skeletal, their bodies in such odd relationship with each other. It's as if the boy's bones are internally unbound
and completely unstable, and it is only the force of the girl's embrace
that keeps him from splaying apart, a loosed bunch of pickup sticks. The
girl leans down, whispers something in his ear, and then kisses his filthy-
looking head with great tenderness.

Gaelan catches Bethan looking at them, too. She's wearing glasses and
her hair is pulled back into a sloppy ponytail. He realizes that they
haven't been alone together for sixteen years.

"Thanks for being here," he says. It seems like a harmless enough introit.

"I want to tell you about my marriage," she replies, still staring at the
sad pair of lovers.

Gaelan has the sensation that a sudden upsurging geographical event
is occurring within his torso, tectonic plates crashing together to form a
ragged mountain range. "What?"

Bethan turns her eyes to him. "My marriage," she repeats. "My
husband, Leo. Can I tell you about him? Not tonight, maybe, but
sometime?"

"Hey!" someone calls. It's one of the trio of men in overalls. "Aren't
you that guy from TV? The weatherman?"

It is not always a major event or decision that stands as a signpost,
and it is a wise person indeed who recognizes that small moments, too—
such as this one, set in a hospital waiting room in Lincoln, Nebraska—
can afford a choice between two possible and very different versions of
the future. Gaelan sees clearly that the portals to these two possible fu-
tures will be opened through the use of two words: *yes* and *no*.

In one version, he has never been so grateful for the way his on-screen
appearance aligns with his up-close-and-personal one: *Yes,* he says, *yes,
I'm the weatherman.* This future has him spending the next several minutes chatting with his fellow waiting-room occupants, autographing
pamphlets—informational leaflets with title like "STD: You're at Risk,"
"AIDS: Not Just a Homosexual Disease," "The Warning Signs of Cancer," and "Who Needs a Mammogram?" Eventually a man in scrubs
appears and says, "Dr. Ellis?" and he and Bethan move into the future
with the identities that this scenario provides.

Gaelan is as surprised as anyone when he chooses the other version.

"No," he says to the young man in overalls who cannot see how frightened his father is, how frightened his brother is, how frightened he himself is—for Gaelan somehow knows that they all have good reason to be frightened. "No," he says again, making sure that there is kindness in his voice. "I'm not the weatherman."

He turns then to Bethan. She is looking at him from behind smudged lenses, her eyes slightly widened. "I'd like that," he answers. "I'd like to hear about your life."

"Dr. Ellis?" the man in scrubs announces. "Mr. Jones?"

"So from what I can tell, there's nothing systemic going on here," the doctor says, referring to the CT images he's brought with him into Viney's ER room; she's still fast asleep. "No sign of a major brain bleed or even a small infarction." He flips through Viney's chart. "Has she been under any stress lately?"

"Her husband died suddenly last August," Bethan replies. Gaelan loves her for this: referring to his father as Viney's husband.

"Well, that could certainly account for the depression, but the agitated speech . . . the personality changes . . . Given her age, I'd like to keep her overnight for observation. You'll need to fill out some forms at the front desk, and then we'll get her admitted upstairs."

Bethan telephones Viney's house while Gaelan deals with paperwork.

"That's taken care of, at least," she says, once she's off the phone. "Bonnie can stay the night with Eli. Now, let's get you up to Radiology."

"What are you talking about?"

"Don't be ridiculous. I've been watching you all night, Gaelan. I saw your face when you picked her up."

She leads him down a long featureless hall to an elevator. They ride up two floors, emerge, wind along another nondescript passageway— this one under construction—and then arrive at a larger bank of elevators and go down three floors. Gaelan hates hospitals. They seem expressly designed to make people feel confused, paranoid, and helpless. At least he has a knowledgeable guide; Bethan's pace is so brisk and purposeful that he almost has to jog to keep up with her.

"What is it they're going to do?" he asks.

"It's called an arthrogram: a type of X-ray. It involves injecting a special dye into your shoulder joint first so we can get a good look at what's going on in there."

His stomach lurches.

"Don't worry," she says, softening her tone. "I know how you feel about needles, so I'll do the injections myself."

When it's over, Bethan studies the X-rays, her face grim. "This is pretty much what I thought," she says. "You've got a minor tear in your rotator cuff."

"What does that mean?" he asks, feigning ignorance.

She peers at him over the tops of her glasses. "It means that you're going to have to stop doing whatever it is that you've been doing, use a combination of ice and heat compression therapy, take the pain meds I'm going to prescribe for you, and stop lifting weights. Before we leave, I'll copy some literature for you to take home."

"I can't do that. Give up lifting."

"Then I guess I'll be scheduling you for a surgical repair?" He's never seen her in physician mode. She's very cute. "Don't be stupid, Gaelan," she goes on. "I'll show you some exercises you can do and get you set up with a physical therapist."

"Okay, Doc."

She is unamused. "Let's go check on Viney. She should be settled in by now."

It's three in the morning when they get to Viney's room; a nurse is checking her vital signs. Bethan introduces herself and then starts looking through Viney's medical records. Gaelan pulls up a chair.

Viney's eyes flutter open. "Welly?" she murmurs.

"Good morning, Mrs. Closs," the nurse says. "My name is Herman and I'll be taking care of you today."

"Where's Welly?" Viney asks fearfully.

Gaelan takes her hand. "Hi, Viney."

"Gaelan, honey! Where am I?"

"You're in the hospital." She looks so confused, so tiny, so aged. "Bethan and I brought you up to Lincoln because you weren't feeling well."

"Bethan's here, too?"

"Hello, Viney." Bethan comes around to the other side of the bed and smoothes Viney's hair away from her face.

The nurse finishes listening to Viney's heart. "I'll be back later," he says.

Viney watches him go and then starts to cry. She reaches for Gaelan's hand.

"I miss him so much."

"Of course you do," Gaelan answers. "You and Dad were married a long time."

Her eyes brighten, focus, and she grips his hand tighter. "Was it a marriage, honey?" she asks eagerly, plaintively. "Did you really think of it like that?"

"Of course we did, Viney," Gaelan answers, surprised and sad that she would need to ask this question. "How could it have been anything else?"

"Oh!" she cries. "Thank you for saying that, sweetheart. Thank you."

She closes her eyes. Her hand relaxes, continuing to make restless movements in his for a while, and then eventually she goes back to sleep.

At the nurses' station, they're reassured that Mrs. Closs is stable and that the doctor will call if there's any change. They walk together to the parking lot.

"You wanna come over to my place before you head back?" Gaelan asks. "I could cook some eggs or something if you're hungry."

Bethan looks at her watch. "Well, they're all asleep, so . . . Yeah, sure. I could use some coffee."

"You wanna go in one car?"

Her brow furrows; a sudden muscular tic causes her eyelids to quiver. She starts blinking furiously. "No," she answers, looking away from him. "That's okay." After squeezing her eyes shut for a moment, she retrieves a prescription pad and pencil from her purse. When she looks at him again, her gaze is unperturbed. "What's the address?"

She assays the condo without comment, deposits her coat and purse on the sofa, and then excuses herself to the bathroom. Gaelan busies himself in the kitchen, hoping to discover something suitable to serve to a guest at four in the morning. He's not hopeful. For weeks (actually, *months*) there's been no one but him and the cats in residence, day or night, so mostly he's been eating out. The fridge contents are pathetically spare and dismal: a couple of naval oranges, an oily carton of take-out fettucini, a saucepan of leftover oatmeal, a couple of hard-boiled eggs, a jar of capers, and some hummus that's gone green around the edges. There might be some rice cakes in the cupboard. Low-fat refried beans. Something canned from Healthy Choice.

At least there's alcohol.

"Beer or wine?" he shouts.

"Just coffee if you have it," she shouts back. "Instant is fine. I should probably get going pretty soon."

He could put on a CD, but he's embarrassed to; his collection is still dominated by the music of their youth—1980s vintage Springsteen mostly—and he realizes how sad that is, how telling. Surely Bethan's musical tastes have advanced into the twenty-first century, if for no other reason than that she has a kid—although Eli doesn't strike him as the kind of boy who's on the cultural cutting edge. To listen with Bethan to any other music but Springsteen feels wrong; but to do that might seem like trying to get something back. After all, they're different people now, aren't they? It would feel desperate. Even turning on the radio seems trivial somehow, sullying.

Gaelan experiences a sorrowful realization: It will never be possible to sit in a room with Bethan Ellis and converse casually to a score of *background music*.

"Thanks," she says, emerging from the bathroom and receiving her coffee. She must have washed her face (dampened wisps of hair are clinging to her forehead) and cleaned her eyeglasses; they are now smudge-free.

He sits on the sofa; she doesn't. This makes him nervous.

She ambles through the corner of the room where he keeps his work-out equipment. "Scene of the crime, then," she mutters.

How is he to respond to this? He makes a show of shifting his weight on the sofa, pretending not to have heard her.

"You going somewhere?" she asks offhandedly.

"What? Oh . . ." He shrugs out of the right half of his coat, then unpeels the left sleeve to his wrist but finds he can't extricate his arm. So he sits there, a one-armed man half-encased in an eiderdown jacket.

She seems to be studying the digital readout on his treadmill when she says, "I can't decide if we have too much to talk about or too little."

Do we have to talk at all? he wonders. Maybe he *should* put on some music.

"How long have you lived here?" she adds, thankfully, as if this segue to idle chitchat is perfectly natural.

"Let's see . . . fifteen years, maybe? No, sixteen."

She looks at him. "So right after you graduated, then?"

"Pretty much, yeah. Right after I got the job at the station."

She nods. "You've done well."

Kate and Spencer come out, mewling and posing. She pets them, makes purring noises. They succumb to her touch with sluttish abandon, swooning to their sides, stretching, yawning, exposing their bellies. She always was good with animals.

"I've had sex with a lot of women," Gaelan blurts.

She gives him a puzzled look. "Yes? So? Why wouldn't you?"

This is not the reaction he expected. Judgment, yes; a blasé acceptance, never. "I just thought you should know."

"Why?" She shrugs. "It's none of my business."

She plops down on the sofa, as far from him as possible. Still, she could have chosen the chair. Kate and Spencer join them.

Bethan continues to assess the room in a studious manner, squinting intently at the white ceiling and beige walls as if determining how best to restore the ancient frescoes beneath.

"Tell me about your husband," Gaelan says. "If you want to."

"Not now. Tell me why you never got married."

She probably thinks this is a difficult subject, but it's not. "I've just never met the right person."

"That's a pretty stock answer," she remarks.

"Well, it's true."

"I slept with a lot of people, too, after we broke up," she announces, her voice determinedly sanguine. "Revenge fucking, I think they call it. I didn't enjoy it much."

"Sorry."

She looks at him, waits.

"I'm sorry," he repeats, giving weight to the words, certain that, at this moment anyway, their inner monologues are roughly aligned. "Can you forgive me?"

Her silence—not an unresponsive silence, but one that is dense and somehow palpably connected to his words—reminds him of something else he's always loved, and missed, about her: the way she makes no effort to answer questions that are unanswerable.

"It's too bad, what happened to us," she says finally, "and I thought I'd never get over it. But I did. I have." She abruptly extracts a thick, folded sheaf of papers from her purse and snaps them open. He's revisited by that sharp upsurging feeling in his chest; she has the resolved look of someone who's about to deliver a prepared, villifying indictment of his sins and transgressions.

Instead, she launches into a description of the subscapularis, supraspinatus, infraspinatus, and teres minor, followed by a lecture on rotator cuff injuries.

"This is some information I printed up for you about shoulder injuries in general," she concludes. "Treatment protocols, physical therapy, self-care measures . . . Here."

"Thanks." Gaelan notes with amusement that the front page of this prospectus is a page from *The Anatomy Coloring Book*. He wonders if the next thing out of her purse will be a box of Crayolas.

"Read that," she insists, "so I can answer any questions before I leave. I want to show you some of the exercises. Do you have any ice packs?"

"I don't think so."

She gets up. "How about frozen vegetables?"

"Maybe." He remains on the sofa reading while she goes into the kitchen. There's a lot in here that concerns him, specifically the part about how he's supposed to stop heavy lifting and/or overhead activity and how physical therapy may take from three weeks to *several months*.

He gets up and joins her. "It says here that steroid injections can also be used to relieve the pain."

"That's one treatment option."

"So?"

She helps him take off the rest of his coat. "I don't recommend that for you."

"I can get used to needles," he says, unconvincingly, even to himself.

"That's not the reason."

"Then why?"

"Because steroidal injections can give you a false sense of confidence. If you're not experiencing some degree of pain you're more likely to do something stupid. Overdo. Reinjure. Bodybuilders are notoriously reckless that way. I've seen it over and over again. Now stand here. I'm going to help you take this off."

He complies. Reaching inside his sweater, she presses his shoulder so that it's stabilized against the surface of the fridge. He'd forgotten the feeling in her hands; how she really is gifted with a healer's touch.

"Why did you become a radiologist?" he asks.

She frowns.

"This might hurt," she says. "Breathe." She starts easing his left arm out of the sweater. It only hurts a little.

"You okay?" she asks.

"Yeah."

She takes the papers out of his hand and pulls his other arm out of the sleeve. His head is now the only part of him still extruding. He feels like an incapable toddler.

But as she starts gathering up the sweater, slowly, carefully, taking it over his head—the moment is a defining example of déjà vu—he registers the proximity of their bodies—it is a very small kitchen—and after months of success at playing dead, his penis finally comes out of *svasana*.

In the brief second when she's left standing with her arms extended overhead, focus directed upward, he reaches around her waist and pulls her body close. She looks surprised, but unafraid, willing.

He does not want to remember the exact circumstances of their last kiss, but he knows that it has been sixteen years since he encountered this mouth, these lips, this tongue—his first mouth, and the only one he knew from the time he was fourteen years old until he was twenty-two.

Time begins to rewind, and it *is* that last kiss, not the sad, guilty, perfunctory kiss he surely gave her on the church steps that Christmas Eve right before they broke up, but another: the kiss at the airport on the day she flew away to med school, their cheeks wet, their mouths full of salt; it is a kiss on the corner of Tenth and G on a wintry Saturday morning outside Klein's bakery, lips dusted with confectioners' sugar, holding paper cups of steaming black coffee and a bag of pastries—the nice German ladies loved them so, they used to give them strudel right out of the oven for free; it is the kiss on the state Capitol steps in spring as busloads of children streamed by, pointing and teasing; on a secluded grassy spot in Pioneer Park before they were rousted by a cop; in the middle of his family's field, or hers, hidden among the corn rows; it is many kisses in his car, making out while Bruce sings about *a barefoot girls sitting on the hood of a Dodge, drinking warm beer in the soft summer rain;* it is prom night, in front of his sisters, who keep making them kiss for the camera; it is their first kiss under the old railroad bridge over the ravine where they used to meet: They were twelve and fourteen and he was so worried about her braces but she said afterward that it didn't hurt at all.

After a while, she eases away and pivots within the circle of his arms so that her back is to him.

"Stay the night," he says.

"I don't know if I can, Gae."

"Why not?"

"I still miss my husband." She tilts her head upward and emits a heavy, ragged exhale; he knows that she's trying not to cry. "It's so funny, for a long time I slept with people because I missed you."

"I've missed you, too," he says, and not just because that response forms the next logical stepping-stone to the bedroom, but because it's the truth. He enfolds her with his right arm and draws her into his good side, resting his chin lightly on the top of her head. He feels her body relax.

"There's a gesture," she says, "something you did, long ago, when we were kids, after we moved to Lincoln and I showed you the kitchen of my apartment for the first time. Those sky blue cupboards in the kitchen, the yellow linoleum. Do you remember?"

That word, how he fears it sometimes.

"I loved that kitchen," Bethan goes on. "That's really why I took that apartment, I think, for that kitchen. So bright and happy. I was so nervous, the first time you came over, and I think you were, too, you were so quiet, so serious. Looking at everything, making sure it was sound, I guess, and safe, or something. The leaky sink, the pilot light . . . Remember?"

He does.

"I wanted so badly for you to like it because it was where we were going to, you know, surrender up our virginities, and I started opening and closing drawers and cupboards in that foolish, compulsive way people do, even when they know there's nothing inside. The cupboards had been painted and repainted so many times that they were hard to open and one of them—way up high—was stuck. I struggled with it for awhile, and then you came up behind me and reached around me and opened it."

He doesn't recall this, and yet, because their bodies are aligned in just the way she's describing, he starts to create the memory, imprint the image in a way that will allow him to speak of it from this moment on as something that he, too, *remembers*.

"We just stood there," she says, her voice high, young, "not touching, looking into that empty cupboard. I can't tell you how many times I've dreamed about that moment, that gesture, especially since Leo died. For the longest time I didn't know why, but now I think I do."

She is crying now. He turns her around so that they're face-to-face again.

"It's such a simple dream, really," she says, "just a replay of that moment without its sexual heat. But it's so powerful, the feeling it gives me. The comfort. I've wanted to thank you for it, that's all."

He smooths away her tears, takes her hand, and starts leading her out of the kitchen. "Come to bed," he says. "Sleep with me."

"I told you, I don't know if it's right. I still miss my husband."

He smiles. "I don't mind being a stand-in." He means it as a tease, but a worried look comes over her face.

"You should mind," she says emphatically. "How can you say that? You should never be a stand-in. Not for anyone. Not ever." Her tone is insistent, even angry. And then her face unfolds into a look of terrible realization. "Is that how it's been for you, Gae?"

He ignores the question. "Be with me." He is pulling her lightly by the hand, backing down the hall toward the bedroom.

She doesn't resist. But when they reach the door to the bedroom, her expression reflects a sudden shock.

"What? What is it?" he says, alarmed, turning around.

There's nothing. Just the bed.

"That quilt," she says, her face astonished, and he realizes that she is one of the only people in the world who knows it to be a replica. "That can't be the one your mom made . . . How?"

"I paid a fabric artist to make it."

She's still scowling. "It's extraordinary." Her voice is expressionless.

"What?" he asks.

"Why is it in here?"

"What do you mean?"

"You could have put it somewhere else."

"It's a quilt. It belongs on a bed."

She looks at him. All the softness is gone from her face. "It's more than that, Gae. Don't pretend that it isn't. You could have"—she gestures vaguely—"hung it on a wall or something."

"I didn't want it on a wall," he says, angered. Why is she making such a big deal about this? "I wanted it . . ."

"Yes?"

"I wanted it to be . . ." She stares at him, and her eyes become projection screens on which he watches all the encounters with all women he's had in this room over the years: same scene, same dialogue, different actresses, one long screen test.

He sees her make all the mental connections between the quilt—the ultimate trump card—and his sex life, the way he's traded on his family story, exploiting the quilt's beauty.

"How sad they must all feel," Bethan remarks, "the women who come into this room, when you tell them that your mother is dead."

She waits, but when he doesn't speak, she lowers her gaze and nods her head—as if his silence confirms some sorry truth she was hoping to disprove.

"I can't, Gae," she says finally. "I have to go."

She leaves behind a used coffee cup. There's not even an imprint of lipstick on its rim. He pulls the quilt off the bed and stuffs it into the closet. He pours a beer, puts on the *Nebraska* album, sits on the sofa, and closes his eyes.

In his mind he plays another movie—one of the two of them when they were young. There's nothing sad about that movie or the characters in it. The future hasn't happened yet. They haven't made any choice but the choice to be in love for the first time and with each other.

Hope's Diary, 1970:
Hide-and-Seek

I'm thinking about things that are hidden: in the back of the closet, in the back of the drawer, under the stairs, behind the door, up in the attic, down in the basement, deep in the earth, in plain sight. That which is hidden acquires power, the size and scope of its power in direct proportion to the time elapsed.

How can human remains stay hidden for so long? I'm talking about the missing-in-action in Vietnam (thank God Viney was at least spared that horror), the mammoth skeleton found in its totality by a family wandering the Siberian plains in the dead of winter, murder victims, the hellish game of hide-and-seek that police detectives must engage in. How is it possible? How can things stay hidden for so long?

What is hidden has power—but where is the power lodged?

In Emlyn Springs, we hide the mirrors in times of grief.

We hide our faces in moments of shame.

We hide our children from things too awful to take in with the eyes.

We hide from the reality of death, if we can.

If what is hidden acquires power, then revealing it should rob it of its power.

Come out, come out, wherever you are.

After reading "Farenheit 451," I wondered where I'd hide the books when the Thought Police came to burn them. And after reading the diary of Anne Frank, I wondered where would I have hidden the Jews? Would Anne and her family have survived in my house?

Things, objects hide from me; I know this without a doubt. And then they reappear, having had their secret adventures. They reinsert themselves into the landscape of my desk, my dresser drawer.

Marital infidelity, yes. One hides those for obvious reasons.

But the body's truth?

"He knows where all the bodies are buried," they say, not only about assassins and hit men, but about anyone who has illicit knowledge of dastardly deeds. Embezzlers, civil servants on the take, crooked cops.

Physicians, too, it turns out.

When I revealed what I thought was happy news to Llewellyn tonight after putting the children to bed, his face was anything but happy.

"What's wrong?"

He hemmed and hawed for a while, finally coming out with this: "Hope, I don't think it's a good idea for you to have this baby."

The words—and his tone—chilled me so much that for a moment I couldn't speak. "What?"

"I just . . . you seem worn out so much of the time with just two. So frazzled and exhausted. How are you going to have the energy for another child?"

"Are you saying I'm a bad mother?"

"No! No, Hope, I'm not saying that at all. Please don't get defensive."

I couldn't believe it. "You're telling me that you don't think I should have our baby. What reaction do you think is appropriate?"

"I'm just saying, think about how tired you are."

"That's your argument? That's ridiculous. There's not a mother I know who doesn't wish she could lie down for a couple of hours every day and take a nap."

"You know what I mean."

"No. I don't, Llewellyn. What are you talking about?"

In the silence, he got this look. I can hardly describe it. His face hardened in a way I'd never seen before. That was when I started to be afraid that he was hiding something, that something was really wrong.

The phone rang—a convenient excuse for L. to cut short our discussion.

"I have to go," he said after he hung up. "We'll talk about this later. Will you please call Viney? Let her know I'm going to need her tonight. We've got an emergency and I'm on my way."

He rushed out the door, leaving me here with my heart pounding.

Hours later I'm still waiting for him to get home, holding my hand to my belly as I write this, trying not to imagine what it is about my having this baby that would make my husband terrified—for that was what the look on his face reflected.

Fell asleep in the children's room last night waiting to hear from L. He finally called around one A.M. to say that he and Viney were at the hospital in Lincoln with the family of a boy who'd been severely injured in a car accident. The boy was in surgery, they were awaiting news. Told me he'd call again later this morning.

No mention of last night's exchange, which didn't surprise me.

Got the kids off to school. When the phone rang again, it was Viney letting me know that they were still up in Lincoln. Llewellyn wanted to stay the afternoon, possibly all night, to be with the boy's family and make sure he was stable.

BULLSHIT! I wanted to shout, and yet calling into question the Good Doctor's motives would be tantamount to blasphemy.

"Viney, what's wrong with me?"

"What?" Viney sputtered.

"Is there something wrong with me?" I repeated. "Physically?"

"What do you mean?'

"I'm pregnant again," I said, and let the remark hang. There was just enough silence on the other end before she chirped, "Oh, Hope, that's wonderful!" to make me realize that whatever Llewellyn knew, Viney did as well.

I went on. "Llewellyn doesn't want me to have it." More silence.

"Why, Viney? What wouldn't Llewellyn want me to have this baby?"

She started crying.

"Oh, honey, I don't know," she said finally. "I can't imagine why he'd say that. When he gets back from Lincoln, I'll make sure he—"

I hung up on her.

Thus stonewalled by my best friend—who is such a terrible liar—and with my husband conveniently unavailable—I got in the car, sped into town, and sought out the only person I knew would answer my questions honestly.

Dr. Williams was in his garage as usual, hunched over one of his creations, carefully, methodically applying brilliant glossy red enamel paint to the wings of a whirligig cardinal.

All it took was that dear old gentleman saying "Hope! What a lovely surprise! Come in and let me fix us some tea" for me to start crying uncontrollably.

After pulling myself together, I recounted Llewellyn's odd reaction to my announcement, his comments about my fatigue. Dr. Williams looked genuinely puzzled. He asked if I minded answering some health-related questions, I said no, and he went

on to inquire if I'd experienced anything besides
fatigue, did I sometimes feel that the fatigue was
debilitating, did it keep me from participating
in the normal activities of daily life, had I experienced numbness in my limbs, changes in my vision? To which, of course, the answers were all
"yes."

"Do you usually feel very well when you're pregnant?" he asked.

"Yes. I mean, aside from the miscarriages."

He nodded. "And in the months after birth, are
you very tired?"

"Yes, but who isn't?" I replied.

He nodded again. It was a long time before he
spoke.

"I suspect—and I cannot be sure, it would be terribly wrong of me to suggest that this is anything
but an educated guess, but based upon what you've
told me—the loss of feeling in your feet and legs
and hands, the blurred vision you've experienced
over the years, the sudden loss—and then return—of
your vision yesterday morning, the way all these
symptoms come and go, the way your fatigue is ex-
acerbated by heat. . . . This constellation of findings indicates that you might be suffering from a
neurological disease."

Constellation of findings. Lovely phrase.

"Such as?" I prodded.

"I couldn't say. There are many things that would
need to be ruled out."

"Name one."

He hesitated. "Well, MS for one. Multiple sclerosis."

I thought back to Larken's birth, the OB's persistent and annoying questions about my vision.

"How long do you think Llewellyn has known
something's wrong?" I asked.

Dr. Williams shrugged.

"Did you know?"

"No," he said emphatically, and I could tell it was the truth.

He tried to soften my anger, explaining that the medical ethics of these times dictate that physicians hide the truth when it comes to illnesses like this.

"This was the case when I was a young doctor, too," he said, "and when I was new to my practice, I withheld information from my patients as well. It takes time and experience to know when these rules need to be bent, or even ignored. I'm sure Llewellyn thought he was doing the right thing in keeping this from you, Hope. I'm sure this deceit on his part comes from a place of real love, from a desire to protect you."

That sounded about right, but it didn't lessen my anger.

"Is there any danger to the baby?" I asked.

"No."

"Is it inherited? Can I pass it on?"

"No one thinks so, no."

"Why did you ask about my pregnancies?"

"Some women with MS feel very well when they're pregnant, their symptoms lessen or even disappear completely, but after they give birth the exacerbations come back worse than before. I'm sure that's what Lwellyn is worried about."

I thanked Dr. Williams and left, and now I'm home, waiting, still not comprehending.

What right did any of them have to hide this from me?

Never mind "any of them"—the generalized world of ethics-adherent physicians. What I mean is my husband—and, it would seem, his nurse.

All this time—years and years—the insidious march of the disease, as if the disease and I were not one and the same.

I am the disease. I should never have been hidden from myself.

I am having this baby.

I may never be able to forgive him.

Chapter 22

The Widow Finds Her Story

There's a special kind of pretending that goes on in small towns. It involves neither willful ignorance nor blindness. It is the opposite of gossip: a pretense of not-knowing.

This pretending is what allows small-town people to continue living in such close proximity. How else could they mingle on a daily basis with the sinners among them? Without the practice of not-knowing, it wouldn't be possible. Were a stranger to enter the societal cocoon of a not-knowing town such as Emlyn Springs and start asking questions like "Shouldn't he be in jail?" or "Did they ever get married?" or "Has she put on some weight?" the answers will come back *I can't say, You're asking the wrong person, You make a good point,* or *That's a very interesting observation.*

This kind of forgetting can occur within an individual as well. After all, a single life might come to contain many identities, a whole community of selves one has inhabited over the course of, say, seventy-five years. In order for all those selves to cohabitate, one must occasionally direct the power of not-knowing inwardly; for example, should one self ask, *When exactly did I start sleeping with my best friend's husband?* another self could answer with conscienable ease and genuine wonderment, *Why, after she gave me permission to do so, of course!* For years, Alvina Closs has managed internal conversations like this with perfect poise.

But now she is the last surviving member of a charterless two-person club dedicated to the not-knowing about and abetting of certain burdensome domestic crimes. The other member of this club is gone, and this has left her with an aching loneliness.

What's the point? has been the dominant conversational question among the town of selves that constitute Alvina Closs.

To which the not-knowing replies have been, *Gosh, I can't really say* or *You're asking the wrong person.*

And so here she is: confined to a hospital bed miles from home, exhibiting symptoms that no X-ray can account for and no physician (except for Welly, of course) can diagnose.

Of course it was a marriage, Gaelan said. *How could it have been anything else?*

It is difficult, so difficult for the aggrieved to open themselves to the complexity of feeling that follows a loss—and many cannot. There is a commonly held misconception that we must only speak well of the dead, encountering them in our hearts and minds with abiding love and unperturbed kindness, fabricating a revisionist view of personal history that excludes pain, suffering, and sin.

And yet grief cannot proceed and healing cannot occur without a willingness to speak truthfully of the dead and of our relationship with them. Expressing the full range of feelings toward those who've abandoned us has a scouring effect—and a strengthening one, too; it allows us to stand with firmess on the terra incognita of a vastly reconfigured future—possibly a long one. "Till death do us part" is a terrible vow to force upon a married couple. Death doesn't end a thing. What was imperfect in life will remain imperfect after death, whatever was unmended cannot be repaired, unuttered words will echo like a curse, unsaid words will become a cancer, and yet this must all be acknowledged and spoken of, in one's own heart at least, if nowhere else.

It wasn't in 1976, when Hope told them they could.

It wasn't in 1967, when Wally Jr. died (*no, not even then*), although when she thinks about it, that could be when it started. It depends on how you look at it.

One thing that's sure: She made something of herself, *by* herself, after her husband died. Maybe that's where it really began: widowed, without question, when she was thirty-one.

There was grief, of course, but she was still peppery and strong-willed, *a real ball of fire* as Llewellyn Jones said. She'd been rebellious since childhood, a staunch nonconforming little girl who preferred jeans to dresses and who was mortified by tears—hers or anyone else's. Most folks expected that she'd grow out of this in time, become more compliant. Maybe there were even some who believed that Alvina Closs had gotten her comeuppance when her husband died so sudden like that. And so young.

But Viney refused to shrink to fit what the town expected of her: a stoic period of mourning during which she'd be the beneficiary of pitying looks, noodle casseroles, and visits by elderly church ladies spouting Bible verses; this followed by a decorous reentry into polite society via church socials, Fancy Egg Days dances, and St. David's *te bachs;* and then eventually there would emerge some bland, flabby, balding male— a widower, a middle-aged bachelor, or one of those types who lives with his mother. He'd take her daughters out for ice cream a couple of times, toss a football around with Wally Jr., and expect that would be enough, because after all, as used goods and the thirtysomething mother of four she wasn't much of a catch. She'd be so thankful for his kindness and fatherly instincts, his health benefits, his life insurance, his pension, and his paycheck that she'd willingly, *gratefully* take his arm at the front of the Bethel Welsh Methodist Church, wearing a modest veiled pillbox hat and a matronly suit in pink or pale yellow or even off-white with matching pumps, say *I do* with a look of utter admiration, and spread her legs whenever called upon to do so.

No. Not that.

Never that.

Long before *Ms.* magazine found its way into her life and the term *feminist* became common conversational currency, Alvina Closs understood that, although the hand that rocks the cradle might indeed be the hand that rules the world, it doesn't hurt if that hand's owner also earns the paycheck.

She married and had her first baby at seventeen—not because she got *knocked up*, as the saying goes (and goodness knows there were plenty of girls of Viney's generation for whom that was the story). She was a smart girl, a *nice* girl, and she was a virgin on her wedding night. Getting married young and having babies early was what she chose. And she wasn't about to stop making choices just because chance—or fate, or God, or whatever you want to call it—had thrown her a curveball. As Viney has aged, she's been amazed by how many people go through life without making choices—*as if that's any way to live!* She can't stand them.

And so after Waldo died she chose again—to go back to school, to become a nurse. She stood firm and proud on the rightness of that decision, even though it meant sacrifice: She went into debt, took out a loan; her children had to become more responsible, more self-sufficient.

She studied nights after the kids were in bed, and there was terrible weariness during that time, the house constantly messy, meals made from boxes or cans. But there was always love. And she knew that at some point Wally Jr. and the girls would understand what she'd done. Maybe even admire it.

On graduation day, they all stood together: Viney and her four kids and Hope and Welly and their two toddlers. There's proof: a photograph buried in a box somewhere in the basement. Maybe she'll try to find it, get it framed.

There were three happy unencumbered years after that. She had a dear friend in Hope and a fine employer in Welly—although he was *Dr. Jones* then in the office and *Llewellyn* in social settings. Not only was she his nurse; she ran the office, too, since he couldn't afford a full-time clerical salary.

So it was Viney who sat at the front desk when the bell jingled that afternoon. She didn't look up right away; she was doing the books. Her first thought: *Why would two such healthy-looking young men need to see a doctor?* She didn't even register the fact that they were wearing uniforms, not right away; it was cold that November. They'd removed their hats but were still wearing their overcoats.

Her history from that moment through the next few months is a construct, a collage of images and linguistic fragments—*forward operations base, Dak To, recon mission for armed escort, engaged the gun, hit in the aft, tail boom separated, explosion, fire, unable to extract both pilots, graves registration team, metal and ashes, bone fragments, teeth, but nothing more, nothing more.*

One of the youngest pilots to die in combat.
A folded flag, a grateful nation.

Eventually she started to borrow images from other *Gymanfas*—because she wasn't present at Wally Jr.'s, not really. When she attended other funerals, she would think, *it must have been this way for Wally* and from there she assembled something, a fleshed-out fabrication that now passes for a memory of her son's burial.

Welly sang at the church service. That's one thing that really happened. He had the most beautiful voice.

So in time she was able to believe that she saw her son buried, but she was never able to reconstruct his death, and that was crazy, it was *unacceptable,* because to have been present at Wally Jr.'s birth and his *Gymanfa* and his funeral but not his death just made no sense whatsoever.

Welly started taking her with him on emergency calls. Her children were old enough, they could be left alone, so he would pick her up, often in the middle of the night because most of the carnage occurred after closing time.

There were so many car accidents in those days, more than now, so many drunk drivers. This was before the admen got together and invented all those catchy PSA phrases: *watch out for the other guy, friends don't let friends drive drunk, be a designated driver, buzzed driving is drunk driving.* Back then, everyone drank and drove, and when parents spent the next day in the bathroom throwing up, they told their children it was the flu, and of course those children watched carefully and eventually learned the truth and so drove drunk, too, and wrapped their cars around trees and on those nights Viney would get a phone call and it would be Llewellyn saying he was on his way, he needed her, *he needed her,* although in the beginning he didn't really. She just stood nearby, a numb spectator handing him whatever he required, her sangfroid passing for what it was not but counteracting any hysteria on the scene and there was a lot of that.

Welly always pretended to be sleepy on the way back home. *Would you mind driving, Viney?* he'd ask. *I'm dead on my feet.*

She didn't mind. She was never sleepy, even though she never slept. How could she when all the lights had to stay on? She couldn't let Wally Jr. come home to a dark house.

They'd arrive in the middle of nowhere—which is where these accidents always happened, on some unpaved, unlit country road hemmed in by corn or milo, a no-man's-land of uncertain jurisdiction. City? County? State? People could die in the amount of time it took to figure out who to call, but if they phoned that young doc from Emlyn Springs and his nurse, they'd come, they'd come right away, they'd be there in no time.

One night, someone, some grateful farmer said, *You two, you're like one of them mobile army surgical teams we had overseas,* and Viney wondered, *What's the time difference between Nebraska and Vietnam?* and from that night on she wasn't here, she was over there, and she and Welly, they only looked like civilians: they were really on standby, waiting to work a mission, and when the calls came, they were summoned to the Dak To runway, to the burn unit of the evac hospitals in Vung Tau, to Brigade Headquarters in Pleiku City.

She replaced the family Bible with Webster's and her vocabulary grew and grew; on the same page as *Vietnam* was *vignetting: a reduction in intensity of illumination at the edge of a field of view,* and as more boys died over there, what she did was, she started saving them over here, they were all Wally, and she was grateful, *grateful* when one of them lost a leg or an eye because then they'd be 4F, they couldn't go. Their mothers and fathers would rather have them home and disfigured than gone forever, bones and teeth and nothing more.

From then on and for some time, it only looked like Nebraska to everyone else. Where other people saw overturned threshers and mangled cars and dense fields of cattle crops, Viney saw a landscape of bomb craters and burned helicopters.

There were no cornfields after that, only rice paddies.

It was the night Hope told Llewellyn she was pregnant again: 1970 then, had to be, because Bonnie was born in April of '71.

So that's when it was. That's when it happened.

There's been an emergency, Hope said. *Llewellyn is on his way.*

By this time, Viney had logged so many hours that she could tell from the first syllable whether Hope was calling as a friend or a dispatch officer. It's true that Hope's voice sounded especially tight, strained, but Viney didn't remember that until later, when Llewellyn told her that they'd had a fight.

Viney hung up, got into uniform, left a note for the girls, and took up her medical kit. She was already waiting outside for Llewellyn when he pulled up in the van and off they sped.

On the way—they'd be driving well north of Emlyn Springs, on two-lane highways and back roads—Llewellyn shared what little he knew: car crash, single vehicle, possible amputation, possible fatality. They fell silent after that. That was usual. There was nothing out of the ordinary about his behavior.

It took nearly an hour to get where they were going. The boy had lost a lot of blood. Wasn't wearing a seat belt, had been thrown from the car. One of his legs was crushed, the other severed above the knee.

No military service in this one's future, Viney thought.

They did what they could, got him ready to travel. Even though it was obvious that reattachment would not be an option, for the family's sake they collected the leg and packed it in ice and then headed to Lincoln.

Llewellyn rode with the boy in the back of the van; Viney drove; the family followed. The boy died en route.

Viney expected them to go back to Emlyn Springs once they'd spent some time with the family.

And yet, when she returned from the cafeteria with fresh cups of coffee, she found Welly on the phone with Hope, saying nothing of the fact that their patient was DOA—*severely injured* were the words he used.

"Viney and I are going to spend the night at the hospital," he was saying, "stay with the family while he's in surgery, make sure he's stable."

Maybe he didn't die after all, Viney thought. This made more sense than believing she was listening to Dr. Jones lie to his wife.

Llewellyn went on to say that either he or Viney would check in with her in the morning, give her an update, let her know when they'd be coming home.

"I can't go back tonight," he explained after he hung up.

"I'll drive if you're too tired," Viney offered.

"No, it's not that." He'd looked at her then, and she could tell that he was genuinely exhausted—but more than that: afraid. Of what? "I can't see her tonight," he said. "We had a terrible fight before I left, she's pregnant again, and . . ."

"What? Llewellyn, what is it?"

"I can't face her, Viney. I can't. Let's just find someplace to spend the night."

Did they plan for it to happen?

No. They did not. They were just tired, both of them. It had been a long, terrible night. They needed to get some sleep. They needed a rest.

And yet, Llewellyn *had* lied, and she *could* have chosen a motel in town, close to the hospital and to the southbound route they'd take when they drove back to Emlyn Springs, but instead she took them out on West O, to the outskirts of Lincoln, where there were big noisy clubs with live road bands that attracted a rough crowd, a seedy crowd; where if the wind was right you could smell the packing plant; where they were sure to pass under the radar.

He'd barely managed a few steps into the room before sinking onto the edge of one of the beds. "Hope is sick," he said. "She has MS."

He sat slumped, with his back bowed like an old man, eyes downcast. The room had stained red indoor/outdoor carpet and smelled faintly of beer, ammonia, and feces.

"She doesn't know," Viney said.

"No, but she's starting to suspect something's wrong."

She'd been sick a long time, he told her, ever since Larken was born, maybe even longer, and it would get worse and worse and now she was pregnant again—it was *his* carelessness, *his* fault—and she wanted this baby, of course she did, but when she came to him with the news he couldn't pretend to be happy. Not this time. Not again.

"I couldn't tell her, how could I?" he asked, over and over. "And now she's guessed something is wrong, she knows I've been hiding something from her, and she hates me, Viney. Hope hates me. We'll never get past this, I know it . . ."

Viney could hear drunks carousing in the parking lot outside, a couple in the next room having a fight.

My wife, back home, he said, or something like it, and that was when Viney realized that they had passed into yet another country together, one where civilian rules did not apply. "My wife, back home, she despises me."

The room was small and dark and closed and there was so much feeling in it, too much, and it had to go somewhere so it went into her body.

"How could anyone despise you?" she said, kneeling beside the bed and pulling his hands away from his face. "You're a doctor."

She examined his hands. A field surgeon's hands, she had seen them in action. He could do anything with these hands. He could stanch blood, set bones, reattach limbs, transplant hearts probably, given the opportunity, and then suddenly he was pulling her heart out of her chest because he'd seen right away that she needed a new one.

There was blood on his clothes, blood of the dead. He needed to get out of them.

Home and wives and children were so far away. They'd lost that boy tonight in spite of everything and didn't they have the right? Hadn't they earned some comfort?

And then she was aware that they were both of them tearing at cloth, grasping hunks of muscle and healthy flesh that was alive with arterial blood, venous blood, bruising each other's bodies with the bone-on-bone force of this, their first time. She had never been with her husband like this, but it was right, this violence. It was what she had needed. Love and gentleness is a luxury of peacetime and they were living in a country at war.

And the next morning, when Viney called to say they were still in Lincoln and would be staying for a while longer, and Hope asked, *Is there something wrong with me?* Viney took her to mean, *Is that why you and Llewellyn slept together?* and an icy panic assaulted her. She could barely speak.

But of course that wasn't it. That wasn't what Hope meant at all.

Such good fortune for them, the new adulterers! At the precise moment when the wronged wife might have sensed, might have guessed (and Viney in her raw fear might even have given them away had Hope not hung up on her), she was preoccupied with the only other thing that could supplant such intuitions: She was pregnant with a baby her husband didn't want her to have. Why would that be?

They'd mastered without trying the magicians' art of redirection. They got away with it.

So they stayed in that rank-smelling room with the DO NOT DISTURB sign on the door and had sex all afternoon. They weren't fooling anyone, the couple registered as *Mr. and Mrs. Jones,* but then, they didn't need to. They could make as much noise as they wanted. They were comrades-in-arms, off-duty, on leave. It was only R&R. It meant nothing.

And that's how it went, for years: It was just the guiltless screwing of soldiers in wartime. They felt affection for each other, of course, but it was their relationship on the battlefield, not in bed, that defined them: a *paradigm* of morality and professionalism.

When Hope encouraged them to have an affair—even though she didn't know she was lending her support for something they'd begun long ago—it felt as though they'd been forgiven. They could start over. They could reinvent their first time.

They came to each other differently after that, with tenderness, with joy.

This is why Alvina Closs has not-remembered the truth. In her mind, she and Welly had their real beginning years later, in 1976, when Hope made possible the thing that would never have happened otherwise, and that none of them, least of all Hope, ever expected. It was Hope who released Viney and Welly from their tour of duty, allowing them to finally fall in love.

The phone in Viney's hospital room starts ringing. It's the children calling, one after another, asking what happened, is she all right, does she need them.

They are good children, caring, responsible children, and they are behaving exactly as they should.

But Viney hears the fear in their voices as well. She senses a level of play-acting in their collective behavior. Underpinning their mature concern is fear—the primal fear of childhood: They are calling to see if she still belongs to them, if she is still their mother, alive and well in mind and body. Adults all, they still need reassurance that their world is stable and safe.

She tells them that she's fine, really, there's nothing to worry about, she just hasn't been taking good care of herself, let herself get run down. Stupid, foolish. The doctors are keeping her for twenty-fours, for observation, to perform a few tests, but it's likely she'll be home this evening. No, they needn't come to the hospital. She'll call again later, give them an update, let them know if and when she needs to be picked up.

When Bud Humphries calls, Viney is reminded that he is the most guile-less, least nosy person she knows, and so she asks him to do her a favor.

He arrives about an hour later, carrying a grocery bag containing fresh fruit, a change of clothing, and a file folder she directed him to track down in Welly's study.

Bud stays with her for a while, holding her hand, saying little—it is just the thing she needs—and then lumbers away when the nurse comes to take her vital signs, reminding her that he expects a phone call when the hospital releases her. It's no trouble. He'll turn right around and come get her whenever she's ready to come home.

Viney extracts the file folder.

NOBODY'S GODDAMN BUSINESS BUT YOURS AND MINE . . .

She stares at the angry words, the barricade of exclamation points, scrawled with such vehemence that they seem to represent a "Do Not Enter" injunction.

She remembers writing those words. She remembers how she felt. She might be asking for trouble by opening this file, inviting that ter-rible anger back into her body. There's really no way to know.

The newest addition to the file is exactly where it should be, right on top. It was printed out at the Beatrice library with the help of Viney's new ally in the world of computer technology and online communica-tion: Sad Bison at Gee Mail Dot Com. Viney gave this document only the most cursory read before remanding it to the darkened file cabinet in Welly's study.

Dear Mrs. Closs, the e-mail begins. I was deeply saddened to learn of the death of Mayor Jones.

Viney steadies her gaze, forces herself to read slowly.

Thank you so much for letting me know of Dr. Jones' passing. Odd as it may seem, in spite of the fact that Llewellyn and I never met face-to-face, I consider him to be one of my dearest friends. I shall miss him more than I can say.

The stark appearance of the letter, with its To: From: Received: Date: Subject format and its narrow, unadorned font, strikes Viney as cold, officious, entirely at odds with its content, and (she now allows) with the person who authored it.

It is true that Llewellyn longed to deepen the relationship between our communities . . .

Viney realizes that every other letter of consolation came from someone she knows, someone she's met, someone she can put a face and voice and body to.

. . . I've taken the liberty of forwarding your kind invitation to the financial committee for their consideration. They will surely be in touch with you soon . . .

Maybe she could ask Brother Henry to send a photograph.

Although the original impetus for the correspondence between Llewellyn and me was businesslike in nature, over the years our discourse became concerned with personal matters . . .

Or maybe she'll just imagine what he looks like.

Our friendship has exerted a profound influence upon my spiritual life—and will continue to do so, I am sure. I owe a great deal to Llewellyn for sharing the tribulations of his heart, and for posing questions that cannot be easily answered.

Yes, No, Maybe. Not Likely. Try Again. Wait and See . . .

Beginnings are so important. Enduring, deep relationships are forged in many ways—over cups of coffee, at football matches . . .

At the scene of fatal accidents . . .

. . . I've always suspected that Llewellyn would never have explored the deeper, darker places were it not for the fact that our relationship was epistolary in nature. Just as some people need the sanctuary of the darkened confessional in order to speak the truth, others can only reveal themselves freely on the page . . .

Viney imagines Brother Henry's hair as fuzzy, like unspun mohair.

You know better than anyone I am sure what an intensely private man he was, how he struggled with the limits of his powers as a physician. More than once I was compelled to remind Llewellyn that the promise of "eternal life" does not apply to the body . . .

She shakes Brother Henry's hand. It is fleshy and large, like a farmer's.

Viney finishes reading this letter, and then travels back in time through the others, born into the past on page after page of handwritten correspondence, through words of harsh inquiry, comfort, condemnation.

There can be no forgiveness for what I did . . . How could your God have let this happen? . . . I speak of these things with no one but you . . .

Words of intended comfort . . .

You faced extraordinarily difficult circumstances, and did so with love and bravery and pain. No one can ask more than that . . .

These words, for better or worse, belong to her now. They are what Welly left.

Did he mean for her to have them? Does it matter? Whether they represent kindness or callousness is for her to decide. Maybe she'll decide one thing today, another tomorrow.

Viney lets her gaze drift to the window. The clouds are gathered up in a scalloping formation, like bunting, and underlit with intense shades of orange and purple. Why do we always refer to the sun as *rising,* she wonders, when in fact it is the earth's rotation that makes a sky like this possible? *We,* as the earth's passengers, not the sun, are the bodies in motion.

She presses the Call button and picks up the telephone. Bud did say he'd turn around and come right back whenever she needed him.

She's ready to go home.

Hope's Diary, 1971:
"Gwnewch Y Pathau Bychain."

It is St. David's Day, on which we partake of leek broth, adjudicate the longest leek in town, humorously, and with many sly references to male anatomy.

The children in Wales are out of school on this day. Not so here, but there was a special assembly at school, so I drove Larken and Gaelan into town this morning. They immediately forgot all about me, flinging themselves into that untamed territory known as the Playground—the tribal force of children loosed from civility and parental influence is always a revelation—and I was left loitering on the fringes with the other disenfranchised mothers.

Never comfortable in this setting. Conversations always seem to turn immediately to achievements and special abilities—theirs, or their children's. It's that highly specialized form of territorial grandstanding that women do so nicely, smiling all the while. I never feel as though my efforts quite measure up. And of course there were the natural questions about how I'm feeling, when is the baby due, have we picked out names yet, and so on. I'm still reflexively superstitious when it comes to talking about my unborn babies. Wish Viney was still a playground mother.

Anyway, made some excuse about forgetting something in the car, absented myself from the throng, and found a nice, sheltered, out-of-sight place next to the parking lot to sit and wait in peace for the bell to ring.

March in like a lion this year—high winds, dramatic sky.

It's a lie what they say about spring, that it's the time of new life and rebirth. Plants know the truth. Yes, there is all that new growth, those shocking shades of yellow-green, and the smells, but there are also the seeds emerging—and what are seeds but the symbols of desperation? Seeds represent foreknowledge of death like nothing else. It's life admitting that death is not far off. Replication is required. Plants know the real story.

Spring bouquets no longer cheer me; a vase of dead grass would be welcome.

"Do the little things that you have seen me do," the saint enjoined us during his last sermon, as he lay dying. I imagine his voice as reedy, but not unpleasantly so. Nothing bombastic, just a pious, politely spoken suggestion: *"Gwnewch y pathau bychain."*

What will be my dying words, I wonder? Or will I be past language by then? Likely. The swallowing mechanism goes, so must all other controls involving the tongue, the lips, the teeth, and the jaw . . . I will be silent at my death, then.

Will thought be possible, that's the real question. Does the brain survive an incapacitated body? Can it keep from going mad, denied all outward forms of expression? And isn't madness unexpressed a kind of triple hell?

Maybe L. was right to keep it from me. What good is knowing? I have been so bitter toward him since learning of this thing he has hidden. After all, he didn't give me the disease, he only knew about it and—out of good intentions, out of love, I suppose (and I'm realizing now that it had to have cost him something)—kept it from me.

"Do the little things" will be my slogan then. And they shall grow littler and littler until . . . what? What in the end will I be able to do? What little thing?

*   *   *

Today at least I managed a big thing, the last big thing this body is likely to manage in this lifetime.

It's hard to consider the possibility that, at thirty-one, I may have just performed my corporeal grand finale, but at this moment, no one could be prouder of this diseased body and what we've accomplished than me.

My last-born child is a girl: Bonnie Ebrilla.

No C-section this time: My little pedaler, so spritely and busy in the womb, announced her intention to arrive with a theatrical downpour—my water breaking as I hung out the laundry this morning on one of the first warm days of spring. Looking down at my soaked clothing and the wet earth, I thought about the never-to-be children I've buried in our field over the years. Always beneath my feet, whenever I walk this land I feel them: the wispy remains of the lost ones, and yet they are of one flesh with this earth that I so love, and with me, and I have never stopped speaking with them; they are no less real to me for having never been born.

By announcing her arrival this way, Bonnie seemed to be saying, "I know who lives here. I know what this place means to you." Standing there, I felt the force of her will, the strength of her spirit, her faith. I felt her choose that moment: She watered those remains believing she could bring them to life, as if her older brothers and sisters were seeds that could still germinate if only they were given the right nourishment.

An hour later, she was in my arms. Llewellyn didn't even make it home in time—he was forty miles away on an emergency house call. Viney was my midwife. A blessing for us both. And so we're home instead of at the hospital. Just the two of us; Llewellyn left to go into town to pick up Gaelan and Larken from school and bring them home to meet their baby sister.

She's so calm and alert. And so completely of my body in the way she is shaped: long (twenty-three inches!), fine-boned, completely different from the two stocky boxers the OB extracted from my womb six and seven years ago!

Whatever else the future brings, this child will always remind me of my body's triumphs instead of its failures.

PART THREE

Fancy Egg Days

I had spent years attempting to find him and had not. He never wanted me crawling around in the grave of his self. He wanted me to find him elsewhere—in the face of the Bearded Priest, in people rising and falling through space . . . In the face of the woman who now set a coffee before me.
                                        —from *The Face of a Naked Lady*
                                                        by Michael Rips

Hope's Diary, 1972:
Amaze and Amuse Your Friends

Bit tired today. Handwriting an effort, so before L. left on a house call, I asked him to bring my IBM Selectric—old friend!—down from the attic. We'll see how it goes. It's been a long time since college essays, even longer since ninth-grade typing class, but I used to be quite the speed demon.

The quick brown fox jumps over the lazy dog.

The quick brown fox isn't as quick as she used to be.

I've been trying to regularly schedule time alone with each of the children. Today it's Gaelan's turn. Viney has the baby at her house and Larken is at Bluebirds.

Right now we're having "quiet time," me doing this, Gaelan on the sofa looking through one of the science books I got him for his birthday. It's the Amaze and Amuse Your Friends! series; there's one on air experiments, one on jets and rockets, one on magnets, and another on seeds.

We've been very interested in air lately. Earlier today we did an experiment called "What Is in the Empty Glass?" which involved stuffing a piece of paper inside a glass, turning the glass upside down, pushing it straight down into a pan of water, and then lifting it out. When the paper comes out dry, it really does seem like a magic trick. I don't think I ever quite contemplated the relationship between magic and science—or at least, what we perceive as magic—before my curious son started taking an interest in such things.

Gaelan has been reading to me on the days when my vision fails and/or when my eyesight is blurry. He took this on without anyone asking. So like him. He reads the newspaper sometimes, or from one of his chapter books, or poetry if I ask for that. He reads to Bonnie, too, which is so sweet I can hardly bear it.

This morning he read an article about the winner of the Nobel Peace Prize, some Russian named Ilya whose last name sounds like a form of pasta. He's come up with a new form of chaos theory, something to do with dissipating forms re-creating themselves into something new. Gaelan understood more of it than I did, but I can certainly appreciate both chaos and dissipation.

My presence as lab and/or magician's assistant is required. G. informs me that, for our next trick, we're going to make water flow uphill. (!)

Chapter 23

Coddling the Slacker

"Have a seat, Gaelan."

The conference room is crowded with the men he's come to expect in this setting—his news director, the sponsors, the suits (although they've clearly relaxed the dress code since their previous gathering)—plus an individual who's introduced as KLAN-KHAM's legal counsel and whose name sounds so much like the station's call letters (*Ken Clam? Clem Lamb? Cam Clapp?*) that Gaelan immediately forgets it.

"We're sorry to have to bring you in like this," the suits-in-shirts begin, "but something has come up . . ."

Gaelan realizes that he may finally get his wish: At long last he'll be allowed to predict the weather wearing clothes that accentuate his biceps.

". . . something rather serious that we needed to discuss ASAP."

True, he's lost a lot of tone and symmetry since his injury—prohibited as he is from doing any left-sided lifting—but he'll get it back. He'll be better than ever. Imagining his new televised look, Gaelan feels a mild surge of exuberance.

And yet the prevailing mood is hardly jovial. The news director is staring at the floor; the sponsors are biting their lips.

"Now understand," the suits are saying, emphatically, "there's been nothing formal, but . . ."

Gaelan suddenly notes that the sideboard is conspicuously empty: no lavish floral arrangements, no catered displays of condiments and deli meat. If there's a dead person in the room, his passing is not being celebrated.

"... an allegation of misconduct has been brought by one of our employees ..."

A criminal, then, or one of those John Doe types whose remains have gone unclaimed and who'll be laid to rest in a cheap pine coffin in some potter's field without being sung even a single hymn.

"... and as we're sure you can understand, it is incumbent upon us to regard any allegations of this nature as extremely serious."

There is a pause. This must be a prompt for him to speak.

"Allegations," Gaelan says, aware that his attention has been wandering and that the safest thing to do is repeat the last few words of the previous speaker. "Extremely serious," he adds, nodding.

The suits regard him with a squinting wariness. "We have to act on this, Gaelan. Right away. Before it leaks. Before there's any damage to the station's image."

"I'm sorry," Gaelan says, "what?"

When the reply is made—and even though it comes (surprisingly) from Ken-Clem-Cam, Esquire—Gaelan has the sensation that the roomful of men is speaking in chorus:

"Ms. Calder believes that she was the victim of sexual harassment."

He doesn't say *Who?*—although he's tempted; his contact with *Ms. Calder* was so short-lived that it really does take a moment for him to realize who they're talking about.

The lawyer goes on. "She alleges that the harassment—in the form of inappropriate touching and sexually demeaning jokes—occurred during the time you were training her as your replacement."

Gaelan doesn't say *What?*—even though that, too, comes to mind as an appropriate response, since *she* was the one who made a habit of hemming him in—on the lounge sofa, by the coffee machine, at his computer desk—making sure that her liposuctioned ass was angled in his direction and her implants were never more than a few inches from his eye line. He has never shown her anything but professional and completely asexual courtesy.

"It's going to be a difficult charge to discredit, Mr. Jones, given what I understand to be your lifestyle."

"My lifestyle?"

"I thought it prudent to investigate your personal life when Ms. Calder came to us, in order to assess whether her charges had any validity."

They're having him on. They've got to be.

So Gaelan laughs and says, "You're kidding."

This does not please them.

The dreary scene that follows makes Gaelan suspect that these fellows have been watching way too many TV courtroom dramas. They've lost their sense of humor. They've abandoned their sense of reality and thus have no interest in anything as complex as the truth.

Above all, Gaelan realizes, they are frightened, and frightened men can feel neither love nor loyalty. There's not a Joe Dinsdale among the lot.

You'll never get any respect being a weatherman, Joe said, *but if you can laugh about it—because think about it, son, how many people in the world get paid to predict the unpredictable?—you'll have a lot of fun.*

In his last official act as a KLAN-KHAM employee, Gaelan Jones, weatherman, asks, "What are you prepared to offer in terms of a severance package?" and when he's negotiated those particulars to his satisfaction, he leaves, marveling at how easy it was.

And yet, as he starts emptying his locker, he finds himself regretting that he didn't leave behind some final symbol, a display of rebellion, a loyal weatherman's equivalent of the gun and badge the wronged police officer always leaves on the lieutenant's desk when he's been leveraged into an unjust resignation.

What could it be?

Passing the glass-walled conference room on his way out, he notes that the suits et al. are still in session—having been joined by the cosmetically altered Ms. Calder and another person, presumably her litigator. There's a lot of smiling and nodding going on.

Gaelan asks the receptionist for a piece of paper. On it he scrawls the "Bad Coriolis" Web site logo—a teardrop shape enclosed in a circle with a slash through it—and then he slaps it against the glass. When everyone looks up, clearly alarmed, he blows Riley Calder a kiss, and then strides out to his car, completely unaware that he's walking like a farmer.

What he tells himself is this: In eighteen years, he's never taken a vacation, and Viney needs him.

In Gaelan's mind, it is for these reasons—not because his condo holds one too many memories of failure and humiliation, and not because the city of Lincoln is too large to practice small-town pretending—that he packs up his cats and his free weights and his CD and DVD collections and moves to Emlyn Springs.

He doesn't need to tell anyone about losing his job right away, certainly not Viney. It would only worry her. He can just go on as if nothing has happened—at least until he figures out what's next.

Who knows? Maybe this will turn out to be the luckiest thing that's ever happened to him.

He's been here for almost two months.

It was a very kind and self-sacrificing thing for him to do, and Viney was grateful for his presence at first. He took care of her, cooked for her, saw that she ate and rested properly. He got her out of the house on days when the weather was fine enough for walks. He took her up to Beatrice a couple of times to the movies. She's loved having this time with him.

But now that she's feeling better she's started to worry about him, and frankly (there's just no other way to put it) he's *underfoot* in that annoying, unwelcome way that surly teenagers and unemployed men have. Not that he's surly, just quiet. Nor is he lazy, not exactly—he works out with those weights for hours every day; Viney hears him up in his room, huffing and puffing to that rock-and-roll music he likes so much. It's more like a lack of direction. She wonders when he's going back to *work*, because there's a special quality men have when they're working, when they have the feeling of self-importance that comes when they *consider* themselves to be working—whatever that means to them. It's almost like an odor they put out.

"Are you going to study after the show is over?" she asks.

They're sitting on the living room sofa, watching *The Guiding Light.* Viney wishes now that she hadn't introduced Gaelan to soap operas. He's grown very invested in the lives of the characters.

"Gaelan, honey," she repeats. "Are you going to study before dinner?"

"No," he replies. "Al Gore's on *Oprah,* and after that I'm going for a run."

Again? Viney thinks, because this will make the third time today. But she keeps her mouth shut.

"I'll study tonight," Gaelan adds.

"Oh, well, you'll have the house to yourself. I'm meeting Hazel Williams at The Little Cheerful in a few minutes, then I'm having dinner at the club with Bud and Vonda, and after that I've got a Fancy Egg Days committee meeting."

"Great, Viney," he replies, his eyes never leaving the television. "That's great."

"Maybe you could call Bonnie," she suggests. "You kids could watch a movie together or something."

"Yeah, Viney, that's a great idea. Maybe I'll do that."

When it comes to men, unemployment, retirement, and partially paid leaves of absence are the worst ideas ever invented. They really lose their dignity if they aren't required to labor for a paycheck.

Viney wonders if she shouldn't start demanding that Gaelan do chores and give him an allowance. Maybe she should see about getting Internet access at the house so he could do his online studying here.

Something has to be done, because his presence is turning her into the worst, most stereotypical kind of hag. Every day she catches herself saying things like *Why don't you call up Bethan Ellis?* or *Have you thought about volunteering at the school?* or *We could sure use your help with Fancy Egg Days.* Imperatives veiled as polite suggestions.

Who knew that having a grown unemployed son at home would feel so much like being married?

After Viney leaves, Gaelan decides to skip Al Gore's good-natured fear-mongering and plug in one of Arnold's early movies instead. He lights up a joint.

His shoulder feels great, fully recovered. It's time to start lifting again. He'll just watch a little more TV, have a quick run, and then head up to his room to work out.

He's wondering how much weight to start with when the doorbell rings.

The appearance of this unlikely visitor should surprise him, but it doesn't. In the narrow history of their relationship, Eli Ellis Weissman has established himself as someone with an uncanny gift for materializing at highly inconvenient and/or embarrassing moments.

"Hello," Eli says. Is it possible that he's even smaller than he was the last time Gaelan saw him?

"Hello."

Perhaps some undiscovered scientific law is at work here, one that causes underdeveloped, hormonally fluctuating twelve-year-old boys to shrink.

"How did you get here?" Gaelan asks.

"I rode," Eli replies. Looking past him, Gaelan notices the new-looking bicycle propped against Viney's porch. It's one of the models Bonnie sells in her shop.

"Where's your helmet?" he asks.

"Nobody in Emlyn Springs wears a *helmet,*" he says disdainfully.

"But you have one, right?"

"Yes."

"You need to wear it," Gaelan admonishes. "Just because kids around here don't wear them doesn't mean that you shouldn't. You could set an example."

Eli stares with an abashed expression, and Gaelan realizes how inappropriate it is for him to speak in such paternalistic tones to this boy he barely knows. "Besides," he amends, "your mom would want you to."

Eli swallows hard and looks at his feet. "I was wondering if you could help me with a project."

"What?"

"I'm doing a unit on meteorology as part of my homeschool curriculum, and I was thinking you might be willing to help me since that's your area of expertise."

Not anymore, Gaelan thinks. "I'm sure you'll do just fine without my help. What's the project?"

"Building a wind vane."

Gaelan nods.

Eli sniffs. He tries to peer past Gaelan into the living room. Gaelan blocks his view.

"Have you been diligent about your physical therapy?" Eli asks.

There must be another scientific principle informing this exchange, one related to magnetic mental fields and extrasensory perception because it's clear that Eli not only knows what Gaelan has been *doing* but what he's been *thinking.*

"Why?"

"My mom has been wondering is all."

"Oh."

"I see you running by our house sometimes. You sure run a lot."

They've been watching me, Gaelan thinks, his paranoia intensifying. *I'll have to change my route.*

"Anyway, my mom's afraid that you're lifting."

"Well, I'm not. You can tell her."

"Tell her yourself. You're out by our house often enough. Just stop by."

"Okay," Gaelan lies. "I might just do that sometime."

"Well, good-bye, then."

"Bye."

Gaelan shuts the door, greatly relieved that he can finally contain the distinct, overpoweringly sweet smell of dope. Moving to the window, he peers out through a tiny slit in the living room curtains.

After looking around to make sure no one is watching, Eli fastens on his helmet and then pedals off, wobbling alarmingly, looking as though he's only just stopped using training wheels.

The days pass.

Gaelan does not lift.

He runs in town, he runs out on the highway, through corn and milo fields, and—despite Eli's disturbing revelation that his movements are being watched—he continues to run along the highway, past the land from whence his mother ascended, past the Ellis farmhouse.

He cannot get used to the idea that he will no longer come upon his father in this landscape, won't round a corner and discover him kneeling over some pilot who crashed his crop duster, performing mouth-to-mouth resuscitation on a drowning victim, doing compressions in order to reignite some fallen soul's stilled heart.

Sometimes he even expects to encounter an earlier version of himself and Bethan.

He's not depressed; he's just taking a break.

One positive thing that's come out of all this is that he's in the best shape of his life. He started running because he no longer has access to the cardio machines at the gym, and ever since UPS delivered his Boflex home gym last month, he doesn't miss the Y, doesn't really even need it. Maybe he'll move back here for good.

At home, Viney has left a note: She won't be here for dinner, there's a frozen entrée if he wants something easy, leftovers if he feels like cooking.

The doorbell rings.

Eli again.

At least Gaelan wasn't smoking dope or about to violate his physical therapist's orders.

"Hello."

"Hello."

"I was wondering if you're ready for auditions. I wanted to answer any questions you might have, about the character, or whatever."

"Auditions for what?"

"The Fancy Egg Days Pageant." Eli frowns. "You forgot, didn't you?"

"Oh. Right."

"Do you still have those sides?"

"Sides?"

"The ones I gave you back in December."

"Um, no. I don't think so."

Eli nods knowingly. He unloads a large backpack from his shoulders, places it on the porch, and starts rummaging through it.

"Listen, Eli," Gaelan begins, looking down at the top of the boy's head, which is covered today by a black yarmulke that's secured with multiple bobby pins. "I feel really honored that you want me to be in your play, but—"

"If you don't audition," Eli says, continuing to forage, "I'm pretty sure the director is going to cast Mr. Canaerfan." He eventually extracts a large three-ring notebook. "I mean, I'm sure Mr. Canaerfan is a really fine teacher and all but he's *totally* wrong for the part, so please try out, okay?"

Eli holds out the notebook; Gaelan accepts it without comment. For some reason he cannot bring himself to equivocate in this child's presence.

"Good-bye," Eli says.

"Good-bye," Gaelan replies.

Eli fits his helmet over his yarmulke and pedals away. He's looking more confident now, a fact that Gaelan finds reassuring.

After fixing himself dinner, Gaelan retreats to his room, lights up, and gives over the entire evening to reading the winning entry in the Fancy Egg Days play competition.

Entitled *Our Little Wales,* Eli's script has three very long acts, is loaded with challenging technical, scenic, and costume elements, and is extremely ambitious in scope—beginning in prehistory and moving through time to the present day. The play calls for the appearance of wooly mammoths and saber-toothed tigers. A wind machine will be used to suggest the tornado that blew Emlyn Halopeter off course, causing him to lose his bearings and homestead here instead of in Wymore. Indian tribes will hunt bison. Sod houses will be built. The Battle of Midway will be reenacted. Gaelan wonders if Eli's imaginative talents might be better served by the movies.

Throughout the script Eli has highlighted the role of the Custodian. He has also inserted a two-page, single-spaced letter to Gaelan, supplying him with detailed notes on the character.

The letter begins: *The role of the Custodian is <u>absolutely crucial</u> to the success of the play. He must have a special quality: outgoing but not overly friendly, charming but professional; he has to show both authority and kindness, like a father.*

Why can't everybody just leave me alone? Gaelan wonders.

Hearing Viney come home, he quickly puts out the joint, turns on the fan, turns off the light, and burrows under the covers.

Hope's Diary, 1973:
Raising Liars

It's a joke at our house. Whenever the phone rings we must ask Llewellyn, "Are you home?" before picking up. This is because nine out of ten times the person on the other end of the line is calling to ask, "Is Dr. Jones there?"

Usually the secretary of the moment gets a nod. "Yes, he's here, just a moment, please." Dr. Jones's patients all have his home phone number, they always know where to find him, it's part of what makes him so beloved, no one is more ethical than Llewellyn Jones, M.D., when it comes to responding to other people's crises and we'd have to be bleeding from our eyeballs before he'd choose us over them.

However, there are times—rare, but they do happen—when he doesn't want to be disturbed. If he's in one of his dark moods, say, or if he's been out all night on an emergency and is trying to get some rest. In such a case the secretary says, "No, he's not here now. May I take a message?"

In waffling circumstances—when Llewellyn can't immediately assess whether the caller is indeed experiencing an emergency, a post-op complication, or something else requiring his immediate attention—L. prompts the secretary by mouthing "Who is it?" whereupon the secretary will say, "He's not available at the moment. Who's calling please?" After the secretary extracts a bit more information and then whispers it, Dr. Jones might decide to be available.

Both larken and Gaelan possess impeccable phone-answering etiquette. They've been well-schooled in this complex form of deceit.

These are the kinds of things mommies and daddies

don't share with their children: how often mommy thinks about divorce, how marriage is a weight unlike anything and it's not even about freedom it's about distance, removal, the horrible treachery conveyed without a raised voice or threatening hand. It's the weight of silence and old voices, saying, "You were always selfish. You should never have married. You are bad, bad, bad, and you will ruin these children before you're done."

I try to maintain a benevolent silence at least—although in the end it makes me so very tired, because suppressing all that subtext takes energy, and energy is a commodity I cannot afford to spend. In the end my silence isn't really about anything: There is no hidden subtext, just a great emptiness, a terrific nonthoughtfulness.

Maybe Mommy and Daddy are all right, I hope the children are thinking. Maybe they're just being quiet, the way we are sometimes.

Who knows what the hell they think? I only hope the damage is not too great.

Marry someone you can talk to, I will advise them, if I live long enough. There is nothing lonelier than the silence of marriage.

I wonder what L. is thinking. Maybe he, too, is simply being dragged under by fatigue.

Part of me wants to be out with it, though: "Must we stay married?" I want to ask, without vehemence or ire, just a simple question. "Do we have to keep on doing this? If you are only bound to me by pity, or by the anchor of obligation, then please, please, let us let it go."

But I cannot bring myself to say the words. I can only sit and watch the children color—Larken confidently applying unique, nonnaturalstic color choices to complexions and hair; Gaelan, so intent on staying in the lines; Bonnie scribbling madly and altering the narrative of the coloring books to include all manner of magical creatures.

The phone rings.

"Daddy, are you home?" Larken asks before picking up.

"No," he might answer, and remain—with us, and yet not with us.

Tonight he answers "Yes," signaling (to me anyway) his desire to get out.

"Joneses' residence, Larken speaking," I hear her say—so grown-up, my little girl—and then, "Yes, just a moment please."

And then he goes.

Tell a lie and Daddy stays. Tell the truth and Daddy leaves.

Such interesting lessons we're teaching them.

Chapter 24

Ex-pats en Route

After months of catching as catch can—quickies snatched between teaching and grading obligations; late-night trysts during Esmé's weekend visits; never waking up together, never experiencing the slow, in-sync breaths of a couple in love, a couple who has *time*—it was supposed to go like this:

She and Jon, arriving early afternoon, would put in a perfunctory appearance at Viney's; Larken would show Jon off to her siblings; he'd charm everyone with his Anglo wit and exotic accent; they'd share a meal, lingering just long enough to be polite; and then the two of them would hasten away to Dad's house, burrow in, and commence their university-subsidized, spring break holiday: a kind of adulterer's honeymoon during which they'd spend the entire week engaged in nonstop fucking, taking only the briefest of interludes to eat, drink, and watch Merchant Ivory films.

However, after dinner—during which Bonnie is distant and Gaelan is stoned—Viney insists that they all go for a drive.

"I bet Jon would enjoy seeing some of the sights before it gets dark," she offers.

Sights? Larken thinks. *What sights?* "That's nice, Viney, but Jon and I have already seen the countryside. On the way here."

"Oh, I know that, but—"

"Besides, Jon has work to do," Larken says pointedly. Jon gives her a quizzical look. "On your novel?" she prompts.

"Oh. Right," he replies, weakly.

Obviously she'll have to teach him the decoding skills this kind of situation requires.

"But you're going to be here all week, aren't you?" Viney asks. "Come on, let's just take a little drive. It'll be fun."

The expression on Viney's face is so deadpan and the layers of subtext are so labyrinthine and inscrutable that Larken begins to wonder if her wish for an evil stepmother has finally come true.

It's unprecedented for Larken to find herself piloting a High-Occupancy Vehicle. The last time she traveled with more than one other person in the car was in childhood, during the days of Going-Away Clover-Leaf-in-Sunshine Daddy and Coming-Home Cherry-Float Hope.

It's March, and even though the air still feels wintry and damp, the roadside ditches are showing signs of life: flowerlet-shaped clumps of leaves, fuzzy and whitish-green, have just broken the surface of the earth and are squatting atop the mud; from their centers, tall verbascum stalks will arise in mid-summer: slender, dotted with yellow flowers the size of small buttons, heavy with bees.

"I've never lived anywhere but Emlyn Springs," Viney is saying from her position in the front passenger seat; Gaelan, Bonnie, and Jon are wedged together in the back. "It's nothing fancy, but it's home. I can't imagine what it would be like to live so far away from where you were born."

"Well, it definitely gives you a distinct perspective," Jon replies. "The good and the bad are cast in sharp relief, that's sure."

Larken checks her watch again. She wishes she could get to the two-pound bag of M&M's in her purse, *melts in your mouth, not in your hands*. She doesn't usually think about food when she's with Jon, but at this moment she could use the sedating effects of refined sugar to take the edge off her impatience and boredom.

They've already toured the pathetic sights of town, with Viney narrating bits of Emlyn Springs history, pointing out the school, the library, the churches, the historic buildings that the community hopes to renovate in partnership with their sister city, blah-blah . . .

Now—and again at Viney's request—they're on the highway, traveling toward Lincoln. Larken has begun to feel as though she's been unwittingly enlisted to drive the getaway car for a cell block of escaping felons. Her siblings are awfully quiet back there.

Jon, on the other hand, is being extremely polite, charming, indulgent—all the things Larken expected, and which under different circumstances she'd find charming. And yet, his infallibly good manners are beginning to irritate; it is his apparent interest in all this shit that's encouraging Viney to persist in her newfound role as tour guide. More to the point, it's keeping the two of them from getting between the sheets.

"Do you ever miss England?" Viney asks.

"Yes," Jon replies without hesitation. Larken is surprised; she's never heard Jon express anything but contempt—albeit gentle—for his homeland. Also, the expediency and sureness of his response troubles her. "Certainly not the government policies or the way Britain's PM seem to be in bed with America. Sorry, Mrs. Closs. No offense."

"None taken," Viney replies, airily. "Please call me Viney."

"What I *do* miss is hard to articulate," Jon goes on. "I suppose it has to do with how memories reside in place. Does that make sense?"

"You bet."

"I don't think it's possible to ever have the same deep feeling for place that we had in childhood."

Viney hums and nods. Clearly, she likes Jon very much. This should be a good thing, but it's becoming harder and harder for Larken to stoke the sparks of illicit lust for a man who insists on being so *nice*.

Briefly inclining her left temple against the cool window glass, Larken looks up and out. Overhead, the geese are migrating: large flocks pass over them, one after another. Their formations look raggedy, disorganized—as though their V has been penned by a weak, unsteady hand.

They're approaching the Vance farm, with its long bordering row of cedar trees minus one. It occurs to Larken that no one besides the people of Emlyn Springs knows the history behind this stand of trees and its absent fellow—and sometimes even they forget.

"Why don't we turn around here," Larken suggests. "Head back."

"That would be fine," Viney replies. "But oh! I haven't seen Clara for a long time. Do you mine if we stop? Just for a minute so I can say hello?"

The question seems to be directed at Larken, so she replies, "No, of course not."

She parks the car. Gaelan and Jon are quickly unhooked from their seat belts and standing outside, stretching, chatting. Bonnie remains huddled in the center backseat.

"I'm sure Clara would love to see you, too," Viney says to Larken. "Come on up to the house with me."

Larken sighs. "Sure." But Viney is out of the car and hippety-hopping away before she can even unbuckle her seat belt. She turns to face Bonnie. "You coming, Bon?"

"No," Bonnie snips. She's pouting, mad about who knows what, engaged in a sullen stare-down with her kneecaps.

Larken sighs again, feeling more and more beaten down by the way the day's events have played out. "Fine."

Her body no longer buzzing with lustful intent, she heaves herself out of the car and starts plodding toward the farmhouse. Behind her, there's a burst of laughter from Jon. Up ahead, Viney has already arrived and is ringing the doorbell, gesturing Larken to hurry up. Her big, scooping, come-hither movements have the effect of warping time and space: The front door suddenly appears to be miles and miles away instead of only a few hundred feet.

Larken trudges on.

Jon's right: The smells of this landscape have had an imprinting effect—regardless of how she feels about the landscape itself. The scent of the air today—damp, undercut with the heavy warm odors of manure and wet hay—has become an unaccustomed one for Larken, and yet it is so familiar that she is enveloped with a longing that is both potent and beyond the ability of language to describe.

Clara Vance is standing at the open door chatting with Viney as Larken makes her approach.

"Larken!" she cries. "How nice to see you!" Mrs. Vance is in her sixties—a contemporary of Larken's parents—and she still bears a slight disfiguring scar on her upper lip where Larken's father removed and biopsied a large mole thirty-some years ago.

"Hello, Mrs. Vance," Larken says. "It's good to see you, too. How's Mr. Vance?"

"Oh, fine, just fine. He's over at the Co-op. He'll be so sorry he missed you."

Larken still remembers what Mrs. Vance's mole meant to Gae and her: It was a terrifying possibility that exploded into their lives in the form of a new and ugly-sounding word—*cancer*—and threatened to change everything, because after all, if Mrs. Vance could get cancer, so could anybody's mom or dad. But the mole turned out to be benign: a meteor that unaccountably veered off course just as it was about to obliterate the earth.

She was lucky, Dad said, in a voice that made it sound like he wasn't sure this luck would last.

But it did. And here she still is.

"How are the grandkids?" Larken asks.

"Oh, thanks for asking. I was just telling Viney, they're wonderful . . ."

Harold Vance was so grateful—as if Dad himself were responsible for the happy outcome—that he gifted the Jones family with a side of venison that took up the better part of their freezer for over two years, constantly reminding Larken that gratitude = food and food = gratitude.

"We don't see them nearly enough now that the kids have moved away," Mrs. Vance continues. "I don't think there's a grandparent in the world who feels like they get enough of their grandchildren—but they get back at Christmas and during the summer, and Harold and I try to get away and see them whenever we can."

Maybe there's only so much good luck in the world, Larken thought at the time. *Maybe luck is like a pie, and if you get a big piece it means somebody else gets a little piece, or none at all.* That's how it felt anyway, because just a little while after Mrs. Vance's mole was pronounced *benign*—another word whose sounds are so perfectly suited to its meaning—they found out that Hope was sick. Their mother, as it turned out, was *not* lucky.

Realizing that Mrs. Vance is looking past her, Larken turns; Gaelan and Jon are leaning against the car in an attitude of nonchalant vigilance—the way teenage boys stand when they're sharing a joint in the school parking lot. Gaelan looks past Jon's shoulder and waves. "Hi, Mrs. Vance!" he calls happily.

Mrs. Vance waves back. "Hi, Gaelan!" Returning her sweet lopsided smile to Larken, she remarks, "It looks like you have a visitor."

"That's Larken's friend, Jonathan," Viney interjects. "He's visiting for the week."

Larken can actually *see* Mrs. Vance formulating—and then rejecting—dozens of questions before she nods and remarks, "How nice."

"Well, we won't keep you, Clara," Viney says. "But I did want to invite you to that planning commmitte meeting I told you about."

"I've been meaning to get more involved," Mrs. Vance says apologetically. "I'll definitely try to be there."

"Planning committee? For what?" Larken asks once she and Viney start heading back. With suspicious suddenness, Jon and Gaelan move away from the car, toward the stand of cedars and the fields beyond. Jon makes a show of shouldering his camera and starts taking photos. Maybe they really *were* sharing a joint.

"Fancy Egg Days," Vine replies. "Everyone's very excited about putting our best foot forward."

"Right." Bonnie is getting out of the backseat. She starts strolling in the opposite direction from Jon and Gaelan.

"Don't be surprised if someone tries to get you to sign up for something while you're here," she adds, taking Larken by the arm and nudging her playfully. "Maybe even me."

"Thanks for the warning."

Bonnie stops, kneels. She's found one of those makeshift roadside shrines.

"Your dad would be real happy," Viney adds wistfully. "Hope, too."

Returning the flimsy toppled cross to its vertical position, Bonnie firms some earth around its base, rearranges the plastic flowers.

"What's the matter, honey?" Viney asks. "Are you upset about something?"

"No, I'm fine. I'm just gonna wait in the car."

Gaelan has hiked out to the bumpy stretch of land they used to call Babe's Meadow Muffins; heroically backlit by the sunset, he's straddling the space between two mounds and is staring at the sky; Viney starts toward him. Bonnie is still on her knees. Jon is wandering around taking photos of the pines, the small withered hillocks, the empty fields.

Could there be a more depressing landscape than that of Nebraska in mid-March? Larken wonders.

Retrieving her purse, she settles into the driver's seat, pulls out the M&M's, and begins to self-medicate.

It is May 1978, and the eldest daughter of Hope and Llewellyn Jones is once again—and for the last time thank God since she'll be too old next year—adamantly resisting her parents' suggestion that she enter the Little Miss Emlyn Springs pageant. Ever optimistic, but, Larken can tell, increasingly desperate, it's a suggestion they've made every June since 1975.

Honey, you're smart, you're pretty, you're gifted, they'd say in a script they seemed to drag out every year and perform with slight variations. *I/We just don't understand why you don't want to.*

That year they've each found occasion to appeal to her in private:

Do it for Daddy, Hope enjoined her with forced gaity. *You know how much he loves seeing you get all pretty and dressed up.*

Do it for your mother, her father pleaded—and then added darkly, *This may be the last year she can come.*

Usually Larken has been able to put them off after a few attempts, but this year, Hope has been especially persistent. She will not let it go.

At the moment, Larken is sitting at her mother's writing desk, flat-out ignoring her. The household bills are due and Mom's right hand is taking one of its impromptu vacations, so Larken is writing the checks this month. This means that she's cornered, literally, a captive audience.

"I just don't understand why you don't want to be part of this," Hope is saying, "especially since it's your last chance."

"You do, too," Larken says tersely. Sitting around nagging her about the Little Miss Emlyn Springs pageant seems to be the only thing Hope has any energy for. The house is a mess. She really wishes her mother would shut up and leave her alone so she can get done with this; there's still a load of laundry to get started and then she has to figure out what to fix for supper. "Is Dad gonna be home tonight?" she mumbles, hoping to lead her mother to another subject.

"No," Hope replies.

Larken is relieved. Her father's presence at the dinner table— infrequent as it is—always ups the ante at suppertime and means she has to fix something special. With him gone, they can make do with Hamburger Helper or something.

"You're right," Hope admits. She falls silent long enough for Larken to hope that the discussion is finally over. "But that doesn't mean we can't address your concerns!" she adds, rallying.

Larken has two objections: First, she's watched enough Miss America pageants to know that she does not now nor is she ever likely to have beauty queen proportions, never mind that Little Miss Emlyn Springs contestants are between the ages of twelve and fourteen and in many cases still don't even have *breasts* (although this is not Larken's situation; she got her period, her size six feet, her five-foot, two-inch height, and her big stupid tits before anyone else, at the age of eleven). They're not, thank God, required to participate in a swimsuit competition, but they *are* required to demonstrate runway modeling skills while wearing *princess heels* and *nylon stockings* and some kind of bridesmaid-type dress with lots of ditz and froo-froo. And no matter what anybody says to the contrary, Larken knows that no one's going to give a Miss Anything crown to a short pudgy girl with big boobs because there's no way they can look anything but stupid and even pudgier wearing spaghetti straps and ruffles.

Then there's the talent. Larken already knows most of the other contestants and can easily guess what their talents will be: Mary Margaret Ellsworth will play the piano, Vicky Davies will do ballet, Jennifer McAllister will do gymnastics, and Tracey Hindemuth will sing or dance or act or all three; she can do everything and everybody knows she's going to win anyway, so why bother?

"My point is," her mother is saying, "the same kind of girls enter these contests year after year, and I don't mean to sound unkind, but you know what I mean, doing the same kinds of talents, and . . . well, you're *different,* Larken, and don't smirk, I know you hate hearing that, but it's true, and one day you'll thank me for pointing it out."

Larken hears her mother get to her feet and—with the aid of the aluminum walker Larken picked up at Beatrice Medical Supply last week—start shuffling across the room. Larken experiences a familiar self-hatred born out of the fact that she can write checks, drive a car, fix dinner, and walk across a room without any assistance.

Hope starts petting her hair. "I just wish you'd stop . . . hiding your light under a bushel basket, that's all."

"The same girls always win because they're good, Mom. And they're pretty, not different."

Larken feels her mother lean against the back of the chair. "First of all, we can design a dress that you like, a dress that looks fantastic on you and has no ruffles whatsoever. Draw a picture for me."

"Mom."

"No, now listen. We don't have to go up to Beatrice and get something off the rack, I can make something."

Larken closes the checkbook and turns to face her. "How are you gonna make a dress, Mom? You barely have enough energy to walk across the room." Larken knows it's a cruel thing to say, but she doesn't care. She just wants her mother to shut up and if being mean to her is what it will take, then so be it.

"I appreciate your concern," Hope says, her voice even and devoid of irony, "but you let me worry about that. Now"—the floor creaks as Hope shifts her weight—"the talent. I've been thinking about this. You're plenty good at piano—"

"Mom—"

"—but I know you don't want to play piano, or sing, or anything like that, so I was thinking"—Hope reaches into Larken's field of view and presents a book: *The Norton Anthology of American Poetry*—"how about reciting a poem?"

"What?" Larken has never heard a more stupid idea.

"You have such a strong speaking voice, honey."

"No, I don't," Larken replies, horrified. "Who says?"

"It's plenty strong when you believe what you're saying, when you want to make a point."

"Like when?"

"Like when you ran for student council."

"And lost," Larken reminds her.

Hope toddles to the nearest chair and sits.

". . . or when you're at one of Gaelan's games . . ."

"Mom . . ."

". . . or when you're walking out of the house wearing the same outfit you've worn three days this week and your mother is trying to get you to put on something else."

Hope is deadpan for a moment; then she laughs. Larken hates this. Most of her fourteen-year-old peers are constantly engaged in mother-daughter battles; it's hard to fight with your mom when she finds everything all so *funny,* not to mention the fact that she's a cripple.

Hope starts looking through the book. It's painful to see. Hope's hands—whether they were playing piano or sewing or unscrewing a lid or plucking a spear of asparagus from a dinner plate—used to be graceful. They were elegant, like a movie star's. Now they're hesitant and bumbling, as if she's old. While Larken watches her mother struggle to turn the pages, a feeling stronger than pain emerges: anger. She is angry at her mother for her senile hands, and this anger makes her ashamed.

Hope's hands continue to fumble with the book. It smells musty, as if it's been buried in a compost pile.

"What about this one?" Hope says. "'Stopping by Woods on a Snowy Evening' by . . . Ha! You know, I never noticed that. It's like a joke, isn't it? His name being Frost . . . Here," she says, handing the book out for Larken. "Take a look and see what you think."

"Reciting poetry isn't a talent, Mom," Larken says, in spite of the fact that she hopes it is. Now that Hope has suggested it, Larken suspects that she might be good at reciting poetry.

"Of course it's a talent, darling. Nobody values poetry more than the Welsh, you know that. And doing a poem for your talent is no different than what's-her-name, that girl who won last year doing a speech from *Romeo and Juliet.*"

"Anne Gottberg. It *is* different, Mom. That's acting a part, a character. This is just . . . poetry."

"Oh, come on. Just read it out loud and see if you like it. Go slowly. Speak it the way you'd sing it."

She begins.

"Slower," Hope says. "Exaggerate the sounds."

Larken starts again.

"Slower still, sweetheart. Think of it maybe as a primer, you know? As if you're learning the words as you read them."

Larken slows way down. It feels silly at first, but at least there's just the two of them. Hope smiles and nods. Eventually she closes her eyes and before long Larken has the sensation of being alone in the room.

She lingers less self-consciously now over words like *miles* and *snow* and *deep,* reexperiencing the strange way words look on the page, becoming aware of the way that they call upon the use of muscles: mouth, tongue, cheeks, lips. She never thought about that before, how speaking words requires physical assistance, how ideas can't be expressed aloud if the body doesn't go along.

"Well?" Hope says, her eyes still closed. Her voice is fairly expressionless, but she must be clenching her teeth because Larken can see the muscles of her jaw working beneath her thin skin.

"It's okay," Larken says.

"Good," Hope replies. "That's settled, then. Be thinking about your dress. We'll talk about it after dinner." She fumbles briefly and ineffectually with the edges of her cardigan—Larken can't tell if she's trying to take it off or do up the buttons—and then emits an expulsive huffing sound and gives up.

"I just *love* solving problems," she mutters, "don't you?"

But the comment doesn't seem to be directed to Larken, and Hope's voice is strangely bitter.

Larken realizes that bringing Jon to a setting with no familial associations allows him to complete his emotional recovery—not a bad thing in and of itself, but during the week they're in Emlyn Springs, his need for dedicated therapeutic fucking definitely diminishes.

Jon also reveals himself as someone who's far more of an extrovert than she realized. He's very interested in the history of the town, in chatting up the townsfolk. He likes to get *out.*

It makes sense when she thinks about it. Jon's a novelist, after all, and a teacher of contemporary literature—not an art history professor and book-bound scholar like she is. His work requires contact with people who are still alive. She's just glad he's feeling better. He doesn't mention Mia or Esmé the entire week.

As far as the rest of the town is concerned, the not-knowing principle is fully in play. If discussions take place at all, they don't extend beyond *Doc's oldest daughter Larken is in town for the week, professor at the university on spring break, not staying at Viney's, though, she's at her dad's house. Got a friend with her, English fella, writer, colleague.* No one asks any questions that might require Jon to speak the dreaded phrases *my wife* or *my daughter.*

They take walks, have malts and burgers and fries at The Little Cheerful, drink beers and watch college basketball at Grumpy's. They visit the Co-op so Jon can study the colloquial speech of Nebraska farmers and learn about irrigation and cattle feed. They spend an entire afternoon at the Historical Society with Jon sandwiched between the Miss Williamses examining the town archives. These include a photo of *Miss Larken Jones, age 14, Little Miss Emlyn Springs, 1978.*

"You're adorable!" Jon remarks. "Larken, come here. Have a look at this."

"No thanks."

Everywhere they go Jon strikes up conversations, asks history questions, liberally bestowing his charms.

In public, they're as asexual as first cousins.

They do manage to screw, but not nearly as often as Larken had hoped, and the quality of their couplings is only slightly less restrained than it would be if Esmé were sleeping in the next room.

Larken consents to be one of the Little Miss Emlyn Springs judges, and the first meeting of the Pageant Planning Committee is held at Viney's house.

"Who should we ask to build the chair this year?" Miss Williams asks.

"Sorry," Jon interjects. "The chair?"

"It's a tradition we borrow from the *Eisteddfod,*" Miss Williams explains, "the national poetry and song competition that has been held in Wales since medieval times. *Eisteiddfod* literally means 'the chairing' and in olden times the bardic winner was allowed to sit at the royal table. Every Little Miss Emlyn Springs receives a special, one-of-a-kind chair."

"Miss Williams's father used to build them," Larken adds, remembering her own chair. Whimsical and brightly painted, as were all of Doc Williams's constructions, the chair seat and back were carved in a curving, sloped shape, made to look like a quilted hammock. Positioned along its edges, colorful carved birds held the cloth in their beaks, as if whoever sat there could expect to be lifted up.

"I think yours was the best one he ever made," Hazel muses.

Missing from most of these gatherings are Bonnie and Gaelan; Bonnie's reclusive behavior is normal, but Gaelan's reluctance to come out is concerning. He seems depressed.

On Saturday, the night before she and Jon are to head back to Lincoln, Larken invites her siblings over to her father's house to watch a movie and eat pizza.

"So what's up, Gae?" Larken asks. They're pouring drinks in the kitchen while the pizza is baking and Bonnie and Jon are setting up TV trays in the living room. "How's the studying going?"

"I quit."

"What? School?"

"No. I quit my job."

"When?"

"Last month."

"Why?"

"It's a long story."

"Viney never said a thing about it."

"That's because she doesn't know. I haven't told her."

"Gaelan—" Larken begins, but then Bonnie comes in holding the DVD case.

"This movie is rated 'R,'" she announces.

The timer goes off. "I'll get it," Gaelan says, arming himself with oven mitts.

"Yes? So?"

Bonnie reads. "'For graphic violence, strong language, and explicit sexuality.'"

"It's supposed to be good, Bon. It won an Oscar."

"I just don't think I want to stay and watch it."

"Bonnie," Larken says, taking her hand, trying to placate her, "this is our last night in town. We don't have to watch the movie if you don't want to. We can do something else. Play cards, or Scrabble, or just sit around and talk. Whatever you want."

"It's not just that," she says, avoiding Larken's eyes.

"Who wants vegetarian?" Gaelan yells.

"Not me!" Jon yells back.

Bonnie sets her jaw, looks at Larken coldly, and delivers a line that Larken senses she's been rehearsing. "I'm not comfortable with the two of you."

"You're not–?"

"You might have fooled everyone else about who he is," she whispers ferociously, "but you haven't fooled me."

Gaelan sighs. "I'm gonna step out on the porch for a minute," he says, fumbling in the pocket of his sweatshirt. "Call me when you're ready."

"I'm not trying to fool anyone," Larken says.

"He's your neighbor, isn't he? The one with the little girl?"

"Bonnie, you don't know anything about the situation."

"I know he's married."

"Yes, and you've been flat-out rude to him all week," Larken says. "And to me. What is your problem?"

Bonnie's face crumples. "What's *my* problem?" she shrieks. "I haven't got any problems! My life is just fine! My life is perfect! At least I'm not a slut! At least I'm not shacking up with some married man in Dad's house!"

She storms out onto the porch. Larken follows.

"And you!" Bonnie says to Gaelan, as she mounts her bike. "You're turning into a drug addict!"

Larken and Gaelan watch her speed away and then share a few tokes.

"She really is becoming an old maid before our very eyes," Larken observes.

Gaelan shrugs. "I can see her point."

"What do you mean?"

"It's just, well, I worry about you, being involved with a guy like that."

"'A guy like that'? That's just great, coming from you."

Gaelan's expression is hurt. "Here," he says quietly, handing her the joint. "You and Jon can finish this. I better go after her. Make sure she's okay."

So she and Jon spend the last night of their honeymoon smoking a joint, eating two large pizzas, and watching a science-fiction movie about the end of the world. They fall asleep without fooling around.

*　*　*

Sunday morning, they pack up the car first thing and then drive to Viney's to say good-bye.

Gaelan is still in bed.

"You should go upstairs and wake him," Viney says. "He'll be sad if you leave without seeing him."

Larken knocks on his door. "Gae? It's me. Can I come in?"

"Yeah," he says, his voice groggy.

The state of his room—cluttered, messy, pungent—makes her realize that there really is something wrong. "I'm sorry about last night," she says. "I want to hear more about . . . well, everything, so call me, okay?"

When she emerges from the house, Jon is across the street, pacing back and forth, listening to his cell phone, his face grim. She waves to him, gets in the car, waits. It's another five minutes before he joins her.

"Everything all right?" she asks.

"Yeah. Fine," he says, buckling in. "Let's go." His voice is reassuringly full and decisive.

They're really going now, back to their real lives, their real selves. With great relief, Larken starts speeding north.

"I had a funny dream last night," she begins, conversationally. "It was about Mia. She was—"

"Don't," Jon cuts in sharply. His tone is unequivocal, punitive, reproving—the voice of an angry Old Testament God. "Please don't speak about Mia."

Larken is terrified, so terrified that she has no idea how many miles go by before he speaks again.

"Sorry," he says more gently. "Let's just talk about something else."

And yet, even though they've always been able to speak fluently on any number of subjects besides Mia, Jon's reprimand has stolen every ounce of breath from her body.

They spend the trip back in silence.

They spend the night fucking loudly.

Hope's Diary, 1974:
Women's Lib

Funny thing happened today.

Viney and L. and the children were up in Lincoln for a football game. (I really can't bear going anymore, the noise, the crowds, the heat. I enjoy staying behind in my quiet, temperate house, sitting on the sofa wearing my red cardigan and watching the games on TV, Bloody Mary in hand. Viney doesn't really like them that much either, but she goes for L.'s sake. She told me that she's perfected a way of leaning forward into her hand and taking cat naps without L. knowing!)

Anyway, L. took the kids out for ice cream after they all had dinner and Viney went to the university bookstore. She's my book-buying emissary; I reimburse her whenever she finds something new and noteworthy.

Standing in line with Joyce Carol Oates and Philip Roth in hand, something caught her eye.

"You know the way magazines are overlapped," she said later, "so you can only see the title? I was about to check out when I spotted this. I couldn't believe it. 'Hope will be so interested,' I thought. 'A whole magazine devoted to MS!'"

We laughed so hard we cried.

"I might not have bought it," she said, "except right then Welly and the kids found me and Welly got this sour look on his face" (she demonstrated this perfectly) "and grumbled, 'You're not gonna get that, are you?' And so of course I did."

God love her.

The two of us had a gay old time filling out subscription cards: one for each of us, one for Llwelyn's office, and (anonymously, as a gift) one for Estella Axthelm. Viney joked that she'd love

to lurk outside her house every day at mail delivery time for the next few weeks, just to see the
look on her face.

It was good to have a laugh.

MS Magazine.

In truth, I can't imagine anything duller or more
depressing than a magazine devoted to this damn
disease.

There is a way in which one can know a person in-
timately for a long time, love them, and then something happens, it needn't be life-shattering, just
some little thing, a face they might make at an odd
moment, a look of impatience that is never even
given language but reveals an underside they haven't
shown—not to you anyway.

Viney is in love with Llewellyn.

It was just a moment: I saw her looking at him in
a certain way. I'm not saying that she's aware of
being in love with him—I don't think she is—or of
L. reciprocating. Two more morally upright people
don't exist, and although my husband is guilty of
sins against me—just as I've wronged him—an adulterer he is not.

Sad to say, the thought that came to mind was
this: "Alvina Closs is a tramp."

This must be what people mean by the presence of
the Devil. What else could have put such a thought
in my head?

Chapter 25

The Last Artifact

Bonnie awakens one morning in April knowing that a storm—a really big one, one as dangerous as that one in the 1800s they still talk about, *the children's blizzard,* because it caught unawares and killed so many little ones—is moving into southeastern Nebraska.

She puts on snow boots and steps out of the woodshed. The sky is laundry-softener blue, infused with sunshine, cloudless. No wind. Temps in the low fifties.

After a snowy, subzero winter, it will feel so warm to the kids that some of them—especially the teenagers—will leave their jackets at home. Never mind hats and gloves.

Bonnie closes her eyes, gets quiet, sniffs.

An hour. Maybe an hour and a half. That's when it will start to change.

They are hers, all of them, even if she did not give birth to them. Why else would she have this gift, this painful sensitivity to the wind and the weather it foretells, if not for this: to protect the embodiment of her town's hopes from harm?

Quickly, she gets dressed. She checks on the Williams girls and lets them know that they shouldn't worry if she doesn't get back to the woodshed tonight; a snowstorm is coming and she may end up staying the night at the shop.

"Goodness!" Hazel says, looking up. "Do you really think it's going to snow? So late in the year?"

"I'm sure of it, Miss Williams," Bonnie says. "Do you have everything you need in case the power goes out?"

"Oh, yes," Wauneeta says. "How about you?"

"I'm fine, but I'm wondering if you have any extra warm hats and gloves I could borrow?"

"Certainly. Get a bag from the kitchen, will you, Wauneeta?" Wauneeta waddles down the hall while Hazel opens the hall closet and starts pulling out numerous scarves and hats and gloves and mittens. The Williams girls are big knitters. "What do you need them for?"

"I'm on my way over to school. If the weather does turn, have a feeling that some of the children might need them."

"Oh! Of course!"

Wauneeta returns with a big plastic garbage bag that the three of them stuff to capacity. Bonnie slings it over her shoulder. *"Diolch yn fawr!"* she calls.

"Croeso!" Hazel and Wauneeta reply.

The Emlyn Springs K–12 School is several blocks away. Weighed down with the large bag of woolens, Bonnie moves more slowly than she expected, so when she passes through downtown, she stops at the grocery and asks Gwilym Moore if she can borrow a cart.

"Sure, Bonnie. What's in the bag?"

"Scarves and hats," she says, breathlessly. *"Faint o'r gloch yw hi,* Mr. Moore?"

"Mae hi'n ddeg o'r gloch," he says. "Maybe five past."

She slings the bag into the cart. *"Diolch!"* she calls, already hurrying away.

"Pob hwyl, Bonnie!" he replies.

Soon after, the sky begins to change color. The clouds materialize out of nowhere, as if they've amassed far above the jet stream and then been dropped over town: a gray, stain-mottled tent ceiling.

The storm moves in with frightening rapidity after that; she makes it to school just as the blizzard starts to show itself for the blinding, malevolent threat it really is. The wind is knifelike now and willful; once inside, Bonnie has to lean into the door, driving her body sideways against it to get it closed again.

As she heaves the plastic bag out of the cart and into the school office, she hears the school secretary, Carys Janssen, talking on the two-
way radio. She's speaking with Lars Gruffudd, Emlyn Springs' bus
driver. He's on his way. The principal, Gareth Peterson, is on the PA
system, announcing that school will be closing and students and teachers should get home as quickly as possible.

"Bonnie," Carys says when she gets off the two-way. "What are you
doing here? This isn't one of your tutoring days."

"No, I know; I was just worried about the kids getting home."

Carys looks puzzled. "Well, everybody's folks have been notified and
Lars is on his way. The roads aren't bad yet, so it should be fine. You
really oughta get yourself on home. These spring storms, you know how
they are."

"I think I'll stay in case you need another adult around."

"Fine with me, honey, but we're gonna get everybody out of here as
soon as we can."

Parents begin arriving; students and teachers start to leave. Bonnie
stations herself and her bag of woolens at the main entrance, making
certain that all exiting children are properly weatherproofed.

Mr. Peterson rounds up the bus riders and herds them into the cafeteria. "Why don't you head on home, Carys?" he says. "I know you've
got a good ways to go."

"Oh, thanks, Gareth," she replies with relief, and she's in her coat and
out the door.

"I'll start calling these kids' folks," Bonnie offers. "Let them know
they'll be late."

She goes into the office and pulls out a school directory. The phone
rings just as she's about to pick it up: It's the police calling to say that
Lars hit an icy patch making a turn off Bridge Street and slid halfway
down the slope of the ravine. He's okay, just a few cuts and bruises, but
the paramedics are taking him to Beatrice.

Bonnie heads to the cafeteria. The children are sitting around in small
groups, faces flushed and shiny from being bundled up so long in the
heat. Mr. Peterson is sitting on the edge of the stage floor with a couple
of the older kids, playing cards. Bonnie catches his eye and signals him
closer. His face turns somber when he hears the news.

"That means we've got twelve children here who don't have a way to get home tonight."

"I'll take them," Bonnie offers. "I'll walk them over to the shop—it's just a couple of blocks—and they can wait with me there until their folks come."

"Are you sure?" Mr. Peterson looks dubious. "I'd let them stay here, you know, but I still need to get over to Wymore and pick up my wife at work; we've only got the one car."

"We'll be fine."

Mr. Peterson buttons coats and turns up collars. Bonnie distributes hats and gloves and mittens to those who need them. Then the adults begin tethering the children firmly to one another using the Misses Williamses' woolen scarves until they form a long, colorful line. Finally, Bonnie lashes herself to the front—like the lead sled dog in an Iditarod.

And so they make their way, heads down against the tantrum-throwing wind and the spitting snow. It takes them ten minutes to go two blocks.

Bonnie ushers the children inside, cranks up the electric heater, and puts the kettle on. They're safe now. While waiting for the water to boil, she massages cold hands and faces and feet.

Blind Tom greets them and starts bringing in armfuls of felted wool piano covers for the children to wrap themselves in.

Bonnie makes hot chocolate and Jiffy Pop. When a discussion about which video to watch leads to a standoff, Blind Tom makes an executive decision.

"We're watching *Monsters, Inc.,*" he proclaims. "There's something in there for everybody."

By one o'clock, the worst of the blizzard is over; by two, the snow stops falling, and by three, Hal Sigurdson, city employee and operator of Emlyn Springs' sole snow plow, is on the job and making his way down Main Street.

"You know how to drive in snow?" Blind Tom asks.

"Absolutely. My sister taught me."

"Let's take these kids home, then."

Bonnie puts twelve-year-old Alyssa Critchfield in charge of getting everyone ready while she and Blind Tom go out through the back door and start digging out the van. He's so competent that she half-forgets about his disability.

They load up the children, head out on Main Street to the highway, and then follow the DOT snowplow that's already clearing the highway.

"This van drives nice," Bonnie remarks.

"You're a good driver," Blind Tom replies.

By the time they deliver all the children and get back to the bike shop, it's nearly seven o'clock.

"Would you like to join me and Sergei for dinner?" Blind Tom asks.

Bonnie finally notices what it is that is so different about Blind Tom tonight: He's not wearing dark glasses. His eyes do not look like the eyes of a blind man. There is no distortion of the musculature surrounding them, no disfiguring scars. Blind Tom's eyes are blue and perfect.

"Sure," she says. "I'm not in any hurry."

"Canned soup okay?"

"You bet. I can make smoothies, too, if you like. I'll just make sure the kids got everything out of the van."

"See you inside, then."

Children leave so many traces of themselves, and in such a short time: The seats are a mess of crumbs and unmated mittens and forgotten homework and gum wrappers. Wondering if there might be some cleaning supplies on board, Bonnie opens up the back of the van. She finds a broom and a dustpan and an empty box, which she converts to a "lost and found" bin.

When she comes through the back door into the storage area, she finds that the shop is pitch black.

"Tom?"

"The power went out," he calls out from somewhere in the building. "Do you mind having cold sandwiches?"

How would he know the power is out? Bonnie wonders. She starts feeling her way toward his voice. "Where are you?"

"Keep coming."

In the dark, what was once a clear, navigable path connecting the storage area to the front of the store has become a minefield. Bonnie's feet come down on what feels like blocks of wood; she turns an ankle. Her swinging arm collides against a table edge; she bruises a wrist.

"Ow!" she cries. Rebounding against one unseen obstacle after another, a hapless human pinball, she finally comes to rest after bumping into a piano.

Then she hears Blind Tom. His footsteps sound rushed, oddly urgent. "Wait!" he calls out warningly, the way one would speak to someone who's about to step into the path of an oncoming car, or trod in bare feet across a floor littered with broken glass.

"What's wrong?"

"Just . . . wait where you are," he says, his voice unsteady. "I'll come get you."

And yet he doesn't. He stays where he is. He sounds as though he's close, just across from her. As the moments tick by, she begins to sense that his hands are on the piano, too.

Using the keyboard to orient herself, she starts trailing her fingers across the keys, from the upper register to the lower. All ivories on this one. She can tell the difference.

"Wait," he says. "It's not ready yet. It's not finished. Please wait. I'm not—" and the quality of his voice has changed; it almost sounds as though—

Wait.

Wait.

Her fingers retrace their steps. Where was it?

Here?

Here?

No, here. This one.

Bonnie closes her eyes.

Hope is in the room.

This key is called middle C, Hope says. *It's an important key on the piano and when we play, we put our bodies right in front of it. Right even with our belly buttons.*

Because it's in the middle, Bonnie answers.

Now, it's true that you can find it with your eyes, Hope says—and Bonnie remembers studying it, noticing its relationship to the black keys, but that confused her—*and you can find it with your ears*—and Bonnie remembers Hope's voice singing the note, but she cannot hold the sound in her head—*but on this piano, we're especially lucky, because there's another way to find it.*

How?
You can feel middle C with your hands.
What do you mean?
Close your eyes now, and feel. Can you tell the difference?
Bonnie's fingers explore the key. *It's not flat.*
That's right.
It's like a spoon, or the inside of a seashell, or a dish.
Yes! It's worn there, by people's fingers, can you believe that? This piano has had a very long life and been played by many, many people. And they all started as children, just like you, learning how to find middle C.
Our middle C is special.
Yes, Hope laughs. *It is.*

"Tell me your name," Bonnie says. He doesn't answer, but she can hear small, irregular intakes of breath, receding. She has the feeling now that he is backing away from her. "Stop," she commands, "stop moving please."

Sliding quickly around the piano's contours, her hands note scratches in the sleek, oiled finish, deep gouges in places, evidence of old scars, sustained injuries.

She continues feeling her way along the curved edges of the piano's flank—its top is open, its strings are exposed—until she finds him and brings her hands to his face.

"Why are you crying?"

"I forgot," he says. "It's been so long since I started working on it. I let myself forget."

"Forget what?"

"That it's for you. All along. From the beginning. I've been doing it for you."

Pulling his face toward her own, she feels the passage of years, a future lifetime unfolding, one that will be filled with this gesture and others like it.

"Don't be afraid,"she whispers, and when she kisses him, she realizes that the last artifact is not even this piano—her mother's piano, conjured into rebirth by this man in this place and that is a story she will ask him to tell—but no. It is not even that.

The last artifact she will ever need to cherish is her body with his; the last miraculous discovery, one flesh.

Hope's Diary, 1975:
The Indians Say It's a Scouring

There was a tornado in Omaha this week. Horrible destruction. A malevolence that seemed to possess consciousness. It cut a straight swath down a major street. And in a city. Tornadoes usually give the impression that they prefer small towns like ours, but if they do decide to visit more densely populated areas, they stay on the fringes, picking off the mobile-home dwellers, the poorly built structures, the marginalized abodes.

They are snobby and elitist, these tornadoes. They have a cruelty that seems class-driven.

The Indians used to say that a tornado appeared because a cleansing was needed, a scouring. No one knows what causes them. There are theories, but no real answers.

When L. and I went up to Omaha last month, the specialist asked many questions about my birthplace and then chattered on about latitudinal forces. Did I experience much illness as a child? Was I prone to fevers?

The truth is I'm not interested in being the subject of research. I don't give a good goddamn about the other people who contract this disease in the future. I have three children and I want help now.

"You have the relapsing-remitting form, as we've discussed," the specialist said, and then added cheerily—as if I needed a dumbed-down translation—"You'll have good days and you'll have bad days. Just like the rest of us."

If something happened to one of them (oh say what you mean, you coward), if one of them died, I would see them everywhere: in the bits of gravel they bring me and dying bouquets of clover and dandelions ("This is for you, Mom")—I align them along the windowsill, these gifts, along with rocks that look gorgeously colored in the rain but become ordinary in their dried-out condition, but I can't bear the children to know, so I periodically spritz them with the laundry sprinkler; their drawings, their stray socks. Even if the house were scoured of all traces, the absence of them would scream incessantly.

So when I imagine my own death, I imagine the traces I'd leave for them, things that would take on significance beyond what they would normally have.

I have a terrible impulse during the day—when Larken and Gaelan are gone and Viney's daughter is watching Bonnie and there's nothing to distract me from the clutter, the chaos, the chores I'm too tired to do, the visual reminders everywhere that I have failed, failed, failed to go about with a large bag and start emptying the house of everything. Throw it all away.

Erasure, that's what I long for. If I leave nothing of myself behind, mightn't I lessen their grief?

If I could, I'd just disappear, evaporate. Poof! A magic trick! I don't want them looking for me after I'm dead. I don't want them remembering me with the assist of scrapbooks or photo albums. I want them to carry me in the air they breathe.

When I think of baby time—and it wasn't that long ago—my mind relaxes. Even last week seems simpler and less cluttered than this one. One minute ago the mountain of laundry was smaller, the stack of dirty dishes didn't tower so. Piles of clothes and toys and books and papers and bills and envelopes and lists and toys. So much clutter. I feel myself becoming walled in by all of it, and yet I have no strength to tear it down. Ironically, a counterbalance to all this acquisition is taking place within my body. The insulation is coming off. The equivalent of shedding skin except it is nerve ends that are being exposed.

Maybe I could train my eyes to stay firmly focused on one small spot, one tiny area of the house that needs tending. One pile. One stack.

L. keeps asking me if I don't want him to hire a cleaning lady. I keep refusing.

I am still angry at him. I will, I fear, always be angry at him.

And so even though one part of me wants the house to reflect this inner condition, to be as bare and denuded as my nerve cells, another part of me wants my husband to walk in the door every single day on his two perfectly functioning finely turned legs and be reminded that his wife is wasting away from a disease that he hid from her for years.

Nothing is hiding now. It's all out in the open. The whole damn mess.

What's easiest, though, is not to scour everything away or be angry but simply lie down—and that's what I'll probably do—and sleep, and then reanimate, like Sleeping Beauty, when the children come home.

Company is becoming unbearable. Of course, intentions are good and worthy and of the highest Christian caliber, but still, the dynamic of normal social interaction has been obliterated by this stupid, stupid disease. Conversation—any attempt at small talk—is overtaken by context, the context of me, dying, albeit slowly and beautifully.

"But you don't look sick!" is the favored refrain from my visitors. They all arrive at this

pronouncement, sooner or later. Who can blame them
for their confusion? Aren't dying people supposed
to have an unsavory smell, manifest a certain toxic
green tinge around their parameters, like bad
beef?

I say that I crave normal social interaction, but
that's a lie. Once we manage to get beyond the "how
are you feeling is there anything I can do for you"
litany, there's not much left but for me to listen.
And then, whenever someone tries to tell me honestly about their life, about whatever challenges
they face—and we both sense it—I can't help but
become uppity.

"Your husband's arthritis makes it impossible for
him to mow the grass?" I want to scoff. "Your son
is failing algebra? Your daughter is smoking mari-
juana? Oh come on. Don't waste my time. Come back
when you have REAL problems to talk about . . ."

I hate being this way but in most instances it's
true: I do have it worse than almost anyone who
comes through the front door. Sometimes I long for
the company of a cancer patient, a Vietnam vet. I'd
enjoy sitting in an ICU with someone who's brain-
dead. At least we could coexist honestly.

The children are the only ones whose problems are
bigger than mine. To live with the foreknowledge
of your mother's death, what could be worse than
that?

"Why do we need to tell them?" Llewellyn implored,
when I insisted that we not keep it to ourselves
any longer. "Can't we wait?"

"Wait until what?" I countered, pulling that card
that is always in hand. "Until I'm dead?"

Talk about uppity. He'll never have anything to
trump the fact that he lied to me for years. It is
a wonderful, terrible thing, having this kind of
power in a marriage. I've grown into a villainess,

a pickled caricature, emasculating my husband by refusing to forgive him.

"Wait until you can reinvent me however you please?" I went on. "Until I'm not here to contradict you, to speak for myself? Wait until I'm so far gone that I have no sight, no words, no ability to explain myself?"

You jest. You joke. You are so full of shit.

How far I've come in these pages from Dear Diary and cooing over my sweet babies.

Poor me, poor me.

And so we told them. We did it together one night last week after dinner—and believe me, I made sure the phone was off the hook that night! We presented a unified front, although I was the one who did all the talking and I'm sure that fact did not escape the children's notice. They see everything.

The thing is—and maybe I sensed this, maybe this is the real reason I wanted them to know—the children are the only ones I can really talk to about the illness. They haven't yet been spoiled by the veneer of civility. Their emotions on the subject of death are still raw and untempered. They don't spare my feelings. They don't pussyfoot around my disability or pretend that having a sick mother isn't the biggest pain in the ass imaginable. I'm still Mommy.

Bonnie even still has the residue of my actual flesh and blood swimming around in her tissues, and will until she's eight. I read that somewhere, or heard it.

"When are you going to die?" Larken asked. Their questions, and their respective styles of inquiry reveal so much about who they are.

"I don't know. Sorry. I wish I did."

"Will I have to cook for everybody when you're dead?"

"Probably. Even before that, maybe. You and Gaelan."

"And pay bills and do laundry and stuff like that?"

"I expect so. That's one of my jobs, and some days, you know, my hands don't work so well."

"That stinks."

"I agree."

Gaelan has been mostly quiet this past week, observant. He likes to fix snacks for me, bring me glasses of water.

"Read to me," I ask him.

"What do you want to hear?"

"How about the comics?"

He pins me down with those soul-deep eyes, ignores my request, and instead reads to me of medical miracles, human interest stories.

"You're not going anywhere," Bonnie said last night. "I won't let you."

Crack goes the heart. The crack heard round the world.

Chapter 26

Bar Mitzvah

It's been easy to avoid her since that night back in January. He's changed his running route so that he no longer passes their farm. If he sees her car—at the grocery store, say, or the bank—he simply executes a covert about-face.

His continuing ability to give her the slip has ceased to be a relief, however, and instead becomes a worry. He's realized that success at this kind of long-term evasion wouldn't be possible in a town as small as Emlyn Springs unless she, too, is successfully employing evasive tactics; the likelihood that she doesn't want to see him as much as he's pretending to not want to see her is depressing.

All of this means that when he answers the door one rainy afternoon in late May, the last person he expects to see is Bethan Ellis.

"I'm returning books to the library, that's why I'm here," she announces.

"Okay."

"That's why I'm in town."

"You wanna come in?"

"No thank you," she says, but then she casts a few nervous glances over her shoulder as if she's afraid someone might see her. "At least, not to stay." She steps into the living room, but doesn't venture off the doormat. "Is Viney home?"

"No, she's taking a class at the community center."

Bethan nods.

Gaelan indicates his appearance. "Sorry I'm so . . . I've been work-ing out."

Her face hardens.

"You sure you don't want to sit down?" Gaelan adds.

"I've really struggled with this," she begins, eyes downcast, arms folded in a way that makes her look like a truculent, unrepentant school-girl who's been sent to the corner for no good reason. "He'd be so upset if he knew I was here."

"He who?"

She works her lips against her teeth for a few seconds, clearly ex-pressing some inner mind-versus-body conflict before finally coming out with it:

"Are you going to audition for the play?"

"What?"

"Eli's play. *Our Little Wales.* The one they're doing for Fancy Egg Days. The one he's been talking to you about since Christmas. Are you going to try out?"

Gaelan has been imagining a number of reasons to account for her presence, scripting possible exchanges. For example:

B: *How is your shoulder feeling? Have you been doing your physical therapy?*

G: *I have. It's feeling really good.*

Or possibly,

B: *Do you remember what I asked you in the ER waiting room? Can I tell you about my marriage now?*

G: *I do. Absolutely.*

Or finally,

B: *Do you still want to sleep with me?*

G: *Yes. Yes. Yes.*

He's not prepared for this.

"Gaelan," Bethan says. "A simple yes or no is all that's required."

"No."

She bites her lip. "Okay. You need to tell him."

"Why?"

"Why? Because he's twelve years old, that's why. Because his father is inconveniently dead at the very time he's trying to understand what it means to be a man. Because he obviously wrote the role hoping that . . ."

She's been accelerating in volume and intensity, but with another exertion of will, she brings herself to a full stop.

"Because he signed you up," she concludes. "This Sunday at four-fifteen."

"And I was going to learn about this how?"

She sighs. "I don't know, Gaelan. He doesn't really talk to me all that much these days. Maybe he was going to call you. Maybe he was going to come over here again. Maybe he was planning an abduction. I have no idea. I only just happened to see a copy of the audition list on his desk when I brought his laundry into his room."

"I'm sorry," Gaelan begins, "I wish I—"

"Listen," she breaks in, "you don't have to do the play, that's not what I'm asking. But you do have to give him an answer, Gaelan. Being evasive . . . it's just not what he needs right now, or even understands. So please, just look him in the eye and tell him that you can't do it. Say whatever you want about why—you're too busy studying, you don't think you can do the role justice, being on stage is different from being on television, whatever—just tell him. Can you do that?"

"Yes," he says, even though he doesn't think he can.

"Thank you. That's all I came by to say really."

Turning up the collar of her raincoat, she starts to leave, but before she can step off the porch she turns back to face him.

"Here's what you should know. I think he's trying to do *gemilut chasadim*."

"A what? What does that mean?"

"He's studying to be bar mitzvah, you know that, right?"

"Yes."

She smiles for a moment, accessing some private memory. "He and Leo used to talk about this a lot . . . One of the things being bar mitzvah means is that you can't just do nice things for people when you feel like it; once you're a man, you're *commanded* to do good deeds, *mitzvot*."

"How do you know all this?"

"I converted. You didn't know that, I guess."

It's not phrased as a question, but he answers anyway. "No," he says, beginning to take in the extent of what he doesn't know about her.

"Anyway, one type of mitzvah is called *gemilut chasadim*—acts of loving-kindness—and one of those acts involves visiting someone who has lost a loved one. It's the mitzvah of *nichum aveilim*. The mitzvah of comforting mourners. So all these visits to you, these overtures, they're his way of . . . I don't know. Just let him know about the play, okay?"

She hurries off the porch and into her car before he can make a reply. It's only after he watches her drive away that he wonders if anyone is performing this loving kindness, this mitzvah of comfort, for her, or for her son.

The school year nears its end. Arthur has recovered his speech and partial use of his left side—although he's still using a walker. He's been home for several months. Larken hasn't yet been invited to visit—recovery from a stroke is surely a long, laborious process, one that precludes social visits—but Arthur and Eloise have started putting in an occasional appearance on campus, so she sees them there.

She's still teaching Arthur's classes, but with the return of his strength, he's offered to lighten her load by grading quizzes and exams. It's a huge help, and clearly it cheers him to feel useful.

Out of the hospital, their encounters have been brief. Larken stops by his office whenever she notices that he and Eloise are in residence. Eloise greets her in her usual, chirpy manner—"Hello, dear! How goes the battle? Do you have time for a cup of tea?"—while Arthur's acknowledgments are less effusive: "Larken. Good to see you." He does tend to speak in slow, truncated sentences, and the grandiose quality of his voice is slightly diminished—but his mind seems as sharp as ever and his eyes have regained their familiar, reassuring brilliance.

She has not queried him on the topic of the department chairmanship—Arthur is on the selection committee and it would be inappropriate to do so—but presumably he is well enough to have participated in the voting process. He'll be one of the first to know the outcome.

Each time Larken sees him she examines his expression closely, trying to detect a mischievous twinkle, a suppression of pride. She's been the beneficiary of such looks from Arthur before—when she was awarded a position on the faculty, when she passed her orals for her MFA, when she received her doctorate—so she knows exactly what to look for.

So far, she has not found it.

On an afternoon in mid-May, she is summoned to the chairman's office.

"You probably know why you're here," he begins, once Larken settles into the chair across from his desk. "It was a tough decision, but the committee went with Mirabella."

"Sorry?" She's sure she's misheard him.

"Of course you were on the short list, Larken," he says amendingly, his tone a parody of unctuousness, "and you shouldn't take this as any kind of affront. Your contribution to the faculty is hugely important."

"I don't understand. Can you explain the committee's thinking?"

"Well, your scholarship is unquestionably first rate, and of course you've been here longer than anyone except Arthur, but the committee felt it was important to have a chairperson who demonstrates a certain flexibility, as well as strength under duress."

What is this bullshit?

"To be honest," he continues, "your performance this year hasn't exactly been up to its usual level of excellence. I know you've had some personal issues . . ."

Hell YES personal issues! she wants to shout. *My father died, my stepmother had a nervous breakdown, my brother quit his job, my sister is a nut case . . .*

". . . and all of that was taken into account, but at the same time, you've never shown any interest in traveling—"

"I don't remember 'must be willing to fly' being part of the job description," she remarks, making no effort to excise the sarcasm from her voice.

Richard brings one of his hands up to his mouth and rubs at the lower part of his face as if erasing an inappropriate, telling expression. When he lowers his hand and speaks again, his look is one of diplomatic blandness. "I'm sure you can understand how that kind of handicap would make it difficult for you to fulfill some of the responsibilities required of the department chair. I'm speaking, of course, about the trip to England."

"Oh, right," Larken says, holding fast to bitterness because if she doesn't she might crumble. "That's *really* what this is all about, isn't it?

That trip. After all I've done for this department and these students. I can't believe this . . ."

He smiles, folds his hands, leans toward her. "It's not the fear of flying per se, Larken, it's the way you mishandled the situation, the fact that you signed on for the trip knowing that you had this handicap—"

"I signed on because Eloise asked me to." Larken hates the pleading tone in her voice. "I signed on," she repeats, with forced restraint, "out of loyalty."

"I understand that, Larken, and yet you didn't make any effort to handle your condition with medication, or whatever it would have required. Mirabella did an admirable job, considering the situation . . ."

". . . I'm sure she did . . ."

". . . but nonetheless, those students and their parents were short-changed. I took a lot of heat over the fact that what those families were promised—not to mention *paid for*—and what they received was very different."

"So what you're saying is that this is really all about you."

He speaks with a weary patience. "No, Larken. I wasn't on the committee. You know that."

"But I'm sure you managed to make your viewpoint known."

He sighs. "I daresay the person who was the most disappointed by all this was Arthur."

The space containing her lungs and heart collapses. "What?"

"He was the one who expressed doubts that you'd be able to handle the chairmanship after what happened in December. You must know that that was very, very difficult for him."

"Arthur?" she says, dazed. "Arthur?"

"I'm sorry, Larken. This must be hard news to hear."

Larken thinks back to the hospital, to Eloise standing next to him, holding his hand, asking, *Will you go?*

It was a test, Larken realizes, incredulous. All these years, she's misunderstood. She's never been special or beloved. The question— this one (*Will you go?*), maybe all of them—was posed not to a surrogate daughter, but to an intellect-in-training, a malleable protégée, a candidate.

Richard stands and makes his way to the door. "As I said, I hope in time that you'll understand . . ." He continues to speechify politely even as he's giving her the boot. After she leaves, he'll surely open up his grade book and inscribe an F next to her name.

Kris is at her desk, giving Larken an aggressively sympathetic smile, an intensely *Christian* smile. "Kiss?" she offers.

Fuck off, Larken thinks.

She starts making her way to the small room at the other end of the building where she teaches her last class of the day, a graduate seminar on the Flemish masters.

There are clusters of students lining the long hallway. They're animated, happy, passionate. As Larken passes by, a few of them lift their heads, wave, say hello, acknowledge her, but most of them are distracted and self-absorbed in the way of the young.

She becomes aware of an unusual conformity in their speech, almost a choral quality—as if their conversations are making use of a shared palette of words, as if they're all talking about the same thing.

Professor Piacenti, the students are singing.
Isn't it exciting?
Elegant Mirabella.
Italian leather shoes.
Sooo beautiful.
Chairman, chairman
Soooo authentic.
She's perfect!
Perfect
Piacenti
Chairman Piacenti
Chairman Piacenti

Larken realizes that she was never in the running for professional advancement, and not because of her slacker performance or her fear of flying. How could she have been so self-deluded? She was doomed to a failing grade by flat shoes and obesity and the most mundane and inelegant of appellations.

Chairman Jones. Could there be a less euphonic title?

After class, she skips out on her office hours. On her way to the parking lot, she sees Arthur and Eloise walking through the sculpture garden, arm in arm.

They see her. They wave.

She rushes away, without waving back.

He's running. It's Thursday—three days since Bethan's visit, three days until the audition Eli has signed him up for. He's picked up the phone numerous times, even dialed all but the last digit, and then hung up.

Why did she have to say *look him in the eye?*

He's practiced a speech, and he reviews it now:

Eli, I'm extremely flattered that you've asked me to try out for your play. You are an excellent writer. It's very good.

These statements are absolutely true. He can speak them with confidence.

Coming up with a truth beyond this has been difficult.

But I'm going to have to . . . I can't try out because . . . I'm sure there's someone else who . . . I can't do it . . . I could, but I can't . . .

And then he hits upon something:

But I'm not going to try out.

I'm not going to try.

That's true. That's straightforward. He can say that.

Gaelan checks his watch. It's nearly one, they'll be done with dinner, so he takes the turnoff he's been skipping for the past few weeks and jogs toward the Ellis farm.

He arrives just as the work hands are heading back out to the field with Bethan's father.

"*Prynhawn da,* Mr. Ellis," Gaelan says. "*Sut wyt chi?*"

"*Yn dda iawn,*" he answers formally. "*Diolch.*"

"*Mae hi'n braf heddiw,*" Gaelan adds.

Mr. Ellis regards the sky, hums doubtfully, and then asks, "*Wyt tichwilio am Bethan?*"

"No. *Rydw i yma gweld Eli.*"

"Ah." His expression is still stern, but it shifts enough for Gaelan to understand that he's more welcome if his purpose involves Eli rather than Bethan. "*Mae ef yn y tŷ,*" Mr. Ellis says, inclining his head toward the house. "*Mae ef yn dysgu bar mitzvah.*"

"*Diolch yn fawr,* Mr. Ellis."

"*Croeso.*"

Bethan answers the door. "Hello," she says, using the same laconic delivery and wearing the same indecipherable expression as her dad. Gaelan had forgotten how alike they are. "He's in Bryn's old room, the one at the front of the house."

Gaelan nods, makes his way upstairs, knocks.

"I'm studying, Mom." Eli's voice is higher than he remembered.

"It's me. Gaelan."

When Eli opens the door, he looks frankly flabbergasted. Gaelan realizes that this is the first time in the history of their encounters that Eli hasn't been prepared to see him.

"Hi."

"Hi."

"Can I come in?"

"Sure."

Eli steps aside. His room isn't the tidy habitat Gaelan had somehow expected; it's as messy as that of any twelve-year-old male. It's as messy as Gaelan's room, for that matter.

"I'm sorry I interrupted your studying," Gaelan says. "Is this a bad time?"

"No," Eli says, excavating a chair from beneath a pile of clothing and books. "You wanna sit down?"

"Thanks. Did you mom mention that I might be coming over?"

"My mom? No." Eli regards him suspiciously, and Gaelan suddenly remembers that he was supposed to keep Bethan's visit a secret.

He backpedals. "So what are you studying?"

"Oh, the usual seventh-grade stuff. Plus Hebrew."

Gaelan looks at the Xeroxed pages laid out on Eli's desk—the odd, foreign letters with their boxy, architectural shapes. He has a strong impulse to pick up the pages and turn them upside down, suspecting they'd make more visual sense to him if viewed that way. "This looks really hard."

Eli shrugs. "It's a lot like Welsh, actually."

"How so?"

"No vowels."

Gaelan nods. "You seem a little . . . down today."

"I'm fine."

"So what does this say?"

"It's my Torah portion, the section I have to recite from the book of Genesis. It's about Joseph. You've probably heard of him. You know: *Joseph and the Amazing Technicolor Dreamcoat*."

"Oh. *That* Joseph. Yeah, I've heard of him."

Eli looks down at his desk. "Joseph is the child of Jacob's old age."

It's at this moment that Gaelan notices the family photograph on the shelf next to Eli's desk. Eli wears a carefree, mischievous expression that Gaelan has never seen; it's impossible to know whether this is because he's younger, ten maybe, or because he's being contained within the circle of his parents' arms. They're all laughing. They must be at a baseball game.

"I'm sorry about your dad," Gaelan says. "I mean, I didn't know him, but he must have been really special."

"His name was Leo Mordecai Weissman. He was a professor of religious studies at the University of Washington."

"You must miss him. I know I miss my dad."

Eli looks quizzically at Gaelan for a moment and then follows his gaze to the photo. "He was a lot older than Mom, but funnier."

"It works that way sometimes."

"He taught me a lot of jokes. You wanna hear one?"

"Sure."

"Okay," Eli begins, with renewed energy. "President Bush, the pope, and the Lubavitcher rebbe are on an airplane flight to a conference of the world's most powerful and spiritual people. Suddenly, the engines fail! The captain comes to the passenger cabin and shouts, 'We're going down, and there are only three parachutes, and I'm taking this one. Good luck!'"

Gaelan watches and listens, trying to identify which parts of this funny small boy derive from Bethan, who he knows so well, and which parts are inherited from his father, who he knows not at all.

"'I'm the most powerful man in the world! I must be saved!' says President Bush. He grabs on to a parachute and jumps out the door of the plane . . ."

—and yet he does know Eli's father, somehow, because in recognizing what is *not* Bethan he sees what *is* Leo, and by the end of Eli's joke he discovers that he likes Leo Mordecai Weissman very much. He must have made Bethan very happy.

Eli is revving up for the punch line. ". . . 'Not to worry,'" says the rebbe. 'The most powerful man in the world just jumped out of the plane holding my tallis.'" He throws himself back with such hilarity that Gaelan has to reach around the back of his chair to keep him from toppling over.

"You're not much of a joke person, are you?" Eli observes.

"Oh, it's a great joke. I'm just not much of a laugher."

"So, why did you come over anyway?"

"Oh, well, I wanted to tell you, I mean, *ask* you about the tryout on Sunday. Do you have any advice? I've never auditioned for a play before."

"Not really. I'm not an actor. I'm a writer. But one of my friends back in Washington—he's been in a bunch of plays—he says that the most important thing is just to go in and have fun. Pretend you've already got the part."

"Okay. Thanks. I'll do that. Good luck with your studying."

"Good luck to you, too."

Bethan is in the kitchen; he calls good-bye to her on his way to the front door.

"Did you tell him?" she asks.

"It's all good," he replies.

As he bounds out of the house, he sees Mr. Ellis and his work hands in the field. Unconscious of the fact that he hasn't been capable of the gesture for many months, Gaelan lifts his arm in a broad, exultant wave.

In response to feelings of intense shame and self-loathing, Larken would normally collaborate with the fast-food industry; there is both punishment and comfort to be found in ingesting excessive amounts of trans fat.

But in this case, she knows that Jon is waiting for her at home. She called him on her cell phone and shared the bad news. At the very least, she'll have the gift of a shoulder to cry on; at best, she'll be rewarded with a curative screw. There's no Happy Meal in the world that beats being in love.

When he answers the door, she rushes into his arms.

"I'm so sorry, Larken," he says, but instead of the usual sensation of sinking into him, she experiences his body at an odd, insulated remove, as if he's encased in heavy-duty bubble wrap. "Nobody deserves the chair more than you."

Then she looks beyond his shoulder into the apartment.

"What's going on?"

"Come in. I have some news for you as well."

"I guess so."

"You want some tea or wine or something?"

"No. I want to know why you're packing."

"Always the forthright girl," he tries to joke. "I'm moving. We're moving." He sighs. "Mia and I are getting back together."

"What?"

"We're going to try again."

"Why on earth would you want to do that?"

"What do you mean, why?"

"She dumped you. She dumped you in the worst, most hurtful way imaginable, and you know she'll do it again. She's a toxic, self-absorbed, self-centered—"

He interrupts her. "Stop. Please. For the sake of our friendship—"

"Our *friendship*?"

"—please stop. Mia and I are married, Larken, that's why. We made promises and we're going to try to keep them."

As the possible ramifications of his words begin to take shape, Larken feels a sudden weakening in her legs. She has to sit down. "What about Esmé?"

"What about her?"

"I would think that Esmé is the best reason for you and Mia *not* trying to get back together."

He doesn't reply.

"And what about the three of us? You and Esmé and I have been playing family every weekend for months now. Is all of that going to stop?" An even more terrifying thought occurs to her. "Am I going to get to see her at all?"

"Mia and I haven't talked about that." His body slumps, his chin falls to his chest, he runs his fingers through his hair. This series of gestures conveys an impotent helplessness that she finds infuriating. All the things that she has loved and cherished about him suddenly repulse and anger her.

"*Please* don't tell me that this is about staying together for the sake of the child," she says with lashing force. "And please don't evoke that sanctity of marriage bullshit. You haven't exactly held up your end of the bargain, have you? You've broken just as many promises as she has." She has a thought that makes him even more repellent. "You haven't told her about us, have you?"

Jon starts to cry, but she is merciless.

"You haven't, have you?" she rushes on, hearing herself from a distance, because it cannot be her, speaking like this; she has never spoken like this to anyone. "You son of a bitch. You really think you can *try again* when you've neglected to tell your wife that you've been fucking your downstairs neighbor, your *friend,* your *babysitter,* from the moment she vacated the premises? What kind of future marital bliss do you think you're going to be able to build on that, Jon? Answer me."

Jon swipes at his eyes and then sits down on the sofa next to her.

"I *have* told her, Larken. I couldn't call myself much of a man otherwise, could I?"

His words not only bring the accelerating tension in her body to a full stop, but reverse it to such an extent that she feels frightened: It is not just her muscles that release, but tendons, sinews, cartilage, whatever attaches bone to bone, organ to peritoneum, heart to mediastinal space. He takes hold of the pile of bones that until moments before were her hands.

"Marriage doesn't exist in a vacuum," he says. "Mia's infidelity is as much my fault as much as it is hers. I'm very, very sorry that I brought you into all this."

He told her about me, Larken thinks wonderingly, still barely able to grasp the concept. None of the married men she's been with have ever told their wives about her. She's been their secret, their sin, a diversion. She's been a nonentity.

The fact that Jon told his wife about her means that Larken exists. It makes everything that she and Jon have been through together real. It makes it all important. His honesty redeems him, but it condemns her, because if Mia can forgive him, then she and Jon will never have a life together. And Esmé will be lost to her forever.

It is moving day. Larken is being allowed to host Esmé for however long it takes Jon and Mia to load up the U-Haul.

Afterward they will drive their belongings to their new abode, wherever it is. Larken hasn't been made privy to that information, although she has been told that they will still reside in Lincoln and their phone listing will remain the same.

When Mia arrives at Larken's door, she is surprisingly cordial. Whatever has occurred in her world over the past few months has softened her; she may have even put on a few pounds. Clearly she is a woman unaccustomed to shame or guilt or any of the normal human tendencies involved in a situation like this.

Of all of them, Mia is the one person who seems to be doing just fine.

"Thank you for helping us, Larken," she says. She speaks with such emphasis and apparent sincerity that Larken cannot help but suspect a deeper subtext.

You're welcome, she thinks. *It is always my great pleasure to do whatever I can to help fucked-up married couples get back together.*

"Larkee!" Esmé yells, and the two of them are alone.

Larken does what she can to keep them busy—they bake, they read, they conduct a treasure hunt—designed to gather up any of Esmé's remaining possessions that may have been left behind in Larken's apartment.

She wishes she could cherish this time with undivided attention, but throughout, Larken finds herself keeping one ear tuned to the comings and goings of Jon and Mia, up and down the stairs with furniture and boxes, working together with such cooperative efficiency that it is easy to imagine that they'll live to celebrate their fiftieth wedding anniversary after all.

Esmé is in the kitchen putting the cookies on a paper plate when Larken hears the dishearteningly conclusive sound of a door being pulled shut upstairs.

Moments later, Jon arrives. "Hi," he says.

"Hello." Larken hasn't seen him yet this morning. She'd rather not have seen him at all.

"We've got everything loaded up," he adds.

"Okay." She will not smile, she will not accept his kiss with grace, she will not let her body soften to his platonic hug.

"Time to go, princess!" Jon calls.

"Look, Da!" Esmé cries. "Larkee and I made cookies!"

"I see that. They look fantastic. May I have one?"

"No," she says firmly. "They're a housewarming present. We have to have them in our new house."

Jon takes up the box Larken has filled with Esmé's things and the three of them head outside.

"Are you ready to ride in the big truck with Mommy and Daddy?" Larken asks.

Jon hands the box off to Mia, who wedges it into the back of the truck. The two of them enter into a negotiation about which route they plan to take and should they stop and get some food first.

Larken takes Esmé's hand, pets her head, removes and tries to replace a pink plastic and rhinestone barrette that is about to fall out of her fine, flyaway hair. She could make this easy—and undoubtedly should, for Esmé's sake. But this is a good-bye she is unwilling to expedite.

"Larkee?" Esmé says, thoughtfully.

"Yes, button."

"I have a question for you."

"What is it, sweetie?"

"When will it come?" Esmé removes a cookie from the plate. She absentmindedly takes a few nibbles and then offers it to Larken. "I've been waiting a long time."

"Mmmm," Larken says. "Delicious."

"So," Esmé says. "When will it?"

"What, sweetie?" Jon is making his way to the driver's seat; Mia is coming around to the passenger side. They're really going.

"When will what come?" Larken starts to panic. It's ridiculous to think she can do this, be away from this child. She reaches down and takes Esmé into her arms. She's getting heavy. "Now," Larken says, "say it again, sweet pea. When will what come?"

Mia arrives and stands at the open passenger side door.

"I've been waiting and waiting and *waiting*," Esmé says.

"I don't understand, honey," Larken says. "Waiting for what?"

Mia interrupts, her tone sharp. "Esmé."

"Your *baby*," Esmé says, smoothing her hand over Larken's stomach. "The baby inside your body. When will it come out?"

"Esmé!" Mia repeats. "That's not a polite question."

Esmé puts her face close to Larken's belly. "Hello, baby!" she calls. "Hello! Please come out soon because I want to play with you." She starts singing *Twinkle, twinkle, little star*.

Mia speaks; Larken hears her as if she were underwater.

What is she to say? When *will* it come out?

How I wonder what you are . . .

Larken pulls Esmé close, even as Mia continues to make indecipherable noises of a shushing, apologetic nature and tries to wrest Esmé from Larken's arms.

"I wish I knew, sweetie," Larken whispers, not letting her go, sick already with nostalgia for this moment, as if it's passed into memory and she's looking back on it from a far-distant future: Standing in front of their apartment, Esmé is four years old and singing to the held weight in Larken's body, as if her voice could bring it forth, and that release would be an event so joyous as to be like birth. The smell of her (butter-drenched crumpets, baby cornstarch, warm Crayolas, Elmer's glue)—and the knowledge that Esmé is escaping this moment even as it happens, that she is growing up and away no matter how tightly Larken holds her—fills her so completely and unexpectedly with feeling that she has to close her eyes to contain her tears. Eventually Esmé starts to squirm a little and giggle. "Larkee, you're squishing us!"

Larken sets her down and looks Esmé in the eyes, realizing that the only answer she can give is one that splits the difference between a lie and a truth. "I wish I could tell you when it will come, but I can't."

Esmé takes this in, her brow puckered, her expression considering. "Maybe it just needs a different song," she concludes. Pressing her face once again to Larken's midsection, she sings a snippet from *I've got a loverly bunch of coconuts*.

Larken hears *time to go now button, say good-bye, good-bye* as if dreaming, and then they are gone, with nothing left to show they were ever here except for a small dollar-store barrette at the bottom of her pocket.

Hope's Diary, 1976:
The Changing Shape of Thought

Feel like swearing more, and do. I blame the pharmaceutical industry. My face has also grown big as a balloon. A travesty. Some days the children look at me as if I'm a monster and then I am glad for the days (good days? or bad days?) of blindness.

Should we talk about it some more? Discuss it at the dinner table?

Larken has started cooking most nights. Hamburger Helper, Tuna Helper. I help, too, of course I do! I tear up the iceberg lettuce. Can't be trusted with a knife, or near the stove. Some days (good days, bad days) it takes half a minute for my fork to travel to my mouth. The suspense is riveting.

I can almost see the shape of my thoughts some days. They are oval, generally, and flat, and intricately detailed, like tatted antimacassars.

But just as I'm about to take hold of one of their fine edges and place them appropriately—on the armrest of an overstuffed chair, say, where I can sit down in regal beneficent wise silence—the thought changes shape and quality altogether. It becomes a floor mat in the car smelling of factories, a bristly thing placed next to the back door and used to scrape mud off of work boots.

I should be writing/typing things as soon as they come into my head, I'm realizing. I cannot trust my memory anymore, I can't count on being able to recall anything once it's flown into my mind because chances are it will just as easily fly out.

I'm developing my own language, a one-of-a-kind language that is already extant and will soon be extinct because how can I pass it on to anyone else?

Good days, bad days, the specialist said.
Heartless son of a bitch.

Viney came over today, did housework. A huge help.
I should feel grateful.

"I love making beds," she said.

"Really. I don't."

"Hmmm. I think it's a nurse thing."

The setting was apt—we were in Llewellyn's and my
room—so I blurted, "Have you had relations with
anyone since your husband died?"

She looked at me. "Relations? You mean . . .?"

"Sex."

She laughed, said no, went back to tucking in
perfectly mitered corners, making the crisp, brisk,
efficient movements of the physically competent. I
caught myself hating her. This was a new experience. I thought: "How fascinating, to have the
ability to hate someone and be grateful to them at
the same time." I don't know why it surprised me so
much. God knows I'm acquainted with the way hate
and love coexist in my marriage.

"Have you ever wanted to?"

"Wanted to what?"

"Have sex since you've been a widow?"

"Hope."

"It's been a long time, hasn't it? Since your
husband died?"

"Thirteen years."

Don't you miss it?"

"Not really." She paused, got thoughtful. "Sex
with my husband was, well . . . How can I say this?
It worked, in a reliable, predictable way, like a
well-oiled machine. It's hard to miss something that
never changed. Missing sex with Waldo would be like

missing a tractor." She started laughing again, a little hysterically I thought.

"But you must have . . . urges, or something. You're still young."

Viney snapped out the top sheet. It billowed between us, briefly transecting my view of her body so that I was able to assess her torso and hips separately and appreciate what a good figure she has. "Don't you get lonely?"

"Sure, but my feeling is, you get what you get. I've had a lot."

"So you've given up on ever having any romance in your life again."

She shrugged. "I don't need a man."

I didn't believe her for one minute, so I came right out with it. "Are you attracted to Llewellyn?"

"What?"

"In theory, I mean. Do you think he's attractive?"

She frowned, leaned over, and started bundling up the dirty sheets. "Your husband is a very handsome man," she said, her voice irritated. "Is that what you want to hear? I'm gonna go downstairs and throw these in the machine. When I come back we'll tackle the kids' rooms."

She fled down the stairs on her good legs. I regarded the fresh linens on my marriage bed.

Have I mentioned my new acquisition in these pages yet? A cane. I like to think that it lends an air of sophistication and/or threat. I feel positively monarchial. Virgin queen, that's me.

Pre-cane, only last week, I fell on my face in the country club parking lot on the way into a benefit dinner for—how's this for irony!—the MS Society! I made a fine poster child, with my fresh abrasions, bruises, and cuts. The checkbooks couldn't come out fast enough. The fall put the kabash on any further efforts at unassisted walking.

Today I learned that my cane also doubles as a handy household tool. I used it to dismantle Nurse Closs's work, poking and prodding, undoing all those precisely tucked and mitered sheets.

Huge fight with L. last night. Exhausted today.

I thought it was a reasonable suggestion—that he and Viney sleep together. It's certainly an extremely boring and unoriginal one. The stuff of countless novels and soap operas. Adultery makes the world go round.

What a prude, my husband.

He got home, very late as usual, having missed everything, the whole domestic sweep of after-school and pre-bedtime life.

"You spend all your time with her anyway," I reminded him. "It would be so easy! No one would blink an eye; people are used to seeing the two of you together."

"Shut up, Hope."

"All those nights you're out on house calls together anyway and feel like you have to rush home to me and the children . . . Think about it from a practical standpoint. You could just stay at a motel."

"I said, shut up."

"She's got a helluva figure, don't you think?"

I think I was trying to get him to hit me or something, _engage_ with me in some kind of real, impolite way. I would have welcomed any kind of crack in his veneer. In retrospect, my cane might have come in handy.

He looked at me, cool as ice, and said, "I'm married to you, Hope," he said. My husband, the loyal masochist.

"So, you'd rather stay manacled to the bed of a failed marriage than be happy?"

"Marriage isn't always about being happy."

"It isn't always about suffering either."

"I'm not suffering."

"Really? You don't miss having a wife who can satisfy your physical needs?"

"No."

"Well then, come on, sweetheart!" I said, patting the fresh clean sheets laid down by my sexy, long-suffering friend. "Here I am, ready and willing and waiting." I started struggling with the buttons on my nightgown. Eventually I just gave up and started trying to tear them off. Too weak of course. L. restrained me. I tried to push him away. Too weak for that too.

"No, no, wait please while I slip out of my diaper, darling," I cried. "I can't make any promises, but I'll try my best not to shit the bed."

He held me while I wept. Poor Llewellyn. Poor me. We sat there for a while, loving and hating each other.

When I finally stopped crying and calmed down I was able to speak to him in a reasonable, civilized way.

"I just want the two of you to enjoy each other. It's not a betrayal, not if I want it, don't you see? You can still love and honor me until death parts us."

I've done what I can. They will or they won't, but I think they will because really: what a sublime form of self-punishment it will be for Llewellyn. He won't be able to resist.

Chapter 27

Art Appreciation Redux

At the congratulatory reception—a big to-do at the University Club with the board of regents and the dean and a lot of other high rollers—current chairman Richard Edgerton Gaffney, that slimeball, noted that the decision was cinched when Dr. Piacenti demonstrated such courage under fire earlier in the year, stepping forward to assume all the responsibilities involved in shepherding a group of twelve UNL art students during a three-week overseas trip when her colleague fell suddenly ill with bronchial pneumonia. Cue the applause, lah-dee-dah. Mirabella looked ravishing. Her husband and kids looked ravishing. Larken gorged on canapés and still managed to get drunk. On the way home, she picked up two pints of Häagen-Dazs and ate them while watching the 1986 remake of *The Fly* on cable. Every hardworking, failed academic/adulteress deserves a little treat now and then.

The end of the regular academic year doesn't usually have this kind of finality. For Larken, it has habitually represented just one more caesura in a year full of caesuras: winter break, spring break, pre–summer school break, post–summer school break, et cetera. Long-term separations are not involved; significant good-byes are not required.

But this year, Professor Jones has decided to *vacation* in the fullest possible sense of the verb. She is absenting herself from the University of Nebraska campus, the responsibilities of summer school teaching, the daily sight of the bronze zaftig women in the sculpture garden. She is freeing herself from the entanglements of university politics. She is taking leave of the students, colleagues, and mentors whom she has disappointed so grievously. She is removing herself from the company of the new upstairs tenant—a twenty-seven-year-old female law student from McCook whose political and social leanings make her a likely reincarnate of William Jennings Bryan and who has no social life whatsoever. She is abandoning the capriciously functioning window air conditioner in her apartment—reliable only in its ability to break down during one-hundred-degree heat waves—in order to read the Emlyn Springs library's Harlequin Romance collection in the cool, steady comfort of a residence supplied with central air-conditioning.

This summer, because she can no longer sleep in a place that echoes so loudly with the sound of a child's laughter, Profesor Jones is moving to her fathers' house in Emlyn Springs.

It is early afternoon when Larken arrives; next to the front door she finds a lidded cardboard box held together by a thick rubber band and labeled PAGEANT MATERIALS FOR LARKEN JONES. She leaves it for the time being and starts unpacking everything from the car into the living room.

She telephones Viney. "Hi, I'm here," she speaks into the answering machine. "Gaelan? Viney? Anybody home?"

There's no reason to suspect that the residents of the Closs household are monitoring their calls, but Larken can't remember a single time when Viney hasn't picked up the phone; her failure to do so now makes Larken feel woeful.

"Okay, well, I guess you're out. Call me when you get this. Love you. Bye."

When she calls the Williams girls, they inform her that Bonnie isn't home either, *but you should try Blind Tom's, dear. There's a good chance that she's there.* This is a puzzling suggestion until Larken remembers that the bike shop and the piano hospital share the same warehouse.

The keeping of regular hours by Emlyn Springs' businesspeople—especially her sister—isn't pro forma even when there *hasn't* been a death, so Larken isn't exactly surprised when the phone rings twenty times without an answer. She hangs up.

Alone in the house, Larken is struck by how cold and uninviting it is. There's no physical imprint of her father here. And yet she still feels like an intruder.

She ponders taking up residence in the large master bedroom—it would certainly be nice to spread out—but that's where she and Jon stayed when they visited, and the whole point of coming here is to avoid those ghosts. Because of their proximity, the two other upstairs bedrooms are equally inhospitable.

In the end she decides to move into the basement—which is even more sterile-looking than the rest of the house, not just because of the bland furnishings but because there are no windows; the only light comes from the fluorescent bulbs contained in a low, suspended ceiling.

But the basement does offer a decent-sized bedroom, a half bath, the large rec room with its pool table, an empty refrigerator, and the big-screen color TV. No phone. She has everything she needs down here, and it's completely private. If anybody comes by, they won't even know she's here.

Supper at Viney's house turns out to be a large group affair. Besides her siblings, Blind Tom is there, also Bethan Ellis and her son, Eli.

Larken has trouble acclimating herself to the assembled energy. For much of the meal she feels as though she's walked into the wrong house, or one in which familiar bodies have been taken over by parasitic aliens. Perhaps she's stumbled onto the set of the Christian remake of *Invasion of the Body Snatchers*. This just can't be her family. Everyone—even Bonnie, *especially* Bonnie—is so *happy*.

Gaelan has clearly outed himself about having quit his job. From what Larken can tell, he's completely unconcerned with the minor matter of what he intends to do for the rest of his life. Maybe he'll go to culinary school. Maybe he'll teach. He might even start taking bodybuilding more seriously, consider competing. At the moment, he's just glad to be here with his family. He's very excited about his role in *Our Little Wales*.

As Viney pours the coffee and they hand around a platter of cookies, Bonnie stands. "I have an announcement to make," she begins. Then she looks to Blind Tom, who's sitting next to her. "Actually"—and to Larken's surprise, Blind Tom stands as well and they put their arms around each other—"*Morgan* and I have an announcement to make."

Who's Morgan? Larken wonders.

"We're going to have a baby."

The energetic field in the room transforms instantly, from politely sedate to raucously celebratory. It's as if Bonnie's simple announcement inspires a fireworks display, a spirit-inspiring explosion of lights and colors and emotional pyrotechnics.

Viney springs to her feet. "Oh, honey! That's wonderful!" she says, rushing to deliver hugs.

"Did I miss something?" Larken whispers to her smiling, alien brother.

"What do you mean? Isn't it amazing?"

The idea of Bonnie being pregnant isn't nearly as astonishing to Larken as its corollary implication: Bonnie—their odd, beloved baby sister: recluse, eccentric, spinster-in-training, source of all their worries and much of their conversational content—has an intimate, enduring relationship with someone of the opposite sex. She has acquired that most unexotic and predictable of life's accessories, a *boyfriend,* and Larken hasn't known a thing about it.

Larken responds with all the appropriate behaviors. But inside, she feels nothing but dull confusion, betrayal, abandonment.

Later, as she and Gaelan do the dishes, she eavesdrops on the zestful conversation taking place in the living room: an early planning session for the baby shower.

How could this happen? she wonders, unaware that she's spoken out loud until Gaelan inclines his head close to hers and whispers, "Well, gee, sis, I think they must've had sexual intercourse."

"You know what I mean. They told us in the hospital she couldn't. Dad said she could never—" Larken cuts herself off, repelling away from wherever these words—and her sudden, unpremeditated invocation of her father—are about to lead.

"Be happy for her, Lark," Gaelan says, putting the last of the plates away and then slinging the dish towel over the edge of the sink. "And for us, too. I'm going to be an uncle!" he rejoices. "You're going to be an aunt!"

Aunt. The word is unattractive, uttered as it is in midwestern America: with a short a, nasally, the corners of the mouth pulled sideways as if smiling overzealously or following instructions from a dental hygienist. Nothing like the way it's pronounced by sophisticated East Coasters, or Brits, with that long, luxurious, elegant "aaaaaah."

Aaaaaahunt Augusta. Aaaaaantie Mame.

Ant Larken.

"It's a miracle," Gaelan concludes.

"Yes," Larken concedes, half-hoping that when she gets back to Dad's house, she'll find a large pod containing her happy alien lookalike. "I guess it is."

After dinner, they all drive to the community center for a meeting of the newly formed Downtown Development Association. In preparation for the August visit from what's being called *the Welsh delegation,* the association's mission is to spruce up the falling-down structures of downtown. They also intend to develop a presentation that will be ready for Fancy Egg Days, one that will make this idea of a cultural and financial renaissance (*Dad's* idea, Larken has to keep reminding herself) not just less than ludicrous, but plausible.

Bud Humphries shows an endless series of slides while committee members speculate on whether or not the old egg factory could be refitted to produce the monks' signature cottage industry product (organic snack bars), the train station transformed into a museum and tourist information headquarters, the hotel renovated as a monastic dormitory, and so on. Does the committee have enough money to hire an architect to render their ideas into blueprint form? Or mightn't investing in a few flats of pansies and geraniums and organizing a planting party be just as effective in helping their distinguished visitors envision their cooperative future?

Larken is lulled into a waking trance by the droning voices and the rhythmic shuffling of the slide projector; it's one of those old carousel machines. The slides—photos of Emlyn Springs' downtown streets and buildings—loop endlessly. This must be one version of purgatory.

Larken remembers slide shows like this from elementary school: on birth control, what to do in the event of atomic bombs or tornadoes, auto assembly plants in Michigan, the natural resources of Peru.

Eventually all she sees are the colors, the quiet, unassertive colors of weathered wood, broken pavement, bleached signs; the flat, pale blue of the sky; shadowed alcoves; whitewashed shutters. The only potency is found in the brick of abandoned buildings: variegations of red, the colors of the Virgin's robes.

A slow realization enfolds her, and she begins to dream herself into another room.

There, she sits in the dark next to a younger version of herself: *Jones, Larken? Here. Here. Here!* the girl calls out with irritation, waving at the white-haired man down at the podium (*is he deaf?*), small-town slut, insolent fuckup, motherless daughter, one of a hundred failing small-town freshman girls jonesing for nicotine, self-exiled to the back row of Art History 101 because she needs the credit, wondering *Am I going to have to know this for the test?* and then rendered breathless, transformed forever by the image of that painting on the projection screen. *That's art,* the girl thought, suddenly understanding a commonplace, three-letter word in a completely new way. She spent the next twenty years wondering why it was *that* painting that prompted her epiphany.

It wasn't about radical ideas or political implications, Larken tells the girl, kindly now, as if she could spare her the past and the future and maybe even the present. *It was about the colors. Other things, too, but mostly it was simply that: the colors.*

Library; school; grocery; hotel; McKeever's Funeral Home; the Williams mansion; Tinkham's Five and Dime.

When Robert Campin, a.k.a. the Master of Flémalle, and his unnamed assistants painted the Mérode Triptych, c. 1420–1430, 64.1 X 63.2/ 27.3 cm, Metropolitan Museum of Art, The Cloisters, New York, New York, they used the sad, familiar palette of Larken Jones's hometown.

She stays long enough afterward to have a cup of dilute, soapy coffee; then she excuses herself and walks back to her father's house.

The small box is still on the porch. Inside is a note from Hazel Williams:

"Dear Larken, You'll find copies of all eight contestant essays in this box. The girls have been asked to respond to the question, 'What are my hopes for Emlyn Springs?' They've been told that typed essays are preferable, but a legible handwritten essay is acceptable if an applicant doesn't have access to a keyboard. Thanks for your help, and good luck!"

Larken lifts out the handwritten essay on the top of the pile. The contestants are identified by number, not name, so that the contest judges can read and respond without favoritism. *My biggest hope for Emlyn Springs,* the first essayist begins, *would be to see a McDonald's get bilt here. A MacDonald's would provid jobs for young people here as well as another place for famlys to go for a meal out for not to much money. It would also be a way to bring turrists to town, since everyone knows MacDonald's and if a town has one they are sure to stop even if their on their way to someplace else.*

And almost everyone is, sweetheart, Larken thinks, pitying and at the same time loving this earnest, unnamed girl who can't imagine a greater gift to her hometown than the arrival of a fast-food franchise.

Hope's Diary, 1977:
Movie of the Week

Dreamed of teaching a tap class to a coliseum of people. I was very good. Made it look so easy. The children were there: Bonnie was dressed in a ruffled pinafore, very uncharacteristic, and running a miniature vacuum cleaner as I gave my lecture demonstration.

"Could you do that a bit later, sweetheart?" I asked, shouting over the sound of the vacuum. In another part of the room, Gaelan was doing magic tricks, I think, or else some kind of scientific experiment: There were balloons and kites. Possibly he was trying to re-create a wind tunnel? A wind machine? He was quite a showman, I remember, and had his own audience, all girls, none of them interested in tap dancing. I had trouble locating Larken at first; she was in the shadows, doing something she wasn't supposed to be doing, don't know what it was.

Meanwhile, I danced a single step, repeating it over and over so that everyone in the room could get it. The step was rhythmically simple; the complexity arose from the accents. The adults were impressed; the children weren't paying any attention to me whatsoever. I was happy that they were involved in their own projects; at the same time, I wanted them to see me doing this vital, playful, agile, carefree thing, tap dancing. I wanted them to remember me this way. Their mother, the tap dancer.

I think what I cannot bear above all else is the demise of myself in full view of my children. They will only remember what they see last. The thought that their enduring image of me will be as a withered, incapacitated, speechless, muddled mass of exposed nerve endings is too horrific. I want to take a snapshot of myself for them before that point. I want to freeze their view, short-stop the long decline.

I could keep deluding myself—maybe a cure will be found, maybe I'll live longer than anyone imagines. I could say, "I'm not going to die," like one of those noble types in the movies, whose lives are accompanied by sound tracks and who even in death have a professional hair stylist.

The only thing I might be able to control is how my children remember me. I want them—especially the girls, for the halo of victimhood has been worn too long by women—to remember me as anything but this: the victim of a disease.

The legs—poor stumps, they've been languishing for so long—are really, finally giving up. They will not be coaxed. Dead as felled timber. It seemed to happen overnight, although of course it didn't. We've been on this path for a long time, my legs and I. Now it seems we must go on our way, if we're to go at all, with the assistance of a wheelchair. No more canes or walkers. I will henceforth move through the world waist-high to most adults, eye to eye with six-year-olds.

I am coming up against it now, the knowledge, the dread, the certainty. I am beginning to see my own death.

I have the disease to thank for this clear-sightedness. Without it, I would have gone on like the rest of the world, not believing in death until much later, maybe not until the end itself, whatever that end would have been: a car crash, a stroke, a heart attack. My death will be a pro-longed affair. I could fight. I could resist. I could try to comfort myself by saying things like

"I am just as alive today as any newborn" in a hearty voice.

But that is not my way, and I am not comforted.

There was a great movie-of-the week on TV the other night. It was called "Griffin and Phoenix: A Love Story" and was about these two terminally ill patients who fall in love, but the woman (was she Griffin or Phoenix? I can't remember) makes the man promise he won't be with her when she gets to the end stage of her illness. She refuses to let him see her die.

Usually these things are unbearably sappy and untrue, and parts of this one were, too, but all was redeemed by the ending, which I loved: Peter Falk walking down the street smashing windshields. It was perfect. I found it roaringly funny. L. looked like he'd swallowed a bottle of aspirin. He seemed disgusted. People who aren't living under the shadow of a terminal illness just don't get it, and I'm not talking about the high moral ground of suffering or any nonsense like that, but about how hilarious it can be sometimes.

It's so ironic. L. always used to think me the flighty and impractical one, the one with the romantic notions. And now our sensibilities are reversed. I'm sure he harbors quite a different scenario involving me and my illness and my death—something all Beth-like from "Little Women," hearts and flowers, dewy-eyed children who've already forgiven me for abandoning them, cue the violins.

I much prefer the windshield-smashing approach. Pissed at the Grim Reaper. Turning vandal.

Unfortunately, I've lost my chance to walk down the street or stride out the back door wearing my

carpet slippers. Tomorrow Viney will take me up to
Beatrice to be fitted for a wheelchair.

Can't write anymore.

It all makes sense now: coming upon Llewellyn working on something at his desk, then furtively moving
papers aside and acting nonchalant; numerous phone
calls for L. that didn't send him out of the house
but into another room; Viney's announcement that she
wanted to take me up to Omaha for the day, treat me
to a shopping spree and lunch in the Old Market area.
This proposal did not fill me with glee.

"Why?" I asked. "It's not my birthday."

"It'll be fun," Viney replied. "Don't be such a
stick-in-the-mud."

"Viney," I grumbled, "I really don't think I'm up
for all that." Admittedly, I was playing up my new
status as wheelchair-bound invalid.

"You can rest in the car on the way up if you need
to, and on the way home, too," she said. "I'll help
you get around. You'll be fine."

And then there was Larken's evasiveness whenever
I asked, "Will you be okay this Saturday, alone all
day?" (L. had already informed me of his plans: He
had two OB patients about to give birth and said
he'd be on call all weekend.) "What are you going
to do when Viney and I are up in Omaha?"

"Oh," she shrugged. "I dunno."

"Maybe you and Gaelan and Bonnie would like to
come with us," I suggested.

She scowled, chewed her lip, got quiet. "No thanks,
Mom. We'll be fine. It'll be good for you to have
a kid-free day."

So off we went, at the ungodly hour of 7:00 A.M.

Visited shops and bookstores, had lunch at a cozy
Italian restaurant. Viney practically rearranged

the entire place in order to accommodate me and the
Chair. I'm thinking of giving it a name; perhaps
then I wouldn't hate it so much.

Anyway, I was ready to come home after that, but
Viney insisted that we take in a movie. "Come on,
Hope," she said. "When's the last time you saw
something in Cinerama?" So we went to the Indian
Hills, where they were showing "Close Encounters
of the Third Kind."

I had several close encounters with the inside of
my eyelids (it was a very long movie, and in retrospect I understand that was part of the reason
Viney chose it), but I did manage to wake up in
time to see the end, when the scientists were com-
municating with extraterrestrials through a simple,
Coplandesque series of notes.

Re-mi-do-do-sol. Re-mi-do-do-sol.

It was surprisingly moving and sweet.

Viney and I laughed quite a lot when Richard
Dreyfus was sculpting all those phalluses. "Devil's
Tower" indeed. No one else in the theater seemed to
get it.

After the movie ended, Viney wanted to make one
more stop. "Let's pick up some pastries at that
French bakery we passed," she said. "Get something
special to take home to the kids."

"I'm TIRED, Viney!" I whined in full-out, pain-
in-the-ass, difficult patient mode. "I want to go
HOME!"

Fell asleep the minute we set off, and stayed
asleep until we reached Beatrice. When I woke up,
we were parked at a filling station and Viney was
outside making a call from the pay phone.

"Everything okay?" I asked when she got back.

"Oh, shoot," she said. "I was hoping you'd stay
asleep until we got back."

"What's going on?"

"Go back to sleep or I'm going to have to blind-fold you."

"What?"

"There's a surprise waiting for you at home."

"What kind of surprise?"

"That's all I'm allowed to say about it." She turned to face me. "You have no idea how much you're loved, honey," she said, and there were tears in her eyes.

Originally, L. planned to do it all by himself. About a month ago, during those dark days after I got the chair, he went into Schlake's with a few sketches and a supply list and started asking questions.

Small towns being what they are, Harold Sr. started asking questions of his own, and before long L.'s secret one-man carpentry project became a public community effort.

"I'd trust Doc Jones with my life," Harold whispered to me tonight at supper. "We've all seen him perform all kinds of miracles—he can reattach amputated limbs, for God's sake!—but bless his heart, give the man a hammer and nails and he's a menace."

So Llewellyn and Harold started meeting, sharing ideas, considering design options. Thank goodness for Harold's interference. L.'s original idea was little more than a large piece of plywood affixed to the front porch steps at an angle that would have required me to defy gravity.

All the supplies—lumber, hardware, everything—were donated. The Schlakes wouldn't let Llewellyn pay for anything. They also outfitted every child who showed up with their own tool belt and set of tools.

Harold drew up the plans, cut the lumber, wrote out step-by-step instructions, assembled a crew of skilled volunteer carpenters (almost every man in Emlyn Springs was here) and delegated all the tasks so that everyone—from my famously unhandy husband to the smallest child—would have something important to do, and the build could happen in a single day.

Wauneeta Williams and Kay Ellis took dozens of photos—they both have one of those instant cameras that spit out a picture right away—and while the men and children were involved in construction, the women assembled a big scrapbook documenting the whole day of "ramp-raising" from start to finish. The scrapbook includes not only photos, but the "blue-prints": Llewellyn's initial drawings, all manner of sketches on small bits of notepad paper and cocktail napkins (clearly, many of L. and Harold's planning sessions took place over martinis at the country club), supply lists scrawled on prescrip-tion notepads . . .

Llewellyn has been telling me for years that I'm much more beloved by this community than I real-ize. I guess today he's proven right—although I can't help but feel that their real loyalty is to the good doctor's wife.

It doesn't matter, though. So many people came to help: Roy Klump, Myron Mutter, Ezra Krivosha, Ellis Cockeram, Owen Lloyd, Bud Humphries, Harlan Beck, the Ellises, and of course dear Doc Williams, all were here, and surely many more I've forgotten, so I'm thankful for the photo record. Many thank-yous to write.

Even Estella Axthelm was in attendance, possibly because she couldn't bear the idea of being left out of a community photo. But still, she came.

There was a potluck supper laid out on tables in the front yard and we were blessed with a clear, fine, humid-free evening. By 7:30 or so—after enduring the mortifying experience of having the entire group watch and cheer as I made my inaugural trip up the ramp—everyone cleared out, leaving us blessedly alone again.

After the grand exit, Bonnie wanted to play her favorite card game: spit. We'd gone a couple of rounds and were just starting to get into the spirit of things when the phone rang.

It's so rare that the six of us are together. You could see everyone looking crestfallen—even Larken, who'd moaned and complained about having to play a stupid card game with her family.

"I'll get it," she sighed, getting up from the table and making her way to the phone. "Dad, are you home?"

He peeked over the tops of his playing cards and—surprising us all—shook his head.

The phone call was for me as it turned out, Clara Vance calling to apologize for not being able to come and help today—one of her children was sick with a fever—and wondering if we got the apple pie she sent over.

I wheeled back toward the kitchen. Viney and Larken and Gaelan were making popcorn and pouring drinks.

Bonnie was sitting in Llewellyn's lap, looking at the scrapbook.

Llewellyn—sounding like the world's most experienced carpenter—was pointing at the pages, talking earnestly about ramp construction, geometry, rises and treads and building codes and how human bodies are wonders of construction, too, capable of so many amazing things, when Bonnie interrupted him.

"Daddy," Bonnie asked, her face troubled, "why do you say that?"

"Say what, Bon-bon?"

"That you aren't home. You know, sometimes when the phone rings? I don't understand."

"It's confusing, I know, Daddy saying he isn't

home."

And then she looked him in the eye and said, very seriously, "It's a lie, too. Because you are."

Chapter 28

The Return of Little
Miss Emlyn Springs

The official launch of Fancy Egg
Days occurs with the premiere of *Our Little Wales*.

This evening's performance constitutes the first run-through with
costumes, lights, scenery, sound effects, and the wind machine they
borrowed from the University of Nebraska. Merle Schlake and his son
Harold drove all the way up and back this morning to get it.

The audience is small—the big crowds will arrive for the weekend
performances—and the prevailing mood is very informal:

In addition to the playwright and the director (high school English
teacher Fiona Hughes), there is Bonnie Jones (Fiona wanted to cast her
as Eleanor Thomas, the famous Welsh singer who visited the opera
house before it burned down in 1911, but Bonnie is five months pregnant and so lending her talents as a prop mistress), her sister Larken and
several residents of the St. David's Home for the Elderly. The playwright's mother is also present, but against her son's wishes, so until
curtain time she is hiding in the girls' bathroom.

The lights are turned off, revealing a general illumination on the
playing area. A single figure, dressed in the nondescript clothing of a
school janitor, is leaning against the proscenium.

"Good evening, folks," he begins, addressing the audience directly.
"This play is called *Our Little Wales*. It was written by Eli Ellis Weissman

and produced by the Emlyn Springs Cultural Committee. In it you will see Mr. Brody Canaerfan as Emlyn Halopeter, Mrs. Bess Simpsom as Julia Halopeter . . ."

As Gaelan continues to introduce the characters, they file in behind him. "The Labenz boys, Allan, Peter, and Dylan, will be representing the fine young men of Emlyn Springs who over the years have made the ultimate sacrifice for their country . . ."

What power there is in this ability they have, the dead are thinking admiringly, *to stand together. They should use it more often.*

"And finally," Gaelan says, gesturing toward stage right, "this is our accompanist, Mr. Morgan Geraint Jones, otherwise known as Blind Tom." He checks behind him to make sure all sixty-three cast members are in place, and then turns back to the audience and says, "In Emlyn Springs, there's nothing more important to us than music, so before I tell you some of the other things you need to know about us and our little Wales, we're going to sing a song. Blind Tom, could you start us off?"

Blind Tom plays the opening bars of the Welsh national anthem, they sing, and then the play begins.

The performance is not without gaffes, line flubs, and technical difficulties—the most obvious being the inaugural use of the wind machine at the end of Act One. This occurs shortly after Brody Caenaerfan, in his big moment as Emlyn Halopeter, stands center stage, plants his feet wide, shields his eyes, and looks into an imagined distance with a growing look of intense horror. He utters the cue: "OH GOD IN HEAVEN! IT'S . . . A . . . TORNADO!" and the wind machine is turned on.

Whatever is not nailed down or weighted by sandbags is sent flying. The papier-mâché stump lifts off the floor, tips sideways, and starts careening across the playing area before it exits stage right. Mrs. Julia Halopeter suffers a terrible embarrassment when her dress flies up over her head, revealing undergarments that have not been purchased from a nineteenth-century haberdashery. The Halopeter children start to cry. The team of cardboard horses, in an effect more grisly and realistic than anyone intended, are severed from their sticks, torn into pieces, and scattered in tattered shreds throughout the gym.

Someone backstage eventually realizes what is happening and the Beaufort wind scale is suddenly reduced from 6 to 0.

The Custodian reenters, shoos the distraught actors from the stage, and—using a broom and dustpan—begins to clean up the playing area.

"Why is it," he muses, "that nobody believes us when we talk about the extremes of Nebraska weather?"

The audience laughs, the actors and crew are reassured, and Gaelan goes on to announce a fifteen-minute intermission.

There are a few more technical mishaps—minor in comparison with what's come before—and it does take the better part of three hours to bring the audience from prehistory to the present—several of the elderly audience members fall asleep—but when it's all over, the cast and crew are greeted with riotous applause.

"AUTHOR! AUTHOR!" everyone shouts, but the playwright is hunkered down behind his clipboard.

It is only after the Custodian steps into the audience and speaks a few coaxing words that Eli finds the courage to join the cast and crew on stage and accept his standing ovation with a smile.

Alvina Closs has lived in Nebraska her whole life and she's never seen a sky like this.

Gaelan has told her the names of clouds as set forth by that Quaker fellow in the early 1800s, and these clouds do not fit any of those categories. They're diverse and disorganized-looking, as if several weather systems have butted up against one another and are fighting for supremacy. One part of the sky's canvas has an undulating, edged appearance, like drifted snow or sand dunes; another part has the look of human organs lit from within: balloon-shaped and placental, having a veined appearance, or like marble, or like the oxygenated lingulae of the lungs. Small bursts of light suddenly flare within these structures, now and then, here and there.

"Look at that," folks are saying, looking up for a few moments from time to time, but then they're distracted by whatever next big thing has been arranged for their entertainment, and there is so much to choose from: the band concert, the 4-H style show, the Saddle Club horse exhibition, skating and comedy and juggling acts, the Welsh spelling bee, the Fancy Hen egg-laying contest . . .

Viney sips her Pineapple Protein Booster Smoothie. She's minding the cash box while Bonnie takes a bathroom break. BJ's Brews has reopened for this week only; it's operating out of one of the many tents that have been set up in McClure Park, full of vendors selling food and drinks and crafts. Viney's angels didn't make it to the craft fair this year. They're at home, pouting.

"Look at that sky," someone says again. They point, they interrupt their conversations to check the progress of the front, but when they're reassured by a rolling-in patch of blue ("See over there, this isn't gonna last long . . .") they go back to watching the tractor pull, or buying another hot dog from the Knights of Columbus, in the meanwhile keeping a close eye on the time because the culminating event of Fancy Egg Days—and none of them want to miss it—is this afternoon's Little Miss Emlyn Springs Pageant. And tonight there's the dinner dance with live music in the Masonic Lodge basement, followed by fireworks at the park.

What a week it has been! Everyone agrees it's been the best Fancy Egg Days ever. The Welsh delegation arrived four days ago and have been wined and dined and shown around town. It's clear that they're impressed and interested in collaborating on this idea of the former mayor's; surely they'll return to Wales with a favorable report. Who knows what might happen? This could be the start of a whole new life for their community, and Llewellyn Jones's long-held dream of an enlivened Emlyn Springs might finally come true.

Alvina Closs takes no joy in any of it.

It will be a year next week, she reflects.

"Hi, Viney!" Bonnie calls. "You about ready to close up shop and head inside to the pageant?"

"You go on in, sweetie," Viney says. "I'll take care of everything."

"Well, don't be too long, okay? I can't wait to see Larken's face!"

Viney watches Bonnie walk across the park toward the community center, weaving between the tents, gracefully maneuvering through the dense, jumbled crowd of tourists and townsfolk. Up until now they've been a disorganized, milling throng, indistinct in their T-shirts and flip-flops, straw hats and baseball caps and sunglasses. But as Bonnie passes them, they start to amass, organize, and flow in her wake, as if drawn by the force of her beauty and happiness. They're going inside.

That's fine. Let them go.

Alvina Closs will spend a while longer with her eyes fixed on the sky.

"I need everyone to take their seats again, please," Don Parry croons. Dressed in his signature red, green, and black plaid tuxedo (accented with a bright red cummerbund), Mr. Parry has been the master of ceremonies for the Little Miss Emlyn Springs Pageant since before Larken was crowned.

Why is it, Larken wonders, *that certain men never age?* As she regards Don Parry's tanned, unlined face, she wonders if he doesn't have access to dark magic, a kind of *Picture of Dorian Gray* enchantment working on his behalf. Maybe there's a painting hanging in that RV he drives all over the place. Or maybe there's a dark arts version of London's portrait gallery somewhere that's filled with wall after wall of grotesque, aged likenesses of men like Mr. Parry: Bert Parks, Dick Clark, Alex Trebec, Regis whats-his-name, Clint Eastwood, Warren Beatty.

Last night, she once again sat through the three-hour performance of *Our Little Wales.* Today, she's been on her butt for another three hours watching the Little Miss Emlyn Springs Pageant—but her front-of-the-house position at the judge's table with Hazel Williams and Owen Lloyd has required her to keep a perpetual smile on her face.

Don Parry continues. "The judges have reached their decision and are ready to chair the winner. He gestures broadly to the offstage area. "Alyssa, Heather, Nicole, Kirstin, and Toree, will you all please come out and line up at the front of the stage?"

Jon and Esmé are here. Their visit is a surprise. This morning, while serving pancakes at the Elks' breakfast, Larken felt a pair of small arms encircle her middle. After Esmé's sweet ambush worked its magic— this was a tactical move instigated by Jon, obviously—Jon announced that they drove down from Lincoln for the closing festivities. They're staying the night at the King's Castle Motel.

Larken didn't ask why. She didn't inquire after Mia's whereabouts. She's happy to see Esmé. Jon remains unforgiven.

"Once again," Don Parry resumes as the girls get in place, "I'd like to thank all the sponsors who made this possible and commend them for their generosity. That said, and before I announce the first runner-up and winner, you girls should know that each one of you will be receiving a monetary prize. The twenty-five-dollar entrance fee that each of you paid has been matched by every one of our sponsors and placed in a Certificate of Deposit at the State Bank of Emlyn Springs. This program, "Nest Eggs for Fancy Eggs," was the brainchild of one of our pageant judges and a former Little Miss Emlyn Springs, Larken Jones. Let's give Miss Jones a hand, shall we?"

Larken stands briefly, turns, smiles, and nods to acknowledge the applause. She spots Viney and Bonnie and Blind Tom, but Gaelan, *stinker,* must have left. Then she resumes her seat.

The five contestants—coifed, hair-sprayed, rouged, and lipsticked, wear the outfits they wore during the final competition category: the talent segment.

It's been an embarrassment not of riches but mediocrity. Much of the afternoon has made Larken cringe in sympathy, but the talent presentations were especially hard to watch: Heather Pike and Nicole Cockeram each performed karaoke numbers; Alyssa Critchfield did a gymnastics routine that basically consisted of an endless back-and-forth of cartwheels and round-offs, Kirstin Penkava did a kind of dance of the veils using U.S., Nebraska, and Welsh flags, and Alyssa's older sister, Toree, played an arrangement of Debussy's *Claire de Lune* on her alto sax. They were uniformly dreadful.

And yet she's been surprised, never expecting to feel so much for these girls and their folks. These are not foolish people, deluded people. They know that, in the grand scheme of things, their daughters are undistinguished, ordinary, but that their efforts on this day deserve reward, because it takes courage to put ordinariness in the spotlight. No one grimaced when a flat pitch was sounded, no one shifted cynically in their folding chairs when the twentieth cartwheel was turned, no one sighed and rolled their eyes when they heard another tepid and unoriginal extemporized response to the question, *What are your hopes and dreams for Emlyn Springs?*

The girls are in place, holding hands, their faces flushed and shiny. Behind them, garlands of Mylar stars undulate against a dark blue velvet curtain.

The Chair is brought in by four men and placed on the raised platform at the back of the stage. The mirror ball that is suspended overhead spins slowly for these girls whose dream this is, casting revolving patches of light on all of them. Don Parry announces the runner-up, Kirstin Penkava, and presents her with a bouquet of flowers.

"And now," Don Parry proclaims in his showman's voice, "let's welcome last year's winner, Little Miss Emlyn Springs 2003, Kelly McAllister, to crown her successor!"

The drum is rolled, the audience grows quiet, and in this expectant moment Larken suddenly hears her own long-ago voice, feels it even in her body: *And miles to go before I sleep, and miles to go before I sleep* . . .

"And the winner is . . ."

As Kelly McAllister lifts the crown from her head and places it on the heavily moussed and styled curls of Toree Critchfield, the muscles of Larken's arms tense and release in sympathy, she feels as though she, too, is divesting herself of some small but significant weight.

After a long cloak is settled on Toree's shoulders, she sits in her chair. Then, Bud Humphries, Harold Schlake Jr., Harold Schlake Sr., and Joe Pappas flank her on four sides and, in one smooth motion, lift her up and start carrying her around the room.

The audience applauds, the cameras flash, Wauneeta Williams plays the piano, Don Parry sings.

Larken is about to join Jon and Esmé when Hazel steps up onto the stage, takes one of the microphones, and starts gesturing to the audience to shush and sit down. She's holding what looks like a framed photograph.

"As our new Little Miss Emlyn Springs takes her place of honor, we'd like to make a special surprise presentation to one of our judges, and a former pageant winner." Hazel smiles at Larken in a way that makes her extremely nervous. "Come on up, dear," she says, off-mic. Larken ascends to the stage with dread.

"As many of you know," Hazel continues, putting her arm around Larken's middle, "Larken's chair was lost." She glances at Larken and gives her an extra squeeze; there are tears in her eyes. "But," Hazel sniffs, "thanks to the efforts of our town archivist, Myrtle Burchett—Myrtle, stand up back there—we were able to locate a photograph of Larken that was taken when she won the crown." Hazel holds up the photo. "Between this photo and a collective stroll down memory lane, we were able to create a facsimile." Hazel looks offstage. "Gentlemen?"

Larken is mortified. This can't be happening.

Onstage the men come: Bud Humphries, Alan Everett Jones, Glen Rhys, and *thank God* Gaelan because if they really mean to hoist her one-hundred-and-seventy-eight-pound bulk and that chair—

"No," she protests, "Please, you don't have to—" but before she can say anything more, she is taken aloft.

None of them struggle or grunt or falter. It doesn't seem to cost them anything to carry her, these men.

They do it easily, as if she weighs nothing at all.

"What is it you're trying to tell me, Jon?"

She has to shout; the band is an electric/Celtic group. They're in the basement of the Masonic Lodge—a location for many of Emlyn Springs' wedding receptions, proms, and community dinners like this one, where there's live music and need of a big kitchen and a dance floor.

Jon has been working hard all night to earn something from her; what that is, she can't quite figure out. Trust maybe. She's not sure she has that to give him any longer.

They've interlocked their arms, making a seat for Esmé between them, and are swaying to the music. All night Esmé insisted that the three of them dance together, and now, noisy and crowded as it is, she's fallen asleep. She shifts in their arms, yawns. Her eyes flutter and then she goes back to sleep. Jon looks down at her.

The musicians come to the end of the tune—a frenzy of dueling fiddlers—and the dance-floor crowd cheers and applauds.

"Mia and I," Jon replies once the room has quieted. "We couldn't put it back together. It's over."

"What?" Larken asks.

"We're gonna take a short break now, folks," the singer announces through the PA system. "We'll be back in fifteen minutes so don't go away."

"Listen," Jon says, "there are some things I need to talk to you about, a lot of things, actually." He takes Emsé into his arms. "I'm going to take her over to Viney's—she said she'd watch her for a couple of hours."

"Why?"

"So we could have some time alone." He leans in to kiss her on the cheek, but Larken pulls away.

Jon smiles ruefully. "Just don't disappear, okay? See you soon."

Larken stands in the middle of the dance floor, mentally reviewing Jon's revelations while people jostle past her and head back to their tables.

She heads to the bar for a glass of cheap Chablis. Bonnie joins her.

"Don't you love the way all the kids dressed up?" she asks, scanning the room. "In tuxedos and formals and everything? Like it's prom night or something."

She's never looked more beautiful, Larken thinks. *She's never looked more like Mom.* Beset by a sudden boozy sentimentaily, she blurts, "I love you, Bon," takes Bonnie by her shoulders, and pulls her close. "I'm really, really happy for you. You know that, don't you?"

"Of course I do. Listen, all these people, the noise, and the heat are getting to me, so I'm gonna say good night."

"You want a ride?"

"No thanks, I've got my bike."

"Your bike? Honey, you're five months pregnant."

"I'm not infirm, Larken. I'm having a baby."

Larken sighs. "Okay."

"See you in the morning."

Larken watches her sister join Blind Tom on the piano bench. They talk with an intimate ease, laugh, kiss. In another part of the room, Bethan and Gaelan have their heads together, their bodies forming a portico-like space, a softly peaked Romanesque arch; they, too, are talking intently about something.

All day it seems that time has been rewinding, flowing backward. Larken expects to see her mother and father sitting at one of the tables, chatting and laughing by candlelight. With very little effort, she *does* see them, imagine them. And Viney, too, because that's how she's come to imagine her parents: one father, two mothers.

She sips her wine, plucks a cube of ice from an abandoned glass of water on the bar, and applies it to her wrists and neck. It's really stuffy in here.

She pictures Jon outside, carrying Esmé asleep in his arms through the streets of her spruced-up hometown to Viney's place.

The lights flicker and go out. The teenagers make ooh-ing sounds. Thirty seconds later, the power is back. It must be windy out.

The band returns. Larken watches her brother dance with Bethan. Jon might be heading back now; she imagines him walking along Bridge Street, walking faster now—(would he be? now that Esmé is no longer in his arms?)—yes, he's walking faster. He has things to talk to her about. A lot of things, actually.

The power goes out again, and stays out.

Larken notices the hurricane lamps on the dinner tables; the candle flames have lengthened and attentuated; they start to shimmy in sync, as if a door upstairs opened and a corridor of air has found its way to the basement. In her mind, she checks in with Jon's progress back to her. She can't see him anymore, can't locate him.

Mayor Humphries gets up on the stage in front of the band. "Listen up, folks," he announces. "I just peeked upstairs, and it looks like we're in the middle of a big storm out there. I'm gonna ask everybody to stay down here where it's safe and wait it out."

Big storm, stay in the basement, where it's safe.

People start muttering names, the names of the absent, the newly departed. *How long ago did they leave? Were they headed straight home? Can I use your cell phone? Does anybody have a flashlight?*

They wait. They listen. The air around them becomes strangely pressurized.

Half an hour later, the power comes back on. They climb the stairs and push open the heavy doors to outside.

Half the town is gone.

Chapter 29

Fever of Love, 1978

It's well past midnight and Llewellyn Jones is coming home. Driving alone in the country at night can be an unreal experience, the sky so black, like velvet, without the bleaching effect of artificial light arising from cities that never sleep, the lone lights of farmhouses here and there—where someone might be up paying bills, tending to a sick child, or just plain worried and unable to sleep—like wayward suns unaligned with any planetary system. Black sky and black earth seem to merge; the demarcation between above and below disappears, giving Llewellyn the sensation that he is flying through deep space.

His nurse often accompanies him when he travels to far-flung locations, but tonight one of her daughters is in town for a rare visit, and so he is alone. Llewellyn thinks of Viney primarily in her professional capacity, although their relationship is also characterized by physical intimacy and deep affection. Llewellyn would never have envisioned that his intimate personal relationships would be so complex; he has his wife to thank for that.

His late arrival at his farmhouse is not unusual. What is unusual is that, in addition to the small lamp on the telephone table that his wife habitually leaves on for him, there are lights on in the back of the house, in the kitchen, suggesting that someone else is still awake.

"Larken?" he calls softly, as he settles his medical bag on the chair by the lamp and proceeds down the hall. "Gaelan?"

Because of his wife's illness, she tires easily, goes to bed early, and so Llewellyn assumes the night owl is one of his children. He'd welcome some time alone with them; he sees them so rarely. There's an element of wishful thinking involved in this assumption as well, for Llewellyn Jones is not eager to encounter his wife tonight.

When he looks through the kitchen, where the overhead fixture casts a buttery glow upon the walls, which Hope painted years ago in a daffodil-dense yellow, he sees her through the open screen door, sitting just beyond on the back porch in her wheelchair. He cannot see her face—her back is to him—but he suspects she is looking at the full moon rising above the fields in that direction.

"Hello, Llewellyn," she says over her shoulder, pivoting her head just slightly, isolating the movement so that there is no residual muscular involvement anywhere else.

Llewellyn has noticed that his wife has become very thrifty in her movements lately. Perhaps it's efficiency. Or it could be that she has to focus all of her reserves of energy upon one simple gesture in order to accomplish it. She could simply be tired, or lost in thought. Or she might be having a bad day and the rest of her body is incapable of further participation. When it comes to Hope's physical abilities and the cruel, fickle nature of her disease, there are numerous possible interpretations.

He leans down and kisses her on the top of her head, noting the martini pitcher and the chilled glass on the table next to her.

She notices him notice, smiles up at him, and says, "It's always Happy Hour somewhere."

"How was your day?" he asks, pouring his martini.

"It was a good day. Yours? Were you able to save that boy?"

"Yes," Llewellyn answers tersely. "He'll be all right."

"I'm so glad," she says, without bitterness.

There are many reasons why Llewellyn is tight-lipped when talking about his patients. It is not solely because (as Hope believes) he's rigidly adherent to the code of patient-doctor confidentiality, it's because every time he recounts the story of some success, some disaster averted, a life saved, the unspoken truth rears its head and shames: His wife is one person he cannot, has never been able, to save.

They stare at the moon, the top-lit cornstalks in the distance, the children's sandbox, the laundry on the clothesline, lowered so that it's within Hope's reach. The bottom edges of the sheets don't ripple freely in places, but are stilled by the smallest contact with the earth.

Llewellyn holds to this comforting silence. As long as they are silent their world can stay the same.

"Do you remember the picnic we had on this porch?" she asks. "When you first brought me here?"

The tone in her voice reassures him. It is light, conversational. They are simply a married couple enjoying cocktails and conversation on the back porch of their home while upstairs, their children are sleeping. "God, we were young."

"I wanted you to ravish me out there." She sounds happy. "But you were so upright. Such a pillar of propriety."

"It wasn't as easy as you think," he says, "keeping my hands off you."

They fall silent again. A slight breeze stirs the wings of Bonnie's whirligig.

"Oh!" Hope says, lifting one of her hands—Llewellyn sees at once that it's limp and quavering—and making as if to reach into her cardigan pocket. "The pictures came back." She fumbles around for a while. "Damn," she mutters.

"Here, Hope, let me—"

"I'll do it!" she snips, and tries again. She succeeds in stuffing her hand into the pocket, but either she can't make her fingers close around the packet of photos or she can't get her hand out again. She closes her eyes and sighs. "Sorry. Go ahead."

The photos were taken two days ago, at the end of Fancy Egg Days, when their oldest daughter was crowned Little Miss Emlyn Springs.

"Isn't she beautiful?" Hope asks, looking on. "She remembered everything when she recited that poem, every nuance, every meaning. Everything we talked about."

Llewellyn regards each photo: Larken center stage during the Talent competition—and without a doubt she was the most talented girl there—standing with Don Parry while he held the microphone out to her and she extemporized her answer to the question: "How do you imagine that small-town life is different from living in a city?" walking down the runway in the dress Hope and Viney made—purple is such a pretty color on her—the moment they announced the winner (he was so proud of her, none of that shrieking and jumping up and down and bawling you see sometimes at these things), then the crowning and the chairing.

"Doc Williams really outdid himself this year," Llewellyn remarks. "What an artist he is. Those birds. It's like he knew she was the one who was going to win."

"Hmmm," Hope murmurs.

"These came out nice," Lwellyn goes on. "We'll have to make a special scrapbook for her." He looks through more photos: Larken being carried through the room in her chair, Larken with her best friends Stephanie and Peggy, with the mayor and Don Parry, with her brother and sister.

When he gets to a group photo, Hope reaches out slowly and points. "That one," she says. "Look at that one."

It's the photo Llewellyn had Bud Humphries take of all of them: Larken, Gaelan, Bonnie, Viney, him, and Hope. Hope is in the center, sitting in her wheelchair, holding Bonnie in her lap, while everyone else is lined up around her.

"That's a nice one of all of us," he says, propping it up against the martini pitcher. "We should get a frame for this one."

"No," she says sharply, staring at the photo. "Look at me. Look at my face."

"What?" he says. "You look fine." His voice isn't convincing even to himself.

She stares at him, silent.

"Hope . . ."

"Did you bring me something? Did you do what I asked?" Her voice now is ruthless, demanding, even though her demands are framed as questions. "I think you owe me a little something. I think I've paid for it."

He busies himself with the photographs, stacking them neatly, aligning their edges, sliding them back into the envelope and then placing them on the center of the table, all the while aware of her eyes on him, aware of the millions of precise neuromuscular commands his brain is issuing to his body, allowing him to complete this simple sequence of movements. It took no more than a few seconds.

"We need to talk more about—"

"No. I've done all the talking I'm going to do. You owe me this, Llewellyn." She pauses, looks away from him, clenches down so hard on her teeth that he imagines the dentin in her mouth starting to crumble, like chalk. "It's my choice. Viney understands."

"Viney shouldn't have anything to do wth this."

She turns to face him. "Viney has everything to do with this. Do you think I'd even consider this if she wasn't part of our lives? I love her. The children love her. You love her."

He's finding it hard to speak, to move, as if the force of her will is stripping the insulation off his own nerve cells. "I can't."

"I can," she says in her stony voice. "Did you bring them?"

He nods.

"All right then." She holds out her flaccid hand; weak as it is, it receives the small paper bag he extracts from his jacket pocket and greedily, triumphantly, snatches it away.

Wrapping both of her hands around the bag, she gives it a shake and smiles happily—as if she's a gambler about to roll double sevens. It's cruel, that's what it is, her frivolity.

"Let's see," she says delightedly, bringing out the small cylindrical containers and dropping them in her lap. "Ooooh, there are so many advantages to being married to a physician."

He has a sudden impulse to slap her; instead, he stares at the moon, aware now of its shadowed craters (it's gone dingy, like filthy bulldozed snow at the end of winter) and drinks his martini.

She squints at the labels. "All these pharmaceutical companies with their gifts. Don't they realize how foolish it is to publish all these contraindications and warning labels? They're like blueprints, aren't they? So that what *not* to do becomes the very thing *to* do." She turns to him, her expression no longer teasing. "Thank you."

They sit in silence for a while longer before he realizes that he's started to cry.

"I'm not going to tell you when," she says, her voice low, soft, kind. "I'm just not. It won't be tonight. It might be years. It will be some day of my choosing. And when I do, you won't have to worry about the . . . I'll make sure that"—her voice starts to tremble—"I'll make sure the children are . . ."

He takes her hand.

"No. Don't." She utters the words as if they're weapons, and yet she is crying now, too. "I won't be this. I won't be the Black Queen in my own daughter's fairy tale. Look at this," she insists, snatching the photo off the table, mangling it. "Look, Lllwelyn! Look!" She holds it out to him and he sees her as she sees herself, sunken and sneering, bitter on the day of their Larken's triumph.

He takes the photo from her, plucks the pill bottles from her lap and puts them on the table, kisses her temples, her eyelids, her cheeks, her lips, starts undoing the buttons of her cardigan, her blouse, easing her legs out of the stirrups, her body out of the chair, and then—as if they were young and in love and had just finished a picnic lunch on a fine, clear-skied, earth-warming spring day, and pulling one of their bedsheets from the clothesline as they go—carries her into the fields.

The following morning, Hope is alone in her house, having wheeled herself to her writing desk. She is sitting with the peculiar silence that ensues in the wake of her children's departure.

She's not sure why she feels compelled to make one more entry in her diary when she'll soon be burning it, along with all the others. Habit, perhaps. She's done this kind of talking to herself for years.

This will be a short entry and a typed one; she must conserve her strength for the most important writing she has yet to do:

The Farmer's Almanac says that thunderstorms after St. Bartholomew's Day are more violent. Who makes these kinds of observations, I wonder?

The day is fine, only a few clouds off to the southwest.

Viney and L. are doing their mobile vaccine visits all week, injecting dilute inoculates of various viruses in a hundred-mile radius. It's one of the few times when Llewellyn's workday has a specific scheduled beginning and end.

I called Viney first thing this A.M. while Llewellyn was taking his shower. Suggested that we all have dinner at the club tonight. Viney welcomed the idea, as I knew she would. She offered to have the children come to her after school—her daughter Haley will watch them—and then when she and Llewellyn are done with work, they'll swing by here to get me, we'll pick up the kids, and then all head to the country club for dinner.

So that's done.

It's all working out well.

I do worry about Llewellyn. But Viney is so full of spunk and spirit. She grounds and at the same time leavens him in a way I've never been able to do. Or maybe I was once—I remember thinking long ago that we balanced each other. But my side of the teeter-totter is far too heavy now, my weight obscenely disproportionate. There's not a human force in the world that could lift me.

And yet, at this moment, I feel oddly light, even happy. I've heard of this. The weight of grappling with this decision for so long finally lifted.

Closing her diary now, she brings out some stationery.

In the first hour or so after the children leave, when the house is silent but still reverberating with their energy, she finds it easy to speak to them, even though she's dreaded doing it in this context.

She takes up her pen. Weeks ago she wrote letters to Llewellyn and Viney, but those she typed. She wants her last words to her children to arise from the efforts of her body, as they did.

Dear ones, she writes, slowly, methodically, working hard to keep her penmanship legible. It has already started to mutate, deterioriate.

There are so many ways to begin a letter like this. "If you are reading this, it means that . . ." is one of them. "Please don't blame yourselves" is another.

If there is anything I have learned in my life, it's that so very little is within our control. Our passions arise to surprise us. Our loves jump out at us like boogeymen as we round a dark corner or open the closet. We try and we try to make things fit, to steer the events of our lives a certain way, to create boundaries of experience and feeling, to wall ourselves off from one another, to stop love—which should never be stopped, ever—and my dears, it simply cannot be done.

The only thing I am certain of is this: Someday something will break your heart, something that reminds you of me.

Maybe this will happen often. I hope not, but I don't know and I cannot promise anything. I know nothing of who you will be in the future, or of how my absence from your lives will affect you.

But this heartbreak thing, whatever it is—something seen or heard, something smelled or touched, or something even more out of reach, beyond your ability to articulate, on the fringes of your awareness, maybe even a half-remembered dream—this thing is two-sided. Think of it as a token, a coin.

Viewed this way, heartbreak has a counterpart. Turn it over, and you will know that that which tells you I am gone can tell you just as convincingly that I am here.

My darlings.

Larken Myfanwy. Gaelan Llewellyn. Bonnie Ebrilla.

Turn the coin over. After I am gone, find me on the other side of heart-break. Look and see and know that you are my best beloved, and that I am here, still, and always.

From the back of the locked desk drawer she pulls out the pills.

She told him she would choose the day and not tell him. She didn't tell him that it would be sooner rather than later.

But maybe he knew anyway and that was why he gave her the gift of last night—their last night—in that sad and sanctified place where the spirits of all their losses and joys reside.

One flesh with the man and the land that bred him.

That was what she dreamed of, that is what she's been given. Not everyone is blessed with such abundance.

Mid-morning, during first grade language arts in Miss Greene's class, Bonnie Jones suddenly feels ill. She raises her hand, is sent to the nurse's office, and is found to be running a slight fever. A mother of one of Bonnie's classmates who volunteers at the school offers to give her a ride home. Everyone knows that Hope Jones is house-bound, an invalid in a wheelchair, poor thing, so there's no reason to phone first to make sure that someone's home.

By the time Mrs. McClure delivers Bonnie to her house, a few clouds have started moving in from the southwest.

"You want me to walk you in, honey?" Mrs. McClure asks.

"No, thank you. I'll be fine," Bonnie says. Such a serious little thing.

"All right then. You give my best to your mom, okay? I hope you feel better."

A sudden wind kicks up, and as Bonnie makes her way up the driveway toward Mommy's wheelchair ramp, she notices wisps of smoke arising from the chimney. This is odd. It's still summer, far too warm for a fire in the fireplace.

"Mom! Mommy!" she calls once she's inside. "I'm home! I had a little fever . . ."

Bonnie finds her mother on the sofa Daddy ordered from the Sears catalog and put in one corner of their big kitchen so that she can lie down in there whenever she gets tired and look out toward the fields. Mommy says she likes being here because she loves the view, but Bonnie suspects that her mother is really trying to catch a glimpse of the Farmer Elves.

She's sound asleep. It's not unusual to find Mommy taking a nap, so Bonnie tiptoes around the kitchen, putting some saltines on a plate. They'll help her tummy feel better. When her mother wakes up she'll ask if she can fix herself some soup. In the meantime, she goes to the living room to lie down on the sofa in there.

She'd already forgotten about seeing the smoke from the chimney, but right away she sees the dying fire in the fireplace. Stranger still, something's in there. Mommy's diaries. All of them. Their pages are blackening. Mommy's words are escaping. Bonnie grabs one of the fireplace tools and starts to drag the diaries away from the glowing coals. Who would do this?

Feeling a new afraid kind of feeling that she cannot name, Bonnie goes back into the kitchen and tries to wake her mother to ask why there's a fire in the fireplace when it's still summer, and about the burning diaries. And when she cannot wake her—not even when she yells, not even when she shakes Mommy as hard as she can—she knows that something is very wrong.

Daddy's office number is written next to the phone in the hall, but it would be silly to call there because Daddy and Viney are out in the van today, giving shots to people who need them and who aren't lucky enough to have physicians in their towns.

But Bonnie doesn't panic. She knows just what to do.

And even though what is left of Hope's spirit is crying *No* with increasing desperation (for the birds are quieting and the color of the air is changing), Bonnie Ebrilla Jones goes outside, gets onto her bike, and starts making her way back to town.

Hope is dying. But her dying body contains residual fetal tissue, a physical link that she still shares with this living child. It is this tissue that keeps her tethered to her own spirit, her daughter's body, and to the danger that is fast approaching.

No NO **NO**

When it comes, the sound is something like a freight train, the way they say, but that doesn't describe it because the noise of a freight train is directional, it is contained and external, whereas this sound seems physically impossible, a three-dimensional assault that is more like being inside the cavernous organ of some gigantic rampaging beast.

Hope feels herself pulled up as if by enormously large and powerful arms. She knows that Bonnie is experiencing this feeling as well—how terrified she must be!—and Hope tries calling to her through that tenuous link of fetal flesh and cells and spirit, like tissue paper but still substantive, a thread that connects them even as they are spun up and about along with the sofa cushions and Bonnie's whirligig, Larken's chair, Gaelan's science experiments, the chickens, poor things, rousted from the henhouse, plucked and rendered as Hope and Bonnie rise higher and higher.

A long-dead mother from Emlyn Springs comes to shepherd Hope to her death, but she is not ready. *No!* she cries, fending her off with whirling arms and insistent cries, *NO! Not yet! NOT YET!*

Where will they land? Does Hope have the power to control this?

She tries reaching for Bonnie but cannot; the elemental pull of the winds encasing them is too fierce, but not—will never be—fierce enough to extract surrender.

This is her last act. Not the taking of pills and sacramental wine, the writing of letters and the reading of that poem she took with her as she settled down on the sofa facing the back door, so that her last view would be of the land and imagined elves and children in the sandbox and children in the earth, and laundry like prayer flags, the sanctity of the ordinary all around her. She could not stride out toward Death, but she *could* make her last act a choice of view. That was her plan and if she still had breath enough to laugh she would, knowing she has made *God* laugh.

So no, her last act will be this: saving, if she can, this girl of her flesh.

Can she affix that pair of wings to Bonnie's shoulders? *Peaseblossom! Cobweb! Moth! Mustardseed!* Hope hears a voice intone. But the wings travel on and the question is moot.

At times the base of the funnel opens up like an effacing cervix, revealing glimpses of the landscape where things have already come down: the eggs laid out like perfect pearls, white and brown and blue and speckled and entirely intact, an anecdote for future books on the inexplicable mysteries caused by tornadic behavior; the piano, whirling in space while it could, an elephantine ballerina doing a pirouette, finally dropped into a field miles from here; a red wagon; a nibbled pencil.

Hope is starting to acquire the vision of the dead, and she can see far enough into what the living call *the future* to know that a photographer will take a picture of her ruined piano, it will appear in a story in *National Geographic,* the magazine that Gaelan likes so much. "Nebraska: The Good Life" the story will be called and there will be no mention of who the piano belonged to. By then it will only be emblematic, a symbol of what this good life takes as well as gives.

She looks for other people within the vortex, but it is only them, only she and Bonnie, spinning as if they're on a carnival ride but on opposite sides, always across from each other.

A force of will allows Hope to catch something that is moving at a faster speed (Larken's purple dress, the one she and Viney made); she hitches a ride on the train and gets closer, then grasps at other fast-moving objects as if they are rungs on a spiraling ladder, allowing herself to be pulled closer and closer.

Bonnie Bonnie Bonnie Hope calls to her through the tissue, through the cells.

They say that a mother's voice will rouse a slumbering child more reliably than any fire alarm, and so Bonnie stays awake, even opens her eyes, or imagines doing so—

Baby, Hope says, *Stay awake, baby. No time to nap . . .*

—and sees whirling ribbons and spiraling bolts of fabric and fairy wings fluttering around her mother, and they speak to one another, make promises, and she starts to fade again but then the telephone careens by and Mommy's voice says:

Bonnie! Bon-Bon!

And Bonnie stays with her mother, and then feels herself fading again, and then black discs like Paul Bunyan's buttons cascade around them, all Mommy's records, Rachmaninoff and Copland and Doris Day . . .

QUE SERA SERA! Mommy sings, her voice loud, even louder than Doris Day. *WHATEVER WILL BE, WILL BE!*

and shoes, too, and a hairbrush and a pair of dice and Mommy's sewing machine, wheelchair, typewriter, her bike . . .

That's it! Hope cries, and snags herself, rendered like the poor chickens but still full of will because of that cellular link, that filament of spirit.

HOLD, HOLD, HOLD! she cries, and when Bonnie lands in the tree, it is not the bicycle seat that saves her from being cleaved in two; it is that tough thin membrane of Hope's last gift to her: a mother's protective cushion, an umbilicus of spirit.

Hope's body, useless now, punches a hole in the vortex, escapes, flies on.

The dead fathers—always in readiness for times such as these, arising with the swift efficiency of minutemen militia—interrupt their labors, gathering en mass to catch Hope in their arms and gentle her passage when she finally comes back to earth. Only the dead fathers know where she lands.

Back in the tree, Hope's spirit lingers and waits with Bonnie, until the storm abates, until her absence is noticed, until they all go looking.

And at dusk, when she sees Mr. Armin Koester shuffling along Bridge Street with his walker, the only one to come anywhere near (dear old soul, feeling so useless in this crisis, a lonely widower with his hobbling gait, his cataract-covered eyes), she calls out to him through the voices of the birds.

Mr. Koester looks up then—even an old man who's all but blind can see an upside-down tree. "God in heaven!" he calls. "There she is!" And knowing that his voice must be employed in song if anyone is to hear him, he begins to sing.

They come then, all her townsfolk summoned by song, swarming toward Bonnie in the tree, damaged, but alive, and blessed. They gather together and sing her to life.

Poor Llewellyn and Viney (*oh be true to one another,* Hope longs to cry as the letters she wrote to each of them come down, pulpy, dissipating shreds, settling in streams and drainage ditches and fields, mingling with the ruined pages of her diaries): They will not know that she has forgiven all, that she is grateful. Those words she labored over will never find them, or her children, but she can stay with them for a time, and with Bonnie, and listen to the voices of the good people of Emlyn Springs, and watch Bethan Ellis ride off on her white mare in search of help, and notice on the fringes of the crowd a boy she doesn't know whose name is Morgan. He will find her piano and when he grows up he will give Bonnie that which she wants more than anything.

It will be all right. She sees it now, because she's dead. The dead see everything because after all it is all there.

That strong young fireman brings Bonnie down so tenderly (he's dead now, too) and places her in Llewellyn's arms.

Hope's work is done.

They call her name for weeks after, looking and looking until finally they stop.

Would it comfort them to know that her body slipped easily into a narrow slit in the earth—like a penny into a piggy bank—and from thence into a secret underground cave carved out by ancient springs that still trickle along the floor?

They will never find her, though she is near. It is a perfectly fine place to be. She needs nothing more from them: only that they move on, see differently, find her elsewhere.

If only they knew—for it might be a comfort—that on the day they sang Flying Girl to life, they sang Aneira Hope Jones to her death.

Chapter 30

Afterwinds

The one-half of town that suffered the damage (and the tornado carved an eerily precise path, clean as a scalpel's incision) is dark in the wrong places, illuminated not as it should be with the small lights of porches or fireflies, but with the taunting flashes of heat lightning in retreat, the flashing red lights of ambulances and police cars and fire trucks as they start to arrive.

This is not their town.

Cell phones come out. Calls are made; some go unanswered. Who is missing, who is here? Who is hurt?

They set out from the Masonic Lodge, the lucky protected ones: Gaelen, Larken, Bethan, Blind Tom and Sergei, the mayor, musicians and caterers, the newly crowned Little Miss Emlyn Springs and her predecessor, the boys in their rented tuxes, the girls in their formals, kicking off foolish shoes if they're wearing them, going barefoot if they must.

Some carry flashlights, not remembering who put them in their hands, but they go in darkness if they have to because they know where to go, how to go, they could find home with their eyes closed if they had to and maybe that would be best, because their eyes must be lying, this cannot be happening, a person cannot walk up and away from music and food and laughter and into this.

They go, wishing they could travel all ways at once, trying to make peace with having only this one slow and clumsy body that can only move in one direction, so that *You and Morgan look for Bonnie, I'll go to Viney's* is the way conversations go.

Up and down the streets, names are called.

Eli! Esmé! Bonnie! Viney!

They scramble over rubble, debris—where is the street?—houses with roofs gone, or partially standing, the tornado's mean mischievousness evident in the way some structures have been reduced to rubble while others could be featured on magazine covers, their doors flung open like astonished mouths, wondering how they've earned this luck, why they are still standing when across the street, only minutes ago and for a hundred years there was another door but now there is nothing but empty space.

It's getting dark and searching will be harder then.

Gaelan runs to the Closs house.

God no, Gaelan thinks. There's a mountain of rubble, but a flight of stairs still stands, leading to what's left of the second story. From this, and because Gaelan knows the contours of Viney's house as if it were his own, he locates the approximate area of the steps leading downstairs.

"Here!" he shouts to anyone able to hear and help. "Dig here!"

With whoever else has gathered at his side, Gaelan hurls aside timbers, bricks, a sink, a door. He wrestles away a kitchen sink, furniture he's never seen before, what's left of Viney's spinet, and then there they are, at the bottom of the basement steps.

"Gaelan, honey," Viney cries.

A terrified Esmé, her face streaked with grime and tears, is encased in her father's arms. "Jonafun!" she calls, pushing at him. "Da! Wake up!"

Days from now, newspapers all over the state will carry a photo of Mrs. Alvina Closs, coming down that flight of stairs carrying a shoe box; this photo will appear next to one taken at the other end of town, where Dr. Llewellyn Jones's house looks the same as it did when the State Farm agent took a Polaroid of it in 1978.

"Where would she have gone?" Larken asks. "Where should we look?"

"I don't know," Blind Tom replies, and then, voicing that which neither of them has been able to say, adds, "She left on her bike, Larken. She went out on her bike."

They split up. Blind Tom heads out with Sergei to the house he and Bonnie share, Larken runs to the Williams place, where she finds a group including Bud Humphries and his sister, Vonda.

The roof of Doc Williams's garage has been removed and set down neatly about twenty feet away, in the middle of the yard, as if it was the lid of a gift box. All of Bonnie's whirligigs are still perched on top, largely undamaged. The garage itself is completely destroyed, the street strewn with the mismatched baby shoes and pacifiers that Bonnie hung, like mobiles, from the ceiling. Her scrapbooks are gone. Only the avocado plants remain; three of them in big pots—spindly and standing tall, in spite of the fact that their leaves have been torn off.

Hazel and Wauneeta appear at their door, in flannel nightgowns and bathrobes. Wauneeta is crying, badly shaken; several of their windows blew out and one of the old elms came down on the turret.

Larken moves on. Everywhere, she collides with people she's never seen, stopping long enough to exchange a few words, get information, relay information, point, lead, follow. "Have you seen Bonnie?" she calls to people who know her. "Have you seen a pregnant woman?" she cries to people who don't.

Among these searchers, no one among them feels anything yet. There isn't time for that.

Gaelan leaves Viney and Esmé and Jon in the paramedics' care and runs to the park. He hears Bethan before he sees her, frantically calling his name.

"I can't find Eli," she cries. "God, Gae, oh God." There are others here, also calling, already working at clearing the debris. The bleachers have been flattened like refuse cardboard, stacked one on top of another. The corrugated steel roof of the Emlyn Springs Boosters Club has been partially torn off, its edges warped.

"Eli!" Gaelan calls, joining his voice with Bethan's. "Eli! Eli!"

They hear an answering moan coming from beneath one of the collapsed picnic shelters. Gaelan moves ragged sheaves of metal and wood aside. When they uncover Eli, he's clutching his notebook to his chest. His eyeglasses are broken. One of his legs is badly cut.

"I'm shy at dances," Eli says weakly, and Bethan clasps him to her as if trying to absorb his body into hers.

Gaelan lifts him up and starts carrying him to the paramedics. Bethan walks close by his side, talking to Eli, holding his hand. They climb into the ambulance and Gaelan waves them away.

He heads back into the night, empty-armed, in search of his sisters.

His shoulder is healed now. He can lift anything.

He'll carry anyone who needs carrying.

In the ensuing hours, more is known:

St. David's Home for the Elderly suffered severe damange, and two of its residents, Mr. Robert Norris and Miss Greta Hallock, are dead.

One person, Mrs. Bonnie Jones, is still missing. Mrs. Jones is five months pregnant.

The Bethel Welsh Methodist Church has lost its roof, its steeple, its bell; across the street, the school is missing bricks and windows. Trees have been knocked down, and in places where the tornado hasn't touched structures directly, the damage comes from those felled trees.

Strangers are pouring into town, volunteers from all over the state, the Red Cross, mobile homes and tents, the tents so suggestive of recent Fancy Egg Days that it seems as though all this is merely another phase of the celebration.

Damage is estimated to be in the . . .

The number of people made homeless by the storm is . . .

The sky begins to lighten, revealing more ridiculous miracles: Where Bess and Owen Simpson's house used to stand, a cabinet alone remains, its doors torn off, the wedding china vanished, and yet a single champagne glass etched with the words HARRIET AND LAWRENCE, SEPTEMBER 9, 1951 sits alone and undamaged in the middle of one shelf. Harriet and Lawrence are unknown to anyone here.

What does it mean? Who is missing?

Where is our town?

Where is Flying Girl?

Everyone looks for her, including the children. They are resolute; they will not be stopped, not by doctors or nurses, not by policemen or state troopers or distraught parents. Flying Girl, Miss Jones, now Mrs. Jones, is the heart of their town. She brought them through the blizzard. She belongs to them more than she belongs to anyone.

They set out on their bikes, those who still have them. Those who don't are issued bikes; Blind Tom sees to that, because the newly rechristened piano and bike hospital, KEEP ON TUNIN' KEEP ON TRUIN', survived as well, but Bonnie is not there.

Sergei knows why his master is crying. He retrieves one of Bonnie's jackets from the bike shop and drops it at Blind Tom's feet.

"I didn't know you were a tracking dog," Blind Tom says, petting Sergei's head. "All right, my friend, lead the way."

Larken heads for the bridge, but it has collapsed. She stumbles along the edges of the ravine until she reaches Flying Girl's tree. It's still lodged in place, while others around it have been torn up by the roots. Bonnie is not there.

Larken crosses the ravine, climbs up the other side, walks east, farther than anyone, farther than what makes sense.

Everywhere she notices bits of trash, the kind of things Bonnie would bring home and glue into her scrapbooks: ticket stubs, business cards, the broken earpiece from a pair of glasses. Larken starts picking them up, pocketing them as she goes, these bits of refuse, this roadside trash to which her baby sister assigned such love, such reverence. No one saw these things the way Bonnie did, as artifacts, as evidence of human lives, the smallness and the greatness of human lives contained in detritus.

Here's a grocery list written in an even, tidy hand: *Bacon, yogurt, eggs, raisins, pineapple, cashews, avocado*. The list is written on notepaper printed with the words *When you can laugh at yourself you become more whole*. Larken tries to imagine, as her sister surely would, the person who made this list. She was making a special salad, something exotic for her monthly bridge group, all widows.

Who can do this? Larken wonders. Who can go through life as her baby sister has done, assigning meaning to everything, looking, always looking? Whose heart is this strong, to have this kind of imagination and faith?

Larken picks up and pockets more refuse—a bit of cloth, a carved wooden spoon, a penny.

In this land that once formed the floor of a shallow inland sea, there are no trees to obscure one's view, no forests. Looking for a body here is looking among flattened muddied fields, short crevasses where in places one of the underground springs has emerged for a time, become visible, given solace and drink to a small stand of trees. A body might be hidden in these sorts of places, and they are searched by some of the people who are looking for Bonnie Jones, but Larken does not search there.

She continues to follow the trail of rubbish, the cast-off crumbs that the tornado dropped in its wake. It leads her to Babe's Meadow Muffins.

Because of the sudden downpouring rain, the ground is soft and wet; it has a surprising, unsupported springiness. Larken feels as if she's walking on the floor of a dwelling with faulty foundation framing, or on the top of a sod house, perhaps a whole village of sod houses. Is that possible? Could it be that what she's believed all these years to be hills are really bubbles overlaid with turf?

She finds a golf tee, a prescription pill bottle, a pair of wooden dice. And then she sees up ahead—is it *that* house? The one at the top of the blind driveway? She's disoriented. Usually she only sees this landscape in passing, and from the window of a car. And yet it could be. She's walked that far.

From a distance, it looks like a doll house: Its back wall has been sheared off, revealing a cutaway view of two floors and many rooms, tattered wallpaper, torn curtains.

As Larken draws closer, she sees that there's hardly any furniture inside, only an old sofa with its cushions missing, its coiled springs extruding in places—no sign that anyone has lived here for a long time. It's hard to know if the tornado did this damage or if the house has been this way for years.

Propped against the sofa is a bicycle.

Larken cries out and starts to run, at the same time becoming aware of other sounds—a dog barking, people calling Bonnie's name. Other figures are running with her, all converging on the place to which she is bound.

It is well known by every child in Emlyn Springs that—in case of a tornado and in the absence of a basement—one must seek out the center of the house; if there is a bathroom there, so much the better.

And so it is that—abutted on each side by the walls of two other rooms, in an old, iron, clawfoot bathtub, beneath a stack of sofa cushions and with a copy of *What to Expect When You're Expecting* lying open on her belly—Bonnie Jones is found, sleeping.

They arrive, one by one, breathing hard, their feet muddied: Larken and Gaelan and Blind Tom and Sergei.

They gather in silence and do not speak until she awakens.

"What's wrong?" Flying Girl asks of the kneeling people surrounding her, her voice sleepy and childlike.

And still they cannot speak.

Coming more fully awake, she chuckles, not unkindly. "Why are you crying?" she asks, petting each of them in turn. "You're all so funny. You didn't have to worry. Didn't you think I'd know what to do?"

Standing at attention on the fringes of this scene like defensive linemen guarding the goalpost—heads denuded, stripped bare, bald as cue balls and naked as jaybirds but otherwise intact—are Viney's hymnbook angels.

Epilogue

A Painting Is a Little Lie

South O got hammered pretty good, but by the time the storm got to Omaha, it was a shadow of its former self, nothing but hot air, a blowhard already bragging about the damage it did in its glory days, down there in the southernmost part of Gage County.

Newspapers all over Nebraska report on the devastating tornado that swept through the tiny town of Emlyn Springs, leaving two dead and many homeless. There are photos of gray-haired women in work gloves with their backs to the camera and their arms around each other; an overhead shot of overturned cars lining the streets, looking like vertebral bodies bent in a severe scoliotic curve; kids knee-deep in rubble, laughing.

One caption reads: "Gaelan Jones, former KLAN-KHAM weatherman, and his sister Larken, a University of Nebraska professor, serve a hot meal to Estella Axthem, longtime resident of Emlyn Springs, and one of many people left homeless in the disaster, which destroyed 20 percent of the houses in this tiny southeastern community."

The day after the tornado of 2004, a thousand people converge on Emlyn Springs. Kind people, well-meaning people, people with expertise in everything from registering an insurance claim to pouring a cup of coffee, skills much needed and welcome. The good monks of Emlyn

Springs' sister city wire a sizeable monetary donation. Food and clothing come in by the truckful.

Yes, help pours in from across the state and across the country and they are grateful for it. No mayor of a small dying town will admit to it outright—certainly not Bud Humphries, and especially not when deaths have occurred—but a natural disaster can be a boon, bringing as it does thousands of volunteers into a community, attention, an outpouring of support, and FEMA money. They'll come out of this okay.

Still, none of them are so naive as to believe that, at the end of the day, it won't be they who are left here, deciding whether to stay or go. No one really knows a small town like the people who live there. No one else understands why they stay, maybe not even those who do.

But if they were to try to explain it, the townsfolk of Emlyn Springs would say that—in those days and weeks following the tornado of 2004, as they freed their loved ones, sifted through rubble, helped their neighbors, salvaged what they could, tore down what was irreparable—they found themselves incapable of leaving, bound together by that rare kind of suffering: an abiding love for a place that has been ruined.

She is learning new modes of travel.

She still comes and goes frequently as a soloist—for that is Professor Jones's long-standing habit—but more and more she chooses to move through the world in the company of others: students, colleagues, new acquaintances, old friends.

Now sometimes when she is flying, eyes closed, half-dozing, she imagines landing, disembarking, and finding her parents waiting for her at the other end of the tunnel that bridges plane and terminal. The fantasy is so real as to feel like something that actually happened, a true memory.

Hi, Mom! Hi, Dad!

And she *does* find them now in a sense, more often, often unexpectedly—the best and kindest and most forgiving versions of those two people with whom she shared such complexities of feeling. (Trite as it is, the word *love* is the only one that holds it all. A reduction, as in cooking, their selves caramelized, leaving only a fierce, dense sweetness just this side of scorched, an effort to chew, sticky and adherent.)

She finds them in a face in a car window glimpsed in passing while walking to school; in an unconscious gesture; in the melody in a stranger's voice; in the graceful hands of a woman sitting across the aisle from her, knitting. She allows her heart to open then, accepting the cost.

In late December, the extended family of Hope and Llwelyn Jones is far-flung, standing at great distances from one another on the map of the world:

In the baggage claim area of Heathrow Airport, Larken unrolls a cherry-colored, hand-knit scarf—an imperfect lacework of randomly occurring holes and dropped stitches—and winds it around Esmé while Jon looks on.

In a synagogue in Seattle, Gaelan stands among a large, joyful congregation, singing the Mazel Tov song to Bar Mitzvah Eli Ellis Weissman. Today, he is a man.

And in Emlyn Springs, Nebraska, the firstborn child of Morgan Geraint and Bonnie Jones (midwifed into the world by Alvina Closs) opens her fist to reveal a flat, rectangular piece of ivory.

These improbabilities set something twanging in the pools of their bellies, and as the birds at lucky dusk cry, *Really? Really? Tell me tell me tell me tell me tell me,* they all let forth with laughter.

Acknowledgments

A couple of years ago, during a difficult time, I took part in literary fundraiser that included the wonderful Malachy McCourt. At one point, I was bemoaning the fact that I was an only child. Mr. McCourt replied, in his beautifully lilting voice, "Ah, but you're a *writer* now, dear. You've got *lots* of brothers and sisters." Indeed I do, and it is my great pleasure to offer thanks for the role they played in bringing this book to completion.

My deepest gratitude:

to the many readers and booksellers across the country I've met since the publication of *Broken for You*, without whom the lonely work of writing would be even lonelier;

to Rich Marriott and M. J. McDermott for their knowledge of meteorology; to Alister B. Fraser and the Bad Coriolis Web site for setting me straight on raindrops;

to Larry Jones, for sharing a wealth of wisdom related to Welsh culture, language, and music; to Robert Price, for translating the lyrics to the "Nebraska Fight Song;"

to Dr. Ron Singler, Dr. Mary Case, and Fran Gallo, for providing medical and personal insights into multiple sclerosis;

to Julie Everson, the former mayor of Wymore, Nebraska; to the citizens of Wymore, including Arnold Irvin, Robert Norris, Bud and Vonda Roberts, and Margaret Thomas;

to Judith Wills for her Web site artistry; to Dave Bennett for the joke;

to Dr. Alan Hamlet for his advice on designing a fictional landscape; to Richard Weeks, for explaining the inner workings of the piano;

to the people of Llithfaen and Pwlltheli, North Wales; to Richard and Bethan Ellis of Organic Parc; to the Welsh Language Centre; to the Seattle Welsh Choir;

to Morgan Entrekin, prince of publishing, for his enduring faith in my abilities, and for including me in the amazing community of Grove/Atlantic writers; to all the Grove gang, including Deb Seager, Elizabeth Johnson, Jessica Monahan, Elisabeth Schmitz;

to Cindy Heidemann and Cheryl McKeon, who read an early draft and provided the cheerleading support so needed at the time;

to my fellow writers: Ellen Parker, Craig English, Ron Pellegrino, Lisa Lynch, Heather Barbieri, Jennie Shortridge, Kit Bakke, Mary Guterson, Garth Stein, Randy Sue Coburn, Phil Jennings, Sheri Holman, and the infinitely gracious Sue Monk Kidd;

to Nan Burling, ChiChi Stewart-Singler, and Alexandra Immel, for being in the room on Epiphany night 2006; to Wendy Dell, Lynne McMahan, Kate Zuckerman for assisting me in my quest for the perfect pancake;

to Hedgebrook, where I was gifted with the time and space to write the first chapter, and to the Ragdale Foundation, where I recieved the inspiration to write the last;

to Dan Lazar, for the offhand but insightful comment about Larken's comings-and-goings;

to Simon Lipskar, for saying the hard words that made me write a better book;

to Lauren Wein—beloved friend, teacher, fellow traveler, and cohort in dreams;

to Noah, Sam, and Bill for helping me remember to laugh and—when laughter was impossible—for holding me when I cried;

and finally, to Joan Didion, for her unwitting guidance in navigating the confounding, slippery landscape of grief, and for helping me understand why my mother could never bring herself to get rid of Dad's shoes.